THE AIRSHIPMEN

Praise for the Airshipmen

The Airshipmen is also available as a series as *The Airshipmen Trilogy*. The trilogy version carries a series of photographs for each segment of the epic saga.

*

A riveting story that plays out against the background of one of the most intriguing chapters in aviation history. David Dennington weaves a fascinating web of romance, courage, tragedy and shattered dreams and gives the reader a front row seat to eye-opening, high-stakes political battles on two continents. A real page turner with the constant feeling that something new and unexpected is about to unfold. ***David Wright, Daily Mirror Journalist.***

*

This book is a hidden gem. I found the airship history portrayed, fascinating and what better way of learning about history through this 'Faction' novel. Fiction-based-on-fact. Brilliant. This story is screaming out to be made into a TV miniseries or feature film. Recently, I discovered that this great story has been published as set of three books, with photographs of main characters, airships, crew, passengers, interiors, maps and construction sheds etc. This brings history back to life even more. So pleased to read this great story again, but this time with real images. ***Mike Barden, Editor, Reeth & District Gazette.***

*

A very big novel in every way, unique, beautifully written and perfectly paced ... setting the scene so well ... the first of a true new genre ... weaving us around the events of the great *Airship R101* tragedy, the people and places we know well ... with wonderfully rich characters ... researched in immaculate detail. ***Alastair Lawson, Chairman, Airship Heritage Trust, Cardington.***

*

The whole future of the airship program in Great Britain rests on the famous flight of Cardington R101. Will politics play too large a role? Will Charlotte be able to handle the very real stress of being married to an airshipman? Will her psychopath stalker, Jessup, triumph? Will Princess Marthe say yes to Lord Thomson's proposal of marriage? Dennington deftly handles a blend of fascinating real people with the characters he has created. This story is written on an epic scale and a fine tribute to those who risked everything. *Jeffrey Keeten, Goodreads Top Reviewer.*

*

Hats off! A gripping story masterfully told, the book reverberates in the reader's mind long after it is over. ***Steven Bauer, Hollow Tree Press.***

*

This is a big story, layered and cinematic—one that I did not want to end. It's about a wonderful group of people that I came to love—full of secrets and surprises. I could not put this book down. ***Edith Schorah, Editor.***

*

An impressively crafted multilayered novel, ***The Airshipmen*** is a fully absorbing read from beginning to end and clearly showcases author David Dennington as a gifted storyteller of the first order. ***Midwest Book Review***

*

The Airshipmen is a very human story ... historical fiction based primarily in Britain in the 1920s and follows the sweeping passions and adventures of the airship industry... with beautifully flawed characters. ... an incredibly interesting fictionalized take on an important and experimental time in air travel history ... recommended for fans of history, air travel, and historical fiction with just a touch of fantasy. ***Portland Book Review***

*

An epic read ... a sure feast for those interested in ... pre-World War II aviation history. ***Historical Novel Society.***

*

The Airshipmen is a love story wrapped around politics of the day, woven into a tale that reveals the rise and fall of the great airships of the 20th century. A truly gripping story. ***Kathryn Johnson, Author of The Gentleman Poet.***

*

A marvelous book. I read it through in just a few days and was fascinated, moved and informed. ***Peter Humphris, Goodreads Reviewer.***

*

I am a fan of author Nevil Shute and therefore knew of the R100/R101 adventure since Shute was deeply involved with ship constructed by Vickers. Fascinating subject matter, and well written. Perhaps the closest a person will ever get to the whole story. ***James Reising, Goodreads Reviewer.***

*

I loved this book. It was a very interesting era in Britain and of course, airships are fascinating. If found myself looking up events and characters on Google all the time. ***Ruth Lee, Amazon Reviewer.***

*

A good book is when you must read it whenever you have a spare moment ... and you feel being in a vacuum having finished it. So was this book to me. Thanks for great research and fine writing. ***Claus, Amazon Reviewer.***

*

Very interesting historical novel that weaves fiction and fact into an amazing story of love, ambition and politics. I found myself checking historical events as I read. The characters are full of life and through the tales told of them, you feel that you are experiencing and living in their period of history. I would love to see this story reach the 'big screen'. ***Bob, Amazon Reviewer.***

*

An amazing debut novel! I got so involved with the plot and the intrigues surrounding the characters—never boring for a second. Plots were continually changing and the unexpected happening. It was a wonderful love story ... how you thought it was headed ... and then the final twist. I was sorry it ended, but it left me in a good place. ***Cheryl R, Goodreads Reviewer.***

*

This epic is bursting with devastating, colourful images, great humour, lush storylines, tender love stories, exciting plot twists and a plethora of factual historical information. It is both fiction and non-fiction – 'faction' perhaps!
Lauren Dennington, Editor of The Airshipmen.

*

Two girls study the airship on which their daddies will fly away—perhaps forever. *Cardington R101* at the tower 1929.

THE AIRSHIPMEN

A NOVEL

BASED ON A TRUE STORY

A TALE OF LOVE, BETRAYAL & POLITICAL INTRIGUE

DAVID DENNINGTON

THE CAST OF CHARACTERS

May be found at the back of the book.

ISBN-13: 978-1518642524
ISBN-10: 1518642527

Printed by Amazon.
Available from Amazon.com and other retail outlets.
Also available on Kindle and other retail outlets through Amazon.

BY DAVID DENNINGTON

THE AIRSHIPMEN
As an alternative, this book is now also available as a three-part series with photographs of real characters, airships and maps (see below).

THE AIRSHIPMEN TRILOGY
FROM ASHES   Volume One
LORDS OF THE AIR   Volume Two
TO ASHES   Volume Three
Available in hardback, paperback and Kindle

THE GHOST OF CAPTAIN HINCHLIFFE
Based on a true story
Available in hardback, paperback and Kindle

Audiobook now available.
Narrated by Lauren Dennington

Deepest gratitude to Lauren, my daughter and consulting editor, without whose help and collaboration this book could not have been written.

For my Mother and Father.
And
Jenny, Christian and Ava, with great love.

Also for Richard—my own Lou Remington.

"Airships are the devil's 'andiwork in defiance of God's laws. And we should avoid them like the plague!"

Lord Scunthorpe, House of Lords. July 4th, 1929.

FIRST PROLOGUE

Arras, France. March 1918.

Midnight. The relentless German barrage continues ever closer, shaking the ground under her feet. She pulls back the tent flap and steps into hell. The dreary, foul-smelling casualty clearing station is packed with moaning soldiers. She lights her lamp and holds it out before her, illuminating her breath in the gloom; off duty after countless hours, back to give a sliver of comfort, to wipe a brow, offer water, loosen a dressing.

To one side, a priest administers last rites to a soldier, his leg, his arm, his life gone. She looks at the priest accusingly.

Where is your precious God? What use are your prayers in this miserable place where the devil roams free?

The priest continues his mumbling. "Yea, though I walk through the valley of the shadow of death, I fear no evil: for thou art with me; thy rod and thy staff they comfort me."

Stretcher bearers stand ready. The cot is needed. Dozens more are being brought in from no man's land by the hour. At the end of the tent, fifty yards off, a civilian wearing a black overcoat enters, hat in hand. He is accompanied by two officers in dress khakis. The young nurse frowns.

Another damned politician playing to the press, come to tell them this disgraceful crime is justified.

The man stops for a moment to witness a surgeon at work removing the remains of a young boy's leg. That area is well-lit and attended by orderlies and nurses holding the boy down. He cries out, but it's no use. The surgeon does not dally, proceeding with ruthless precision.

The civilian stands his ground a few more seconds, he can't just turn away. When he does, she sees his shoulders slump, the burden too heavy. As he passes, he glances at her with piercing blue eyes. In them, she sees tears of bewilderment and sorrow. He'd obviously meant to stop and offer words of encouragement to others. Instead, he moves wearily on and out through the entrance through which she had come. She glances at his back, now with respect. His escorts trail behind. They hear him retching outside in the darkness.

"Our future Prime Minister," one of them, a major, says.

"Preposterous!" his companion scoffs.

The nurse moves to sit beside a young soldier barely older than she, her look grave. The boy shakes uncontrollably, tears flowing from wild eyes. She unravels his dressings, caked in dried blood, and sighs.

If they don't get here soon, then God help us!

Lord Thomson's Painting of the Taj Mahal, India.

SECOND PROLOGUE

No. 10 Downing Street, London.
Friday Evening, October 3, 1930.

A t 10 o'clock, Thomson and MacDonald emerge from MacDonald's study on the second floor, having gone over the agenda for the Imperial Conference of Dominion Prime Ministers scheduled to begin later that month. They stand on the wide landing overlooking the grand staircase. MacDonald puts his hand on Thomson's arm, eyes intense.

"Forgo this trip. I need your wise council for this conference. Do this for me, CB."

"Are you ordering me not to go, sir?"

"No, I'm asking you as my dearest friend."

They hold each other's forearms and Thomson looks earnestly into the Prime Minister's face.

"How can I not go? I'm committed. And besides, the troops are expecting me. I need to rally them." Thomson moves to the top of the stairs. "Don't worry. I'll be back for the conference—have I ever let you down, Ramsay?"

MacDonald's eyes, moist earlier, now glisten. Thomson sees this before he starts down the stairs. When he gets to the bottom, he stares up at MacDonald and waves. Thomson crosses the black and white checkered floor, stopping at the door.

"Farewell, my good friend," MacDonald calls down weakly.

Thomson's voice echoes up the stairway. "Don't look so glum, my dear chap. Don't you remember? Our fate is already written."

MacDonald stands hunched like a man watching his brother going off to war. He wipes his eyes with a handkerchief. "Yes, I do," he whispers. "Yes, I do."

"Ramsay, if the worst *should* happen, it'd soon be over."

As Thomson leaves, the door slams behind him, the sound echoing around the great hall like thunder.

Thomson leaves Downing Street and crosses Whitehall to Gwydyr House. He passes the nightwatchman, giving him a curt nod. His office is in darkness. He switches on the picture light over the huge oil painting of the Taj Mahal and sits down, staring at the airship he'd had superimposed upon it by Winston Churchill. He hopes for some sort of divine affirmation. But he gets none. He gets up and goes to the window and peers out over the river, which faintly glimmers under the dim street lamps. The bitter taste and the feeling he has is something akin to buyer's remorse. Brancker's words continue their stinging assault:

I will go CB—and I'll tell you why. I encouraged people to fly in this airship—people like O'Neill and Palstra—believing it'd be built and tested properly. I believed all your rhetoric about 'safety first.' I didn't think you'd use this airship for your own personal aggrandizement, for your own personal agenda, with everything set to meet your own personal schedule. People like O'Neill put their faith in me and my word. I will not abandon them now.

Then he hears the young American's voice like an echo, depressing him further.

You're putting all your chips on black, Lord Thomson... You're putting all your chips on black...

PART ONE

Maiden flight of R38/ZR-2, Cardington, June 23, 1921

YORKSHIRE

1

DEATH ON THE HUMBER

Wednesday August 24, 1921.

T he lighthouse keeper at Flamborough Head checked the time as he
peered at the airship cruising overhead. It was 4:40 p.m. Aside from
him, no one noticed except three carrion crows intent on the carcass
of a rabbit. They paused in their evisceration, following the airship with
blank eyes, as if it were a larger bird of prey and then, after much scolding,
returned to their meal, black beaks tearing at the dead creature's flesh. The
air was humid—a late summer afternoon storm pending. Their instincts knew
the day would end in rain, and wind, and worse.

His Majesty's Airship *R38* swept across the Yorkshire sky at twenty-
five hundred feet. After this last training flight the ship would become the
property of the U.S. Navy. In the control car, crowded with silent British and
American officers and coxswains, Lou Remington, newly promoted chief
petty officer and former marine, anxiously rechecked his watch. He glanced
down at the lighthouse on the headland surrounded by the North Sea, the
salty air and cries of gulls, drifting in an open window. They cruised
smoothly at fifty-five knots on six Cossack engines. The British commodore
turned to Lou.

"Chief Coxswain, find out what Bateman's got to say about the
rudders and elevators. We need to start this last test if we're to land before
dark. Report back to me after the next watch change would you, there's a
good chap."

"Aye, aye, sir. I'll go and talk to him," Lou answered.

Lou left the control car and headed along the catwalk toward the
crewmens' mess. He needed to check on 'New York' Johnny before visiting
Bateman who'd been monitoring the control gear all afternoon in the stern
cockpit. These final tests could soon be over, perhaps within the hour,
depending on Bateman's report.

Maybe we can head home soon—God willing!

Lanky Josh Stone, a blond, Californian rigger, smiled pleasantly as
Lou passed him on the catwalk. "Ready for some o' them good ol' American
hamburgers, sir?"

"You betcha! And a cold one," Lou answered.

"I wish!"

Along the catwalks shouts and jeers in British and American accents echoed from all directions as riggers and engineers mustered for the watch change.

"I'll be glad to get away from you bloody Brits!"

"And your rotten, soggy fish and chips!"

"And yer lousy, warm Limey beer!"

"Tastes like cat's piss."

"*You* bin drinkin' it, ain'tcha!"

"It's better than what you gonna get over there, me old cock!"

Lou suddenly remembered Prohibition had started in the States the year before—a fact most of his crewmen had completely forgotten.

"California, here we come. Yeehaw!"

A Brit had the last word in this exchange, "Good luck to life wiv no beer, boys!"

Lord have mercy!

Lou knew he was going to miss this ragged bunch with their strange expressions and eccentric ways. Many of their foibles had rubbed off on the Americans. Goodness knows what their families would think when they got back to the U.S. These Brits were great guys and England was a manicured wonderland, but he longed to be home. He looked forward to sitting on his parents' porch in balmy Virginia air, playing his guitar, as he'd done as a kid. That all seemed a long time ago.

The atmosphere aboard *R38* was of both nervous tension and exuberance. The banter between the English and American crews had been building over the past few hours. Their elation was only natural—soon the ship would be officially re-designated USS *ZR-2*. Lou had listened to their merciless teasing all afternoon. At twenty-three, he was younger than many of the men under his command, including most of the British crewmen, whom he now outranked.

He rubbed the stubble on his chin while, like adolescents, they jeered and poked fun. They even danced and sang. Lou marched on, though their tempting Providence made him uncomfortable. There was no need to dampen their spirits—for now.

It's nervous bravado—they're damned scared, that's all.

When Lou entered the crewmen's mess, Al Jolson's latest hit, "My Mammy", was belting out from the gramophone and little Jerry Donegan, a lively soul from Kentucky, was doing a perfect mime on one knee, hat in hand, his face smeared with old engine oil.

On the final note, his small audience gave him a round of applause, while New York Johnny, a sandy-haired nineteen-year-old from Brooklyn, sat motionless, staring at the fabric wall. No one paid him any attention.

Lou leaned over him and whispered. "You gonna be okay to do your watch, Johnny?"

"Yes, sir," the boy answered weakly.

"You sure?"

"Yeah 'course."

"I'll come and get you just before five."

"Sir!"

Lou stepped out onto the catwalk and stopped for a moment. He worried about that kid.

This life's definitely not for him!

Lou would've stood him down, but he was a man short. Wiggy, an engineer from Cleveland, hadn't reported for duty at Howden before they took off. Something must have happened to him; he was usually reliable. Lou made his way toward the stern, studying the massive structure around him. He breathed in the odor of gasoline, grease, and dope, as if it were fresh-cut hay. Some days it was like being in church, on others, in the belly of a great whale: six hundred and ninety-nine feet of girders, beams of meccano-like steel, held together with rivets, cables, guy wires, nuts and bolts, shrouded by a silver-painted outer cover of finest linen canvas. Walking this labyrinth was exhilarating.

On completion of construction at Cardington and her launching eight weeks ago, the designers and British command had drawn up a comprehensive schedule of flight tests. After initial testing, *R38* was flown to Howden Air Station where another massive shed waited to house the dirigible. Due to time constraints, both the British and American governments insisted the tests were hastened. Lou had taken part under the command of British captain, Flight Lieutenant Wann; now it was time for the final round under the command of Air Commodore Maitland, Britain's most experienced airshipman.

Speed trials completed an hour ago had been satisfactory, although no testing had been done in inclement weather. To compensate, the Air Ministry decided that rough weather conditions could be simulated by stressful maneuvering at low altitude.

All that remained now was a series of these stress tests to prove her structural integrity, and at the same time, confirm that modifications to the rudder and elevator mechanisms had been carried out successfully.

At the end of September, the weather over the Atlantic would almost certainly deteriorate; another reason for rushing these tests. At first, the urgency wasn't so dire, since the fabulous new shed under construction in New Jersey had not been ready. But after the ship's own construction delays, completion had fallen behind and the shed at Lakehurst stood empty, waiting for its charge like a stable without its promised thoroughbred.

After additional training, they'd be on their way, leaving behind the moist, green hills of England and new friends they'd made—many girls—

and heading for New Jersey. Although they looked forward to going home to their families, the upcoming passage brought a tinge of sadness and, for many, sheer terror at the thought of facing the Atlantic. Still, there'd been rumors of a ticker-tape welcome.

Why, soon we might all be famous!

Lou descended a long cat ladder to the keel and moved toward the stern, past brand new rolls of neatly-coiled rigger's ropes and spare bolts of linen, each with its own smell. Everything was 'ship shape.' Some crewmen sat in specially fitted machine gun nests studying the picturesque view of fields, villages and streams below. One held a message in a tube attached to a tiny parachute. It was common for crewmen to drop messages—sometimes miraculously received by the addressee.

"A love letter to your honey, Bobby?" Lou called.

"You know it, sir."

"She working today?"

"Yes, sir, she's a nurse in Hull."

"What's her name?"

"Elsie, sir ...Elsie Postlethwaite."

"That's quite a mouthful! Is it serious?"

"Absolutely, sir!"

"Maybe you should ship that babe home," Lou said.

"I'm gonna pop the question as soon as I see her. I want her to come to Baltimore ...after the baby's born, sir," Bobby said, holding up a ring box he'd fished out of his pocket.

"Oh ...okay. I see ...Right. Well, er, that's good. That's the message, is it?"

"Yes, sir."

"Perhaps you'll be able to ask her yourself tonight if we finish these last tests."

"That's what I'm hoping, sir."

"Good luck, Bobby!"

A Brit chimed in from another machine gun nest. "Hey, don't you bloody Yanks be stealing all our women!"

"You got a surplus of 'em, buddy!" Bobby yelled back.

"Yeah, and that's the way we like it, mate!"

Lou chuckled and walked on. He made several stops checking on his crewmen, giving words of encouragement, a pat on the shoulder, a smile. He passed rows of water ballast containers and newly fitted bomb racks, and extra banks of petrol storage tanks, installed at the request of the Navy. He made a point of observing the ship's structure, as trained, for signs of loosening fasteners or metal fatigue in the girders. He stared up with satisfaction.

Over the past twelve months he'd personally witnessed every part being hoisted and riveted into place at the Royal Airship Works at Cardington in Bedfordshire, monitoring construction for quality and keeping records and as-built drawings. Satisfied all was well, he climbed back up the ladder to the central level. From there, he made his way aft to get the answer to the commodore's question.

After four hundred feet, Lou reached the stern and opened the flap into a cockpit where Henry Bateman sat bundled in oilskins, pointing a camera at the huge tail structure. This tiny area was like a boat cuddy without a roof. From the ground, Bateman appeared as small as a freckle on a whale. Lou paused while Bateman snapped a picture. He shivered as the air enveloped him.

"It's freezing out here!" he shouted above the wind.

"Hello, Lou. It's bracing Yorkshire air, my boy—breath it in!"

Lou glanced at the patchwork quilt of lush green fields and hedgerows below. Far beyond, across the flat Holderness Plain, he admired the North Sea. It was difficult to distinguish where the ocean merged with the hazy, azure-blue sky on the horizon.

"You're lucky. You've got a decent view," Lou said, moving into the cockpit. He sat down on the built-in wooden bench seat running around the perimeter. He peered up at the small, fluttering American flag attached to the tail fin and the *ZR-2* lettering stenciled on the rudder. Lou smiled broadly, exposing even white teeth.

Bateman laughed. "We're a little premature with the flag, aren't we, Lou? I don't think you've paid for the bloody thing yet."

"Don't know anything about that, pal. I'm only here to deliver the beast."

"You'll soon be on your way."

"How are the elevators and rudders?" Lou asked.

Bateman held up his clipboard. "Everything's working fine now. I've been noting course and altitude changes by the coxswains. Everything's on the money."

"Good."

"She's a fine ship," Bateman said. "Just drop a check into the Bank of England and you can drive her home."

"You sound like a damned car salesman!"

"Just pulling your leg, Lou. You know we like having you blokes around."

"I'll let the commodore know. They're gonna do another test in about half an hour. I've got to make a crew change. I'll check with you later," Lou said, getting up.

While *R38* glided majestically toward the city of Hull, the statuesque, twenty-two-year-old Charlotte Hamilton made her final rounds in the geriatric ward of Hull Infirmary. The cream-colored walls gleamed in the late afternoon sunshine, streaming in the windows overlooking the waterfront. The room was full of sick, elderly women propped up on pillows against ancient, white-railed bedsteads.

Charlotte and the other nurses moved from bed to bed, their black leather shoes squeaking on polished, linoleum floors that reeked of disinfectant. This shift would be over at 5 o'clock, but before they could leave, each patient's needs had to be met, beds straightened, bedpans emptied.

Charlotte went to the window and studied the scene on the busy waterfront and the river estuary beyond. Small ripples on the smooth surface indicated that the river was on the turn. Soon, it'd be a raging torrent rushing seaward. The sky overhead was partly clear, but dark cumulus clouds were building over the high ground in the west. Tiny waves, kicked up by the chilly breeze, slapped the wharf. A hundred yards off, Charlotte spotted her best friend's husband and son in a rowboat.

"Fanny, your Lenny's out there with young Billy," Charlotte said, as Fanny dashed by. "There's a storm brewing by the looks of it."

"Yes, I've seen them. They'd better be packing up and getting home. It's almost five," Fanny called over her shoulder.

On the side street opposite the hospital, five boys, about eight years old, were playing cricket. A lamppost served as a wicket. Two bored girls, around the same age, sat on their mother's front step, babysitting their infant brother. They watched a scruffy lad with close-cropped hair slam the ball down the road with an old cricket bat. The boy whooped. The others scowled, arguing about whose turn it was to go for it.

A safe distance from the boys, a group of girls was skipping, one end of their rope tied to a drainpipe, while one twirled. Two girls jumped in unison, chanting their verses in time with the rope as it kissed the ground.

> *One, two, buckle my shoe,*
> *Three four, knock at the door,*
> *Five, six, pickin' up sticks,*
> *Seven, eight, they're at heaven's gate ...*

Charlotte smiled as she turned from the window and went over to Mrs. Tilly, her favorite patient, who was engrossed in the girls' melody.

> *Up above the world so high,*
> *Like a diamond in the sky ...*

"Oh, I do love to hear their sweet voices," the old lady said.

"They make up their own rhymes as they go along, you know love. They see the airships coming over all the time from Howden. You have to laugh at them really—the girls, I mean. Is there anything you need before I go off duty, Mrs. T?" Charlotte asked.

If she dives, they all might die,
Oh, I wonder, why, why, why?

"Much as I love to hear 'em, I'm feeling a chill right down in my old bones."

Poor ol' Bobby, he's in the drink,
Should we pull him out—what do you fink?

Charlotte closed the steel casement window with a clunk. The chanting grew fainter.

Nine, ten ...

"Can I do anything else for you, love? You only have to ask."
"Don't go to a lot of trouble for me, dear," Mrs. Tilly protested.
"Come on, let me fix this bed for you."
She pulled the old lady gently up into a sitting position. Mrs. Tilly wheezed and coughed while Charlotte fluffed up her pillows and straightened the bedclothes. Charlotte read the birthday card on the side table next to a vase of flowers.
"I hope you've had a nice birthday, Mrs. Tilly."
"Eighty-one years I've been on this earth—it's long enough. I lost my 'usband last year. I'll be glad to join him and my sons in 'eaven."
"You've got a few more years to wait, I'm sure," Charlotte said.
Charlotte eased her frail patient down onto the pillows. The entrance doors to the ward rattled as a young nurse pushed in a tea trolley. Charlotte poured tea and brought it to Mrs. Tilly with a bite to eat.
"Here's a cuppa and a cucumber sandwich. This'll keep your strength up, love."
Mrs. Tilly's face brightened. "You're such a lovely girl."
The factory whistle blew—grating, but always a welcome sound on Prospect Street.
"It must be time for you to go and meet your young man," Mrs. Tilly said.
Charlotte grimaced. "Oh, no. Nothing like that."
"What! Why ever not?"
"Eligible men are scarce nowadays—most of them are buried in France."
"What about them Americans?"
"Oh, no, no. I can't be bothered."
"Why not?"

"I've heard too many stories. A lot of girls I know are in a right sorry state."

"Maybe you could find a nice one."

"No, I don't want to get mixed up in all that. Besides, I read they're all going back to America any day now."

The old lady seemed seriously concerned. "What a pity. Pretty girl like you should have a fella. You could have your pick, I reckon."

"Oh, go on with you!"

"With that marvelous black hair and beautiful figure you could be an actress."

"Bless your heart, Mrs. Tilly."

"You'll find someone special. I just know you will. And when you do, you grab 'im and 'old on to 'im and never let 'im go. I did. My 'usband was a lovely man and he gave me two wonderful sons. Oh, I do miss 'im so," she sobbed. Tears filled Mrs. Tilly's eyes and ran down her cheeks. "They're all gone now. Our first boy at Mons …the second at Ypres. All three of 'em. Make the most of this life, my dear. It's just a flicker of a candle. That's all it is …"

A dark cloud fell over Charlotte's face. She understood perfectly.

"I'm so sorry, Mrs. Tilly," she said.

The old lady stared up at the ceiling for a moment as though looking through a window to the past, or perhaps the future. After a few moments, she became calm and was at peace.

"I'll see you in the morning, love," Charlotte said.

"Don't forget what I said, my girl," Mrs. Tilly called after her. "Some of them Americans are really lovely!"

"Yes, I know they are, Mrs. Tilly," Charlotte whispered to herself.

After getting permission from Matron to leave, Charlotte went to the staff room where several nurses were washing their hands, combing their hair and freshening their makeup before leaving for the day. Others were getting ready to go on duty. Charlotte sensed desperation among some. One girl had been crying. She was starting to show and Charlotte wondered if her condition had escaped Matron's attention.

No chance of that!

Some were going on about their boyfriends. Charlotte frowned.

They're just so irritating!

"I hope they finish their testing today. I wanna be with my Bobby tonight," one said.

"Do you think they will, Elsie?"

"Bobby said they should and, all being well, they might fly over the city this afternoon."

"Oh, I do hope so."

"Bobby told me they're not expecting any problems, but I wish the test would fail so he could stay here for a few more months."

"But you know if they leave in October or November, it'll be everso much more dangerous for 'em, Elsie."

"Yes, you're right, but I love 'im so much. I don't want 'im to go, Minnie."

"I know. I love my Jimmy, too. I'm going over there, though. He's asked me to marry 'im. We're going to be wed next year."

"Oh, you're so lucky, I wish …"

"What love?'

"Oh, I got a feeling tonight Bobby's going to ask me …he did promise …"

The two girls looked up and saw Charlotte and glanced at one another.

"Oh hello, love. Why don't you get yourself a nice chap from the U.S. Navy? They're smashin', aren't they, Elsie? I could listen to my Jimmy talk all night long. He's like a movie star. I've seen 'em in the talkies at the Odeon in Leeds," Minnie said.

"Not me. And if I were you, I'd make sure you get a ring on your finger before you do anything stupid, Minnie Brown," Charlotte snapped.

"It's a bit late for that, love," Elsie scoffed. At that, both girls doubled up, laughing uncontrollably. Charlotte scowled. Taking her make-up compact from her handbag, she peered into the mirror and puckered her full lips to apply a little plum-colored lipstick. Her vivid blue eyes stared back at her questioningly. She thought about what Mrs. Tilly had said.

Maybe a doctor? No, they're all old men around here, or ugly!

After applying a few dabs of her favorite perfume to her neck, she went to the wall mirror and untied her hair. She laid her head to one side and brushed her thick curls out with long strokes. She then flicked her head back, allowing it to cascade to her waist. The other nurses watched.

"Time you had that lot cut off, isn't it, Charlotte?" dumpy, little Minnie said, with a sly grin.

"No, I'm perfectly satisfied the way it is, thank you very much."

"You should go in for one of these, Charlotte. They're all the rage," the well-endowed Elsie said, running her fingers through her bob cut and thrusting out her bosom.

"You'd feel free as a bird," Minnie added.

"Like us!" Elsie exclaimed.

They rocked back and forth cackling again.

Jealous little cows!

"You're much too straight-laced, Charlotte," Elsie said.

"Aye, *straight-laced* is what I am! And *straight-laced* is what'll prevent me from landing myself in the right pickle you two are gonna be in," Charlotte snapped.

Charlotte ignored them further, taking off her white cotton apron. She put her foot on a chair and hoisted her light blue cotton uniform, pulled her black stockings up tight over her long shapely legs and refastened her garters. After smoothing down her skirt to the ankles, she re-tied her headscarf and put on her dark blue cape before making for the door. Elsie and Minnie stared after her, as if *she* were the foolish one.

Lou entered the crewmen's mess at the same time the factory whistle was sounding on Prospect Street (although he couldn't hear it). The lads still appeared to be in high spirits, except for New York Johnny whose mood hadn't changed. He sat in the corner staring at the wall, just as Lou had left him, elbows on the table, chin in his hands.

"Ready, Johnny?"

"Yes, sir," Johnny said.

He got slowly to his feet, without looking up. Lou led him along the catwalk to the opening above engine car No.1 and pulled back the canvas hatch to the exterior ladder. They were buffeted by the cold, noisy wind rushing over the ship's cover. The boy caught his breath.

"Right, Johnny?" Lou shouted.

Johnny nodded without speaking, staring at the fields below. A tiny goods train rushed along its tracks like a kid's toy train, a black smoke cloud billowing behind, while its whistle screamed a warning. Lou had watched the boy climb down this ladder dozens of times, but it got harder each time. Lou knew he'd developed a phobia. He'd seen it before.

This line of work's better suited to circus performers, or barnstormers. Climbing down ladders suspended from airships at two thousand feet isn't for the faint-hearted.

Lou understood phobias only too well. During the war, he'd developed one of his own—claustrophobia.

"Come on, Johnny, it's okay."

With terror in his eyes, the boy gripped the cold steel of the ship's ladder. Lou knew his heart must be beating like a sledgehammer. Clinging on tightly, Johnny gingerly began the twenty-foot descent to the engine car slung in mid-air beneath the ship.

Suddenly, Johnny froze and glared at the huge propeller whirring in a high-speed blur below him. He gasped for breath, his mouth wide open.

"Johnny, don't look down!" Lou yelled. "Look up at me, buddy!"

The boy remained stuck, screwing his eyelids tightly together to shut out the world.

"Look at me, Johnny! Look at me!"

Johnny tilted his head back and slowly opened his eyes. He peered up into Lou's confident blue eyes, assessing him. It was a face people trusted. Lou smiled and after a few moments the boy's terror subsided.

"Okay, Johnny, ease your way down, one step at a time."

The boy, now completely calm, moved one foot onto the next steel rung. Lou willed him down bit by bit, until he'd inched his way to the entrance of the tiny engine car. He slipped inside, as though returning to his mother's womb.

At six feet four inches and physically fit from his army days, Lou lowered himself down after the boy effortlessly. His close-cropped hair, square jaw, and finely shaped head accentuated his muscular physique. But now, Lou's own secret demons grabbed him by the throat. He took a deep breath, gritted his teeth, and wormed his way into the cramped engine gondola. He found it stifling and hard to breathe once inside.

The engine car was a tiny pod, housing one of the six ear-splitting Sunbeam Cossack III 350-horsepower engines. It was the engineer's little haven, smelling of oil, petrol, exhaust fumes, sweat, and sometimes urine. The massive engine generated suffocating heat and took up most of the eight-by-twelve foot space.

On two sides, small portholes allowed light in during the day. Overhead was a light for night-time use. The engineer sat on a small bench keeping vigil over the engine gauges, waiting for instructions from the control car—the telegraph bells would ring while the pointers moved from *IDLE* to *SLOW* to *MEDIUM* or to *FULL POWER,* depending on the captain's whim. Lou entered as Johnny was stuffing plasticine in his ears, the only protection for the eardrums against the deafening roar. Lou patted Johnny on the shoulder.

"Okay, Johnny, you'll be fine. I'll come and get you later," he shouted, knowing Johnny would have to lip-read. The boy gave a half-smile, mouthing a weak 'thanks.'

Lou and the engineer, whom Johnny had relieved, climbed back up the ladder into the hull to be greeted by Fluffy, the ship's long-haired tabby. She rubbed herself against Lou's leg. He picked her up and nuzzled her affectionately.

"Fluffy, you know you're my best girl, don't you?" he said.

He put her down and she ran to her own sheltered spot off the main walkway. On the subject of girls, he suddenly thought of Julia. He hadn't really thought much about her. He'd met plenty of girls in England and been pursued by many, but none had taken his fancy. It'd be nice to see Julia again soon.

Charlotte stepped out onto the hospital entrance porch, pulling her cape around her shoulders. She gave the surrounding area a quick glance—something she did instinctively nowadays. The coast was clear. As she crossed the street toward the waterfront, she stared at the patchy blue sky overhead. It should remain pleasant for a while, though chilly. She eyed dark clouds in the distance which were moving closer.

Charlotte decided to go for a short stroll along the promenade, as she sometimes did on summer evenings. She had no reason to be in a hurry—nothing and no one to rush home to. Her calling was caring for the sick, which she did with dedication. A walk would do her good and help her relax after a hard day.

Workers from the Macey Brothers' factory, makers of fine furniture and mattresses, poured into the street through rusty iron gates, many on bicycles. She studied them. They appeared pathetic, with not many young men among them. Those she saw were disfigured, or had limbs missing. There were a few fourteen and fifteen-year-old boys. They wore cloth caps, jackets, and trousers in similar drab colors. Charlotte felt sorry for them. The bustling crowd was mixed with a higher percentage of women of all ages, their heads wrapped in headscarves tied like turbans.

These poor wretches are trying to get back to a normal life after that bloody awful war—that's if you call living without a son, a brother, a husband, or a father, 'normal'!

These thoughts made her tremble and her eyes moist with tears. She dare not let herself dwell on all that. It was like pulling off a scab. She preferred numbness. She tried to concentrate on the work done to the waterfront as part of a post-war beautification project: new paved walkways and small cherry trees planted with protective metal shields around them. She ambled along the docks toward Victoria Pier with hundreds of others, enjoying the last of the evening sunshine. There was much activity on the river, with work boats being moored at the quay alongside rusty freighters from Holland, Belgium, and as far away as Australia and New Zealand. Charlotte often saw dockers unloading wool, dairy goods, and frozen lamb.

She walked on, leisurely glancing at the tugboats lumbering toward the dock to be moored, their wakes shimmering behind them. Men aboard vessels and on the docks, in grimy dungarees and rubber boots, tended mooring lines and checked everything was secure for the night. They took no notice of passers-by—until their eyes fell on Charlotte. Then their faces lit up and they called out to her.

"Hello, my lovely. You're looking beautiful this evening."

"She's a corker, all right!"

"Oh, to be thirty years younger!"

"What a little smasher!"

They were cheeky, older men, but she didn't mind their harmless flirting. She'd got to know many of them by sight and attended to some of them after accidents on the wharf. She stopped for a minute and peered out across the river at Fanny's husband and son in their rowboat. Lenny was telling the boy to pack up while Billy protested and sulked. Charlotte smiled when Lenny relented. He sat back and lit another one of his Woodbines, snapping his steel lighter shut. He took another drag and blew out the smoke, while Billy went on fishing.

Charlotte thought about the young men she'd known. Though she'd received many proposals, there'd been nothing serious—well, not really. There'd been the encounter with Robert of course; unforgettable, though fleeting. That was an era she'd erased from her mind, with memories too painful and difficult to share—though the brief meeting with Robert had been a pleasant one. That period had changed her life forever, but she couldn't bear to think about it or allow it to be mentioned. Did she regret it? No. She'd do it all again.

Her mind returned to the future and available men. The thought of one, made her wince. Jessup! He'd caused her, and her family, so much trouble—indeed the whole village. After reading up on the subject in medical journals, she realized now he was a psychopath. Her parents had tried to warn her, but she always tried to see the good in people, or to save the bad. She'd found out the hard way. He was obsessive and had a dreadful mean streak, especially after he'd been drinking. She'd gone out with him for only two weeks after her return to the village; that was all it took. Since then—for the last two years—he'd stalked her relentlessly.

God, how I hate him!

But she'd had worse things in life to deal with and she'd survive *him*. She needed to meet someone nice, but choice was practically non-existent. Charlotte knew Americans to be respectful and well-mannered, having been approached by many, but she'd steered clear to avoid complications.

Most of them are out for a good time. And who can blame them?

Charlotte thought if you met a sincere one, what good would that be? He'd soon be gone, back to Grand Rapids or Cincinnati, or some other place with an exotic-sounding name. No, they were not for her, as good-looking and manly as many of them were—and she had to admit, some looked gorgeous in uniform. But most of all, thinking back, she always remembered their sad, pleading eyes.

She'd leave the heartbreak and the muddles to the other girls in Howden and Hull with no common sense. There were girls who'd married after a whirlwind romance. Charlotte realized some might get lucky, but wondered what the chances were of those relationships lasting. They might hate America when they got there. Then what?

No, Charlotte Hamilton will not fall into that trap—better to be an old maid, dedicated to the sick, than endure the plight of those silly fools.

Lou set off down the catwalk behind Fluffy. He went through the officers' dining area and control room, and descended the polished mahogany steps into the control car where Flight Sergeant Walter Potter awaited him. Potter, a gentle soul, had spent a lot of time these past months mentoring the

Americans, including Lou. He reminded Lou of Stan Laurel, the Englishman of the Laurel & Hardy duo who'd made dozens of hilarious short films. At times, his bland face made him appear dazed and befuddled, though he wasn't in the slightest. He made Lou laugh, especially when he played his accordion for the crew during lighter moments. He pumped the bellows, while his fingers glided over the buttons and keys, his face expressionless, except for those smiling eyes. They'd become fast friends.

The mood was somber, more so than before. As Lou entered, everyone briefly nodded in his direction. The American captain, Commander Maxfield, stood stiffly beside Commodore Maitland, the most senior man on the ship and in control of the tests. He appeared pretty relaxed.

That good ol' British stiff upper lip.

The commodore glanced at the clock—it was now 17:11 hours (5:11 p.m.).

Flt. Lt. Wann, the British captain, was positioned between two coxswains. The three officers stood silently, their eyes on the horizon. Lou sensed tension among them.

The windows wrapped around the control car, providing an excellent view. In the distance, ten miles off, Lou could see the City of Hull, a sprawling mass of factories, docklands, freight yards, offices, shops, and homes clustered along the river estuary toward the east.

The control car, about thirty feet long by twelve feet wide, had been finished in varnished mahogany similar to a ship's bridge. From the exterior, it looked like a tramcar on a city street.

The height coxswain stood at a console facing the starboard side. He controlled the altitude of the ship with a turn of the silver wheel in front of him. Lou checked the altimeter above the coxswain's head. It read: 2,500 feet. Everything appeared normal.

The helmsman stood at a similar wheel at the front, near the windows, facing forward. He controlled the rudders, which steered the ship. Both coxswains were American, dressed in white crew-neck sweaters, navy blue trousers, and white soft-soled shoes. A British coxswain stood beside each man, monitoring his activities and coaching him. They, in contrast, wore drab, blue boiler suits and grubby, black shoes.

A battery of telegraphs mounted on the port sidewall was for sending orders to the engine cars beneath the hull. From these, instructions were issued to the engineers controlling each of the six engines. Lou was always fascinated when he entered the control car. The behemoth was controlled from this room—'the bridge'—his favorite place. If the weather was clear, visibility was excellent for 360 degrees with the engine cars in full view in front and behind, their propellers a blur. Lou wondered if anyone in the control car had noticed the incident earlier with Johnny frozen on the ladder. The commodore turned and addressed Lou, surprising him. Lou had begun to think he and Potter had become invisible.

Typical of these Brit officers. Stuck up bunch!

"Chief Coxswain, do you have a report from Mr. Bateman?"

In U.S. parlance, Lou was called a chief petty officer, but the commodore used British terminology.

"Yes, sir. I spoke with Mr. Bateman fifteen minutes ago."

"And?"

"He said the elevator and the rudder cabling gear are working fine now, sir."

"Good," the commodore said, although he didn't appear the least bit happy.

The American captain, Cmdr. Maxfield, stood with his jaw clenched, his lips screwed tightly together.

"These tests have been woefully inadequate, but ..." the commodore began.

"We have our orders, sir," Capt. Maxfield interjected.

"I'm not happy with this situation. I cannot condone shortening these tests—it's a grave mistake."

The American captain didn't reply. Lou was taking note.

Something's not right here.

"We'll start in fifteen minutes," the commodore said. They glanced at the clock on the wall. "That will be at 17:20. We'll come in over Hull on our present course and head out to the middle of the estuary where we'll turn sharply to the north. That will be your salute to the city."

"Yes, sir," Capt. Wann said. He'd been relaying the commodore's orders for the past few hours.

The commodore turned to Lou. "Chief Coxswain ... I'm sorry, your name again?"

"Remington, sir."

"Ah yes, forgive me. Remington, go and quiet down the crew—*both crews*. Put *everybody* on high alert. Station men at fifty-foot intervals throughout the ship. Give them the task of watching for any structural deformity or weakness. Tell them to sound the alarm immediately if they spot the slightest abnormality or sign of failure. Tell them this is the last test and it will be more rigorous than the speed trials we've done."

"Yes sir."

"Report back when everyone's at their stations."

"Yes sir!"

Lou and Potter went straight to the mess. The men, still in a buoyant mood, fell silent as they entered. Everyone gathered around while Lou relayed the commodore's instructions. He did his best not to alarm them, but he needed them to be vigilant.

"Is all that clear, men?" They were unable to conceal their anxiety. "The good news is—this will be the last test." Lou glanced at the American faces. "After this, we get to go home!"

A weak cheer went up.

"All right!" Josh, the Californian, hollered.

"Thank the Lord for that!" a Brit shouted from the back.

Lou and Potter marched up the catwalk with the crewmen, positioning a man every fifty feet, with orders to 'hold on tight.' Along the way, the cat came out to greet Lou, hoping for more attention. Lou picked her up and thrust her into the arms of the sixteen-year-old cabin boy from Louisiana.

"Here, Gladstone, put her in the oil storage room out of the way." Gladstone usually took care of her.

Lou and Potter returned to the control car. "All crewmen are at their stations and on high alert, sir," Lou announced. The three uniformed officers remained grim-faced.

"Then let us proceed with the final test," the commodore said with cool detachment. "We'll make this a tough one. If she survives this, I promise you, she'll survive anything you'll meet over the Atlantic. I absolutely refuse to release an unproven ship into the hands of a green crew."

The American captain didn't respond and Lou wondered what he was thinking. All afternoon, he'd been haunted by the sensation that something was wrong.

Charlotte turned back from her walk along the waterfront and headed toward Victoria Pier. The droning airship in the distance caught her attention. She had an inherent dread of airships. German Zeppelins had bombed Hull during the war, striking terror into the local population. She pulled her cape tightly around her shoulders. The temperature was dropping.

Those horrible things give me the creeps!

When she'd reached her starting point, Charlotte noticed the children still playing cricket and jump rope in the hospital side street. An ominous black shadow swept down the road and over the kids. One girl screamed with delight when she looked up and spotted the airship. As it sped away over the river, Bobby's message tube floated down on its tiny parachute and fell at her feet. She scooped it up and began to run. A boy at the lamppost dropped his bat while the other girl bundled her infant brother into a battered pram. Together, they all dashed helter-skelter for the river, the baby bouncing and giggling along the way. Charlotte turned her attention toward the water when she heard Billy out in the rowboat, yelling to his father, who was laid back, smoking another Woodbine. Billy had leapt to his feet and was pointing at the sky, almost rocking them both into the water.

"Oh look, Dad, an airship!"

"Sit down! Sit down!" the boy's father shouted as he tried to steady the boat.

All around, city folk stood frozen, as though in a trance. Windows opened on upper stories and people stuck out their heads, hands shading their eyes, dazzled by the sun's last gleam. People emerged from shops and offices and raced for the waterfront. Charlotte got caught up in the excitement and found herself on the pier surrounded by the scruffy, breathless kids. Everyone watched the sky.

"Eee, loook at that! It's looovely in't it!" the girl with the pram exclaimed.

In the control car, the commodore calmly issued his first order.

"Full power all engines, Captain Wann."

"Full power all engines," the English captain repeated.

He leaned over and rang the telegraphs and moved six levers on the control panel to 'FULL POWER.' The trainee American engineers in the engine cars would be waiting for this signal, ready to move the throttle levers gently forward as Potter had trained them to do. Lou worried about New York Johnny, the kid who'd cracked earlier. He hoped he was coping all right down in engine car No.1. The engine notes changed to a full-throated roar. Anxiety showed in the officers' eyes. The British and American coxswains exchanged worried glances.

To the crowd, the change in engine note was like a signal. Something was about to happen; a bit of a show perhaps. People on Victoria Pier chattered excitedly above the airship's droning Cossacks. The five gossiping nurses from whom Charlotte had escaped twenty minutes earlier, now joined her. She gave them a dirty look.

Don't you dare embarrass me!

"It's here. It's here! Oh, it's so beautiful," Minnie yelled.

"My Bobby's in that airship," Elsie shouted proudly.

"And my Jimmy, too! We're getting married in America next year," Minnie announced. People turned and smiled, happy for her.

"Oh look, she's flying the American flag," Elsie said pointing to the tiny Stars and Stripes fluttering on the tail. Excitement was building.

"Look how she sparkles in the sunshine!"

"Like a diamond."

"Incredible!"

"Makes yer so proud, don' it!"

"My Bobby told me the airship might fly over this evening to say goodbye," Elsie told the crowd.

People began cheering and madly waving up at the ship. Shouts went from one to another along the waterfront like a recurring echo.

"She's come to say goodbye. She's come to say goodbye!"

Aboard the airship, the commodore issued his second order.

"Reduce altitude to fifteen hundred feet."

Capt. Wann instructed the height coxswain, "Reduce altitude: fifteen hundred feet."

The bow dipped dramatically and the ship gathered speed, aided by gravity. Lou focused on his American skipper, sensing the man's apprehension. His eyes were darting back and forth, from the scene outside, to the instruments, to the coxswains. Lou thought of Bateman, who he'd left minutes ago in the stern cockpit studying the movement of the gigantic elevators and rudders.

The ship flew directly over the city, Welsh slates on rooftops and brick chimneys in plain view. As they raced toward the river, Lou saw factory workers, shop people and office workers running in the streets. Some stopped in their tracks, staring up in wonder as the ship sped toward the estuary. When the commodore gave his third and final order, an uneasy frown passed over the American captain's face.

"Rudders—fifteen degrees to starboard."

"Additional fifteen degrees to starboard, sir."

Capt. Wann watched the rudder coxswain rotate his wheel to implement the radical turn. The compass needle moved rapidly. Alarm and disbelief registered in the American captain's face. The ship, traveling at considerable speed, began a sweeping turn over the estuary, followed by the eyes of thousands on the ground.

Charlotte turned to check on the children, who'd instinctively gathered around her. A small, black Austin came skidding to a halt at the curb and two men jumped out—one in naval uniform, built like a little bull, the other a rotund, lumbering man, about five feet ten. The fat one, unable to keep up with his companion, yelled after him. Charlotte couldn't hear what he was saying above the crowd as they rushed onto the pier.

To the spectators, the airship was an extraordinary sight—a futuristic fantasy, but to these two men, the display clearly meant much more. Although his breathing was labored, the fat man's voice became audible as he stumbled closer.

"Hell, he's giving her a hammering!" he shouted in a broad Scottish accent.

They rushed up and stood close to Charlotte and the children.

"Nah! She can take it, Mac," replied the little bull.

"I don't like it, Scottie. It's bloody suicide! She's not built for this— you know she ain't."

Charlotte took her eyes off the airship and glared at both men. She didn't like that kind of language in front of children, but the desperate anxiety in the fat man's face struck her and she too, became alarmed.

High above them in the control car, the officers gripped handholds on the walls and ceiling. The coxswains clung to their wheels, but the commodore remained cool. Suddenly, a deep, vibrating boom reverberated throughout the ship, like the snapping of a great steel string on a giant bass instrument. Every man felt the awful jolt through their feet and hands.

"What the hell's that?" the American captain shouted.

The rudder coxswain spun his wheel without resistance, shrieking in panic, his face ashen. "Rudder's gone, sir!"

The ship was now in mortal danger. Terror showed in every face, including the commodore's. "Rudder cable's parted," he shouted. "Cut power to all engines!"

The American captain turned and screamed at Lou, "Remington—look to your crew!"

"Aye, aye, sir!" Lou replied over his shoulder as he and Potter raced up the stairs. When they reached the catwalk above the control car, crewmen clamored for answers.

"What happened, sir?" Josh, yelled.

"We've lost the rudders. Get your parachutes on, all of you."

On the pier, Charlotte and the children beside her gazed up at the airship, mesmerized. But then, almost in slow motion, a crease formed in its side, aft of the midsection, behind the control car. With a deep, sickening feeling in pit of her stomach, Charlotte realized she was about to witness something terrible.

"Oh, bloody hell!" Scottie groaned.

The crease grew into a diagonal crack at first, and then a gaping black hole, running from the top to well behind the control car. The five nurses screamed hysterically.

"Aaaaah no!"

"Bobby! Bobby!"

'My Jimmy! My Jimmy!'

"It's breaking! It's breaking!" the children sobbed.

The crowd wailed as the two ends of the airship sagged downwards, the whole thing splitting open like a massive dinosaur egg. Suddenly, a huge explosion knocked the crowd to the ground. Flames and black smoke burst from the opening, and equipment, gas tanks, ballast tanks and men on fire tumbled from the envelope into the sky.

"Sweet Jesus save them!" yelled the fat man as he went down.

When the airship began to separate, Lou was standing twenty feet forward of the breaking point, close to one of the parachute racks. He grabbed the last parachute and held on to it. He'd put it on when he got a chance. Inside the ship everything was carnage and chaos. Struggling to keep his feet, he watched the writhing ship violently pulled apart by invisible forces—its cables and guy wires wrenched from their anchor points like sinews from a chicken's leg. They whipped around with lethal ferocity, decapitating Al Jolson, dismembering many, and lashing the faces and torsos of others—not a soul was left unscathed. Lou received a deep gash down the right side of his face. The dreadful creaking, moaning, and groaning of the steel girders sounded like a prehistoric creature in her death throes.

Wildly sparking electric cables were ripped from their sockets and pipes carrying fuel to the engines broke apart, dousing crewmen who rushed blindly like madmen in all directions. The gasoline erupted, followed by the first hydrogen gasbag. With an ear-splitting explosion, dozens of men enveloped in orange flame were blasted into the sky from the airship, now almost completely severed in two. Lou, Potter and Josh were in the blazing front section. The rear half hadn't yet caught fire, but Lou expected it would very soon.

With blood pouring from his wound, saturating his white jersey, Lou watched the cabin boy rush past him, trying to hold on to the terrified Fluffy. When the explosion came, the cat broke free, leapt the divide, and raced off toward the stern. The screaming cabin boy was blown off the catwalk, falling forty feet through the girders into the sky toward the raging river below.

The canvas cover—much of it on fire—made tearing and popping sounds as it was ripped off like paper. The rushing wind fanned the flames enveloping injured men. Now ablaze like flaming torches, crazy with fear and pain, they ran wildly up and down the catwalks, screaming. Inevitably, each one hurled himself out into the sky toward the icy water. Powerless to help, Lou watched his men perish all around him. Numb to his own physical pain, he felt as though his heart was being ripped from his chest.

As the gap widened between the two halves, something told Lou to make the leap to the other side. He did. Potter was right behind him. They heard a yell as Josh made a running leap. He barely made it before the gap widened and the front half broke away, leaving him clinging to a girder in space. Lou spotted Elsie's boyfriend, too frightened, and now too late, to make the jump. Lou threw his parachute to him.

"Put this on, Bobby!" he yelled.

Bobby caught it and struggled to put it on. Two more attempted the leap, but the gap had become too wide. They fell to their deaths. Josh, still clinging on, turned his head away in horror. Lou lay down and held on to the ship with his left hand and grabbed Josh's outreached hand with the other. Below them, he saw the control car, itself ablaze, separate from the plunging front section and veer off, cart-wheeling in the air. For a split second, Lou thought of the men inside, where he'd been only minutes ago. He noticed the engine pod on the port side—the engineer had managed to get out and was clinging to the struts.

Must be New York Johnny.

His chances looked slim. As Lou mustered the strength to pull Josh up, a girder collapsed, trapping and breaking his left arm. Adrenalin, or a miracle, allowed Lou to haul Josh up to a point where, with help from Potter, he was able to scramble onto the catwalk. Josh and Potter pulled up on the girder, releasing Lou's arm. Lou winced as they lifted him to his feet. Nausea and dizziness swept over him.

On the waterfront, spellbound spectators witnessed the disaster unfolding. Charlotte cried as she tried to comfort the distraught children beside her, while the five nurses clung to one another sobbing uncontrollably. The crowd had become as one in shock and sorrow. The fat man gasped in anguish and closed his eyes, at breaking point.

"Oh, dear God, what have they done?" he cried.

"My Bobby," Elsie whimpered, her face screwed up in anguish.

Another, more powerful detonation knocked the crowd to the ground for a second time. An eerie silence followed after the engines, starved of gasoline, sputtered and quit. All that could be heard now were heartbreaking cries of falling men, echoing over the water, crashing glass dropping from shattered windows across the city, and moaning, weeping people in the crowd.

The second explosion had also occurred in the front half of the ship —the rest of the gas bags exploding in a massive chain reaction. Lou, Potter, and Josh stood at the opening as the blazing front section fell away. Now without hydrogen buoyancy, the severed section fell like a rock with men in flames falling out or throwing themselves out, while the lucky ones, apparently unhurt, floated down in parachutes (one of them, Bobby). But luck is a fickle mistress; large swaths of the river were afire, blazing with gasoline spilled from ignited storage tanks. On Victoria Pier, people lay on the ground, as though dead.

Lou and his two crewmen made their way to check more parachute racks. They were all gone. Close by, an English crewman wearing a parachute was getting ready to jump. Two Americans watched with envy. The man hesitated, taking pity on them.

"Come on, you Yanks. Grab on to me," he hollered.

They rushed to him and wrapped their arms around him.

"Hold tight, boys!"

As they were about to jump, one panicked. "I can't swim! I can't swim!"

"Don't worry, I got you, mate," the Englishman shouted.

All three jumped into space. Lou was skeptical, not sure they'd made a wise decision. At least for now, this half of the airship hadn't caught fire. Lou and his two companions held on, watching the threesome descend. The chute suddenly burst open, breaking their freefall with a jerk, dislodging the non-swimmer. The screaming man fell and splashed into the black water.

Lou stepped back from the opening, wincing and clutching his arm. He looked up at the remaining part of the ship and flapping gas bags. For now, they had hydrogen and therefore, lift—too much lift! All around them, the wind howled. The remains of the outer fabric cover fluttered and loose parts of the structure chattered and vibrated.

"D'ya think she's gonna blow, Lou?" Potter asked, his face dead-pan as usual.

"No—but we're ascending," Lou said, pulling a switchblade from his pocket.

"Damn! You're right," Potter gasped, noticing they were coming up into higher cloud.

"Take this knife and slash the gas bags and open the valves—quickly!"

"I've got a knife," Potter said. Josh pulled out a similar one.

"Good, go help him, Josh," Lou said. "Meet me at the stern cockpit —there may be some parachutes there," Lou said, putting the knife back in his pocket.

Lou held his throbbing arm, and moved carefully along the catwalk, leaving a trail of blood. On the way, he found a thick rope, from which he cut a piece and fashioned a sling. When he got to the stern, Bateman had disappeared, but Fluffy stood on his seat snarling and spitting—her eyes blazing, her back arched in fury. There were no parachutes.

Lou heard someone yelling from outside the cockpit. He cautiously peered over the side where Bateman dangled precariously in space. Lou figured he'd thrown on his parachute in blind panic and hurled himself overboard, his lines hopelessly tangled with the hooks and ropes in the cockpit. Lou leaned over and, with his good arm, pulled the terrified man back on board. The badly shaken Bateman sank down onto the bench seat, shaking his head. They looked up at the rudder swinging freely from side to side.

"Oh, Lou, am I glad to see you, my friend."

"I told you I'd come back, didn't I?"

Lou's relief was mixed—their section of the ship was now *sinking* toward the flaming river. Below them, men with parachutes were descending into the inferno, their chances of survival poor. Lou thought he and the others would probably suffer the same fate.

Better we take our chances here than to be blown out over the North Sea.

On Victoria Pier, everyone struggled to their feet again. Charlotte helped Scottie pull Mac up from the ground. All eyes were glued to the front half of the ship, now a speeding fire ball, heading in their direction. *They* were the ones in danger now. The crowd stampeded toward the road.

One of the girls grabbed her infant brother from the pram and ran off with the other children and screaming nurses. Charlotte got knocked sideways into Scottie and Mac by the rushing mob and all three landed on the ground in a heap yet again. The flaming front half hit the water just short of the dock, spewing more bodies and gasoline into the river and sending a cascade of dirty water over the unfortunate ones still on the pier. The children managed to get clear and stood motionless in the middle of the road with the dazed, weeping nurses.

The river was blazing immediately in front of Charlotte and far out across the estuary. She stood dripping wet, while the parachutists, thought to be safe, dropped into the sea of flames. She watched her friend's husband and son as they clung to their upturned rowboat, not far from the fiery wreck. If they escaped being burned alive, they'd soon die of exposure in the icy river. Minutes later, she saw the rear half of the ship splash down in a flame-free area to the north, but it was soon caught in the clutches of the outward rushing tide. She wondered if anyone was inside.

Charlotte, Scottie, and Mac left the pier, which was strewn with the remnants of panic: shoes, clothing, newspapers, handbags, broken eyeglasses and the kid's pram on its side. They hurried along the wharf in the direction of the infirmary and boats tied up at the dock. They stopped for a moment, not quite knowing what to say. As is common at such times, a bond had developed between them. Storm clouds, accompanied by lightning flashes and rolling thunder had moved closer, adding to the misery. Smoke drifted across the river toward them and raindrops began to cut through the petrol-laden air mixed with burnt odors, which Charlotte pushed from her mind.

Mac spoke first. "What's your name, miss? I'm Fred McWade and this is Major Scott."

"Nurse Charlotte Hamilton."

"You're going to be busy, Nurse Hamilton," Scott said.

"Yes. I must get back to the infirmary."

"Come on, Mac, let's jump into one of these boats," Scott said, eyeing the boatmen along the wharf, already hurriedly untying their mooring lines. Scott called down to them.

"We're airshipmen. Can you take us out there?"

"Come on, guv, climb aboard," one replied.

Charlotte pointed toward the river. "Sir, please hurry and get to the boy and his father—look—clinging to their boat. They're my best friend's family."

Fanny came rushing up. "Oh, help me, help me, I beg you," she pleaded and then with a sob, "It's me 'usband, Lenny, and Billy, me little boy."

"All right, we'll get 'em," Scott said. He pulled out a silver hip flask and gulped down a couple of good mouthfuls before they rushed off down the quay. Charlotte sympathized—any man would need a drink to cope with scenes they were about to encounter. She put her arm around Fanny's frail shoulders as they watched the two men climb aboard an old rusty riverboat.

"Don't worry, love, they'll save them. Come on. Let's sort these kids out."

They went to the children who were standing in the road crying and soaking wet.

"Come on, let's get your pram. Your mum and dad will be worrying about you."

"We ain't got no dad, miss," one girl said, holding a message tube tightly to her chest.

"What's that you've got there, dear?" Charlotte asked.

"It cooome down from airship, miss. I picked it ooop 'ere int' street."

Charlotte recognized the name on the tube in large letters:

ELSIE POSTLETHWAITE C/O Hull Infirmary.

"You'd better give it to *me*, love," Charlotte said, gently removing it from the girl's grip. "Don't worry, I'll see she gets it. I promise."

After retrieving the old blue pram from the pier and sending the kids home, Charlotte and Fanny headed back to the infirmary. Charlotte expected it'd be a long night and though she felt shocked and heartsick she'd steal herself to do her job. She'd seen worse.

Charlotte left Fanny with Matron and hurried to the staff room to dry off. There was no sign of Elsie. After that, she headed to the ward to get instructions. Once there, Charlotte, together with nurses and patients wrapped in blankets, gathered at the windows, watching the awful scene on the river—dozens of boats of all sizes had joined the search for survivors. She breathed a sigh of relief, seeing Scott and McWade had pulled Lenny and son, Billy, to safety. Their boat was now moving toward the middle of the estuary to assist in the search.

The rear half of the airship had landed on the water, raging and rushing toward the sea. At first, it was swept along, bobbing and rolling in the waves, but at the river bend it beached itself on a sandbar. Potter and Josh laid Lou on some blankets near the open severed end of the broken ship. He'd lost a lot of blood. They strapped up his broken arm with strips torn from bed sheets from the still-intact crew berths and gave him a wad to stave the bleeding from the gash to his face.

Josh, Bateman, and Potter, with the cat in his arms and his accordion slung over his back, stood next to Lou, surveying the hellish scene. Swirling red fires blazed on the surface and columns of black smoke rose from piles of twisted wreckage. Menacing clouds continued to close in and the smell of death permeated the air. The southwesterly winds carried the stench across the city.

A hundred yards away, the control car floated on its side, its fire extinguished. Lou presumed the occupants were trapped inside. A rescue boat had turned up to investigate and men were pulling someone out through a window. They couldn't see who it was. Lou and Potter exchanged grim looks. As soon as the man had been extracted, the control car rolled over and sank.

Lou looked across at Potter's accordion and spoke in nonsensical monotones. "Will you teach me to play that thing, Walt?"

Potter looked at him strangely. "Course I will, sir."

But it was a promise he'd never keep, and one Lou would soon forget, at least, for now.

"Look!" Josh exclaimed. A boat was heading in their direction. Within a few minutes, it maneuvered alongside and one of the crewmen threw them a line. Lou recognized Maj. Scott and Inspector McWade from his Cardington days. He'd spoken to McWade a few times—a gruff Scotsman. Scott was legendary. Bateman and Josh helped Lou into the boat, where they eased him into a sitting position.

"Any more men aboard?" the riverboat captain asked.

"Just us, I'm afraid," Bateman answered.

"You boys were bloody lucky!" Scott barked.

"Aye, that you were. Didn't even get your feet wet," McWade said.

The boy and his father from the rowboat were sitting down below, wrapped in blankets. Once on board, Fluffy wriggled from Potter's arms and ran below to the boy. The boat moved off and made for the wharf, checking for life among the floating bodies, some mutilated beyond recognition, many tangled in parachutes. Scott took another swig from his flask. Lou remembered how relieved he'd felt for his crewmen when the "lucky ones" had leapt from the dying ship in the last of the parachutes. Then he spotted Bobby. Like many others, he was burned and covered in oil, but one side of his face was clean and recognizable. He'd managed to get Lou's parachute on.

Fat lot of good it did him! And so much for his marriage proposal.

Lou recognized another victim: New York Johnny, not so badly damaged. He'd appeared so serene and peaceful when he'd last seen him on the ladder. He had the same look about him now. Near him, Gladstone, the cabin boy, lay on his back, his skin as black and shiny as the river. He, too, appeared strangely at peace.

The boat made its way to the wharf and they put Lou, barely conscious, on a stretcher and carried him across the road to the infirmary. The other three survivors along with the young fisherman and his dad, followed.

The six survivors rescued by Scott and McWade wound up on one of the wards cleared of patients ready to accept injured airshipmen. Charlotte had been assigned to the emergency operation by the matron. Her friend Fanny was truly thankful. Billy lay on a bed opposite Lou and kept looking across at him and then at his father on a bed beside him.

Lou, though weak and deathly white, was now fully conscious. His arm had been wrapped and temporary dressings applied to his face and naked torso. They'd each been given a thorough examination by a doctor and it was time for Lou to have the deep gash in his face stitched.

"Your name will be 'Lucky' from now on, sir," Josh said.

"We've *all* been lucky," Potter said.

Charlotte looked at Lou for the first time. She hadn't been paying attention. She glanced at the scars on Lou's upper arm and chest.

"What's all this?" she said.

He nodded to his right shoulder and then down at his chest.

"Belleau Wood … Saint-Mihiel," he answered.

Her face registered no expression, as if she hadn't heard. "Is *that* your name—Lucky?"

"No, it's Lou Remington."

"Lucky Lou!" Charlotte said.

"Those closest call me 'Remy'."

Lou's crewmen appreciated Charlotte's beautiful figure and the long legs that her prim nurse's uniform could not conceal. She leaned in closely to Lou's face, pulling the thread tight, drawing the wound together. When she spoke, Lou felt her warm, sweet breath on his face. He breathed in her lingering perfume.

That scent is heavenly. And my God, so is she!

The distraction helped dull the pain and fill the terrible void in his gut.

"Beautiful perfume," he mumbled, closing his eyes, then becoming immediately annoyed with himself.

"Je Reviens," she said softly.

"Je Reviens," he repeated.

"You're gonna look right manly, with this scar," Charlotte said, her voice husky.

Lou peered into her huge eyes, open wide while she concentrated on her handiwork. For a second, she glanced from the wound and met his eyes, before turning away. He felt a tremor course through his body. If it weren't for her striking blue irises, he would've taken her for Italian or French.

God, she's magnificent and she's totally unaware of me.

And she was. He was just another case.

"She does a beautiful job," Josh said. "How did you learn to stitch like that?"

"Practice," Charlotte replied

"What's your name?" Lou asked.

She pointed to her name badge next to a Red Cross pin. "I suppose you people can read English, can't you?"

Lou squinted at the tiny print on her badge. "Charlotte," he said, nodding with a half smile to himself.

"What's so funny?"

"No—it's my favorite name."

She gave him a disbelieving stare.

"My grandmother's name is Charlotte Remington," Lou said. "You look Italian."

"Black Irish. On my mother's side," Charlotte said. "My grandfather came over to work in the mines."

Charlotte glanced across at Billy who'd been watching and listening to their every word. The boy seemed in awe of Lou. Two orderlies dressed in white arrived at Lou's bedside.

"They're taking you to get a cast put on your arm," Charlotte said.

The orderlies eased Lou into a wheelchair and pushed him out. After the door had swung closed, Potter spoke while Charlotte was gathering up the swabs and dressings.

"If I hadn't stuck with 'im, God knows where I'd be. I'd follow that man anywhere on this earth. God's truth!"

"We *all* owe him, I reckon," Josh said.

Bateman nodded in agreement. Charlotte remained silent. She left the ward sensing Josh watching her as she moved to the door. When she returned, she heard them discussing her behind the curtain. "My God. What a dream that girl is!" the American was saying.

"You might as well take yer eyes off 'er, me old cock. You're wasting your time."

It was Potter, the Englishman, with the rebuke.

"What are you talking about?" the American answered.

"You're looking at Charlotte Remington the Second there, mate."

Charlotte marched past the curtain and glared at them. They gave her a guilty, caught-out look and Josh sighed ruefully. She slid the curtain back roughly against the wall, leaving them no privacy. Charlotte saw Billy was listening intently.

His mother, Fanny, entered the ward. "You and Dad are staying here tonight. We're going to keep an eye on you," she said.

"Oh, that's good," Billy replied.

"Good? You're a funny boy! Snuggle down now. You've had too much excitement, son."

Fanny kissed him and turned to her husband, who was propped up, smoking a cigarette.

"I'm so glad you're all right, Lenny. I don't know what I'd have done if ..."

"Don't you be fretting, Fanny. We're safe and sound, thanks to that major and his Scottish friend."

"Charlotte sent them out to rescue you—God bless that girl!"

Around 2:00 a.m., Lou woke from his nightmare, finding it only too real. His dry mouth tasted of blood and his head throbbed. The cut on his face stung and his arm and shoulder ached. He tried to turn his body, but found it difficult. The smell of burning flesh wafting from the river, hung in the air, tangible and sickly.

In the room's half-light from the windows' glare, he could make out Potter, Bateman, and Josh asleep in their beds. The boy and his father were also dead to the world. The snores rumbled back and forth in unison. It would've been comical if the circumstances weren't so dire. Lenny snored loudly, his lips fluttering as air was expelled with guttural noises followed by long silences, and then spluttering. Answering snores came from down the ward like echoes.

Lou struggled out of bed and hobbled over to the window bumping into a chair, waking Billy. Although night, Lou could see clear across to the other side of the estuary, the river bright with floodlights vividly illuminating search vessels of all types. Some anchored, shone searchlight beams on the dark, fast-running water. Others moved slowly back and forth, scanning the surface. Stationary boats worked on tangled wreckage, trying to dislodge bodies held tightly in its grip. On a tugboat at the wharf, men were unloading covered stretchers, making Lou feel sick. He heard a sound behind him at the door and realized it was *her*. Charlotte came to him at the window. "You need to lie down and get some rest," she whispered. "You've lost a lot of blood."

Lou didn't move. He stood in silence looking toward the river.

"We must have our dead," he said finally. He slowly eased his way back to the bed where he slumped with his head in his hands. "I lost all my men," he said. "I should've done more."

"You did more than enough, I think. The men you saved think you walk on water. You'll feel much better when you get home to America."

"I'm not going home."

"Why ever not?

"I can't go home …not now."

Charlotte stood close to the bed and put her arms around him, holding his head against her breast. She felt his tears on the palm of her hand.

"Hush now. I'm sure you did everything you could. You got three of your mates out, didn't you?"

"Did they bring in any more survivors?"

"They've only found one, so far. The English captain."

"Captain Wann. My God!"

"They said it was amazing," Charlotte said.

"Where is he?"

"In intensive care. He's in a bad way."

"Is he gonna make it?"

She shook her head. "It's very doubtful."

Charlotte gave Lou two sleeping tablets with a glass of water and made him lie down.

She considered for a moment and then said, "One of the girls on the dock picked up a message from the airship. It had one of our nurse's names on it."

"Whose?"

"Elsie …Elsie Postlethwaite."

Lou sighed. "Did you read the message?"

"Yes, I felt I had to, for her sake…"

"What did it say?" But of course, he already knew.

"Marry me and come away. I promise to love you forever. Bobby."

"Did you give it to her?"

"No."

Lou laid his head back and closed his eyes, picturing Bobby holding up the ring box.

"God, it's strange how it goes," he said wearily. He lay still a few minutes, his eyes closed. Charlotte sat watching him. His eyes suddenly opened wide, startling her.

"What the hell's happened to Fluffy?"

"Who's Fluffy?

"The ship's cat. She came back on the boat with us."

"I'll find out what's happened to her. Don't worry," Charlotte said.

He nodded his head thankfully, closing his eyes again. Charlotte sat by the bed holding his hand until he fell asleep. She studied his hand—a strong, beautiful hand. Finally, she reluctantly let it go. She lifted her palm to her lips where his tears had been and kissed it. She stood up and carefully pulled the sheets around him and left the ward. As she left, she noticed Billy wide awake, watching her. He must've seen and heard everything. She put a finger to her lips. He rolled over and went back to sleep. The ward door swung closed behind her.

Damn that little rascal!

Charlotte had been asked to stay on the ward that night, a ward held open with twenty empty beds in case more survivors were brought in. There were none.

She slept on a cot in the nurses' room and two other nurses, one of them Fanny, did the same. In the morning, Charlotte checked on the survivors. They were all sleeping soundly. She then went straight to Mrs. Tilly's bed on her usual ward. Her bed was empty. Charlotte spun around scanning the room—Mrs. Tilly was gone. She knew the old lady had been on her last legs, but it came as a shock. She hurried to the nurses' room where she shed a few tears. Matron found her and sent her back to the ward.

"Get back to your patients. They need you. They all die someday, Charlotte," she said.

2

A COURT OF INQUIRY

May 15, 1922.

A court of inquiry was convened on a warm day the following spring at Howden's court, an old municipal building, far too small for such a gathering. The survivors of the accident attended, with the exception of Josh Stone, who'd been recalled for duty in the United States and Capt. Wann, who'd survived, but not recovered sufficiently to attend.

Lou's face had healed, but the mending of his broken arm had been slow. He sat with Potter and Bateman, also there to give testimony, in the front pew. Lou's companions appeared healthy enough, although they told him they suffered from painful memories and nightmares. It showed.

The stifling courtroom smelled of mildew tempered by cleaning fluid, reminding Lou of his schoolhouse days in Great Falls. It was jam-packed with high-ranking U.S. and British military, government officials, engineers and designers. The whispers and sobs of widows and girlfriends drifted down from the gallery. Maj. Scott sat stony-faced opposite the grieving families. Inspector McWade sat beside him, along with personnel from Cardington's Royal Airship Works, in attendance as expert witnesses. Amongst the hoard of pressmen, Lou recognized George Hunter in his scruffy raincoat. He gave him a nod.

The court rose to its feet as the president of the court, a man with priestly bearing, entered. He was impeccably dressed in a flowing black robe, open at the front revealing an elegant pin-striped suit. He strode to the mahogany desk on the platform and gazed around the room, exuding an aura of omnipotence. He put his hand to his mouth and gently coughed.

"Please be seated," he said.

Everyone obediently sat down. The president remained standing, his face stern, his voice rich—a Cambridge man.

"Good morning, ladies and gentlemen. It is my unpleasant duty to preside over this court of inquiry charged with ascertaining the cause of the tragic accident which occurred on August the twenty-fourth at twenty-seven minutes past five, when His Majesty's Airship *R38*, soon to be re-designated USS *ZR-2*, broke in two and crashed into the River Humber in the City of Hull. On behalf of the court, I wish to express sincere condolences to all those from both sides of the Atlantic who lost relatives and loved ones, colleagues and friends, in this unfortunate event."

The court remained silent, save for the sound of weeping wives and sweethearts who held handkerchiefs to their mouths, trying not to cause disruption. Lou found himself studying his feet. He'd been dreading these proceedings.

"The people of Great Britain are heartbroken over this tragedy which has caused loss of life, not only to our own, but also to our sister nation. This sad event has dealt a terrible blow to the morale and prestige of this country, its military and industry."

During the next four days, Lou listened to the testimony of two dozen expert witnesses, including designers and builders from Howden and Cardington. They discussed problems experienced with the airship during the first test flights. Lou learned much he hadn't known previously, but the questioning appeared to be orchestrated and truth became another casualty. By skilful interrogation, the solicitor general led the court through the events leading up to the accident without really getting to the heart of why the accident happened and how it could have been prevented.

This covered the purchase of the airship by the U.S. Navy for the sum of two million pounds; the design and construction at Cardington; and the arrival of a contingent of American naval airshipmen who were billeted in homes around Cardington and Hull to be trained to fly and maintain the airship, as well as monitor its construction. Lou had been part of that team.

They touched on the early flights only briefly, since the Americans hadn't been allowed to participate, causing a lot of irritation at the time. The subject of "rushing the tests" embarrassed all parties and wasn't dwelt on. Lou didn't have first-hand knowledge concerning this subject, but he and his crewmen realized the ship had not been sufficiently tested.

Lou was sure of one thing: Commodore Maitland hadn't been happy with the tests being cut short. The man had expressed his frustration in Lou's presence. Fierce and irresponsible pressure must have been exerted by both governments to hasten the process.

The three survivors testified at the end of the hearings, Lou being the last. He was to be questioned by the solicitor general, a short, aggressive Yorkshireman with steely, gray eyes and a bald head. Lou got up reluctantly, biting his lip as he buttoned the jacket of his dark blue suit. He marched stiffly across the hushed courtroom to the witness stand, his footsteps echoing on the oak boards. Today, he felt as nervous as New York Johnny. So many people had been waiting to hear Lou's testimony—especially the press —there'd been such a hullaballoo in the newspapers. He was sick and tired of it. Sweating profusely, he delved in his pocket for a handkerchief to wipe his brow, while coughing to loosen the tightness in his throat.

"Good morning, Mr. Remington."

"Morning, sir."

"*Mr.* Remington. Is that how I should address you? I notice you're not in uniform."

"Yes, sir, that'll do just fine."

"You were aboard the airship that afternoon?"

"Yes, sir."

"As an enlisted man?"

"A *senior* enlisted man."

"Not an officer?"

"No, sir."

"What role did you play on the airship?"

"I was chief petty officer, sir. That's similar to chief coxswain over here."

"It sounds like an important job. Were you in charge of a lot of crewmen?"

"That day, ten Americans and twelve British were under my command."

The solicitor general looked surprised. "British, too?"

"Yes, sir. I'd become senior in rank, although still mentored by the British."

Lou could tell by his dubious expression the solicitor general was thinking he'd been in way over his head. "How long had you been a chief petty officer?"

"I was promoted three months before the accident," Lou said.

He didn't much care for the man's tone.

"You're very young—too young, some might say. And I ask you these questions in order to prove your competence—you understand?"

"Perfectly, sir."

"So, prior to your promotion, had you experience in flying airships?"

Lou sensed everyone's eyes upon him, as if they thought he had something to do with the cause of the accident.

"I flew in blimps after the war, sir."

"You joined the Navy, or was it the Army—when?"

"The U.S. Marine Corps in 1914."

"At what age?"

Lou hesitated.

This is complicated.

"Sixteen, sir."

"Sixteen?"

"Yes, on my sixteenth birthday, sir."

The solicitor general frowned.

"What's the minimum age for acceptance into the U.S. Marines?"

"Eighteen, sir."

"How come they accepted you?"

"I lied on my application."

There were looks of surprise and a few raised eyebrows in the courtroom.

"They didn't kick you out?"

"No, they sent me to a special unit."

"They put you on ice, so to speak?"

"Yes, I trained for three and a half years in hand to hand combat and Japanese martial arts, observation and parachute training."

"You must have become a pretty dangerous fellow by that time?"

Lou had become lethal at karate and was on the verge of obtaining his black belt when they shipped him off to war.

"Yes, I became an instructor at Quantico."

Lou glanced up into the gallery and gave a half-smile. He figured someone up there would be paying careful attention.

"They made you a corporal, what the Americans refer to as an E4, before being sent to France in 1918?"

"Yes."

The solicitor general went to the table, poured water into a glass and swallowed a mouthful, pausing to think. He returned to Lou.

"Then after the war, with the rank of sergeant, an E5, you were discharged?"

"Yes."

"What did you do after the war?"

"I joined the Navy, based at Lakehurst, for training in blimps and airships."

"You seem to be a glutton for punishment! Why airships?"

"I thought they were going to be the next big thing, sir."

The solicitor general smirked. "*Cruise ships* in the sky?

Lou smiled faintly. "Yes, I suppose."

"And now?"

"I'm not sure."

The solicitor general peered around the court, searching for a reaction. There was none.

"You came to England when?"

"June, 1920."

"You were based at Cardington during the construction of *R38*?"

"Yes, sir, and then in Howden, after the launching."

"And you've left the Navy?"

"Yes."

"Discharged?"

"Honorably discharged, yes sir."

"Why?"

"I was about to sign on for five more years …"

"And then, this happened. …Are you married?"

"Yes, sir. I am."

"Good. I hope you found a nice, Yorkshire lass."

Lou couldn't help smiling. He peered up into the gallery again, scanning the faces for Charlotte.

"I did, sir."

He spotted her and grinned sheepishly. The solicitor general and everyone else in the court followed his gaze and saw Charlotte smiling down at Lou. Everyone looked happy for a moment.

"I want to say that all of us here in this court congratulate you, not only on your marriage to that lovely girl up there, but on your receiving the Navy Cross. ... You did heroic things that day."

"I did *nothing*, sir."

"Mr. Remington, how many stitches did it take to sew up that gash in your face?"

"Seventy-eight."

"And that young lady stitched you up?"

"She did."

"Most people in court know what you did on that horrible day, but for the benefit of the few who don't, I'll elaborate." The solicitor general turned and addressed the court. "With a cut to your face requiring seventy-eight stitches, you threw your own parachute to one of your desperate crewmen. You led this man ..." he said, pointing at Potter, "... to safety. You pulled Josh Stone, who was hanging on by his fingertips, back on board the airship, which was now torn in two, receiving a severely broken arm in the process. And you then heaved this man ..." pointing to Bateman, "...whom you found dangling from the stern, back on board with your one good arm. No, sir, these actions could not be described as '*nothing*'! We're honored to have you living among us."

Lou wiped his forehead and glanced at the faces. They were all proud of him and one or two people actually shouted and clapped.

"Well done!"

"He's a hero!"

Lou sat shaking his head.

They're all wrong!

The solicitor general paused for the court to take a little pleasure from this moment. Then Lou saw his attitude change back to business. He could tell this lawyer was a skilled and artful interrogator. He'd probably been softening him up. He'd need to keep his guard up.

"Now, going back to the final tests, you and your crew were watching the structure of the ship for signs of weakness. Isn't that so?"

"Yes, sir."

"They told you to *expect* problems?"

"No, but we were instructed to stay alert—keep our eyes open."

Lou glanced around the courtroom. The attention of all was riveted on him. Suddenly, a baby cried out at the back of the court, breaking the stillness. They paused while the young mother in black, soothed the child. Lou glanced at her, and recognized Elsie as one of the nurses from the hospital.

That must be Bobby's child. Poor guy.

"How did you receive this order, Mr. Remington?"

"From the commodore, sir."

This surprised the solicitor general. He put his hand up to his head. Murmurs went up through the gallery. Scott and McWade glanced at one another.

"Really! How so?"

"I'd reported to the control car for instructions."

The solicitor general's eyes opened wide. "You were in the presence of the commodore himself?"

"Yes."

"Did you notice anything abnormal—among the officers, I mean?"

"No, sir. Everything appeared quite normal."

Lou's mind raced back. He remembered the expressions on the faces in the control car.

"Tell the court about the order you were given."

"The commodore said they were due to begin the final test, which would be a tough one. He instructed me to warn the crewmen to be alert and to keep a close eye on all parts of the structure."

"That sounds rather ominous. Did *you* find these tests especially dangerous?"

Lou glanced across at Maj. Scott. He remembered him coming to their rescue on the river estuary. Scott gave him an icy stare. Lou felt ill at ease with these questions. He was torn. He thought of Charlotte and all the English people who'd been good to him over these last months.

They treated me like a son, damn it!

"No. I wouldn't say that."

The solicitor general hesitated, staring out the window toward the quadrangle at the rear of the court. He appeared to be searching for the right words.

"Mr. Remington, there's been a lot of speculation and innuendo in the newspapers about the events of that day. This is a tough question, but one I must ask, I'm afraid. Did you get the impression anyone was trying to impress people gathered at the waterfront with some 'fancy flying'?"

The court fell silent, save for a buzzing sound. Lou gazed up at the clerestory window. A bumblebee was trapped, bumping against the glass. He sympathized with the creature. The droning filled his head, and his mind drifted. He found himself standing in the control car. The tension in the men's faces he'd seen before was now replaced with anguish and horror.

Those expressions—now exaggerated and distorted by months of brooding—seriously disturbed him. He relived the commodore giving him the order and then going up to the crewmen who were waiting for him—waiting to do his bidding, to carry out his orders without question, like faithful dogs! Their trusting faces haunted him. Every damned *day,* they haunted him. Every damned *night* they haunted him. Could he have done more? Could he have done something, *anything*, to save them? His head became full of his own voice, yelling.

When the commodore gave me the order I should have screamed·
"No! No! No! Don't! This damned thing's gonna fall apart!" Any imbecile would've known that—wouldn't they?

Lou remembered the uneasy tightness in his chest as he climbed those stairs.

I just didn't have the guts, damn it! I can never go home. I could
never face their families. I know they'd want to meet me. They'd write and track me down. They'd want a first-hand account of how their sons died. They'd want to know how come I survived while their boys are dead. "What's so damned special about you?" they'd ask.

No longer conscious of anything in the courtroom, Lou heard the American captain shout. *"Remington, look to your crew!"*

Lou put his hand to his throbbing forehead. So many times he'd been woken in the night by the captain's voice out of the darkness. And so many nights Charlotte had consoled him. Lou found himself jarred back from the nightmare by the irritated voice of the solicitor general, his face no longer kindly.

"Mr. Remington. Mr. Remington! Was this about 'fancy flying'?"

Lou glanced up at the clerestory window. The bumblebee was gone.

No question the commodore had made a terrible miscalculation—foolish even, but he wasn't showing off.

"Not at all, sir. It was about a concerned man testing an airship."

The solicitor general's voice became silky—like a blade.

"To destruction?"

"As it happened, yes …to destruction," Lou said softly.

The solicitor general resumed his calm and became chatty. He leaned his elbow on the railing in front of Lou, confiding.

"Did anybody tell you this airship was a copy, an almost *exact* copy of a German Zeppelin 'height climber', not designed to carry out radical maneuvers at low altitude?" He then turned and addressed the U.S. naval officers sitting at the front. *"R38/ZR-2* was a copy of the German *L49* high altitude bomber shot down in France. Those airships were constructed with their weight and strength reduced to get out of the reach of our fighters. In other words, they were *pretty* fragile. So, gentlemen, if you're constructing any more airships, please keep that in mind," he said.

The Americans stared back with faces of stone. He turned back to Lou for a comment. Lou struggled to recover, feeling like he'd been slugged with a baseball bat. He knew they were constructing a sister ship in Lakehurst—*ZR-1*—*Shenandoah*—Josh's ship, another Zeppelin copy!

"Er, I didn't know anything about that, sir, no."

"But you do know now."

"Yes, I do now."

Later, Lou realized he'd been used as a pawn for publicity in British politics by the court and by the press. Although the British had done some calculations, the ship that had come apart had been based on a German Zeppelin not meant to be maneuvered at low altitude in the denser air of the earth's surface, where excessive stress would be put on the ship.

Lou knew her back had broken, pure and simple, due to too much rudder in a diving high-speed turn. He understood now why the officers in the control car had been so tense. But he couldn't bring himself to blame Commodore Maitland. Desperately worried about the testing not being adequate, he'd struggled with the responsibility of sending a 'green' crew off to face the Atlantic in an unproven airship. He'd taken drastic measures to prove the ship's airworthiness—fatal ones, as it turned out. Under the strain of full power and full rudder, it was impossible *not* to break the back of that airship. She'd jackknifed. Lou also knew that this charade, this well-choreographed show, had deflected blame from where it truly belonged and attempted to saddle the commodore with it, but Lou hadn't allowed that. He wondered about the solicitor general—wittingly or unwittingly he'd helped Lou make that possible

After three days of cross examination of eye witnesses, the court was adjourned. Before Lou left, he was surprised to find Scott standing beside him with McWade. They shook hands.

"Major Scott," Lou said.

"Just wanted to thank you for your testimony—and your honesty."

"No problem, sir."

"So, you're sticking around—not going home?"

"No, sir. This is home for me now."

Scott was all ears. "Really! What are you doing?"

Lou hesitated. "I'm working in a garage, pumping gas and fixing trucks."

Scott looked pained. "I see—"

The huge frame of the American commander appeared. Lou brightened on hearing his familiar voice. "Good testimony, Remington," he boomed. Commander Horace Dyer towered over them in dress uniform. He was the most senior officer in charge of the American contingent in Britain. They shook hands.

"Thank you, sir," Lou said.

"I just want to say, as far as the Navy's concerned, the door's always open."

"Kind of you to say, sir."

"We're all gonna be pushing off soon. You should think about coming with us. We'll find you another ship. Bring that beautiful bride with you."

"I'm grateful to you, sir. Maybe one day, but not right now."

Their attention was taken by two grief-stricken, nurses—Elsie and Minnie. Elsie, still rather large, was holding an infant, while Minnie looked ready to give birth at any moment. They waddled by, dabbing their eyes with handkerchiefs, sniffing. Lou pitied them.

"Looks like your boys've been busy," Scott said with a smirk.

"It's a damned shame," Lou said.

"If the silly little cows had kept their drawers on, they wouldn't be in this mess. Maybe you should take them back to the States with you, Commander," Scott said.

"Maybe we should," the commander replied. He turned to Lou and put his hand on his shoulder. "Stay in touch, Lieutenant." He gave a formal nod to Scott. "Major," he said and strode off.

Suddenly, there was a scream. Minnie stood by the door holding on to Elsie. Water poured down between her legs, pooling on the floor.

"Saints preserve us!" Scott muttered in disgust. A few people gathered around Minnie and helped her to a chair out in the reception hall. "Get that woman an ambulance!" Scott yelled.

Someone rushed off to find a phone.

Scott resumed as if nothing had happened. "Look, here's my card. I've heard good things about you. I don't like to see talent go to waste. If there's anything I can do, let me know. The airship industry will survive. Those men were all pioneers. They didn't die in vain. Remember that, son." Scott stuck out his hand again and abruptly marched off with the silent McWade. Lou nodded skeptically as they went.

That's the kind of crap people say at funerals.

Lou knew Charlotte would be waiting outside the courtroom and moved toward the doors. He spotted her from a distance and hesitated for a moment, relishing her beauty. He felt like the luckiest man in the world. He was ridiculously in love and it was mutual, but with the joy came gnawing guilt, which never left him. On seeing Lou, Charlotte's eyes lit up. She came and put her arms around him.

"How are you now, love?" she asked.

"It was all a waste of time."

"You were wonderful. I'm proud of you."

Lou didn't feel so impressed with himself.

"It's over. You can put it all behind you now," Charlotte said.

"That's the end of my Zep days, I guess," Lou said.

"Never mind. Who needs *them!* You've got *me* instead!" Charlotte put her hand to his face, gently tracing the scar with her slender fingers, from his right eye down to his chin. She kissed his mouth tenderly, her lips moist and delicious. While he embraced her, he ran his fingers through the mass of black hair cascading down her back.

"You look so handsome, darling. I told you, you would, didn't I?"

They moved through the reception hall, passing Scott and Cmdr. Dyer who kept glancing in their direction, while deep in conversation. Lou thought nothing of it at the time. Minnie now sat in an old leather chair moaning. Elsie stood beside her, holding her own baby. As Charlotte passed, holding Lou's hand, both women looked at Charlotte, bitterness and envy showing in their weary eyes. Charlotte's face registered a twinge of guilt. Bobby's message to Elsie was still in the drawer at her flat.

Damn! I was only trying to save you more pain, love!

Lou led Charlotte to the curb, where his shiny, black and red Rover motorbike was parked. He kick-started the engine and, after donning their goggles and gloves, they climbed on. Charlotte sat side-saddle hugging Lou tightly around the waist. They drove off hopefully into their shared future, but any contentment Charlotte may have felt was crushed by the sight of Jessup, standing some distance away. He dragged on his cigarette and shot smoke into the air from thick, rubbery lips. Mouthing curses, he glared at Lou and spat on the ground like a cobra spraying venom. He threw the dog-end down, grinding it into the dirt with the heel of his boot. God, she hated him! She wondered if Lou had seen him.

A silly question!

After this awful humiliation, it was vowed 'never again.' The British airship industry came to a complete standstill. Both the government and the public lacked the stomach for these monsters in the sky, unlike the Germans who were making a great success of their own program. And so, the enormous, sheds at Howden and Cardington fell silent and into a state of neglect, overgrown with weeds and ivy ...that is until Brigadier General Christopher Birdwood Thomson came bursting upon the scene.

PART TWO

The Flying Scotsman

SCOTLAND

3

THE BRIGADIER GENERAL & THE FLYING SCOTSMAN

New Year's Eve, December 31, 1923.

Thomson bought a first-class return ticket to Aberdeen at King's Cross Station, costing one pound seven and six pence, money he could ill afford, but it wouldn't be seemly to be seen alighting from a second-class carriage with the future Prime Minister of Great Britain waiting to greet him.

He walked to Platform 10, where each day *The Flying Scotsman* left for Edinburgh at 10 o'clock sharp, stopping in York for a fifteen minute break. He had plenty of time. Dropping in at W.H. Smith, he bought peppermints and two newspapers: The left-leaning *Manchester Guardian* and the conservative *Daily Telegraph*. He liked to read both sides of a story, although he invariably agreed with the *Guardian*.

He strolled down the platform past the carriages—counting eight—until he reached the coal tender and the massive Super-Pacific engine. He looked up at the driver and fireman leaning over the rail in blue boiler suits. The two men stared down at him with sullen indifference.

They'll make disparaging remarks the minute I turn my back, I'm sure.

He lingered while the engine got up steam, admiring the magnificent machine in its traditional apple-green livery and crimson crash bars.

British engineering at its finest! No wonder small boys are fascinated with railway trains.

His mind briefly returned to his Boer War days as a young lieutenant tasked with keeping the railways open for the war effort in South Africa and keeping Kitchener happy. His idle curiosity satisfied, he turned back along the platform and went to his carriage. He climbed into the empty compartment, hoping to remain its sole occupant. He found it torturous to sit for long journeys making polite small talk. Usually, by the end, fellow travelers knew far too much of one's business. Thomson had lots to contemplate, and needed to get his thoughts in order.

Best done in solitude.

After stowing his small suitcase on the overhead luggage rack, he removed his felt Homburg and put it on the seat next to the shabby, leather briefcase. He slipped off his woolen overcoat, folding it with care, though it'd seen better days, and placed it on the rack.

This last morning of December 1923 was damp and chilly, but the carriage was warm enough. It struck him how well appointed trains were nowadays, with corridors leading to the dining car, the bar and the lavatories and even through the coal tender, so crews could be changed without stopping. Transportation fascinated Thomson. This was the Golden Age, not only of fashion, but of luxurious travel by train, by ship, and soon, by air.

Such progress—and so much more to be made, by golly!

The journey to Edinburgh would take eight-and-a-half hours and another two-and-a-half to Aberdeen. He relished it. He'd read his newspapers, write a couple of letters and sit and reflect. He never minded his own company.

Marthe's company is infinitely preferable, of course.

He fished out a peppermint and popped it in his mouth and settled down to scan his newspapers. The price of butter was to be increased by ten percent. A loud blast on a whistle preceded slamming doors. The train lurched forward. No one had entered the compartment at the last moment.

Thank God for that!

He continued updating himself on current events. Both newspapers had run articles summing up the year's political highlights and the recent general election.

Baldwin's Blunder
The Manchester Guardian crowed.

The strategy of calling an election in order to increase the Tory majority had badly backfired. Prime Minister Baldwin already had a substantial majority and the move had been unnecessary.

Stupid fool!

The Conservatives were on the ropes and most likely going to fall. Thomson read the election results in the article, although he knew them by heart:

Tories   258
Labour   191
Liberals 158

If the Labour Party formed a coalition with the Liberals, they'd hold a majority. And with Labour winning more votes, they'd get to choose the leader—almost certainly Ramsay MacDonald—one of three men who'd recently created this new party. Would Labour come to power? That was the question on the nation's mind. Thomson and MacDonald believed their

44 DAVID DENNINGTON

chances were excellent, but nothing in politics was certain. If the Tories collapsed, this would be the first Labour government; a momentous achievement for the radical left—revolution without violence.

The *Guardian* gleefully went on to speculate what Ramsay MacDonald would nationalize and what he might leave alone—the mines and railways being high on the list. Thomson had ideas of his own—the possibilities were infinite, with the sky, quite literally, the limit.

The train sped through St. Albans. Thomson looked up and grimaced. The very name made him squirm. He hated failure. Then, he brightened. If not for St. Albans, he wouldn't be on this train today. He went back to his newspaper. It wasn't long before he was chugging past Cardington toward Grantham through lashing rain. He looked up in time to spot the looming airship sheds in the distance.

To a stranger, at first glance, Christopher Thomson sitting alone next to the window might cut a rather striking figure. A closer look would reveal signs of a man who'd recently been going through hard times—not eating well, not looking after himself, pining for a lost love perhaps. Although his jacket was well pressed, the lapels were threadbare. His face was thin, his cheeks hollow and his close-set, deep blue eyes, which gave the impression of constant scrutiny, were sunken. He stood six feet five, and although slender, his shoulders were broad. His nose, broken by the vicious kick of a horse during a fall, had reshaped his previously symmetrical, angelic face, causing it to have a harsher, granite-like appearance. As a brigadier general, this had only served to enhance his overall demeanor. Under that impressive nose, he had a well-groomed, thick moustache, adding dignity. He could appear menacing when necessary, but congenial, even gentle at times.

Thomson pondered the circumstances bringing him to this point in his life. This was a pivotal moment. He felt certain he'd done the right thing giving up his commission in the Army. During the last twenty-five years he'd reached sufficient heights to satisfy his military ambitions and had played a significant role serving his country. At times, he wished he could do more to improve the lives of others—not a sentiment usually associated with a seasoned brigadier general.

The decision to resign had resulted from his attendance at the Treaty of Versailles as an aide to diplomats of the British delegation. He watched in dismay as European politicians fought over the scraps left after Germany's defeat, a country forced to its knees and made to accept peace terms he thought too harsh.

He decided the time had come to take a stand. He'd witnessed the suffering of people who didn't have the slightest control over their own miserable lives, let alone global events. This damned unnecessary war had been a prime example. 'Lambs led to the slaughter' is what they'd said and in his heart he believed it was a perfect description. He made the decision to enter politics and his journey had begun. The first two years had been a rough ride, in fact, a roller coaster of hellish humiliation.

Leaving the Army after twenty-five years service gave him a stipend of one hundred and fifteen pounds, which he put in his account at Barclays Bank. The grand sum of sixty-four pounds, sixteen shillings and five pence remained. He'd taken a low-priced bedsit in Stockwell, an easy walk to Westminster.

He had a few conservative friends, who thought highly enough of him to get him seated on a panel to advise the government on the wisdom of resuming the airship program. Dennistoun Burney, a director of Vickers Aircraft, had been rigorously promoting a plan for the company to construct six airships to be underwritten and operated by government. Thomson didn't care for Burney's type. A profiteer! The 'Burney Scheme' promoted a program whereby Vickers built *all* Britain's airships—an intolerable situation! Besides, 'state enterprise' would be the wave of the future in the new British Socialist State. Burney's proposal had been accepted by the Conservative Government in principal, although not ratified.

I will certainly put a stop to that!

Thomson pulled out a file from his briefcase which had been passed on to him by Sir Sefton Brancker—a man always in the know, always with one ear to the ground and always ready to help—a bit of a dandy, but a loveable one. The file contained information concerning one Lieutenant Louis Remington, an American airshipman, who happened to be sitting around in Yorkshire doing nothing. "The man might come in useful," Brancker had said, "since we've lost so many of our own people." Thomson glanced at the man's war record. A marine …survived the war …bailed out twice from observation balloons (*that's amazing—I was in observation balloons, too!*) …survived being hit and buried alive for hours in a bunker with twenty-five others …joined the Navy to fly airships …posted to England …survived the *R38* disaster …displayed fine leadership qualities— gave excellent account of himself at the court of inquiry …discharged 1922. Thomson slipped the file back into his briefcase.

If things go well, I'll drop the Secretary of the Navy a line in Washington …or speak to him on the phone, perhaps. Sounds like a useful chap. That other American fellow—Zachary Landsdowne—they said <u>he</u> was a first class fellow when he worked here with us.

Thomson received no salary for serving on the airships panel, but it propelled him into the right circles. Now he needed to get himself elected to Parliament. It came as a surprise to his friends when he chose to join the Labour Party. Many became angry over the betrayal of his own class when he threw in with 'the radical Left.' The road might have been easier had he joined the Tories, but his idealistic notions prevented that.

In truth, Thomson had no real political doctrine or ideology clearly set in his mind. He'd met a few larger-than-life figures in his time, men he had reason to look up to. He begrudgingly admired visionary Cecil Rhodes, but had more in common with Socialists Lenin and Mussolini. Socialism had to be the answer to life's problems and inequalities. He found it seductive.

Thomson put himself up for a seat in Bristol Central. This hadn't been a pleasant experience and he began to question the wisdom of joining this new Labour Party. He went from one committee meeting to another at working men's clubs and women's organizations—all fiercely left wing. The reception he received from party supporters ranged from frigid to downright hostile. They regarded him as one of the enemy, a filthy capitalist, a toff, upper class, or worse, an aristocrat—the very people causing worldwide misery and keeping them down.

He said the words they needed to hear, but delivered in an irritating hoity-toity tone. Often he used words they didn't understand. They jeered and hooted at him, calling him a 'toffee-nosed git.' He couldn't do much about the way he spoke. His deep, gravelly voice made him sound gruff— perhaps too much like the officers who'd ordered men out of their rat-infested trenches into the German guns to die like vermin, to collapse in the mud and filth and left to rot on the endless dumpsite called 'No Man's Land', to later have their bleached bones tilled into the soil like fertilizer. All that, while the senior officers in their fancy uniforms and shiny boots remained in safety well behind the front lines. *They* weren't unwashed and plagued by lice, driven mad by trench foot, sickened by contaminated food and the stench of rotting bodies. That was the way they felt and at the mere mention of the war, they became infuriated and yelled abuse at him.

"Oh, yeah, where were you, then mate, eh? What were you doin' while our lot were dyin' up front?"

Thomson managed to increase Labour's vote count from the last election, although this hadn't been enough to win in that Conservative stronghold. He tried again the following year, putting himself up for a seat in St. Albans. He campaigned hard, said all the right things, but the result was the same. They called him an imposter and a spy. He became demoralized, not used to rejection.

Thomson had always scoffed at politicians, believing them to be a spineless, self-serving lot. Now, he found politics to be a rough business and his respect for its participants grew. Sometimes he questioned his own motives. Was all this really about improving the plight of the downtrodden, or was it more about *her*?

Thomson scratched his head and glanced at the gold watch given him by his mother. An hour had passed. He peered out the window, hoping for an answer in the sopping landscape. The sky had turned dark over what he guessed must be Grantham. In the gloom, his gaunt reflection stared back from the glass. Nagging guilt seized him. He was circumventing the system

—not like him at all. He'd always earned his way—worked for everything he got.

After the crushing defeat in St. Albans, he'd received a letter bearing the Labour Party name with a return address in Lincoln's Inn Fields. It was a short handwritten note from Ramsay MacDonald, leader of the new party, asking him to meet at a tea room at Charing Cross. Thomson knew of it as a place frequented by writers, artists, Fabian Society members and other left-leaning types. Thomson wasted no time writing back.

They met at the café in summer '23. When they shook hands, they took a liking to one another immediately. Everybody knew MacDonald, but here was a new face. Other patrons watched in silence, sensing an important moment. After two or three coffees, they walked along the Thames Embankment. MacDonald told Thomson not to dwell on his election defeats, though he didn't realize it now, his 'baptism of fire' was all to the good; he'd turn out to be a stronger politician.

MacDonald understood the obstacles Thomson had been facing, but there'd be a place for him in the party. He said being surrounded by hot-heads, he needed an ally and a confidante—someone capable of calm, rational thought. An election would be coming soon. MacDonald sensed it in his gut. He urged Thomson to sit tight.

During this time, Thomson served on the airship advisory panel and was befriended by Sir Sefton Brancker, Director of Civil Aviation. Brancker went out of his way to help him, sensing Thomson faced not just financial hardship, but perhaps ruin. He arranged for Thomson to go on a paid speaking tour in Canada, and Thomson gratefully accepted. Thus, another momentous friendship began.

MacDonald's instincts had been right. An election was held December 6, 1923 and the Tories didn't win a clear majority. MacDonald asked Thomson to forgo his visit to Canada and meet him instead at his home in Lossiemouth in the Highlands. Labour's time had come!

The train thundered through Sheffield, then Leeds and on to Doncaster through blinding rain, then toward brightening skies. At ten minutes past two, the train made its fifteen-minute stop in York. Thomson put on his overcoat and paced up and down the platform in the drizzle. He couldn't wait to get to Aberdeen.

Returning to his compartment he took out his fountain pen, and using his briefcase to rest on, made some notes in his bold hand.

        Cardington
        Airships
        Employment
        State Enterprise
        Keep Capitalists (Burney) Under Control

Gov Funding
Links to Empire
Improvement and betterment of mankind

He crossed out the last line.

Too grandiose.

Underneath that, he wrote.

My title?

The train rushed through the counties of Yorkshire and Durham toward the border, where it traveled the long viaduct and over the River Tweed into Scotland. After a brief stop in Edinburgh, it continued toward Aberdeen. Before crossing the Forth Bridge, the train slowed to half speed. At mid span, they were hit by a fierce squall, causing the carriages to shake and creak, rain beating against the windows like gravel. Thomson thought about the Tay Bridge, which had collapsed in a storm. He knew this bridge had been built to new designs by different engineers using steel instead of cast iron. He was unfazed, secure in the belief that British designers had learned their lessons from previous mistakes.

Let it blow all it likes! This bridge is as solid as the Rock of Gibraltar.

It was dark outside. The Flying Scotsman's rapid progress was now impeded by steep gradients and sharp curves of the Highlands. As it climbed, the wheels made a dogged, metallic 'clacking.' Lulled by the sound, Thomson's mind became filled with thoughts of Marthe. What would he do about her? What *could* he do about her? She was his most difficult, and by far, most important problem.

Problem? That's too harsh a term.

If he did call her a problem, she was certainly one he would not wish to be without. She caused him pain—exquisite pain that never went away, clawing at him constantly. He'd been so close in the past, but like a beautiful bird, she always remained just out of reach and ready to fly off.

I'm a man forever in pursuit—that's the mark of a true thoroughbred woman! Why am I—someone who has commanded thousands of men in the worst hells on earth—as docile and compliant as a new born lamb in this delightful creature's hands?

March 24th, 1915 had changed him forever. The Romanian King Ferdinand had hosted a soiree at Cotroceni Palace in Bucharest. There, British diplomats had told Thomson he'd be contacted by an official at the highest level. Thomson had stood in the lower hall of the reception area from which a grand staircase swept up to the galleries above, between cascading fountains and palm trees. While a five-piece orchestra played chamber music, he chatted with British embassy personnel about life in Romania—a mountainous country he found breathtakingly beautiful.

The walls flanking the staircase, lined with paintings of Romanian rulers and warriors from centuries past, reached up to the crystal dome a hundred feet above. He watched as Princess Marthe made her regal entry. Gliding down the stairs, she moved as though suspended in air. He took in every part of her: her beautifully shaped hands and fine fingers on the gleaming brass rail, her slender arms exposed from the three-quarter-length sleeves of a gown that did not hug her body, but hinted with subtlety at what lay beneath. Made of black and dark green satin overlaid with chiffon, the gown had a scooped neck, which perfectly set off a shimmering diamond necklace. He took note of her shapely ankles and delicate feet fitted into the latest-fashion shoes—stylish, black and dark green kid pumps with Louis heels, steel beaded and embroidered—perfectly complementing her dress. Her shining, dark brown hair, gathered and pulled back tightly to her head, accentuated her high cheekbones and fell in a coil at the neck. Her eyes were black and bituminous and her skin as smooth and white as porcelain. Her slightly open, full, red lips, revealed perfect, even, white teeth.

From the moment she put her foot on the top step, her eyes rested upon him, making him feel as though he were the only person in that crowded room. For months he'd been in miserable surroundings in France and Belgium, where the sight and stench of death were an unbearable weight he'd learned to live with. She awakened in him intense joy of living and of love, a sharp contrast after being dead so long in mind and body. Thomson stood and marveled, becoming deaf to all sound in the room—the orchestra and the chatter of people around him. He listened to the soft rustling of her dress as she approached. When she drew close, he realized her eyes were, in fact, dark green, not black. Staring into them for the first time, he saw both joy, and sadness, as well as the thing they most had in common—loneliness.

He was suddenly struck by the recognition that this had happened to him before. There had been a magnificent young creature in an open-topped white carriage on a summer's day in 1902 on Rue de Rivoli. She'd taken his breath away and he still carried the vision of that girl with him to this day. He often dreamed of her. How old would she have been? Fifteen—maybe younger! Surely, this couldn't be her, thirteen years older. He tried to calculate. His mind wouldn't function.

That was Paris. This is Bucharest. Silly romantic notions. Stop it!

His palms sweated. His throat became dry. He smiled at her, as though reuniting with a lost love. He reached out and took her hand and kissed it.

"Princess Marthe, I am—"

Her Parisian accent stunned and captivated him, once again setting off thoughts of the girl in the white carriage.

"My dear Colonel Thomson, I know exactly who you are and why you're here, and naturally, I'll be *completely* at your disposal," she said, fluttering her long, dark eyelashes. From that moment, Thomson was a lost soul. The evening was perfect, the attraction seemingly mutual. They conversed in English and French and even a little Italian and German. They didn't leave each other's side the entire evening. People assumed they were a couple.

Marthe became invaluable to him during his months in Romania, enabling him to accomplish the task that he'd been sent by Lord Kitchener to carry out—to bring Romania into the war—a mission he didn't believe in, since he knew that country was totally unprepared. Marthe had a complete grasp of Romanian politics and access to every politician who mattered—her father the Foreign Minister, the Prime Minister—even the King himself. They saw much of each other and Thomson's attachment grew into blind, unconditional love.

True, she'd been married into the aristocracy at fifteen. To Thomson, this didn't count as marriage, and besides, her husband was an absentee spouse, always in pursuit of fast cars, fast aeroplanes and loose women. Thomson was thankful and prayed the fool wouldn't learn the error of his ways. He soldiered on, hoping one day she'd be his. He couldn't bring himself to face the fact that Marthe, a devout Roman Catholic, would never divorce her negligent husband. But racing cars and aeroplanes were dangerous pastimes—who knew? Fate could intervene.

During that magnificent spring, their love grew with a magical intensity found only in romantic fairytales—'The Soldier and the Princess', this one might have been called. One night, at her home on the banks of the Colentina, thoughts of marriage must have been going through her head. She'd thoughtlessly left her diary open beside her bed:

Kit has been my guardian angel. Oh, to lift the veil to see what might be written in the stars! Tonight, he came to me with special roses and the promise of his eternal devotion.

Had it been thoughtlessness, or had she left it there purposely for him to read? Eight years later and he *still* couldn't fathom that. Thomson often thought about those words written in her beautiful hand, now etched into his brain. Had she been romancing? Or worse, leading him on? Did she believe, as he did, that her husband's activities were too dangerous for his survival? He must surely die in an air crash sometime. Or did she contemplate facing up to the Catholic Church? Most unlikely! At times, he put it down to a young woman's fantasy during a war-time romance brought on by the death of her beloved father. Impossible thoughts! His mind went round and round like a damned carousel and he began to curse the day he'd seen her diary.

That careless or deliberate act had shaped his destiny and sealed his fate. Over the years, he tortured himself with longing, just as he was doing now on this dark night, alone in a railway carriage somewhere in the Scottish Highlands. He'd seen photographs of young, handsome men in ornate gold frames on Marthe's dressing table; one was George, her husband, two she said were beloved cousins, while another was 'a very dear friend'—Prince Charles-Louis, away at the Front.

After Thomson's negotiations with the government, Romania entered the war and in a matter of months Germany invaded and overwhelmed the country, just as he'd predicted. Before supervising the destruction of the country's oil wells (ironically, aided by Marthe's husband, George), Thomson helped Marthe escape to safety. Then he got posted to Palestine, where he spent the remainder of the conflict alone with his bitter sweet memories.

After the war, Thomson took part in the surrender of the Ottoman Empire aboard HMS *Agamemnon* at Moudros Harbor in the Greek Islands. After that, he worked on the Armistice in France until the end of 1919. Throughout the tumultuous years from their meeting to the present day, his romance with Marthe entailed endless separation, relieved by touching letters and all-too-rare meetings in London, Paris and, after the war, Bucharest. He always kept a few of her letters with him. He had some in his briefcase on the seat beside him tonight, along with one her shoes wrapped in white tissue. The letters were tied with one of her blue silk ribbons. He carefully took out one of the worn envelopes, and held it to his nose for traces of her divine scent. He clasped the sacred document, reading her words. He'd written to her constantly and she'd never failed to reply, albeit late sometimes, particularly as time went by. He suspected she must have been forming new attachments, or renewing old ones with 'dear friends' home from the Front.

His thoughts and actions constantly swirled around her. He was a man ensnared, but he'd have it no other way. He was blissfully happy in his unhappiness. If he managed to gain a post in His Majesty's Government, he believed his stock would rise, which might cause things to change dramatically in his favor. Where there was hope, there was life.

Thomson was jolted from his reminiscences as the train slowed and blew its whistle before entering Aberdeen. It eased its way into the quaint country station of damp, gray stone where Ramsay McDonald waited to greet him. Suddenly, he remembered it was New Year's Eve. His spirits rose.

Thomson stepped down from his carriage and the mustachioed McDonald came forward with two hands outstretched. He wasn't as tall as Thomson, but he exuded extraordinary charisma, making him larger than life.

He had an earnest face and his blue eyes sparkled with both passion and with pain.

"My dear Thomson. Happy New Year to you!"

"Mr. MacDonald. Yes, I'm sure it's going to be a very special New Year for you and for us all! But you shouldn't have bothered coming to the station, sir."

"Nonsense! We've not a moment to lose, we've lots to talk about—and please call me Ramsay. Come, I'm in the local cab. One of the few cars we have in Lossie!"

The two men headed for the taxi, and once inside, McDonald pulled the privacy window closed. "Excuse us, Jock," MacDonald called to the driver.

The journey to Lossiemouth took almost two hours, during which time they made small talk. Although it was dark and he could see little, Thomson sensed he was in a desolate place.

"I hope you brought your walking shoes?" MacDonald asked.

"Yes, I remembered."

"We'll get some of this clean Scottish air down your lungs. We'll walk and talk whilst you're here, laddie," MacDonald said. "And we'll make plans."

"I look forward to that. I can't wait to see the beautiful countryside."

"This is God's own country. I promise you'll love it."

The taxi turned into a gravel drive and stopped outside a two-story house nestled between sycamore trees. The wind hissed in their swaying branches. Lights in the windows and on the porch were warm and welcoming. Before getting out of the car, MacDonald gestured toward the house.

"This is our home. Built this for my mother and children in 1909 and she lived here till she died two years later. She loved it and so do we, still. Nothing's changed since Mother's time—except we have electricity now. Ishbel, my daughter, keeps things running smoothly."

They climbed out of the taxi and Thomson attempted to pay the driver, but MacDonald told him to forget it. "I pay Jock for his services each week," he said.

A handsome young woman of about twenty opened the door with a gracious smile, the resemblance to her father clear.

"This is Ishbel. Looks like me, but lucky for her, she has her mother's common sense."

"Mr. Thomson, welcome to 'The Hillocks'. Please come in and make yourself comfortable," Ishbel said, in her distinctive Highland accent. "Come in and get warm. I'll get the tea mashing." She ushered the men into the parlor, where a fire crackled in a large fireplace with a black cast iron surround, incorporating a cooking stove. They stood for a moment warming themselves before removing their coats.

"My close friends call me Christopher, CB, or Kit. So, please, no more Mr. Thomson."

Ishbel smiled. "Very well, I shall call you Christopher," she said, taking the boiling kettle from the fireplace hob. She poured hot water into a brown earthenware teapot and put on the woolen tea cozy.

"And *I'll* call you CB!" MacDonald said.

Over the fireplace, on the two-tiered mantel among the knick-knacks, were family photos Thomson took to be of MacDonald's mother, wife and six children. Thomson listened to the loudly ticking clock at center as it began striking the eleventh hour. The day had been long.

One more hour. Who knows what the New Year will bring?

In a glance, Thomson realized his impression from the exterior had been correct; this was the coziest of places. He felt the presence of MacDonald's wife and mother looking over them, a position now fulfilled by Ishbel—a role she obviously took pleasure in. After several cups of tea and ham sandwiches, MacDonald announced a toast. He opened a bottle of local Scotch and poured out three glasses.

"We welcome you, my dear CB, to Lossiemouth and to our home. Here's to you. We wish you a most pleasant stay," MacDonald said.

"I'm honored to be here in this delightful place," Thomson said, "especially for Hogmanay—a time sacred for Scotsmen. I didn't bring you any coal and now I kick myself. Anyway, from this Indian-born Englishman, please accept sincere wishes to you both for a happy and progressive new year."

The three raised their glasses.

"Don't worry about the coal, CB. We'll soon have plenty, you'll see," MacDonald said.

MacDonald was right. As the clock on the mantel struck twelve, there was a commotion at the front door. Local people crowded into the house carrying lumps of coal and bottles of Scotch. Glasses were poured and toasts proposed. They wished MacDonald luck in his aspirations, though nobody mentioned the words 'Prime Minister.'

The small band of well-wishers was soon gone and Thomson, MacDonald and Ishbel were left alone in the parlor, uplifted, but exhausted. After clearing away the glasses and putting the pieces of coal in the hearth, Ishbel led Thomson upstairs to his bedroom, explaining that this was 'Mother's room' reserved for 'special guests.' Thomson felt honored. The room was spacious, its slanting ceilings contoured to the roof with white painted beams and boards. White bed linens and curtains contrasted with the antique hardwood furniture and dark board flooring. At the center was an inviting single bed, with plenty of fluffed pillows and a matching eiderdown.

Beside a small casement window was a chest with a bowl and water jug with neatly folded towels. Most welcoming of all: a fire in the grate, made him feel warm and secure.

Thomson thanked Ishbel as she left, closing the white, planked door behind her, the metal thumb latch clanking in its keep. This was luxury after his miserable bedsit in Stockwell. He wearily undressed and climbed into bed, the metal springs complaining until he was still. He was pleasantly surprised to find not just one hot water bottle in the bed, but two. He was asleep within seconds, dreaming.

It was Paris, the year 1902 on Rue de Rivoli. As a young lieutenant, he trudged behind a white horse-drawn carriage as it moved slowly up the dirt road, flanked by cloistered stone buildings. He could see the back of a young girl in the carriage. She wore a white dress and a matching wide-brimmed hat. He longed to catch a glimpse of her face, sensing he knew her. No matter how hard he tried, he couldn't keep up. He watched in dismay as the carriage gradually pulled away. The driver, dressed in black livery and a top hat, turned and looked over his shoulder at him with a mocking grin.

4

HIGHLAND WALKS

January 1, 1924.

Thomson didn't stir until Ishbel knocked gently and placed a tea tray on the floor beside the door. Thomson opened his eyes, squinting against the glorious morning sunlight that streamed through the small casement windows.

"It's seven thirty, Christopher. Breakfast will be served at eight," she called.

"Thank you, Ishbel."

"No trouble at all," she said.

Thomson listened to her footsteps receding down the stairs. He jumped out of bed and gazed out at the frosty fields and snowy hills in the distance. He felt marvelous.

Washed and dressed in brown corduroy trousers and a matching woolen sweater, Thomson went down to the parlor. MacDonald was already seated at the oak table drinking tea. He was slightly more formal, wearing a white shirt and a tie with a V-neck tartan jumper.

"Ah, there ye are, laddie. Did'ya sleep all right?" he asked. "Ready to face the day?"

There it was again. Thomson had never been called 'laddie', but took it as a term of endearment. "I've never slept so well in my life, Ramsay."

"After your journey, I expect you could've slept on a clothes line," MacDonald said.

"I actually enjoyed the train. Gave me time to think."

Ishbel put down plates of eggs, bacon and mushrooms in front of them. A young girl in a white apron stood holding a thick slice of bread to the fire on a brass toasting fork.

"Toast is coming. Martha is our helper," Ishbel said.

"Ah, Martha! My favorite name," Thomson said, making the girl smile shyly.

"I'm going to suggest you and I stretch our legs this morning. We have some wonderful walks in Lossie," MacDonald said.

"Splendid. I just peeked out of my window and the view is stunning."

"I like to walk. Clears my head. We can get to know each other."

After breakfast, they wrapped themselves up in warm coats and swallowed a tot of Glenfiddich. The air was cold, but it was sunny and the wind had dropped. Thomson found the calling of the seabirds overhead and the biting fresh air, exhilarating. They set off down the lane toward the little town center. After a few minutes, they stood outside a dilapidated, ridiculously small, stone cottage.

"I was born in this wee one-room house," MacDonald said.

Thomson was intrigued, realizing just how far this man had come. MacDonald led him along the street where people smiled and wished them a 'Happy New Year.' Others, though, crossed the road and passed by on the other side, refusing to look in their direction.

MacDonald chuckled. "You see, not everybody loves me," he said.

Thomson gave him a wry smile. "Apparently not."

After a few minutes they stopped again, this time in front of an ivy-clad house with an overgrown garden. This dwelling was much larger.

"This is where I grew up," MacDonald said.

Thomson was unable to tell if this was pride in MacDonald, or shame. The man was clearly showing him who he was and where he'd come from.

"Our childhoods couldn't have been more different. My earliest recollections are of India. I lived there until I was four," Thomson told him.

They walked to the Lossie River, which meandered lazily into the sea just a few hundred yards away. Crossing over a small wooden footbridge, they wandered down to the beach where the foamy surf at low tide made a soft hiss. Thomson sucked the sea air deep into his lungs. They strolled in silence for a while, wrapped up in their own thoughts. Thomson pondered the question of Marthe and whether he dare broach the subject. He took the plunge.

"Ramsay, there's something I need to mention from the onset."

MacDonald appeared mystified, perhaps a little worried, but waited patiently.

"I'm involved with a woman. Have been for the last eight years. She's married—a princess."

"My word, how splendid. A *princess* no less! My God, man, I thought you were going to tell me you'd committed robbery or murder."

Hugely relieved, Thomson smiled.

I'm a fool. This man already knows all about her. He's done his homework. Canny, old Scotsman!

"And you're in love with this woman?"

"I'm afraid so."

"Afraid so! Don't be afraid. I was in love with the most wonderful woman in the world, but I lost her."

"Yes. I'm sorry."

"My wife was the bravest person I've ever known. She fought for the working class all her short life, championing women's causes and encouraging them to unionize." Thomson knew that when his wife had died, MacDonald was sick with grief for years to the point of total collapse. "She was the sun in my universe. When she went, the world fell into pitch darkness—and it still is for much of the time."

"I hope you can take solace in the children she gave you," Thomson said.

"Yes, there's that to be thankful for," MacDonald turned his face away toward the sea. A squall was building on the horizon. Thomson bowed his head, sharing the man's sorrow. MacDonald suddenly looked up as though he'd received a shot of adrenaline.

"So you're in love, my boy. Wonderful! That's all that matters. Love is all!"

This pleased Thomson. Marthe's beautiful face filled his mind. He knew she'd be delighted to hear MacDonald's words, if only one day she could.

"I'm glad you don't disapprove, Ramsay."

"No, I *wholeheartedly* approve! Every man needs the love of a good woman. When love comes along, grasp it with both hands."

"You don't see this as being a possible hindrance or political embarrassment?"

"Och, no! Most of the people in Parliament have doxies on the side. Same with the Royals—the aristocracy are even worse!"

"And what about you? Do you see yourself marrying again?"

"No, no. Plenty of women show interest, especially now of course. But no one could fill Margaret's shoes. I could never fall in love with another woman. Real love comes only once in a lifetime. You know, there's nothing I wouldn't give to spend one more day with her. Just one day."

"But not your immortal soul?"

"Oh, no! I shall need that for when we're reunited, laddie." They continued along the beach in silence until the sand turned to shingle, then headed inland toward the river and followed the footpath along its bank.

"They said I was a bloody, godless, Commie bastard, you know," MacDonald said suddenly. Thomson showed slight surprise. He'd heard vicious things, but dismissed them. "Wouldn't let me build our home on Prospect Terrace. 'No Red bastard will build up here,' they said. Oh well, I like it where we are. It turned out fine."

"It's a wonderful location," said Thomson.

"Well, they got it partly right. I am a bastard."

"Ramsay!" He'd heard this before and dismissed that, too.

"My mother was a seamstress, God bless her, and my father, a ploughman. She wouldn't marry him." MacDonald laughed, but it sounded hollow. Thomson found himself speechless. MacDonald pointed to the hills in the distance. "See the fairways over there? Moray Golf Club. They expelled me—for my stance on the war. I vehemently opposed it. Truth is, they got me out because I wasn't good enough—no pedigree."

"I'm sorry they treated you badly, Ramsay."

"Are you sure you want to get mixed up with me?" MacDonald asked earnestly.

"Ramsay, it'd be an honor."

The path led into a pine wood and, as they entered, MacDonald pulled out a hip flask and offered it to Thomson who took a swig, savoring the exquisite Scotch.

"Such a wonderful New Year's Day," Thomson said, wiping his mouth as the liquor warmed his belly.

"*This* is Macallan! Best Scotch in the world; distilled right here in Moray," MacDonald exclaimed.

"Mm, excellent!"

"When I opposed the war, they painted 'Traitor' on our front garden wall. Said I was a German sympathizer. I tell you this: I did oppose the bloody war and I'll oppose the next one, too—unless we're attacked, of course."

"I'm a soldier and I despise war myself. Most military men do."

"I may be a pacifist, but I went over to the trenches at the Front in Ypres to see our boys and they threw me out—had me arrested and shipped home," MacDonald said. Thomson was incredulous. "When I got back to England I went straight to Lord Kitchener and complained. He was furious."

"Kitchener was a good man," Thomson said.

"After that, he gave me free reign to go wherever I pleased on all fronts, which I did. Saw some action. It was dreadful—but I don't need to tell *you* that."

MacDonald offered Thomson the flask and he took another drink. MacDonald did the same. "CB, I may be a bastard, but I'm still a patriot— I'm not a bloody Commie. The carnage I saw on that battlefield and in those field hospitals was appalling—broke my heart, I can tell you. Convinced me more than ever: War is evil! I witnessed the slaughter and suffering of our men, driven mad by non-stop shelling, mustard gas, lice, sores, trench-foot, hunger and exhaustion. Just boys most of 'em, up to their thighs in water, filth and body parts. Blown to pieces—dead or maimed in mind and body. I was right to oppose it!"

"You *were* right, Ramsay. I was at Ypres, myself."

"Bless my soul! We may have rubbed shoulders in that hell hole."

They walked on in silence through the leafless woods until MacDonald stopped and took hold of his own coat lapels as if addressing a multitude.

"It was a crime against humanity, that's what it was!"

"Indeed it was."

"I love this little country and our great empire. My goal is to make sure the sun never sets upon it—and it never shall, as long as we honor God and we're faithful to our convictions. Yes, yes, I know this all sounds odd coming from an old left-winger like me. Most Leftists, Progressives and Socialists are Atheists. I'm not one of 'em. I'm not *overly* religious, but I do believe in God. I really fear that if we turn our back on Him, *He* will turn away from us and say, 'Very well, if ye want Satan—then ye shall have him in *abundance*'."

Thomson nodded in agreement. He wasn't sure if MacDonald was quoting from the Bible. It sounded like it.

"You see, I'm not the radical they say I am. There's a vast difference between a Socialist and a Communist. I believe in fairness and opportunity for all people. Everyone deserves a doctor and a roof over their heads. I believe socialism is the best hope for the world."

MacDonald continued tugging his jacket lapels. He strutted around mesmerizing his audience of one. "Marx was right about many things; he said capitalism could never survive. I believe in freedom for all people. Socialism will provide that: freedom from poverty, freedom from hunger, freedom from suffering, freedom from fear and freedom from ruthless employers. The workhouse must be abolished forever! The working class deserves those freedoms. We must stand together behind the state, for state ownership and state enterprise. The wealth of the nation must be shared; it must be spread for the benefit of all. The pie is large and must be cut up into equal parts. I don't believe in revolution—not violent revolution—I'm not a revolutionary! But I *do* believe in change; change by persuasion, by appealing to people's intellect and their better nature. I'm not really an imperialist, or a colonizer, but I do believe, having *inherited* the situation, we have a golden opportunity and an obligation to improve the lot of others in all those far off places. Our goal will be: the betterment of mankind throughout the empire—and the world!"

"And we shall achieve that goal, Ramsay. I'm certain," Thomson assured him. "But when we've made the world into a perfect place, what need of us will they have then?"

"The poor will be always with us, CB. That's not something you need worry about—not in our lifetime."

Thomson listened in wonder, he'd much to learn. They came out of the wood onto a country road and walked to the Garmouth Hotel, a quaint stucco building with gabled roofs.

"You must be ready for lunch. I'm starving," MacDonald said.

The hotel manager greeted MacDonald warmly, obviously expecting them. He led them into a small dining room with low ceilings and a table set with fine linen and sparkling silver. First, they drank beer to quench their thirst. After a splendid lunch, they enjoyed brandy and cigars while they waited for Jock to come and take them back to 'Lossie'.

New Year's Day ended with a cosy evening at 'Hillocks' by the fire, exchanging stories. Ishbel sat crocheting silently in a corner. Thomson perceived Ishbel to be an intelligent young woman whose advice was often sought by her father. After an early nightcap and a cup of cocoa, Thomson excused himself and climbed the stairs to Mother's room.

Three more wonderful days passed, walking and talking and visiting various landmarks. On Thomson's last day during a walk in Quarry Wood, near Elgin, MacDonald stopped in his tracks, as if a thought had just occurred to him.

"What do you want?" he asked, his eyes piercing.

Thomson was taken by surprise. "What do I want?"

"What Ministry do you want? Foreign Ministry? War?"

Canny, old Scot! I like this man.

"Air, I think."

"Air! Why Air?"

"I thought you'd want to take the Foreign Ministry yourself. As for the War Ministry—I think it might ruffle a few feathers. Many of those people were my superiors."

"I suppose you're right. Might set off a few fireworks!"

"I've given this a lot of thought. I think I could do well with the Air Ministry, in view of my time on the airship advisory panel," Thomson said.

"Hmm. The Air Ministry?"

"There's so much potential. Air power will be one of the most important developments in the country's future—the empire's future. It has so much to offer regarding employment—absolutely vital to the success of your government," Thomson said.

"*Our* government!" MacDonald corrected him.

Later that morning, they were driven to the Elgin Hotel, one of the oldest and finest in Moray, where MacDonald had arranged luncheon. Once again, they were warmly welcomed by the manager who seated them at the window in a private Victorian dining room with splendid views of the countryside. Over bowls of mushroom soup, MacDonald raised the question of how Thomson was to be slipped into his government, should they take up the reins of power.

"To bring you in, it'll be necessary for me to raise you to the peerage, I'm afraid," MacDonald said, with an apologetic frown. Thomson had anxiously awaited this discussion. The future—especially where Marthe was concerned—rested on this. He was ready.

MacDonald continued. "So, you'll have to become 'Lord Thomson of something or other.' Any thoughts about that?"

"Of Cardington, I think." Thomson said without hesitation.

"*Cardington!* Where does that come from?"

"Cardington in Bedfordshire. The center of the airship industry, or it was. It will be from there, that we'll begin its revitalization. We'll create thousands of new jobs under this, the cornerstone, of our new state enterprise policy."

"You certainly *have* been giving this a lot of thought. Good. *Air* it is then. As long as you don't go buzzing around all over the place. I need a man with a wise head fixed reliably on his shoulders and his feet planted firmly on the ground."

"Thank you, Ramsay. I'm delighted."

"Airships, eh. I don't know. Aeroplanes are okay, but airships …"

"They've fascinated me since I got bombed by a Zeppelin in Bucharest in 1914," Thomson told him.

"Sounds unpleasant. I hope you're not planning to drop bombs on anyone."

"No. The goal will be the building of a luxurious, mass air transportation system reaching around the globe. The Germans are well ahead in this field and we must catch up."

They sat through the next two courses discussing the nationalization of other industries, banking in particular. MacDonald spoke about the need to build vast tracts of 'state housing' for the working classes. Over dessert, Thomson laid out his ideas for setting up his 'New British Airship Program.'

"I'll propose that the whole scheme be set up as two entities, one being state enterprise, and the other 'private' or 'business—capitalist.' The head of Vickers, Dennistoun Burney, has ideas of private industry taking over the whole future airship industry—with profit being his sordid motive, of course. I plan to head Burney off and keep him contained. My intent is to show the country once and for all that we should look to government to do things properly—and fairly. Once we prove this point by building the best airships, the most luxurious and the safest in the world, the profiteers will never be able to compete, because government won't have the burden of profit built into the cost. They, on the other hand, will be shackled by the need to make money for greedy shareholders eager for their dividends. This will be a contest. A contest they can never win."

"Most interesting and challenging! Well thought out. The world will be watching," MacDonald said. "We shall drink a brandy to your success."

"Burney knew I was on the airship panel. He must have known of my political leanings. He probably contributed money to the campaign funds of my opponents in my two election attempts," Thomson complained.

"He did nothing illegal. To capitalists, money is like mother's milk. Welcome to the cruel, rough-and-tumble world of politics, dear boy. But he didn't win did he? You're going to be the one in the driver's seat!"

"Yes, I'll defeat him and leave him in the dust. I plan to bury him along with capitalism."

"That's the spirit, CB!"

When Thomson inquired about a bill, it was brushed off. No bill was presented to the table—not that Thomson had much money to pay. He only had four pounds in his wallet.

"Your English money is no good here," MacDonald said.

"You're too kind, Ramsay," Thomson replied. "Now I must get ready for my journey home tomorrow."

MacDonald studied him kindly for a moment.

"I hope you'll forgive me for saying so, but I know you've been alittle down at heel …living in that Stockwell bedsit …" MacDonald began. Thomson had seen him glance at his threadbare jacket lapels and felt ashamed. "…But all that's about to change. I know your pain. When I came to London before I was married, I was starving—no I mean, *literally* starving! My mother used to send me oatmeal by mail. My wife saved me in every sense. She was middle class and my life changed, and so will yours. I must also tell you I never had much respect for military men, but you have caused me to change my views. It's not fair that you should be hard up after all you've done for your country."

The next morning, MacDonald, always the gracious host, took Thomson in his taxi to Aberdeen Station. Two reporters and a photographer were waiting on the platform, presumably arranged by MacDonald. They asked a few questions and MacDonald answered them, though not in detail. After shaking hands—a moment caught on camera—Thomson climbed on board. After doffing his hat to a woman sitting with her young son, he sat next to the window and waved to MacDonald as his train pulled away. He sat back contentedly and gave his companions a beaming smile. The boy was dressed in his Sunday best—a grey jacket and short trousers with a matching flat cap.

"Is this your son?" he asked.

"Yes," said the Scottish woman proudly.

"What's your name, son?" he asked the boy.

The child looked at the floor not answering, but kept banging his foot against the paneling on the side of the carriage.

"His name's Stuart," the boy's mother said.

"And how old are you, Stuart?" Thomson asked.

"He's six. He's a little shy."

"Thomson pulled out the bag of peppermints still in his pocket from W H Smiths and held it out. "Here sonny, would you like a peppermint?"

"No."

"Stuart! Don't' be rude to the nice gentleman."

Thomson held the bag out to her. She took one to be polite.

"Do you like trains, son? Thomson asked.

"No, I hate 'em," the kid snapped, still looking at the floor as he swung his foot to and fro. The woman chimed in with an apologetic smile.

"I'm sorry. His grandfather was killed in the Tay Bridge Disaster. It's all he's ever heard about when it comes to trains."

"Oh dear, I *am* sorry," Thomson said.

There was an awkward silence. "Visiting Scotland are you? Business?" she asked finally.

"Oh, just a little holiday, visiting a dear friend."

Thomson looked at the boy again. "What about airships, son? Do you like airships?"

"No, I hate 'em. They're stupid and they always crash and burn," the kid sneered.

Two days later, most London newspapers carried the photograph of MacDonald and Thomson shaking hands at Aberdeen Station. They seemed to approve of Thomson being in the running for a cabinet post, if Labour should be victorious. Some conservative newspapers, not wishing to miss an opportunity, grumbled that he'd be getting in 'by the back door'—unable to get himself elected, as legitimate people are required to do. Over the photographs of the two men, they led with headlines:

THOMSON A POSSIBLE CABINET PICK?

And

ENTER LORD THOMSON OF CARDINGTON!

They reported if Labour came to power, Thomson would likely become Secretary of State for Air. The title bearing the name 'Cardington' had been leaked. This led to speculation about the resurrection of the airship industry—a good prospect for those in need of work—but for others, another inevitable disaster in the making.

PART THREE

St. Cuthbert's Church, Ackworth, Yorkshire.

THE RISE OF THE
PHOENIX TWINS

5

LOU AND CHARLOTTE

August - October 1921.

It was 10:50 a.m. November 11, 1918. Lou was moving forward with his platoon, his brothers-in-arms, his buddies. What had started as gleeful morning was ending disastrously; they'd first been ordered to stay in their trenches and keep their heads down. They'd survived the war and the slaughter would finally end at 11:00 a.m. But later, orders came down for them to attack. Incredulous and angry, the soldiers reluctantly climbed the ladders up and out on to the battlefield. They moved forward, keeping as low as they could. Lou couldn't see the enemy, but he heard the whine of the bullets slicing the air and hitting the bodies of men close to him—sop-sop-sop—sop-sop-sop.

The Germans were calling out. "Go back Yankee dogs, go home. It's over!"

He peered through the fog and smoke recognizing the uniforms of English and American crewmen from *R38*. Those in front and beside him, including Potter, Bateman and Josh were mowed down by machine guns or blown to pieces with deafening artillery shells. They fell writhing in pain into the mud, crying out for their mothers, guts hanging out, faces blown away, legs and arms blown off.

Some cried out to him, "Lou, help me. Help me, *please.*"

He moved on, miraculously unscathed and untouched. He stepped over the bodies of New York Johnnie, Bobby in his parachute, Gladstone, Al Jolson—not Jerry Donegan, the real Al Jolson in black-face—and then the dead German boy who lay staring up at him with cold, accusing eyes, babbling in German, "*Sie morder! Sie morder!* Murderer! Murderer!"

Lou turned to see Charlotte behind him, a shaft of sunlight falling upon her. She appeared pristine and beautiful in her perfect white apron and headscarf. She stood amongst the officers of *R38* in dress uniform, in the battered control car resting on the battlefield. Charlotte reached for him, imploring him not to go forward, but the others urged him on. Capt. Wann stood nearby, his face burnt and stony, his uniform saturated in blood.

"You could've warned us, Remington! March forward and die, you bastard!" the commodore shouted.

"He knew this would happen," Capt. Maxfield sneered.

"He knew all right. Let him die," Capt. Wann said coolly.

And lastly, off to one side, was Lou's father, about forty, hands on hips, hair receding, face angular. His penetrating eyes were mean and accusing, his lips drawn back in contempt. He said nothing. *He* didn't have to.

Lou woke, crying out, wretched and confused. He sat up and looked across the dark ward, not knowing where he was or when it was. Charlotte rushed into the ward and turned on a light beside his bed. She put her arms around him, putting her face close to his. "There, there, my dear. It's all right. Don't fret—you're safe," she said.

The dead men in Lou's mind were out of control. Lou's injuries were healing satisfactorily, but at night he had terrible nightmares, many of them about New York Johnny. He sometimes dreamed he was over the cat ladder coaxing the boy down to the engine car, below them the river estuary, its surface a sea of molten lava like a scene from Dante's Inferno.

"Come on, Johnnie! You can do it," Lou would yell.

"I don't want to. Please don't make me, sir. *Please!*"

Lou would wake up and lie there unable to go back to sleep. The doctors told him these dreams might get worse for a time. And they did. In another dream, he stood at the divide as the airship began to break in two, he on the flaming side, Charlotte on the other. No matter how hard he tried, he couldn't make the leap across the widening chasm. He watched Charlotte as he fell away from her, descending into the dark abyss.

Long before the inquiry, just after the crash of *R38*, Lou's decision to remain in Hull became firm. His dread of returning to the United States stayed with him, although he sorely missed his parents and his brother and sister. He wrote from the hospital, asking them to forgive him for not coming home just now; he needed to sort himself out. He also let them know about the matter of a certain nurse he'd become rather taken with. "Smitten" would've been more accurate.

He'd never encountered a creature so exquisite. It wasn't only her beauty; she had a wonderful intellect. She brought her favorite books in for him to read, and he became an ardent reader of British classics. If he returned to the U.S., Charlotte would have to be at his side. Lou stayed in hospital for three weeks where Charlotte nursed him. During this time, their affection grew to a level of intensity neither could have imagined. Old Mrs. Tilly would've been delighted.

Josh, Bateman and Potter left the hospital after a couple of days, their physical injuries only slight, but they visited Lou each day. They marveled at the relationship between Lou and Charlotte and boasted they'd seen it coming. Lou and Charlotte couldn't disagree, but Lou was filled with questions about life in general.

The 'Wiggy thing' got to him and would become a bizarre, recurring thing in his life. By a twist of fate, Wiggins, the engineer, who failed to report the day they took off, had escaped death. He visited Lou in hospital and apologized. His car had broken down and he'd arrived as the ship was lifting from the ground. Lou smiled, telling him he'd been miffed at the time, but glad for him now.

"Somebody up there likes you, Wiggins," Lou told him.

A week after the crash, a massive funeral procession for British victims passed by the hospital on its way to Western Cemetery. While church bells tolled across the city, patients and nurses crowded at the windows, watching in silence. Charlotte allowed Lou to get up and stood beside him. They saw Potter and Bateman marching solemnly in the procession, their heads bowed. After twenty minutes, Lou went back to bed. A few days after that, he was informed that the bodies of the dead American officers and crewmen were being sent to Davenport and then by sea to Brooklyn Naval Yard. Three, including the captain, would be buried in Arlington National Cemetery, overlooking Washington D.C.—a place Lou regarded as home.

Before August 24th, Lou had intended to extend his Navy enlistment when he got back to the States. After the crash, everything changed. The Navy told him to take as much time as he needed to recuperate. He'd served his country well, and whatever he decided, the Navy would respect his decision. All this was conveyed to Lou by Lt. Jensen, his immediate senior officer.

The lieutenant also told Lou that the newspapers wanted an interview and it might be a good idea, if he was well enough. Lou agreed and they sat and discussed an outline of what would be divulged. Only the human side of the tragedy could be talked about: the cause of the crash and events on board the airship were 'off limits.' The two men met with reporters next day, including the unshaven George Hunter, from the *Daily Express* who left him a business card.

Matron surprised Lou a couple of days later, announcing he'd be receiving visitors within the hour. 'Top brass' she said, from the U.S. Navy would be 'on deck' (as they put it), to pay him a visit. The nurses got Lou looking spiffy, sat him up, and wheeled his bed to an open area of the ward. Within the hour, a magnificent troupe of fifteen U.S. Navy men in dress uniform marched solemnly in step into the ward and stood at each side of Lou's bed. Among them were Cmdr. Horace Dyer, Maj. Scott, Walter Potter, Henry Bateman, Josh Stone, five reporters, and four photographers. The nurses and patients who were well enough gathered around Lou's bed.

Charlotte stood beside Lou at the head. The voice of the imposing Cmdr. Dyer boomed down the ward.

"Chief Petty Officer Remington volunteered for the U.S. Marines in 1916 and served with distinction in the Belleau Wood and Saint-Mihiel offensives in France where he ended the fight in the Verdun sector until the last day of the war. After that, he joined the U.S. Navy and served with the Airships Division in Lakehurst before coming to England where he took a crucial role in the development of the U.S. Airship Program. It is an honor, Chief Petty Officer Remington, on behalf of the United States Navy, to award you the Navy Cross for bravery, exhibited at the time of the tragic accident that occurred to Airship *ZR-2* at 17:29 hours on August 24th of this year. This medal is awarded for heroic, unselfish action taken in saving lives of your crewmen, as well as the ship's cat Fluffy." There were titters and smiles at mention of the cat.

"You showed resolve and leadership and by your actions three men were saved, while 44 regrettably perished. You sir, by order of President Warren G. Harding, the Commander-in-Chief, are now promoted to the rank of lieutenant. On behalf of the United States Navy and the Government of the United States, I now say, thank you and God bless you, Lieutenant Louis Remington!"

Cmdr. Dyer moved closer to Lou, and Lt. Jensen handed him the medal. He towered over Lou like a giant, pinning the cross to his chest over his pajamas. He stepped back and saluted Lou.

"Lieutenant!" he snapped.

Lou stared at the commander in astonishment. The cameras flashed, and everyone gathered around the bed and down the ward, cheered and clapped. Lou was unable to speak. Charlotte stood with tears flowing down her cheeks. After handshakes all round, the contingent marched out with the press ordered not to linger. However, George Hunter from the *Daily Express* did linger, and chatted with Lou for a few minutes. The following day, stories and photographs appeared in the British and American newspapers about Lou and he became an international hero. And Fluffy became famous.

After three weeks, Lou got discharged and returned to his digs on Castle Street. His face healed rapidly, but his arm was still in a cast, making it impossible to ride his motorbike. Frustratingly, there was little he could do but rest up at his flat and read novels, but at least he got to meet Charlotte at the end of her shift each day.

They usually walked along the waterfront for an hour, regardless of weather. Those walks were harrowing, with Lou staring out at the swirling black water. But Charlotte was determined they face their fears. Afterwards, they would go to Charlotte's flat where she prepared a meal while Lou fed Fluffy (whom Charlotte had managed to retrieve from the unhappy boat captain) and lit a coal fire in the tiny fireplace.

After their meal, Charlotte would light a candle and they'd snuggle down on the sofa—chaperoned by Fluffy, who supervised from the sofa arm. They often chatted well into the night, until the fire had become a flicker, and the room chilly. Charlotte asked about his family and he told her about growing up on his grandfather's farm in Great Falls. He spoke of his folks proudly, although she sensed there was friction between Lou and his father. Charlotte told him how she'd begun nursing and how she'd been sent to London for training—there, she'd seen her first airship, but she didn't elaborate. Lou noticed her cringe as she spoke of it.

They touched on their previous brushes with the opposite sex. Charlotte told him about meeting Robert on a bus and how they'd spent the day ambling around the city together stopping at various cafés and an art gallery. Robert was leaving for the Front the following day. He asked for her address and she gave it to him. She never heard from him again. She said besides Lou, he was the only decent boy she'd ever met. She told him there was no need to be jealous. Robert was most likely dead like all the rest. Just 'passing ships', she said. Lou sensed her loss, but understood.

All too soon, it came time for Lou to trudge back to his own flat through the misty night. Their kissing and cuddling often became intense and Lou wished he could stay over, but never suggested it. His respect for Charlotte never waned; that would've been unthinkable. But it got to the point where they could hardly bear to be out of one another's sight, or out of each other's arms. Charlotte made up her mind—she wanted his children one day—one day soon.

In October, Lou's sling came off and he took the motorbike for a spin around the city while Charlotte was at work. It felt good to be back in the saddle. The next day, he rode to Howden Air Station where his Navy friends came out to welcome him. They made a fuss, shaking hands and patting him on the back, genuinely proud of him. They told him they were cleaning the place up and removing all their stuff and going home at the end of the month. "Nothing to stick around here for," they said. Lou knew he'd be sorry when they went. The massive, double-bayed shed, covering more than seven acres, stood eerily quiet. It was completely empty, save for a toolbox and a few bits of scaffolding. Out front, a mountain of debris and scrap metal had been piled, ready to be hauled off.

After chatting for an hour, Lou rode off, feeling pretty damned low. When he met Charlotte later in the day, she sensed his mood and tried to buck him up, obviously worried he might up and leave, too. He put his arms around her and reassured her he'd never run out on her.

A couple of weeks later, Lou wore his new dress blues and went back to the Howden shed where three charabancs waited for Americans from the surrounding area. They were bound for Southampton to board a U.S. Navy destroyer. More than two hundred people were gathered, many of them young women come to say tearful goodbyes—a few temporary, most, forever.

Josh was in uniform like the rest, and he and Lou said their farewells.

"I just got my orders, sir," Josh said, as pleased as punch.

"Where are they sending you?" Lou asked.

"I've been assigned to the *Shenandoah* under construction at Lakehurst."

Lou looked apprehensive.

"Hey, don't worry about me, sir. It can't happen twice—not to *me*!"

"Be careful, Josh."

"I'm golden now—indestructible—and that ship's gonna be using helium—no danger of fire, sir."

"Just the same, don't take chances."

"Sir, do you think you might head back home soon? Maybe you'd be assigned to the *Shenandoah,* too."

"I'm not sure yet. I'm gonna rest up here for a while."

"I don't blame you for that, sir. You certainly are lucky …"

Lou knew he wasn't just alluding to their miraculous escape.

"I owe you my life, sir. I'll always be grateful."

"Don't be silly, Josh."

"I'll make sure and get down and see your folks in Virginia."

"I'd appreciate that. They'd love it if you did," Lou said.

"If there's anything I can do for you—let me know, sir."

"I will. Stay in touch."

"Good luck to you and Charlotte. She's very fine, sir."

Josh stepped back, stood stiffly to attention and saluted Lou, looking him squarely in the eye. A feeling of dread passed over Lou as he returned the salute.

"Remember what I said," Lou told him.

"Don't you worry, sir, I'll be fine."

Lou had a sinking feeling as he watched those little green buses drive away. He thought about his family in Virginia and felt like a deserter. And unbearably lonely.

6

LOW ACKWORTH VILLAGE

October 1921.

L ater that month, Lou and Charlotte took a train to Charlotte's home in Low Ackworth, near Pontefract, fifty miles from Hull. "Where they make the liquorice sticks," Charlotte told him proudly. They tramped along Station Road in the sunshine over a carpet of gold and yellow rustling at their feet. Lou was taken by the beauty of the stone village set among the farms and streams and had a sense of déjà vu. Perhaps it was that exquisite painting of rural England he'd seen in the National Gallery in Washington when his parents took him as a kid. He remembered the cows, the river and tall oaks around lush green pastures. Even then, he knew he wanted to see this place. It must have been a Turner, a Constable, a Gainsborough—he wasn't up on that stuff.

After a twenty minute walk, they arrived at a terrace of four three-storey houses surrounded by giant oaks. Each dwelling had a Welsh slate roof, secure behind high walls of matching blackened stone. Radiantly happy, Charlotte opened the wooden gate and pointed to the window on the ground floor overlooking the front garden.

"That's where I was born, Lou," she said. "Right there in that front room!"

"Wow!"

Charlotte pointed to ropes hanging from the bow of one of the oaks. "And here's my swing!" she said, settling into its seat and swaying back and forth. The door burst open and Charlotte's excited parents rushed out with open arms and welcoming smiles. The resemblance between Charlotte and her mother was striking: same height, bone structure, hair color, though her mother's was a little faded.

A good-looking lady.

Father was tall, with graying hair and strong features.

And this man works in the mines.

Lou shook his large, rough hand. Both were finely dressed, as though going to church—Charlotte's mother in a blue, flowered dress, father in a neatly ironed white shirt, plain blue tie, tan jacket.

"Charlotte, you look so well, my darling. This must be Lou. Oh, he *is* handsome—just like you said," Mrs. Hamilton said. "We saw the pictures in the paper, your poor face covered in bandages and Charlotte standing beside you. We were so proud!"

"Welcome to Ackworth, Lou," Mr. Hamilton said. "I'm pleased to meet you, son."

Charlotte grabbed Lou's arm, anxious to show him the house and make sure nothing had changed. They entered a small vestibule and stepped into the spacious living room with beige carpeting, a flowery couch and comfortable matching armchairs. As soon as they went in, Lou smelled the glowing coal fire in the grate. Charlotte noticed his glance.

"When we're home, we keep the fire going every day, winter or summer," she said.

Lou's eyes swept the room. The heavy drapes at the Georgian windows also had a floral pattern, similar to the couches and wallpaper. An upright piano stood at one end, polished brass candlesticks on its front panel, several framed family photos on its top. One of Charlotte as a child caught Lou's eye. She knelt on a beach, her arms around a small, white dog. He picked up the frame for a closer look.

"That was Charlotte at the seaside at Scarborough with Snowy. She's seven in that photo," Mrs. Hamilton said. "Oh, how she loved that little dog!"

"I want another dog just like him, one day," Charlotte said.

Lou carefully replaced the picture frame. "A dog … what about one of these?" Lou said, running his hand along the top of the piano. "This is real nice."

"Charlotte plays. She's very good. She had lessons at the Quaker School since she was little. Perhaps you'll play for Lou," Charlotte's mother said.

"Oh Mum, I haven't played in ages. Don't embarrass me."

"I hope you'll knock out a tune for me, honey. I love the old Joanna," Lou said.

Charlotte opened the lid and ran her fingers over the keys, picking out "My Mammy."

"It's out of tune Mother," Charlotte said.

Lou grimaced, remembering little Jerry Donegan in blackface aboard *R38*.

Any song but that one!

The white mantel over the fireplace surround was loaded with knick-knacks and more photos. The armchairs were arranged on each side of the hearth, one obviously 'father's chair.' Lou made a mental note. Beside it, between the fire-breast and the wall, was a half-height built-in cabinet with a mahogany wireless on top.

I guess this is where Father sits and smokes, listening to the BBC evening news and then a play before bed.

"Sit down and make yourselves comfortable," Mrs. Hamilton said, rushing off to the kitchen. She returned within minutes with tea and sandwiches and set them down on the coffee table. Starving, Lou and Charlotte tucked in. There was a knock at the back door accompanied by, "Oowoooh, oowooh, it's only me, love."

This was a sort of a British bird call now familiar to Lou, meaning: 'Is anybody home?' Of course, one always knew exactly who 'me' was. Lou grinned.

"It's Madge from next door," Mrs. Hamilton explained. "They'll all be by, you'll see."

Lou soon realized entering by the front door was pretty unusual. A procession of neighbors, relatives and friends came to the back door on one pretext or another; the main reason to inspect Charlotte's young man. Each one entered smiling shyly, ready to be introduced. They took to him on sight. They'd read the newspaper articles about the American hero who'd saved some of his fellow airshipmen and been injured and then taken to Hull Infirmary to be nursed back to health by 'our very own Charlotte.' A fairy tale!

"Oooooh! 'ees loovly, 'int 'ee?" (Which Lou figured meant, "Oh! He's lovely, isn't he?") they said, one after another on entering the living room, where Charlotte sat proudly beside Lou on the couch. Lou drank endless cups of tea, something he'd never done before, but found palatable enough—a British ritual. He could live with that.

Mr. Hamilton didn't say much. He listened and smiled. Charlotte had talked a lot about him during their evenings together. "He is the gentlest of men," Charlotte told him and Lou could quite believe it. Lou remained the center of attention for the afternoon, by which time the room had filled with people: Mrs. Scargill, Auntie Betty, who had a face full of kindness, Auntie Jean and her five kids, Auntie Mary from the Brown Cow (a pub, they explained), Auntie Rose from the fish shop ont' corner, Auntie Ethel from the dairy and Mrs. Hendry from the farm across the road, and many more.

Soon, after their shift at Ackworth Colliery, a troop of miners filed in. Lou wasn't sure if they'd give him the same reception, but they did. Lou had one problem, however; when they talked fast, he couldn't understand a word. So, he sat nodding, feeling like a parrot.

They're not speaking French, but they might just as well be.

After most visitors had left, one of Charlotte's girlfriends, Angela, came in and the two girls hugged. She shook hands with Lou, but seemed unable to look him in the eye.

"A crowd of us are meeting at the Mason's Arms tomorrow night. Why don't you come?" Angela said. "The old gang will be there."

Charlotte turned to Lou.

"Sure thing, as long as your parents are going," he said.

More villagers to meet!

Exhausted by conversation and sated by a beautiful roast dinner, Lou fell asleep in the attic room as soon as his head hit the crisp, white pillow case.

The next day was cloudy and cool. Charlotte and Lou spent the day walking across the fields to the viaduct and down to the river. It was a magical place, reminding Lou again of his favorite childhood painting.

The Mason's Arms was a chilly mile's walk just off the main Ackworth road. With its low, beamed ceilings and wood floors, the pub was welcoming and cozy. The publican greeted them from behind the bar as they entered. Lou was led around by Charlotte and introduced to everyone, including her cousin Geoff, who hadn't shown up at the house the day before. He was a handsome young man, about twenty-four, with a pleasant smile and beautiful teeth. Lou received the same friendly reception as at the house and wasn't allowed to buy any drinks. The publican grinned when he tried to pay. "Yer money's no good 'ere, son," he said.

Many pints were drunk by the men while the women sipped gin, or some fizzy, champagne-like drink. Just before closing time, a disturbance erupted in the adjacent private bar, with much shouting and swearing. A man in his mid-twenties appeared at the doorway to a collective moan of disgust from the public bar. He was Lou's height and build with lank, greasy hair hanging down one side of his pockmarked face. Murderous brown eyes blazed and thick lips drawn back in a sneer, revealed large, uneven, wolf-like teeth.

"Oh no, it's Jessup," someone said.

The drunk tried to focus on the man who'd dared to speak. "You shut your bloody mouth, Alfred Braithwaite, or I'll shut it for yer!"

Lou stared at the fool, unimpressed.

"So where's our American hero?" the man snarled, staggering into the center of the room. The drinkers scattered, leaving Lou alone with Jessup. Charlotte stood horrified, off to one side with her mother and Angela. "What's *he* doing here?" she asked. And then to Angela, "Did *you* know your brother was coming?"

"No, er …" Angela stuttered.

"She knew alright! She told me you'd be 'ere, my lovely," Jessup shouted over his shoulder. "So this is your pretty boy Yank? Oh I'm *so* in love," he said, in falsetto and puckering his lips to Lou. "Ah, give me a kiss, pretty boy."

Lou didn't move, his face blank, eyes alert. Charlotte's father stood mortified while the publican seemed to have his feet nailed to the floor.

"Now look 'ere, fella, why don't you go on back in yer balloon to bumsnot New York or whatever rat-infested dump you crawled out of and stay there! This girl's mine. I 'ad her first—yes, that's what I said—*I 'ad her first*—and she'll always be mine! Got that, Yankee Doodle Dandy?"

In a matter of moments, Lou had become a stranger alone in a foreign land. He didn't lose eye contact with Jessup, enraging the drunk even more. He ran at Lou and punched him in the face twice, knocking him to the boards. Lou didn't raise a hand to defend himself. Jessup swung round and leaned over the bar-top to seize a brown beer bottle. He smashed it on the edge of the bar and turned back to Lou with the jagged weapon.

Before Jessup managed to reach Lou, cousin Geoff grabbed a long shard of broken glass from the floor and with a sweep of his hand, slashed the left side of Jessup's face, piercing the flesh through to his mouth and ripping his tongue. Jessup screamed and fell down, blood gushing from his cheek and babbling mouth. Belatedly, the publican leapt over the bar. He grabbed Jessup's feet and dragged him across the floor into the other bar, like a bleeding dead horse, leaving a thick trail of blood. Angela rushed in to her brother. Charlotte sank down to her knees over Lou and took his hand.

"Oh Lou, my poor love, are you all right?"

"I'm fine. Who the hell was that knucklehead?" he said, sitting up.

Charlotte was at a loss. Mr. Hamilton leaned over Lou.

"Come on, Lou, let's get you home, son," he said, taking his hand and pulling him to his feet. Everyone in the bar was shocked and sorry this had happened to a visitor to their village. Each of them came offering apologies.

Lou, Charlotte and her parents trudged home in silence. Once there, Mrs. Hamilton went to the kitchen with her husband, leaving Lou and Charlotte alone in the living room.

"Charlotte, tell me, what the hell was that all about?"

"Lou, I swear to you, he means nothing to me. I went out with him for a couple of weeks, that's all. That was two years ago."

"Sounds like the boy's pretty stuck on you."

"He seemed nice at first, but then he started to get fresh. And when he was drunk he got mean, like a rabid dog. He wouldn't leave me alone. He's tracked me ever since. I had to get out of the village. That's why I'm working in Hull. He's made my life hell."

"He seems to think he's got a claim on you."

"What he said is a filthy lie! And if you don't believe me, you can get out of this house right now!" Charlotte stormed as her father entered the room.

"Please don't argue. You've been so happy together and you've made us happy. Don't end a beautiful day like this. Go to bed and sleep on it and talk in the morning. Lou, Charlotte is a good girl. That boy's a real problem in this village. He's always been a bully, just like his father before him—he used to terrorize this whole area—and *he* died in the hangman's noose; killed the boy's mother. I've no doubt this one'll die a violent death, too."

"I'll say goodnight. Thank you for your hospitality," Lou said, making for the door.

Later, in the attic bedroom, Lou took his bag from the closet and was busy unzipping it as Charlotte entered.

"W-What ... are you doing, Remy?" she stammered.

"It's best I go. Perhaps we need time to think about all this."

"Lou, I'm sorry. I didn't mean it. Please don't go. I'd die if you left me. I love you so much."

He dropped the bag in the corner of the room.

"All right, we'll talk tomorrow. Leave now."

Charlotte went out, closing the door silently behind her.

7

ST. CUTHBERT'S

October 1921 – April 1924.

Lou lay on the bed without undressing, staring at the stars through the skylight for most of the night. He fell asleep as the sun was painting the leaves gold and the birds were bursting into song. The room took on an orange glow as the chickens on the farm next door started kicking up a fuss. But Lou was dead to the world.

He went down to the kitchen about ten thirty. Agitated and embarrassed, Charlotte's mother leaned over the coal-fired stove, cooking breakfast. "Lou, I don't know what to say …" she began.

"Mrs. Hamilton, please don't feel bad. Nothing that happened last night was your fault. The man is obviously deranged," Lou said, sitting down at the table.

"Evil is what 'ee is," Mr. Hamilton said.

"Against our wishes, he took Charlotte out a few times. We were horrified. She had no idea what a bad lot he was, but it didn't take long," Mrs. Hamilton explained. When Charlotte entered the room, Lou could tell she hadn't slept well either. He stood and she came to him and kissed his cheek. They sat down at the kitchen table and ate bacon and eggs—except Charlotte who had no appetite. Later, Lou and Charlotte sat in the living room.

"Lou, I'm so sorry for what happened," she said.

"You should've warned me—why did you keep it from me?"

"Lou, I had no idea this would happen. I know he keeps tabs on me. He comes to Hull and skulks around. He knows I won't even *look* at him— let alone speak to him."

"I wish you'd told me, that's all."

"Lou, why didn't you defend yourself?"

"A couple of blows to the head are the least of my problems. I guess I need to keep an eye over my shoulder from now on," he said with an edge of sarcasm.

"I don't know why you didn't stand up to him, Lou. It was like you were scared. That madman could have gouged your eye out."

Lou's eyes narrowed. "He's got more to fear from *me*, I assure you."

Charlotte looked skeptical. "Lou, at times I don't understand you."

"Don't worry about me, sweetheart."

"It was that Angela's fault—she obviously told her brother we'd be there. He never goes in that pub."

"Why d'you hang around with her? There was something I didn't like about her. She's got lyin' eyes."

"She seemed like a decent girl and wanted to be friends and I felt sorry for her—you know, because of her father."

"Sounds like she comes from a bad lot."

"You do believe what I said last night, don't you, love?" Charlotte asked.

"Of course I do. I have no doubts, Charlotte."

"Oh, Remy." Charlotte kissed him. He took a handful of her hair and ran it through his fingers—something he loved to do when they embraced.

"Will you please excuse me, honey? I need to speak to your dad," Lou said. Charlotte frowned. He left the room and went to the kitchen where Mr. Hamilton sat alone, listening to the wireless drinking tea. Lou stopped respectfully and listened while the BBC news continued.

'It was announced today in the House of Commons that a proposal has been put forward to the Conservative Government by Mr. Dennistoun Burney, member of Parliament for Uxbridge and managing director of Vickers Aircraft Corporation's Airship Division, for the company to build six airships to be owned and operated by the government....'

Mr. Hamilton turned off the radio. "They want to build more of them airships ..."

"Sir, I wonder if I could talk to you for a moment," Lou said.

"What is it, lad?" Mr. Hamilton's face fell. He obviously thought Lou wanted to talk about Jessup. "Let's go in the other room," he said, getting up. Charlotte had gone upstairs. It felt more formal in the living room.

"Mr. Hamilton, I know this is rather sudden, but I'd like permission to marry your daughter," Lou said. Mr. Hamilton's face lit up.

"We'd be honored to have you in the family. We've not seen our Charlotte looking so happy for such a long, long time." They shook hands and Mr. Hamilton reached up and took hold of Lou's shoulders. "You're a right good lad. She couldn't do better—and nor could you. I know I'm her dad, but it's true."

"Thank you, sir. I'll take good care of her, I promise."

"I know you will, son. This calls for a celebration drink," Mr. Hamilton said, making for the door to fetch some glasses. He opened the door to find Charlotte, her mother and Auntie Betty, listening. Everyone laughed.

"Come in, all of you," Mr. Hamilton said. "It's time for a toast."

There was another sound at the back door it was Auntie Jean and Auntie Mary. The faces of the women were filled with excitement. Mrs. Hamilton loaded a tray in the kitchen with gin, whisky, brown ale and tonic water, and marched in with the new arrivals.

"We've an announcement. Lou has asked permission to marry our Charlotte," Mr. Hamilton said.

"And what did you say, Harry?" the ladies all said at once, surging forward. Charlotte looked at her dad.

"I said we'd be delighted to have him as our son-in-law."

A cheer went up and some clapped. Lou stepped into the center of the room. He delved into his pocket and pulled out a small black box.

"Charlotte, I hope you like this," he said, opening and offering it.

Charlotte carefully removed the diamond ring from its red velvet cushion, her hand shaking a little. She held it out to him to slip on her finger. Every one cheered again, as he did so.

"It fits!" they said.

Charlotte held up her hand to show the small diamond for all to see, clearly ecstatic. Jessup's name wasn't mentioned again. The rest of the visit was joyful and Charlotte even played the piano for Lou. She was a bit rusty, but he was impressed. Maybe one day they'd have a dog *and* a piano.

Lou and Charlotte made a second visit to Ackworth over Christmas. On Christmas Eve they attended midnight mass with the family at St. Cuthbert's, located not far from the Hamilton home. The old Gothic church was covered in ivy and surrounded by gravestones, bearing the names of villagers from centuries past. After the service, they walked home as a powdery snow began to fall, turning the village and surrounding countryside into a silent wonderland.

On Christmas Day, the usual procession of neighbors, family and friends came by, each bearing a small Christmas gift—a cake or dish they'd made, a small bottle of brandy or whisky. Traditionally, this was a lazy day, with lots of eating. Lou left about eight thirty that evening to stay at Auntie Betty's home on the Wakefield road, where he'd been billeted this time.

Lou and Charlotte were married at St. Cuthbert's the following day, Boxing Day. It was cold but sunny, the fields laden with snow. Lou's family had sent a telegram wishing them the best for their future with 'great love.' They also said they hoped the couple would visit the U.S. before long. Potter, smartly dressed in a grey flannel suit, acted as usher, while Bateman, in naval uniform, performed duties of best man. (Lou and Potter were closer, but Lou knew Potter was too shy and wouldn't be comfortable.)

Lou wore his officer's dress blues with the rank of lieutenant. Charlotte suggested he wear his Navy Star, but he refused. She understood and didn't press it, although she longed to see it pinned on his chest. With or without it, he possessed the looks and charisma of an American movie star, making Charlotte remember poor, broken-hearted Minnie Brown.

Lou got to the church early, after Bateman and Potter picked him up in Bateman's Morris. They waited nervously in front of the altar rail. A couple of times Lou turned around and winked at Billy who sat with his father, Lenny. Lou made Bateman check three times to make sure he had the two rings in his pocket and each time the answer was same: "Oh my God, what did I do with them?"

Before Charlotte arrived, a commotion started at the church doors where a gang of twelve burly miners had gathered, a fact that had been kept from Lou. Lou found out later Mr. Hamilton had told his workmates from Ackworth Colliery about Lou's dust-up with Jessup at the Mason's Arms. Jessup arrived on the scene with two other unsavory characters, stinking of beer. They hadn't come to say prayers, or to leave offerings. Lou rushed to the church door as four miners frog-marched Jessup toward the steps at the foot of the graveyard. Jessup turned and saw Lou and flew into a rage.

"I've not finished with you—you bastard!" he screamed.

Lou watched the miners manhandle him to the top of the icy steps and throw him down. He slipped and landed in a heap at the bottom, bruised and bleeding, the deep wound to his slashed face, reopened. The men stood with their hands on their hips. Jessup's friends had already scarpered.

"Try it again, mate, and we'll break yer bloody neck—just like yer old man's!" One of the miners turned to Lou, "You can go back and wait for her now, son. Don't worry; we'll be at the door."

Lou returned to the altar rail amid anxious murmuring in the pews, relieved the miners were on guard, although Jessup didn't scare *him*. His only concern was for Charlotte. Her day wasn't to be spoiled. Presently, someone whispered that Charlotte had arrived. Lou turned and stood facing the back of the church in anticipation.

As she entered, a gasp went up from the packed pews. Charlotte was radiant, and when she saw Lou waiting, her face was joyous. She looked stunning in a full-length, high-necked, white lace over satin dress that fitted snugly at her narrow waist and around her shapely bosom. Fanny followed behind as maid of honor.

Charlotte carried a simple bouquet of red roses. Lou watched her make her entry and walk down the aisle on her father's arm. She was all he ever wanted in a bride. He only wished his family could be here. And then, for a brief moment, he thought of Julia.

After the service, in biting air, they hastily posed for pictures in the snowy church grounds, their new gold rings glinting in the winter sunshine. They drove to the Workingmen's Club in Pontefract in the shiny black Daimler that had carried Charlotte to the church. It was decked out with traditional, flowing, white silk ribbons.

At the wedding breakfast, Bateman read telegrams sent by well-wishers. One came from Maj. Scott, at the Cardington Royal Airship Works. This puzzled Lou; he wondered how Scott knew about their marriage, but thought it kind of him to take the trouble. No one told Charlotte about Jessup showing up at the church.

The wedding guests spent a long afternoon at Mrs. Scargill's quaint home next door to Charlotte's parents' house. In the evening, celebrations continued in the upstairs rooms of the Brown Cow, where Potter, with laughing eyes and a cigarette between his lips, delighted everyone by playing hit songs and polkas on his accordion. It created a fun, French atmosphere in the Yorkshire pub that night.

"You make that thing sound beautiful, Walt," Lou called across the room.

"If anything 'appens to me, it's yours, sir," Potter replied, out the side of his mouth.

Later that night, Bateman drove the newly-weds to Monk Fryston Hall, a stately manor house in the Vale of York, where they spent a blissfully happy four-day honeymoon. Charlotte was a shy virgin—about that, there was no doubt—but after a day or two, she became a tigress. The wait had been worth it. When not in their sumptuous room making passionate love or ravenously eating meals brought up to them, they wandered the thirteenth century building with its stone mullioned windows, inglenook fireplaces and ornate, paneled rooms. At other times, they strolled, arm-in-arm in the delightful gardens among stone lions and statues set in acres of frosty woodlands and frozen ponds.

The honeymoon was almost spoiled. Jessup showed up in Monk Fryston Village. He had another dressing on his face after his nasty fall in St. Cuthbert's graveyard. Lou spotted him lurking behind a tree as they left the hotel and then later, skulking around in the gardens, gazing up at the windows. He didn't tell Charlotte,

Once back in Hull, they consolidated themselves in Lou's ground floor one-bedroom flat, which was larger than Charlotte's bedsit. They took Fluffy with them. Lou, still on disability, decided it was time to notify the Navy he wouldn't be extending his service due to end in March. He found a job in a country garage where he worked as a mechanic and pumped petrol for customers. The people of Hull treated him like one of their own. His new employer appreciated him and they got on well. Lou was content doing this job—a welcome change, and therapeutic.

Around this time, Charlotte got word that her cousin Geoff, who'd slashed Jessup's face, had been rushed to hospital. He'd been set upon by four thugs wearing balaclavas who stole his wallet. He'd been stabbed and his face cut with a stiletto, his arm broken and all his front teeth knocked out. He couldn't identify his attackers. Lou and Charlotte visited Geoff in hospital. The identity of the 'robbers' wasn't hard to guess. Powerless, Lou filed the episode away for another day.

He still had bad dreams and thought about his dead crewmen much of the time. All this was entwined with his war experiences, which had previously subsided, but this latest catastrophic accident revived everything, giving old memories new life.

Lou often drove his motorbike to Howden Air Station, now an abandoned, lonely place. He sat outside the huge doors on an old chair he'd found in one of the scavenged, dilapidated offices. He'd sit searching for answers, wishing he could find peace. The crash of the *Roma* in his home state of Virginia that February caused him more distress. That airship, flying from Langley, near Great Falls, to Norfolk, hit overhead power lines and caught fire. Thirty-four men perished in the flames. He and Charlotte could not discuss it.

The air station became like hallowed ground. He went there often over the next three years, witnessing the ever-changing, rural landscape through the seasons—in rolling October mist from the river marshes, winter snow, April rain showers and summer sunshine. He sat outside the shed where he befriended the animals: squirrels, rabbits, deer, foxes, stoats, badgers and pheasant. Sometimes he brought them food and they became tame, scampering at his feet.

When he couldn't sleep, he slid out of bed without disturbing Charlotte. It wasn't until she heard his motorbike start up down the road and move away, that she woke up. She knew his destination and didn't worry, confident he'd get over it in time.

Lou liked to light a fire in an old oil drum and sit studying the stars over the old aerodrome, while owls and foxes and other nocturnal creatures made their eerie sounds. If the winds were howling across the desolate plain, he'd find a sheltered spot where he'd listen to the ghostly noise of the building's skin of loose corrugated sheeting chatter and whine, like a living thing, while the gigantic structure creaked and groaned like a ship at sea. He always returned home before dawn and crawled back into bed with Charlotte, who turned over sleepily, drawing him close. He felt safe entwined with her, and so did she.

No children came along, which made Lou thankful. They needed more time together and he wasn't earning enough to start a family. Charlotte was desperate for a child, but knew he was right. It was important they get established first.

8

CHEQUERS

January 1924.

A procession of Rolls-Royces, Bentleys, Daimlers, Mercedes and other luxury sedans made its way from Missenden along the winding lanes to the wrought iron entrance gates of Chequers, the Prime Minister's country residence.

Situated forty miles west of Ten Downing Street, Chequers sat below Beacon Hill, nestling inconspicuously in the Buckinghamshire countryside among the towns of Princes Risborough, Great Missenden and Wendover. From atop the hill, on a clear day, one could take in a sweeping panorama of the Berkshire Downs, the Cotswolds and Salisbury Plain, although there were no good views from the house itself. To the south, the ancient, well-trodden Ridgeway Trail crossed open parkland.

The ancient, russet brick Elizabethan manor with its multi-gabled roofs, leaded windows and tall chimneys was surrounded by high, stone-capped walls and boxwood hedges. The cars passed into the walled courtyard situated on the east side. They made their way on the gravel drive around the quatrefoil-shaped lawn at whose center stood the lead statue of Hygeia, the health goddess, who posed close to a giant tulip tree—said to be the finest in England.

At the imposing entrance, each vehicle disgorged a set of dignitaries, many enjoying a new-found status. They were led to the front door by servants holding umbrellas to protect them from the gently falling snow. This afternoon, the house looked especially magical, like a painting of a winter scene on a Christmas card. Light shone from the windows in the grey gloom, accentuating the Welsh slate roofs, lawns, surrounding hedges and trees, draped in snow.

In the December election, the Tories had failed to obtain a clear majority and after losing a confidence vote in January, Conservative Prime Minister Stanley Baldwin had resigned. Labour joined with the Liberal Party and took up the reins of power and Ramsay MacDonald became Prime Minister. To celebrate this momentous occasion, MacDonald threw a party for Labour Party supporters and trade union bosses.

Thomson had arrived two days earlier and, at MacDonald's insistence, moved into the state bedroom. This room, with its ornate,

Elizabethan four-poster bed, complete with carved, oak lions, was usually reserved for distinguished guests and heads of state. A coal fire burned in the grate under a marble mantel. The view from the windows faced south over Chequers Park and the driveway toward Missenden.

Thomson felt at home at once and found the historical residence had the same effect on other visitors. After his bedsit in Stockwell, his fortunes had taken an extraordinary turn for the better and he considered himself truly blessed. He and MacDonald had been going over matters of state for the past two days, and although they were still in the 'honeymoon period,' they appeared to make an excellent team—both were committed to improving the lives of ordinary people. MacDonald had already begun crafting the Housing Act, designed to set in motion the building of half a million homes for working-class families at affordable rents.

They had got off to a cracking start and now, this very afternoon, Thomson would lay the foundation stone of his brainchild. He liked to manage his time efficiently and today he'd do many things simultaneously: celebrate the success of the first Labour Party victory, hire a genius to head up the program, make friends with people who couldn't relate to him, and lastly, drive the first nail into the coffin of Dennistoun Burney and the rest of those money-grubbing profiteers.

In order to get the airship industry back on its feet, the negative image would first have to be overcome. To do this, he'd move in a new direction, starting with hiring some new people—the best people. Changes would be made in the way things were managed. The process of selling the program to the public would need to be carefully controlled.

The celebration was held in the Great Hall, an imposing room, thirty feet high, with a gallery on the east side adjacent to a huge stone and brick fireplace, alive with blazing logs. An impressive brass chandelier hung at center, casting its glow over a pale green carpet, overlaid with exquisite Persian rugs. Original art covered the walls, and coats of arms, ranging from Lord Lee back to William Hawtrey, adorned all corners of the room.

Thomson stood chatting with MacDonald under a painting of *The Mathematician* (thought to be a Rembrandt) opposite the galleried end of the room, close to the entrance. Thomson oozed confidence, every inch a polished politician, debonair in a borrowed black tuxedo, stylish wing-tipped collar and silver tie. He was at his most seductive. He'd *need* to be.

Ishbel, at MacDonald's right, acted as 'hostess' while Thomson stood at his left. The three of them greeted guests as they arrived: first MacDonald, then Ishbel, then Thomson. This gave Thomson immediate status, or so it was hoped. He saw the pleasure of being at last, close to the center of power written on the faces of all who entered—that is, until their eyes fell on *him*. They gave him inquiring glances, and he sensed their burning resentment. He read their minds.

Who is this man who has leapfrogged into the inner circle? What has he done to get MacDonald elected? Nothing! We're the ones who've worked hard all these years to build this party. Now, from nowhere, here comes this interloper—this upper class fraud!

Thomson gritted his teeth and smiled as he greeted them, but they turned away, openly hostile. Thomson knew he had mountains to climb. He'd need to be patient. He listened to barbed comments—meant for his ears.

"I 'eard 'ee killed a lot of Germans in France, Bulgaria *and* Romania."

"*I* 'eard 'ee's having an affair with some 'ot blooded, gypsy woman over there."

"Bloody disgusting!"

"The movement can do without the likes of *'im!* "

"We need to cleanse the party."

"We can't have our people 'obnobbing with the upper-classes."

"We must be vigilant!"

Thomson had made sure Barnes Wallis's name was included on the guest list and had briefed MacDonald. He was keeping an eye on the door.

If only Marthe were here. I could confide in her. She understands the common people so well. She has those peasants in her village eating out of her hand. She'd love this place and my goodness, what a hit she'd be—even with this surly bunch!

He put Marthe out of his mind as a man stepped into the Stone Hall just inside the entrance vestibule.

This could be him.

The man took off his black overcoat and handed it to one of the servants, who brushed snow from its shoulders, before taking it to the cloakroom. Dressed in a grey suit and a somber blue tie, he walked into the room, as though stepping into a minefield. His name was boldly announced. "Mr. Barnes Wallis of the Vickers Aircraft Company, Prime Minister!" All eyes fell on Wallis as if he were Satan, himself. Wallis showed no reaction.

"Ah, yes, we've been expecting you, sir. I know Lord Thomson here has been looking forward to your visit," MacDonald said, glancing at Thomson who studied Wallis intently. He was thirty-seven, average height and build, possessed a stony face and expressionless, steely blue eyes; eyes that revealed nothing, but which seemed to take in everything in one sweep with camera-like precision, to file away. His stern demeanor and full head of prematurely graying hair, made Wallis appear older than his years and formidable.

A man easily under-estimated. A good poker player, no doubt.

"Thank you, Prime Minister, and congratulations to you," Wallis said, with calm assurance. His grey suit was a metaphor for his personality—

blending in without calling attention—but it *did* call attention, since every man in the room was dressed in black.

Maybe he's making a statement—not one to run with the herd!

Thomson stepped forward, hand outstretched. Wallis's hand was more delicate than his own—more like that of a violinist—but his handshake was firm enough. "I'm honored to meet you, Wallis. We've heard so much about you. Come let me introduce you to everybody, then I'd like to show you the house."

After presenting Wallis to Ishbel, Thomson led him around the room, introducing him. For a rag-tag bunch of rabble rousers, the guests were well turned out, Thomson thought. Not in every case, but generally he was impressed. Women were adorned in the latest fashions of delicate silks and colorful fabrics, loose fitting at the waist, some short at the knee, others to the ankle. The men wore tuxedoes or lounge suits.

These people have gone into debt to be here today.

Thomson knew how that went. The group included government civil servants, party members, party workers and hangers-on, along with several balding trade union bosses from the docks, mines and transportation industries, wearing steel rimmed spectacles. Thomson called them 'Lenin-look-alikes.'

Thomson cast his eye across the room. He'd done his homework memorizing the names of everyone on the guest list, positions held, names of their wives, children and girlfriends. Through research he'd learned of their ambitions and hobbies. After spending a polite and reasonable amount of time on pleasantries, Thomson led Wallis up the staircase to the gallery overlooking the Great Hall.

"This building is a special place," he began. "Only two other Prime Ministers have resided here—usually at weekends—Baldwin, and before him, Lloyd George, of course. And now here *we* are."

Thomson perceived Wallis's eyebrows raise slightly as he injected the '*we*'.

"That's nice," Wallis uttered coolly.

Thomson leaned on the railing and stared grandly up at the ornate ceiling with its octagonal glazed cupola and then down at the gathering below. He waved to MacDonald.

 "Seven years ago, Lord Lee of Fareham bequeathed his stately home to the nation for use of future Prime Ministers, for rest and relaxation, to confer with heads of state and distinguished guests."

"That was awfully generous of him," said Wallis.

"You know there's history attached to the name, too. It's thought to have been the home of the King's Minister of the Exchequer during the twelfth century."

"Interesting."

Suddenly, a blast of bagpipes took everyone by surprise—much to MacDonald's evident delight. A small band of Scots Guardsmen, in full dress of the Black Watch, filed into the Great Hall and gathered at the center of the room. They were followed by four dancers carrying swords. Thomson glanced down at them, shouting above the din.

"Come, let me show you the library. We must endeavor to preserve our eardrums." Thomson led the way down the steps. They moved along a corridor to an ornate wooden door, opening onto what Thomson called 'The Long Gallery', a room running the length of the west side of the house. The place smelled of smoke and damp logs. On one side, seven-foot-high mahogany bookcases were stacked with ancient, leather-bound books, many of them first editions. The bookcase was interrupted at the center by a carved stone fireplace where another log fire blazed. Soft, comfortable chairs and occasional tables had been positioned for cosy chats, a well-stocked bar within easy reach. Then Thomson had a thought.

"Ah, I know—this'll interest you," he said, again leading Wallis away. Wallis obediently followed. Thomson went to the bookcase and opened a section, complete with dummy books. Behind, was another door.

Thomson pushed it open with a flourish. "Voilà!"

"My goodness!"

"Isn't that fun?" Thomson said. "This is the Cromwell Passage. I should warn you, they say this place is haunted. At least, Lloyd George's dog thought so. He used to bark like mad in the Long Gallery. Do let me know if you spot any ghosts!"

Wallis stared at him blandly, as if he were mad. Thomson pointed to the paintings hung along one side of the corridor.

"Here's Cromwell as a child. He's two years old in this one. Cute little fellow, isn't he! Here he is again at the Battle of Marsden Moor. Now, that was a strong man—and altogether quite unpleasant!"

Wallis studied the painting intently. Cromwell sat on a black horse with a sword in one hand, his other arm in a sling. They proceeded along the corridor and Thomson showed him more portraits of Cromwell and his family. Wallis seemed mildly interested, but exhibited no sign of being in awe, as others might. But his eyes missed nothing.

"Ah, and look here, Cromwell's death mask," Thomson said, pointing to a cast lying on a side table. Wallis peered down at it, without comment. At the end of the corridor, Thomson stopped and slowly turned. "I expect you can guess why I invited you here, Wallis?"

Thomson had thoroughly reviewed Wallis's background. Wallis had the reputation for being the finest and most experienced airship designer in the country. The only thing was—what were his political leanings? If he leaned left, it should be easy, but if he was a dyed in the wool Dennistoun Burney disciple, things might prove difficult—or impossible.

If he's just a regular Conservative, I expect we can seduce him—they're all for sale. All they think about is money. But this man's hard to read.

Unusual for Thomson.

"My guess is—something to do with engineering?" Wallis answered.

Thomson chuckled. "Let's go back to the library, shall we?" he said, leading the way to the warm hearth. The sun's last rays were shining through the stained glass windows at the end of the room. Thomson went to the bar and poured two large glasses of twelve year-old Macallan. He handed one to Wallis.

"I'm glad you came, Wallis," he said, holding up his own glass.

"My pleasure, sir. Thank you for the tour." Wallis held up his Scotch, but did not drink. Thomson wasn't sure what to make of him.

Is he being sarcastic? Perhaps he doesn't drink.

"I must congratulate you, on your government's victory and your appointment as Air Minister," Wallis said.

Ah, that's more encouraging.

"Thank you, Wallis. That's why you're here. We're hoping to do great things. We must get started on a grand new global transportation scheme." They sat facing each other over the coffee table.

"Sounds exciting," Wallis said. This pleased Thomson. Finally, a sign of interest.

"It's a matter of national security for us to revitalize the airship industry without delay. The Germans have got too far ahead of us," Thomson said.

"Indeed they have."

"We must seize the initiative, Wallis."

"I must agree, sir."

"I attended the Treaty of Versailles and I can tell you quite bluntly, we were too hard on Germany. I said it then, and I say today: This peace will not hold!" Thomson said.

"That would be most unfortunate."

"If there is another war, which I think is likely, we must be prepared, Wallis!"

"I hope not, but you're right, of course—war might be inevitable. It's more likely though, that it'd be because we weren't *hard enough* on Germany."

Thomson was surprised Wallis had the temerity to contradict him.

"That's your considered opinion, is it, Wallis?" he said.

"One general warned we'd have to 'do it over' if we allowed them to walk away from the battlefield with their army intact and Germany left totally unscathed."

Thomson frowned. "Who said that?"

"General Pershing."

"Old 'Black Jack' said that, did he? He would!" Thomson snorted.

What the hell do you know, Wallis? You weren't there!

There was a long pause and then at last, Thomson spoke again.

"I want someone to head up the New Imperial Airship Program. The industry shall rise again like the proverbial phoenix," Thomson said, getting away from the subject of war.

"Yes, you'll need the right man."

"This is where you come in. I believe *you're* that man."

"You understand my position with Vickers Aircraft, Lord Thomson?" Wallis said, with slight discomfort.

"Yes, I do, Wallis, but this is all much too important. It's my belief Vickers's intention is to monopolize the airship industry, and we certainly can't allow that. This has got to be more about the good of the country—not just about profit. There are people out there ..." Thomson jerked his thumb toward the sound of the bagpipes, "...hell-bent on nationalizing Vickers and just about every other company in the land. To them, 'profit' is a *very dirty* word. Private business has its usefulness, but it must be held in check for the 'common good'. You do understand, don't you, Wallis?"

Wallis showed no sign of what he was thinking. "I think I understand perfectly, sir, yes."

"Government took the lead in the production of airships until the unfortunate accident, but it's time to put all that behind us and restart the program. Vickers will have its role to play—an important role. Our new government will not only undertake the design and construction of airships of its own, but will oversee airships built by Vickers under contract to us. And this is where you come in, Wallis."

"What are you saying *exactly*, sir?"

"I want you to oversee the entire program, as Secretary of the Airship Committee."

Wallis showed emotion for the first time. He was aghast.

"You're planning to build airships by committee?"

"Yes, why not?"

"Well, I, I ..."

"You *are* the best man we've got after all—or so I've been led to believe." Thomson paused. "Now your country needs you, Wallis."

Wallis sat and stared down at his shiny, black lace-up shoes. Thomson waited, while the fire crackled in the grate. "I take it I'd be at liberty to pick and choose my own teams on both government and private sector projects?"

Thomson hadn't seen this coming. He stared away at a painting of Charles I, searching for the right words. This was a loaded question.

This man is his own master. He'd certainly be strong enough for the job.

"Yes, to some extent, but naturally, I'd require you to take over the team at the Royal Airship Works at Cardington," Thomson answered.

"The same people who built *R38*?"

Thomson tried to slough that off. "Well, yes."

"The same team that built the airship that plunged into the Humber three years ago?"

The man's tone is becoming irritating.

"As I said, they'd be working under your direction, yes."

"I cannot believe you'd actually contemplate keeping those people employed—they're totally incompetent. If I were in the position to, I'd sack the lot tomorrow. Some of them should've gone to prison. They shouldn't be rewarded with another airship to build. That'd put more peoples' lives in danger. It'd be a serious mistake indeed, sir!" Wallis said.

Stunned, Thomson stared down into his whisky and then slowly raised his head, his eyes boring into Wallis's. "I take that, sir, as a refusal of your government's offer?"

"I refuse to be part of another major airship disaster," Wallis answered.

"I was rather hoping you would *prevent* one," Thomson said with finality.

There was a long awkward silence. Wallis put down his untouched glass of whisky and both men got up and moved toward the door. A footman stood in the corridor waiting for instructions.

"Kindly fetch Mr. Wallis's coat from the Stone Hall cloakroom and show him out through the west door to his car. Mr. Wallis, please wait here. I bid you good day, sir." Wallis showed no emotion whatever as they parted without shaking hands. Thomson went up the main staircase to his room. He needed to unwind. This had been a disaster.

An unmitigated damned disaster!

He went to the sink and splashed his face with water. He trembled as if he'd been punched in the stomach. He hadn't anticipated this reaction from Wallis and felt he'd misjudged him—mishandled the whole thing. He was furious, mostly with himself—his first important task and he'd failed miserably. It left him questioning the way the program was to be set up. Wallis's sarcastic jibe kept running through his mind.

You're planning to build airships by committee?

Thomson gradually calmed down and went to the window in time to see Wallis trudging to his car. He watched him climb in and white puffs shot from the exhaust. The car moved off unsurely in the snow toward the sun disappearing below the tree line. Thomson sat down in an armchair, staring at the fireplace until he felt composed. He thought about what Wallis had said about the Cardington people. The truth was, the design people who'd been responsible for *R38* had perished with the airship. He concluded Wallis must have been ranting about government enterprise—his sacred cow!

Later, he went down to the Great Hall where the Scottish Guards and the dancers were finishing their performance. He slipped into the room as the servants were turning on table lamps and wall sconces. He moved to where MacDonald stood with a group around him.

Sensing Thomson's disappointment, MacDonald's glance showed he instinctively knew the interview had been a failure. As the guardsmen and dancers wrapped up, MacDonald started the applause and everyone joined in. He eased his way over to Thomson and they went under the galleried arches into the White Parlor.

"Why so glum, CB?"

"It didn't go well with Wallis. He seemed quite receptive at first. But then he said his first task would be to fire all the staff at the Royal Airship Works."

"My goodness!"

"The nerve of the fellow," Thomson said.

"We're supposed to be creating jobs, not laying everybody off!"

"He may be the greatest engineer in the world, but we can't have someone like that going around laying down the law, telling us what's what!"

"You don't really know if he *is* the best engineer available. There must be others, surely?" MacDonald said.

"Time will tell, Ramsay."

"Well, old chap, don't let this little hiccup spoil this wonderful party. Let's go in there and tell them about all our plans," MacDonald said.

They reentered the Great Hall and Thomson picked out one of the Lenin look-a-likes and went to work.

"George Casewell, isn't it? I'm Christopher Thomson," he said, thrusting out his hand. "You're with the Yorkshire Miners Union. The future is looking bright indeed. We have plans afoot to nationalize the coal mines and introduce more safety regulations, you know."

The rough-and-ready Casewell peered at Thomson as if assessing him for the first time, obviously surprised to hear such sweet words coming from someone of his sort. Thomson sensed the man melt. His manner changed before Thomson's eyes—yes, he was being reappraised.

Progress indeed!

9

OUT OF THE BLUE

Lou enjoyed working at the garage. John Bull, the owner, was a gentle man with hands that tremored and words that faltered. He stood six feet tall, with sad blue eyes and a full head of grey hair and a matching, close-cropped beard. His disarming smile, though rarely seen, hinted at his inner goodness. Lou sensed he possessed a strong business acumen, but clearly his heart wasn't in it; perhaps once it had been, but not anymore. Lou didn't ask questions. It wasn't hard to figure. If Mr. Bull wanted him to know, he'd tell him in his own time.

Lou guessed John had read about him in the newspapers from a few things he'd said. One day while Lou was working on a truck in the shop, John brought in two mugs of steaming tea and leaned on the bench.

"My son was in France, too," he said.

Lou shook his head, sadly.

"Died at Passchendaele with hundreds of thousands of other young boys," John said, staring at the ground, the memory raw and unbearable.

"Awful," Lou said, remembering that indescribable horror.

"Blown to bits, I suppose, or drowned in the mud. They said he was 'missing.' No body, no funeral. No *nothing!*"

Lou screwed up his face, recalling the macabre faces of the dead. He'd encountered many gruesome skeletons in rags wearing helmets, propped against barbed wire, grinning—their faces eaten away by rats.

"When we got the news, it was the most miserable day of our lives."

"I'm so very, very sorry, sir," Lou said.

"So many of our young boys are gone—*thousands and thousands* of them from around here—gone forever. It just wasn't right!"

"It was all a waste, Mr. Bull. A terrible waste."

"Please call me John. No more sirs, or Mr. Bull, eh lad?"

"All right then …John."

John went silent for a few moments as though deciding whether to ask—not sure if he really wanted to know. In the end he spoke.

"Tell me, what was it like for you? Where were you?"

"I was in Belleau Wood and then Saint-Mihiel with the Marines. I started out in observation balloons until they were shot down by enemy planes."

"What happened to you?"

"I bailed out twice, but I was okay."

"You were bloody lucky!"

"That's what they called me, especially later," Lou said.

"Why what happened?"

"Once the balloons were down they sent me to the trenches. I got blown up by German artillery in a deep bunker with twenty-five others and buried."

John was horrified at the thought. "How long were you buried?"

Lou grimaced. "Six hours."

"Six hours! Oh no! Were you okay?"

"Yeah, I was a bit banged up. They sent me to the field hospital for a few days."

"You're okay now though?"

"Well, it stayed with me. I can't bear being shut in—gives me the horrors."

"What about the other men?"

"All dead."

"Oh, dear God. What happened to you then, son? Did they send you back to the trenches?"

"I requested to be sent back with my Army buddies. But that wasn't the worst of it."

John looked at Lou with compassion. "Tell me what happened to you, I want to know."

"On eleven, eleven ..."

"The last day of the war?"

"Yeah. After first standing us down, we were ordered to attack. We climbed the ladders out of the trenches into No Man's Land. There were waves of us. It was pretty quiet for a long time—the Germans were holding their fire."

John was mortified. "What time was this?"

"We got to the German line about ten minutes to eleven."

"Dear God! Then what?"

"The Germans kept shouting: 'Go back, Yanks. Go home!'"

"But you advanced?"

"Yes. They fired over our heads at first. They wanted no part of it."

"And then?"

"Finally, they understood we meant business and were coming to kill them."

"And you would've?"

"Yes. We were under orders to kill them to the last second. They started firing at us. I saw my buddies to my left going down and then they all went down."

"What about you?"

Lou paused for a long time, unable to answer.

"I went down, too," he said finally.

"You were hit?"

Lou hesitated. "I guess I blacked out."

John was reliving this with Lou who'd turned white. "What happened then?"

"I came to, lying beside my friends." Lou wrapped his hands around his head trying to banish the memory.

"They were all dead?"

"Yes."

Lou saw the look of thankfulness on John's face. "But you were alive!"

Lou nodded, ashamed.

"Then I heard bugles sounding, claxtons going off and cheering."

"What was the commotion?"

"It was the cease fire signal. The war was over. I walked back to camp.

"You must've been happy."

"It was the saddest day of my life," Lou said.

Lou noticed a slight change in John over the coming weeks. He was a little brighter and his hands shook less. John had taken to Lou. He could never take the place of his son, but having Lou around seemed to help ease the pain. For Lou, he had someone to talk to. He confided in John about his own demons from the war and the *R38* debacle.

A couple of weeks later, John asked Lou to take a ride with him in his car. "I've got something to show you," he said.

They drove in silence to the village of Peacehaven, about seven miles away. Stopping outside an old but very beautiful stone cottage, they climbed out and John opened the squeaky wooden gate. The sign beside the front door, its paint peeling, read: 'Candlestick Cottage'.

"I wanted you to see the cottage we bought for our son before he went off to war." John reverently opened the front door and they entered the musty-smelling living room. Lou glanced around. The room was cosy with black beamed ceilings and a quaint, stone fireplace. "He loved this place. He only came here once. In his letters he promised he'd come back and live here," John said bitterly. "I thought if we bought it, somehow he'd return. He *would* survive—he'd *have to survive*! …All I did was put a *jinx* on him."

"Your son would've been happy here," Lou said.

"We want you and Charlotte to live here. You can have it for whatever rent you are paying now."

Lou hesitated, not sure what to say.

"Hell, you can live here for nothing," John said, his voice faltering, his eyes filling with tears.

Lou put his hand on John's shoulder. "John, we couldn't possibly. This place is too important to you and Mary."

"Yes, that's the point. Lou, I want you to talk to your wife. In fact, I'd like to speak to her myself. We'll bring Charlotte over here tomorrow and see what she thinks."

Charlotte fell in love with the cottage immediately. She particularly liked the box room next to the bedroom—perfect for a baby's crib. Perhaps it was a sign! But she had reservations.

"We'd be taking advantage of these lovely people," she whispered.

John would have none of it.

"I have to tell you honestly. Mary and I'd be thrilled if you lived here —it'd give us peace of mind," he said. "And it needs to be lived in … it needs life!"

Charlotte relented on the understanding they'd pay a fair rent. Lou and Charlotte moved into Candlestick Cottage a week later, where they settled into a dreamy contentment and as newlyweds, they were blissfully happy. It was a dream come true. John and Lou got to work repainting the place and fixing things. They sanded and refinished the wood floors. Lou touched up the peeling sign at the door. Charlotte worked hard with Mary to make it comfortable with colorful curtains and soft chairs bought from Friedman's Second Hand Furniture & Removals in Hull.

Charlotte's parents had their piano delivered ('on loan') to the cottage by the same company for Charlotte. Delighted, she rushed out and picked up the sheet music for Irving Berlin's "What'll I Do?" It was all the rage. She practiced playing and singing the mournful song every day until she was perfect. Money was short, but that didn't spoil their happiness. Charlotte made the twenty-minute ride to the hospital in Hull each morning on a little green bus and Lou continued at the garage.

A few weeks later, Charlotte took Lou with her to the music shop in Hull to buy a couple more songs. Lou noticed a second-hand guitar in the window and asked to see it. It was a Martin guitar, more than twenty years old, made in Nazareth, Pennsylvania. The back and sides were of Brazilian rosewood, the front, white spruce. Lou really knew a thing or two about guitars and was taken with the inlaid ivory rosette, bridge pins and knobs. He adjusted the gut strings and tuned it. Suddenly, the shop was filled with beautiful, melodious sound. Charlotte was amazed.

This was a talent she never realized he possessed—he'd never mentioned it. Lou asked the shopkeeper the price. It was five pounds. Lou knew it was well worth it, but reluctantly handed it back. Charlotte resolved that somehow that guitar would be his. The next day, she put down half-a-crown to hold it. Over the next two months she worked extra shifts and paid down more. In the end, the shopkeeper told her to take it home and continue making weekly payments. Charlotte gleefully hid it under the bed in its black, coffin-like case until Lou's birthday that June, when she presented it to him wrapped in brown paper. He was thrilled. Charlotte was delighted when he sung country songs—cowboy music! Sometimes, he accompanied her when she played the piano, and he began writing his own songs.

That spring, Charlotte started a vegetable garden, which she tended at weekends. She proved to have a green thumb. Soon, colorful flowers and vines were blooming around the cottage in beds, rockeries, trellises, and hanging baskets. John often came by, cheered by the new life in this little home. His demeanor improved and he and his wife began to think of them as more than friends. Lou was content, especially now the court of inquiry was behind him. He missed his family in Virginia, but at least they exchanged letters every week.

Life moved along pleasantly until April of 1924. One bright Saturday morning, Charlotte, in headscarf, long apron and rubber boots was preparing a patch in the garden to plant carrots and potatoes, while Fluffy sat on the stone wall, watching.

"Mrs. Remington?" a man's voice called over the front gate.

Charlotte stood up, shielding her eyes from the sun. He wore British Airshipmen's blues, resembling a naval uniform.

"Oh hello, Major …er," Charlotte said.

"Scott," he said. "I wasn't sure if that was you in the wellies."

"Ah, yes, Major *Scott*. How are you?" she asked, puzzled.

"I was in Hull on official business and thought I'd drop by. I hope you don't mind."

"No, but how did you find us?"

"You stop the first person you meet and ask for 'the American.'"

Charlotte laughed. "I suppose that's true."

Scott peered over her shoulder. "Is he about?"

"He's at work—should be home in half an hour."

"All right, I can come back, if that's all right?"

"Why don't you come in and wait. I'll make you a cup of tea, if you like."

"Wonderful! I could murder a nice cuppa."

Charlotte led Scott through the planked front door into the living room with Fluffy following. A coal fire glowed in the fireplace. She was pleased when Scott glanced around appreciating their work: painted black beams, a colorful rug over highly polished wood flooring, throw-covers and the dozens of cushions of all colors and sizes strewn haphazardly about.

"My, what a lovely room," Scott exclaimed. "Hey, I recognize that cat!"

"That's Fluffy. I had a fight with the boat captain. He wanted to keep her."

"Ah yes, the famous Fluffy!"

Scott's eyes fell on the bottle of sherry on the sideboard and then on Charlotte—perhaps lingering a little too long. She could overlook that. He'd done a lot for all of them that day—she'd never forget *that*. His face was red and she caught a whiff of alcohol. She remembered him taking a swig from his flask before rushing off to the boat.

Must've had a heavy session in Hull last night!

Charlotte gestured toward one of the soft armchairs.

"Make yourself comfortable, Major."

Before disappearing into the kitchen, Charlotte picked up her knitting and bent over the couch and put it in a basket out of sight. She sensed him watching her.

She soon reappeared with a tea tray, which she placed on the low table in front of the couch. Scott looked up pleased. "Good. We can chat before Lou comes in. How is he—in himself, I mean?"

"He's much better," Charlotte said as she poured the tea. "He's getting over the accident pretty well."

"Is he happy?"

"Yes, *very* happy."

"Working?"

"He works in a garage."

"Oh, yes I remember. He told me at the inquiry."

Charlotte got up to poke the fire and add a few shovels of coal from a brass scuttle. They sat and chatted for half an hour. Scott was interested to know about all aspects of their lives, including Charlotte's folks in Ackworth and their own plans to start a family. In the end, he came to the point.

"I have a proposal for Lou and in some ways it's good I talk to you first, because if you're not in favor, it wouldn't work. 'Behind every good man …'—you know the old saying. He'd be able to put his valuable knowledge and experience to good use," Scott said.

Suspicion showed in Charlotte's face. "What sort of proposal?"

"I expect you've heard. The British Airship Industry is about to be revitalized and Lou could play an important role."

Charlotte and Lou had, in fact, heard things on their new wireless and read glowing reports in the *Daily Mirror*. They'd listened to a speech given by the new Minister of State for Air, a rather pompous-sounding Lord something-or-other with a voice like a gravel pit.

Charlotte screwed up her face and shook her head. "Oh, I don't know."

"You want him to be happy, don't you?"

Charlotte sipped her tea and thought for a moment, staring out the window into the garden.

Damn! Why did he have to show up here?

"Yes, of course I do—but those contraptions are too dangerous."

"They won't be," Scott said.

"Another one went down in America. Killed 34 men. All of them burned to death. That was in Virginia—Lou's home state."

"You're talking about the *Roma*. That thing was just an Italian sausage balloon—stone-age technology. *That* can't happen again."

"I'd be too worried."

"No need to worry. Government is drawing up massive new safety regulations."

"I don't like them."

"Airships will be as safe as houses. Huge new industry—thing of the future."

Charlotte shook her head, unconvinced.

"The pay will be substantial for officers in the fleet—a good living indeed!"

"I'll talk to my husband," Charlotte said.

"Yes, yes, of course. He'd be working only down the road from here at Howden. You wouldn't need to move—not for three or four years anyway. I think you'd both be very happy."

They heard the front door opening and Lou walked in, looking surprised. "Major Scott! What brings you here, sir? I wondered whose car it was outside."

Lou kissed Charlotte and Scott jumped up to shake hands.

"I had business in Hull, Lieutenant. Just thought I'd drop by."

They sat down around the low table. Charlotte poured tea for Lou. "More tea, Major?"

Scott hesitated and glanced at the sherry bottle. "I tell you what. A glass of your sherry would be nice."

"Of course." Lou went to the sideboard, poured out a glass and handed it to Scott.

Scott raised the glass. "Here's to both of you." He took a polite sip and leaned forward in his chair, stroking Fluffy purring at his feet.

"Were you happy in the Navy, Lou?"

"I loved the Navy, sir."

"How would you like to be back in?"

Lou glanced at Charlotte. "I don't understand how that could be possible, sir."

"I was telling your wife, things are opening back up at Howden. I don't suppose you want to work in a country garage for the rest of your life?"

Lou hesitated. "Er, well I suppose not."

"If you want back in, it can be arranged. In fact, it's *already* arranged. If you're both interested—just say the word," Scott said, swallowing the rest of his sherry.

Charlotte shot Scott a look of surprise. He hadn't told her that earlier.

"I can't believe this," Lou said.

"The Minister has spoken with the Secretary of the Navy in Washington. You'd be seconded by the Air Ministry to work on the New British Airship Program."

"Where?"

"You'd be based here in Howden as part of the Royal Airship Works team, which is totally responsible for the ship Vickers Aircraft Company will construct. You'd monitor the construction and report to us at the R.A.W. I know you did the same job when you were based in Cardington—I remember you very well.

"Sounds interesting," Lou said, refilling Scott's glass.

"You'd be here full time until this ship is completed. Then you'd move to Cardington—a beautiful little village, by the way," Scott added, giving Charlotte a reassuring glance.

"Wouldn't all this be unusual, me being in the U.S. Navy and ..."

"Not as unusual as you might think. Allies often second members of the each other's military for training and assistance. Commander Zachary Lansdowne was trained here and worked with us. He flew with me as American observer when I made the first return flight to the United States. He was awarded the Navy Cross and I received the Royal Air Force Cross. ..." Then he added wryly, "Others got knighted for less."

"I served under Commander Landsdowne for a short time," Lou said.

"Yes, so I understand. He's just taken over command of the *Shenandoah*," Scott said.

"We know someone else on that ship—one of Lou's crewmen," Charlotte said, without enthusiasm.

"These are exciting times. It's up to you," Scott said.

Lou sat stunned at this opportunity out of the blue. "I don't know what to say, sir."

"Don't say anything yet. You and Charlotte need to talk things over and think about your future and your new family." Charlotte saw Scott's eyes go in the direction of her knitting basket behind the couch and he nodded. She dropped her eyes—he'd noticed her hide her knitting. "Bedford will become one of the biggest travel centers in Britain, with regularly scheduled flights to the United States, Canada, India, Australia and New Zealand—it'll be known as 'Airship City.'"

"Sounds like they've got big plans," Lou said.

"Your first job would be to manage the re-commissioning of Howden Air Station, including repairs to the shed. That'll take a couple of years and should be interesting," Scott said.

Lou pondered that. He'd been sorry to see that place fall into ruin.

"Sounds great, sir."

"Howden used to be the biggest airship base in the country. Oh, and another thing. You'd be working with one of the finest airship engineers in the country—fella by the name of Wallis, Barnes Wallis."

While he stroked Fluffy, Scott talked generally about the airship industry and Lou's future prospects. Finally, he stood up and took out his wallet.

"Here's my card. Give me a call next week. If you decide against it, that's fine. I'll totally understand. You're under no obligation. I must be going—and thanks for the sherry—and the tea."

Scott shook hands with them and they watched him drive off in his little, black Ford. They closed the door after he'd gone and Charlotte cleared away the tea things in silence. The prospects were exciting—though much less for her.

"I guess there's not much to think about, is there?" Lou said.

Charlotte couldn't stop him. It'd make him happy and might be therapeutic. There'd be benefits, too: a better standard of living, a house of their own, they could seriously think of starting a family—maybe even get a little dog named Snowy!

"It's too good to turn down," Lou said

Charlotte reluctantly agreed, forcing herself to put negative emotions aside. It'd be years before any of these airships would be ready to fly. She could always talk him out of it later.

On Monday morning Lou had the unpleasant task of breaking the news to John Bull.

"John, something has come up, completely out of the blue," Lou told him. There was disappointment in John's eyes.

"What is it, Lou?"

One of the Air Ministry guys came by the cottage Saturday ..."

"And offered you a job?"

"Yes."

"Airships?" John tried to hide his dread.

"Yeah. They're gonna be building one at the Howden shed."

"That would be so handy for you, son."

"Long term it looks good and they've already squared things with the U.S. Navy. They're talking about me becoming a ship's officer—maybe even a captain, one day."

"My goodness! They must really want you."

"They asked me to manage fixing up the air station—that'll take a couple of years."

"I'm really excited for you, Lou. Sounds like a wonderful opportunity."

"Yes, but I'd hate to leave. I love working here with you, John."

"Lou, you must do what you must. You've got your whole life ahead of you. Mary and I want the best for you. You can't stay here all your life, can you?"

"I don't know, John …Charlotte and I have been very happy."

"No harm in trying things out. We'll still be close by. You're like a son to us."

Tears formed in John's eyes, making Lou feel wretched.

"And if things don't work out there'll always be a job here if you need one—and perhaps a lot more …" John said, taking Lou's hand between his own.

"The cottage …" Lou began.

"The cottage is yours as long as you want, my son, you know that."

Lou went home to Charlotte, his mind in turmoil.

The following week, Lou called Scott with their decision. He'd take the job. Scott told him to 'sit tight.' Two weeks later, Lou received a letter from Scott saying the offer had been approved; Lou would be hearing from the U.S. Navy and he'd be seconded by the Air Ministry, as discussed. A week later, Lou received a wire from the Navy confirming he'd been reinstated and would receive the rate of pay for a U.S. lieutenant based overseas, with travel and housing allowances. He was to take orders from Maj. Scott and Wing Cmdr. Colmore at the Royal Airship Works at Cardington under control of the British Air Ministry. He would observe British military ranks.

Scott was in Hull again two weeks later and he and Lou visited the Howden shed to make an inspection. Scott was interested to view the condition of the property since money would need to be allotted for renovations and additional equipment to turn the place back into a habitable working facility.

While the skylarks sang in surrounding fields, they drove around the thousand acres of low-lying ground, stopping at various dilapidated buildings. Their movements were watched by a herd of grazing cows, and scattered sheep bleating in the distance.

"The first thing you'll need to do is to reclaim this place from all these bloody animals!" Scott declared.

In the main shed, Lou showed Scott a vixen's den under the concrete slab in the hydrogen pipe ducts where she lived with her cubs. The shed floor was covered with chicken's feathers. They had a good laugh about that before driving off to The Railway Station pub in Howden where they ordered ham sandwiches and pints of Tetley's Best Bitter. Amused, Lou watched the barman pull up their beers with the bar pump handle. It frothed and overflowed, running down the glasses and over the bar.

I reckon these people would take a bath in this stuff if they could.

"I think you're going to do well here, Lou," Scott said, after taking a long swallow, half emptying his glass. He licked his lips. "Ah, that's much better."

"I'm looking forward to it, sir."

"You'll become a ship's officer in no time if you study hard."

They tucked into their sandwiches and Scott ordered more beers. Lou hadn't finished his first. "No, no more for me, sir."

"Come on, man, have another. It'll put hair on your chest," Scott said, and to the barman, "Give him another." Scott drained his first pint and went on. "You'll need to come down to Cardington next month to discuss your duties here and your relationship with Vickers."

"Okay, sir. When?"

"I'll let you know. Lord Thomson, the new Secretary of State, will be holding a press conference and making a public announcement about the program. They'll be broadcasting his speech on the wireless."

"You don't say!"

"I want you to attend. I'll introduce you to him."

"Great," Lou said with both awe and apprehension.

"I'll check and give you the exact date. You'd better arrange to get the telephones reconnected at the shed and get one installed at your cottage. We'll need to be in touch constantly. Oh, there's someone I must warn you about."

Lou was intrigued.

"Fella by the name of Dennistoun Burney. He's the man who heads up Vickers airship division. He's a royal pain in the arse. So, when you meet him, be polite, but don't take orders from him. Just say, you'll discuss the matter with your superiors."

"Right. Thanks for the warning, sir," Lou said.

"The others are okay. Barnes Wallis is a good man. Norway I've never met. He's with deHaviland Aircraft, but I understand he'll be joining their team as chief calculator this year. I don't think he knows anything about airships."

"I look forward to meeting everyone," Lou said.

Scott sank his second pint, while Lou struggled with his.

"Well, I must be going," Scott said, jumping up. "Come on, I'll drop you off."

10

BACK IN BEDFORD

During the first week of May, Lou traveled to Bedford. He was familiar with the area from his days working on *R38* in 1920 and '21. Lou felt the optimism in the air as soon as he got off the train. He sensed it on the familiar, old, green bus on the way to the Cardington gate. Though it was good to be back, he felt pangs of grief and as well as nostalgia. Passengers noticed his uniform and his American insignias. They smiled sympathetically.

The bus conductor remembered him. "Hello, sir. Lovely to have you back," he said. Lou forced a grin and looked out the window. They were passing Rowe's Tobacconist Shop, also known as the 'corner store,' where his buddies used to buy cigarettes and newspapers.

"We were all so choked up about what happened to you and your shipmates," the conductor said. Lou said nothing. He watched the people hurrying along the high street. The sun blazed and new leaves shone fresh and green. There was no evidence of his compatriots ever living or working here. Life had moved on. He looked out and saw a good-looking girl. Oh, those girls! They used to go mad for him and his buddies. It used to make the Bedford boys so angry. The haunting lyrics of Irving Berlin's "What'll I Do?" came into his mind. Charlotte had been playing that damned song all week. Desolation washed over him.

"I've been following you in the papers, sir. You didn't go home with the others, then?" the bus conductor said.

"This is home," Lou answered.

He thought about Charlotte and realized how much better he'd been since he got married. Lou held out a shilling for his fare. The conductor refused his money and winked. "Welcome home, son," he said, walking to the other end of the bus. Lou looked out the window again. His thoughts were disturbed by a plaintive voice behind him.

"Excuse me, sir."

Lou turned around to find a young man about twenty-six, skinny and angular with a fine nose and earnest, small, blue eyes. He removed his cap and held it in his hands, prayer-like.

"I couldn't help overhearing you're going up to Cardington, sir."

"Yes, why?" Lou noticed his right eye and cheek. He had a nervous twitch.

"I'm interested to find work, sir, and wondered if you might be able to help me in that regard."

"I'm not sure I can. This is my first day here, and I'm really only a visitor. What d'you do?" Lou asked.

"I'd like to work on the construction and I'm very good with engines. I'm a very 'ard worker, sir, 'an I'm very, very faithful."

"What's your name?"

"Joseph H. Binks, sir, but everybody calls me Joe."

Lou took out a small notepad and wrote down his name. "I'll see what I can do. Can't promise anything. Here, write down your address."

"I understand, sir. Work's scarce, you know, and I've got two young'uns at 'ome. Since I came out the Navy fings 'av been very 'ard," Binks said.

The bus came up to the gate and Lou got off with Binks behind him.

"Well, thank you, sir," Binks said, thrusting out his hand and bowing at the same time. "Lovely to have met you, sir."

"And you, too, Mr. Binks," Lou said, shaking his hand.

"God bless you, sir," Binks called after him, still holding his cap and bowing. Lou looked back, smiling. Binks trudged off and joined a long queue of men who, Lou presumed, were waiting for day work. As he walked toward the gate, he spotted Walter Potter standing by the gatehouse. Lou grinned, happy to see his old shipmate.

"Walter!"

"Sir! They said you was coming down. I couldn't wait to see you," Potter said, grasping Lou's hand. "I thought I'd wait and say hello."

"That's nice of you, Walter. How've you been? Are you working?"

"No. There's not much to do around here yet." Potter gestured to the line of men looking for work.

"Haven't you had enough of airships for one lifetime, Walter?"

Potter threw his head back and snorted. "Yeah, I have, but it's all I know. It's work. And a job is what I desperately need right now. Can you help me, sir?"

"You know I will, if I can. You live close by?"

Potter indicated with a sideways nod. "Shortstown. Just up the road."

Lou got out his pad again. "Write down your address. I'll see what I can do. I'm sure they'll find you something," Lou said. They chatted for a few minutes. Lou checked his watch. "I'd better go. They're waiting for me up there."

"Okay, sir, I hope we'll meet again soon."

"I'll be down every month. We'll have a pint. I'll see what I can do for you, don't worry." Lou gave him an assuring wink as they parted.

The guardhouse had been painted and the flower beds at the gate freshly planted with daffodils, making the place look spic-and-span. The gatekeeper greeted him warmly.

"Lieutenant Remington! How are you, sir? They told me to expect you," he said. "I'll get you a lift. Wait a mo.'" He held his hand up to a car coming through the gate. "Hey, Harry can you drop off our old friend the Lieutenant at the Admin?"

"Sure," the driver said, peering at Lou with a spark of recognition. Lou climbed in and they traveled up the driveway lined with flowering cherry trees. "I remember you, sir. My name's Harry, Harry Leech. I'm one of the engineering foremen."

"Your face is familiar. You're the engine wizard," Lou said. "Looks like this place is coming back to life."

"You bet! This bloke Thomson might be our savior," Leech said.

"Never can tell," said Lou.

The enormous sheds dominated the skyline and the surrounding area with all their ancillary buildings—housing machine shops, a gasbag factory, a hydrogen plant, electricity generators and warehouses. The area bustled with activity. Contractors' vehicles passed by—builders, painters, plumbers, electricians and landscapers, while others delivered scaffolding, planks, lumber, and assorted building materials.

In the distance, at the sheds, men stood on ladders fixing lighting while others painted the areas around the entrance doors. The weeds and brush, which had taken over, were being cleared and loaded onto a lorry.

"Good to see the ol' place resurrected," Leech said. "I'll be glad to get back to work." Lou nodded, realizing the enormity of his own task at Howden—that property being older and far more run down. He also had twenty derelict homes to renovate on the base for use by staff and their families. Cardington was years ahead in getting their facilities back in commission. Vickers' Howden team would be at a disadvantage from day one.

They traveled up the gravel road to Cardington House, an imposing stately home, previously owned by a wealthy industrialist and philanthropist. He'd made the property a gift to the government for the sake of airship research and development. The classical stucco great-house, set in magnificent gardens, now served as the headquarters for the Royal Airship Works (the R.A.W.). The building stood in a sea of daffodils with a backdrop of flowering tulip trees, magnolia trees, azaleas and rhododendrons. The place was a bird sanctuary with magpies, swallows, robins, pigeons and sparrows flying busily from tree to tree. Fragrances from this colorful paradise were overpowering. Lou paused to take it all in, not noticing the three black crows cawing and blinking slyly at him from their low branch.

Scott met Lou in the entrance hall of Cardington House and took him to meet Wing Cmdr. Colmore, Deputy Director of Airship Development in his ground floor office which looked out across the airfield. Lou had only been in the building a few times in the past, usually to deliver a communication or memo from the U.S. Navy to the R.A.W. brass.

Colmore, a charming man of forty-five, had graying hair, very short at the back and sides. He put Lou at ease immediately and confirmed Lou would begin restoration work at Howden as soon as possible, so Vickers could get started. The money had been budgeted and was available immediately. After the air station was up and running, Lou would continue to be based at Howden, assisting Vickers with the airship's construction and keeping records of progress as one of the general overseers—'not as a watchdog, but as a pair of eyes for the R.A.W. and there to assist Vickers in any way necessary.' He would not betray confidences from either side.

This relieved Lou. He didn't want the Vickers staff to think of him as a spy in the camp. Lou would visit Cardington once a month to report on progress and relay anything Vickers needed. Lou got a further boost when Colmore told him he'd be his 'special assistant'—a liaison officer. He winked at Lou and told him there'd be an increase in his salary paid by the Air Ministry. To Lou's amusement, Colmore reiterated the warning about Dennistoun Burney, who Colmore said was a bit of a 'bloody nuisance.'

After lunch in the dining room with Colmore and Scott, the building came alive. The heavy, white paneled office doors opened and closed constantly and people dashed in and out of the marble reception hall where Thomson's press conference was scheduled to take place. Broadcasting equipment and microphones were being set up and tested. Thomson would be on the air in two hours.

Suddenly, there was a great fuss at the entrance—Thomson's limousine had arrived. Lou went out with Scott and Colmore and other R.A.W. staff to greet him. Thomson got out and climbed the steps, his military bearing evident, though he appeared pale and gaunt. He came across initially as a forceful, energetic man. Word had traveled fast—the new Minister of State from Whitehall was on base. Everyone was anxious to catch a glimpse.

Inside the majestic reception hall, Thomson peered around at the seating, nodding with pleasure at the preparations. He was led to the conference room by Colmore and Scott, and the door closed behind them. Lou went and sat in the reception hall. Thirty minutes later, Lou was sent for and taken to the conference room to meet 'the man'. He entered in time to see the chief steward receiving generous praise for the 'delicious cucumber sandwiches' he'd served Thomson with his tea.

Thomson, long-necked and vulture-like, stood with his slender hand extended. His sagging, weary eyes and hollow cheeks made his nose prominent and beak-like. His shoulders were stooped and his threadbare, black coat ill-fitting and loose around the collar. Lou assessed him as a man who'd seen rough times. Though Thomson was courteous, Lou couldn't help feeling intimidated, but at the same time sympathetic. At times like this, he remembered what his grandmother once told him: 'Remember, son, inside every man there's a small boy'. Her words floated down from the ether at this moment.

"Lieutenant Remington! I'm pleased to meet you," Thomson said, shaking Lou's hand, the grip of his long, delicate fingers firm, but not overly so.

"Likewise, sir."

"I've had conversations about you with your people in Washington. Are you happy with the set up?"

"Yes, sir, I'm very pleased."

"We're honored to have you with us. You're highly thought of, both here and at home. I think this arrangement will be beneficial to both countries," Thomson said.

"Thank you, sir."

Thomson seemed about to end the conversation, but had an afterthought.

"You were at the Front?"

"Yes, sir—Belleau Wood and Saint-Mihiel."

"And thank God you were, Lieutenant. I was at Ypres. I read your war record. You were buried alive with twenty-five other men, weren't you?"

"Yes, sir."

"Awful business. Any ill effects?"

"No, sir. I'm fine," Lou lied.

"What about the others?"

"All dead, sir."

Thomson nodded sadly. "Well, welcome aboard. We'll be changing the world together. These new airships will be the next big thing," Thomson said, looking from Lou to Colmore and Scott.

After more small talk, Lou left the conference room to find the reception hall filling up. Those gathering appeared to be the well-to-do from the local area: businessmen, bankers, solicitors, doctors, accountants—mostly professionals. Others included Whitehall civil servants, members of Parliament and military personnel in uniform. Two dozen reporters and about twenty photographers were also present. Lou took a seat off to one side. Some reporters recognized him. A nerdy-looking young man in a Harris Tweed jacket, sitting nearby, also seemed to be taking quite an interest in him.

11

THE DIE IS CAST

May 1924

At ten minutes to three, Thomson marched in and mounted the low podium where he was joined by Colmore, Scott and another R.A.W. man Lou hadn't seen before. Thomson took a sip from a glass of water. After testing the microphones, a BBC technician wearing headphones told Thomson he'd be on in four minutes. As the time came up, the man held up his fingers, counting down seconds. Thomson cleared his throat and began in his gravelly, baritone voice.

"Good afternoon, ladies and gentlemen and listeners. It gives me great pleasure to speak to you from the Royal Airship Works at Cardington, in Bedfordshire—home of the British airship industry for more than ten years."

The two hundred people in the audience listened with rapt attention. "It is with pride that I announce today the beginning of the New British Imperial Airship Program and I'm here to describe my vision of a future fleet of luxurious airships that will compete globally with ocean liners."

Thomson smiled benevolently into the flashing cameras while reporters scribbled. "The proposal I put to the Cabinet was approved by the Prime Minister, who put it to the House of Commons where it was overwhelmingly approved. I presented this proposal to the House of Lords, explaining how this program will be the most ambitious airship building program ever undertaken. Once again, the program received enthusiastic support."

Thomson paused to make sure he had everyone's attention.

"After careful deliberation, I've decided the government will underwrite the construction of two airships at a cost of one million, four hundred thousand pounds. Each will have the capacity of five million cubic feet of hydrogen, giving a lifting capacity of one hundred and fifty tons." Thomson paused again for reporters to write the numbers down.

"Weight shall not exceed ninety tons—leaving sixty tons of lift for passengers, fuel, stores and ballast. The top speed will not exceed seventy miles per hour—four times the speed of a passenger liner! High fuel loads and high speeds will give these airships the range and power necessary to reach all corners of the globe.

"The first ship, designated *Howden R100*, will be constructed for the government by Vickers Aircraft at Howden in Yorkshire under a fixed-price contract. Those in charge of constructing *Howden R100* will report directly to, and be administered by, the Royal Airship Works Staff."

Thomson paused, remembering his meeting with Wallis as he gestured grandly to the three men standing with him at the podium. They smiled serenely while a series of camera flashes started again.

"The second ship, designated *Cardington R101*, will be built by the government team here at the Royal Airship Works."

Murmurs of excitement were building.

"This ship will be one of a new class in design. Now, before introducing the Royal Airship Works team, I will say this: The acceptance of the New British Airship Program is a rejection of the 'Burney Scheme,' which proposed Vickers build six airships costing tax payers a whopping four million eight hundred thousand pounds. A proposal far too grandiose, and meaning Vickers would have a complete monopoly—an unacceptable state of affairs, if I may say so."

Thomson seemed to have the approval of most, but not all.

"In the early stages, it will be my intention to enlist the help of private enterprise—not in competition, but in a spirit of cooperation—each assisting and improving the performance of the other."

He paused and looked down for a moment. "I may take a risk when I say I don't believe even the most aggressive businessmen will be wholly inspired by sordid motives—in other words, by greed—when they assist the government in the conquest of the air! The earlier pioneers in aviation made sacrifices at first, but in the end, they made money—lots of money. In order to make a success of this venture, sacrifices will have to be made by private enterprise—for the *Common Good."*

There were a few shouts of "Hear, hear" and weak applause.

"Under the Burney Scheme, if the first ship crashed, all would be lost. Under our plan, if we lose one of the ships, we will still have the other ship plus the experts, the designers and the engineers. We would still have our air routes, our infrastructure and the will and determination to carry on with this project to see it through."

There were frowns on some faces. Some found his line of reasoning hard to follow, but they'd go along—jobs were all that mattered.

"At the end of the day, we'll learn that state enterprise in industry, business, finance, transportation and communication will be enormously more efficient than private enterprise. This program will be a learning experience. State enterprise will be the cornerstone of our socialist policies. I will now introduce you to the team."

Thomson gestured grandly toward the three men standing behind him. "Wing Commander Reginald Colmore as Deputy Director of Airship Development and will be overall administrator of the Airship Program.

Colmore has had fifteen years experience in this industry. During the war, he developed an effective anti-submarine patrol strategy using airships in conjunction with surface ships and aeroplanes to hunt down the enemy. So effective was his brainchild that the system was set up around the entire coast of Britain. Wing Commander Colmore has been involved from the inception of this program and assisted in writing the specifications. He has a proven track record as a fine leader."

Colmore stepped forward and bowed his head slightly while receiving gentle applause. Thomson had assessed him to be a rather humble, well-bred man of grace and charm. They said Colmore didn't possess a mean bone in his body. Thomson had reservations—perhaps he wasn't forceful enough. Furthermore, although Colmore thoroughly understood airships, he'd made it known he believed they had their limitations.

Can he give me one hundred percent?

"Now I introduce Major Herbert Scott. Most of you know this man and why he is such a valuable asset." Thomson smiled and so did Scott, who took a pace forward. Thomson thought of him as hard driving when the going got tough, but he had a reputation for recklessness. Thomson was well aware of past instances of this. He'd been in command of the Parseval PL-18 when she crashed into her shed in Barrow in 1915. That was in fog—ages ago. He'd also been in command of R36 when she was badly damaged during mooring operations at Pulham in 1921.

Despite all that, he's a man who'll inject momentum into this team. He'll need holding in check. Men like this—prepared to take risks—built the Empire.

"This man is a true pioneer in British aviation and a man to whom we owe a debt of gratitude. He was the *first* man to fly the Atlantic, as the captain of *Airship R34*, making the return journey between Scotland and the United States in 1919. Major Scott will be in charge of testing and flying the aircraft and training personnel. He'll make sure we have the best men in our fleet."

Thomson looked across briefly at Lou who showed no reaction. The applause this time was loud, with a few cheers, delighting Scott who waved to the audience.

"Last, but not least, I want to introduce Colonel Vincent Richmond, who will head up management of the design team. The design of *Cardington R101* will be in this man's hands."

Richmond, average height, slightly rounded, with a head of dark, shiny, Brylcreemed hair, stepped forward to give the audience a curt nod and a begrudging, crooked smile from thin lips. Thomson also had reservations about Richmond. He sensed the man was confident, perhaps overconfident. His colleagues considered him pompous. Thomson knew he was ambitious, which made him glad. He really didn't care about his other traits.

He has a high opinion of himself, no doubt. We'll see what he's made of. What good would these people be, if they weren't confident and ambitious? Competence and leadership are what we need.

This position would carry not only immense responsibility and pressure, but the stigma of failures by previous government designers. None of this seemed to phase Richmond. This was a man who sensed his time had come and was ready for the challenge. Richmond received meager applause. Thomson went on, squinting over his pince-nez spectacles, smiling at reporters.

"As soon as construction and testing are complete, each ship will be required to make an intercontinental flight—*Howden R100* to Canada, *Cardington R101* to India."

This caused a buzz of excitement. Thomson beamed with pleasure.

At this point, the BBC technician signaled that the broadcast segment was coming to an end. Thomson paused while the radio announcer wrapped things up with a few words to the radio audience after which, Thomson continued with his press conference.

"If you have any questions, gentlemen, I'd be pleased to answer them."

An eager reporter leapt to his feet.

"Tom Brewer, *Daily Telegraph*. Lord Thomson, the feeling in this country, after so many crashes and loss of life, is that airships are totally unsafe."

Thomson held up his right hand as though directing traffic and lifted his chin defiantly, staring over the reporter's head. The man had become invisible.

"Good, good. A wise, thoughtful question, indeed, sir—one this government will take seriously. One thing I stress above *all else*: 'Safety First' is the unbreakable rule!" Thomson put on a determined frown and shook his finger at the ceiling. "*And 'Safety Second' as well, by Jove!*"

An overweight reporter in a khaki raincoat stood up next.

"Bill Hagan, *Daily Mail*. Lord Thomson, there were reports that Barnes Wallis was going to head up this program. What happened? He *is* the best airship engineer in the country, is he not?"

Thomson's memory of his encounter with Wallis at Chequers tasted like acid reflux in his throat. He covered his mouth and coughed, carefully formulating an answer. He hadn't realized that meeting had got out.

"We considered a lot of people for the position and discussed all possibilities at length. We have a wonderful team of experienced men and I know the two teams will work well together toward a successful outcome." Thomson hoped no one sensed any lack of conviction.

A thin, well-dressed reporter in a Savile Row suit was next.

"William Haines, *The Times*. My question is directed to Colonel Richmond," he said, turning the pages of his notepad. "What do you think about having jurisdiction over Vickers? Are you confident in overseeing Barnes Wallis?"

Ouch!

Richmond glanced at Thomson as though for help. Thomson ignored him. "I don't think this will be an issue. Mr. Wallis will not need *supervision* from me, or this team. As you say, he's a superb engineer and we can all expect wonderful things from him."

This answer seemed to satisfy everybody. Richmond had been magnanimous. Thomson noticed him biting his lip and screwing up his eyes as he stepped away from the podium. Another reporter raised his hand. He had a Yorkshire accent.

"You say Vickers is building their ship for a contract sum. Do you know 'ow much your airship will cost and will you be able to build it for the same money?"

Thomson answered. "We don't know exactly, no. The airship has not even been designed, but the Cardington ship will certainly cost less—since it's being built at cost with no *profit* involved." He spat out 'profit,' grimacing. He pointed at the next reporter. A short, rotund Londoner stood up.

"Edmund Jones, *Daily Mirror.* Colonel Richmond, the last airship broke in half, killing forty-four people. How do you know your airship won't do the same?"

Richmond stepped forward. "I've spent a great deal of time studying the *R38* mishap. It's possible that sacrifices were made for lightness. I assure you, the strength of this airship will be our *top priority*. We'll go back to basics. Through strength we shall achieve safety—and, I should add, absolutely no expense will be spared in that regard."

A tall reporter wearing a scruffy raincoat and a five o'clock shadow had been pacing around impatiently at the back of the hall. It was George Hunter. Thomson pointed to him.

"George Hunter, *Daily Express.* Lord Thomson, you say you don't care much for the idea of Vickers getting a monopoly on the airship business. The way you've set all this up means *government* will have the monopoly. Is there *really* any difference?"

Thomson tried to hide his irritation. "Certainly. Government is entirely different. We represent the people and the *Common Good*—that's Common with a capital C and Good with a capital G."

George Hunter followed up. "But if a private company messes up, they go out of business, or are not hired again—ever! Things don't work that way with government, do they? Government just carries on as if nothing happened."

This infuriated Thomson.

Who is this man? Must be one of Burney's people!

"I'm not sure if I should dignify your statement with a rebuttal, sir."

The team on the podium appeared distinctly uncomfortable, nervously shuffling their feet. Tension became palpable. The angry reporter wouldn't let it go. He stalked down the center aisle to the foot of the podium, raising his arms and yelling up at Thomson.

"Do any of you people remember the horror of *R38*—any of you?"

Thomson recovered and did a commendable job of composing himself, his expression heartsick. "Yes, sir. All of us do. In fact we have someone in this room who remembers that awful day only too well."

Many of the reporters had already turned to gauge Lou's reaction. Thomson's gaze was followed by the rest of the people in the room, including Inspector Fred McWade, whom Lou noticed for the first time at the front. The man in the Harris Tweed jacket stared intensely at Lou. Their eyes met.

Who the hell is this guy?

"I want to present Lieutenant Louis Remington of the United States Navy, who has graciously agreed to be here today and who will be assisting us with these projects. Would you be kind enough to stand up, Lieutenant?"

Thomson didn't mention Lou's connection with *R38*. It wasn't necessary. Lou got out of his chair, standing as though for inspection. He didn't smile and hadn't been expecting this. Thomson continued. "We take this whole matter very seriously indeed, especially concerning safety. As I said, safety in the design of these airships will be our main concern. I don't think the lieutenant would be working with us if he didn't believe that to be true. Thank you, Lieutenant Remington."

Lou sat down.

"Now, one final thing I wish to say: If I thought the ships being constructed under this program were unsafe, I wouldn't fly in them myself. It's my intention to be on board *Cardington R101* for her maiden voyage to India. You can put that in your diaries gentlemen. And you can take it to the bank!"

A boffin-like reporter in a striped shirt and tussled frizzy hair stood up and referred to notes through gold wire glasses. "Sir—John Jacobs, *Aeroplane Magazine*. What did you say the useful lift will be?"

"Sixty tons," Thomson answered.

"*Sixty tons?*"

"Yes," Thomson said.

"*Sixty tons,*" the reporter repeated, scribbling the number down. "When you spoke of the government's *Cardington R101*, I got the impression you were saying this ship would be the more advanced ship—hence the higher designation number—with more innovation—a different class to *Howden R100*. Is that the case?"

"Oh no, I didn't mean to imply that at all, no, no. I'm sure the Howden ship will be as strong and as safe," Thomson replied. The *Aeroplane Magazine* reporter didn't seem entirely satisfied with the answer, skepticism registering in his face as he began to sit down. But he had another thought and stood up again, referring to his notes. "You said, 'In the early stages you'd enlist the help of private enterprise.' What will you do after that—*nationalize them?*"

This was irritating. "No, no. That's all too far off to contemplate," Thomson said with a wave of his hand. The reporter scratched his head and sat down again. A few less serious questions were asked and Thomson answered with patience and humility until all topics were exhausted. He began a series of closing statements, but before he'd finished, photographers were packing up their equipment and reporters were snapping their notepads shut, ready to head for the telephones to file their reports.

"Thank you for coming, gentlemen," Thomson shouted over their noisy departure. He smiled happily, watching them rush off, not irritated by their rude exit. He knew there'd be a big spread in the papers the next morning. And that was really all that mattered.

After the conference, Colmore introduced Lou to Col. Richmond whom Lou found aloof and cold. Lou wasn't sure of the reason. Perhaps it was Lou's connection with *R38*, which they didn't discuss, or maybe it was because he was based in Howden with 'the enemy.' Later, he put it down to the man's nature combined with the superior attitude of design engineers. While Lou was talking with Richmond, he noticed the Harris Tweed guy hovering near the door, looking his way. He seemed to have something on his mind. The next time Lou looked, the man had disappeared.

After that, Lou spent an hour with Scott going over the Howden renovations. He'd draw up a preliminary schedule of items to submit within two weeks for review. It'd be necessary to meet with Vickers to introduce Lou and to discuss these improvements. After that, estimates would be submitted. Lou pulled out his notepad and tore off the top sheet.

"Major, here are two names and addresses. One is Walter Potter who flew with me on *R38*. The other is a fella named Binks—I like the looks of him. They both need jobs."

"Potter, oh yes, I remember him. We'll certainly fit him in somewhere."

"What about Binks?"

"Yes, all right, give it to me. I'll take care of them both," Scott said gruffly, taking the sheet of paper.

Although irritated at being used by Thomson as a prop, Lou left Cardington in good spirits. These were heady days, but he knew the euphoria couldn't last. In the meantime, he'd make the most of it. Close to the cottage, he could even pop home for lunch and make love to Charlotte! The coming months would pass without much pressure. This was going to be fun.

While Lou was riding the bus to Bedford Station to catch his train home, Charlotte was on her way to Ackworth Station from her parents' house. She'd listened to Thomson's speech on the wireless with her mother. The sky was threatening. As she walked along Station Road, she recognized the figure approaching, shoulders hunched, hands in his pockets. From a distance, except for his posture, he had an uncanny resemblance to her husband. Her heart thumping, she doubted this encounter was an accident. As he drew close, he stopped and leered, his eyes bulging and bloodshot.

"Hello, my lovely."

"Get away from me, Jessup!"

"No baby yet, then? Been a long time now, hasn't it?"

"Shut up and go away."

"I heard you've been tryin'. They bin talkin' about you in the village. My sister's been tellin' me all about it."

That little bitch Angela. I'll strangle her!

"Now I'd like to help you out, my love. I guess he just ain't doin' you right."

"Leave me alone! You evil bast—"

"Uh-uh-uh! Mummy wouldn't like you using that kind of language. Come on, sweet pea, give me a kiss. You know you find me irresistible. Try me. I'll have you knocked up in a week."

Jessup took her by the upper arm and leaned in to kiss her. Charlotte, repulsed by his beery breath and body odor, wrenched herself away, breaking her heel. With the broken shoe in one hand, she ran awkwardly toward the station. Jessup roared with laughter as she fled.

"I'll get you, don't you worry. You high and mighty little cow!" he screamed after her.

12

OH, SHENANDOAH!

May 1924 – October 1924,

As soon as Lou got back to Howden things moved rapidly. He arranged for a caravan to be delivered as a temporary office and for telephones to be installed in accordance with Scott's instructions. A couple of weeks later, Barnes Wallis showed up unannounced. Lou liked him. He appeared quiet and unassuming. Lou had the feeling he was a man easily misjudged on first impression. Wallis and Lou went around the aerodrome as he'd done with Scott, but more thoroughly. Wallis took in every detail. They examined the buildings and utilities in need of refurbishment or replacement, including the sewage plant, water treatment plant, water storage tower and electrical generating shop. Wallis surveyed a brick building he'd use to manufacture helical tubing for framing the ship. They inspected the hydrogen plant located next to the shed. That needed work.

Lou coordinated between Cardington, Vickers at Westminster (where Wallis was presently based), Yorkshire County and many contractors. A crew of twenty men came up from London to make the shed watertight; thousands of sheets of corrugated iron cladding had rusted or become loose and in need of replacement. Lou also organized local contractors to complete the renovation of the brick-built offices located inside, down one side of the shed. He put these same companies to work restoring the twenty bungalows situated along the boundary of the aerodrome. These would be home to design and engineering staff, including Wallis and Burney and their families.

For Lou and Charlotte, this was the happiest period of their lives. Sometimes, if Charlotte wasn't working, Lou dropped by the cottage for lunch, or Charlotte came by the caravan on the bus. The work crews were pleasant and everyone was on familiar terms.

One time, Charlotte came by the caravan with Lou's lunch and it turned into a passionate exchange. The caravan shook and rocked, squeaking on its chassis and Charlotte cried out. Afterwards, they lay in the bunk exhausted. Some time passed before they registered the knocking. Lou scrambled to make himself respectable and went to the door, red-faced and embarrassed. A delivery truck driver stood outside. He took off his cap and gave Lou a knowing smile.

"I was just taking a nap," Lou said.

"Sorry to disturb you, gov.' I 'spect you was 'avin a bad dream," the driver said.

"Er, well ..."

"Got a load of timber 'ere. Where d'yer want it?"

Lou came out of the caravan and pointed to the shed doors.

"Drive inside the shed and find a dry spot."

The driver hesitated a moment. "Er, you might like to know, sir, there was a bloke 'ere, right 'ere, looking in the window of your caravan. When he saw me, he scarpered right quick."

"What'd he look like?"

"A lot like you, actually. Same height, same build, 'cept he was an ugly, mean-looking sod with thick greasy 'air and a scar on his face like you—blimey you could be twins!"

"Where'd he go?"

"In them woods over yonder. He must've been on a motorbike. I heard it start up and drive off down the trail."

"Thanks, I'll be on the lookout."

Lou went back inside the caravan, but said nothing to Charlotte about the 'peeping Tom.' Later, he asked the workmen if they'd seen anyone lurking around. They told him they'd noticed a man at the edge of the wood staring at the caravan once or twice, but thought he might be someone looking for work.

In July, trouble was brewing in London for Thomson and the Labour Government, but he failed to appreciate its seriousness. Since Labour didn't have a majority, it was difficult for the more radical social issues to be moved forward, but MacDonald's bill promoting the construction of 'council housing' passed through the House without fuss.

With Thomson acting as his confidante and council, MacDonald put much energy into international affairs in his role as Foreign Secretary in addition to being Prime Minister. He did his best to repair damage done by the Treaty of Versailles, tackling reparations issues and shaping agreeable terms with Germany concerning the French occupation of the Rhur—actions some saw as appeasement. The 'London Settlement' was signed and an Anglo-German Commercial Treaty put into effect. MacDonald's main goal was the disarmament of Europe and though noble, it was not one Germany would later share.

As soon as he'd assumed office, MacDonald set about normalizing relations with the Russian revolutionaries. On February 1st, The government recognized the Soviet Union and negotiated a treaty guaranteeing loans to the Bolsheviks. Large segments of the public, previously willing to give MacDonald the benefit of the doubt, became suspicious, believing him to be a communist after all. These treaties were unpopular, not only with Conservatives, but with Liberals who shored up his hold on power.

Another nail in the coffin came in July when J.R. Campbell, the communist editor of the *Worker's Weekly,* wrote a highly inflammatory article. Thomson went to No. 10 Downing Street to discuss the matter with MacDonald. He'd heard about the article, but paid little attention to it. These were people out on the fringe—every country had them. Thomson entered the Prime Minister's study overlooking the gardens. A small, mahogany desk and a couple of chairs had been placed in the room, which was otherwise bare; there were no photographs of MacDonald's family on the walls, no pictures. MacDonald looked up from his desk while Thomson stared at the boxes stacked around the walls.

"Good morning, Ramsay."

"Don't bother looking at all that, CB. It's hardly worth unpacking."

"Why not?"

"I expect you've read this rubbish?" MacDonald said, pointing at a copy of *Worker's Weekly* on the desk.

"No, but I heard the rumpus."

Thomson picked up the paper and scanned it quickly, reading aloud.

" '*Open letter to our Fighting Forces. Comrades:* '"

Thomson looked up at MacDonald. "That's a good start!"

"'*You never joined the army because you were in love with war ...In most cases you were compelled by poverty or misery of unemployment ... when war is declared you are expected to kill the enemy. The enemy are working people just like you, living in slavery ... So, I say soldiers, sailors, airmen, flesh of our flesh, bone of our bone—The Communist Party calls on you to let it be known, in war, be it class war or military war, you will not turn your guns on your fellow workers, but will instead, line up with your comrades and attack the exploiters and capitalists. Refuse to fight for profits! Turn your weapons on your oppressors!*' "

Thomson's jaw dropped. "He's telling them to shoot their officers!"

"The Attorney General has announced that this editor and some of his cronies are to be prosecuted under the *Incitement to Mutiny Act of 1797.* We're under tremendous pressure from our backbenchers to put a stop to legal action against these fools. What's your opinion?" MacDonald asked.

"If you let the prosecution go ahead, we'll have rebellion in the party. Me personally, I think these people should go to prison, or be shot. This is treason, no question. If you quash this, there'll be hell to pay from Conservatives and Liberals. We'll be finished," Thomson replied. He suddenly thought of Marthe and his hopes for the future. He put his hand to his head.

Damn! Things had started off so well.

"Point is, CB, these are just a bunch of silly fools no one's listening to. The more fuss we make, the more we empower them."

"You and I know that, Ramsay, but some people are up in arms. I'd hate to see them get away with this. If they'd been in my regiment, they would've been executed."

"But they're *not* in your regiment, CB."

"More's the pity," Thomson sniffed.

"There was a time when you would've had to shoot me, too!"

"I suppose so," Thomson begrudgingly agreed.

"The people pressuring me are the ones who have supported me from the beginning. I cannot desert them now."

Thomson got up to leave. "You must do as your conscience dictates, Ramsay. Whatever you decide, naturally, I'll support you without reservation."

"I'll need time to think," MacDonald said. "Come back tomorrow morning."

Thomson descended the imposing staircase troubled and disappointed.

Life knocks you down—just when things couldn't be better.

Re-commissioning progressed well at Howden. Another crew was sent from the south to refurbish the hydrogen plant and would finish next spring. Inside the shed, contractors rewired the offices and made general repairs while others worked on the bungalows.

Lou started making his monthly visits to Cardington as required. He reported on expenditures and submitted budgets for renovations. Fifty thousand pounds was a lot of money and the Air Ministry was anxious the budget wasn't exceeded. While in Cardington, Lou saw no progress at all and was told that team was working furiously on revolutionary 'state of the art' designs. The Air Ministry gave the press the same story. Articles were published regularly in glowing terms, describing what the public could expect to see rolling out from the Cardington shed in the future—marvels designed by geniuses. By comparison, *Howden R100* was rarely mentioned. That suited Wallis.

Thomson returned to No.10 Downing Street the following morning. MacDonald looked grave and got to the point as Thomson sat down.

"I've decided to drop the prosecution of the editor."

"I see," Thomson said, trying his damnedest to hide his disappointment.

"With our friendly attitude toward the Soviets on trade and now this, we'll be up against severe criticism. They're saying the party is under the control of the radical Left," MacDonald said.

"Yes, they are."

"In any case, I'm not going to allow these people to be put on trial."

Thomson appeared skeptical. "They're talking about a motion of no confidence."

"Yes, I know—but I think we can weather the storm. I believe the British people know we're their best hope. I'll announce my decision in the House next week."

Surely, a baby must come soon!

That would make everything perfect. Charlotte continued making baby clothes and wrapping and folding them neatly in the chest of drawers in the bedroom. She daren't think about the airship and its completion.

That's years down the road.

Charlotte's friend Fanny had become a frequent visitor to the cottage. When off duty, she came during the week while Billy was at school and Lenny was at the saw-mill in Hull. Some Sundays, Fanny's family, the Bunyans, came over for tea and the boy made a big fuss of Fluffy. Billy, now thirteen, idolized Lou and they often played football in the garden, while Lenny leaned on the damp, stone wall smoking Woodbines. Fanny knew Charlotte was mad for a child and constantly gave her advice.

"God will make you pregnant when He's good and ready. Don't be in such a rush, love," Fanny would say. And then laughing, "Meanwhile, enjoy all that good lovin'!" But this didn't satisfy Charlotte's obsessive longing.

In August, the Prime Minister announced charges against the editor of the communist *Worker's Weekly* would be dropped. A storm of outrage, both in the House and in the press, erupted immediately. The Conservatives entered a censure motion while Liberals entered an amendment of their own. These motions were put to a vote of "no confidence" which carried, and Parliament was dissolved. A general election was set for October 29.

In September, while Charlotte was doing housework, Fanny arrived at the cottage, rapping furiously on the front door. Charlotte answered, carrying her dusting pan and brush. Fanny rushed in, in great distress.

"Oh, Charlotte. Have you heard?"

"What's happened, Fanny?" Charlotte asked with growing panic.

"The *Shenandoah's* gone down in America. The BBC announced it."

"Oh, no." Charlotte's eyes filled with tears. "Josh is on that ship."

"Yes, I know, love. That's why I came straight here."

Charlotte threw the dusting pan and brush at the wall. "Damn, damn, damn! I hate bloody airships!"

Charlotte and Fanny spent the rest of the afternoon sobbing in between cups of tea—the English cure-all—until Fanny had to leave.

When Lou arrived, he'd obviously heard the news.
"Was Josh on the ship?"
"Yes."
"He's dead, isn't he?"
"Yes."
Charlotte screwed up her eyes and her tears flowed again. Lou slumped down onto the couch, his head in his hands. "I knew three of the others, too. Fourteen were killed. I called the Washington Navy Yard and got the full story. They were on their way from Lakehurst to Ohio. The ship broke up in a storm."
"Oh Lou, I'm so sorry. I know they were your mates, love."
"Josh said he was golden," Lou said, bitterly.
"He was such a lovely fella."
Lou didn't speak for some time. "It's amazing—twenty nine actually survived. I served under Landsdowne for a short time. He died, too."
"Major Scott will be upset," Charlotte said. "He'll be drowning his sorrows I expect."
Charlotte spoke no more about it, but all her fears had been re-awakened with a vengeance. It was a sleepless night.
They all die someday, Charlotte.

A cloud of grief hung over the Howden shed. They were all brothers, these airshipmen. Lou knew this had come as a severe blow to Charlotte, jarring her out of the vacuum. But there were no more explosions or hysteria, just a tacit agreement never to mention the *Shenandoah* again.

The election campaign was spirited and MacDonald believed Labour would pull it off. However, another issue reared up, complicating matters further. Thomson was summoned to Chequers. And so, on a damp autumnal morning in October, while mist rolled across the Berkshire Downs, Thomson was driven up the gravel drive. He entered the Prime Minister's study, a comfortable room lined with leather-bound books and ticking clocks. MacDonald sat looking out the window into the mist. He turned on hearing Thomson enter.
"Ah, CB, thank you for coming. More problems, I'm afraid. The foreign office received a letter addressed to the Central Committee of the British Communist Party purported to have been sent by a Mr. Zinoviev."
"Who the hell's he?"
"A Bolshevik revolutionary in the Communist Party in Moscow. He's calling for agitation in Britain."

"You mean revolution?"

"Yes. In concert with the Bolsheviks, promoting Leninism in England and the colonies."

"Damn these people!"

"It's probably a forgery perpetrated by the Tories, or the White Russian intelligence, or both."

"This couldn't have come at a worse time," Thomson said.

"This is no accident," MacDonald said.

"When was it written?"

"It's dated September 15th. Received by the Foreign Office October 10th."

"If this gets out …"

"Oh, it *will* get out. I'm sure the newspapers already have a copy of this letter."

"Surely they won't publish it, if it's a forgery?"

"CB—don't be naïve! Of course they'll publish it! I've sent a letter of protest to the government in Moscow. I intend to beat the conservative newspapers to the punch and make an announcement to the House and the press exposing the matter, with a copy of my letter. With luck, this'll blow up in their faces and help us in next week's elections."

Thomson puffed up his cheeks and blew the pent up air from his lungs. It'd be close. "When are you going to do this, Ramsay?"

"Ten o'clock tomorrow morning."

Thomson returned to Ashley Gardens.

The next morning he sat at his dining table while Gwen served him scrambled eggs on toast. She brought the newspapers to the table. By her expression, she'd already caught the *Daily Mail* headline. Thomson held it up, hardly believing his eyes.

LETTER FROM RUSSIAN COMMUNIST PARTY PRESIDENT ENCOURAGES BOLSHEVIC REVOLUTION IN BRITAIN & COLONIES

A letter has come into this newspaper's hands which is purported to have been written by the president of the Russian Communist International, Mr. Grigory Zinoviev, a radical Bolshevik revolutionary

…

Thomson scanned the article, laid down the paper and put his hands to his head.

Damn! It's all over!

He called to the housekeeper, who'd made herself scarce.

"Gwen, I'm leaving. I'll be at No.10."

"What about your breakfast, sir? You've hardly eaten anything!"

"No time," Thomson said, dashing out the door.
And I don't have any appetite now!

At No.10 there was an atmosphere of panic. An usher waved
Thomson to go up. He bounded up the stairs and knocked on the Prime
Minister's door.

"Come in," MacDonald's dull voice replied from within.

"Ramsay ..."

"Yes, yes, yes. They beat us to it."

"Now what do we do?"

"Our chances are slim to none. We'll make the case it's a forgery and
a conspiracy, but with four days to go, it's unlikely we'll convince anyone.
The Foreign Office thinks the damned thing's genuine."

"Who leaked it?"

"It really doesn't matter, CB."

The day after the elections Thomson went to Chequers to help
MacDonald collect his belongings and enjoy the place for a couple of hours
before Baldwin's people arrived. They took coffee in the Great Hall and sat
analyzing the election results. The Conservatives had won a stunning victory,
gaining 155 seats, giving them a total of 413. The liberals had been crushed,
with the number of seats held slashed from 158 to 40. MacDonald thought,
overall, Labour hadn't done badly, losing 40 seats, holding on to 151.

"I'd hoped we'd hang on, but it wasn't to be, laddie."

"What will you do now?" Thomson asked.

"I'm going to fly up to Lossie and do a lot of walking, golfing,
fishing, thinking and writing. I'm gonna be planning our future! Why don't
you come?"

"Good idea."

"We'll fly with my new pilot—chap named Hinchliffe."

"Where did you find him?"

"Sefton Brancker recommended him."

"Good old Sefton."

"He'll put us down in the field near the house. I'll pick you up
tomorrow at nine."

"Right."

"After a spell at Lossie, I suggest you go and see your lady-love in
Romania."

"Perhaps I shall."

"Main thing is—don't give up. We'll be back. Count on it!"

"I *am*," Thomson said.

"Write a book or something whilst we bide our time."

"I've been planning to do that. I've already chosen the title."

"Well, what is it?"

"Smaranda," Thomson said.

"Sounds like a fascinating story about a Romanian Princess."

While Thomson and MacDonald were clearing out their possessions from Chequers, a small ceremony was taking place at Howden Air Station celebrating the formation of Vickers's Airship Guarantee Company to handle design and construction of *Howden R100*. The contract had just been ratified. A little 'sign planting' party was arranged to commemorate the occasion.

Those gathered in the drizzle at the entrance under umbrellas included, Wing Cmdr. Colmore, Maj. Scott, Dennistoun Burney, Barnes Wallis, newcomer Nevil Shute Norway and Lt. Lou Remington. George Hunter, the *Daily Express* reporter and angry journalist at the Cardington press conference, had traveled up from London. The local Hull newspaper sent a reporter and a photographer. Norway, Lou remembered as being the guy in the Harris Tweed jacket who'd taken such an interest in him. When they were introduced, neither acknowledged prior contact.

Two holes had been dug for the posts on one side of the driveway at a location chosen by Lou. While the group waited for the truck to arrive with the sign, Burney fussed around and decided the location was all wrong. Two new holes were dug and another thirty minutes of standing in the rain was endured until the sign was duly erected. It read:

Airship Guarantee Company
A Subsidiary of Vickers Aircraft Corp.

A meager round of applause went up from the party of bored souls. Lou opened a couple of bottles of champagne and poured it into fancy glasses on a small, wet table. Hurried toasts were drunk and a few words said. No one wanted to be there, but it was a ceremony which seemed necessary at the time. It contrasted strongly in Lou's mind with the kick-off meeting conducted by Thomson at Cardington in May, and he said as much to Wallis and Norway.

Wallis smiled. "Let them have their pomp and circumstance. We have no need of it here," he said.

PART FOUR

An Airship Under Construction in her shed.

HOWDEN

13

A SLEEPLESS NIGHT

April 1929.

Lou stared at the ceiling, listening to the clock's 'tick, tick, tick', beside him, while the wind whistled through the tall elms outside. He rolled over and checked the time. It was 2.30 a.m. He could tell by her restlessness Charlotte was awake, too. Neither spoke. This'd be their last night at the cottage. Lou had been posted to Cardington and they'd travel to Bedford on the train in the morning. A deal had been struck with the devil and payment was due. Was he being unfair to Charlotte? He felt selfish to the core, but confident they were doing the right thing. He thought of his dead *R38* buddies. It always came back to that, as if he were tied to them for eternity.

The price of being a survivor.

This was his second chance, a way of redeeming himself. Or was he being overly dramatic? Then there was John Bull. He felt miserable about leaving him—and disloyal. Everything went around in his head. He lay in the gloom considering the events of the past three years…

14

THE WALLISES

B y summer of 1926, the air station had been restored to a functioning facility—not as modern as Cardington, but good enough for the Howden people, who were always at a disadvantage; like relatives from the wrong side of the tracks. Renovations of the twenty bungalows were complete and freshly painted. Design staff and senior personnel, including Barnes Wallis, his new bride, Molly, and their three-month-old son moved in. Burney and his wife took one, though absent most of the time. Burney was busy much of the time with his duties as a Conservative Member of Parliament. He also traveled abroad extensively.

The offices were also ready and Lou furnished them with second-hand furniture from Hull, much of it the worse for wear, but 'perfectly adequate', as Wallis put it. A week after everyone had settled in, Wallis called a meeting with his staff. Lou was first to arrive and Wallis expressed satisfaction with his office, which smelled of new, white distemper and an almost-new piece of brown carpet.

Ten team members sat at the old, chipped conference table and the remaining seventeen squeezed in around the walls. The group was mixed, with male and female staff from the drawing offices and workshops, including shop foremen, engineers, engineering draftsmen, Norway's calculators, and lastly, Philip Teed, the chemist, and his assistants, who looked after gas management and purity. Wallis stood at the head of the table dressed in a dark blue suit. He smiled at the enthusiastic faces—rare for him.

"I called this meeting to welcome you to Howden and to let you know what I expect—to lay down ground rules and give you my opinions about certain matters. I'm calling this a 'meeting of mutual understanding.'"

Wallis raised his hand toward Lou.

"First, I know by now you've all met this man, but I want to introduce you officially to Lt. Louis Remington of the United States Navy. I'd personally like to thank the lieutenant for his work in getting this old, broken-down aerodrome into working order. He's done a great job. Thank you, Lieutenant."

There was a spontaneous round of applause.

"He has considerable experience in airship construction and in flying them—you all know his history. He's familiar with this air station and with Cardington. Please understand I have absolute trust in the lieutenant. He's a man of the highest integrity. We shall keep no secrets from him and treat him as one of our own. Besides assisting our team, he's also here on behalf of the Air Ministry and the oversight group in Cardington."

There were a few questioning glances in Lou's direction.

"Cardington is overseeing this operation. That was the mandate and it's something we have to live with. Personally, I'd *rather* have oversight, as long as it is thoughtful and intelligent. Lieutenant Remington will use his discretion as to what information he will pass on to Cardington. Technical data, much of which will become patented, I'm sure he will not divulge until we're ready to release it. As well as assisting us here in monitoring the work, Lieutenant Remington will make monthly visits to Cardington where he'll give the Deputy Director of Airship Development a report covering our progress for the month, a schedule for the upcoming month and detailed costs of work to date."

Lou was relieved Wallis had got this out of the way. He and Wallis understood one another perfectly.

"Now, what are we all doing here in the backwoods of Yorkshire? Ladies and gentlemen, this is our mission: We have the task of delivering an airship built to concise specifications, for a stipulated contract sum, by a certain date, ready for an intercontinental voyage. No more. No less."

Wallis paused. His eyes swept the room.

"This airship will be the best we can design and build. We will not pay attention to what others are doing, or saying. What they do is *their* business. We shall stay focused right here in this shed and not be sidetracked or upset by politicians and news hounds."

Everyone nodded their heads in agreement.

"We must always remember our awesome responsibility. Peoples' lives are at stake. It's not just about our survival as a company, not about looking good and trying hard—that won't be good enough. This is true of all things in life. Just showing you're trying to do a good job won't enable you to survive an Atlantic crossing. Nice appointments, nice berths, nice showers, nice tables and nice white table cloths with glistening silverware are things which look good in the shed—but none of that stuff will get us to Montreal. In a matter of only a few years, we're attempting to build ocean liners in the sky—vessels that took hundreds of years to develop. We must *not* forget these aircraft are experimental!"

Wallis stopped and rubbed his chin thoughtfully.

"I must inform you of my opinions on certain matters—and this is confidential. Only one team will survive this ridiculous competition. I believe that's always been the intention of the Air Minister. I know he's gone, but everything in politics is temporary. I'm sure he'll be back. His intent is to show how much better government can do things. The ultimate goal is our demise. Both teams are essentially supposed to be building the same airship, at least if you read the specification requirements you might think so. For two reasons, they won't be the same; our two philosophies are different, and they have unlimited money—but *that* could be their undoing. Although we're the underdog, we shall win this competition. We came here to win, and win it we shall!"

There was an enthusiastic round of applause and cheers. The meeting made a big impression on Lou.

Wallis began holding weekly progress meetings with key members of his team. Attendees included Lou, Norway and Teed. Burney attended rarely. At the first meeting, Lou learned what the team had been doing in the south for the past eighteen months while he'd been managing the re-commissioning of Howden. Wallis had the concept of the airship developing in his head during the summer of '24 and by Christmas, had the engineering details worked out down to the smallest details.

Wallis decided to get away from the Zeppelin design, which he considered fatally flawed, and began from first principles. Much of what Wallis said went over Lou's head. He spoke of longitudinal shear, bending moments, aerodynamic forces, point loads, geodetic design, changes in buoyancy and lift behavior due to atmospheric changes. Lou did, however, fully understand the meaning of 'catastrophic failure.'

Wallis mysteriously seemed to be able to feel every force within the airship while working on design, which he now had down on the drawing boards. He had an uncanny instinct, enabling him to pinpoint forces in girders, transverse frames, guy wires, fabric meshing and gas bag supports, as well as in every rivet, nut and bolt! He sensed these forces as if they were in his own body—forces that would be forever changing due to effects of weather, gravity, aerodynamics and cataclysmic events.

Lou had no clue what 'geodetic design' meant, but after patient explanation by Wallis, he understood that when one part of the structure became overstressed, or broken, its load would be taken up by another part. These principles were also applied to the gas bag harnessing system. Wallis lived and breathed internal structural forces. The man was a genius.

Wallis seemed to be able to go to that place where great composers or distinguished writers go for inspiration and answers—*the wellspring*. Many times, Wallis came into the shed early in the morning with a bright smile, announcing he'd dreamed of the answer to some inscrutable riddle he'd been wrestling with for weeks. He'd be as excited as a schoolboy, charging into his office to write it all down and make sketches. When this happened, Lou shared his euphoria.

Wallis was hard to get to know. His puritanical nature was softened by a willingness to have fun, especially with his wife, Molly, now pregnant with their second child. One day in the autumn of 1926, at sunset, when the shed cast its giant shadow across the field, Lou approached after hearing strange sounds coming from inside. He went to the door and found Wallis zooming Molly around wildly in a workmen's wheelbarrow, while they both childishly shrieked and howled like wolves. Every so often, they stopped and listened to echoes receding down the shed, counting to fifteen each time, until the vast space descended into silence. Lou watched for a few minutes until they became aware of him. They were embarrassed at first, and then they all burst out laughing.

Wallis, the outdoor type, taught Molly how to skate and play golf. Often, they went out camping in all kinds of weather with only a side and top to their tent—Wallis's way of toughening them up; learning to live with and understand the elements.

In the autumn of that year, the Wallises knocked on the cottage door during a terrible rainstorm. Wallis and Molly liked to go on long hikes visiting neighbors and friends. They'd travel five miles by road and five miles across country 'as the crow flies', using a compass to guide them. They came inside like drowned rats, staying until they'd dried out by the fire and had been served (despite their protestations) a meal of sausages, baked beans and coffee.

During their surprise visit, Lou and Charlotte learned Wallis and Molly were cousins-in-law, having been married the previous year after an agonizing courtship. Their marriage had been strongly opposed by Molly's father due to their sixteen-year age difference. When they'd met, Wallis had loved her on sight and stayed close by, coaching her in mathematics, usually by mail. Now, all appeared to be well. They'd been left alone to enjoy their lives together in this desolate place in Yorkshire.

The Wallises, like Lou and Charlotte, seemed blissfully happy, except that *they* had a baby and another on the way. The only blight on their happiness was the managing director of the company, Dennistoun Burney. Lou and Charlotte learned much from the Wallises about various people and their relationships that rainy afternoon.

Burney owned everybody who worked for him and they were not allowed to forget it. Any successful task they performed became *his* doing. During his visits to Howden, Burney made everyone's life miserable by his sheer arrogance. The greater the distance from Westminster out of the public eye, the more obnoxious he became.

At the end of the day or at weekends when in residence, Burney liked to call on the Wallises to discuss work without regard to convenience. His wife, just as annoying, showed up on Molly's doorstep at all hours to make camp. Wallis couldn't stand the woman's powdery smell, and whatever she put on her hair made him sneeze.

Scott also offended Wallis's puritanical sensibilities, but at least his visits were infrequent. When he came up by train, Lou fetched him from the station in the works truck and he'd stay overnight at the Railway Station Pub or the Grand Hotel in Hull. Wallis had a high regard for Scott's flying skills, but abhorred his drinking and hell raising.

If Scott showed up at the cottage, he usually demanded gin, and when Wallis requested a 'drink' allowance from Burney for these unwelcome visits, the request was denied. When Burney and Scott were both in town, the drinking got out of hand, much to Wallis's annoyance—especially when they drank in his home and *he* was footing the bill.

That summer of '26, Wallis's factory began producing duralumin tubing. By Christmas, they'd built one of the central transverse frames and hung it from the roof decked in Christmas lights. To complete the festive ambience, a pine tree from the nearby forest was installed in the shed with decorations and a nativity scene.

That first Christmas had been a happy occasion. Lou and Charlotte went to the Wallises' bungalow on Christmas morning and Wallis poured them Bristol Cream Sherry. Charlotte took a baby's white, knitted sleepsuit she'd made for her own longed-for child. When she handed Molly the present wrapped in tissue, Molly embraced Charlotte after seeing tears in her eyes.

Lou's role at Howden had changed. With the renovations finished, his task now was to monitor activities and make daily reports. These were typed and filed by a young secretary named Monica. He also kept a deficiency log after reading and filing the inspectors' reports. These records were kept current and discussed at Wallis's weekly meetings.

Howden Airship Station became a happy place, not unlike a British holiday camp, and to Lou, it remained special. The management personnel worked hard and played hard together, forming life-long friendships. Lou and Charlotte spent countless hours socializing with them. People understood their time in Howden to be temporary. They were far from home in pleasant, country surroundings. Most had grown up as city folk and this was an adventure. In this 'unreal' atmosphere, inevitably, one or two affairs got started.

They enjoyed being close to the animals, too. Molly told Charlotte she liked to watch the rabbits hopping around their garden and see cows poking their heads through their windows, except when they chewed her flowers on the windowsill and broke her vases. This community was a separate place, divorced from the outside world. They played soccer and rugby on the airfield, keeping it mowed and rolled. Wallis had a tennis court set up with a low perimeter fence where he and Molly practiced. In summer, they had Sunday tea parties and the wives brought homemade pies, cakes, jellies and blancmanges, while their men played cricket. The 'shed people' never attended these get-togethers, not being invited. On rare occasions, shop foremen received a special invitation.

The atmosphere was always pleasant, as long as Burney and his wife weren't in attendance; they would bust their way into every conversation and lord it over all, talking non-stop shop. Burney had the gift of being able to turn his employees against each other. Lou thought this must be caused by some survival instinct people have when in the company of individuals with power over them. If the Burneys showed up on these Sunday afternoons, most people drifted away early, whereas the games and socializing normally carried on until dark.

Burney was never impolite or bombastic toward Lou or Charlotte. Perhaps he saw Lou rising in the Naval hierarchy in Washington where he'd become a useful contact for his airship business. During the times Burney was in residence, a nasty cloud hung over the place and the backbiting became unpleasant. On his departure, the sun came out and a state of tranquility descended across the plain, peace restored. Lou heard him referred to as a little prick, a nuisance, a hemorrhoid, a pillock, and an arsehole, though he never made comments about the man himself. But Charlotte did.

15

'MR. SHUTE' & FRIENDS

Autumn 1926 and onwards,

One day in autumn of '26, Lou and Charlotte invited Norway to Candlestick Cottage for dinner. It was customary for families to eat a roast late in the afternoon on Sundays. Lou had come to enjoy these feasts, especially in the dreary months of late autumn and winter. A log fire crackling in the grate and a glass or two of frothy Yorkshire ale always made it special and the cottage extra cozy.

Norway, an Oxford graduate, had been hired by Wallis as chief calculator to head the team of mathematicians who would sit for years calculating the stresses and sizes of each girder for manufacture in the metal shop. Norway had left de Havilands to join Vickers. He'd worked down in Kent at an office in Crayford until Howden was ready. Although well versed in aeronautical engineering, he had no airship experience whatsoever and made no bones about it. He loved to fly aeroplanes.

At ten minutes to three, they perceived a gentle knock. Charlotte opened the front door to find Norway every inch the intellectual, comically boffin-like, and hating herself for thinking this—no beauty. He was of average height and build and, though a year younger than Lou, seemed older. He wore a green and brown Harris Tweed jacket with leather elbow patches, which they'd learn he wore in all weathers for all activities. He carried with him the smell of aromatic pipe tobacco, which Charlotte found quite pleasing.

Norway's beady, blue eyes peered out from under bushy eyebrows. When working on his endless calculations or poring over drawings, his hooked nose supported thick, horn-rimmed glasses. Capping everything, Norway had a stutter—a real doozy. Lou and Charlotte wanted to help him by finishing his sentences, but forced themselves to resist. Lou noticed the more they got to know each other, the less Norway stuttered. At times, it disappeared altogether.

He stood stiffly to attention on the step under the porch roof, clutching a bottle of wine.

"Hello! You must be Mr. Norway," Charlotte said, putting out her hand.

Norway became flustered, overcome by her beauty. She wore a stunning red dress and her favorite perfume. He thrust the bottle into her outstretched hand.

"Er, p-p-please c-call me N-Nevil," he said.

"Right then, Nevil! Oh, you shouldn't have done that," she said, examining the bottle. "Oh, it's red. My favorite! Thank you so much. Come in and make yourself comfortable."

Norway peered around the room, at the crackling fire and the round table, beautifully laid for dinner, overlooking the damp, autumnal garden. Norway breathed in the smell of roast lamb, mint sauce and scorched Yorkshire puddings.

"S-smells w-wonderful and what a l-lovely c-cottage …And I m-must say I do like your p-perfume."

"*Je Reviens!*" Lou shouted from the kitchen. He then appeared. Norway looked visibly relieved to see him.

"It means, 'I w-will r-return.'"

"Charlotte told me the name of it when we met. I never thought about what it meant. I wish we could speak French," Lou said.

"Glad you could come, Nevil. I've cooked a roast. Hope you like lamb?" Charlotte said.

"Oh, yes, I d-do. M-marvelous. Yes, thank you."

Charlotte picked up the bottle and squinted at the label. "Nevil's brought us a bottle of wine. It's called Chateau er, neuf du P-P- er …er …"

"Pape!" Norway blurted out. They all roared with laughter, Norway revealing all his large, crooked teeth, reminding Charlotte of a horse. She felt dreadful again.

"Looks so expensive. We'll have this with dinner," Charlotte said.

"I got a crate of pale ale from the pub. Would you like one before dinner, Nevil?" Lou said, giving Norway a wink.

"Oh, yes s-splendid."

Lou and Nevil drank their beers and chatted while Charlotte put the finishing touches to the meal.

"D-Dinner smells t-t-temptingly d-delicious and one f-f-feels so at home here," Norway said, his eyelids fluttering under the strain of trying his best not to stutter.

"Charlotte grows all our vegetables. I'm real proud of her," Lou said.

After a couple of beers Norway settled down and talked about himself. He obviously felt comfortable and, as a young man away from home, appreciative of their hospitality. Norway told them he didn't want to live on the aerodrome close to work and his bosses and had therefore taken rooms over a pub in Howden with two colleagues. He'd settled down to life in Yorkshire and joined a flying club in Sherburn-in-Elmet.

Over an excellent meal, washed down by Norway's fine wine, they learned that joyriding in aeroplanes wasn't all Norway did for fun. After packing his pipe with Balkan Sobranie and filling the room with sweet-smelling clouds of smoke, Norway told them that, for his own amusement, he'd written a novel in his spare time. And, to his amazement, a draft had been accepted by a London publisher. Since Norway thought his employers might think he wasn't taking his day job seriously, he'd had the book published under his middle name, 'Shute.' He was now working on a second novel in the evenings. This intrigued Lou and Charlotte. They'd never met a writer before.

Norway was interested in Lou's experience and his survival of the *R38* crash. He told Lou he'd attended Thomson's press conference in Cardington, incognito. He said he'd badly wanted to talk to Lou about that ship, but in the end decided not to intrude. Lou nodded and smiled, telling him he *had* wondered—Norway didn't look like a reporter. Norway said, before moving to Howden, he'd made a study of *R38* and was horrified to learn it was basically a copy of a Zeppelin without fresh calculations. He said he believed her factor of safety had been less than 1. He explained that it should have been at least 1.5, that is to say, designed for one and a half times the stress it was likely to encounter. From this, Lou realized neither *R38* nor *Shenandoah* had stood an earthly chance of survival.

During the months that followed, usually over dinner, they had many conversations about *R38*. This wasn't a subject Charlotte enjoyed talking about, and even though the first piece of structure hadn't been erected, *Howden R100* was becoming a reality. The airship would soon encroach upon their lives. The subject of *Shenandoah* never came up—Lou had warned Norway not to speak of it. Despite all the talk of airships, Charlotte came to adore Norway, pleased to have a writer for a friend, especially when he asked them both to critique his second book. Charlotte liked the title: '*So Disdained.*' They laughed when Norway was coming over to talk about his writing, referring to him as 'Mr. Shute.' It was their little secret.

One weekend, Charlotte and Fanny had a heart-to-heart talk while they sat at the dining room table watching Lou and Billy playing soccer in the garden. Billy and Lou scrambled and dribbled, while Lenny leaned on the stone wall coughing and wheezing as he tried to light another Woodbine.

"Your boy's growing fast, Fanny."

"Yes, he is. He idolizes your husband, you know."

"You're right, he does," Charlotte said.

"I tell him, 'You should try and be like your Dad,' and d'you know what he says?"

"What, love?"

"He says, 'I want to be like Lou.' It really upsets me. His dad's been through so much. They gassed him in the trenches at the Somme, you know."

Charlotte winced. She felt Lenny's agony.

Fanny began to cry. "He got TB after the war and now look at 'im, poor love. He's having trouble smoking a fag. He suffers with his nerves and melancholia and oh, 'ee loves that boy *so* much."

Charlotte was overcome by sadness.

"You mustn't talk about that bloody awful war to the boy, Fanny," she said bitterly.

"No, I don't want to upset him with all that horror." Fanny changed the subject and perked up. "Anyway Charlotte, no news yet?" she said, dabbing her eyes and then patting Charlotte's tummy.

"I don't think it's ever going to happen."

"Be patient. When the Good Lord's ready, it'll happen, you'll see," Fanny said, forcing a smile.

"I've been to the doctor and he said it's not me. *He* won't go. I'm sure it's his fault," Charlotte said, looking in Lou's direction.

"Charlotte, you don't know that!"

"Then what's wrong with us?"

"Things have to be right. Don't get so desperate."

"Desperate! We've been married five years now. He's more interested in that bloody airship."

"You mustn't nag him about it—entice him," Fanny said. Charlotte sighed and stared out the window at Lou, she watched him for a while. She'd thought he was gorgeous when she first saw him on that ward—and he was still gorgeous. After a moment, she turned back to Fanny.

"I guess I fell in love with Lou the moment I laid eyes on him, you know, Fanny."

"Yes, I know you did, love. We *all* knew."

Over the following months, the stream of visitors to the cottage at weekends increased. Sometimes everyone showed up at once: John and his wife, Mary, Fanny, Lenny and Billy, Norway, and sometimes the Wallises and Charlotte's parents. Everyone in this diverse group got on well and these get-togethers usually ended with a sing-song. Charlotte sat at the piano playing all the latest hits: "Tea for Two," "Yes Sir, That's My Baby," and "What'll I Do?" She was banned from playing "Mammy." Sometimes, Lou accompanied her on the guitar and played a few country songs from the Deep South which delighted Billy. Charlotte always encouraged Molly to bring the children, though it made her both happy and sad. She and Molly became close over the next four years.

16

CARDINGTON VISITS

December 1926 and onwards.

L ou visited Cardington each month. It was usually a day trip. He showed Colmore and Scott drawings and photographs of the work executed during the last month and work projected for the next. He also submitted a schedule of costs to date. Lou found most of the R.A.W. staff polite, but sensed underlying hostility—not toward him, but Howden.

Lou got to know Col. Richmond over the three-year period of construction and his arrogant manner confirmed Lou's earlier impression. Around Christmas that first year, Lou arrived at Cardington House only to be informed Colmore and Scott were away and Col. Richmond would be available in half an hour or so. Lou waited in the reception area for ninety minutes before being sent to Richmond's office on the second floor. Lou knocked on the door and entered. Richmond rose from behind a fine mahogany desk, well-dressed in a blue serge suit and red tie.

"Ah, Lieutenant Remington, thank you for coming," Richmond said. After slight hesitation, they shook hands and sat down. Richmond stared at Lou for some moments without speaking.

"So, what's happening in that mud hole up north?"

Lou opened his briefcase and pulled out drawings of *Howden R100* with photographs of the metal fabrication shop. Richmond held up his hands.

"I don't need to look at all that stuff, just tell me what's going on."

"The ship's pretty well engineered. They're using a geodetic design. They're still working on the tail, the elevators and rudder configurations."

Richmond appeared uninterested, but Lou continued, his demeanor pleasant.

"The metal factory is set up and is producing components. The central frames are being fabbed and ..."

"Fabbed! What is this word 'fabbed'?"

"Prefabricated, sir."

"Ah, it's one of your Americanisms. You people love to shorten everything, don't you."

"The first of the central frames is set in place. I can show you ..." Lou said, opening a drawing of the ship's frame.

Richmond waved it off, wrinkling his nose.

"I don't need the details. What about gas bag harnesses?"

"Gas bag harnesses? Oh yes, they're designed. Mr. Wallis seems happy with them."

"*Is* he indeed?" Richmond grimaced. "And gas valves?"

"Yes, they're designed, too."

"Really?"

"Yes, in Germany."

"What you mean is: They're using the ones the Germans have been using for donkey's years."

"Well, yes. Mr. Shute …er Mr. Norway said they're tried and tested."

"Tried and tested!" Richmond guffawed. "Who is this Mr. Shute?"

"He's nobody, sir. I misspoke. I'm sorry. I meant Norway."

"The gas valves are coming from Norway?"

"No, sir, I meant *Mr.* Norway. Not Mr. Shute."

"Ah, I see. And who is this Norway person?"

"Howden's chief calculator, sir."

"How much airship experience does *he* have?"

"None, sir."

"None! And where did they drag *him* up from?"

"He came from de Havilands. I understand he's an aeronautical engineer, sir."

"But with no airship experience?"

"None whatsoever, no."

"What are they doing about gas bags?"

"They're being ordered from Germany, too."

"Yes, of course. They don't have facilities to make their own, do they?" Richmond sneered.

"No sir, they are not as fortunate."

"What else are the Germans doing for our Howden friends?"

"I believe that's about it, sir."

"Perhaps Wallis should have the Germans build the whole ship for him. They would've stood a better chance, I should've thought."

Lou played dumb. "I'm sorry, sir, I don't follow."

"Well, I don't suppose you do, Lieutenant."

Lou sat and waited for Richmond, who rested his chin in his hand pouting at the wall. "This whole thing's all a bit of a farce, Remington, let's face it."

"How do you mean, sir, exactly?"

"Vickers's people are all up there scratching around in that broken-down old shed. To be honest, I feel *sorry* for them. They're not going to be able to compete with us. We've got a state of the art facility, unlimited funds, Bolton and Paul's engineering department with their steel works just down the street—not to mention the resources of the entire British Government—all at our disposal!"

"That's a real nice position to be in, Colonel."

"And d'you know what's best of all, Remington? Time is on our side—time to get it right. They're stuck with a schedule and an impossible set of conditions they can't possibly hope to fulfill. No, they're up a creek without a paddle, I'm afraid."

Lou said nothing. Richmond got fidgety. "What do *you* think, Remington—honestly?"

"Oh, me, sir, I'm not qualified to give an opinion, not being an engineer."

Richmond paused and looked away, mulling it over.

"No, bit unfair of me to ask, really. Well, our goal here is to construct the finest airship ever built, *anywhere*. Better than anything the Germans have produced and certainly better than anything the Howden people could conceive of. *Cardington R101* will be cutting edge—as comfortable and as smooth as any luxury liner that ever put to sea—and the *safest*, of course."

"That will be a wonderful thing, sir."

"Yes, and no doubt you'll be aboard her as an officer, one day."

"I look forward to that."

"And so you should, Lieutenant. And so you should!"

Lou left the building turning their conversation over in his mind.

If these people have all the advantages, why the hell is he so uptight?

In the coming months, Lou had more contact with Richmond. He was even invited to his home office where he met Richmond's wife, Florence, or 'Florry', as he called her. Lou found her to be a classy lady and they seemed devoted. In those surroundings and in Colmore's absence, Richmond became more amenable. He clearly hoped to get a feel for how *he, Richmond*, was doing compared to Wallis. Lou sometimes thought Richmond was torturing himself. Naturally, despite what Richmond said previously, Lou was there to be pumped for information about *Howden R100*.

Lou couldn't help comparing the two men leading the teams. They were complete opposites. Richmond seemed to be more of a manager, whereas Wallis was himself the hands-on engineer and designer. He was a perfectionist, and like all perfectionists, kept absolute control over all things. In Cardington, it was a project being managed by a committee. Lou hoped the airship wouldn't turn out like the proverbial camel. He realized the Cardington team's goals couldn't be more different than Wallis's. It seemed to be more about being the best for the sake of it.

The other motivation for Cardington was to not repeat the old mistakes—a sensible goal. The attitude was: No matter how long it takes, and at whatever cost, *Cardington R101* will be built not just state of the art, but to the state of perfection. They weren't under the same restrictions and operated with virtually no oversight—they were their own judge and jury. This made the government types—be they military men, government bureaucrats, or airship works employees—arrogant and condescending toward Howden.

In the early part of 1927, Richmond took Lou into the shed before construction had started and proudly showed him a mock-up of a forty-foot section of the airship, complete with a gasbag. This sample had been fabricated by Bolton and Paul to prove their structural theories. After study and inspection, it was demolished. This experiment, Richmond proudly told him, had cost the British taxpayers forty thousand pounds. Lou thought it was a good idea but knew Howden couldn't afford such experiments to prove Wallis's theories or Norway's calculations.

Later that year, Richmond shared their designs for gas bag harnesses, gas valves and servo mechanisms (to assist in steering the airship), designed by his assistant, Squadron Leader Rope. Richmond also showed him pictures of the Beardmore diesel engines on order from Scotland, due for delivery next spring.

Lou couldn't tell whether all this was an attempt to demoralize Howden, thinking Lou would divulge these details and they'd be overcome by their brilliance. Or, maybe, Richmond was looking for Lou's reactions, which were always congenial and reassuring—perhaps even a tad patronizing. Richmond, like most English people, was unable to appreciate the subtle nuances of American polite conversation. It wouldn't have occurred to him such a thing existed in American culture—after all, Americans could hardly speak the language.

Richmond asked Lou not to mention these things at Howden and he didn't. He knew Wallis wouldn't be the slightest bit interested anyway. Lou felt the petty jealousy and rivalry increasing between the teams, but refused to pick sides or let himself be drawn in. He and Charlotte had their own growing personal problem to contend with—*Jessup!*

17

'BURNEY'S MEETING'

Spring 1927.

By spring of '27, work in the Howden shed was in full swing. The noise struck visitors first—the crash of steel against steel, banging, shouting and often, laughter and singing. Half the transverse frames, up to 130 feet in diameter, had been hung from the ceiling beams from center toward bow and stern. The place was alive with men everywhere like ants—on dangling bosun's chairs, swings, webs of scaffold and swaying firemen's ladders.

While working at Howden and visiting Cardington, Lou sensed this mounting tension between the two teams. He saw increasing strain in other quarters, too—within Howden itself. During a visit to Howden, Burney attended one of Wallis's meetings after enjoying one of his liquid lunches at The Railway Station pub. He made a point of sitting at the head of the table, in Wallis's chair. Wallis sat at the opposite end with Lou, Norway and Teed. Burney, the purple veins in his cheeks pronounced, sat hunched forward over the table like a greyhound. The room soon smelled of Burney's beer and whisky breath.

"I called this meeting to discuss where we stand on all components of the airship. I'm concerned we're falling behind," Burney announced.

Wallis said nothing. This was one of Wallis's regularly scheduled meetings held in his office every Monday afternoon. Burney hadn't called it —he'd merely shown up.

"Let's start with gas bag harnesses, gas bags and valves. Where are we on those items?" Burney asked, looking around the table.

"The harnesses are designed. I'm satisfied with them. As for the gas bags and gas valves, we'll get them from Zeppelin. We don't have the means to manufacture gas bags here, and I suggest we don't try to get them from Cardington," Wallis said.

"Absolutely not," Burney agreed. "They'd string us out 'til kingdom come."

"The German gas valves can't be improved on and the price is reasonable," Teed said.

"No point in reinventing the wheel," Wallis said.

"Quite. What about weight? Where do we stand?" Burney glanced sharply at Wallis. "This is critical."

"We're on target," Wallis answered.

"And what about factor of safety? What are we working to?"

"Around 4.5. Which means we have plenty of margin of safety," Wallis answered.

"I don't need *you* to tell me what it means." Burney snapped. "What about the servo assistance for the elevators and rudders? A little bird told me Cardington has designed elaborate systems for their ship. I'm disturbed to hear we haven't done so. Why not?"

Norway leaned forward. "I s-studied this for m-months. M-my c-calculations sh-show we don't n-n-need them."

"Are you *absolutely* sure?"

"Y-y-yes."

"Come on, spit it out, man!"

"Y-y-yes."

"I want you to go through all your calculations again and when you've done *that,* check them again. After that, have them checked by Professors Bairstow and Pippard," Burney demanded. Wallis often consulted the two professors with the Airworthiness Panel on various structural issues. Wallis grimaced and his face began to flush.

"Now I want to talk about procedure," Burney said, looking accusingly at Wallis. "I want you to make a habit of visiting the engineers on a daily basis at the same time of day. I'm seeing too much rework in the machine shop which could've been avoided if you'd caught these mistakes on the drawing board."

"I don't need *you* to come here telling me how to manage operations. I'm the design engineer and I'll run things the way I see fit!" Wallis said, his face beet red.

Burney was unfazed. "The deficiency lists are too long. The rework in the shops is costing me a fortune. This is stuff you should've caught before shop drawings were issued."

There was an angry silence. Burney leaned back in his chair with his hands behind his head. "I see it's necessary for me to teach you people the facts of life. Money is what makes the world go round. This ship will be a financial loss to this company. We're fighting a war of attrition here, but you seem not to understand. We knew it'd be a loss before we started, but it's an investment in our future. We want to build a successful airship, not a bloody pie in the sky like those silly arses at Cardington."

Burney leaned forward again, elbows on the table. "So gentlemen, this is why I'm intent on guarding against waste—wasted man hours, wasted research, costing money we don't have. Let's talk about the engines: Where are we with them?" Burney looked from one to the other.

"We looked into d-developing a k-kerosene-hydrogen engine—"

"And?"

"That's years away in development and I've dropped the idea," Wallis said.

"*That's what I'm talking about.* Don't just drop ideas without talking to me first," Burney fumed. "Working on ideas costs me money!"

"I-I've been doing research on the B-Beardmore diesels developed for the C-Canadian railway—"

Norway's stutter was irritating Burney. He kept rolling his eyes. "Railway engines?" he exclaimed, glaring at Norway.

"They weigh t-t-twelve hundred pounds each," Norway said.

"Forget them," Wallis said.

"What do *you* propose then?" Burney asked, turning on Wallis.

"We'll use Rolls-Royce Condors," Wallis said. "I've already made up my mind."

"Petrol?" Burney queried.

"We'll never get off the ground with diesel engines!" Wallis answered.

"Okay, Condors it is then. We'll get reconditioned ones. They'll be half the price and be as good as new," Burney said. "Any objections?" He glared at the group, daring them to oppose him.

"The government may not be happy with us using second-hand engines," Teed said. Wallis shook his head in disbelief.

"Doesn't say anywhere in our contract we can't use re-conditioned engines."

"We'd b-be breaking Lord Thomson's r-rules. He wouldn't be p-pleased. He wanted us to use d-d-diesels."

"To hell with Thomson and his rules. He's long gone—along with all his *comrades*."

Lou thought about the events leading to Thomson's departure last October. Since then, the communist editor and his henchmen had been tried and thrown in jail. "Poor Lord Thomson," he muttered.

Burney exploded. "That genius stole all *my* visionary ideas and took them for his own and then dreamed up this crackpot competition! The Conservative Government had agreed to my scheme long before that clown came on the scene and reneged on everything."

Lou choked into his fist.

Oh dear, now I've upset him.

"All for the sake of increasing the size of government and squashing private enterprise. It was for his own personal aggrandizement—to satisfy his wild ambitions! Not to mention he was trying to impress some bloody Romanian princess he's been after. Every inbred, royal, blue-blood European has been sniffing at that woman's drawers for years, like mongrels. She's like a bitch on heat. Now he's a lord, he thinks *he's* royalty. The woman's a siren. *She'll be the death of him!* No, he deserved to be kicked out. He's a bloody

Marxist radical, a hypocritical bastard like the rest of those conmen—out for himself. Everything about those people is just one great big lie!"

Lou glanced at Wallis apologetically. No use; Wallis was seething.

Holy cow, that set him off! I wonder who this dame is. Must be quite some broad!

"Thomson might be back," Teed interjected lamely, but no one was listening.

"And where did *you* get all *your* great visionary ideas, *Mr.* Burney?" Wallis said glaring at Burney.

A painful pause ensued. Everyone waited for the next explosion.

"Now, you just wait a minute! You *did* work on the *R80*, a moderately successful airship and a few other small ones, but the building of six great airships was *my* idea!" Burney blustered.

"Fuelled by *me!*" Wallis answered.

"Okay, you kicked around the idea of building a bigger airship. Without *my* vision you wouldn't be sitting here, in your cocoon, working on a five-million-cubic-foot airship. It was *my* dream. It was *I* who conceived the building of six gigantic airships. It was *I* who made all this happen. Not *you*! Not even *Thomson*! You're forgetting your place, Wallis. Without *me,* you wouldn't have a job." Burney's bloodshot eyes swept around the table to Norway and Teed. "None of you would!"

Wallis pushed back his chair and stood up, buttoning his jacket. Burney looked up incredulously. "What are you doing? Where do you think *you're* going?" he shouted.

"I've heard enough." Wallis said as he walked out, closing the door quietly behind him. Lou stared after him with admiration.

That's class! Most guys would've slammed the door.

"Come back here at once!" Burney yelled.

Teed and Norway gave each other embarrassed looks. Burney got up.

"All right, gentlemen. We'll finish it there. I'll deal with Mr. Wallis later." They trooped back to their own rooms in silence. Wallis had gone across the field to his bungalow. He wasn't seen for the rest of the day. Lou figured he must've quit.

Much to everyone's relief, Wallis appeared in his office next morning as usual. Nothing came of this altercation except that relations between the two men grew steadily worse. In coming months and years, things deteriorated to the point where they were working against each other, with Wallis looking for another, more peaceful, avenue to pursue and Burney publicly tearing down the design of both *R100* and *R101* in books and interviews. They were too small, he declared, and not the right shape—they needed to be flatter and oval shaped. His belief in the concept of airships hadn't waned.

18

'NERVOUS NICK'

Spring 1927

During spring of 1927, the airship's frame steadily took shape with more workers being hired every day. One morning, a young man about twenty-five, came into the shed. He was very thin, roughly dressed and unshaven. Lou, Norway and the shop foreman stood talking at the foot of one of the fireman's ladders. He waited humbly by, until they'd finished speaking. At last, the foreman turned to him.

"What do *you* want?"

"Looking for work, sir."

"As what?"

"A rigger, sir."

"Done it before, 'ave yer?"

"Well, no sir, but I can learn."

"What's yer name?"

"Nick, sir, Nick Steele."

"Got nerves to match, 'ave yer?"

"Beggin' your pardon, sir?"

"Not nervous are yer?"

"No, sir. Not at all."

The foreman pointed to the ladder, which seemed to reach the roof.

"See this? It's 110 foot."

"Yes, sir."

"Any problem?"

"No problem at all, sir."

"Ever climbed one before?"

"Er, no, sir."

"Up you go then, lad. Show us what you're made of."

Nick walked boldly to the foot of the ladder, grabbed the rails and peered up the treads. The top was almost invisible. He set his jaw. Lou and Norway glanced at one another. This was going to be interesting. They'd been through this themselves. Nick set off suddenly at a vertical run, trying to overcome fears he didn't know he had until this moment. When he got about a third of the way up, he stopped, the ladder swaying wildly from side to side.

"Don't stop, lad. Keep going!" the foreman yelled. But it was useless. Nick reluctantly came down. "I'm sorry, gov'. I just couldn't go any further," he said, painfully out of breath and unable to hide his bitter disappointment.

It was lunchtime and Lou felt sorry for the man. "Hungry, Nick?"

"No, sir. I'm good, thanks."

Lou put his hand on the man's scrawny shoulder. "Come on, pal, we'll get you something to eat," he said.

Nick didn't protest and the four men trooped over to the nearby canteen, full of workmen in overalls eating bread rolls and drinking beer. Lou bought the despondent Nick a cheese sandwich and gave him a bottle of John Smith's ale. The others chose their eats and they sat at a wooden table, where Nick, between ravenous bites, told them he'd been unemployed for five months and things were desperate at home what with his wife and three kids and sick mother. After lunch they trooped back to the shed.

"Can I give it another go, sir?" Nick asked, looking at each of them in desperation. Please let me try it again."

"I used to be afraid w-when I f-first got here," Norway said. "Now I run around on the c-catwalks in the roof and climb the c-cat ladders without a second thought. Maybe you can get over your f-fear."

Once inside the shed, Nick made for the ladder again and went bounding up. He passed the point where he'd frozen the first time and kept going, but he slowed down with every step as the ladder swayed more the higher he got. He stopped three quarters of the way up. Norway and the foreman yelled up at him, "Go on! Go on! You can do it!"

"That was an improvement," Lou said.

Nick stood there for some moments, trying to find the courage and for the ladder to become still. He slowly started the descent and when he reached bottom, he burst into tears.

"What am I going to do?" he sobbed.

"Come on, buddy, I'll buy you another beer," Lou said, grabbing him by the arm and leading him away. "We'll be back shortly and he'll try again," Lou called over his shoulder.

Fifteen minutes later, Lou and Nick came back, Nick smiling. A crowd had gathered. Nick made for the ladder and without hesitation and with the crowd shouting "Go, go, go!" he made it to the top where he gave a triumphant yell and took a bow. Below, everyone cheered and gave him a big round of applause which filled the shed and echoed fifteen times.

"The trouble was, 'Nervous Nick' wasn't drunk enough!" Lou said. And from that day on, the name stuck—'Nervous Nick', the man who owed everything to John Smith (and Lou Remington).

19

JESSUP

Summer 1927,

J essup had become ingrained in their lives—someone they had to live with—like a third member in their marriage. He continued to follow Charlotte around and loitered near the hospital in plain view. Nothing had changed since Lou and Charlotte were married; in fact, things had become a whole lot worse. Lou went to the police station and filed a report. He was told Jessup had the right to stand wherever he liked in the street, as long as he didn't interfere physically with anyone, and, if he did, it'd be necessary to produce witnesses. It put a strain on Lou and Charlotte's relationship.

A couple of times after they'd gone to bed—once when making love and another after they'd fallen asleep—they were disturbed by sounds in the living room. Lou crept into the other room thinking they had a burglar. He found the bedroom door ajar—which they both swore had been closed—and the front door wide open. Lou heard the garden gate squeak, a cackling laugh, running footsteps, and moments later, a motorcycle kick-started. Lou knew the sound of a 490 cc Norton—the motorbike Jessup rode.

The situation continued to become more serious, perhaps even dangerous. Lou went to the police again, but after a polite interview and making a report, things went nowhere. Nothing had been stolen, no one had been hurt, no damage had been done, and Lou couldn't prove Jessup was the culprit.

Jessup filled Lou's thoughts incessantly. He worried about Charlotte, especially when he was away at Cardington. Powerless, he wondered how much their marriage could take. He didn't mention the problem to his colleagues at Howden. The whole business seemed too juvenile and embarrassing; the thought of bringing it up with them he found humiliating. Just when he thought things couldn't get worse, they did. He returned from Cardington to find Jessup in the shed, working alongside the riggers as a laborer with two of his yobos. Lou went to the foreman, trying his best to appear casual.

"New faces?"

"Took 'em on this morning," the foreman said.

"Who are they?"

"They're from Moortop over in Ackworth. Seem like decent lads. Very polite and they've been working pretty good."

"I see."

"They seemed desperate for work."

"Is that so?" Lou frowned.

"Do you have a problem with them?"

"Er, no."

"You sure?"

"Not at all."

Devastated, Lou stood glaring at Jessup who kept his eyes down. But Lou could see the smirk on his face as he worked. Lou knew his game: He'd lie low and not make trouble—the perfect employee—for the time being. Lou was in a quandary. He couldn't discuss the problem with anyone at the air station, but he'd have to tell Charlotte.

Lou went home after work and sat down heavily on the couch with a sigh of frustration.

"What's up, love?" Charlotte said, leaning over and kissing him. "Is everything all right?"

"No, it's not."

"What's the matter?"

"They've hired Jessup."

"What!"

"While I was down south yesterday."

"Oh no! What are you going to do?"

"That son of a bitch must've known I was in Cardington."

"You must tell them he's evil and should be sacked."

"I can't do that. They don't fire people for being evil. Perhaps they should, but they don't."

"You've got to go and explain what he's done to us."

"Charlotte, they'll tell me to go to the police and we've been all through that."

"You'll have to see him *every day*. You've got to talk to them."

"Charlotte, I'm not sure they'll believe us. The whole thing's bizarre. No question he's a mental case, but they might think it's you, I mean *we*, who have the problem."

"What do you mean? *I* don't have a problem!"

"Sorry, my darling. You don't, but you know how people are."

"Lou, do you remember the time I came home with a bruise on my arm?" Lou glared at Charlotte. Instinctively, he knew before she said any more.

"Yes, and you said an elderly lady grabbed you in the ward."

"Jessup did that to me. He said a lot of dirty things and laid his hands on me when I was walking to Ackworth Station."

"That must have been when the heel of your shoe broke off?"

"Yes."

"And you don't tell me until now!"

"I didn't want to upset you. I was afraid what you might do."

"But now you're not afraid?"

"I just want you to get him fired. That's all."

Lou was silent for a few moments. "Charlotte, I killed a man once."

Charlotte was dumbstruck.

"A German," he said quietly.

"What happened?"

"I'd shot a lot of Germans …" Charlotte was horrified. He'd not told her he'd even shot at anybody, although he had told her about the last day of the war. "But this was different. He was a POW who'd escaped. He came at me with a bayonet, terrified, babbling in German. He was just a kid …" Lou hung his head, "no more than sixteen."

"What did you do?"

"He had no chance. I snapped his neck in a second," Lou said, gesturing the action with his hands.

Charlotte turned her face away, sickened. "Oh, Lou, that's awful. My God!"

"It's hard to live with, Charlotte."

"You poor love. I understand," she said, turning back to him.

"I didn't need to kill him—not really. It was sadistic and it came natural. I regret it every day." Lou put his hands to his head, remorse tearing him up inside.

"I'm so sorry, Lou."

"When I was young, I was cocky and aggressive. I loved karate and the thought of meting out punishment to those I thought deserved it."

"That's natural, love."

"Sometimes when I look at Jessup, I see myself. I can't explain it."

"Oh no, Lou. That's silly."

"Charlotte, I can't describe to you the desolation I felt on eleven-eleven when I walked away from the battlefield leaving all my buddies lying dead in the mud. All I could think about was them …and that German boy. I wanted no part of violence after that. I vowed not to hurt anyone again."

He looked into Charlotte's eyes. Even though it was impossible, she had an uncanny way of understanding all he'd been through; another reason why he loved her so much, though they usually avoided the subject of war. It upset her too much.

"When I joined the Marines I was angry; when I left, all that was gone. I have an ugly side I'm not proud of, Charlotte, especially when someone close to me is threatened. In those days, I was always in a rage. My father told me over and over—I was a pussy and I'd never amount to anything."

"He must have caused it then. Perhaps he was jealous of you. Some fathers are."

"That's as maybe, but it's why I don't want to get into it with Jessup. It'd be too easy. I always remember what old Jeb tried to instill in me as a kid —respect for life. It took a while, but it finally took hold. Forgive and forget, he always said."

"Who's Jeb?"

"A great guy who stays on my Gran's farm. Known him all my life. I love the man."

"So, what are we going to do?"

"We'll wait. Things will be better when I get posted to Cardington."

The dirty secret hung over them—suffocating—like a filthy blanket. Lou didn't speak of it to Wallis or Norway, and Jessup and his friends kept their noses clean. To make matters worse, in the noisy turmoil in the shed where men shouted directions from the roof to the floor, while swinging around like stuntmen, Jessup's stature rose. He displayed extraordinary athletic ability and fearlessness as he climbed the massive webs of scaffolding. He dangled from the bosun's chair, raced up flimsy ladders and climbed ropes to great heights—as good as any high wire circus performer. All this was accompanied by annoying, shrill, two-finger whistles to his buddies signaling them to 'get up here' or bring something to him. It became one of his trademark mannerisms; part of his successful bid to dominate the shed. He became feared by all.

Wallis and Norway noticed him. He was a hard worker who got things done and could make the others jump to it. Bit by bit, he became brazen and smiled at Lou in his cocksure way. Now it was Lou's turn not to look at Jessup directly, feeling those wicked bug-eyes always on him. Jessup had got the upper hand. Over the coming months, Jessup became increasingly mouthy. He'd joined the union and been promoted to charge-hand foreman over his three buddies and three others. One day, a delivery of duralumin arrived on a truck and Lou went out to check it.

"Hey boys, here's the lieutenant." Jessup pronounced 'lieutenant' the American way – 'looootenant' instead of 'leftenant.'

"Where would you like to stick this, sir? Anywhere special? I can think of a place, if you can't!"

"Cut the crap, Jessup. Stack the stuff over there," Lou answered.

"Oooooh. Cut the crap, eh? You 'eard the lieutenant, boys. Put the stuff over there and cut the crap—we mustn't upset the brave lieutenant, must we."

Lou went to the driver and signed his delivery slip and returned to his office. This was the first time Jessup had stepped out of line on the job, and it caught him by surprise. Lou wasn't sure what to do and assumed the insults would escalate. A week later, a load of timber arrived for cribbage and shoring. The truck pulled into the shed and Lou went out to the driver. Jessup, his gang of apes in tow, surrounded Lou as the driver got down from the cab. The driver, a heavy-set man, had become friendly with Lou since the caravan incident. His brother, a rigger, had been aboard *R38* when it crashed, and Lou remembered him. He gave Lou a bright smile.

"Hello, governor. How are you today?"

"Not bad, Bill," Lou answered.

" 'Ere, you wanted a description of that peeping Tom trying look in your caravan that time. Remember?" the driver said, pointing his index finger in Jessup's face, whose bulbous eyes blazed in fury. "This is 'im right here!"

"Now you watch it, cock! Your health could take a nasty turn," Jessup yelled.

"Oh, yeah? Is that right, you pockmarked, grease ball? I'll cut yer dick off—if I can find it," the driver shouted back.

The foreman, hearing the commotion, came rushing over. "What's going on?" he demanded, glaring at the driver.

"It's not his fault," Lou said.

"What's all this about, then?"

"I saw this man here, peeking in the lieutenant's caravan window a while ago," the driver said. "Stinking little pervert."

"I'd come to find a job, that's all. But this bloke," Jessup pointed at Lou, "was inside with a woman. He must have bin havin' 'er away. The caravan was rockin' about an' she was screamin' like a wild woman. "

Jessup's crew laughed and sniggered. "Wo!" they yelled.

"That wasn't right. Not on *government* property," Jessup declared, puffing out his chest.

"All right, all right!" the foreman growled. "Bugger off, the lot of yer. Get to the other end of the shed. Report to the foreman down there."

"I'm going to report this to the shop steward," Jessup hissed.

"You can go and tell the Pope, for all I care," the foreman shouted.

After they were out of earshot, he turned to Lou. "Is any of this true, sir?"

"It was during the time of reconstruction. My wife had brought me my lunch …and she was giving me dancing lessons. We were doing the Charleston."

"And what was Jessup doing?"

"He was trying to look in the window," the driver said.

"Maybe he *was* looking for a job, like he said," the foreman said.

"You could be right," Lou said. "Let's forget about the whole thing."

The foreman shrugged and walked off to bring another crew to unload the truck.

"I'm sorry, sir. I didn't think …" the driver began.

"Don't worry. It wasn't your fault, Bill."

"I just wanted you to know, it was *him*. Dirty little wanker!"

"I knew exactly who it was," Lou said.
"Do you want me to do 'im for yer, sir?"
"No, please don't. I don't like violence."
"What are you going to do, guv?" the driver asked.
"I'm working on it."

A few weeks later, in the middle of summer, Jessup showed up uninvited to one of the Sunday afternoon picnics. He slunk around, trying to blend in. Charlotte spotted him and watched him sidle up to one of the wives who lived in a staff bungalow with her husband, a wispy-looking design engineer who was on the field playing cricket. Charlotte was on to them immediately. The woman was older than Jessup, obviously flattered by his attention. Charlotte nodded to Lou who quickly grasped the situation. He walked over to Jessup who, seeing him coming, moved toward Wallis and Molly and stood close to them.
"What are *you* doing here?" Lou asked.
"I'm sorry, sir. I thought this was a general thing for the workers on government property," Jessup said pleasantly.
"You're wrong and you know it, Jessup."
Wallis was listening.
"I'm awfully sorry, sir. I wouldn't have dreamt of coming—I was just tryin' to be sociable," Jessup said humbly, looking at Lou while shooting appealing sideways glances at Wallis.
"You need to leave, right now!" Lou barked.
"Wait. Don't be too hard on the man," Wallis said. "Let him stay today." Lou glared at Jessup, who stared meekly back at him with a hint of pleasure.
"Well, that's awfully kind of you, sir," Jessup said, smiling at Wallis. "I *will* stay a while. I think I'll try some of the ladies' English trifle. Looks awfully delicious." He looked at Lou, smiling sweetly, and then with a wink, "I'm awfully sorry, sir. I really had no idea—honest!" Jessup snuck off and took up again with the woman he was trying to bed.
Lou and Charlotte went home.

The following week, Jessup tipped the scales, putting his own health in serious jeopardy. As Lou walked to the other end of the shed searching for one of the foreman, Jessup came up behind him with his gang. "Look who's here, boys. It's our great American hero—hero my arse!"
"Get back to work, Jessup!"
"This is the man who deserted his shipmates, boys. They came up with a big story for the papers. He saved *this one* and he saved *that one*. He was hiding in the tail of his balloon wiv all them other gutless Yanks," Jessup yelled. "He ain't no bleedin' hero. He just got lucky! Then, what do they do?

They give him a job here so he can knock off his old woman in a bloody government caravan—right here. Talk about benefits on the job!"

Lou went to Jessup and stood close. Jessup stared at Lou in surprise. Lou spoke quietly and the others gathered around trying to hear above the construction din. "Jessup, look at me. Look at me." They stood, their noses almost touching. Lou continued, while Jessup smirked. "Now listen. I'm going to ask you to knock it off, for your own good. I don't want anything bad to happen to you."

Jessup whooped. "Oh, listen to 'im, boys. He doesn't want anything bad to 'appen. And it's all for me own good!"

"Just don't say I didn't warn you. It'll be bad. D'you understand?" Lou said.

Jessup grinned. "Nothing's gonna change, Yank. I'm gonna keep on 'til you're gone from 'ere and you and yer wife are history."

"Okay, Jessup, this is how it's going to be."

Jessup put his hands on his hips. "Come on, tell me, Yankee boy."

"Old Hinkley's Farm."

"Yeah, what about Hinkley's Farm?"

"One hour. Be there. Bring *one* of these knuckleheads with you. You're gonna need help. But *only* one," Lou said, holding up one finger and glaring at the three stooges gathered around Jessup.

"Blimey. What d'yer know. I do believe he wants to fight. All right. One hour, then."

Jessup was thrilled. Lou turned away, making for his office.

"We got 'im now, boys. Damn! We got 'im now!" Jessup crowed.

20

OLD HINKLEY'S FARM

Summer 1927.

Lou put on his construction boots. In the bottom drawer of his desk he had an old black T-shirt and a pair of dungarees. He pulled them out and slipped them on. He left the shed and crossed the old railway line toward the perimeter of the field, walking briskly to loosen up. Lou trotted and walked alternately along the edge of the airfield toward the wood on the well-trodden path. Stepping along a fallen log, he crossed a small stream and disappeared into the forest, passing a bevy of deer.

Inside the tree line, the sound of birdsong increased. So did the drumming of rain drops from leaves overhead. He turned and retraced his steps after a mile or two and ran back past the animals. Feeling good, he jogged toward the aerodrome, re-crossing the spur railway line and onto the muddy field. His head and chest were clear, his blood pumping steadily, pushed by a strong heart. He took deep breaths of the damp, misty air drifting over the marshes from the river.

During his exercise, which was as much about psyching himself up to fight as anything, Lou planned his strategy. He must stay in control. Not lose his temper. Not kill anyone—although that might be difficult. He didn't want to be responsible for another man's death and go to jail, or worse. He had too much to live for: to be with Charlotte and take care of her. He hated this. He thought he'd left it all behind. He ran to the end of the air station and back across the field. It started to drizzle again. He entered his office in the shed and was putting on his motorcycle jacket when Norway appeared in the doorway.

"Lou, oh, are you leaving?"

"I'm gonna pop out for twenty minutes. Anything important?"

"No. I wanted to ask if you and Charlotte…"

"Nevil. I've got a meeting with someone. I don't want to keep him waiting. Can we go in your car? We can talk on the way. It'll save me getting wet on the bike." They headed for Norway's green three-wheeler parked outside the shed. Lou looked at it and smiled. Norway was so proud of this funny little car. They climbed in. It smelled of Balkan Sobrani.

This thing fits Nevil's personality perfectly and he's just so content.

Norway turned the key. After a few attempts, the engine sputtered to life. They chugged jerkily down the road, leaving a trail of blue smoke from the tail pipe. "She'll be all right in a minute," Norway said.

"Follow this road for two miles. So, what's up, Nev?"

"I wondered if I could take you and Charlotte to dinner this evening. They've just opened a new restaurant in Hull. I can take you in the car."

"What's the occasion?"

"I want to celebrate. My new novel's been accepted by the publisher."

"'Hey, Nev, that's great. Well done!"

"I also wanted to ask if you've read my new manuscript."

"As a matter of fact, we both have. We liked it. Sure, we can meet up for a chat. You know you should think about doing a story about building the two airships—you know, like rivals—a big adventure and all that."

"Hmm, maybe. We'll see how this saga turns out, but I expect it'd be dreadfully dull," Norway replied. They followed the road to the junction known as Old Hinkley's Farm.

"Here, Nev. Pull over on the grass, if you don't mind."

They were deafened by the roar of four motorcycles wildly revving up behind them. "W-what the heck is going on?" Norway said. "I b-believe they're t-trying to int-t-timidate us."

"Oh, don't worry. It's my guy. They're having a bit of fun that's all. He and I are going to have a little talk. Wait here. I won't be long." Norway peered uncertainly at the four hostile bikers. They kept looking over at the car and laughing as they pulled their motorbikes up onto their stands.

"Brought yer protection with yer then, Lieutenant?" Jessup said, grinning.

"Hey, Jessie, that's 'is armored car," one with rodent features shouted.

"It's right sporty!" said the tall one with no hair and snake eyes.

Lou saw Norway becoming increasingly unnerved. "I told you to bring *one* knucklehead, Jessup, not three," Lou growled.

"Yeah, well, they all wanted to come. They wanna see your guts splattered all over this field," Jessup said, pulling out a pack of Gold Flake. He lit one with a steel lighter and sauntered after Lou, the cigarette dangling from his mouth. Lou climbed over the five bar gate, pulled off his motorcycle jacket and carefully hung it on the gatepost. The gang of four followed Lou, who looked back at Norway leaning nervously on the gate. Lou spent the next seven minutes meting out punishment to Jessup and two of his gang. He allowed one to escape injury so he could render assistance to the others.

After Lou had done his worst, he ambled back to the gate. Norway looked sick.

"What's up, old buddy?" Lou asked.

"I heard that man's leg snap," Norway answered. "Lou, what the hell are you d-d-doing? Have you gone m-mad?"

Lou put on his jacket. "It's a long story, Nev. But you know, you really should think about doing a book about the airship business. Could be a best seller."

"Let's g-get away from here," Norway said, scurrying off to the car, "b-before you kill somebody." Once inside the car Lou did his best to calm Norway down.

"Look Nev, don't be alarmed. These low-down, dirty rats deserved what they got. That last one has been harassing and following Charlotte around for seven years and he's broken into our house at least twice—not to mention beating up and robbing Charlotte's cousin."

"Why didn't you go to the p-police?"

"I did. There was nothing they could do."

"Maybe I *will* write that b-book and *y-you'll* be in it," Norway muttered. He turned the key in the starter. The engine started after five or six tries.

"You know this is one hell of a car, Nev," Lou said.

"She'll be all right in a minute, when she's warmed up again."

"If your book's a success, maybe you'll be able to afford another wheel."

The car sputtered and took off merrily along the road to the Howden shed where Lou worked the rest of the day without further distraction, save for the sounds of ambulance bells ringing as they sped along the Selby Road toward Old Hinkley's Farm.

Jessup's recovery was slow. He spent six months in the hospital in Hull. Charlotte stopped by his ward every so often without him seeing her. He looked as though he'd been in a dreadful traffic accident. His jaw had been wired up and his head wrapped in bandages with only his eyes visible. His left leg was in plaster from the ankle to the hip and suspended from the ceiling. His arm was in a sling due to his broken collarbone and his right hand was wrapped in bandages, his fingers in splints. He complained of pains in his abdomen caused by a massive blow to the solar plexus. Jessup's bald friend was in the next bed for a week before being sent home on crutches. During his hospital stay, Jessup had a few visitors, including his sister Angela, as well as a few toughs from Moortop.

Most of the nurses knew of Charlotte's troubles with Jessup and kept her abreast of his progress and what he said to his visitors. For a month, he kept quiet, his jaw being wired up tightly. Jessup wasn't a happy man and took his fury out on the nurses. After that month, Charlotte was sent to work on Jessup's ward and when he caught sight of her, he became enraged.

"You see what he did to me, bitch? You see what he did! He's gonna pay for this. Just you wait. I'm gonna kill him!" Jessup hissed and spat through clenched teeth like an incoherent madman. Hearing the outburst, the matron came rushing down the ward.

"You listen to me, *Mr.* Jessup, one more peep out of you and I'll have you thrown out on the street! In the meantime, I'll inform the police of your threats," she said.

At that moment, Angela came into the ward to visit her brother and overheard the matron's bollocking. She glared at Charlotte with bitter hatred. Charlotte was sent to another ward. Later in the evening, she told Lou what Jessup had said. Lou shrugged and said he wasn't surprised—Jessup was a slow learner. A couple of weeks after the beatings, Jessup's friend with the rat-face, showed up for work at the shed with the unharmed member of their gang. He wore a dressing over his nose which covered most of his face. In comical nasal tones, he told the foreman he and his mates had been set upon by soldiers from the barracks in York. He said the other two were recovering.

Jessup returned to work with his bald friend nine months after their 'little talk' at Hinkley's Farm. He acted docile and the foreman let them work even though both limped badly. Lou learned Jessup was back and sought him out on the shop floor. When Jessup saw Lou coming, his face became mask of terror.

"Ah Jessie, I've been really worried about you, big guy," Lou said, taking his hand and giving him the smile of a caring friend. "I heard you got into a bit of a dust-up. Are you okay now?"

The shop foreman listened with interest.

"Yes, sir. I'm pretty good now," Jessup said, in a weird voice, his speech affected by his crooked jaw.

"They said you and your friends were set upon by a platoon of soldiers. Is that true?"

"No, sir, only six, not a platoon," Jessup answered.

"Well, that's mighty unfair. Anyway, keep me informed of your progress. I'm gonna be taking a close interest in your welfare from now on." Lou moved in close to Jessup and spoke in his ear. "Remember what I said, you little shit. You're on probation—you'll *always* be on probation."

"Yes, sir. I understand, sir."

"Now, the things you've been saying in the hospital about …well, I don't need to repeat all of it, do I?"

"I'm so, so sorry. I was saying crazy things for a time. I was out of my head with the pain. You understand, sir. Please forgive me."

"All right, Jessup, we'll see how you shape up," Lou said.

21

Ⲁ ⲤⲎⲀⲚⲄⲈ ⲒⲚ ⲀⲦⲦⲒⲦⲨⲆⲈ

B y 1928, the skeletons of both ships had been fully framed. Shed No.1 at Cardington had been lengthened to provide more than adequate room, whereas at Howden they had only eighteen inches to spare each side. Lou realized the sheds had served as huge templates for the airships, growing like giant grubs inside their pods. The press continued to follow every detail during the construction of *Cardington R101*, which they considered the main story. *Howden R100* was second-rate in comparison and not paid nearly as much attention. George Hunter from the *Daily Express* however, didn't write the Howden ship off so quickly, remaining quiet on the subject. He visited Howden a couple of times a year where he usually met with Norway and Lou. He and Norway became friends. Wallis shunned the press.

In the autumn of '28, Lou made one of his monthly visits to Cardington. In Colmore and Scott's absence, he'd arranged to meet Richmond. Before doing so, he dropped in on Captain Carmichael Irwin in his site office in Shed No. 1. Scott had brought Irwin on board as the skipper of *Cardington R101* and, for the time being, he was familiarizing himself with the engineered drawings of the airship, its power and mechanical systems. Four years older than Lou, Irwin was unmistakably Irish, that is 'Black Irish', good-looking with jet-black hair and blue eyes, tall and somewhat shy. His nickname was 'Blackbird' or just 'Bird'. He was also known as 'the Crow', which would later become a *Cardington R101* call sign. They talked briefly about the war. Irwin had served with the Royal Naval Air Service as a commander of non-rigid airships in the Home Waters and East Mediterranean. Now, he was with the Royal Air Force with the rank of flight lieutenant. He was also a fine athlete, having represented Great Britain as a long distance runner in the 1920s Olympics in Belgium. Lou found the soft-spoken captain to be a genuine and decent fellow. Knowing the Remingtons would be posted to Cardington early in the coming year, Irwin offered his help in finding them somewhere to live. Later in the year, he sent newspaper cuttings of homes for rent in the area with names of reputable estate agents.

After leaving Irwin, Lou met Richmond at his office in Cardington House. He found him slumped in his leather chair, shirt rumpled, sleeves rolled up, Air Force tie loose at the neck. His scoffing superiority seemed to have vanished."Oh, Remington, come in," he said wearily.

"Are you well, sir?" Lou asked.

"Rather tired, actually."

"Burning the midnight oil, are we?"

"That's about it. So much to be done," Richmond sighed.

"Always the way, sir."

"I shouldn't complain. I'm doing what I love most …I suppose. I can't seem to get any satisfaction out of it these days. I'm exhausted." Richmond leaned back in his chair, meeting Lou's eyes. "Just how are things at Howden? I want you to tell me *everything*. When we first met, you told me they were using 'geodetic' construction. Tell me more about that. I have my own ideas of course, but I'd like to hear *you* to explain it."

"For technical information you might want to speak with Mr. Wallis or Mr. Norway. You could pay them a visit. I'm sure they'd be more than glad to consult with you, sir."

"I doubt that very much," Richmond said, shaking his head.

"Perhaps you should try."

Richmond turned away, as though thinking about it. "We'll see. *You* tell me."

"The best way I can put it is—if one part of the ship fails, or is under stress, say like a girder or something, then other parts take up the load. They ride in to save the day, like the cavalry, so to speak." Lou put his fist to his mouth and made a bugle sound and grinned. "I'm sure Squadron Leader Rope's familiar with all that stuff."

Richmond puffed up his cheeks and blew out a long breath. "Fascinating. Tell me about their engines; I understand they're using petrol."

Lou had spoken to Wallis before coming down and asked if he should remain tight-lipped. Wallis's answer had surprised him. "Tell them whatever they want to know. Richmond's committed now. He can't change a thing—government won't allow it. They're overspent. And as far as my knowing what Cardington is doing—which is of no interest to me—I only have to read the papers. The Air Ministry puts out propaganda every day."

"Howden's using six Rolls-Royce Condors, two of which can reverse for maneuvering," Lou said.

Richmond's pain was obvious. *Cardington R101* had five engines, underpowered and overweight. One, a permanent reversing engine, was just dead weight ninety-nine percent of the time.

"I wish we could switch to petrol. We'd save tons. What about gas bags and harnesses?"

"As you know, the bags are coming from Germany. The harnesses are made and everybody's happy with them," Lou said.

"And the gas valves?"

"They should be in from Zeppelin any time."

"Well, ours are built. I hope they work." Richmond peered gloomily out the window.

"Oh, I'm sure they will, sir."

"What about servo assistance?" Richmond said, studying the wintry scene outside his window.

"They don't have any."

Richmond suddenly sat up and glared at Lou. "What! Why not?"

"Mr. Norway found it unnecessary."

"I can't believe *that!*"

Lou read his disappointment. "They've been through the numbers countless times."

"Rope said just the opposite. That damned gear weighs a ton!"

"If I may be so bold, sir, how is the weight coming out?" Lou asked innocently.

"Heavier than expected. I can't say anything now. We're working on it."

Underpowered and heavy. No wonder he's up at night. He's a pompous ass, but you can't help feeling sorry for the guy.

Lou remembered Wallis telling him and Norway the Cardington ship was bound to come out heavy. "They'll be depending on dynamic lift to stay airborne, you'll see," he'd said.

"How much did you say they'd spent so far?" Richmond asked.

"Actually, I didn't, but it's under two hundred and ninety thousand pounds."

Richmond was incredulous. "Under two ninety!" He put his hand to his brow, staring at his untidy desktop. "We've spent over two million pounds."

No wonder you look glum, pal.

Lou knew that at the end of the day, Vickers estimated they'd be at least a hundred thousand pounds over budget, but they knew that going in.

Richmond continued, "That's confidential. I shouldn't have told you."

"I shan't say anything, sir."

"How the hell does he do it?"

"How does who do what, sir?" Lou asked.

"Wallis. How does he do it?"

"It's all in his head, sir."

"Just like that?"

"Yep. He has a pretty amazing mind."

"Look, Remington, we've been talking openly. Keep all this to yourself. Don't divulge anything to Howden."

"Sir, I never do and they never ask. They're good like that."

"Quite."

"They have their own designs and ways of doing things."

"Yes, yes, I know. They're not going to steal our ideas."

"No chance of that."

"I just don't want information to get out, especially in the press."

"I understand perfectly, sir."

"Their confidence is astonishing," Richmond said.

"One thing I can tell you, sir. They're glad of oversight."

Richmond pondered this, puzzled. "You know, I'm a *chemist*," he said suddenly.

"Really, sir?"

"I expect they joke about me up there, don't they?"

Lou had heard them call him 'Dopey', but he couldn't remember who said it.

No point in upsetting the poor guy.

"I've heard nothing of the sort."

Richmond looked embarrassed for opening up the way he had.

"I depend on Bolton and Paul's engineers," he said.

"I guess they've got aeronautical design staff over there?"

"They're very experienced. They've done stout work here. I think highly of them and Rope oversees a lot of this stuff, of course—he's exceptional," Richmond said.

"The newspapers can't say enough about the guy," Lou agreed.

Richmond opened his bottom drawer and pulled out a sheaf of papers. He buzzed his secretary and asked her to bring in 'one of the special envelopes.' A young woman appeared moments later with a brown envelope. Richmond slid the papers inside and wound the string around its fasteners.

"I'd like you to give this to Mr. Wallis, with my compliments. It's a copy of our gas valve design. I'd be most interested to hear his opinion." Lou took the envelope wondering if this could be a new beginning; an era of cooperation.

In Howden the next morning, Lou handed Wallis the envelope, relaying Richmond's message. Wallis read the words 'TOP SECRET' on the front. He handed it back to Lou.

"Aren't you going to open it, sir?"

Wallis's answer was brief. "Send this back by special courier immediately. We don't have anywhere secure enough at Howden to store such valuable, high-level, top secret documents."

Lou was disappointed—this was Wallis's unforgiving, stubborn side.

"Don't look like that, Lou. These people are on the ropes. Do you think they'd afford us the same consideration if the situation were reversed? They've been kicking us around for the last four years and now they want to play nice. Don't be soft."

"Right you are, sir," Lou said.

22

GOODBYE LENNY

Autumn 1928.

L ate in summer of '28, afternoon tea was arranged at Candlestick Cottage. Wallis was present with Molly and their two children and Norway showed up with an unexpected guest—a new lady friend. Frances was a quietly spoken girl who worked as a medical practitioner in York. He'd met her at the flying club. John Bull dropped by with Mary and chatted with Charlotte's parents while Billy played darts with Lou and his dad in the garden. Lenny did his level best to play, squinting through his specs, a Woodbine in his mouth while he tried to suppress a chesty cough full of phlegm. But his darts kept falling short into the dirt. Charlotte stood inside at the window with Molly, each holding a baby. Fanny began to cry, her shoulders heaving. She held a handkerchief up to her eyes, her heart breaking.

"Fanny, love, what's the matter?"
"It's terrible," Fanny sobbed.
"What?"
"He's only got three months."
"Oh Fanny, what do you mean?" Molly gasped.
"He's got lung cancer. They said it's spreading—to his brain."
After that news, it became impossible to enjoy the afternoon. Fanny and her family soon left after tearful goodbyes. Everyone realized Lenny was a very sick man and when they were gone, Charlotte broke the news.

Lenny died two weeks later. Those present at the Sunday afternoon tea at the cottage attended the funeral at Western Cemetery, which brought back sad memories to Lou and Charlotte. They watched the autumn leaves fall on Lenny's coffin as it was lowered into the ground, while the distraught Fanny held on to her mother and Billy. After the service, the mourners returned to the cottage—everyone except Fanny and Billy, who went to Fanny's mother's in Selby.

Wallis told Lou that if the boy needed a job in order to help his mother financially, there'd be a place for him at Howden. Billy reported for work two weeks later. Lou took him to the shop foreman and told him to take good care of him. He earned twelve shillings a week—not bad for a boy of fifteen.

After a couple of months, Billy was shinning up and down the ladders and climbing the scaffolds and ropes with the best of them. Lou was glad he had a job; it'd keep his mind off his father's death. Fanny left their rented place near Hull and went with Billy to live in Selby. A position had been found for her at Goole Hospital.

23

LEAVING 'CANDLESTICK'

April 1929.

L
ou hadn't slept at all. It was now 4:30 a.m. He rolled over and sat up on the side of the bed. The wind had strengthened and continued to howl through the trees and rattle the windows.

"What time is it?" Charlotte asked.

"Half past four."

"Suppose I might as well get up, too."

"Not much point in lying here."

"I'll make tea," Charlotte said.

Lou got up and dressed and went into the living room where boxes were piled high. He lit the fire in the grate. It was chilly. They sat around the fireplace drinking tea and eating toast, enjoying a couple more hours in this room they both loved. Charlotte held her cup to her lips, withdrew it, and stared into the fire.

"Oh, Lou, I don't want to leave Candlestick."

"Neither do I honey. I love this place as much as you. But once we get down there, we'll make new friends, you'll see. Remember, I already know lots of people."

"Yes, and you'll be off flying around the world in that bloody airship. And I'll be stuck at home on my own. … Oh Lou, …"

"Come on, Charlie. We'll give it a try and I promise if you're not happy, I'll quit."

"You promise?"

"I promise."

"I don't want to leave this place. I'd hate it if anything happened to you."

"Don't worry, nothing's gonna happen."

"What will John do with this place?"

"Perhaps he'll sell it."

At 8 o'clock, John arrived to take them to Hull Railway Station. They'd arranged with him to pick up their belongings and transport them down to Bedford at the weekend in his van. Lou had sold his motorbike and planned to buy a newer one in Bedford. He was looking forward to shopping around.

After putting two small suitcases in the boot of John's car, Charlotte and Lou went back inside the cottage for one last look and to make sure Fluffy was all right with plenty of food and milk. John would send her down with the furniture in her cage. He was going to look in on her in the meantime. Charlotte cried and Lou put his arms around her.

"Don't be sad, love," Lou pleaded.

Charlotte said nothing. She stared out the window at the rear garden and fond memories of their friends came back to her. Her snowdrops and shrubs were just starting to bloom and she wondered who'd care for them now. She remembered all the things they'd done in this house—their first real home together. It had always been full of friends and laughter. She could hear it now—so many happy memories, and some sad ones, too. She thought of Lenny, the baby that never came, and the box room where she hoped to put the crib—but which had gradually become full of junk. She was heartbroken, and for the first time in her life, bitter.

Charlotte walked to the car while Lou turned the key in the deadlock on the front door. Charlotte climbed into the back seat. John turned to her from the driver's seat and forced a smile.

"Come on, love, it won't be so bad. You're off on a new adventure."

Charlotte said nothing. She felt empty.

Lou climbed into the passenger front seat and handed the keys to John who slid them into his pocket with a final sad nod. They pulled away. Charlotte stared at the cottage until it disappeared from view. She believed she could never feel more miserable than this. But she was wrong.

PART FIVE

Cardington Shed No. 1.

CARDINGTON

24

THE IN-BETWEEN YEARS

1924 – 1929.

W hen the Labour Party had been kicked out of office, Thomson didn't sit around feeling sorry for himself. He visited MacDonald once or twice a year, traveling up by air with their good friend Capt. Hinchliffe, chief pilot with a Dutch airline. 'Hinch' sometimes rented a two or four-seater plane and flew Thomson and MacDonald to Lossiemouth on one of his days off. Thomson usually stayed for a week or two at The Hillocks, during which time they went for long walks, fished or played golf. They also visited local Highland beauty spots and dined at favorite hotels.

On their walks, Thomson and MacDonald strategized, devising new policies to get Britain on a permanent socialist footing once they regained power. MacDonald assured Thomson it would happen soon. Thomson believed him.

Thomson became 'a man in waiting'—a role he'd learned to live with for years. Besides Marthe, getting back in office was all he thought about. He yearned to be back behind his ornate desk at Gwydyr House.

Taking up residence in that mansion on Whitehall and setting up the New British Airship Program—his creation!—had been the greatest thrill of his professional life. He believed it to be his destiny. He loved his Air Ministry position and all it entailed—it remained key in his plan to win Marthe for good. She was the ultimate prize; his cabinet seat and elevation in stature were the means to that end and so obviously preordained—all he had to do was be patient.

For the first two years after leaving office, Thomson started his memoirs and got on with writing *Smaranda*, in part, a book about Marthe. During a visit to Bucharest, he presented it to her as soon as he alighted from the train with a note inscribed on the inside cover describing it as 'a testament of his devotion.'

Since his rise, Marthe had become more accessible—hard for him to admit, but true. She had her own life, a husband, and position—maybe even a lover or two. He tried not to dwell on that unbearable thought, reminding himself she had little or no interest in sex. As an acclaimed writer, possessing the gift of words, she'd won the highest honors and praise for her literary works in Paris. He'd been nothing but a soldier and a mere student of history, art and languages. A brigadier general wouldn't be considered lofty enough in her social circles. For her to have become 'Mrs. Thomson' would have been too embarrassing to even contemplate.

Now everything had changed, as he'd hoped and prayed it would. He'd become someone—a close friend and confidante of the British Prime Minister, a man who'd be in that position again soon enough. She asked after MacDonald constantly, which he noted. He was aware she adored powerful men.

Maybe one day, I myself might aspire

He met Marthe in Paris two or three times a year at her apartment on the fashionable Rue du Faubourg Saint-Honoré. He also visited her in Romania, where he stayed with her at Mogosoëa for ten blissful days. Thomson took pleasure in the beautiful gardens of the Romanian Renaissance palace with its magnificent courtyards, chapel, Venetian palace, ponds and lily pads, all set on the rolling banks of Mogosoëa Lake. They took romantic walks, picnicking beside the whispering waters, a perfect place to relax and prepare before re-entering the rough and tumble of British politics.

While in Bucharest, Thomson met Marthe's husband Prince George again. The last time they'd met was when they worked together in the war, destroying Romania's oil wells. George came by with his mistress and in the most civilized manner, the four had dinner together in the grand dining room. Although Thomson found it strange and offensive to his sensibilities, he accepted the situation—*she* was sitting beside *him*. That was all that mattered.

Thomson thought it ironic that he and Marthe's husband shared the same interest in aviation, although George was a highly skilled pilot. Thomson had no intention of ever being at the controls of an aircraft. After dinner, George, a little drunk, drove off in his Mercedes with his mistress to the house they shared, while Thomson and Marthe retired to their adjoining rooms.

Thomson served on several committees at the Royal Aero Club in London for a couple of years and was later voted chairman. This gave him stature and contact with the most influential people in aviation, keeping him in the eye of the top brass in the RAF and the Air Ministry. They regarded him as the next Minister of State for Air, assuming Labour regained power, which most thought inevitable.

During these years, Thomson traveled the United States and Canada from coast to coast, giving speeches on aviation and trade between the continents. These speaking engagements supplemented his income from the House of Lords, helping to finance his trips to Paris and Bucharest.

Marthe met him at the luxurious Willard Hotel on Pennsylvania Avenue in Washington, D.C. in December of 1928 where, as chairman of the

Royal Aero Club of the United Kingdom, he headed a British delegation at the International Aviation Conference.

The circumstances were, once again, bizarre. As chairman of the Romanian Aviation Society, Marthe's husband had also been invited and had brought his mistress along. They too, stayed at the Willard, but in a luxurious suite. Thankfully, Thomson's and Marthe's adjoining rooms were on a different floor.

For Marthe, this trip had a dual purpose: to spend time with Thomson and to promote her latest book—already well received in the United States, Canada and Great Britain.

25

MOVING SOUTH

April 1929.

W hen Scott mentioned Lou had been posted to Cardington, Captain Irwin volunteered to put him and his wife up until they'd settled in. Lou had met him many times over the past year during his visits to Cardington. Lou and Charlotte had visited Bedford the previous month for Charlotte to inspect a property Lou had been offered for rent which, although expensive, looked promising. The house was on a terrace of homes on Kelsey Street close to Bedford, near the parade of shops Lou knew well. Bay windows ran up the front on three levels from the half buried basement to the third story bedrooms.

Concrete steps led from the parking area up to the entrance door at mid-level. On that level, the living room was at front, dining room at rear, overlooking a long narrow garden. The room below ground level at the front was protected by a retaining wall with a large railed open area, allowing light in the bay windows. That room was ideal for a workshop and storage.

The large main bedroom, situated on the third floor at the rear, had space for a wardrobe, dressing table and a chest of drawers. Two smaller bedrooms overlooked the street. Charlotte chose one she'd decorate as baby's room. The kitchen, located on the bottom floor had French doors opening onto the rear garden.

Charlotte thought the house had potential for entertaining and gardening. The drawbacks were the beige flowery wallpaper and green linoleum. At least the building had electricity and an inside bathroom on the top floor, unlike other places they'd viewed with gas lighting and no inside lavatory. For hot water, there was a gas geezer over the kitchen sink and bathtub. Although the amenities were better, the place wasn't as nice as Candlestick, but nothing ever could be. They took the house.

On arrival at Bedford Station, Lou and Charlotte took a cab to the Irwins' on Putroe Lane, a spacious, pebble-dashed bungalow with a slate roof. Being there was awkward for Charlotte in her unhappy state of mind. Olivia Irwin, tall, attractive, with blond hair and hazel eyes, and a bewitching Scottish accent, sensed Charlotte's discomfort and went out of her way to be kind. Soon, they were sharing confidences. Charlotte told her how she longed for a child and how she was on the verge of giving up. Olivia too, wanted a baby, but she and her husband had decided to wait just a little longer. She urged Charlotte not to be bitter and not to give up. Charlotte was relieved she had someone she could talk to now Fanny wasn't around.

Lou took a bus to Cardington and met the captain while Charlotte and Olivia were getting acquainted. Irwin explained he'd been reviewing blueprints and preparing flight manuals for *Cardington R101*. A wood-framed office had been built in the shed, which he and First Officer, Lieutenant Commander Noël Atherstone shared. Another office had also been set up for officers at the base of the tower for use when ships were moored there.

The three men went into the shed, where *Cardington R101* appeared to be at about the same stage as *Howden R100*. Both ships had been completely framed, with interior accommodations and finishings well underway. They climbed aboard via a stepladder, moved through the control car and went upstairs to the chartroom overlooking the control car. The layout was different from the Howden ship and the control car smaller. From there, they showed him the officer's cabins, crew berths and mess, dining room, lounge and promenade decks. Lou was impressed, but he remembered Wallis's words about things 'looking good in the shed.'

During the afternoon, Charlotte and Olivia took a bus to the house on Kelsey Street and Charlotte showed Olivia around. Mrs. Jones, a kindly neighbor, knocked on the door offering them tea. Close to the main street, the house was handy for shops and buses. Charlotte told Olivia she'd written for a job at Bedford hospital and was awaiting a reply. She didn't expect to start work immediately, as Lou would be spending time at Howden when they installed gasbags in *Howden R100*. Charlotte planned to accompany him and spend time with her parents during that time.

The Royal Airship Works folks at Cardington greeted Lou cordially, making him welcome. He bumped into Walter Potter and Joe Binks, now both gainfully employed on construction of *Cardington R101*, thanks to Lou. They'd heard Lou and Charlotte were moving down and offered their services. Lou told them he'd be glad of their help.

The Remingtons stayed two days at the Irwin bungalow, with Lou and the captain at Cardington most of that time. Olivia and Charlotte spent time in Bedford buying furniture. They had two pleasant evenings at Putroe Lane when the conversation focused on airships and Lou's career in the airship service. Charlotte put on a brave face.

On the third day, a Saturday, Lou and Charlotte went to No. 58 Kelsey Street to wait for John Bull's van. Potter arrived at 10 o'clock with three other young men, anxious to help. Charlotte answered the door, delighted to find Potter on the front step, his face cracking into one of his familiar half-smiles, although she sensed he still bore the effects of *R38*.

"Walter, lovely to see you! Come in, all of you," Charlotte said.

Potter took Charlotte's hand and kissed her cheek. They trooped into the empty living room. Lou hung back while Charlotte was introduced.

"I've been looking forward to seeing you, Charlotte. It's been eight years!" Potter said. He cast his eye around the room. "Hey, this is nice."

"It will be when it's painted," Charlotte said.

"This is Joe Binks' cousin, Freddie. Joe's not here yet—he's always late." Potter pointed out Freddie who stepped forward and shook Charlotte's hand. Freddie looked pretty scruffy. Her mind went back to the pathetic souls she used to see leaving Macy's factory. His jumper was full of holes, shoes worn out and falling apart. She noticed him limp as he walked in. He probably had short leg syndrome, caused in the womb or during birth. She couldn't get over how much he reminded her of Robert, the young man she'd met during the war. He was much younger of course, but the resemblance was striking.

Such a sweet boy. What a lovely face! I'll take him under my wing.

"And I brought Arthur Disley along, our electrician," Potter said.

"Call me 'Dizzy'," Disley said, with a droll grin. Charlotte shook his hand. His grip was firm.

A 'cool customer'—not at all 'dizzy'—the reliable type.

"This is Cameron—one of the coxswains. His wife, Rosie, works in the gasbag factory."

Cameron smiled pleasantly.

The picture of innocence. An open, trusting face—he seems like a happy man indeed!

"We mustn't forget old 'Bad-Luck' Sammy Church, over there," Potter said, pointing at a tall, twenty-four-year-old dressed in a gray sports jacket, white shirt and red tie. His shoes were well shined. He was shy and soft-spoken, with strong features. He had a head of thick brown hair with that just-combed look. He nodded and smiled, not quite looking Charlotte in the eye.

He's proud of that hair. Loves his Brylcreem!

"Why *Bad-Luck?*" she asked.

"Just don't play cards with him. As he scoops up yer money he always says, 'Oh, bad luck, mate.'" Charlotte laughed. "And he'll show you a few card tricks, too," Potter said.

Church pulled out a new deck and held it up. "Glad to know you missus," he said.

Lou stepped into the middle and was shaking hands all round as a rat-a-tat-tat came at the front door.

"Our stuff should be here any minute. My old boss is trucking it down," Lou told them while Charlotte opened the door to a breathless Joe Binks.

"Sorry I'm a bit, late, missus," Binks said.

"Come on Joe, where you bin—lyin' in bed?" Potter chided.

"No, no, something came up," Binks stammered.

Charlotte greeted Binks. He'd made a hurried effort to dress and his hair was a mess. He appeared jittery, his right eye twitching, which made her smile.

This one wouldn't make a good fibber.

Ten minutes later, the van drew up and John Bull climbed out of the driver's seat. Surprised to see him, Lou and Charlotte rushed out to greet him at the curb.

"John, what happened? We thought one of the mechanics was driving down."

"I couldn't resist. I had to make sure you're all right, didn't I?" John said.

"You shouldn't have done that," Charlotte said. "But I'm so pleased you did!" Her eyes filled with tears.

John winked and put his arms around her. "I've got big surprises for both of you. Follow me." John led everyone to the back of the van. "Close your eyes, Lou," he said. While Lou closed his eyes, John opened the van doors, revealing an object covered with a sheet. John climbed up and untied it.

"Okay Lou, open your eyes." As Lou did so, John removed the sheet with a flourish. There stood a gleaming black motorcycle with two enormous chrome-plated tail pipes.

"What the devil's this?" Lou asked.

"A 1000cc *Brough Superior.* It came into my shop yesterday. Fella wanted me to sell it for him. Had your name written all over it didn't it?"

"It's gorgeous! And yes, I want it. How much does he want?"

"Nothing. It's a present from me to you."

Lou was dumbfounded. John pulled a plank down from the van and the six men carefully rolled the bike down. Lou climbed on.

"It's you all right, sir," Binks said.

"It's smashin'!" Freddie exclaimed.

"This is the motorbike Lawrence rides," John told them.

"Who's Lawrence?" Freddie asked.

"Lawrence of Arabia. You know the fella who rode around on a camel during the war. Well, he's traded in his camel and rides one of these now."

"Looks bloomin' powerful," Charlotte said. "You be careful, Lou Remington!"

"John, I don't know what to say," Lou said.

"Don't say anything, just take care, like Charlotte says," John replied. "And I have a little housewarming present for our Charlotte."

Further back in the van a larger object stood covered with another sheet, which John removed, revealing a brand new piano.

Charlotte's eyes lit up. "Oh, John! I don't believe it!"

"I took the other one back to your parents. Now you've one of your own," John said.

The six men carefully eased the piano down into the road. Charlotte lifted the lid and with one finger tinkled "Blue Skies".

"Grey skies—let's hope they've all gone," John sang.

"Do you play, Charlotte?" Freddie asked.

"Does she play!" John said.

John climbed back into the van and held up the cat in her cage. Fluffy let out a loud meow. "And last but not least, here's our Miss Fluffy!"

They spent the next couple of hours bringing in boxes and furniture and setting it up under Charlotte's direction. Finally, they sat down in the living room for tea and sandwiches brought in by Mrs. Jones from next door. Afterwards, Charlotte tried out her new piano which, after her mother's, sounded sweet indeed.

The house was beginning to look more like a home, Charlotte pleased to have her things around her. As for the piano—it took her breath away. Before everyone from Cardington left, Charlotte asked them round for Sunday afternoon tea with their wives and girlfriends. John stayed for a couple more hours chatting. Charlotte hugged him tightly and thanked him before he headed back up north. She thought things mightn't be so bad— she'd met some nice folks and they were finally free of Jessup.

The following weekend, Potter brought an army of fifteen men to the house and they painted the interior white from top to bottom. Charlotte plied them with tea and sandwiches while they worked and Lou provided paint, paintbrushes and beer. By Sunday evening, the house gleamed and smelled of fresh paint. Charlotte was delighted.

A week later, her upbeat mood was soured again. Lou learned that Jessup, at his own request, had been posted to Cardington for training, along with two greasy cohorts. They'd rented a place in Bedford. Lou didn't expect trouble and wasn't unduly worried. Charlotte was skeptical; the beating might have made him worse. She knew the people of Ackworth would be pleased to see the back of him.

26

VICEROY TO INDIA

June 1929.

The mood in Britain during the early months of 1929 was bleak. With the General Strike not long over, unemployment and living standards worsening and the government's popularity plummeting, a general election became inevitable.

Labour won the most seats, with 287 against the Conservatives' 260, but still lacked a majority to form a government. The leader of the Liberal Party, Lloyd-George, whose party had won 59 seats, threw his lot in with MacDonald and Labour took over on June 5th. Just prior to taking office, Thomson was summoned to Lossiemouth. During their last few days of solitude, he and MacDonald made plans and chose cabinet members and staff for the new government. Thomson would be back at the Air Ministry.

MacDonald and Thomson also had the sad task of finding a new pilot to fly them back and forth to Lossiemouth. Captain Hinchliffe had gone off in a bid to fly the Atlantic from east to west, in an attempt to seize the record, as many others had previously tried (and failed) to do. Neither he nor his copilot had been heard from since—at least not in the flesh.

Thomson felt a little guilty, but he really *had* done all he could after receiving an urgent call from Hinchliffe, pleading for help. He and his heiress copilot were being evicted from Cranwell Aerodrome, their base of operations, due to strings being pulled by powerful people. Thomson had called his friend, the previous Air Minister, Sir Samuel Hoare, for assistance.

In an effort to save his daughter's life, the copilot's father had already spoken with Sir Samuel and got the eviction notice served. Sir Samuel told Thomson there was no way he'd intervene. Sadly, their eviction deadline, instead of causing the pioneer aviators to give up on their plan, pushed them into flying off prematurely into a horrendous storm.

At the beginning of June, Thomson moved back into Gwydyr House and MacDonald moved his staff and his furnishings into No.10 Downing Street, this time with the intention of a longer stay. To Thomson's delight, McDonald also took up residence at Chequers at weekends, as before.

During a visit to No. 10, Thomson received a surprise. Thinking he'd been called in to discuss policy, he stood at the window overlooking the colorful rear gardens, while MacDonald sat musing behind his desk. Unlike Thomson's last visit to this room, it was orderly, with pictures of MacDonald's family and Highland landscapes adorning the walls—no unpacked boxes lying around. Thomson's head was full of thoughts concerning the airship program, but while he spoke, MacDonald's mind appeared to be elsewhere.

"How I love this room, Ramsay—it's the heart and soul of the Empire, you know."

MacDonald remained silent. Thomson continued. "I'm planning a trip to Cardington next week. I can't wait to see what progress they've made. We have to get those intercontinental voyages organized. There'll be lots to do in those far off lands to prepare for our mighty ships. The schedules have slipped badly—I need to get things back on track."

MacDonald remained silent. Thomson turned back to the window and studied the lush green lawns. Several minutes later, MacDonald spoke.

"The post of Viceroy to India will be vacant soon. I need to make a nomination to the King to fill that position."

"Do you have anyone in mind?"

"Yes"

"Who?"

"You!"

Thomson hadn't seen this coming. His mind went into a turmoil.

"Ramsay, that's impossible! The airship program will be in full swing. And if I'm gone, who will watch your back? Those jackals on the left will run amuck!"

"True, CB, but I'll manage. And my dear fellow, what could be more fitting than for you to return to the land of your birth as viceroy? Why, you'd be King of India and Marthe, your queen!"

This came like a hammer-blow. Thomson suddenly had a throbbing headache and put his hand to his temple. A spontaneous vision exploded in his mind.

He stood on a balcony dressed in a magnificent black tuxedo, vivid blue sash across his chest, Marthe at his side in a flowing silver gown, a diamond tiara upon her head. They waved to adoring crowds below, flanked by elephants and a sea of Indian soldiers in dazzling red uniforms under a dusty, orange sun ...

"Ramsay, I beg you not to say such things. That couldn't happen, at least, not as long as her husband's alive—and no doubt he'll outlive me."

Ramsay is like a brother who wants the best for me.

MacDonald's knowing blue eyes twinkled.

"My dear CB, as viceroy, you'll lay the crown at her feet. Nothing will be refused you. Rome would almost certainly grant an annulment."

"I seriously doubt *that,* after all these years. She was fifteen when she was married off and they have a child! It's true they aren't married in the real sense of the word …"

"Well, there you are then!"

"You fill my head with things I dare not even dream about."

This wasn't true, of course. It was *all* he dreamed about.

"Marthe is a strict Catholic. She has a priest who's been her spiritual advisor since she was a girl in Paris," Thomson said. "He knows about me—in fact, I've met him. He always advises her against divorce."

"Then you will need to be more forceful, won't you. It's usual for a viceroy to be married. There'll be ceremonial duties for his wife to perform. Look, you're getting on in years. You deserve some real happiness. You'll have much to offer. This could be the chance of a lifetime, CB. Think about that."

Charlotte surprised herself, settling in rapidly. They had lots of Cardington folks around on Saturday and Sunday afternoons for tea. After the third week, they had a housewarming party with many of the crewmen and some officers and their wives or girlfriends, including Potter, Binks, Freddie, Church, Disley, Cameron and Leech. Capt. Irwin and Olivia and First Officer Atherstone and his wife showed up and stayed for a couple of hours.

At these little soirées, Charlotte usually gave Freddie something to wear, which she'd bought in Bedford—a pair of second-hand shoes or a sweater, or something Lou didn't wear anymore—a shirt or a pair of trousers (after she'd made alterations). Freddie was grateful and came to adore Charlotte. His face would light up whenever she entered the room.

Charlotte had been to the music shop in Bedford and picked up a few songs in sheet music and practiced them when Lou was at work as a surprise for him. He loved to hear her play the classics, which she did rarely. Everyone fell for Charlotte, especially men; besides being beautiful, she was a good listener and easy to talk to. After coaxing, Charlotte played the piano, sometimes with Potter on the accordion and Lou on guitar. Everyone gathered round and sang the latest hits. As usual at these gatherings, Disley sat in a corner quietly playing chess with challengers. Church dazzled the crowd by rolling pennies over his knuckles, performing card tricks and cutting and shuffling like a pro. Toward the end of the evening, he invariably managed to talk a few into a bait-and-switch bet or a game of brag, during which time he was heard to mutter, 'Oh, bad luck, mate,' as he pulled his winnings across the table.

Binks, as it turned out, was an accomplished artist. He usually brought a sketch pad and sat making pencil sketches and portraits of anyone who cared to sit for him. Lou was surprised by his quiet talent. Many, including Lou and Charlotte, had them framed.

He did one of Lou and two of Charlotte: Lou the flying ace in his navy cap and leather greatcoat, collar up, an airship in the sky behind him; Charlotte, a short-haired, ravishing twenties flapper, in a tight-fitting, black, knee-length dress, a silver beaded necklace down to the waist. She stood beside a grand piano, long cigarette holder in one hand, champagne glass in the other. In a close-up, Binks showed Charlotte again with short hair under a sequined, beaded skull cap, huge eyes wide, her sensuous, full lipped mouth and gorgeous smile, stunning—a movie star! That portrait caused quite a stir.

During the week, Lou had homework in the evenings. He reviewed drawings and new operating manuals for *Cardington R101*. Sometimes, he worked on a navigation course under the tutelage of Squadron Leader Ernest Johnston, who also attended their parties with his wife. Johnston, the most highly experienced navigator in the country, had made many landmark flights around the world and would serve as navigator for both ships. Lou got a kick out of Johnston—he was a hell of a wag.

Now he was based at Cardington, it became necessary for Lou to travel to Howden once a month. He was still responsible for ensuring documentation and as-built drawings for the Howden ship were updated and filed correctly. Lou would also be required to assist Wallis and Norway with not only the installation of the gasbags, but also with the engine trials in the shed—a subject he never dared discuss with Charlotte.

During the first week at Cardington, Lou sat down with Colmore and Scott a couple of times and once with Richmond. Richmond appeared to be in a more anxious state than when he'd last seen him. Lou couldn't understand why Cardington was so worried about the schedule. Richmond had said 'time was on their side.'

It became apparent that there were two factors pressuring Cardington. The first was the Germans: the Graf Zeppelin had made a successful maiden voyage to Lakehurst from Friedrichshafen in October and a round-the-world trip was scheduled in August via Russia, Tokyo and San Francisco. The second was Thomson: he was back at the Air Ministry and had let his displeasure over the slow progress of the airship program be known. He'd soon be here to assess the situation for himself. Cardington was filled with dread. In him, they began to sense a hard taskmaster who'd be on the warpath. They couldn't say this with certainty, since he'd been ousted in October 1924 before they'd built anything, but here they were in 1929, still fiddling around in the shed—at least, that's how they thought he'd perceive things. On the bright side though, Howden was no further along—or so it seemed.

On the day before Thomson's planned visit, Lou realized there was a third factor upsetting Cardington, more troubling than the other two. He went to Richmond's office to discuss matters concerning Shed No. 2 where *Howden R100* would be housed after her arrival later in the year. When he walked in, Richmond and Rope were huddled over Richmond's drawing board deep in conversation. Lou raised his hand and backed away, as if to leave.

Richmond looked up. "No, come in Lieutenant Remington. You're just as much a part of this team as anyone. We keep nothing from you."

This surprised Lou. "Okay, sir," he said and joined them.

"We're discussing her weight. We've done separate final calculations. After 20 tons for crew, ballast and stores, we only have 13 tons left for lift, d'you agree, Rope?"

"Yes, my figures agree," Rope said.

"Bugger! We should have built her another bay longer. We had plenty of room in the shed," Richmond exclaimed. He walked to the window scratching his head. "We've known for a long time she was coming out heavy."

I figured that's why you've become so stressed.

"Any suggestions, Remington?" Richmond asked.

"Lighten her, sir, and increase her lift," Lou replied.

"Quite. Quite." Richmond stuck his hands in his pockets, trying to look nonchalant. "Let's deal with the Air Minister's visit first. I won't dwell on the weight issue. I'll have to *touch* on the subject, of course. When he's gone, we'll give the subject our full attention. In the meantime, we'll keep it right here," Richmond said, looking from Lou to Rope.

"Absolutely, sir," Lou said, realizing why he'd been invited in.

"I'm sure these problems can be overcome," Rope said.

Lou glanced at Rope.

He looks confident enough.

27

THE FISHING PARTY

June 19, 1929.

The bedroom was dark, Charlotte sound asleep. Lou slid out of bed noiselessly and, taking his clothes with him, went down to the kitchen. He dressed while his coffee was brewing. After munching on a couple of slices of toast, Lou returned to the bedroom and opened the wardrobe door. His fishing rod was in the back corner for some silly reason. Wishing he'd retrieved it the night before, he leaned in and pulled it out. In the half-light, Charlotte raised her head from the pillow.

"Lou?"

"It's all right, love."

"What are you doing?"

"I'm meeting some of the guys. I promised I'd go fishing with them before going up to the shed," he whispered.

'What time will you be back?"

"About five."

"Five!"

"The Old Man's coming up from London. Everything's got to be perfect."

"Damn it, Lou, it's Saturday! I wanted us to spend the day together."

"We'll be together tomorrow, Charlie. I'm sorry; I can't help it."

Charlotte rolled onto her back, her hair spread across the pillow like a mane.

"Come back to bed for half an hour. I need you, love."

"I can't. The guys are waiting for me, honey."

"I suppose tomorrow you'll be studying, or fiddling with your damned motorbike."

"I mentioned in the week he was coming. You forgot."

Lou leaned over her to kiss her, but she rolled back on her side with a sigh, her hair cascading across her face. Lou went downstairs, put on his short black coat and went down to the motorbike. He strapped on his fishing rod, kick-started it and drove off sleepily toward the parade of shops where the 'boys' were waiting outside the corner store.

At St. Pancras Railway Station in London, Thomson marched down the platform, a walking stick hooked over his arm. This added accoutrement lent a certain gravitas. He was flanked by the two men closest to him at the Ministry. All three wore raincoats and hats. The air was chilly, but the morning sunshine streamed through the roof skylights, brightly lighting the station. The first man, Sefton Brancker, a staunch friend, had done much to help Thomson and further his career. It was *he* who, in those lean years of '21 and '22, had introduced him to people connected with aviation and was influential in him getting a seat on the Airships Advisory Panel. And during his time out of office, it'd been *Brancker* who'd arranged for Thomson to go on lecture tours throughout Canada and the United States, boosting Thomson's income. Thomson had been immensely grateful. He owed much to Brancker.

Brancker's looks were sometimes deceiving. In his early fifties and of average height, he appeared unkempt and ill-bred in rough tweed jackets —almost like a farm laborer. Though he seemed slack-jawed, his voice was rich and deep and he spoke the most beautiful King's English, as only the most well-bred could. To cover his baldness, he wore a toupée. He loved the ladies and they loved *him*—and his rakish mustache. They adored his vibrant personality and infectious enthusiasm, and the pains he took with them. He had an aura of self assurance and power. For Brancker's friends, nothing was ever too much trouble, especially if it enhanced the cause of aviation—his other great passion. Thomson liked having him around because he was such a positive force. At Gwydyr House, Brancker occupied the large office above his own.

Thomson's second companion was his personal secretary, Rupert Knoxwood, a tall, wiry fellow who had difficulty pronouncing his 'Rs', making him sound foppish when saying words like 'fwankly' or 'fwightfully', which he insisted on using. To Thomson, he was the consummate bureaucrat who understood him perfectly, anticipating his every need. As the three men strode down the station, Thomson spotted a uniformed railwayman heading in their direction. Thomson gazed at him, smiling like an old friend.

A potential voter!

The man, compelled to acknowledge Thomson, touched his cap. "Mornin', sir," he said.

"And a *very* good morning to *you*, my dear sir!" Thomson gushed.

"What carriage are you in, sir? Perhaps I can be of assistance." Knoxwood pulled out their tickets. "That's first class. Right this way, gentlemen," the railwayman said, leading them along the platform.

He stopped abruptly and opened their carriage door. They piled in while Knoxwood dropped a coin into the man's hand. They stashed their briefcases and raincoats in the overhead racks and got comfortable. Thomson gleefully rubbed his hands together like a schoolboy off to the seaside. A few minutes later, the doors slammed down the platform and the guard's whistle blew. The train jolted forward.

"Well, here we are again, Sefton. Back where it counts!"

"I can't tell you how pleased I am, CB," Brancker said.

"We'll need to visit Egypt. We must make sure everything's on schedule with the mooring mast and shed. Pity we lost our man, Hinchliffe. He'd have been ideal to fly us out there."

Brancker shook his head sadly. "Such a loss!"

"Perhaps you'll come back with another magic carpet," Knoxwood said, brightly. He knew one of Thomson's most prized possessions was a Persian rug presented to him in Iraq.

"Our magic carpet, Knoxwood, will be *Cardington R101* which will transport us first to Egypt and then on to India."

"Well put, CB," Brancker said.

"Perhaps the ship should be named *The Magic Carpet*," Knoxwood said, laughing.

"No, no. No fancy names," Thomson declared. He leaned his head on the headrest and relaxed. The train glided unhurriedly through grimy rows of terraced houses, wheels clacking rhythmically over the tracks. Thomson loved that sound. Train rides always put him in a good mood.

"Now, gentlemen, let's see what's what, shall we?" he said, delving into his red ministerial box. After reading his memoranda a few moments, he looked up suddenly, shooting a glance at Brancker, who was busy studying the form of a young woman pegging out the washing in her back yard.

"What happened to those trial flights to Egypt? We were going to use R33 and R36 for that purpose. What happened?"

Brancker turned back to Thomson. "Er, er, the trials got scrapped—budget cuts. Well er, ...not budget cuts exactly ...R36 and R33 needed a lot of money spending on them—especially after R33 got wrecked."

"Got wrecked! How?"

"Collided with her shed ..."

"Collided with her shed! Who was in command?"

"Scott, of course."

Thomson looked away in exasperation. "Whatever is the matter with that man?"

Brancker raised his eyebrows and made no comment.

"Well, they should have rebuilt those ships," Thomson said.

"The funding just wasn't there CB," Brancker replied.

"Budget cuts? Damn the Tories! Wish I'd been around. What else did they cut?"

"Nothing I can think of, but the emphasis is on heavier-than-air aircraft nowadays. Many in government don't like airships," Brancker replied.

"We'll see about *that!* I hope we don't live to regret cutting those test flights with the older ships. We could've learned a thing or two from a few trial runs to the Middle East. My main concern is the schedule. The Germans are getting way out in front. Our ships should've been in the air by now."

"Quite so, Minister," Knoxwood agreed.

The train rushed into a tunnel and they sat in the dark while Thomson continued. "So let's recap. Both ships are running three years late. We've taken twice as long to reach this stage. But on the brighter side, we've only spent half as much again. So, I suppose we can say we've given employment to more people, for a longer period of time. Fair assessment, Sefton?"

"I suppose you could put it like that, CB, yes."

Even in the dark, Thomson sensed Brancker was amused by his nutty logic. The train rushed out of the tunnel into sunshine, revealing lush green fields and blue skies. A happy omen.

"India by Christmas then!" Thomson exclaimed. Brancker and Knoxwood exchanged knowing glances.

28

THE BRIEFING

June 19, 1929.

O n the edge of Bedford, crewmen had gathered at Rowe's Tobacconists, the 'corner store,' adjacent to Munn's Dairy. Lou drew up at the curb and parked his motorbike alongside others. Potter was waiting with Disley, Church, Binks and Freddie. Cameron hadn't arrived. Lou noticed Capt. Irwin's Austin Seven approaching. The car stopped some distance away and Irwin climbed out. He cut a striking figure in his dark blue officer's uniform. This man had the keys to the city, admired and loved by all, especially his crewmen. Then Cameron appeared, his face tired and drawn.

"You all right, Doug?" Lou asked.

"No, but I don't wanna talk about it if you don't mind, sir."

Binks glanced across at Lou, shaking his head. He then turned to his cousin.

"Freddie, guess what? You know the lieutenant got me a job on the construction? Well, now I just got promoted," Binks said.

"To what?" Freddie asked.

"Engineer. I'll be in one of them engine cars."

"You liar!" Freddie exclaimed.

"God's honest truth. I'm set for life. Ain't that right, sir?"

Lou smiled. This week, he'd interviewed and recommended a few men from the construction team for jobs in the crew. Church, who'd finished a spell cutting and shuffling his cards and springing them from one hand to the other, was now busy combing his hair. "Yeah, and I'm gonna be a rigger. How about that!" he said.

Freddie gritted his teeth. "You lucky sods!"

Lou felt sorry for him.

"That's not all. Old Bad-Luck Sammy over there's doin' all right—ain'tcha, Sammy. Show 'em the picture of your new girl," Binks said.

Church stuck the comb between his teeth, pulled out his wallet and produced a photograph. He handed it to Freddie who scrutinized the well-endowed blond in a tight-fitting jumper with a pretty face. Everyone gathered round.

"What's her name then?" someone demanded.

"Irene," Church said proudly, stuffing the comb in his top pocket.

"Oooo, nice tits!" Freddie shrieked, holding the photo up close.

"Give it 'ere, you little sod!" Church yelled, grabbing Freddie's collar.

Freddie handed back the photograph. "Sorry, Sammy. No offense. I didn't realize it was serious." He peered up at Lou, meekly. "Lou, er sir, do you fink you could get me a job ... please?"

"Give it a year or two, Freddie," Lou answered.

"Oh, come on, sir. He's me cousin, twice removed, and he's ever so old for 'is age," Binks pleaded.

Lou glanced away toward Irwin, closing on them. The group parted, respectfully for the captain.

"Good morning, men," Irwin said in his soft Irish brogue giving them all a smile.

"Mornin', sir," they said together.

Irwin proceeded to the shop doorway and went in, the bell inside jangling.

"Who was that?" Freddie asked innocently.

Leech, the foreman engineer, now joined them. "That, my son, is the captain of *Cardington R101*," he said.

It was Leech who'd given Lou a lift up to the main house from the guard gate on his first day. Lou was pleased to see him here with the younger crowd. He wouldn't miss a fishing party at the river, Leech had told them. Lou followed Irwin into the shop. The bell inside tinkled again as he stepped onto the well-worn floor boards. The sweet smell of confectionery, tobacco, and newsprint, reminded him of his days here with his *R38* crewmen. Irwin was at the counter.

"Ten Players, if you'd be kind enough, Mr. Rowe," Irwin said.

The shopkeeper reached for the cigarettes from the shelf behind him. "That'll be one and tuppence, sir."

"Oh, and a box of Swan and the *Daily Mirror*."

"Certainly, Captain." The shopkeeper reverently laid the cigarettes and the red-tipped matches on the counter. "They say it's gonna be a warm one today, sir," he said.

"Yes, indeed. Thank you," Irwin said.

Irwin gathered up his change and took a newspaper, glancing at Lou as some of the group came in. Lou realized the captain wanted to speak to him. He picked up the *Daily Mail* and a pack of Juicy Fruit, paid, and went into the street. Irwin walked to his car and climbed in, pausing to light a cigarette. Lou popped the Juicy Fruit in his mouth, watching Irwin's car move closer. Lou got to the curb as Irwin rolled down his window.

"You're going in later, right Lou?"

"Yes, sir. We're gonna fish for a couple of hours first."

"The Air Minister is scheduled to visit the shed at 2 o'clock."

"That'll give us plenty of time. We'll finish this morning and make sure everything's perfect."

"Wing Commander Colmore's anxious the Minister leaves with a good impression."

"You bet, sir."

They were disturbed by a noisy group across the street, yelling and attracting attention. Lou turned and saw Jessup and his cronies—three originals and two new faces. They hadn't spotted Lou, leaning down talking to Capt. Irwin.

"They're Howden crewmen. I see you've pitched in with the Cardington lads," Irwin said.

"Oh, no sir. They were all invited, but the Howden lot don't wanna mix."

"I've noticed that. I hope we're not going to have trouble with all these different groups—different ships—different construction crews."

"They *are* rivals, sir," said Lou.

"Yes, I suppose they are. Dumb really, isn't it!"

Jessup's crowd continued making a fuss—looking over and laughing. Jessup limped off, smirking while his gang laughed and whooped. They jeered at Cameron, who was on the verge of tears.

"Give it to 'er, Jessie," one of the gang shouted.

Jessup gave Cameron one of his two-finger whistles and pumped his fist in a crude gesture.

That son of a bitch is up to his tricks again, dammit!

"When they're not busy, they get into mischief, sir," Lou said.

"I don't like the looks of that one—could be a troublemaker. You know him?"

"I've had a few dealings with him."

"I'd better get moving, Lieutenant."

"Okay, Captain."

"It's good you're taking an interest in these men. They'll think the world of you for it."

"Thank you."

"Make sure you're in uniform this afternoon."

"Yes sir."

Irwin drove off. Lou went back to his group and they ambled to the river carrying rods and tackle. They spent two hours fishing. Freddie caught a couple of trout and Leech hooked a pike. After that, Lou left the river, arranging to meet Potter, Binks, Disley and Church at Shed No.1. Cameron didn't look up to it.

Thomson was still in high spirits when his train rolled into Bedford Station. The chauffeur-driven Airship Works Humber was waiting. He had fond memories of Cardington House and couldn't wait to see the place again. The driver touched his cap and opened the doors for the three men. Thomson settled down with a sigh of contentment beside Brancker.

"Ah yes, it's nice to be back in this city," Thomson said. "What's that wonderful smell in the air, Sefton, hm?"

"I don't smell anything, CB."

"I smell optimism, my dear fellow. That's what I smell—*optimism!*"

"Ah yes," Brancker said, smiling.

"Have the press been informed of my visit, Knoxwood?" Thomson asked.

"Absolutely, sir. I'm sure they're eagerly awaiting your awival."

"I'm getting hungry and we've been promised a bang-up lunch by all accounts," Thomson said.

The driver pulled out onto the high street. Twenty minutes later, they reached the Cardington gate, stopping at the guard house.

"Lord Thomson, we've been expecting you, sir," the gatekeeper gushed, grabbing the phone. The car glided smoothly up the winding driveway. Thomson savored every moment—like the returning warrior. They drew up outside the great house where Thomson leapt out and stood for a few moments surveying the building in its lush surroundings.

Ah yes, it's as beautiful as ever.

On seeing his team gathered with a dozen press people at the top of the steps, he handed his walking stick to Knoxwood. He bounded up two at a time like a man half his age, the photographers, catching the moment. What would they think of him? It'd been five years since they'd seen him. He looked fit and had put on weight, banishing the under-nourished look. He wondered how they'd fared under the strain. He made straight for Colmore, at center.

"My dear Colmore!" he said, taking his hand.

"We're so pleased to have you back, sir," Colmore lied.

"A few more grey hairs, I see. I'm sure you've earned them," Thomson said.

"Oh, yes, sir, we've had a few mountains to climb."

He turned to Cardington's head of design. "I hear you've been achieving great things, Richmond."

"We've been doing our best, sir," Richmond replied.

"Well, don't look so glum, man! The best is yet to come. All your hard work's about to pay off!"

Not so cock-sure by the looks of him. Must have all been tougher than he thought.

He held his hand out to Scott who appeared a little the worse for wear.

Looks like the drink's catching up with him!

"Scottie, my dear fellow! You're looking well. Wonderful to see you. You all know the Director of Civil Aviation, Sir Sefton Brancker, and my private secretary, Rupert Knoxwood." Everyone shook hands and made pleasantries and Colmore led the way into the grand, marble entrance hall. Thomson retrieved his walking stick from Knoxwood. Their voices and footsteps echoed as though they were in a museum. Thomson paused, remembering that glorious day when he stood here between these great columns at the foot of the sweeping, stone stairs and announced his plans to the nation.

What a day that was! Well, there'll be plenty more days like that.

Thomson stopped and leaned on his walking stick peering at the ensign hanging forty feet up from the ornate, coffered ceiling, among gold leaf scrollwork and classical paintings of British battles on land and sea—a blaze of red, white and blue, cannons and muskets, blood, mud, fire and raging seas. Scott stepped forward and pointed to the ensign.

"We plan to fly that from the stern on her maiden voyage, Lord Thomson."

Sounds tipsy ...yes, I can smell it.

"What a splendid idea. It'll look superb fluttering in the wind from the world's mightiest airship. Bravo, Scott! I'm planning to be on that voyage, in case you've forgotten."

"None of us have forgotten your pledge," Colmore said.

"I'm looking forward to that," Thomson said. "You're coming, too, eh Sefton?"

"Oh yes, rather, CB. Wouldn't miss *that* show for the world!"

The group filed into the reception room for Earl Grey tea served in bone china cups with digestive biscuits and snacks, while the chief steward hovered. The engineering and design staff of the Royal Airship Works trooped in to shake hands with Thomson, who treated them like old friends. He remembered their faces and names from his visit in 1924 and the roles they played. This impressed them greatly. Naturally, he'd consulted a staff list he kept at the flat the night before.

After tea, and the opportunity to get re-acquainted, the group of forty-two moved to the conference room. The table seated thirty and the rest sat around the perimeter walls. Brancker and Knoxwood sat next to Thomson at the table. Anticipation was high: shades drawn, projector on, nerves on edge. Thomson had this effect on people, individually or en mass. It was time to crack the whip. They'd all had it too easy for too long—they'd fallen asleep at the switch. No excuse for that.

Richmond stood stiffly at the front, waiting for the room to settle down. People lit cigarettes and pipes. Soon the air was laden with smoke drifting across the projector's beam. For some, it became hard to breath.

"All right, Colonel Richmond, proceed. Perhaps you won't mind if occasionally I butt in with a question or two," Thomson said.

The lights were dimmed and a picture of *Cardington R101* appeared on a screen behind Richmond, who cleared his throat nervously.

"This is a side-view. Strength of the hull has been our first concern."

"Excellent!" Thomson said.

Richmond traced the outline of the ship with his pointer.

"*Cardington R101* is 734 feet long, 134 feet in diameter. You'll notice she's fatter than previous airships. This makes her more resilient and with a stainless steel skeleton, she'll be the strongest airship ever built."

"Good. Now tell me about progress."

The picture on the screen changed to one showing the gas bag harnesses hanging from the ship's interior.

"There have been some delays, but the features of this airship are, if I may say so, unique and innovative. We have designed a revolutionary new gasbag harnessing system—"

"What have you done to cut down the risk of fire?"

"We cannot eliminate the risk completely. Even static electricity can be deadly and is an *ever-present* threat—that's why it's necessary for groundcrewmen to *always* use rubber mats when picking up lines dropped from the ship. Static electricity can be deadly; it's a danger to the men and could cause fire. It's another reason we're using diesel engines in accordance with the original specification requirements, though they've turned out to be less powerful and heavier than expected."

"Is that so?" Thomson's tone was level.

I smell trouble. This man isn't telling me the full story.

"Of course, I expect you've already been informed Howden is using lighter petrol engines from Rolls-Royce which, by the way, I hear are second-hand."

"Second-hand petrol engines? No, I *didn't* know that," Thomson said flatly.

Thomson sensed Richmond's discomfort over the weight of the engines. Now he seemed to be alluding to the diesel versus petrol issue as a distraction. Thomson wondered if Wallis had got one over on the Air Ministry.

Damn Wallis! But at least he had sense enough to do some arithmetic first.

Thomson made an effort to hide his irritation, but his eyes narrowed. This was a dilemma. Richmond was a military man who'd followed the edict Thomson had laid down himself. He'd need to give the matter more thought later. Richmond continued, mentioning that the gasbags were manufactured by the workers of Cardington and ready to install—unlike Howden, who'd imported theirs from Germany. He talked about the new and complex design of the gas valves and servo assistance mechanism necessary for a craft of such immense proportions. Lastly, he explained the revolutionary approach to the process of doping the ship's outer cover, which he himself, had developed.

When the briefing was over, everyone was ushered into the dining room. Roast leg of lamb smothered in mint sauce, baked potatoes, and garden peas were served by immaculate stewards in white jackets and gloves under the watchful eye of the fussy chief steward. A Beaujolais was offered and Thomson and Colmore had a glass each; Scott drank more. Treacle tart followed the main course and then coffee, cheese, and biscuits. By the end of the meal, Thomson had mellowed somewhat. He turned to Colmore.

"How's the American doing? I expected him to be here."

"He's down in the shed supervising the finishing touches to the mock-ups for your inspection. He thought that was more important than lunch, sir."

"He's a conscientious chap."

"He's been a great asset and a fine liaison officer between the teams."

"So I've been given to understand," Thomson said, noting the chief steward perk up at the mention of 'the American.'

"It's just before two. Perhaps we should make a move, sir," Colmore said.

"Yes, I can't wait!" Thomson said, jumping to his feet.

29

'SHOW ME YOUR SHIP, MY CAPTAIN.'

June 19, 1929.

The lunch party made its way to one of the huge green buildings in convoy, led by Thomson's Humber. He was always amazed by the size of this structure and how ridiculously tiny the staff entrance doors looked. He stepped inside, where silence was absolute. The reverent atmosphere surrounding the enormous space reminded him of a cathedral or even his favorite building—Westminster Hall.

Lou had been on board the airship with Potter, Binks, Disley and Church since 9:30 a.m. Using a layout issued by the drawing office, they'd placed furniture in the lounge, dining room, and smoking room, with setups of couches and easy chairs positioned around coffee tables and card tables. Deck chairs were arranged on the promenade decks with side tables. In the dining room, tables were laid with white linen, dinnerware and cutlery, shined to perfection. Two typical cabins were set up with bunks, chairs, linens and blankets. Once they'd finished, Lou sent the others home.

During the morning, while they worked, he'd asked them about Cameron. "What's up with Doug?"

"He's having trouble with Rosie," Potter said.

"What sort of trouble?" Lou asked.

"She's messing around with one of them Yorkshire blokes," Church answered.

"And he found out?"

"He did."

"Which one?"

"The ugly bastard with the pockmarks and eyes like lollypops," Binks replied.

Lou grimaced. This explained what he'd witnessed earlier.

"It's a bloody shame. They were really 'appy. Next we know she's gone overboard for that crazy lunatic," Potter said.

After they left, Lou made final adjustments to some of the lamps and cushions in the lounge. He thought about the change in Cameron. He and

Rosie had been laughing and joking at the house-warming party. He'd need to keep an eye on that situation.

Damn Jessup!

Lou took a last look around the airship. Satisfied, he wearily sat down for a few moments in one of the comfortable easy chairs. He dozed off.

Thomson walked from the shed door toward the ship, mesmerized.

By Jove, what a sight!

Beaming with pleasure, he stared up at the massive skeleton. The structure was completely visible from bow to stern, her gas bags and cover, not yet installed. The stainless steel girders gleamed, giving the ship an aura of indestructibility.

We'll have no more structural problems like R38!

Thomson's gaze swept across the faces gathered around him.

"Where's our captain?"

Irwin, standing modestly four rows back in the crowd, raised his hand.

"Ah, there you are, my dear Captain Irwin. Show me over your ship, if you don't mind,"

Irwin edged forward in his unassuming way. "Not at all, sir. Please follow me."

Irwin led Thomson to a stepladder and they disappeared inside the control car. People in the entourage shuffled their feet and gave sideways glances, some slighted. Scott stood next to Richmond rattling loose change in his pocket, while Brancker stood beside Colmore and Knoxwood making polite conversation. Colmore showed no emotion—affable as always.

Lou came to, awakened by voices in the shed. He glanced at his watch and went to the promenade deck and peered down at the group gathered below. He'd planned to make his way down before Thomson arrived. Time had slipped away. He moved to the chartroom where he heard the voices of Irwin and Thomson. He stood and listened, unable to help himself.

This was the first time Thomson had been on an airship. He stared at one of the shiny ship's wheels in the control car. "For steering?"

Irwin pointed to the other wheel. "This one is, yes, sir. It controls the rudders. That one controls the elevators—the altitude." Irwin pointed to three valves attached from pipes from above. "And here, beside the height coxswain, are the valves for releasing water ballast."

"And these?" Thomson gestured to the telegraph equipment.

"These are telegraphs for sending instructions to the engine cars."

Thomson feasted his eyes on the hardwood wainscot, the floor and coxswain's consuls.

"It's like a ship, Captain, but the instrumentation reminds me of a submarine."

"It does, indeed, sir."

Thomson ran his fingers along the shiny hardwood windowsill.

"The workmanship is superb," he said, thoughts about weight and engines banished from his mind. Thomson looked out the windows wrapped around the control car.

"You'll have a pretty good view from here."

"Yes, sir. All five engine cars are visible and we'll be able to see where we're going."

"Always good to know!"

"Yes, sir."

"I look forward to standing here beside you, Captain, sailing the lofty skies."

"'Tis a nice thought, to be sure."

"I'm expecting great things from you, Irwin," Thomson said. "I know you're a man I can count on."

"I'll do my best, sir."

"Let's go up, shall we? Lead the way."

Irwin started up the mahogany steps. The spacious area above the control car doubled as control room and chartroom and was situated within the ship's envelope. A railing allowed officers and navigators to look down into the control car below. A high hardwood table had been built along the back wall for studying maps and charts with plenty of pigeonholes for storage. Irwin described the room's function.

"This is where the navigator will chart the ship's course and the officers will work on calculations and suchlike. You'll see it's convenient for keeping the officer on watch informed of their position and for him to call down new bearings."

"Very impressive, Captain. I can't wait to see the dining room and lounge."

"And don't forget the smoking room, sir," Irwin said with a smile.

Lou, having heard a good deal of their conversation, decided to stay put until he could slip out undetected. He stayed out of sight, but he caught a glimpse of Thomson, remembering the last time he'd seen him. He saw a big change. Thomson certainly looked healthier, and sounded self assured.

These last five years must have been good to him.

Irwin led Thomson to the lounge, which measured sixty feet by forty. Linoleum flooring, replicating hardwood, gleamed in the subdued lighting of table lamps and wall sconces, powered up by Disley and Lou earlier. Thomson admired the room and furniture.

"This is stunning! And tastefully done. Look at the size of it!"

He rushed to the middle of the floor and spun around, marveling at the fluted columns at the perimeter with their gold-leaf ornamental heads.

"I'm delighted. It's better than I could have ever imagined. Why, they'll be able to dance all the way to India in this fabulous room!"

"I do believe you could be right, sir."

Thomson spotted the promenade deck and raced off to the polished wood guardrail in front of the huge plate glass windows and stared out into the shadows of the shed, oblivious to his entourage below. Irwin followed him.

"Oh, this is exceptional, Irwin. Can you imagine the view of the Mediterranean coast? The French Riviera! The Italian Riviera! My goodness, what a sight that'll be."

"Yes, it'll be grand, sir."

Thomson was deeply preoccupied with his vision of the future.

One day, I shall travel with Marthe in this beautiful airship. We'll arrive as husband and wife!

He turned and saw the captain patiently waiting.

"Do forgive me, Irwin. I was lost in thought. I look forward to returning in this airship to the land of my birth."

"India?"

"Yes, India. And confidentially, Irwin I hope to be taking a very special lady with me as my wife, one day."

"That'll be very nice, sir."

"It's fate, Irwin. Do you believe in fate?"

"I suppose I do."

"Yes, our fate is written."

"I'm sure you're right about that, sir."

Thomson grabbed Irwin's hand and clasped it, warmly in two hands.

"This ship will be the making of us, my dear Captain. *All* of us!"

30

THE OLD GASBAG

A fter reviewing the dining room, cabins and smoking room—which everyone had made so much fuss about—Thomson posed for a few photographs before making for the gasbag factory. The fabric shop, another cavernous, corrugated iron building, stood among a group of utility buildings near the two main sheds. Within, eighty-seven excited women patiently waited, singing to relieve their boredom. On his arrival, Thomson was greeted by the sound of their voices drifting through the windows. He paused to listen. He'd heard the song a thousand times before.

> *Good-bye, Dolly, I must leave you, though it breaks my heart to go,*
> *Something tells me I am needed at the Front to fight the foe,*
> *See the boys in blue are marching and I can no longer stay,*
> *Hark I heard the bugle calling, good-bye, Dolly Gray.*

The haunting melody reminded him of France. Suddenly, he was back in Ypres listening to the soldiers. He heard the boom of guns, the whine of shells, explosions thundering in the distance. He became morbid—so much death. He shook it off and turned to Colmore and Brancker.

"Let's go in."

As they entered, the anticipation was palpable. The sun on the metal building made the interior oppressive, despite the open windows. A few electric fans placed in strategic locations did little to dispel the smell of rotting animals' intestines, dampness, body odor and glue. The women went silent, as if on cue from an invisible conductor, as Thomson's towering frame appeared in the doorway.

Members of his entourage silently eased their way in behind him, as though late for church. Lou, now in uniform, stood next to Scott. Photographers clutched their cameras, ready for a spread in tomorrow's papers. Seeing their eagerness, Thomson's face lit up, captivating the women. He stepped forward into the open space and took off his hat to survey the scene. Down one side, dozens sat on stools in rows, six deep, at tiny scraping boards working on wet, slimy substances with wooden-handled scrapers.

Although dressed in protective smocks and unglamorous hats, he noticed they were wearing makeup.

Must be for me—how nice—I'm very flattered.

He unconsciously began to fan himself with his hat before he caught himself and stopped. On the floor, huge sheets of fabric were laid out with women on their knees joining the pieces together. It reminded him of parachutes being spread out for assembly, or the cutting and sewing of great yacht sails. Thomson raised his arms in a grand gesture and gave them one of his paralyzing smiles.

"Ladies! I beg you, please don't stop. I should enjoy to hear you sing. I love that you are so happy in your work, which I know is arduous— but so vital to this great undertaking."

A stocky, sergeant-major-like woman stepped forward and stood beside him. Thomson observed her closely. Even to him, she was intimidating. She wore a starched, sharply pressed, blue boiler suit, bright red headscarf tied in knots over her tightly cropped hair and shiny black boots. She placed her hands on her hips, ready for business.

"You 'eard the Lord, girls!" she bawled and then, pointing to one young woman in the middle, yelled, "Okay, sing, Millicent!"

Clearly struggling with her nerves, the one called Millicent took a few moments, but soon the great space was filled with the most beautiful operatic sound, continuing the song Thomson had heard outside. It took his breath away.

> *I have come to say good-bye, Dolly Gray,*
> *It's no use to ask me why, Dolly Gray,*
> *There's a murmur in the air, you can hear it everywhere,*
> *It's time to do and dare, Dolly Gray.*
> *So if you hear the sound of feet, Dolly Gray,*
> *Sounding through the village street, Dolly Gray,*
> *It's the tramp of soldiers true, in their uniforms so blue,*
> *I must say good-bye to you, Dolly Gray.*

At this point, all the women joined the chorus, producing a harmony enough to warm any choirmaster's heart; they sounded like a choir of heavenly angels.

> *Good bye, Dolly, I must leave you though it breaks my heart to go,*
> *Something tells me I am needed at the Front to fight the foe,*
> *See the boys in blue are marching and I can no longer stay,*
> *Hark I heard the bugle calling, goodbye, Dolly Gray.*

It was Thomson's turn to be smitten. He almost choked up, not believing such a wonderful sound could come from this ragged-looking bunch of women. He stepped forward with his hand out to the forewoman.

"Welcome to the fabric shop, your Lordship," she bellowed.

"You're in charge?"

"I am indeed."

"And what's your name, if I may ask?"

My goodness, what a scary woman—must be a communist!

"Yes, you may. It's 'ilda, sir."

"'Ilda?" Thomson repeated.

The embarrassed women tried to hold back their laughter. He'd pronounced her name in Cockney. The forewoman corrected him.

"No, sir. 'Haych' as in H–ilda," she said, emphasizing the H with much heavy breathing.

"All right you lot, that's enough," she hollered.

"Oh, *Hilda*, of course! Do forgive me."

"Quite all right, me lord."

"Would you be kind enough to show me around and educate me on what these fine ladies are doing?"

"It would be my pleasure, sir. In this 'ere place, we make gasbags and canvas covers for the airships. First of all, what we call the 'goldbeater's skins' are shipped from Argentina and Chicago—that's in America." Hilda led Thomson along the rows of women perched on stools, pointing at the skins on their scraping boards.

"What are they made of, these goldbeater's skins?"

"Cattles' bellies, sir."

Thomson already knew some of this, but wanted to give the woman her head. He wrinkled his nose, as though all this was completely new to him.   "Cattle's bellies. Fascinating!"

Hilda picked up a sloppy, dripping skin and held it up, a respectable distance from Thomson, careful not to splash his face or his pinstriped suit.

"Then we take 'em and we stick 'em together on that there table over there. Then we glue 'em on them linen sheets on them slantin' boards what you see and then make 'em into big sheets on the floor," Hilda said, pointing at the women on their knees.

"Well, bless my soul. How many skins will you need for this airship, Hilda?"

"More than a million, actually."

"More than a million! Good Lord! You don't say."

Hilda flopped the skin down onto one of the women's boards, wiped her hands on a cloth, and threw it down. Thomson marched across to a petite, middle-aged woman perched on her stool. She had an impish face and big brown eyes.

"Now, please introduce me to this lovely lady."

"This 'ere is Nellie. She's bin 'ere longer than any of my girls, 'Eaven knows how many skins she's 'andled, this one!"

Giggling broke out across the factory floor; first among the women and then the entourage. Thomson's face showed no emotion, as if he didn't get the joke. But he did. Overcome by his intimidating presence, Nellie became painfully shy, blushing and perspiring like a sixteen-year-old. For Thomson, the experience of getting down to these people's level was exhilarating. He felt wholesome and good. He fawned over Nellie, knowing the effect he had on her. His interest was genuine and knew she completely understood that.

"Nellie, show me exactly what you're doing."

"She's wettin' 'er drawers is what she's doin'," a woman whispered behind him.

For the next few minutes, it was as if he and Nellie were the only two in that stifling shed. "I must tell you, it's good to see such wonderful work," he said.

"Oh, sir, it's ever such a pleasure, sir." Nellie was steeling herself to respond and squirming on her seat as he squatted down closely beside her, his voice soothing and seductive.

"Show me how you do it, Nellie."

Nellie became calm, reached into a barrel beside her and pulled out a skin dripping with fluid.

"What's that?"

"Oh, that's brine, what they come in," Nellie said.

"They're very slippery, aren't they?"

"Oh, yes, sir, they are!"

"As slippery as your willie, mate," someone said.

"Show me your technique," Thomson said.

"She'll show 'im 'er technique all right," another woman guffawed.

Nellie started working furiously and expertly with her tool, and in no time the skin was scraped as clean as a whistle. She held it proudly in the air for all to see. Thomson got up from his crouching position, applauding enthusiastically. Cameras flashed, the women cheered and clapped, while those in the entourage suppressed their laughter. Thomson spent the next fifteen minutes moving around the shed shaking hands, making eye contact and smiling at the workers like a campaigning politician.

"Now ladies, before I go, I want you to do one more thing. Will you sing for me again?"

Hilda was ready—as if she had control of the Moscow Women Workers' Choir.

"All right, *Millicent!*"

Millicent's haunting voice began the mournful intro to "What'll I Do"—an ode to, and chosen especially for, Thomson. He again became totally mesmerized.

At the chorus all the women on the floor joined in. Thomson stood enraptured until Knoxwood signaled it was time to leave. With a wave of his fine, long fingers and a gentlemanly bow, he put on his hat, turned toward the door and was gone. His people followed.

Before Scott left the building he leaned close to Lou and whispered in his ear. "This lot would have his trousers off in seconds flat, if we weren't here. Poor bugger wouldn't stand a chance." Lou smiled. He was the last to leave.

The women were staring at the empty space where Thomson had stood, as though it'd all been a dream—the spell now broken. They stopped singing and went wild with excitement, swarming around Nellie, the woman who'd handled so many skins. She was suffering the infatuation of a pubescent girl—beet red and sweating profusely.

"Oh my good Gawd, I ain't never talked to no lawd before! Oh my good Gawd," she kept mumbling over and over.

" 'Ee definitely fancied you, love," one shouted.

"You'd like to clean 'is skin for 'im, Nellie, eh!"

"Oh, 'ee was so lovely," Nellie swooned.

"Ah, look at the state of 'er, she's in love!"

Before he left, Lou noticed a girl waving to him and smiling. It took him a moment to figure out it was Rosie Cameron. He hadn't recognized her in her work clothes and protective hat.

I guess this is where Jessup met her.

31

SPEECHES & SURPRISES

June 19, 1929,

Lou left the gas bag factory laughing to himself—it'd been an education. He followed the rest of the party to Cardington House, where the press was being directed to the rear gardens. Afternoon tea was served by the men in white jackets in the reception hall—an assortment of sandwiches, followed by buttered scones with fresh cream and strawberry jam. The chief steward ensured cucumber sandwiches were on the table, remembering Thomson's favorable comments back in '24. He hovered around while Thomson munched and nodded his approval.

In the gardens below the open windows, the murmur of the assembling crowd drowned out the gentle splash of an ornate fountain—a romantic creation, peopled by stone cherubs clutching bows and arrows, presumably arrows of love. Toward the end of tea-time, Thomson gently tapped a silver spoon against his cup. The room fell silent.

"Last year, I had the honor, as chairman of the Royal Aero Club, to represent Great Britain at the International Conference on Aviation in Washington, D.C. Whilst there, I had the pleasure of meeting the Secretary of the United States Navy." Thomson's eyes fell on Lou, at whom he smiled benignly. "We spoke of many things concerning aviation and the Secretary takes quite an interest in their man over here—Lieutenant Louis Remington —who has diligently assisted in our endeavors over these past five years."

All eyes turned toward Lou. Thomson continued. "The Secretary asked me to personally convey his thanks to the lieutenant, along with his warmest personal regards. Captain Irwin, I would be grateful if you will do the honors."

On cue, Irwin walked to the top of the room and stood with Thomson who glanced at Lou. "Lieutenant, if you would kindly step forward," Thomson said. Surprised, Lou joined Thomson and Irwin. Thomson held something in his hand which he handed to Irwin who spoke next.

"Lieutenant Remington, it is my pleasure to inform you that your rank has been raised by the United States Navy to that of Lieutenant Commander."

Lou stood to attention while Irwin pinned the insignia to his collar. Irwin then stepped back and saluted. Lou returned the salute and everyone applauded. Lou glanced around the room at Colmore, Scott, Irwin and Atherstone—all in dress uniform.

Whaddya know, these guys all knew in advance!

"Thank you, sir," Lou said to Irwin, and then to Thomson as they shook hands, "I'm very grateful, sir."

Thomson smiled, pleased. He loved these occasions. The chief steward appeared to be swooning and nodding enthusiastically at Lou as he pointed to an iced cake on the front table.

"Now, if you will kindly move to the garden, I'd like to say a few words to you and the good people of Cardington and Bedford," Thomson said.

Thomson's entourage moved from the entrance hall down the stone steps into the garden, an area some two hundred feet square flanked by boxwood hedges and flowering trees. This had once been the previous philanthropic owner's outdoor theater, complete with a stage built of stone where Shakespearean tragedies were performed. Rough cut flagstone paving covered much of the area and two hundred steel folding chairs were occupied by a group of people similar to those who'd been present when Thomson made his announcement in '24: Royal Airship Works personnel, local bankers, businessmen, and solicitors. In addition, there were contractors, and general workers from the factories and sheds connected with the airship program with their families.

Crewmen and construction workers stood along the sides and at the rear of the gathering, leaving seats for VIPs and the elderly. The first four rows had been reserved for those emerging from the reception room. Journalists were seated in the front row with photographers positioned down each side in the aisles.

There were two in the audience of note, sitting at the front: Sir Arthur Conan Doyle and Mrs. Emily Hinchliffe, the wife of Thomson's pilot, dressed in black. A buzz went around the crowd as people noticed them. Lou had no idea who the portly, older gentleman was until someone told him he was the most popular author in the world. (He'd get a kick out of telling Norway about that!). Lou had met Mrs. Hinchliffe the previous year, during one of his monthly visits to Cardington.

A lectern had been set up on the stage with a microphone and six chairs. The crowd chattered excitedly. Thomson was pleased with the size of the gathering. They were all here out of self-interest. Times were tough and work was scarce. It was satisfying for Thomson to know he'd created jobs in two counties.

These people love me now, posh accent or not—they know on which side their bread's buttered!

Thomson sipped the last of his Earl Grey and replaced his bone china cup carefully on its saucer. He went out through the French doors, held open for him by the fawning chief steward and descended the steps like a conquering hero to enthusiastic applause. He walked stiffly down the center aisle to the stage where Colmore, Brancker, Knoxwood, Scott and Richmond sat. As he approached, they got to their feet, applauding and smiling. Thomson sat down. Colmore went to the lectern and waited for the applause to die down. All seats were occupied and the aisles down each side were filled with people standing between the chairs and hedges.

Lou stood at the rear of the garden with his crewmen, foremen, construction workers, and of course, Freddie. Chief Coxswain 'Sky' Hunt stood behind them. Lou had known Hunt for years and had great respect for him. He'd trained Lou for his job as chief petty officer aboard *R38*. He was gruff, but well-loved, known for a bark worse than his bite. Lou noticed Jessup standing with a group of six at the back on the other side. Jessup kept his eyes down. Murmuring in the crowd grew as tension increased. Binks found all the fuss amusing.

"Wonder what the old gasbag's got to say for 'imself," he said.

Sky Hunt turned to Binks. "Keep yer mouth shut, Mr. Binks," he growled.

Colmore cleared his throat and adjusted the microphone, causing a screeching whine from the speakers on each side of the podium.

"Good afternoon, ladies and gentlemen. It is my distinct pleasure to introduce the Minister of State for Air, Lord Thomson of Cardington, whom we all know and admire. He'd like to say a few words concerning our progress and the future of the British Airship Program. Before I turn over the microphone, I'd like to say, all of us owe him a debt of gratitude, not only for revitalizing the airship program, but for making the Royal Airship Works central to his great vision." There was more enthusiastic applause.

Thomson got up from his chair and stepped up to the lectern. He adjusted the microphone up six inches, causing another earsplitting screech.

"Wing Commander Colmore is much too kind," Thomson said. "I'm just one man doing my small part. It is *you* who will make this program a success, not I. My job is to jolly things along. This great endeavor that you've worked upon with such selfless dedication—and I must say, I've seen it with my own eyes today—is one that will open the skies for the benefit of all mankind."

Binks was unable to resist. "Yeah, right, mate," he said under his breath. Lou frowned. Binks shut up.

"We've reached a critical stage in the development of the program. In some ways we're out in front—from the technology standpoint—but in other ways—on the practical front—we're falling behind. The Germans made their maiden flight last year, crossing the Atlantic in their Graf Zeppelin. They're preparing to make a round-the-world trip in August, and if we're not careful, we'll be in a position where we cannot keep pace."

Everyone now looked concerned. "With this in mind, I say to you: We must push hard to produce results as quickly as possible. We must show the world what we can do. It's been more than five years since I announced the start of the program and our ships are still in the sheds. I'll leave it there. I know you appreciate what I'm saying, and why."

Thomson was careful not to single anyone out with his icy stare, but could see the audience understood only too well. Richmond and Colmore had taken his words to heart. It was time to build them back up.

"Having said that, I'm certain we'll come out on top. When this ship emerges from her shed this year, she'll be the finest airship ever built—about that, I have no doubt." Thomson looked reassuringly at Richmond, but Richmond didn't exude confidence. Thomson went on.

"Now, we've embarked upon a great journey, you and I, and I look forward to the day when we fly together in this magnificent airship down the route of Marco Polo to India. And thereafter, we shall press forward with airship services linking our great empire around the globe and build bigger, more advanced airships that'll become technological marvels of the world."

Thomson stepped back and the crowd was on its feet, applauding. He'd rallied the troops. Everyone was smiling except Richmond. Success, or failure, rested with him. It was at this point that Mrs. Hinchliffe stood up and started saying something. Everyone turned in her direction. Lou couldn't hear what she was saying, but judging by the embarrassed looks, she must have been making some sort of protest. Thomson switched off the microphone and replied to her statements. This exchange lasted some minutes until Thomson, clearly irritated, descended from the platform and marched down the center aisle, followed by those on the stage.

They reached the throng of people at the top of the aisle, which parted like the Red Sea. Thomson climbed the steps, followed by the multitude. When he reached the top, he gave the crowd a jubilant wave. He swept through the reception room, out the main entrance and down the front steps to the Humber, where the driver held the doors open. They drove off slowly, the driver tooting his horn and Thomson waving his royal wave.

"Well, I think that went off all right, except for that damned Hinchliffe woman at the end. We'll need to keep an eye on her," Thomson said.

"Fwankly Minister, you were marvelous. I shouldn't worry about her," Knoxwood said.

"Top hole!" Brancker exclaimed.

Later, Lou jumped on his motorcycle and rode over to Shed No.1 to meet Irwin, who'd requested to see him. He waited beside the control car and soon heard the captain's approaching footsteps echoing across the shed.

"Ah, Lou. Let's go aboard," he said.

They climbed on board and Irwin led the way up to the lounge where they sat in the wicker easy chairs at one of the card tables. Lou wasn't sure why Irwin wanted to see him and worried perhaps he'd known Lou was on board earlier.

"You and the crew did a great job, Lou. The Old Man was thrilled."

"Thank you, sir," Lou said, relieved.

"Perhaps you should be an interior decorator!"

"No, all we did was set it up. He ought to be pleased; it's a beautiful ship."

"Looks can be deceiving," Irwin said. "We'll see what she's made of when we take her up." Irwin glanced down at the table for a moment, then back at Lou.

"Congratulations on your promotion today."

"Thank you, sir. That came as a big surprise."

"Everyone was pleased about it. You've done a great job at Howden. You're a natural diplomat and you've helped keep the peace."

"Thanks."

"How's Charlotte? Is she taking kindly to all this?"

"I think she'll be pleased with my promotion, and proud. She's settled down fairly well here now. She really didn't want to come south."

"Yes, I got that impression."

"She's been worried about safety, naturally, but everyone's assured her these new ships will be safe."

"Let's hope so," Irwin said.

"Charlotte's pleased I'm happy and doing what I like. I think once we've got a few trips under our belt, she'll be okay."

"She's a wonderful girl."

"What Charlotte needs is a child. In fact, she wants lots of children! But no luck so far. That's what makes her most unhappy," Lou said.

"We want a family one day—we've even chosen a name for our first," Irwin said.

"What is it, sir?"

Irwin looked away, concentrating on an image in his mind. "D'you know, when I close my eyes sometimes, I can see that child. His name will be Christian. I see his black hair and blue eyes."

"Just like his dad."

"It's all up to the good Lord," Irwin said.

"I guess so."

Irwin turned his eyes back on Lou, his expression now business-like.

"Lou, I'm going to propose you for another promotion—to third officer—if you want it. You'll be under my command aboard this ship and Captain Booth on *Howden R100*."

"Thank you. I don't know what to say, sir."

"You've got a good head on your shoulders and the crewmen look up to you."

"I suppose they do."

"You survived *R38* and that experience will make you careful."

"That was just luck."

"Nothing wrong with that. I need men with good luck on my ship."

"Kind of you to say, sir."

"If all the things the Old Man says come true, the sky's the limit. He'll be in need of captains for the fleet."

They got up and shook hands, went down to the shed floor and stood alongside the ship.

"Oh, one more thing, Lou. I like to see my officers and crew in church on Sundays." Irwin looked up at the ship, a hint of skepticism in his eyes. "We'll need all the help we can get," he said, before abruptly marching off toward the exit.

32

DINING ALONE

June 19, 1929.

Thomson sat at the roll-top desk in the front lounge of his Westminster flat. Though pleased with himself and his trip to Cardington, he had a gnawing feeling something wasn't right with that airship. Richmond had seemed gloomy. Thomson hoped there were no major concerns, but supposed all would be revealed when they launched her this year.

The Hinchliffe woman had put a damper on things. He tried to put it out of his mind. He wondered about Barnes Wallis and his group. They were a secretive bunch up there. He set these thoughts aside and picked up his most recent letter from Marthe. He needed to inform her of today's events—tell her about his triumphant return! She smiled down from a silver picture frame on top of the desk.

The long, austere room had ornate ceilings and cornice work with cream-painted walls and moldings similar to the rest of the flat. Although comfortable, the place lacked a woman's touch. The tall, Georgian windows overlooked the street where Saturday night traffic passed to and fro with a gentle hum. The furniture, various shades of browns and beiges, was second-hand, but passable. A brown, woven-wool couch faced the fireplace, complemented by a mahogany coffee table with a black leather top. He liked it when he found it in the furniture shop in Stockwell and the dealer threw it in for an extra ten bob.

A huge oil painting of the Taj Mahal in a chipped gilt frame had also caught his eye, and when the dealer offered to splash a coat of gold paint on the frame for an extra half crown, Thomson jumped at it. He thought it must be a sign. The picture now hung over the living room fireplace in all its glory. He decided he'd have Buck install it in his office at Gwydyr House the following week. The whole lot had cost twelve pounds fifteen shillings, including the slightly worn, blue silk chaise longue and delivery by a man with a horse and cart.

He paused looking at the Taj with satisfaction—he suddenly had a great idea. He'd speak to Winston Churchill about it when he next saw him—he'd heard he was something of an artist. Meanwhile, he must write to Marthe. He picked up his fountain pen and began in his bold, beautiful script.

My Dearest Smaranda,
Just home from Cardington. It was a great day and wonderful to be back up
there. What an enthusiastic crowd they are—dedicated and determined to
make R101 all that she can be. Airships! They are my pride and joy—my
phoenix twins, rising from the ashes—I am so passionate about them. There
is of course only one precious thing I am more passionate about. No need to
remind you of that!

His thoughts were interrupted by a gentle knock on the door. Gwen,
his housekeeper, popped her head in; mid-fifties and well rounded, she wore
a white apron and matching headscarf.

"Lord Thomson, dinner's ready to be served, if convenient, sir," she
said in her R-rolling Devonshire accent. Thomson slipped his unfinished
letter into the top drawer.

"Very well, Gwen, I'll come now."

He'd burned a lot of energy today and felt hungry again. Later, after
dinner, Thomson sat alone with his thoughts. Gwen's chop had been
delicious, even though he'd already had lamb for lunch. He didn't tell her of
course. She reappeared as he was finishing his apple pie and custard.

"Will there be anything else, Lord Thomson? Would you like
coffee?"

"You know what? I think I'd like a glass of port, if you don't mind."

Gwen beetled off and brought back a bottle of port and a wine glass
on a tray and placed them on the table in front of him. She poured out a
decent measure.

"Thank you, Gwen. That will be all for tonight."

"Are you sure, sir?"

"Oh yes, I'll be fine."

"Good night, Lord Thomson."

"Good night, Gwen."

Thomson put on his red and black silk smoking jacket and moved
back into the front lounge. He put some music on the gramophone, enjoying
his favorite pieces while sipping the delicious port. Hearing the music,
Sammie, Thomson's huge black cat, strode into the room with a big meow,
jumped onto one of the soft arm chairs and settled down, purring like a
tractor.

"That's what I like—a cat who appreciates opera," Thomson said.

The cat rolled on its side, understanding perfectly. Thomson took
another sip and placed the glass on the coffee table. He put on his favorite
recording—V*esti la giubba*—sung by the great Enrico Caruso. He turned up
the volume and sat down on the chaise, where he rummaged through his
dispatch box. Beside him, on a side table, stood another picture frame from
which Marthe peered at him from the steps of Mogosoëa. Thomson looked

up from his documents and rested his eyes on her and laid his head back on the chaise, allowing his mind to wander. Marthe would be in London in a couple of weeks.

Dear God, how I long to see her!

He remembered how he'd comforted her in her boudoir in Mogosoëa, in 1915. It was a bitter sweet memory. Within seconds, while Pagliacci's heart was breaking, Thomson fell asleep.

He found himself drinking coffee at his usual table by the window of a popular café on Rue de Rivoli—one of the most fashionable streets in Paris. In British Army uniform with the rank of lieutenant, he gazed at the beautiful girl sitting in an open-top carriage under a white parasol, shading her unblemished, white skin from the blazing sun. She fanned herself with a cream and white rice-paper fan. A matching wide-brimmed hat partially obscured her face and her shoulder-length, dark brown hair. She sat with aristocratic grace, her black eyes—or dark green?—revealed intelligence and innocence.

Much of what he took in was not only by sight, but by clairvoyance. He seemed to know so much about her—as if they were close. Perhaps he'd known her in some previous lifetime. But to her, *he* was always invisible.

Thomson realized he had to seize the moment—she'd soon be gone and an encounter might never come again. There was always this kind of desperation. He jumped from his seat, almost tipping over his chair and ran out the glazed wood doors into the street, just in time to see the driver snap the reins and loudly click his tongue, signaling the two magnificent white horses to pull out and move in slow motion toward him.

Thomson stood poised at the curb, hoping for some communication or acknowledgment, but the girl remained oblivious to his existence, staring straight ahead, so close, he could have reached out and touched her—and he had a burning desire to do so. As he dreamed (and he realized this was a dream), he knew he'd seen her many times before in other dreams such as this on Rue de Rivoli. As the carriage drew level, the driver looked down at Thomson with evil, piggy eyes and smiled his cruel smile. Thomson remembered him also—only too well.

You always smile at me with devilish intent. Damn you! You do it to torment me, injure me, torture me, aggravate me, toy with me, tantalize me— yes, all of those things!

Overcome by blinding love, his heart sinking, Thomson watched helplessly as the carriage slowly moved away between white, cloistered buildings, its grinding wheels and thumping hooves churning the gritty dirt. When at last it disappeared, the previously immaculate dress uniform in which he stood was now completely covered in white dust from head to toe. He looked and felt like Caruso's pathetic clown, Pagliacci, the all-too-familiar pain of longing burning like a knife in his gut.

Thomson woke with a snort, coughing and spluttering, tasting the grit in his mouth. The gramophone turntable revolved like the wheels on her carriage, the needle swinging back and forth in the grooves beside the label, making a dreadful scratching sound. Thomson reluctantly opened his eyes, his gold pinz-nez spectacles at the end of his nose, barely hanging on.

He came round in the awful moment of realization: this wasn't Paris, not the year 1902, but 1929. He was in London as the Secretary of State for Air. He shook off the nostalgia and his Cardington visit flooded back into his mind like water bursting from a dam. He glanced down. Sammie sat on his lap among his ministerial papers guiltily staring up at him, purring as softly as he dare. Thomson reached down, pulled the cat up to his face and nuzzled him affectionately.

"Oh, Sammie, you're such a naughty boy. But I know I can always count on *you* to tell me the truth, can't I!"

The cat meowed a loud response, sounding human—uncannily so.

After meeting Irwin, Lou went home with the chief steward's iced cake. Before he could even put the key in the front door, Charlotte opened it with a flourish. He stepped inside and she threw her arms around him, kissing him feverishly.

"Oh, Remy, my darling. I love you so much. I'm sorry I was so mean to you this morning. You will forgive me, won't you?"

Lou was surprised, but relieved.

"Of course, Charlie. You must've been tired. I'm sorry I had to be out all day."

"I want to talk to you tonight about things," Charlotte said.

"What about?"

"Well, about '*us—and things*'."

They went downstairs to the lower level to the breakfast table looking out into the garden. It was still sunny and a few of Charlotte's flowers were in bloom. Lou unwrapped and placed the chief steward's cake on the table.

"What's that?" Charlotte asked, reading the icing."'Congratulations!' What for?"

"I'll tell you in a minute. It's a present from the chief steward," Lou said, trying his best to remain expressionless.

"Oh, I see. What's his name?"

"Er, I don't know."

Charlotte batted her eyes and pursed her lips, taunting.

"Oooh, should I be jealous?"

Lou chuckled, not biting. She opened a bottle of white wine and poured two glasses. She held one out to him. The kitchen was warm. He breathed in the dinner cooking in the oven.

"Smells good," he said.

"Roast beef and Yorkshire pudding—your favorite."

"Mmm, lovely."

"Well, how did it go today?"

Lou's face lit up. "So much to tell!"

She was intrigued. "Why? What happened? Tell me!"

"We fished for a while, and before that, the captain came by and spoke to us at the corner store." He didn't mention Jessup or Cameron. "We went to the ship and finished setting up the furniture and I must say, it looked pretty damned good! Then the Old Man arrived. I was stuck on board while Irwin showed him over the ship. I stayed out of sight—I couldn't very well announce my presence. I heard everything they said. It was pretty damned embarrassing."

"What did they say?"

"Well, Lord Thomson got a bit flowery about the ship and the future and how he was depending on the captain—and a lot of stuff I should never have heard."

"What sort of stuff?"

"He talked about a woman he hopes to marry one day."

"Goodness! Did the captain know you were there?"

"Nobody knew and I won't say anything. Anyway, they all went off to the gasbag factory. I put on my uniform and joined them. The Old Man had them old gals eatin' out of his hand. Funny as hell."

"What did he say?"

"Oh, he told them they were special and doing important work and all that *old jaboni*. He gave them all a boost. They were tickled to death."

"That's good. He must be a very nice man," Charlotte said.

"Yeah, he's all right, I guess. Anyway we all went to the big house for afternoon tea and sandwiches. And then, you can't imagine what happened!"

Charlotte couldn't contain herself, "Well, tell me then!"

"The Old Man got up and gave a short speech."

"What about?"

"*Me!*" Lou said, cracking up.

"*What!*"

"He said he'd been speaking to the Secretary of the Navy in Washington and he'd asked about me and how I was doing over here."

Her eyes had become saucers. "Oh go on! ... Really?"

"Yes, and then everyone stood up and Captain Irwin did the honors and I got promoted! I'm now Lieutenant Commander Louis Remington! Ta da!" Lou stood to attention, saluted and then bowed with a flourish, as though to the Queen.

"Oh, Lou, I don't believe it! So what is a lieutenant commander?"

"It's the same rank as a major in the army."

"That's amazing!"

"But that's not all. The captain talked to me afterwards."

"What did he say?"

"He said I'd done a great job not only with the furniture and how the Old Man was pleased, which of course I already knew because I'd heard him with my own ears—but he said I'd done a good job at Howden and with the liaison work between them and Cardington."

"Well, it's true. You've done a bloody good job!"

"Anyway, he's nominating me for promotion to Third Officer."

"Two promotions in one day! Lou, I'm so, so proud of you."

Lou finished his wine and put the glass down on the table.

"You said you wanted to talk about *'us and things'*," Lou said.

"Oh, it doesn't matter. It was nothing important."

He looked at her, puzzled. She wrapped her arms around him and put her luscious, wet lips over his mouth, kissing him gently—at first. Then things rapidly got out of hand.

"I think we'd better turn the oven down low—we'll eat later," Lou said, and then taking her hand, he led her up the stairs to the bedroom.

PART SIX

Cardington R101 Over London. October 16, 1929.

THEIR TRIALS BEGIN

33

ENTER THE PRINCESS

July 4, 1929.

It was July 4th, 1929. The rain had stopped. Clouds were dissipating and the sun beginning to show itself after a succession of miserable, grey days. The longed-for moment had finally arrived. The train bearing Princess Marthe Bibesco glided into Victoria Station. As it did, a debate regarding the British Airship Program was raging in the House of Lords. Naturally, Thomson's attendance was required. Six months had passed since Thomson had seen Marthe. She knew he'd be bitterly disappointed, not being able to meet her.

Dust-laden shafts of sunlight, interrupted by clouds of steam, shone down from the skylights onto the platform. The train came to a gentle stop, exhaling a huge sigh. All doors swung open and Marthe stepped onto the platform, preceded by Isadora, her maidservant. A thin young man with a pencil moustache peered at her. She studied him for a moment. James Buck, Thomson's valet, would be meeting her. He wore a green check suit, a yellow tie, and a narrow-brimmed grey bowler, in accordance with the description provided. Not exactly her choice in men's clothing. But this had to be him.

"Princess Bibesco?" he asked.

"Yes, indeed," Marthe said. "This is my maidservant, Isadora."

Buck nodded to the dumpy, non-descript Slavic woman in her fifties wearing a headscarf. She ignored him. She was invisible. Buck turned back to Marthe.

"Honored to meet you, madam. I'm James Buck, Lord Thomson's valet. I trust the journey's been satisfactory?"

Marthe adored his accent. It was what she described as 'upper-class Cockney', and it was amusing.

"It was fine, Mr. Buck. Now, if you'll kindly bring my bags from the guards' van …"

"Certainly, Princess." Buck summoned a couple of porters. Soon, they appeared with Marthe's luggage piled on a trolley.

"Lord Thomson's limousine awaits you, Princess," Buck said.

"You're most kind," Marthe said, her half smile melting Buck. He led the way to the station entrance where a black Daimler was waiting. The chauffeur opened the rear door and Marthe and Isadora climbed in. Marthe settled down, breathing in the luxurious, beige leather.

Kit's doing well. I'm so pleased for him.

They loaded her baggage into the boot and Buck thrust some coins into the porters' hands. They peered in, smiling and touching their caps.

The British are so decent. Like dear Kit, always anxious to make one comfortable.

The chauffeur got in with Buck beside him. Buck pulled back the glass divider. "The Ritz as usual, Princess Marthe?"

"Yes, if you wouldn't mind, thank you, Mr. Buck."

"No trouble at all, ma'am."

"Can we go by the Palace?"

"Oh, absolutely, ma'am."

Buck closed the partition glass and Marthe relaxed, looking out of the window in the total silence. They entered the main road and moved along Buckingham Palace Road, past Rubin's Hotel. The cobblestone roads glistened, steam rising in the sunshine.

The streets of London washed clean especially for me!

As an acclaimed writer, Marthe habitually documented her impressions of people and places when she traveled. It was one of her passions. She wrote everything down as soon as she reached her destination before her memories faded. She studied pedestrians; most appeared down at heel. Once in a while she spotted a well-dressed, professional type, a lawyer or a politician, perhaps.

Marthe enjoyed London, a bustling city with its red omnibuses and black and blue taxis. Not Paris, but she could get to love this city every bit as much, with all its nooks and crannies steeped in history. Getting to know London would take many lifetimes.

Horse-drawn vehicles laden with goods, building materials, coal, and junk, accounted for the piles of horse manure everywhere. Soon, she guessed, the evil-smelling combustion engines would take over the city and the manure would disappear. The odor was not so unpleasant, unlike foul black smoke emitted from ten thousand tailpipes.

That will be progress. Such a pity!

An old chestnut mare was being allowed to drink at a granite trough. Marthe was thankful. She felt for the poor creature.

At least the combustion engine will spare their suffering.

Her mind drifted to Thomson. She wished she was sexually attracted to him, though that might be futile. She thought back to the time before the war and his mission in Bucharest. Her husband had brought news of her father's death—her greatest hero and friend. The loss, on top of her disastrous marriage, had almost destroyed her. She'd passively given herself up to Thomson. Sadly though, his efforts had been clumsy and lacking in expertise, leaving them both miserable. But despite that, his love and tenderness had carried her through inconsolable grief. He was such a dear man—a wonderful man, whose friendship she treasured.

Yes, no question he was a guardian angel sent to save me and nurse me back to life.

She remembered how Thomson had got her to safety during the German advance. She smiled when she thought of the shoe she'd left in his car in her haste to escape—a delicate, Louis-heeled shoe. She'd been wearing those shoes the night they'd met. He said it reminded him of *Cinderella* from the Italian folk tale. *Cinderella* seemed apt.

Unrecognized, unloved, and lonely at the time—that was me.

He treasured that shoe, keeping it polished and wrapped in tissue paper. He'd still have it somewhere—probably in his top drawer.

Such a small price to pay—that shoe gives him so much pleasure.

The fact remained: no chemistry existed for her regarding the subject of love. He was a gentleman—always attentive and considerate, unlike many of the men she'd had in her life, before and since 1915. But she *had* experienced real passion and sexual fulfillment, thank God, and been deeply in love—but not with Kit.

She remembered how her husband had almost ruined her on her wedding night—her fifteenth birthday—a mere child. Such a brute! The thought of it made her shudder to this day. During her betrothal, she'd had such romantic dreams of marrying her prince and their two aristocratic families being joined. It'd been a fairytale, but one which soon turned into a nightmare. Within weeks of their splendid marriage, the rage of Bucharest high society, he'd gone off with another woman—in fact, many other women, leaving her heartbroken and lonely. And nothing had changed since.

Oh, well, that's George. I don't hold anything against him—he has his good side. Although, it's a wonder I survived to make love ever again.

But she had. In matters of passion, Prince Charles-Louis de Beauvau-Craon was the man who saved her—becoming the love of her life. She thought of the abuse she'd suffered, when compared to Charles-Louis's magnificent, loving treatment of her.

If my body were a Stradivarius, then Charles-Louis was a maestro. He taught me about sex and love. Oh my God, those nights with him were pure ecstasy! For him, I would've given up everything.

Marthe had been madly in love, but his mother had put her foot down, refusing to allow him to marry a divorced woman.

And thank God she did! I should hate to be living in abject poverty now. Sex and love are all very well, but ...

No man had abused her since her marriage. In fact, during her numerous affairs she'd tantalized many a man for her own amusement. Marthe wondered about the future. She was still a beautiful woman, adored and pursued by powerful men.

She thought about this visit and supposed she'd have to succumb to Thomson's advances at some point. Maybe she could manage to hold him off until the last night. She usually did. This naturally left him thirsting for more. Sex with him was a chore to be endured, but thank God, always soon over. But he really was such a dear, dear man though! She told Thomson she'd been totally ruined on her wedding night. He thought of her as a passionless, injured flower. All he ever wanted to do was protect and nurture her.

Bless his heart!

Isadora would play her part. She'd taken care of Marthe in Romania since the age of ten, as her surrogate mother. Isadora certainly cared for her as much as Marthe's mother—probably a lot more—and Marthe adored her. But Marthe couldn't be too hard on her mother. The poor woman was in a perpetual state of grief over the loss of her only son, Georges, to typhoid fever and then later, of Marthe's older sister to cholera. After her father's death and Thomson's departure for Palestine, her younger sister killed herself. Soon after that, both her mother and favorite cousin also committed suicide. Marthe had been very much alone in the world, but for Isadora.

Soon after Marthe's marriage, Isadora had nursed her through near-death during childbirth. Thank God for Isadora! There were two people Marthe kept no secrets from—her priest and Isadora. She and the old Slav woman laughed together and cried together—in private. In public, she became her maidservant, rarely noticed—never heard.

Marthe was terribly fond of the old priest. He was the second pillar in her life. He'd converted her to Catholicism as a girl of twelve, after she'd been sent to Paris by her father. He instructed her in the faith, becoming her confessor and spiritual adviser. He was modern, open-minded and witty, especially for a priest. That chubby little man in his threadbare habit, living a life of poverty—except for the good food and wine lavished upon him by doting parishioners—was extraordinarily well-read. She told him about all the goings on in her life, including details of her affairs, and he usually chuckled. He advised against divorce—under no circumstance would he approve contravention of God's laws, except when violence played a role.

The Daimler passed Stable Row on the palace grounds, where the king's horses were kept. At the top of Buckingham Palace Road, they turned in front of the palace. Marthe was thrilled at the sight of the mounted King's Guard on its way from Wellington Barracks on Birdcage Walk. They looked so fine in their red tunics, gold tassels swinging from side to side. The horses glistened beautifully, like the soldiers' boots and the wet tarmacadam streets. Police held up their limousine as the riders turned and entered the palace gate. Outside the iron railings, Marthe witnessed the changing of the guard.

Such timing! Such splendor! A perfect start to a pleasant interlude in England.

After the horsemen had passed, the police allowed them to proceed around the Victoria Memorial and up the Mall. Soon they turned on to St. James's Street, passing St. James's Palace. The car moved up the hill, in front of Boodle's and White's gentleman's clubs, well known to Marthe. Some of her male friends were members. How she wished she could set foot inside them. Now, here was Brooks's conservative club on the left. Kit wouldn't be a member, but he'd certainly have been invited as a guest. At the top of the street, before entering Piccadilly, the car drew up outside the Ritz. It was immediately descended upon by hotel staff.

The hotel manager escorted Marthe through the marble hall to the lift and up to room 627, a magnificent suite furnished with Louis XVI antique furniture with a balcony overlooking the Royal Gardens in Green Park. As soon as the door swung open, she was enveloped by the scent of roses—*Variété Général Jacqueminot*—in cut glass vases placed around the room.

"Lord Thomson came this morning, Princess, to inspect the flower arrangements," the manager gushed. Excited, Marthe went to the vase containing the largest and most beautiful bouquet, placed on the round table at the center of the room. She plucked out the envelope wedged between the stems and removed the engraved card.

"Ooo la la!" she exclaimed.

Welcome back to England, my dearest Marthe.
Our special roses come with my deepest love.
Until eight, tonight—Your ever devoted Kit.

Thomson arranged for flowers to be placed in her room every time she returned to London, but like a young girl, she always expressed surprise and appreciation. He'd certainly out-done himself this time, though. She called for Isadora. A scented bath would help soothe her for a couple of hours before he arrived.

34

THE WRATH OF LORD SCUNTHORPE

July 4, 1929.

Thomson was indeed vexed. He hated not being at the station to meet her. It was such a thrill when her train came steaming in, her face at the window, her uplifting smile. Alas, today it couldn't be helped—the debate in the Lords concerned the future of the airship program and his presence was of paramount importance. Many on both sides were bitterly opposed to 'lighter than air' and out to sabotage the program. They'd cut funding given the slightest opportunity. He must fend off attacks—give them some stick. There were rumors of a showdown.

Thomson entered the magnificent chamber of the House of Lords, which formed part of the Palace of Westminster. The King's throne, the highest seat in the room was modeled on the fourteenth century coronation chair in Westminster Abbey. The area was shrouded by a canopy clad in gold and supported by ornamental columns. Oil paintings, depicting Britain's glorious past, hung above the throne up to the ceiling. The rest of the walls, clad in Elizabethan paneling, ran up to the Gothic stone window surrounds just beneath the beamed roof. Stained-glass leaded windows lent a holy atmosphere. The great space was lit by gold chandeliers hanging from the roof and by candelabras on ornamental columns in front of the throne.

Visitors and the press, which included reporters who'd attended Thomson's first press conference at Cardington, stood on the high gallery running around the room. Today, more than a dozen were present, including George Hunter from the *Daily Express*. As Thomson strode in, he listened to the chatter of finely dressed, white-haired lords. They twisted and turned in their red leather banquettes and leaned over chairbacks, talking. Thomson knew they liked fireworks. They wouldn't be disappointed.

He took his seat in the front row, on the left side of the Lord Chancellor's empty chair. Despite the charged atmosphere, Thomson was preoccupied with thoughts of Marthe—thoughts that gave him butterflies. Everyone stood as the Lord Chancellor entered through the ornate doors. He strode to his seat in front of the throne and sat down. The lords sat down in unison.

After preliminary remarks, the Lord Chancellor indicated Lord Scunthorpe would speak first. Lord Scunthorpe, an imposing man in his sixties, heavily jowled with flowing, white locks had taken his name from the city south of Howden, which was also his family name—making him Lord Scunthorpe of Scunthorpe. He stood up and glared in Thomson's direction for a long moment, before speaking.

"I've never flown in a dirigible and I never will …that is, whilst I'm still in my right mind!" he boomed in his heavy Yorkshire brogue. A chorus went up and many of the heads of white hair shook from side to side.

"Hell would freeze over before that 'appened!" he added.

"Hear, hear!"

"Nor I!"

"Airships are the *devil's* 'andiwork in defiance of God's laws and we should avoid them like the plague!"

"Quite right!"

"Where in the world are we going to find people crazy enough to fly in these diabolically dangerous contraptions? From which lunatic asylum will they be dragged?"

Lord Scunthorpe stared at Thomson as the jeering and heckling continued. Thomson's face was expressionless. Inside he seethed.

"This is not a matter of party politics—of left versus right. It's a matter of common sense verses *sheer stupidity*. A matter of *life and death*. What we're dealing with 'ere is a *flight of fantasy*!"

"Hear! Hear!"

"I agree!"

"Now, let us examine the Air Ministry's achievements to date and the track record of these floating 'ydrogen bombs. We'll start with the *R33*, although there are of course, many earlier horror stories. That airship cost three 'undred and forty-six thousand pounds and blew away to Germany—luckily, no one was killed in that one."

Thomson had seen the newsreels. The ship had been torn away from its mooring in Norfolk and blown to the Continent. It limped all the way home flying backwards after the storm.

"The *R34* cost three 'undred and sixty thousand and was scrapped after an argument with the Yorkshire Moors and getting blown out over the North Sea."

This infuriated Thomson. Scunthorpe failed to mention the ship had made a historic return flight to Long Island, New York in 1919 (with Scott in command).

"Now let me see. The *R35* cost three 'undred and seventy thousand and ended in disaster. While 'undreds were 'oldin' 'er down, she took off with scores of men still clinging on. Men died that day—*for absolutely no good reason whatsoever*!"

"Shame! Shame!"

Thomson remained stony-faced.

"This brings us to another monumental failure—the *R37*. It cost three 'undred and ninety thousand pounds and was smashed into the shed by the wind, destroying the airship and the shed. Luckily, 'undreds of men escaped injury or death."

Thomson folded his arms.

How much longer must we endure this?

"Now we come to the *R38*." Lord Scunthorpe stopped and gazed around the chamber at the faces. No smiles now. Lord Scunthorpe's accusing eyes burned into Thomson.

Carry on, you visionless-fool.

"Yes, we all remember *R38*, don't we? That miracle of British engineering cost a whopping five 'undred thousand pounds. And that's not all it cost—it cost forty-four men their lives. That monstrosity broke in 'alf, exploded in flames and crashed into the River 'Umber." He raised his hands to the heavens as if imploring the Almighty. "I seem to remember after that little mis'ap we all said, 'Never again!' Didn't we? …Well, *didn't we?*"

"Yes, we did!"

"We did!"

"Now, we mustn't forget our American friends—yes, they 'ave their share of great 'visionaries' too, wanting to build airships as big as their egos. After *R38,* in 1922, the *Roma* went down in Virginia. Thirty-four men got roasted alive in that one. In 1925, the *Shenandoah* broke to bits in a storm over Ohio, costing fourteen more lives. The same thing 'appened to the French *Dixmude.* That thing blew up and fell to pieces in a storm over the Mediterranean with the loss of another forty-four men. It's obvious to me these ridiculous machines are even more useless in bad weather and, I submit, we will *always* 'ave bad weather!"

"Of course we will!"

"Yes, indeed!"

Scunthorpe peered round the chamber with his hands on his hips.

"India …" The word trailed off into silence, his timing impeccable. He stared up at the chandeliers, shaking his head, his lips pursed. Everyone waited. "…you know …I think …you've got more chance of flying to the moon on a *witch's bloody broomstick!*"

The chamber erupted. The Lord Chancellor banged his gavel.

"Order! Order!"

"Ha, ha!"

"Stupid fools!"

"They've got no chance!"

"Let us turn our attention to the Air Minister's *latest folly.* The engineering feat he calls the *Cardington R101,* designed by 'the experts' at Cardington, has been under construction for five years now, costing the taxpayer four 'undred and sixty thousand pounds, which by any stretch of the imagination, could not take to the air *this year* ...*next year* ...or *the year after that!*"

The chamber was now bedlam. Members stood banging the banquette chair backs while the Lord Chancellor furiously hammered his gavel. "Order! Order!"

When order was restored, Lord Scunthorpe resumed softly.

"Finally, I have just one question. When will the British Government come to its senses and put an end to this madness and *stop pouring money down the drain!*"

This crescendo exhausted him. With a red face and bulging veins, Lord Scunthorpe sank into his seat. All eyes turned and rested on Thomson, who remained motionless for what seemed ages, glaring at Lord Scunthorpe. Eventually, he rose and the room fell silent.

"The honorable gentleman may mock ...but God gave men vision to better their lot—to use logic and reason and engineering skill to overcome the obstacles of gravity and distance—and yes, *weather*. God did not give us brains for us to behave like *shrinking violets*! Men shall break the bonds of earth and take to the air to fly like eagles, despite what the honorable gentleman from the North would have us believe. The trouble with the noble lord is ...he doesn't get out of Scunthorpe enough!"

It was the turn of the supporters of the program to jeer and for Thomson to give Lord Scunthorpe a withering glare.

"All the brave pioneers in aviation who lost their lives shall not have died in vain. From the ashes of *R38* these mighty airships shall rise like the phoenix—*bigger* and *stronger* and *safer*—capable of flying enormous distances in *any kind of weather*. Airships are the wave of the future and they'll forge air routes around the world, binding our empire and improving the lives of millions. Mark my words, sir. Mark my words!"

Thomson bowed to the Lord Chancellor and marched stiffly from the chamber.

35

BITTER SWEET

W hile Thomson was doing battle with Lord Scunthorpe at the House of Lords, Marthe was being bathed by Isadora in the magnificent, marble bath. After sending her away, Marthe allowed herself to soak and contemplate for an hour in the warm, perfumed water. She thought about the roses.

So many this time! He's always generous, but is there more to it?

She hoped not.

By 8 o'clock Marthe was well-rested and Isadora assisted her in putting the final touches to her makeup, hair and dressing. She wore a black chiffon dress and black goatskin shoes. To complement the dress, she wore a magnificent string of pearls given to her by Kronprinz Wilhelm of Germany, an ardent admirer for years. She twirled in front of the mirror like a dancer. At forty-three, she looked as beautiful as the day Thomson had first seen her in Bucharest: her skin still smooth and white as china, without the first sign of a wrinkle; her hair, rich, dark brown with highlights of red, shone with health. Tonight, as on the first night he'd met her, she had her hair fastened up and drawn tightly to the back, accentuating her bone structure and slightly hollow cheeks.

There was a knock at the door. Isadora opened it. Thomson stood dressed in a black evening suit, winged collar and bow tie. He'd known Isadora since 1915. She never changed. She appeared old to him then. Always silent. *Sullen* he thought. She annoyed him, but he knew it was unreasonable to feel that way about a servant. She seemed constantly present.

"Ah, good evening, Isadora," Thomson said. "May I come in?"

Isadora stepped aside without a word, allowing him to enter. Marthe appeared from her bedroom, smiling. Isadora hovered.

"Kit!"

Thomson was overjoyed and rushed forward. She allowed him to kiss her on both cheeks and to kiss her hands. He longed to take her in his arms and kiss her lips, but now wasn't the time. Each time they were reunited he had to court her all over again. He was resigned to the fact that Marthe was not a passionate woman—she'd always been that way; affectionate and friendly, but never *passionate*.

"God, I've missed you, Marthe," Thomson said, clasping her hands.

"Thank you for all these lovely flowers. You shouldn't have gone to so much trouble."

"It gives me great pleasure, my dearest," Thomson beamed.

"We must go if we don't want to be late," Marthe said.

Isadora removed Marthe's evening coat from the closet and held it up. He let go of Marthe's hands.

They were driven in Thomson's limousine to His Majesty's Theater in the Haymarket where 'Bitter Sweet,' an operetta by Noël Coward, was playing. Marthe had expressed an interest in seeing it and Thomson had obtained the Royal Box. The musical was popular and the theater filled rapidly. Marthe appreciated the building, admiring the burgundy walls and fluted columns with gold relief. She slipped into one of the red velvet chairs with Thomson beside her. He was in heaven.

'Bitter Sweet.' How appropriate.

If only he were able to freeze these moments and relish them over and over. "I dreamed about you again the other night, Marthe."

"And what did you dream this time?" she said with a teasing smile.

"The same dream. You are as lovely tonight as the first time I saw you on Rue de Rivoli in that fine, white carriage. You're the girl in my dream."

"And what year was that?" she said with an artful stare.

"1902."

"My dear Kit, I've told you a dozen times. That girl wasn't me. I would've only been fourteen!"

Thomson knew this wasn't an excuse, but didn't argue. "Then you more than fulfill that vision of beauty I've carried with me all these years, dear heart."

He held her hand throughout the evening and they enjoyed the play like a tender, young couple. On arrival back at The Ritz, Marthe said she was tired and after escorting her to her suite, Thomson left. It'd been an enchanting evening, though frustrating. He'd need to exercise patience.

The next day, Thomson took Marthe to Wimbledon for the ladies' finals. They watched Helen Wills Moody beat Helen Jacobs in two sets. Their arrival had created mild interest. People suspected they were 'somebody,' but not sure who. Tennis bored him. Heads turned back and forth like a thousand metronomes, but not Thomson's. Only Marthe was on his mind. He stole discreet looks at her throughout the afternoon.

The following day, they drove to Heston Aerodrome where they watched sky racing around pylons. This was one of Marthe's husband's favorite pastimes. Thomson studied her reaction feeling a stab of jealousy.

She obviously found it exciting, spending much of the time on her feet. At the end of the races, Thomson presented silver cups to the winners.

They spent the next few days visiting and dining with friends at their country estates. Marthe was wonderful to be with on these occasions and Thomson was happy, except for the gnawing deep inside that grew painful as time wore on—she'd soon be gone. One sunny afternoon, Thomson took Marthe to visit his chambers in the House of Lords and to pick up his dispatches. He'd taken her to the main chamber before, but now he had his own office. The room was ornate, smelling of wood and leather —'wonderfully masculine,' she told him.

Marthe kicked off her shoes and sank into a leather armchair opposite his desk, curling up like a kitten, delighting him. After studying the surroundings, she stared at him coquettishly while, like a schoolmaster, he studied his papers through half spectacles.

"Look at you, Kit. Lord Thomson of Cardington, Minister of State— so aristocratic, so royal!" she said.

"Splendidly put, my dear princess."

"All those years ago in Romania, who could've pictured *this*?" she marveled.

Thomson got up from his chair.

"Come, let's walk to the lake. The ducks are waiting."

Thomson had bread in his pocket; he'd made sure Gwen put some in a bag. He'd planned this stroll in the park for weeks and waited for a beautiful afternoon. He felt certain this was the right moment. They left the House of Lords. Thomson was unable to resist taking Marthe through Westminster Hall, forming part of the Palace of Westminster, on the way.

Their footsteps echoed across stone paving in the cavernous building. Thomson always waxed poetic here, seeming to have a spiritual connection with the place.

"Do you know this is my most favorite Gothic room in all England, Marthe?" he said, staring up at the massive wooden roof beams which rested on stone abutments.

"I should, Kit. You tell me each time we pass through it!"

"This is where they tried King Charles the First," he said. He'd told her this many times over the years. In his mind he was now back in January of 1649. "You can just see it, can't you, Marthe? King Charles standing there on a platform, his once pristine white, ruffled shirt, scruffy and dirty, his head held high, despite being tried by a filthy mob led by that scoundrel, Oliver Cromwell, thirsting for his blood—and his throne." Thomson waved his arms grandly. He sensed the crowd around them and now so did Marthe. She became distraught.

"Before they dragged him away and chopped off the poor man's head! Oh Kit, this place gives me the chills. It reeks of despair. Let's get out of here!"

Thomson was surprised—she hadn't acted this way before, but she was right. No question, this place carried an aura of death. They stepped out into the sunshine to stroll arm in arm, enjoying each other's company. On reaching the Horse Guards Parade, they crossed the road and admired the two mounted guardsmen in gleaming, thigh-length, black boots, crimson coats and black capes that fell across their horses' backs.

Marthe made a fuss of the horses before they ambled into the cobblestone yard and across the gravel parade ground toward St. James's Park, where indeed, the ducks *were* waiting. Thomson fished around in his pocket for the brown bag of bread while the ducks watched in anticipation. Together, Thomson and Marthe threw bread into the pond and the splashing birds fought noisily for it. They chatted idly until the bread was gone. When calm was restored on the water and the greedy ducks had disbursed, Thomson became serious. The moment had come.

"Marthe, I have something to tell you which is very hush-hush."

"What is it, Kit?" Marthe asked, alarmed.

"Ramsay is going to put my name forward to the King for consideration for the post of Viceroy to India. Most likely, I'll be offered the job."

"Oh Kit, that's wonderful! I am so proud of you. Congratulations." she said, kissing his cheek.

Thomson was disappointed at Marthe's reaction. Unless …

"Perhaps he's asking rather a lot of … us … Don't you think?"

"What's the difference? I can always visit you in India," she said, with an encouraging smile. "That would be rather fun."

She was too flippant.

"I thought this might be an opportunity for us to be together … perhaps … permanently."

"*Whatever* do you mean?"

"I thought maybe we might … marry."

"But you know I'm *already* married."

That was cold and sarcastic, not the reaction he'd hoped for.

He plunged on. "In my position, I think we'd get Rome's blessing."

"*Rome's blessing!* For what?"

"An annulment."

"I'm married because I *choose* to be married. In *my* position, even an annulment wouldn't be acceptable to society—I'd become an outcast!"

"Marthe, you cannot live your whole life just to please society."

"I live my life the way I *choose* to live it," Marthe snapped.

"How can you go on being married to a man who doesn't love you?"

"This may sound strange, but he does love me—in his own way."

"You lead separate lives. He has a mistress whom you tolerate."

"I'd do nothing to hurt or embarrass him. He's like a brother to me."

"And *I* want to be a *husband* to you!"

"Look, I don't blame him—and what's more, neither will *you*."

"I'm not blaming anyone. I'm simply asking you to end this arrangement and enter a normal loving marriage with *me*," he said.

"Enough!" Marthe cried.

Totally deflated, Thomson stared across the pond, and after a long pause, spoke softly. "Marthe, I've waited fifteen long years … and now, perhaps, we have the opportunity."

Marthe was silent. Thomson sensed her pondering the possibilities, perhaps for the first time. He waited patiently.

"At the moment, all this is mere speculation," she said.

Her tone had the air of finality and Thomson knew to press no more.

After two weeks in England, it was almost time for Marthe to return to Paris. The second week had been strained. For the first time in their relationship, there'd been awkward moments. Thomson's proposal hung over them like a black cloud. The day before Marthe's departure, they had tea on the terrace of the House of Lords with the Prime Minister. MacDonald had invited them so he could meet the woman who'd had such an effect on Thomson for so many years. Thomson had been longing to introduce Marthe to him.

"Prime Minister, may I present Princess Marthe Bibesco," Thomson said.

MacDonald's eyes lit up on seeing Marthe, and she appeared to be just as delighted.

"Prime Minister, it's such a pleasure," she said, her long eyelashes fluttering.

MacDonald took her hand between his and delicately raised it to his lips, kissing it as though it were fine china. Thomson closely watched their every movement and expression, remembering distinctly the night, he himself, had fallen under Marthe's spell at the foot of the staircase in Cotroceni Palace. He felt a twinge of jealousy.

"You don't know how long I've wanted to meet the darling of Paris," MacDonald said.

"Prime Minister," she purred.

"Please call me Ramsay; all my closest friends do. CB is one of them and now I hope you will be, too."

Thomson remained silent. This was a meeting of intellectual Titans.

"You're so kind, Ramsay," Marthe said, gracing him with one of her most gorgeous smiles.

"If I say I'm honored, I mean it. For me to meet as talented a writer as you is a great thrill. I know you're the toast of the salons of Paris. Even Monsieur Proust himself heaps lavish praise upon you."

"Oh, they exaggerate, Ramsay."

"No, no. I've read *Catherine-Paris* and *Les Huits Paradis* and the critics praised you as a delicious and learned writer—and I can attest to both. No wonder Thomson's in love with you. Everybody is!"

"You yourself are much accomplished. I've read your works, and although I may not agree with some of the principles of your political thought, there's so much I *do* agree with," Marthe gushed.

Thomson couldn't help but marvel. He knew Marthe to be conservative through and through, but here she was displaying her humanitarian side, which he knew MacDonald would find irresistible. She'd never mentioned reading MacDonald's writings—and neither had he, hers—that was new and interesting. He could see MacDonald was enchanted.

They took their seats around a wooden table overlooking the Thames and chatted for half an hour over cream tea and buttered scones. There were no references to the future or their relationship. It was a pleasant interlude and Marthe was thrilled to meet the man who currently managed the greatest and most powerful empire on earth, with a yearly budget greater than the United States, Soviet Russia and Germany. Finally, MacDonald stood up and graciously bid Marthe farewell with a courteous bow and a kiss on each cheek.

"When you come back, you must both come to Chequers. The gardens are beautiful. I know you'll enjoy them. When will you come?"

"I am not sure, Ramsay—perhaps not until next year."

MacDonald chuckled. Thomson knew Marthe was admiring his stature: his shock of white hair, like an old lion's mane, and the bushy white moustache that gave him character and made him so striking.

She studies people intensely. It's the nature of writers—Marthe especially; she's like a sponge. Nothing escapes her.

"That's a pity. I'm not sure I'll be in residence at Chequers by then, Marthe."

"Oh yes you will, Ramsay," Thomson said, turning to Marthe. "He always cracks that joke. He'll be spending weekends at Chequers for years to come."

"Then we shall see. But I'd like you to come. Both of you," MacDonald said.

"Yes, and during Marthe's next visit we'll dine at my flat," Thomson said. "You must bring Lady Wilson."

MacDonald hurried off to attend to matters of state.

"What a wonderful-looking man. He has such charisma!" Marthe exclaimed, watching MacDonald striding away.

"Thank you, Marthe. You made him feel special today. He loved you."

"You're such a good person, Kit. I can understand why you're such close friends. Does he see much of Lady Wilson?" she asked, looking away across the river.

The next day, Thomson took Marthe to Victoria Station to catch the train to Dover. From there, she'd take the ferry to Boulogne. They walked down the platform in silence, amid hissing steam and the echoing of slamming doors. Isadora trailed at a discreet distance.

Thomson was depressed. Everything seemed different. To make matters worse, after her meeting with MacDonald, he felt diminished. Marthe was difficult to read at the best of times. Perhaps he'd pushed her too hard. He'd lain awake all night alone in his flat thinking of what to say this morning.

At the assigned first-class carriage, Thomson went on board and stashed Marthe's hand luggage on the overhead rack. From there, he went back to the platform and stood at the door. Isadora disappeared down the corridor out of the way. Marthe stood at the open window above Thomson. A picture of unattainable beauty.

"Think about what I said," Thomson said.

Marthe stared down like the Sphinx. Suddenly, there was the guard's deafening whistle screaming in his head, signaling loneliness and grief to come. As the train began to move, she put her hand to her mouth and cleared her throat. She spoke softly.

"All right, I will," he thought she said.

He looked at her, unsure; it was hard to hear over all the damned noise in the station. With a half smile, she moved away from the window and sat down. He watched her departing train until it was out of sight, before trudging away with that familiar sinking feeling in his stomach.

What did she say? All right, I will—I will what?

Her muffled words kept going round in his mind on the way back to the flat. He'd need to write and find out exactly what she meant, but it might take weeks to get an answer, if then.

36

GAS BAGS & ENGINES

August & September 1929.

The dreaded engine trials began in August—dreaded because they were both absurdly dangerous and unnecessary. Barnes Wallis stood at one end of the shed with his bullhorn. The three engine cars had been attached to the underside of the airship's hull. Each car housed two reconditioned Rolls-Royce Condor engines in tandem, totaling six and the gas bags, having a total capacity of almost six million cubic feet had been charged with hydrogen. The more expensive helium—not available in Europe—was a safer gas, but produced less lift, making it less effective. Lou often thought about this—helium hadn't helped Josh aboard *Shenandoah*.

The installation of the gas bags and their charging by the hydrogen plant had been a massive and expensive undertaking. Wallis, the absolute perfectionist, had supervised the operation himself, with assistance from Norway, Lou and Teed, as well as the drawing office and technical staff.

Lou and Charlotte traveled up on the motorbike and stayed at Charlotte's parents' house in Ackworth. Ironically, Jessup had also been summoned to assist, joined by his two Yorkshire cohorts, now recovered. On the road north, the three had flashed by at high speed, passing too close, after swerving around Lou and Charlotte at the last second. Charlotte was shaken. Jessup would require further reining in.

Wallis showed signs of stress; often irritable, his eyes heavy due to vicious migraines. Lou realized this wasn't just about having Burney for a boss, nor the sheer enormity of his task. It came down to his nature—the need for absolute control.

During the gas bag installation, Wallis's booming commands filled the shed. Things had gone perfectly until the last bag suffered a small tear, not bad, just a few inches long. The shed became filled with Wallis's fury. Lou took no notice; he knew the performance of all concerned had been practically flawless.

The gas bag installation and filling operations occurred during a two-week period when Molly was absent (the family having been wisely sent away). During that time, Wallis, Teed, Norway and Lou went over to Wallis's bungalow for tea, lunch and dinner. Often Burney and his perfumed, powdery wife knocked on the door, itching to be allowed in. On spotting the troublesome pair, Teed would wedge a pencil behind the doorbell, while Norway turned up the wireless. After a few minutes leaning on the bell and thumping furiously, they gave up and trudged away.

Lou and Charlotte visited John and Mary Bull during their time up north. News of Lou's promotion made them proud. Charlotte saw the promise of a successful future for Lou, but potential danger overshadowed everything. Charlotte also visited Fanny, still pining for Lenny. Charlotte doubted she'd get over the loss. Billy had done well at Howden and was highly thought of. His future looked bright. He'd be posted to Cardington after the engine tests and promoted to 'rigger' within a couple of months. Lou arranged for Billy to be billeted with Freddie's family for a reasonable price for bed and board. Lou thought it'd be good for Billy to be with a family, with a boy his own age.

Lou rewarded Freddie and his family by getting him a place in the ground crew. Freddie's father had already been a casual member of walking parties for previous airships over the years, including *R38*. In that position, Freddie would graduate toward becoming a crewman one day. For now, he'd work in the walking party when time came to launch and assist in mooring operations.

During their time up north, Lou and Charlotte had dinner with Mr. Shute at the Brown Cow. As soon as they sat down, Norway stunned them.

"Wallis is l-leaving us," he said.

"What do you mean?" Lou asked.

"Switching to aeroplanes."

Lou's jaw dropped and Charlotte gasped, putting her hand to her chest.

"I thought he was committed to airships," Lou said.

"I think he still is, but he'll do anything to get away from Burney. Things are pretty bad."

"That's a damned shame," Lou said.

Then Norway dropped the other shoe. "Burney's now written a book, which in essence says these two airships as designed are a lost cause," Norway said. "I'm not sure if it's to annoy Wallis or Thomson, or if he truly believes it—all three most likely."

"Sounds like they're both baling out," Charlotte said.

"No, Burney's not b-baling. He's suggesting designing elliptical shaped ships, which is a damned neat concept, actually," Norway said.

"So what's Wallis gonna do?" Lou asked.

"Design aeroplanes. He's moving to Weybridge."

"Wow! How long before he goes?" Lou asked.

"I think he'll be here until this ship's launched. He told me he definitely wants to make the trip to Canada, though."

"Which I guess'll be sometime next year," said Lou.

"It turns out that for the past year Wallis has been visiting a workshop in Brough, just up the road from here. There's an engineer building a great big seaplane and Barnes is completely taken with it. Of course, he says they don't know what they're doing, but now he's all fired up about aeroplanes."

"Rotten traitor!" Charlotte said suddenly.

"Gives him a second string to his bow," Lou said.

"If airships don't work out, he's got another avenue," Norway said.

Charlotte, said nothing. She stared down at her Dover sole.

Perhaps he's come to his senses.

She felt empty. She'd thought these men knew what they were doing and they'd get things right. Now Wallis was abandoning them and Burney was questioning the basic designs.

Why?

To her, 'If airships don't work out' meant: 'If they crash and burn, again'. Lou lifted his glass showing no feelings of betrayal. "Here's to Barnes Wallis and to his future endeavors—whatever they may be."

"Yes, to a great engineer," Norway said. They raised their glasses.

"You don't seem bothered in the least," Charlotte said, glaring at Norway.

"No, he's happy about it—*he's* moving up. He'll be the new chief, right, Nev?" Lou said.

"Could be, but I tell you this: Wallis needs to get away from here. His health has suffered terribly. The migraines are killing him. Changing the subject: I have more news," Norway said with a toothy grin.

"What?" Charlotte asked.

"They liked my, er *our* last book *So Disdained*. It's coming out this year."

"Congratulations, Mr. Shute!" Lou exclaimed.

"Thank you both. You don't know how much you've helped me."

"Okay, put our cut toward another wheel for that car of yours."

"And when you're famous, I want to be your editor—don't forget," Charlotte said.

"I'll drink to that," Norway replied.

Wallis lifted the bullhorn to his mouth. "Okay, start engine No.1."

Lou stood in the Howden shed beside engine car No.1. Norway was at No.2. Lou watched the engineer start the engine through the car window. Once they were running, the noise was deafening. The bullhorn now became useless. Wallis put it down. After that, everything was done by hand signals and thumbs up or down. Each engine was run for two hours forward and thirty minutes in reverse.

The eighteen-foot propellers whirled two feet above the concrete floor, causing the airship to surge forward and up and down due to air currents generated—like a massive fan. Lou knew their lives would never be in greater peril. If the restraining cables gave way it would mean certain death for all, not to mention complete demolition of the seven acre shed. Lou looked at the engineer in the car next to him. The man gave him a beaming smile and a thumbs-up. Lou smiled back.

This is so damned phony. No one's fooling anyone.

He hadn't told Charlotte about the danger and when the tests were over, he was glad he'd kept his mouth shut. Engine trials were completed within three days and were a total success. To Lou, the whole exercise was sheer madness and he thought a much safer method could have been devised.

He and Charlotte headed south to Cardington for more of the same in Shed No.1. Similar trials were conducted on the *Cardington R101* engines with Richmond and Scott in attendance, assisted by Lou and Rope. Everyone cheated death once more, and Lou again said nothing to Charlotte. He figured he'd used up two more lives—if he were a cat, he had three left.

37

THE QUARREL

September 1929.

Lou spent less time up at Howden now the gas bags were installed and the engine tests completed. *Howden R100* floated in her shed, her suspension wires slack. Bedford Hospital offered Charlotte a nursing position and she was happy to go back to work. She hoped this was temporary, still desperate for a child. She and Lou kept trying, although Lou became increasingly wrapped up with his job. This sometimes irritated Charlotte. He didn't understand—having a baby was the most important thing in her life. He was either at the shed or studying at home.

Things erupted in September. Lou was at the dining table poring over navigation books loaned by Johnston. Charlotte came up behind him, leaned over and put her arms around his neck. "Lou," she whispered.

He felt her warm breath on his neck. "What d'you want, Charlie?"

"You."

She bit his ear, playfully. He felt her tongue slide invitingly into his ear. It felt good, but this wasn't the time. He had too much on his mind.

"Charlotte, I've got to study this stuff. It's important. You don't want me to get lost over the Atlantic, do you?"

"Come to bed, Remy," her voice husky and seductive.

"Not now. I must finish this. Johnny's gonna test me in the morning."

"*Saturday!*"

"So?"

"Come to bed."

"Look, I've got to do this and I'm really tired, honey."

Charlotte leapt back and straightened up. "Damn! All you care about is that bloody airship. I'm sick and tired of it!"

"That's not true."

"We were so happy up north. Now it's all about the airship. You don't care about me."

"Stop being melodramatic. I have to work on this."

"For all your dead buddies—including Josh of the '*Good Ship Shenandoah*'! Right?"

"That's enough, Charlotte!"

Her eyes blazed. "Sometimes I feel like I'm living in a house full of *dead people!*"

"Will you shut the hell up!"

"I'm alive. You should care about your *wife!*"

"Look, I can't help it if you can't get pregnant."

"Perhaps you're just not *man* enough!"

"*I said*, it's not *my* fault you can't get pregnant."

"How do you know that? You won't go to a bloody doctor to find out!"

"Dammit Charlotte! You never stop. There's no need to behave like a damned prostitute in the back bar of some Yorkshire dockside pub."

"You rotten bastard! How dare you!"

Lou swung around in his chair to get up. Charlotte drew her arm back to slap his face. He grabbed her wrists. "Stop it, you bitch!"

She broke free and stormed out, slamming the door, causing a framed photograph of Candlestick Cottage to fall to the floor and break into pieces. Lou cleaned up the glass and tried to go back to studying for his test, but it was impossible. He lay down on the couch, refusing to go up to the bedroom. He slept fitfully until awakened by Charlotte's voice. He'd no idea how long she'd been sitting next to him in the dark, but he was glad. She took his hand.

"I'm sorry, Lou. It was all my fault. You didn't deserve it. Please forgive me. I don't know what's the matter with me. There's so much hurting me deep inside and I worry about you all the time … and I want a baby so much and—"

"Honey *what's* hurting you?"

She didn't answer. She sat looking down shaking her head. Lou knew he'd gone too far last night. He'd been a brute.

"Charlie, I'm sorry for what I called you." He screwed up his face, unable to believe he'd said those things.

"I deserved it. I was a perfect bitch."

"Don't say that … but you're right about one thing. I do much of it for *them*. It seems crazy, but it tears me up to be the one left alive. When I survived the war, it was the same. The chaplain told me my life had been spared for a reason and it was up to me to discover that reason. So, I do this, thinking maybe this is why. Charlotte, I can't let them down—remember that."

Charlotte put her arms around him, drawing him close. "I do understand, Lou. I'm a mess, too. I get so desperate. Sometimes I think this is the day it's gonna happen—I'm gonna fall. It's a hundred million-to-one chance, and I hate to see the moment slip away."

Lou looked at her questioningly. Was there more to all her sadness? Something deeper. He was at a loss. "We'll keep trying," he said finally.

"I thought you were going to see Johnny this morning."

"I didn't finish. I'll see him later."

Charlotte put her hand to his face running her fingertips down his scar. "I'm sorry."

"Don't worry, baby."

Charlotte's face brightened. "I want us to have a big launching party."

"You don't have to do that, sweetheart."

"They'll be pulling it out soon, won't they? I want to have a really big bash. We'll invite everyone. We'll have Walter and Sammy Church and Irene, and Joe Binks and Ginger Bell and their wives – I don't know their names—and Freddie and Billy and Cameron and his dear wife—if they're still speaking—and Dizzy and Polly and Mr. Leech and his wife, he's married isn't he? And ..."

"Charlie, these are folks we have round all the time."

"I know, but I want this to be really special—a big celebration. We can get Captain Irwin and Olivia—if they'll come—and Mr. Atherstone and his wife and Johnny Johnston, oh I do like Johnny, and he can bring his wife —what's her name?"

"Janita."

"Oh, and Major Scott—thank God for Major Scott—and we'll get Inspector McWade. Oh, I do like that man, thank God for him, too!"

"You're forgetting Wing Commander Colmore—my boss—he's the most important guy in the joint!"

"Oh yes, and him, too. And your friend the steward who likes you."

"What about Lord Thomson, you're leaving him out," Lou said, chuckling.

"We'll invite him, too, if you want. Do you think he'd come?"

"Yes, and he'll bring Princess Marthe Bibesco and Prime Minister MacDonald, no doubt. Charlie, Charlie. You're being silly."

Lou led Charlotte to the bedroom.

"I'm loopy aren't I," she said.

"No, you're not loopy."

As she lay down she said, "Lou, we will have that launching party, won't we? I'll bake a cake and you can play them some of your mountain music and some of your own songs. You can sing the one you wrote for me —"Oh Charlotte, My Charlotte"."

"Yes all right, we'll invite them all, but it's a bit short notice. I doubt the Prime Minister will be able to make it."

"Oh Lou, I do love you so."

38

LIGHTEN HER LOAD

L ater that morning, not wanting to appear rude, Lou went to Cardington House and found Johnston in his office. "Hi, Johnny, I'm real sorry about this morning. I had trouble studying last night and then I couldn't sleep," Lou said.

Well, technically it was true.

"Don't worry, Lou. We'll do it when you're ready."

Lou went and stood by the window. He could see a lot of activity beyond the Cardington airfield. There were countless trucks laden with metal parts being unloaded by dozens of people.

"What the heck's all that metal framing for?" Lou asked.

"It's the fair. They always come to the village in the autumn. It's good timing. There'll be thousands of people here for the launching—they'll make a few bob."

"What's the latest?" Lou asked.

"We should have the temporary permit to fly this week. The launch is set for Thursday, subject to weather. They're desperate to get her out before Howden."

"The race is on!"

"Silly buggers!" Johnston sneered.

"Charlotte wants to have a launching party."

"Good. I hope she'll play the piano. I like a good old singsong—presuming I'm invited!"

"Of course you are. I'm sure she'll play all your favorites."

Johnston sang a verse of "Yes Sir, That's My Baby" and jigged around the office.

"Johnny, you're a star. But don't give up your day job, ol' buddy."

Lou left and as he walked past Richmond's office, someone called his name. He poked his nose around the door. Rope and Colmore were standing at the drawing board with Richmond.

"Ah, come in, Lou," Richmond said.

Lou gave a polite nod to Richmond and Rope and smiled at Colmore.

"Morning, gentlemen," he said.

"Rope and I have completed our calculations. As you know, we've been doing lift and trim tests all week."

"How's it look?" Lou asked.

"Our suspicions have been confirmed, I'm afraid," Richmond said.

Colmore looked grim. "We have thirty-two tons of useful lift," he said.

"And we're supposed to have sixty, right?" Lou queried.

"Quite," Richmond said.

"We've made a list of dispensable items," Rope said, handing Lou a sheet of paper. He began reading.

"Servo assistance, bunks, lavatories, windows, ballast tanks …"

"We'll reduce the number of cabins from twenty-eight to sixteen, remove some washing facilities, and replace the glass on the promenade decks with Plexiglas," Richmond explained.

"And the ballast tanks?"

"We think we can dispense with two of them. We're also looking at loosening the gas bag harnesses—in fact they've started that," Richmond said, pausing for Lou's reaction.

"That's risky! The gas bags'll get torn up," Lou warned.

"It's damned risky!" Colmore muttered. "I don't like it."

"She's 106,000 cubic feet short of the five million we designed her for," Rope said.

"How much do you expect to gain by letting out the harnesses?" Lou asked.

"We'll pick up another 100,000 cubic feet," Richmond answered.

"Won't the bags chafe?" Lou asked.

The topic was depressing Colmore, who was chewing his fist.

"We'll need to make sure they don't. Simple truth is: without radical changes, a voyage to India will be *completely* out of the question," Richmond said. At least they were facing the truth. Lou was relieved about that.

"What do you propose to do now, sir?" he asked Colmore.

"We'll do some test flights after the launch and then reassess the situation."

"We'll find out if she's manageable without the steering servo. If so, we'll remove that, too," Rope said.

"If these changes are made, we'll increase lift by 6 tons—not enough. Damn! I wish we'd made her a bay longer. We had room in Shed No. 1." Richmond said.

"Maybe it's not too late," Lou said.

Billy arrived from Howden the following day, now assigned to Cardington. Lou met him at the station on the motorbike and took him home for a few hours to see Charlotte before delivering him to Freddie's. Charlotte made a fuss of the boy and gave him a Sunday roast dinner. He was now sixteen, tall and wiry like his dad. He was also smoking Woodbines like his dad.

"Seen anything of Mr. Norway and Mr. Wallis?" Lou asked over lunch.

"We see quite a bit of Mr. Norway, but Mr. Wallis hasn't been around. They say he's working at Weybridge now," Billy replied.

"How's your mum? Hope you've been taking good care of her," Lou asked.

"She's all right. We've been staying with me nan."

"Now you're a working man, I expect you've been helping her out a bit, eh?"

"Nah, she's all right. She's workin.' How's *your* mum? Are you takin' care of her?" Billy asked with a sly smile. Lou knew Billy was joking, but the jibe stung. He'd conscientiously written every week but, thanks to Billy, realized he'd neglected his mother. He knew his brother and sister were still at home and they'd make sure she was all right. It gave Lou license to do as he liked, but he wasn't proud of that. He pondered the idea of getting down to Virginia on the train, if fortunate enough to be chosen for the Montreal flight. He'd work on that idea.

"Yes, Lou, we should go to see your mum one day," Charlotte said.

"She'd love to meet you, honey. You know she always goes on about you in her letters."

"I'd love to see Virginia."

"God's country!" Lou said.

"Well, I'll be …I've never heard you say that before," Charlotte said.

39

THE SIGNAL

October 12, 1929.

I t was 3:30 a.m. and very dark. This would surely be the most wonderful day in Freddie Marsh's young life. Here he was on the corner of Crawshay Road on the outskirts of Bedford with a hundred other men ready to form part of the walking party. The group looked sadly pathetic, with Freddie and his father no exceptions—down and out like the rest, dressed in rags and old overcoats, cloth caps and worn out boots.

The British economy, like that of the United States, was in dire straits. The men were hunched on this damp street corner smoking cigarettes. They desperately needed work. Their breath came out in smoky clouds under the streetlamp, their nervous eyes darting back and forth to the sky. They were waiting for the confirmation signal. The previous night, the searchlight beam lit up the sky, indicating a walking party would be required at dawn. Three short bursts this morning would be confirmation. They'd been on standby the last two nights for an early morning launch, but stood down due to increasing winds both mornings. Things looked good for a launch today; the sky was clear, wind dead calm. Freddie was keyed up.

"Relax, son," his father said. "We'll see it in a minute, don't you worry."

At 3:40 a.m. a beam of light shot into the sky over Cardington, prompting a cheer from the men. This happened three times—three short blasts, three cheers. They'd earn a little money today—enough to put food on the table for a day or two.

"There it is, Dad!" Freddie exclaimed.

"Take your time, son. I'll go and get seats. Remember, easy does it." Freddie's father rushed off to one of the five waiting buses to save two seats. Freddie limped after his father at his own pace.

Lou got to Cardington at 3:00 a.m. in his newly-issued, dark blue uniform (his with U.S. Navy insignia). The other officers would be dressed similarly. On his way to the shed, Lou glanced at the fair, which had been going all night. Its colorful flashing lights, carousel steam organ, and carnival atmosphere, spilled over the new chain-link fence, across the aerodrome, creating a mood of gaiety and celebration. Newspapers said people were traveling from all over the country to witness the launching of the world's greatest airship.

Thousands had been at the fence when Lou left last night and thousands more had shown up overnight. They kept vigil, all eyes glued on the shed doors. Would they open to reveal the shed's secrets for the first time at daybreak? Spectators watched ground crewmen and airshipmen going to and fro all night. No one wanted to miss this historic event—the first sighting of the mighty *Cardington R101.*

Lou made his way to the control car. Irwin and Atherstone had already arrived. Above, in the chartroom, Johnston leaned on the rail. Lou gave him a wave. He responded with a grin. There were no journeys to be plotted, but everyone was on board and ready, just in case the ship should break away. It would be disastrous to be aloft involuntarily without charts, a navigator, sufficient crewmen, or fuel. Lou knew that feeling first hand from the *R38* accident, as did Sky Hunt and Capt. Booth after *R33* had been ripped from its mast and blown away to the Continent a few years previously.

Airships can be unpredictable creatures.

Lou recalled the thrill of flying in *R38* those first months—feelings of elation during the flight over Yorkshire; the wonder of looking down at the world in miniature; living, eating and sleeping in the clouds. It'd been a whole new way of life with its own terminology. Even small things—the smell of a new airship and the antics of the ship's cat, Fluffy, intrepid rat and mouse killer—had sparked excitement in him. And then came the crash. It'd been eight years. Would those good feelings ever return? He was skeptical.

"Good morning, sir," Lou said, looking at Irwin.

"Morning, Commander," Irwin said with a nod.

Lou smiled at Atherstone. "Today's the day!" Atherstone said.

"I'm early, sir. All right if I go ashore for a while? I'd like to see what's happening on the field," Lou said.

"Sure you can. It's organized chaos out there," Irwin replied.

He got outside in time to see Scott give the order to shine the searchlight into the air to signal the walking party groups around the region. A cheer went up at the fence. Many had been on the field since Thursday night and were now confident they'd catch a glimpse of the ship today. Lou studied the faces; in addition to genuine excitement, he perceived hope.

The transport of five hundred men by bus and positioning them on the field would take a good hour or two. Lou hung around near the front of the shed where Scott stood with a bullhorn in one hand. He was giving orders to two gangs engaged in opening the shed doors, which stood over a hundred and fifty feet high. Six men pulled ropes turning two capstans, easing the doors open, inch by inch. As the gleaming ship's bow was revealed, another louder cheer went up. A steel curtain was opening on an exciting drama—a contest of leviathans! Scott appeared pleased with the crowd's reaction, as though he were some great conductor.

Lou scanned the field. White lines had been painted on the grass as guidelines for the walking party to follow from the shed to the tower. Down the field, a man on horseback was driving a flock of sheep into a nearby pasture. Lou smiled.

The captain was right. It's chaos all right!

Around the fence, car headlights illuminated people boiling up water for tea on primus stoves and cooking eggs and bacon—it was like camping out. For others, it was too early; they slept under blankets in the backs of cars, snoring with their mouths wide open. Not everyone cooked for themselves. Vendors had set up along the fence, roasting chestnuts and potatoes. Others sold cheese sandwiches, bread and dripping, and cups of tea or cocoa. Hawkers yelled enticements to the crowd to buy souvenirs commemorating this day; postcards, photographs, flags and trinkets were all on sale at inflated prices. In the distance, the brightly lit Ferris wheel slowly turned, while sounds of the carousel organ drifted their way.

"Morning, sir."

Lou spun around to see Billy behind him.

"Ah, Billy, you're bright and early. What are you up to this morning?"

"The foreman told me to muck in with the walking party when it gets 'ere and then 'elp out the ground crew."

"Good. Have you had something to eat?"

"Yes, I 'ad a bacon an' egg sandwich before I left Freddie's."

"They taking good care of you?"

"Yes, they're nice to me, especially his mum."

"Good. You're gonna need them muscles this morning, kid."

"Yes, sir."

"I'm taking some of the crew to the fair later. Why don't you and Freddie come."

Billy broke into a grin. "Oh yes, Lou. We'll come, all right."

Thirty minutes later, at 5:00 a.m. a convoy of buses drew up to the gates and hundreds of men poured onto the field and ambled toward the shed, among them Freddie and his father. Another cheer went up from the crowd and Lou spotted a black limousine approaching, followed by three other official-looking cars. The windows of the limousine were open and the interior lights on, allowing the crowd to view the occupants. The motorcade moved toward the tower, and when it stopped Lou saw Thomson, Brancker and Knoxwood climb out. He realized they must have stayed overnight at Cardington House. Lou had to give the old man his due. He took a personal interest in the program he'd put in motion. He was also a master at managing public relations—and this was an opportunity not to be missed.

By now, ropes had been stretched out by the ground crews from the pulling rings on the airship and laid across the grass along the lines toward the mooring tower. Scott addressed the walking party.

"Good morning, gentlemen," he boomed. "I want you to form four lines across the field. Space yourselves six feet apart. The rest of you take up the lines at the stern and along the port and starboard sides as she comes out."

The men took up their positions, most of them old hands. Lou walked along the line to where Thomson stood. Brancker poured coffee from a thermos flask into a cup held by Thomson. Next to them was a BBC van and a radio announcer. Lou listened.

"This is Donald Carpenter, speaking to you from the airfield at Cardington, home of the giant airship *Cardington R101.* This is an historic occasion indeed, for today she'll be pulled from her shed where she's been under construction. Beside me, I have the architect of the British Imperial Airship Program, the honorable Lord Thomson of Cardington. Sir, this must be a very proud day for you?"

"Yes, indeed it is. The fine people of Bedfordshire have toiled with great dedication for five long years—since I announced the beginning of the airship program in 1924—and we are about to see the results of all their efforts ..."

As a brass band struck up "Soldiers of the King", Lou decided to return to the ship and marched briskly to the shed. He'd heard all this stuff before. It was still flat calm and cool—about 50 degrees—just right. He climbed the ladder into the hull and made his way to the control car. Nothing had changed there. The skipper was still standing with his hands tucked in his jacket pockets. Atherstone held a mug of coffee. Cameron was on this watch as height coxswain. Another man was on the rudder wheel. Providing there were no mishaps, neither coxswain would be required to do anything. The men in the control car peered forward as dawn began casting its eerie glow over the field. The four columns of ant-like men waited for orders. Lou spotted Freddie behind his father, forward of the control car.

Scott put the bullhorn to his mouth. His orders echoed across the field and into the shed. "Take up the ropes." Men in the walking party reached down and grabbed their ropes. "Take the strain." The four lines became taut. "Forward march on the count of three ...slowly ...one ...two ... three!"

The columns moved as one, expertly in step. The airship, floating in well-balanced equilibrium, moved gently forward. At the first movement, there were cheers and applause and then the sound of car and truck horns from around the field. The din got louder with every step as the airship, almost the size of *Titanic,* was drawn from her shell, like a great sea creature. Once clear of the shed, the noise rose to a crescendo, drowning out the band, except for the thump, thump, thump! Ropes were attached to all sides and stern, and the crew held them tightly, keeping them taut to prevent the ship moving in the wrong direction, should there be an unexpected puff. These men were also there as ballast to prevent the ship lifting into the sky, should a sudden change in temperature cause an increase in lift. (This, as Lord Scunthorpe had eloquently pointed out in the House of Lords, hadn't always worked out for the best!)

Within minutes, the ship had been walked to the center of the field and tethered to mooring rings set in the ground. From there, she was allowed to rise to eight hundred feet by dropping water ballast. The shining, silver ship floated in the sky for all to see for two hours, after which time, she was winched down and moved to the tower, where she was attached to the mooring cone at the top of the mast. Irwin had posted a watch list for a skeleton crew of ten men to remain on board at all times. He included himself on the ship's first watch. Lou, Johnston and Atherstone disembarked with the crewmen.

40

THE GYPSY FORTUNE TELLER

October 12, 1929,

Later that morning, Lou met some of his crewmen at the fair. After the success of the launching, everyone was in high spirits. First, they rode horses on the carousel and then they split up. Lou took Billy and Freddie on the Ferris wheel—it was all they could talk about. Binks, Church and Cameron made their way around the attractions. Disley and Potter grabbed a hot dog.

From high atop the wheel, Lou and the two boys admired the scene. They got a good view of *Cardington R101* at the tower and the aerodrome surrounded by sightseers. Lou noticed Binks and company had found the coconut shy and had made it their mission to dislodge the big hairy nuts. When the ride was over, they joined the others. Binks and Church were very upset.

"Better luck next time boys," the fairground attendant said to Binks with a smirk.

"Yeah, right! Don't give me all this 'better luck next time' bollocks."

"They've got them things glued in," Church yelled. He had one foot on the top rail about to jump over and prove his point.

Lou grabbed him by the arm. "Steady on there, Mr. Church."

"We've hit the coconuts six times and they won't budge," Binks said.

"Calm down, guys. Come on, let's go this way," Lou said. Freddie spotted a clown's head lit up in a glass display case on a stand. He went over to it and the others followed.

"Look at this," Freddie said. "He looks real. Er, maybe he *is* real!"

The clown's eyes were closed, but then he opened them briefly and blinked a couple of times. He had long white hair, a bald head and a bulbous red nose planted on his vivid white face. The lips were open, revealing a row of yellowed teeth. The caption read:

PUT A PENNY IN THE SLOT & MAKE HIM LAUGH

Freddie stood, fascinated. "Go on, Freddie, put a penny in then," Church said.

Freddie hesitated. Lou figured the kid only had his bus fare in his pocket and handed him a penny. Freddie inserted it in the slot. They heard it drop. The clown suddenly came alive and Freddie jumped backwards in shock. Its bloodshot eyes opened wide, glaring at him, and then the head tilted back and its mouth exploded into crazy laughter. Everybody, save Freddie, joined the clown's frivolity. The boy was visibly shaken. Lou put his arm around his shoulder and gave him a little shake. "Hey kid, don't worry about it. It's just a machine," he said.

After they'd watched the clown, Billy came rushing up. A sign outside a red tent had caught his eye. "Hey, sir, I'd like to go in," he said, pointing at the sign.

LET THE WORLD'S GREATEST CLAIRVOYANT
MADAM HARANDAH
THE ROMANIAN GYPSY
TELL YOUR FORTUNE
PSYCHIC READING
PALM READING
TAROT CARDS
3d EACH

Lou chuckled. "Come on then, guys."

They piled into the gloomy tent, which smelled of damp grass and cow manure. Lou was last one in and smiled on seeing the reactions of his crewmen. Binks peered suspiciously up at the ceiling and walls. "This tent's a lot bigger than it looks from outside," he said. "It's kinda strange!"

Freddie, still visibly shaken by the clown's head, stood at a table covered with a green, baize cloth, peering at a collection of items: a polished wood block cradling a crystal ball, a rabbit's foot, a deck of tarot cards, and a china bowl with burning incense. "Blimey, this place gives me the creeps," he mumbled.

"Don't be silly. It's only a witch's tent. Oh look, there's her transport," Billy said, pointing to a broomstick hanging over them next to a dim, red bulb dangling from an electric wire. Wisps of smoking incense in the eerie glow added to the weirdness. Lou laughed. Madame Harandah was obviously a joker—or was she? He didn't have to wait long to find out.

Church, Disley and Potter gathered under a photograph of a beautiful woman in a blue headscarf hung on the fabric tent wall. It'd been colored and touched up by hand.

"She's a smasher! Wonder if that's her," Church said.

"It's me if you wanna know," a voice growled from behind a black curtain. Billy was in the act of reaching out to touch the rabbit's foot. "Don't touch that, you little bugger!" the voice bellowed, scaring the life out of the boy.

A scruffy woman suddenly burst through the dark curtains. She seemed caught off guard by so many entering her tent. The crewmen were speechless, trying to take in this vision. Her eyes were glutinous, black pools set in a sea of bright blue eye shadow, glowering at them from under ridiculous, false eyelashes. Her eyebrows had been plucked out entirely and repainted in thin black lines, at once comical and frightening, and her puffy cheeks were rouged in a red blush almost as bright as her thick, ruby lips. Shiny, silver bangle earrings dangled from her lobes, as large as those on her wrists. She wore a purple headscarf from which graying, auburn hair sprouted and hung in ringlets to her waist. Her well-worn clothes—a ruffled, dark green blouse and an ankle-length black skirt—reeked of eau de cologne, cigarettes and mothballs.

"*Gordon Bennett!*" Binks exclaimed.

"What d'you lot want?" the woman demanded.

"We thought this was where you got your fortunes told," Church said.

"You've come to the right place," she bellowed.

"'Ere, you ain't the gypsy in that picture! Where's she?" Binks demanded.

"I certainly am! That was taken in Southend-on-Sea ten years ago. Any objections?"

"Forty years ago, more like," Disley grumbled.

"Next you'll want to see me bleedin' birf certificate!"

"We thought you were supposed to be Romanian," Potter said.

"I'm from the Elephant and Castle. Me dad was from Bucharest. So that makes me a Romanian gypsy—all right? If you don't like it, you can sod off—the lot of yer!"

"Keep yer bleedin' wool on, lady," Binks said.

. "Okay, if you're stayin', that'll be sixpence each. Show me yer money."

"The sign outside says threepence," Freddie objected.

"All right, all right! Give me one and nine pence."

"We should get a discount. You ought to do us all for one and six, the lot," Church said.

"All right, all right! One and six. Put it right here," she demanded, her craggy hand with long, purple fingernails outstretched.

"Oooh, cross me palm with silver," Binks said.

Lou was thoroughly enjoying himself. He pulled out a shilling and a sixpence and put the coins in the old hag's palm. They all held back while she sat down.

"Okay, whose gonna shuffle the cards?" she said.

"Give 'em to Sammy," someone said.

Church went into action, his hands a blur, cutting and shuffling, cards flying from one hand to the other. Everyone whooped and whistled until the old dear was thoroughly irritated.

"All right! All right! That's enough!" she shouted, grabbing the cards back.

"Go on Dizzy, you go first," Church said. Disley slipped into the chair opposite Madam Harandah, who spread her cards into a fan on the table.

"I see you're going on a journey," she said.

"Oooooh, you don't say," Binks said, eyeing Lou's uniform.

"Shut up, Joe. Let her tell me."

She turned over another card. "I see you high in the sky."

"This woman's *bloody amazin'*!" Church said.

She turned over another.

"Ah, you're the cool one. Electricity is your friend. You will deliver a message when the great game is over. Next!"

Disley screwed up his face in annoyance.

"What the hell does that mean, 'Deliver a message when the great game is over'? What *great game*? Is that all I get for thra'pence? What a bloody swindle!"

"Come on, let me have a go," Freddie said. Disley reluctantly got up out of the chair, shaking his head.

"Now you! You need to be more careful, Sunny Jim," the gypsy said, poking Freddie in the heart with a long, skinny finger. "You know what I'm talkin' about, doncha?"

Freddie became sheepish. "S'pose I do."

"You've had big ideas coming in your silly little 'ead lately, haven't you, son?" He glanced down at the table, unable to look into her all-seeing eyes. "You need to be careful. Electricity is not *your* friend. So stay away from it! Now get up and let him have his turn," she said pointing to Church. Church slid into the seat. Madame Harandah turned over more cards.

"Ah, here's a boy lucky in love," she purred. She smiled for the first time, revealing two rows of sparkling white dentures. The boys jeered, making Church blush.

"It's true love I see, all right. But I feel such an ache in my heart. Like him over there," she said, pointing at Freddie. "So you better settle down, my lad, and be good to your lady. Stay home! If you don't, she'll marry another. And she *will* do that I promise you—do you hear me?"

Church had heard enough. He got up from the table.

"No flying around for you, Sammy, me old cock-sparra!" Binks crowed.

She looked up at Binks. "The one who's always late—thirty days late being born. You must've given your mother a right fit!"

"Me mum said I was late."

"Better late than never! Ah, and you're an artist. And I see you have the gift, like me. But you've always got far too much to say for yerself, 'aven't yer," she said with a sneer. "Hmm, I see you walking through fire, rain and fog."

"Walking through *fire, rain and fog*? Sounds bloody daft, if you ask me," Binks said.

"Well, I ain't askin' you, am I? But you remember this—'ee who hesitates, is *not* always lost. Next!"

"What's she talkin' about?" Binks moaned.

Billy was standing next to her. She took his hand.

"Now, here's a young man whose father follows him around everywhere. Do you know that, son?" Billy pulled his hand away, rattled.

"He does *not!* Me Dad's dead, so how could he?"

"He might be dead to you, sunshine, but he ain't no more dead than I am! He wishes you well and says 'Go and break a leg, my darlin' boy'," the gypsy said.

Billy became infuriated. "That's rotten. You're makin' all this up."

Lou had listened intently. He'd talk to Billy later. The gypsy peered up at Cameron.

"Come on, Gunga Din, sit down." She spread the cards again. Cameron gingerly did as he was told. "It's very sad …she's a silly little cow, and she'll pay the price—and so will 'ee. My 'ead explodes at the thought of it!" she said, melodramatically throwing her hands from her head into the air as if it'd exploded all over the tent. No one spoke. Cameron jumped up and went outside in a fury. Everyone turned to Lou.

"Come on, sir, it's your turn," Potter said.

"What about you?" Lou said.

"No. I don't wanna know," Potter said. Lou understood perfectly.

"*No, you don't!*" the gypsy snapped, glaring at Potter, her dreadful eyes blazing like fire.

Lou eyed the woman carefully as he sat down and rested his hands on the table. Madam Harandah briefly held both his hands in hers and closed her eyes. He felt his hands tingle. She then took the cards, shuffled them and laid them out in a fan again.

"Ah, I see you have an evil twin. You'd better watch out for that one. You're a lucky man though—like a cat. Six times you've been lucky I see. Question is: Will your luck 'old out? And are you lucky in love? We'll have to see about that, won't we? I see here in the cards you believe there's something you must do. Do you know what it is? You *think* you know— don'tcha? But you've got a lot of questions hanging over you." Lou smiled, giving away nothing. "I'm gonna tell you just this, mister—you're in grave danger of losing everything you 'old dear."

"Well, tell him what you *mean* then. You talk in *bloody riddles*, woman!" Binks growled.

"Come on boys, let's get the hell out of here," Lou said, getting up. They moved out to join Cameron who was still agitated, smoking a cigarette. Lou sensed the gypsy's knowing, black eyes on him and turned to look back at her.

"We'll meet again soon," she said.

"If you say so, lady."

"That woman of yours has some real issues you know—*deep issues!*"

Lou hesitated. What was the old crone talking about now?

"And *try* to keep that bunch out of trouble," she added with a crafty smile.

Outside, Lou and the boys walked straight into Jessup and his pals. On seeing Cameron, Jessup sniggered. Cameron rushed at him, grabbing his throat and leaning him over a chestnut fence, which promptly collapsed. They fell in a heap. Jessup's face turned red and he was having trouble breathing. His five friends grabbed Cameron by anything they could, and pulled. Lou and his crew did the same till everyone was pulling on somebody and throwing punches.

Lou stepped back. "Okay, all of you. That's enough!" He grabbed two of Jessup's gang and pushed them away. "Walk that way, all of you. You and I will be talking, Mr. Jessup."

Jessup and his cronies slunk away.

"Okay, lads. Charlotte's launching party's tonight. Make sure you're all there," Lou said.

"Yes, sir, we'll be there," Potter said. "We're going back in the fair, for a bit."

"Starts at five. Come on Billy and you, Freddie. Charlotte needs our help." They ambled off toward the sheds and the airship floating at the tower.

"Just look. What a sight," Billy said.

Lou turned to him. "So, what did you think of the fortune teller?"

"Didn't like her. She was daft."

"Why?"

"Talkin' about me dad like that."

"Perhaps she *was* able to see him. Maybe he *is* still around you."

"Nah! It's a lot of nonsense. Saying he wishes I'd break me leg. That's silly."

"Billy, it's just an expression." Billy looked puzzled. "When you tell someone to break a leg, it means you wish them good luck," Lou said.

"How could it mean that? If I broke a leg it wouldn't be good luck, would it?"

"I don't know, but it does. Billy, your dad thought the world of you."

"Yeah, I s'pose you're right. I miss 'im."

"He was a brave man. He suffered real bad in the war. I never heard him complain once—*ever*. Remember—he did it all for *you,* kid"

It all came down like a flood on Billy. "Yeah, I know. I wish he was still 'ere." He began to sob. They heard running feet behind them. It was Binks and Church, laughing like madmen. Church had something under his arm.

"Here, look. I told you they was glued in sir. I told yer!"

"He jumped over and knocked it loose with a chunk of wood," Binks said. Church held a coconut high above his head in two hands. They all laughed. Lou turned to Billy and Freddie.

"Come on let's go. Charlotte's waiting for us."

41

A WORD WITH MR. JESSUP

October 12, 1929.

At the crew's locker room, Billy and Freddie showered and got changed for the party. Lou went to the officers' locker room where he changed out of uniform and put on work clothes. He then went to the crewmen's locker rooms to pick up the two boys. Jessup and his gang had finished changing and Jessup was looking into a mirror over the sink, combing his lank, greasy hair. On seeing Lou, fear clouded his face, though his eyes harbored bitter hatred. He looked more brutish after having his jaw wired up and reconstructed. Lou stood behind him, blocking his escape. He glanced into the mirror and for a split second thought Jessup's reflection was his own. It brought out irrational anger in him.

"Okay, you lot—out! Jessup and I need to have words," Lou said. Jessup made a move to leave. "Stay right there, Jessup," Lou snarled.

The other five left without a fuss.

"Don't you touch me," Jessup whined, not turning around.

"I told you, you were on probation. I see you're up to your old tricks again. I don't think you took me seriously." Lou grabbed Jessup by the back of the neck and slammed his head into the mirror. His face was flattened, his breath steaming up the glass.

"I did. I did."

"You've been messing around with people's wives. You think you can go around doing this stuff and get away with it?"

"I don't know wocha talkin' about." Jessup had difficulty speaking. Spit was running out the corner of his mouth and down the mirror.

"I see you're drooling again, Jessup—not becoming a gentleman. I'm talking about *Cameron's wife*! It's common knowledge. You go out of your way to humiliate the man."

"What are you, the bleedin' judge and jury? You told me to stay away from Charlotte and I did. You didn't say anything about other people's wives, didya?"

"You really are a piece of crap. I'm gonna have to kick it out of you. Since they made you a rigger, you've gotten back to your cocky self again."

Lou pulled Jessup away from the mirror and pushed him across the room. Jessup saw his chance to escape and rushed full speed into the metal lockers, causing a deafening crash.

"You stay away from me. I'll report yer. I'll have you up for assault, I will. You have no right …I can see whoever I want. It's a free country."

"I'll be watching you, Jessup. Now get lost!"

Jessup bolted from the room as Billy and Freddie came out of the showers. Billy looked questioningly at Lou, but Lou said nothing.

"We heard him talkin', Lou," Billy said.

"What'd he say?"

"He said you thought you'd got rid of 'im, but you aven't."

Freddie cut in. "He stood right there combing 'is hair and 'ee said, 'I'm gonna kill that bastard one day. I swear on my father's cold, dead eyes. You just see if I don't.' And then 'ee said, 'My daddy'll be right proud o' me then'."

42

CHARLOTTE'S PARTY

October 12, 1929.

L ou, Billy and Freddie arrived at the house as a man from the local off-license was delivering dozens of wooden crates of beer. Charlotte came to the door in her apron and stood aside while they carried the crates inside.

"Ah good, now you lads can move the furniture for me. We need to make lots of room," Charlotte said, after kissing Lou.

They followed her down to the kitchen, where the women had been working furiously. Olivia Irwin, the captain's wife, had made a pile of small, triangular sandwiches of fish-paste and watercress and Mrs. Jones, the neighbor, had made a stack with egg and cucumber. On the table was a large, square cake Charlotte had baked and just finished icing with a picture of an airship on top.

"Hey, look at this!" Freddie said. "What's the fish on top for?"

Billy rushed over. "It's not a fish—it's the *R101*, you daft sod."

"Looks like you ladies've been busy. Mind if we have a sandwich? We're famished," Lou asked.

"Lou!" Charlotte exclaimed.

"Launching airships makes a man hungry," Olivia said. "Come on, help yourselves."

Charlotte pointed at Freddie. "Watch out for this one, he'll eat 'em faster than you can make 'em," she said. She put her arms around him and squeezed him tight, making him blush. "I'm only kidding, Freddie. I love you, really," she said. "He's such a lovely boy, isn't he!"

"I'll pour you boys some tea," Mrs. Jones said.

"How did it go, love?" Charlotte asked Lou.

"Everything went without a hitch. She's up there, floating at the mast. The crowd's going nuts. I took the lads over to the fairground for a while afterwards," Lou replied.

"How smashing!" Charlotte said.

"You're good to the crewmen," Olivia said.

"Yeah and we 'ad our fortunes told by a gypsy," Freddie said.

"You did? Oh, *I* want to go! What did she say?" Charlotte asked, excitedly.

"She talked a lot of nonsense. Said my dad keeps following me around and 'e wishes I'd break me leg," Billy sneered.

"How weird," Charlotte said.

"She could be right. Perhaps he does follow you about. Them gypsies have special powers. Very psychic, they are you know," Mrs. Jones said.

Charlotte was filled with curiosity. "Tell me what she said, Lou."

"Hmm. I've forgotten already. I wasn't paying attention. It was just a lark, that's all."

"Come on, Lou, tell us," Olivia said.

"Oh, I remember, she said I'm lucky—" Lou said.

"She said six times he's bin lucky—" Billy interjected.

"Yes, that's about it," Lou said, glaring at Billy, who took the hint.

"Promise you'll take me after church tomorrow. I love fortune tellers," Charlotte pleaded.

Lou knew exactly what was going on in Charlotte's head. "You mustn't let those people mess with your mind, Charlie."

"I know how you feel, Charlotte. I can never resist myself," Olivia said. "My husband won't go anywhere near them. Well, I'd better go home and get changed. I'll be back with my Blackbird later. We won't be able to stay long. We've got three launching parties to go to. I hope you'll play for us, Charlotte."

"Of course I will. Thank you for all your help."

"Bird loves Al Jolson. Will you play "Blue Skies" for him?"

"If he'll sing it, I'll play it," Charlotte promised.

Lou was setting up the bar in the living room when Charlotte came down from the bedroom. He handed her a glass of sherry and she took a good sip. She wore a black chiffon dress in the latest fashion, skinny at the waist and delicate.

Freddie was swept off his feet. "Oh, Charlotte, you do look smashin'!"

"He's got a right crush on you, Charlotte. Lou's gonna have to watch out," Billy said.

Charlotte drank the rest of her sherry and put the glass down. It was making her woozy. "Come here and give me a big hug you beautiful boy," she said. Lou laughed as Charlotte gathered Freddie into her arms and squeezed him to her bosom, making him blush and sweat all over again.

"It's your birthday on Wednesday and I've got a present for you, Robert …er, Freddie," Charlotte said, becoming flustered and then, "Come with me."

Lou pretended not to notice Charlotte's gaff. Billy whooped as Charlotte led Freddie up to the bedroom. She went to the wardrobe and took out a brown paper bag and handed it to him. "Here, something you need, now you're a fine, working man," she said. "Try them on."

Freddie opened the bag to find a pair of black boots. After she'd bought them, Charlotte had taken them to a shoe-mender and had them soled and heeled, asking the cobbler to make the sole thicker on the right shoe. She said nothing to Freddie about that. "They're second-hand. I found them in the market, Freddie," Charlotte said.

"They're smashin'," he said, after slipping them on. They fit perfectly and he was thrilled. When he walked around, his limp was less noticeable. Freddie was pleased, but also puzzled.

"Why did you call me Robert just now?" he asked.

Charlotte shook her head, slightly embarrassed and a little light-headed. "I'm going to let you into a little secret. I met a soldier once. His name was Robert. And you remind me of him, that's all."

"Did you love him?"

"Oh no. I only knew him for one day—but he was very, very nice."

"What happened to him?"

Sadness swept over her. "I don't know. I expect he was killed. Our little secret, right?"

"Yes, yes. I won't say anything to anyone, Charlotte, honest."

When they got downstairs, he kissed Charlotte's cheek and thanked Lou with a handshake.

By the time the crewmen and regular crowd trickled in, Billy and Freddie had put a sign up in the living room, which they'd colored with kids' crayons. Everyone admired it, and though child-like, the sentiment was right.

GOOD LUCK CARDINGTON AIRSHIP R101
LAUNCHED OCTOBER 12th 1929

Some brought bottles of beer and wine and boxes of chocolates. Many drank tea, ably served by Mrs. Jones and her husband. Johnston, the navigator, and his wife came in around 6 o'clock and had tea and sandwiches. The crewmen were on their best behavior and took turns playing darts in the garden where they started a competition. Church turned out to be the expert, winning every game and taking everyone's money. They stood around, relaxed, chatting and sipping drinks. At 7 o'clock Capt. Irwin and Olivia arrived. Most were informally dressed, but well turned out. After the sandwiches were gone, they made a big fuss while Charlotte cut the cake and they enjoyed a slice for good luck.

"Come on, Charlotte. Play for us," someone said.

Charlotte went to the piano and burst into "Toot, Toot, Tootsie, Goodbye." Everybody joined in, Johnston singing the loudest. At the end of the song, Olivia made her own request. "Can we have "Blue Skies" please," she called.

Charlotte obliged, while Lou strummed the guitar and Potter played his accordion. It seemed the perfect tune for a perfect day. Everyone sang along. While they were singing, Doug Cameron and Rosie showed up. Their presence made others uncomfortable. The couple were at odds, not looking at each other or speaking.

About half an hour later, Scott, carrying a bottle of gin, arrived with Fred McWade. Lou was surprised, but thought it a nice gesture. Scott, already 'well on the way', happily joined in the singing. Shortly after, Capt. Irwin and Olivia expressed their thanks and bid everyone goodnight. By nine, the alcohol had run out and the gathering dispersed. Scott said he'd another party to go to and he and the Atherstones went off together, leaving Disley finishing a chess game with Ginger Bell. McWade stayed on a little longer and Charlotte made a big fuss of him.

Later, while Charlotte was lighting a candle before slipping into bed she remembered something. "What happened to your chief steward friend? I was looking forward to meeting him."

"Oh, sorry, I forgot to ask him, honey," Lou said, as they snuggled down.

"You forgot Lord Thomson and the Prime Minister, too, I suppose?"

"Yes, my love I plain forgot," he answered.

"Okay, but just don't forget about the gypsy tomorrow," she said.

"Charlotte, let's think about us," he said, gently lifting her so she was straddling him.

"Yes, yes, all right, my darling. I can do that," she whispered, settling over him.

He loved to see her like this in the candlelight, smiling down at him, hands behind her head, hair tumbling around her shoulders to the waist. She began to writhe.

"I can certainly do that …" she said, closing her eyes.

"It was a wonderful party, Charlotte. Thank you."

"You're very welcome, my darling."

"I'm the luckiest man in the world," he said

"Yes, you are, and just don't you forget it, Lieutenant Commander Remington."

At times like this, Lou felt really and truly blessed to have Charlotte as his wife.

43

ST. MARY'S

THE BLESSING & HARVEST THANKSGIVING

October 13, 1929.

The next morning, everyone, with the exception of Rosie Cameron, attended St. Mary's Church. Her absence didn't go unnoticed. Lou wondered if she was with Jessup. All officers and crewmen of *Cardington R101* were in their smart, new Airship Service uniforms. This was a special service to bless the airship and to give thanks as part of the Harvest Festival. The church, with the aroma of a garden market, had been decked out in a colorful display of locally-grown fruits and vegetables: sweet onions, cabbages, huge, polished marrows, potatoes and carrots scrubbed clean; all collected and donated by school children, later to be given to the poor.

On their way to the old, brick church, worshipers lifted their eyes in wonder to the airship tethered to the tower, glistening in the sun. They trooped into the church to thank God and ask for His protection. The organ played softly while everyone took their seats in wooden pews, which smelled of lemon polish. They sat with their heads bowed amid hushed whispers. A baby cried in the rear of the church, close to Freddie and Billy. Charlotte waved to them and Lou gave them a nod as they passed before sitting down toward the front.

Suddenly, the organist became energized and the congregation stood for the singing of "All Things Bright and Beautiful"—the cue for the vicar, choir and assistants to file down the aisle toward the altar, holding their hymn books high in front of them as they sang. Lou and Charlotte sat in a row near the Atherstones, Irwins and Johnstons. Scott and his wife sat in front of them with Wing Cmdr. Colmore, recently promoted from Assistant Director to Director of Airship Development. Colmore's wife sat proudly beside him. They looked at each other fondly from time to time, like sweethearts. The Richmonds sat nearby with Rope and his wife. Lou was struck when Richmond turned to acknowledge them, by how much he'd aged this past four years. Scott appeared jaded, but no doubt he'd recover by noon.

Staff from the Royal Airship Works design offices and machine shops sat in nearby pews, intermingled with strangers—here for the launch. By the time the vicar started the service, the church was full. During a long pause after prayers, the sound of children mumbling to their parents and people clearing their throats echoed around the building. Irwin got up and moved to the front of the church. He climbed the pulpit steps to the lectern, where an enormous Bible lay open with the lesson marked. He read beautifully, in his rich Irish dialect, the opening passages of 'Jonah and the Whale'. The captain's soft voice was mesmerizing, gently floating around the church as he related the story of Jonah disobeying God's commands and fleeing aboard ship. In an ensuing violent storm, the crew, blaming him for bringing bad luck upon them, cast him into the sea.

" ...*Then Jonah prayed unto the Lord his God out of the fish's belly and said, 'I cried by reason of mine affliction unto the Lord and He heard me; out of hell cried I and Thou heard my voice. For Thou had cast me in the midst of the seas; and the floods encompassed me about and Thy waves passed over me ...*"

Lou glanced at Charlotte. He wondered if he had a connection to this story. By Charlotte's returning stare, she was wondering the same thing. He squeezed her hand.

"*...but I will sacrifice unto thee with the voice of thanksgiving; I will pay that that I have vowed. And the Lord spake unto the fish, and it vomited out Jonah upon the land.*"

To Lou, the text chosen by the vicar was ironic—perhaps too ironic!

Maybe that whale out there's gonna swallow us all and spit us out!

Irwin reverently closed the Bible and returned to his seat. The vicar moved to the center of the church to face his flock. "Tomorrow is an important day in our lives—the maiden flight of our great airship. I want you to remember the words read to you by Captain Irwin. Remember always that in times of trouble, you must pray to the Lord and ask for his help and deliverance. At this wonderful time of Harvest Thanksgiving we now see the fruits of all your labor—*Cardington R101* floats out there at the mast for the world to see. Similarly, we experience the fruits of the labor of our farmers and those who tend our fields and gardens. The harvest has indeed been bountiful. Let us give thanks to God and ask Him to bless this airship and all those who fly in her." The vicar signaled for the congregation to kneel and began his prayer. "Oh, Heavenly Father we thank You and humbly beseech You ..."

The faint sounds of the carousel and the girls' screams from the fairground drifted from across the road behind the graveyard. Lou looked at Charlotte, who seemed far away in a dark place—a place she inhabited too often these days. He wondered where her mind was at times like these.

She noticed him studying her and returned from her brooding. Lou winked and she forced a smile. He took her hand, signaling, no, he hadn't forgotten—they'd walk over to the fair and see the damned gypsy. The organ struck up again for the last hymn—a rousing one to lift all spirits: "Jerusalem."

> *And did those feet in ancient time*
> *Walk upon England's mountains green:*
> *And was the holy Lamb of God*
> *On England's pleasant pastures seen!*

Lou made a point of looking at all the faces, particularly the ones he knew. Everyone sang, except poor Cameron. Even Binks seemed to be taking things seriously for once. Freddie and Billy, were giving it their very best.

> *Bring me my Bow of burning gold;*
> *Bring me my Arrows of desire:*
> *Bring me my Spear: O clouds unfold!*
> *Bring me my Chariot of fire!*

The organist at this point, pulled out all the stops, giving it everything. The church came alive, the enthusiasm tangible—the usual Sunday morning drowsiness swept away with everyone singing at the top of their lungs. The vicar and his brethren marched out grandly, uplifted.

> *I will not cease from Mental Fight,*
> *Nor shall my sword sleep in my hand:*
> *Till we have built Jerusalem*
> *In England's green and pleasant Land.*

Lou and Charlotte followed Irwin and Olivia down the aisle.

"That was some hymn, Charlotte. I've never heard it before," Lou said as they filed past the vicar, smiling and shaking his hand at the door.

"The hymn is fairly new, I think. There's something magical about it," Charlotte said.

"Is there a story behind it?" Lou asked.

Overhearing, Olivia turned to them. "'Jerusalem' is about the legend of Jesus' lost years. They say He came to England during that time and went to Glastonbury," she said.

"Wow! Interesting to think He may have walked this 'green and pleasant land.'"

Outside the church, Lou and Charlotte socialized for a short time, but Charlotte was anxious to get over to the fairground. As they strolled along

Church Lane, Lou couldn't resist pulling her leg. "Out of the church and into the soothsayer's tent! It all seems a bit sinful, if you ask me, missus!"

"Oh Remy, it's just a bit of fun, love."

"I'm sure there's something in the Bible about fortune tellers," Lou said. They turned into the gap in the chestnut fence and walked toward the Ferris wheel.

"Do you want to go on some rides first?" Lou asked.

"No, I want to see the gypsy!"

"All right, this way." Moments later, they were outside the red tent where Madam Harandah stood at the entrance. Charlotte studied her, suddenly unnerved.

"Waiting for us?" Lou said, smirking.

"Yes, I was. Come in, my dear. My, what a lovely girl you are. You *are* a lucky man," she said looking from Charlotte to Lou. Inside, Lou took out a shilling and put it in the old woman's hand. He was about to sit down.

"You'd better go for a walk, young fella," the gypsy said.

Lou was surprised. He glanced at Charlotte.

"Oh Lou, do you mind? Do as she asks, please, my darling."

Lou left the tent. He regretted bringing Charlotte now.

Oh Damn! This was a mistake.

He hoped the gypsy didn't upset Charlotte; that was all he cared about. He walked over to the chestnut fence and bought the *Sunday Pictorial* from a paperboy and a coffee from a vendor. He sat down in the sunshine to read about the launching and drink his coffee—which tasted like crap. The article told how wonderfully advanced the Cardington airship was; how much like an ocean liner; the wave of the future; blah, blah, blah; a good write-up—propaganda, nonetheless.

Charlotte appeared forty minutes later. She seemed more cheerful.

"There you are," she said.

"How did it go?"

"I couldn't understand half of it."

"She talks in confusing riddles. That's her technique," Lou said.

"But she did say I'd have a child. In fact, she said 'You *will* have *children.*' But she said I needed to get my house in order first. There are things I must do."

Lou frowned. "Like what?"

Charlotte looked away, evasive.

"Well, she could be right… You might and you might not," Lou said.

"No. She said *I would,* one day." Her eyes brightened at the thought.

"Yes, I'm sure you will, Charlotte ... I'm sure you will."

He swallowed the last of his coffee and stared across the field at the airship.

Let's hope they're mine.

44

OVER LONDON

October 14 & 16, 1929.

The next day, with her blessing bestowed, *Cardington R101* rose into the air in perfect weather conditions, watched by an enthusiastic crowd and a friendly press. The ship, under the command of Capt. Irwin and his officers, Lt. Cmdr. Atherstone, Flying Officer Steff, Johnston the navigator and Lou as third officer, made a short flight around Bedford and then on toward the outskirts of London before returning home. When the airship passed over Bedford, Charlotte came out into the street with dozens of other nurses to catch a glimpse. To most of those who saw her, the airship appeared as a thing of awesome beauty.

Cardington R101 had proved she could fly. Thomson was invited to make a flight two days later. As with the launching, Thomson, Brancker and Knoxwood stayed overnight at Cardington House so they could be at the field early next morning. At 6:30 a.m. the crowd cheered Thomson as he climbed out of the car. This event, seen as the 'official' maiden flight, appeared as a bright spot on the otherwise chaotic, depressing world-wide economic front and spectators made the most of it. Thomson waved to the crowd and then marched along the line of ground crewmen to the tower, nodding and smiling to each man. He noticed Freddie standing next to Billy.

"My, my, you've been working hard on those boots, young man," he said, placing his hand on Freddie's shoulder. "Good work, son."

Thomson knew the boy must have spent a lot of time the night before polishing those old boots. They shone like black-gloss paint. He took pains to notice things like that. When he reached Irwin, waiting at the foot of the tower, he took his hand between his and greeted him warmly.

"My dear Captain Irwin. This is a momentous occasion."

"Welcome aboard, sir." While the captain shook hands with Brancker and Knoxwood, Thomson stepped back to look up and study the gleaming airship. "Give me a moment," he said.

"Please, take your time, sir," Irwin said.

Freddie and Billy followed Thomson at a discreet distance and stood watching and listening. After a few minutes, Thomson turned to them and smiled again.

Two young lads witnessing history in the making—future airshipmen of the fleet!

Thomson and his party squeezed into the elevator and the operator closed the accordion gates. There was a stiff breeze at the top of the tower and, although sunny, it was chilly. Thomson was glad he'd worn his overcoat. He stood for a moment taking in the scene across the field toward the sheds and beyond to Cardington House. He held onto his hat as Irwin allowed them to go aboard. Church stood rigidly to attention inside the entrance ramp and as Thomson passed he greeted him with a polite half smile.

"Good morning, young man," he said.

Thomson and his group were led by Irwin along the catwalks from the rounded bow. Crewmen and engineers had been posted at intervals. He passed Binks, who stood ramrod straight.

These chaps are not military and here they were doing their best to appear so.

This showed respect and he liked that. He wore his benevolent headmaster expression as he moved along. Disley stood at the door of the electrical room. He nodded to Thomson.

Not so servile, this one. Probably intelligent!

Then there was Sky Hunt, the chief coxswain. Thomson had taken the trouble to find out who was who. He'd heard about Hunt's no-nonsense reputation and his bravery concerning the *R33* breakaway, for which he'd earned the Air Force Medal. Thomson reached out and took Hunt's hand, surprising and pleasing the man. Thomson moved on, noting the areas leading to the passengers' section were somewhat spartan. This would need to be a topic for discussion.

Not as luxurious as a real ship, but we'll soon fix that.

Colmore, Scott, Richmond, Johnston, Rope and Lou, all in uniform, waited for Thomson in the lounge in a line with eight well-dressed civilians from the Royal Airship Works and the Air Ministry. As Thomson entered, they broke into applause and he went down the line shaking hands, saying a few well-rehearsed words while they praised him as the great architect of it all. Colmore and Scott took over the handling of Thomson from Irwin, who went to the control car with Lou to join Atherstone. Thomson was led out to the promenade deck where he could appreciate the extraordinary view and witness take off from the enormous windows.

In the control car, Irwin picked up the phone and gave orders to the tower crew foreman to be on standby for cast off.

"Is everybody ready in the control car?" he asked.

"All ready, sir!" Cameron, on elevators, and Potter, on rudders, answered together.

Irwin turned to Lou. "Let's pull up the gangplank and close the forward hatch."

Lou picked up the speaking tube to Church. "Bring in the gangplank and close the hatch."

"Right away, sir. Yes, sir!" Church answered in Lou's ear.

Lou glanced up at Johnston, leaning over the chartroom rail, who winked and smiled. Irwin turned to Lou again.

"Start engine Nos.1 and 2 and idle."

Lou passed this order to the engine cars via the telegraphs. They rang faintly below in the cars. This was followed by puffs of smoke from the starter engine exhausts. As the diesel engines kicked over, the propellers began to turn after slight hesitation. In a few moments, plumes of black smoke and diesel fumes spewed from the engines and drifted down the field. Moments later, the engines settled down and ran smoothly.

"Engines 1 and 2 are idling, sir," Lou said.

"Start engines 3 and 4," the captain ordered.

Lou went through the same process until all four were running.

Irwin picked up the phone to the tower again and held it. "Be ready on ballast. Ready on rudders. Start engine No. 5."

"Ready on ballast. Ready on rudders, sir," Atherstone repeated.

"Starting engine No. 5," Lou said, relaying the order to Binks and Bell, who were anxiously standing by. Lou caught a flash of Binks five years ago standing at Cardington gate, cap in hand. He'd come a long way.

Mr. Humble Pie!

Lou smiled. A puff of smoke came from the exhaust and the propeller started moving. The critical moment had arrived. Irwin put the phone to his mouth.

"Standby to slip."

Lou was impressed with Irwin. He'd studied him closely on Monday's short maiden flight. "Ready on reversing engine No. 2?" Irwin asked.

"Ready on No. 2, sir!" Lou confirmed.

"Be ready to increase revs on No. 2 to four hundred."

Irwin spoke loudly into the phone. "*R101* ready to slip." He listened for a second, then spoke again forcefully. "Slip now! Thank you, Cardington Tower."

The bow dipped after disconnection from the tower. The ship did nothing for a few moments, being suspended in air.

"We're free and clear of the tower, sir," Atherstone announced.

"Okay increase revs on reversing engine No. 2 to four hundred."

Lou passed the order to the engineers in No. 2 and the revs went up. The ship pulled back, her nose down.

"Increase revs on No. 2 to six hundred. Dump two tons at Frame 4," Irwin ordered. Atherstone released water ballast. The bow came up. Not nearly enough.

"Shut down reversing engine No. 2 and increase revs on the rest to six hundred."

"Shut down reversing engine. Increase revs all engines to six hundred, sir," Lou repeated.

The power on the four forward running engines increased and the ship turned smoothly away on a starboard tack toward the perimeter fence. She cast a giant shadow over the crowd gathered a hundred feet below, nose still dangerously low, wallowing like a whale in the shallows.

"Drop emergency ballast. Now!"

Lou grabbed the speaking tube to Church at the bow.

"Drop emergency ballast. *Right now!*"

Water cascaded from under the ship's bow and even though the amount of water was small, the effect was dramatic. The bow came up, but still not enough. The crowd below got soaked. The ship lumbered on, hovering over the country road toward a school where children waved handkerchiefs and scarves as the great monster approached. Still she wallowed. More water ballast was dropped from the forward frames. This time the children got wet, but it did nothing to dampen their spirits—quite the opposite; this was a wonderful game. They ran off screaming and laughing in all directions. The bow came up, at last, until she was flying straight and level.

On the promenade deck, Thomson was in good spirits. He and his entourage waved back at the crowd at the fence initially, and then to the children in the schoolyard. He was elated, relishing Irwin's maneuvering, which he presumed to be flawless.

"Superb getaway! Well done, Captain Irwin," Thomson exclaimed.

"Hear, hear!" Brancker and Knoxwood seconded. Not everyone was so sure. Some mumbled under their breaths. "We're too close to the damned ground for my liking," one R.A.W. engineer grumbled.

"I'd of thought we'd be a lot higher by now," another complained.

Scott peered out the window, his expression sullen.

The airship slowly gained altitude and, after reaching eight hundred feet, turned toward Bedford to show herself a second time. So many in this city were counting on the success of this vessel. Thirty minutes later, they turned south toward London. The chief steward approached Thomson.

"Good morning, sir. Breakfast will be served in the dining room in ten minutes, if that suits you, my Lord." He addressed Thomson a little more tenderly than he would've preferred.

"Splendid," Thomson said with a weak smile. "All this excitement makes one very hungry."

After a delicious breakfast of ham and eggs and freshly ground coffee, everyone gathered on the promenade deck to get a good view of the London skyline from a cloudless sky. The ship, now at twelve hundred feet, approached from the north, passing over Lord's Cricket Ground, close to Regent's Park, and then followed Edgeware Road along the edge of Hyde Park, bursting with vivid, autumn colors. At Hyde Park Corner, the ship turned toward Buckingham Palace. Its rooftop flag was absent.

The effect the ship had on the streets below Thomson thought was magical. Traffic came to a halt. Open-mouthed Londoners stopped in their tracks. *Cardington R101* traveled over Birdcage Walk to Westminster Palace, the heart of the British Government. The panorama was a beautiful sight: Westminster Hall, the House of Commons and Big Ben, now striking the bottom of the hour—8:30 a.m. Thomson gazed at the House of Commons. He thought of Lord Scunthorpe and his scathing remarks.

Now we shall find out who's right.

He didn't dare crow, even to himself. He wondered what Scunthorpe would think if he came out of the House of Lords at this moment and looked up.

Would he be inspired? No. Of course not!

Thomson glanced down at the spot on the quadrangle where he and Marthe had recently had tea with MacDonald by the river. Seeing that place was gut-wrenching. Everywhere he turned was a reminder of her. The ship made its way along Whitehall, over the Horse Guards Parade, on to St. James's Park Lake, and the Ritz Hotel. He'd requested they pass over these landmarks. For him it was enjoyable, masochistic torture. They traveled along Piccadilly to Piccadilly Circus. During this time, Thomson and Brancker stood together, separate from the others. They'd often talked about Marthe—not in depth as he did with MacDonald—but Brancker was aware of Thomson's devotion. Brancker had met Marthe a few times at the Ministry.

"I wish Marthe were able to witness this," Thomson confided.

"All in good time, CB. No doubt, she'll be impressed."

Brancker, in a well-cut, pinstripe suit today, appeared refined, not his usual rustic, country-gentleman self. He leaned on the promenade deck rail, monocle planted in his left eye, voice deep, accent rich and upper-class, toupée smartly combed and greased down.

"It's been a long time coming, but worth the wait, CB. You must feel very, very proud indeed," Brancker said.

"I do. I can't help myself. It's unjustified. I've had so little to do with it all really."

"You had *everything* to do with it."

The ship pressed on over the Strand, along Fleet Street, home of the British press. Thomson had an idea. Press photographers were out in droves this morning; he'd made sure of that. Tomorrow there'd be photographs of *Cardington R101* over every landmark. Sunday newspapers would be full of it, with whole pages and center spreads devoted to her maiden flight.

Marthe will read about it soon enough.

Thomson decided to address the Lord Scunthorpe situation head on. He beckoned everyone over. "Gather round. I have an announcement." He held his hand out toward the press buildings below as they formed a circle around him. "I hope after today we'll get full support from the Government and the press," he said.

"I should jolly-well think so, sir," Scott said.

"I want to announce that we're inviting one hundred Members of Parliament to make a flight in this airship," Thomson said. Everyone was surprised and most faces lit up.

"What a splendid, original idea," somebody said.

"A hundred MPs over how m-many flights, sir?" Richmond stammered.

"One, of course! That ought to shut the critics up," Thomson replied.

"Are you sure about this, CB?" Brancker asked, taking down his monocle and polishing it thoughtfully.

"Don't worry; nothing like a hundred will take us up on it. But our confidence will speak volumes!" Thomson noted Richmond doing his best not to appear negative, while Colmore, by his demeanor lacked confidence in the idea.

Damn, that man is weak!

"Trust me. This'll be a good move," Thomson assured them.

The airship passed by St. Paul's, Tower Bridge and the Tower of London. The time was nine-thirty. Having seen the sights, and London having seen the sight of her, *Cardington R101* headed over northeast London toward the Essex countryside, then Cambridge and Sandringham. Thomson had looked forward to spending time on the airship, working on his papers.

"There are some matters of state that cannot wait," he said grandly, excusing himself. "Come Knoxwood, we must earn our keep."

They headed to the promenade deck on the starboard side where a privacy curtain had been hung across the opening to form a makeshift office with an imposing desk and a leather executive chair.

45

SANDRINGHAM

October 16, 1929.

While the ship cruised silently at twelve hundred feet, Thomson sat and read through the papers in his dispatch box and ministerial files, glancing up every so often to appreciate the countryside. The surroundings and the silence made him calm and confident—just how he'd always imagined it. Knoxwood sat at a table preparing documents for Thomson to sign. He got up and brought them to Thomson.

"Can't beat this, what?" Thomson said.

"Smoother than a liner, sir," Knoxwood replied.

"This makes the perfect office, such peace and quiet."

While Scott and Richmond chatted with the rest of the VIP's, Brancker and Colmore paid a visit to the control car, where they found Irwin and Lou with two coxswains. As Brancker entered, he threw up his arms in exultation.

"This is magnificent!" He ran his hands over the hardwood and his eyes over the instrumentation. "The workmanship and finish are extraordinary. We should call her HMAS *Victory II*, or HMAS *Queen Victoria*, or some such splendid thing!" After a few minutes, Brancker, an experienced pilot, couldn't resist. "May I?" he asked.

"Of course you can, sir," Irwin replied. He instructed both coxswains to leave the control car and for Lou to take over the elevators. Brancker took the rudder and turned the wheel gently around from port to starboard. He then turned the ship through twenty degrees, the massive bulk, moving like a great sea galleon under canvas.

"I say, she seems responsive. What do you say, Irwin?"

"She's responsive to the helm all right, but she's underpowered and grossly overweight." Colmore sighed in exasperation. Irwin was confirming everything Richmond and Rope feared—but were things even *worse* than they thought?

"You mean *seriously* overweight?" Brancker asked.

"Fully loaded, this ship wouldn't get off the ground, sir."

"Hell, you don't say!" Brancker exploded. "He's all set to go charging off to India before Christmas!"

"That'd be suicide. This ship's quite unserviceable at the moment, sir," Irwin replied.

Lots of questions went through Lou's mind.

Would the lightening help to any significant degree?

Would they need to push for an extra bay?

Even then, would that really be enough?

Irwin's pronouncement was devastating to Colmore. Brancker raised his hand, indicating Thomson's location on the promenade deck above them.

"We'll need to keep his Lordship in check somehow. We must develop a strategy for dealing with the problem before things get out of hand. Damn it all! He's talking about inviting a hundred politicians to go on a flight *next week*."

"Oh dear," Colmore said, his sad eyes searching the countryside.

After circling Cambridge University for ten minutes, the airship sailed on toward the North Sea coast and by 11:00 a.m. they'd arrived at the King's country home at Sandringham, a magnificent red brick house, quoined in white stone, set in manicured gardens. While gardeners raked the lawns, pleasant smells of burning autumn leaves wafted heavenward, permeating the airship.

The ship was flown slowly in wide circles, showing herself to the King and Queen who had emerged from the French doors onto the stone terrace. The royal couple slowly walked down the steps to the gravel path and stopped. The Queen waved a red silk handkerchief, while the King stood motionless at her side, his right hand raised. Thomson was thrilled they'd been noticed by the royals.

"God save the King!" he exclaimed.

"God save the King, indeed, sir!" Brancker echoed, and then under his breath to Lou, now at his side, "God save us all!"

After a final wave, the King and Queen made their way unsteadily back up the steps and re-entered the building. The airship was turned toward the bay of the North Sea. Twenty minutes later, they crossed the water and traveled toward Boston and Nottingham.

A luncheon of tomato soup, Dover sole, gooseberry tart and custard was served in the dining room at noon, accompanied by a Beaujolais '22. Thomson was conservative in his drinking, especially during the day. After two or three glasses of wine, Scott requested brandy and after one or two of them he stood up. "Would anyone care to join me in smoking a fine cigar in the smoking room? We can find out if it's air-tight," he said with a broad grin.

The chief steward wasn't amused, but Thomson's face also broke into a grin. "What a smashing idea, Scottie. I find the idea of lighting up and smoking a cigar, surrounded by five million cubic feet of hydrogen, quite *irresistible!"*

The stewards looked from one to the other.

"Can we bring you coffee, gentlemen?" the chief steward asked.

Thomson stood. "Yes, please. And lead us to the smoking room. We'll take coffee there. That room needs christening."

The chief steward looked down his nose. "Very well, sir. Follow me."

He led the way with Thomson, Brancker and Scott, close behind. Only one of the R.A.W. people joined them. Knoxwood excused himself, saying he had more work to do. The rest returned to the promenade deck to admire the view of Nottingham.

Thomson was a little disappointed once in the smoking room—depressing without windows and not terribly well-lit. He thought now perhaps his own bravado had been overdone. The chief steward poured coffee and then brandy from a drinks trolley. He then brought drinks on a silver tray. He passed round a box of Cubans. Each man solemnly took one, as if it might be his last, cut the end with the cutter and lit up with a lighter, (prudently chained to the trolley). The room soon filled with smoke, which the extractor fan fought bravely to overcome.

"You may leave now, steward, if you like," Thomson told him.

"It's quite all right, sir. I'll be here, if you need anything," the chief steward said between coughing fits. He then slunk away and sat on a chair in the corner. Thomson suspected the poor man was afraid to open the door. The truth was that Lou had instructed him to stay and keep a watchful eye on the smokers.

While Thomson smoked his cigar, Lou inspected the ship, running into Sky Hunt as he moved along the catwalk.

"Hi, Chief, what do you think?" Lou asked.

"It's flat calm out there, even so, the bags are rubbing. Let me show you," Hunt said. He led Lou to the stern and from there, they moved down the length of the ship to the bow. Hunt pointed out locations where gas bags were in contact with the ship's frame.

"In rough weather, they'd really be getting ripped up," Hunt said.

"I think she's getting heavy," Lou said.

Hunt gestured toward the bags. "Here's the reason: the bags are getting full of holes and the valves are discharging gas—she's losing lift all the time." They walked past the hissing gas valves and Hunt continued. "I'm not happy with these valves. In bumpy weather they'll be discharging even more gas."

Richmond appeared. "Discharging! What do you mean?"

"Gas. Lots of it, sir, from the valves and the bags," Hunt explained, but obviously Richmond already knew. Lou returned to the control car.

Later, Thomson and the cigar-reeking smokers returned to the promenade deck. The chief steward immersed all their cigar butts in a bowl of water before allowing them out. By now, Richmond was back from his own inspection.

"Well, as you can tell, the smoking room experiment was a complete success," Thomson declared as he rejoined the others. "Where are we now, Richmond?"

"Leaving Leicester and approaching Birmingham, Lord Thomson."

Over Birmingham the passengers peered down at the tight-knit masses of tiny houses. Once again, traffic came to a halt. Elated citizens got out and waved and honked their horns.

46

MISHAP AT CARDINGTON TOWER

October 16, 1929.

S oon, they were over Northampton, heading toward Bedfordshire. At 2 o'clock passengers were served afternoon tea, digestive biscuits, and Thomson's favorite cucumber sandwiches. They were nearing Cardington. In the control car, with Atherstone and Lou at his side, Irwin was becoming concerned. Lou had briefed him on Hunt's comments.

"She's getting heavy and losing gas doesn't help. It's happening so rapidly," Irwin said.

"Do you want to dump ballast yet, sir?" Lou asked.

"Yes. Dump five tons from Frame 2 and five tons from Frame 8."

"Right you are, sir," Atherstone said, grabbing ballast release valves.

"I'm going to drive her hard and keep her nose up. Increase all engines to eight hundred."

"All engines to eight hundred, sir." Lou sent the message to all cars and the engine notes increased.

"How are we off for fuel?" Irwin asked.

"We got plenty. Enough for eighteen hours," Atherstone replied.

"Dump water ballast on Frames 3 and 6," Irwin ordered.

"Dumping ballast on 3 and 6, Captain. We're down to five tons of water ballast," Atherstone said.

"Save that. We might need it at the tower. Damn. She's sinking like a rock. Dump five tons of fuel from Frame 5."

"Did you say *fuel,* sir?" Lou asked.

"Affirmative. Start dumping *fuel.*"

Atherstone carried out the order. From the control car they watched diesel fuel cascading over the fields.

"That's good for the animals and crops," Atherstone said.

"Can't be helped," Irwin muttered.

Lou imagined what the farm would smell like when the cows came home tonight. Soon, they were within three miles of Cardington at an altitude of four hundred feet. They were surprised by a voice from above.

"Okay, I'll take over now," Scott shouted from the chartroom, his speech slurred. Lou, Irwin and Atherstone stared up in disbelief.

"Steer off forty degrees—" Irwin began.

"Steer straight in from here," Scott barked. "Don't you change course!"

"I was planning to avoid the fairground, sir," Irwin said.

"No, we've got plenty of height. Go straight across the fairground to the tower. We can't mess around. Daft place for a fair anyway."

"But sir, that would be—"

"Just do as I say, Irwin," Scott hollered, bounding down the stairs. "Make room, Atherstone. Go upstairs and wait for my orders." Atherstone reluctantly did as ordered, mounted the stairs and stood with Johnston at the chartroom rail.

"Cut power to dead slow all engines," Scott ordered.

"Dead slow all engines," Lou repeated looking to Irwin for confirmation. The captain merely nodded. Lou relayed orders to the four forward driving engine cars, 1, 3, 4 and 5, via telegraph.

"Start reversing engine No. 2 to idling speed," Scott shouted. Lou relayed that order. Potter on rudders instinctively steered away from the fairground. Scott leaned across and grabbed the wheel. "Hold your course I told you!"

"Yes, sir," Potter mumbled. A few minutes later they were over the fairground. The music drifted up to the control car. Lou glanced down and saw the gypsy at the opening of her tent. She stood looking up, her hands on her hips. He didn't know if she could see him, but felt her eyes on him. Moments later, she'd disappeared. He thought perhaps it'd been his imagination. The people at the fairground were thrilled at the spectacle, waving furiously. Those on the Ferris wheel yelled like crazy people, from what appeared to be eye level.

"Okay, increase revs on reversing engine No.2 to four hundred," Scott ordered. "Cut all other engines to dead slow."

"They're already at dead slow," Irwin said.

"Er, right. Continue on. We'll coast in from here."

The airship passed over the Cardington fence where the crowd had doubled in size since morning. Cars sounded their horns; flags, handkerchiefs and scarves were waved, resembling a soccer crowd. The ship wasn't aligned with the tower and their altitude had been misjudged.

"We're not gonna make it. We'll have to go around again, sir," Irwin said.

"Er, yes. I think you're right, Irwin. That coxswain messed up. Get us out of here. We'll start over."

Irwin took a deep breath. "Go to full power on 1 and 3—cut power on 2!" The ship swung away from the tower and, when safely clear, Irwin fired up engines 4 and 5 to bring the ship up with dynamic lift. They climbed to four hundred feet and traveled toward the east, making a huge circle in preparation for another attempt.

Twenty minutes later, they were in position to try again. As soon as Irwin had the engines set at the right revs, Scott stepped in again and took over. Precisely the same thing happened and again they had to start from scratch. After dumping more fuel, the third attempt went slightly better, and as they approached the tower, Irwin gave instructions for the mooring line to be dropped. Lou communicated with Church at the bow.

"Church, drop the mooring line."

Church shouted a 'Yes, sir' back to him. Lou knew he'd have the hatch open, ready to drop the line. The ground crewmen were also at the ready. Then Lou saw Freddie, like a sprinter coming out of the starting blocks. He'd never seen the boy run before. He seemed to hop and run at the same time, but even with his limp, he was swift. Freddie raced under the airship toward the bow, where he knew the line would be dropped. Lou saw the other crewmen running after him waving their arms frantically—to stop him. Freddie turned, and seeing the others chasing him, ran all the harder, throwing back his head and laughing hysterically. Lou couldn't hear them; Freddie's laughter and their warning shouts were drowned by the engines, carousel music and spectators. The frustrating scene was like a hideous mime on some great stage. Lou saw the line thrown down and Freddie, like a whippet go for it.

Why didn't anyone tell the kid to use the damned mat!

As Freddie grabbed the line, an arc of static electricity hit him and his body arched. He stiffened and fell backwards, striking his head on the ground where he lay motionless. Lou had seen everything. He was totally distracted.

Damn, is he dead? Oh, no, please!

He was jarred back by Irwin's voice.

"She's sinking fast! Dump the last five tons of ballast at Frame 7 and five tons of fuel from Frame 8!"

Lou hesitated for a second, looking at Irwin, questioning his order.

Surely not. We can't dump fuel and water on Freddie!

"Do it! *Right now!*" Irwin yelled. Lou came out of his stupor and grabbed the ballast discharge valves. Scott did the same with the fuel dump lever. Freddie lay on his back, eyes wide open, legs spread apart. Water ballast and diesel fuel cascaded over his body, fresh, young face and shiny boots.

"Pay attention, we're closing in," Irwin said.

"I'm going to the bow to direct the operations," Scott said, climbing the stairs. "Atherstone, you come back down to the control car."

Docking and locking onto the tower took another hour, due to Scott's continued meddling. Lou watched the ground-crew foreman yelling at his men to get away from Freddie and attend to lines dropped from the ship.

On the promenade deck, Thomson was oblivious to the calamity below, but suspected the docking operation wasn't going well. He calmly addressed the Royal Airship Works staff standing stiffly before him, while the ship lurched and bumped against the tower. They looked uncertainly at Thomson in the surreal lighting emanating from the fairground.

"I want to congratulate you, Colmore, and your staff, for the successful culmination of all your years of hard work. This has been a great day. This is the beginning of a new era in British aviation …"

From the control car, Lou watched an ambulance draw up alongside the airship. Freddie's body, draped with a sheet, was placed on a stretcher, carried to the ambulance and loaded into the back. Lou winced as the ambulance men slammed the doors, guilty that he'd got Freddie the job in the ground crew. This was bizarre. He couldn't understand it. And how the hell was he going to break the news to Charlotte?

The ship was locked onto the tower just after 6 o'clock. The throbbing engines were shut down and the sounds of shouting and confusion grew faint, allowing the carousel organ and screams from the rides to wash over the field. Lou and the other officers went ashore where Thomson was already speaking to the press, surrounded by R.A.W. personnel. As soon as the elevator doors had slid open, flashbulbs had popped. Thomson was delighted the journalists had turned up on schedule.

"How was your flight, Lord Thomson?" a reporter called.

"I must say, I've rarely had a more pleasant experience than I've had today—with a feeling of safety and well-being. We've all been comfortable and dined like kings amid luxurious surroundings. I spent some hours working in peaceful seclusion. This has been a wonderful day, gentlemen. The views from the ship have been magnificent. We even watched a fox hunt —and what a colorful sight that was!"

"Do you look forward to going on a voyage soon, sir?"

"I'm hoping to make the trip to India during the Christmas recess and that, I can tell you, will be a welcome interlude, where one can relax and read, or work with the comforts of an ocean liner."

"You said Christmas, sir? Did you mean this coming Christmas? That's less than three months away."

"Look, there are more trials to be done and all sorts of tests. I refuse to put any pressure on our Cardington team. I want to make one thing perfectly clear. As I said in 1924 when I introduced the program, no long distance flights will be undertaken until the staff is ready and testing is complete. I said then: 'Safety first and safety second, as well.' We shall live and die by that policy. Good night, gentlemen."

An unknown reporter shouted from the back of the group.

"Sir, are you aware that a young ground crewman died this evening?"

Thomson's pleasant mood was shattered. This would put a damper on the weekend newspaper stories. He looked round helplessly at his people.

Damn, why didn't someone tell me!

They shuffled around in embarrassment.

"What happened?"

"We believe he was electrocuted, sir."

"My goodness. Er, …this is the first I've heard of it. I'm deeply saddened. My condolences and my prayers go out to the young man's family."

Lou watched Thomson walk to the car, his pain evident. It all seemed such a shame after what had appeared to be a good day—except for Irwin's reservations (also unknown to Thomson, as yet). Thomson climbed into the car and the door was slammed shut. Everyone dispersed.

Lou went home. Behind him, the carousel music played on, the girls on the Ferris wheel squealed with delight and the hideous clown in its glass box threw back its head and laughed hysterically.

47

BLACK TUESDAY

October 29, 1929

Freddie was buried in St. Mary's graveyard on October 29—a day of misery that became known around the world as 'Black Tuesday.' The American stock market crashed almost as soon as Wall Street opened and panic ran its course. There were stories that afternoon of people throwing themselves out of high-rise windows in New York.

Burial had been delayed due to the requirement of an autopsy—Freddie's death occurring in unusual circumstances, they said. Attendees were not concerned with world finance, but it added to the mood of despair; their focus was on Freddie's poor family. The funeral was heavily attended with crewmen, officers and their wives present. Freddie's grave had been dug at the back of the cemetery, farthest from the road, almost in the shadow of Shed No.1. The higher echelon of the R.A.W. didn't attend, in case the program garnered too much adverse publicity. Billy stood in the drizzle with Lou and Charlotte, still badly shaken. The boys had become inseparable. Billy, though traumatized, decided to remain at Freddie's home for the time being, since his presence gave the family some comfort.

Lou had entered the house around 7 o'clock the evening Freddie died. He walked into the living room, his face ashen. Charlotte looked up from her sewing and knew instinctively something was seriously wrong. She jumped to her feet.

"Lou. What's the matter?"

"Freddie."

"What's happened to him?"

"He's dead."

"Oh, my God, no!" she sobbed. "What happened?" Her voice trailed off in despair.

"He ran and grabbed the mooring line and fell down dead."

"No!" Charlotte sank back onto the couch again, screwing up her face.

"It made no sense. None of us could understand it. I feel terrible."

"Damn these airships!"

"Joe Binks told me later Freddie had a weak heart."

"Damn these *rotten, bloody* airships!"

"He should never have been in that crew. That family kept his condition from us."

"That ship is cursed!"

"If I'd known, I swear he'd never have been on that field."

"And this *city* is cursed."

"Charlotte, please don't."

"And now *we're* cursed, too ...Don't you see that, Lou?" she said, as though entranced.

"It was just unfortunate—nothing to do with the airship."

"Just unfortunate! *The boy's dead!* He was here with us in this room only last week. Poor Freddie ...oh, that poor boy, he was just a child. I loved him so much." She was inconsolable and floods of tears flowed down her cheeks. Lou felt wretched and powerless. Freddie had become like her own child.

"You came in the door with that same look on your face when Josh died. How many more times do I have to see it? I can't take this anymore!"

Lou sat beside her and put his arm around her. "Charlotte, Freddie had a bad heart, my darling."

"What about Billy? He'll be next. I shouldn't have allowed you to bring him into this dreadful business. That ship is cursed!"

"It's not *cursed*."

"Oh, it's cursed all right. They're *all* cursed!" Charlotte sneered. Everything was crystal clear now. Only hell lay ahead. She stopped crying, wiped the tears and stared out the window into the darkness. After a few moments, she got up, left the room and went upstairs.

Charlotte took to her bed, where she stayed for three days, unable to return to work. The morning of the funeral she put on the black frock Freddie had admired at the party and a black, heavy topcoat with a matching hat, lent by Mrs. Jones. It was cold and windy at the grave site. She was chilled to the marrow and practically catatonic. Freddie's father told her they'd dressed him to look nice in the clothes she'd bought him, including the boots. He thanked her for being kind to him.

The following week, ill and deathly white—accentuated by her black mourning garb—Charlotte trudged to Putroe Lane in the rain and knocked on the Irwins' door.

"Olivia, may I come in?"

Olivia held out her arms and hugged Charlotte. "Oh, Charlotte, you poor dear. Come in and sit down by the fire. Give me your wet things."

Charlotte took off her coat and headscarf. Olivia hung them over a chair to dry by the fire. "Here, sit and warm yourself. I'm going to make you some coffee," Olivia said.

While Olivia was in the kitchen, Charlotte sat staring into the flaming coals. Soon, Olivia reentered the room with a tray of coffee and homemade cake.

"I needed someone to talk to," Charlotte said.

"I'm glad you came."

"I've been so miserable."

"Poor, wee Freddie. *Everybody's* sick about it."

"I'm so worried, not just for Lou—but there's Billy, my best friend's boy—and everyone else. We've got to know everybody here now."

"You're worried about the airships?"

"Yes, of course, aren't *you?*" Charlotte asked, in disbelief.

"Freddie's death wasn't due to the airship. Bird said Scott made a balls-up of the mooring, but none of that had anything to do with the poor, wee lad's death."

"People said he'd been electrocuted," Charlotte said.

"Bird told me there's always a kick of static electricity, but not enough to kill anyone. They're trained to stand on a rubber mat when they take hold of the line so they don't feel it. Freddie had a weak heart. They did an autopsy. Chasing after the line must have killed him. He wasn't even supposed to touch the line—it wasn't *his* job. They said he bashed his head when he fell down, too. Someone even said he broke his neck."

Charlotte wasn't listening. "I don't think these airships will ever be safe, Olivia."

"I'm *sure* they will, dear gel."

"How do we know that?"

"Bird isn't satisfied, but he thinks they'll get the problems sorted out, eventually."

"*Eventually!* A man was on the radio this week talking about an article in the *Aeroplane* magazine saying these airships are experimental and we must *expect* many more disasters."

"There're always going to be naysayers forecasting doom and gloom, pet. We must look on the bright side. We're officer's wives. We've got to give them our support."

"Yes, I know, but ..."

"You seemed so happy at the party. Then you went to see the gypsy, didn't you?" Charlotte looked sheepish. "What did she tell you?"

"She didn't say, exactly."

"But she's upset you, hasn't she?"

"I suppose she has. She gave me a bad feeling about the airship—as if she knew something. She kept talking about 'their big game' and said there'll be no winners—only *losers.*"

"She gave you the impression something bad would happen?"

"Yes. Perhaps it's already happened with Freddie dying—or maybe this is only the beginning ...Oh, Olivia, I don't know ..."

"She's told you nothing really, has she? Now you're worrying yourself to death."

"That's not all. She told me I would have a baby … one day."

"Well, that's good, isn't it?"

"In a way, yes, I suppose. She gave me the impression this would be after my life had changed ...after huge things happening ...after all the things making me miserable were resolved ...the decks cleared ...when all things unspoken were spoken ...when I'm *free* ...I will become whole again ...and only then, will I conceive." Charlotte shook her head from side to side. "I don't know how any of *that* can happen ...there're just too many things! ...I'm at my wit's end."

Olivia, although obviously burning with curiosity, didn't press it, lest she upset Charlotte further. "My poor, wee bairn. You need to get away for a rest. Couldn't you go to your mum's place for a while?"

"I thought about that. Lou even suggested it. He's going to be away a lot doing tests."

"Then you must go. I'll come with you to the station. They already know you're sick at the hospital. You need rest. You're drained."

48

OVER YORKSHIRE

November 1929.

Two days later, Olivia put Charlotte on the train to Wakefield, where she made the connection to Ackworth. While she recuperated at her parents' home, Lou took part in test flights aboard *Cardington R101*. The weather was perfect for these tests and, although pleasant, not useful for testing her durability.

The engines proved troublesome on two trips, but not as troublesome as Scott during docking operations. His ham-fisted interference created havoc, causing them to run into or over the tower several times. On a couple of occasions, he dropped ballast without Irwin knowing, sending the bow shooting upward. The officers grew sick and tired of him and by the end of the fourth test, were showing signs of strain. Any one of these botched attempts at docking could have easily resulted in the loss of the airship and everyone on board.

The Air Ministry also caused unnecessary stress by insisting they take government officials, MPs and civilian VIP's for pleasure trips around the countryside. These flights were intended to give the public the impression that the Cardington airship was *'as safe as houses'*—a phrase bureaucrats liked to bandy about. Once, they carried forty-four crew and forty passengers, plus the additional weight of a wet cover from the previous night's rain. This broke all records for being the largest number of people ever carried in the air, a fact proudly reported in the newspapers the next day. During the flight, *Cardington R101* flopped around the vicinity, barely able to stay afloat. Lou credited Irwin's flying skill and good luck for their safe return. Its confidence bolstered, the Air Ministry decided to go ahead with Thomson's plan to take a hundred MPs on a 'demonstration flight,' scheduling it for November 16[th.]

Ten members of Parliament on board for one of these joy rides had a serious scare one afternoon. No one knew the lift and trim equipment at the mast was out of adjustment. After casting off, the bow shot skyward at twenty-five degrees, and VIPs seated in the dining room ended up with their lunch in their laps. The sound of breaking crockery frightened them out of their wits.

That same week, a storm hit Bedfordshire without sufficient warning to get the ship put away in her shed. Lou was on board with the watchcrew while 80 mph winds battered the ship. Many thought she'd be wrenched off the mast and blown away, as R33 had been from Pulham. She remained, held fast by the mooring gear—a credit to Scott, who'd designed it. Officials were pleased with the ship's performance, but disappointed when they discovered the state of the gas bags. Adding to their dismay, the valves had expelled gas at an alarming rate, while the cover leaked like a sieve.

The night before the ship was to carry the hundred MPs, the weather deteriorated and the trip was postponed until the following week. In the meantime, *Cardington R101* sailed off to carry out her thirty-hour endurance test. The pleasure of it was that they were unburdened by politicians or Air Ministry bigwigs and able to consume the food and drink put on board for the MP's flight. With no one aboard to impress, Scott behaved himself most of the time. Lou witnessed Irwin make the best take-off so far without any drama. The weather, once again perfect, caused minimal gas loss from the valves, but the bags were still full of holes. The flight took them up the east coast over Lincoln, Darlington, York and Durham.

Over Yorkshire, after passing Scunthorpe, Scott came down to the control car. He called up to Johnston for the bearing to Howden. Johnston checked the map. "Three hundred and twenty degrees. About fourteen miles, sir," he replied.

"Okay, let's drop in on our friends at Howden," Scott said.

Capt. Irwin turned to the rudder coxswain. "Steer three-twenty."

The ship veered to port. Irwin raised his eyebrows to Lou.

"We'll show them what a real airship looks like," Scott said with a crafty smile. "Bring her down to six hundred feet, five miles out and then bring her down till you can see the whites of their eyes!"

Lou glanced at Scott before he disappeared upstairs. He didn't think Scott was being malicious—mischievous perhaps, reckless certainly—probably hoping to tweak Burney's nose. It made Lou uncomfortable.

The sky was clear and soon Howden Air Station loomed in the distance. They'd reduced altitude and were still descending. Lou, although pleased to see the old place, worried that the appearance of *Cardington R101* would infuriate Wallis—like a detested neighbor showing up on his doorstep uninvited, but a whole lot worse. When he raised his binoculars, his fears were realized. As they approached the dilapidated shed at 400 feet, Norway came out and stood at the doors in his tweeds, hands on hips. Wallis joined him, followed by *Howden R100's* Capt. Booth. Norway showed no emotion, except wonder, perhaps. He held up one hand, shielding his eyes, clenching his unlit pipe between his teeth. His mouth was set in that peculiar grin he wore when concentrating. Wallis scowled up at them, rubbing his temples. Lou knew he'd take this as a personal insult—which, of course, it was.

His migraine's gonna get a whole lot worse!

Norway removed his pipe and shouted something above the noise, cupping his hand over Wallis's ear. Wallis nodded his head vigorously up and down and replied with a grimace. Lou could see Wallis was seething and wondered what Norway had said to him.

I must remember to ask Nev when I see him.

Scott and the R.A.W. staff were content to sail on, confident they'd annoyed the hell out of their rivals in their own backyard. Lou knew Colmore wouldn't have allowed this stunt. It was bad form, and he, too much of a gentleman. Richmond would've felt the same. Both men were busy at Cardington House, working on a report to present to Thomson, addressing the ship's weight problems. This 'in your face' detour had been childish and fate-tempting. Repercussions would be *incalculable.*

Why go out of your way to make enemies?

Irwin grinned at Lou. "They've had their bit of fun. Now it's our turn." Lou was puzzled. The captain glanced up at Johnston leaning on the rail above. "Johnny, give me the bearing for Low Ackworth."

Lou understood. Seeing that beautiful place from the air in perfect weather would be a treat, but hoped it wouldn't upset Charlotte.

"Two hundred seventy-five degrees," Johnston called down. "Nineteen miles, Captain."

"Do you think they'll mind upstairs?" Lou asked Irwin.

"I don't suppose they'll notice. They're too busy tucking into the caviar and champagne," Irwin replied.

Twenty minutes later, the airship was cruising at six hundred feet, closing in on Ackworth Village and its three collieries, each with its own coal mountain. The fields, rivers and pastures appeared as beautiful as ever, even in November with the trees almost bare. Soon they were nearing Station Road. Many residents, hearing the engines, had come out and stood in the street. Lou spotted the obelisk and St. Cuthbert's through his binoculars—and then Charlotte's house. He smiled when he saw a wisp of smoke coming from the chimney. It was a sure sign.

Somebody's home!

"There's her house," Lou said, pointing. "Over there."

The door opened and Charlotte ran out into the front garden.

"Ah, look now, there's your missus," Irwin said.

Charlotte was followed by her parents and then Auntie Betty. Johnston came down to see for himself. "I think she's pleased to see you, mate!" he said. Lou's heart skipped a beat. He slid the window open, took out his handkerchief, and waved it. She spotted him and pointed. He felt relieved. She was looking better and blew him a kiss. As they sailed on, he watched Charlotte until she was out of sight. He hoped she'd come home soon.

The rest of that flight was uneventful, passing over many parts of England, including York and Newcastle, then Edinburgh and Glasgow in Scotland, and Belfast and Dublin in Ireland. Irwin took a detour of his own, steering the ship over his hometown of Bray, on the coast south of Dublin. They returned to England and thick fog over Stafford. Scott didn't interfere and landing was accomplished without mishap. Reporters were waiting when the officers disembarked. Scott was happy to give them a statement.

"This has been a magnificent flight. Everyone's been most comfortable. We've been doing rigorous turning exercises in the air and she's been behaving splendidly."

Scott was trying to say that this airship wouldn't break in two like *R38* had done. He didn't say the ship was overweight and the gas bags were full of holes. That would be broken to the public on another day perhaps—perhaps not.

Charlotte returned to Bedford a week later and went straight back to work. She pushed the worry and grief over Freddie under the surface where it lay with her other torments. At last, it was time for the MP's flight, or in Johnston's words, *'the flight of a hundred old men.'* Although the forecast wasn't favorable, the Air Ministry refused to postpone again; Thomson kept bringing it up. There was no way out.

On the morning of the flight, Lou attempted to climb out of bed, but Charlotte pulled him back. "Stay awhile, love," she implored.

"Let me check the weather first, honey." Naked, Lou climbed out of bed and while Charlotte laid back on her pillows admiring him, he went to the window overlooking the garden. Rain was coming down in torrents, wind howling.

"Great! I don't think anyone'll show up in this weather. I can spare you half an hour." He slipped back under the warm covers and took her in his arms.

"You cheeky dog. I need you for at least an hour," Charlotte said, pulling him closer.

"God, you feel so good, Charlie. Let's make it two."

"See what happens when I'm not around."

"It's been too long, my darling. Much, much too long," Lou whispered.

49

ONE HUNDRED MPS & AN ULTIMATUM

November 23, 1929

L ou put on his waterproofs and drove to Cardington in driving rain two and a half hours later. When he arrived, *Cardington R101* was rolling gently around on the tower while an army of men serviced the ship from below. Hydrogen was being pumped aboard and would continue to be until the last moment before takeoff. Boxes of food and drink were being carried up the tower stairs. Lou stopped Bert Mann to ask why they weren't using the elevator. Mann told him it was broken. Lou climbed the stairs as usual.

This won't please the old boys—if they bother coming.

He went to the control car. "Sorry I'm late, sir. Something came up," Lou said.

"I'm sure it did …nice having the missus back, I expect. No need to worry yourself. Maybe no one'll show up," Irwin said, checking his watch. "Hmm, ten minutes to ten. Boarding's at eleven. *Oh, Jeez.* Will you look at this!"

Lou glanced at the road. Two limousines were driving up to the gate.

"What are you going to do?" Lou asked.

"She's already as heavy as old Sister Malone's heart. Tell Sky Hunt to drain off half the fuel and ballast. Let's hope the weather gets worse," Irwin said, peering at the waterlogged field. "It's beginning to look like Lake Superior out there—I guess they'll be comin' in two by two."

Lou went and found Hunt and relayed Irwin's message.

"Are they gonna fly in this?" Hunt asked.

"Doubtful, I reckon," Lou replied.

"Major Scott might have other ideas," Hunt scoffed.

Half an hour later, twenty more black cars had appeared at the gate. At 10:45 a.m. the gates were opened and they drove across the sodden field to the tower, where ground crewmen in raingear directed MPs to the customs shed. No one was deterred by the weather or the broken elevator. Lou went to the bottom of the stairs to check conditions and attitudes. Waves of huffing, puffing, determined, old men on walking sticks made their way into the tower to begin the slog to the top.

Lou went into the customs office—where many were getting checked for lighters and matches—before the climb. One of the men, a little rotund, fifty-something, Lou recognized as Winston Churchill. He was in the act of removing a leather cigar case from his raincoat and counting his cigars. Lou politely stopped beside him. He peered up at Lou defiantly.

"Sir, you won't be lighting those, will you?" Lou asked

Churchill gave him a haughty stare, mouth drooping, chin out.

"And who the blazes are you?"

"Commander Remington, sir."

Churchill glanced at Lou's insignias. "United States Navy?"

"Affirmative, sir."

Churchill's attitude softened. "Ah, the American." He stuck out his hand, smiling broadly. I'm honored to meet you. I know these things are deathtraps, but I don't intend to prove it—not today."

One or two MPs shuffling past gave Churchill a filthy look.

"Glad to hear that, sir. What's up with those folks?" Lou said.

"Don't worry about them. Not fans of mine, or my party."

Lou grinned. "And you don't have any matches, or lighters, sir?"

"Absolutely not. I've already been interrogated by this bunch."

"Good. Thank you, sir," Lou said. Churchill pulled up his collar and started up the tower stairs beside Lou. He shouted above the drumming rain.

"I hear there's a smoking room on board?"

"Yes, sir."

"Thomson told me he's already christened it, personally."

"That's true. He did."

"He's hung some fifth-rate oil painting on his office wall done by some daubing fool—probably a painter and decorator! He's asked me to brush in an airship for him. God knows why. Anyway, I thought I'd better come here and see the damned thing for myself first.

Lou laughed. "You picked a good day for *that*, sir!"

A massive wind blast made the tower shudder and rattle and rain showered down on them through the open sides.

"Do you think there'll be a flight today in this lot?"Churchill asked, eyeing the weather. Scott, in civilian clothes, was on his way up the stairs.

"Indeed there will, Mr. Churchill," Scott answered. "Even if Remington and I have to fly the bloody thing ourselves." Scott bounded past them two at a time. Lou gave Churchill a crooked half-smile and cocked his brow. Churchill understood.

"We may need to keep an eye on that one. I hope I can get coffee and some decent brandy on this old rust bucket—then at least I can die happy," Churchill said. They continued their ascent of the never-ending steps.

Less than forty miles away, black and silver clouds rolled like breakers across the skies above Gwydyr House. Rain pounded the Georgian windows in Thomson's office and cascaded down the brickwork. He stood peering out into the mist hanging over the river, listening to the hoots of invisible tugs.

He returned to his desk and sat down while the tugs continued sounding their mournful warnings. He felt the dreary dampness in the air due to lack of heat. Six table lamps lit the room in isolated areas, leaving the rest in gloom. He assumed Colmore and Richmond were waiting outside in the reception office. They'd be nervous and soaking wet.

Good. Let them be.

He sat for another ten minutes planning his attack. Marthe's framed photograph smiled up at him from the half-open desk drawer at his side, while the Taj, in its ornate gold frame behind him, dominated the room. Buck had hung it for him and later he'd had a picture light installed over it. He often sat staring at the architectural masterpiece, meditating. It gave him inspiration. He looked forward to Winston visiting with his paint brushes. Finally, he stood and drew himself to his full height and strode to the door. He threw it open with a beaming smile, putting his hand out to Colmore.

"Gentlemen, gentlemen, good of you to come. Come in! Come in!"

Both uniformed men got out of their chairs and shook Thomson's hand. Their dripping raincoats hung on the coat stand by the door.

"Morning, sir," they said together. Thomson noticed their faces brighten.

They're thinking 'He's in a good mood—things won't be so bad.'

"Oh, you shouldn't have got dressed up. There was no need."

This was all insincere banter, of course. They followed him in, carrying briefcases, wet hats under their arms. There was a sitting area with a low table and a couch and easy chairs set around the unlit marble fireplace. Richmond looked in that direction, but Thomson gestured for them to sit in the upright wooden chairs in front of his desk.

No good you looking over there, Richmond. This isn't going to be a cosy, little fireside chat.

They waited for Thomson to sit down. When he'd done so, they stared at the brightly lit painting of the Taj Mahal behind him, impressed.

"How was your train journey?" Thomson said casually.

"The weather's filthy out there, sir, coming down in buckets," Colmore replied as they sat down.

"Cats and dogs, eh? Same up there?"

"Worse actually," Richmond said.

"Not sure they'll be able to make that flight today," Colmore said.

Typical Colmore!

"Why the hell not?"

"Might upset the passengers," Richmond said, not touching the real reason.

"A spin around Bedford'll do them good—blow the cobwebs away! How many showed up?"

"When I spoke with Scott on the phone, he said forty-four had arrived," Colmore said.

"*Forty-four!* We must take them up if they've gone to the trouble of showing up in such foul weather. Excellent. They're as keen as mustard!"

"Forty is the maximum we've carried so far, sir," Colmore said weakly.

"Well, here's the chance to break your own record, man!"

Richmond rummaged around in his briefcase, bringing out a file.

Lou got back to the control car where Irwin was still eyeing the weather.

"How many are there now?"

"I just counted forty-eight. And more cars are arriving."

"Did you talk to Sky Hunt?"

"I did, sir. He's draining down fuel and ballast per your orders."

"It's getting worse," Irwin said.

Atherstone entered the control car. He looked worried.

"I've just looked this boat over from stem to stern," he said.

"And?"

"The canvas cover's leaking and breaking down. I could see daylight in a lot of places."

"What about the bags?"

"They're rubbing all right, sir."

"And leaking?"

"Oh, *yes!*"

"Lou, keep an eye on the passengers and keep a count. We're getting dangerously overweight. Keep me informed every fifteen minutes," Irwin said.

Lou checked his watch. It was 10:30 a.m.

Thomson still appeared amiable and his two airshipmen had achieved a reasonable comfort level. Thomson picked up a sheaf of papers and waved it in the air.

"I read your report. Seems this airship of yours is too heavy?"

"Yes, sir. Heavier than expected," Colmore answered.

"You may remember at the briefing in June I touched on the subject, sir," Richmond said.

"I do remember—and *you* made light of it! How much lift do you have?"

Richmond hesitated. "Around thirty-three tons."

"A bit shy of sixty, isn't it!" Thomson said. He glared at them in silence, while the wind screamed around the rumbling window frames. "It doesn't look as though we'll be getting to India any time soon, does it?"

He let the sense of failure hang in the air.

"The schedule will be delayed, I'm afraid, yes, sir," Colmore said.

Thomson stared at them, saying nothing. During these silences, the ticking of the pendulum clock on the mantel sounded as loud as Big Ben.

"'The schedule will be delayed.' You speak as if we have all the time in the world, Colmore."

"Sir, we deeply regret the delay, but we'd like to discuss solutions," Richmond said.

At this, Thomson brightened and smiled pleasantly.

"I must point out we followed the rules rigidly, especially regarding safety. And we've been innovative to an unprecedented degree. The Howden ship will be using highly flammable petrol, whereas we'll be carrying much safer diesel fuel."

"Yes, yes, you said all that before, Richmond. At least *they'll* have enough lift to carry fuel."

"Sir, we have options."

Thomson thought for a moment. "How much lift does Burney have?"

Richmond looked pained.

"They're saying they've got over fifty-three tons," Colmore answered.

"I doubt that's true," Richmond bristled.

"If *Wallis* is saying it, it probably *is* true, and we're going to look pretty damned silly," Thomson said.

Lou entered the dining room where the stewards had laid out a light buffet of starter dishes and snacks with tea and coffee. MPs were helping themselves, chatting happily, well into their cocktails. Lou counted twenty-three in the dining room, mostly standing. He went to the lounge—another thirty-nine. On the promenade deck on the port side there were eleven and on starboard, eight. Eighty-one total. He wrote it down. He spotted the chief steward.

"Chief, see Mr. Churchill over there, with the cigar?"

"Yes, I do indeed, sir. He's a scary one, that one—like *a ruddy bulldog!*"

"Tell the stewards to keep an eye on him—just in case."

"Ooooh, believe me, sir, we're watching him like a hawk. He makes me very nervous. I'm the nervy type."

"I see, well, I'm sorry to hear that," Lou said.

"Commander, I prefer to be called Pierre if you don't mind—it's Peter really, but I like it the French way, you know…" He smoothed a lock of hair back over his ear. Lou suspected he was wearing an expensive hairpiece.

"Okay, *Pierre* it is."

"How many more should we expect, sir? They're coming on board by the dozen."

"I'm not sure. You got plenty of chow?"

"Enough to feed the five thousand," Pierre answered.

Lou hurried off to the control car.

"How many you got now?" Irwin asked.

"Eighty-one and counting."

"How's Hunt doing?"

"Fuel and ballast drained as instructed, sir."

"There's no sign of a break in the weather. We'll give it thirty minutes. Anyway, make sure our passengers are comfortable."

"Aye, aye, sir."

Thomson leaned back in his chair. "Tell me about these solutions," he said, his tone reasonable.

"I'm proposing we lighten her, as I said in the report. We made a list of items we can live without …it was in the report."

Thomson showed them a look of disgust. He'd studied it.

"You intend to remove cabins and bunks and bathrooms—most disappointing!"

"We've already increased the capacity of the gas bags."

"How did you do that?"

"We slackened the harnesses, sir."

"The harnesses holding the gas bags in place?"

"Yes, sir."

Thomson tried to comprehend this. It was confusing. He glared at Richmond. "Why weren't they adjusted to give maximum capacity in the first place?"

Richmond looked uncomfortable. "It's not the ideal situation, sir."

This part Thomson hadn't properly understood in the report.

"I see," he said vaguely.

"And finally, I'm suggesting we add another bay," Richmond said.

An expression of well-planned incredulity came over Thomson's face. "Just how in the world would you do that?"

"It's in the report, sir. We'll need to part her and insert an extra bay which will carry another gas bag—giving us a further nine tons of lift."

"By 'part her' you mean cut the thing in two pieces?"

"Yes, sir, we'll build an extra section and insert it."

Thomson let them see he was irritated now. "Do you have any idea how embarrassing this is to the government and to me *personally*?"

Lou returned to the dining room. The place was heaving now, the plates picked clean. Tea and coffee were still being served by the stewards, but gin and whisky were in greater demand. In the lounge, Churchill sat with the unlit cigar in his mouth, removing it to take a sip of cognac or coffee once in a while. He looked up at Lou with a precocious smile.

"You see I'm behaving myself, Commander."

"It's much appreciated, sir," Lou responded.

"Besides, you've got all these people in white coats watching me!"

Lou laughed, continuing to count heads. He returned to the control car.

"Eighty-two on board now, sir."

"And they're still coming," Irwin said, pointing at the gates.

"Who was it said 'Nothing like a hundred would show up'?" Atherstone said. More cars were arriving and ground crewmen were escorting occupants to the tower under umbrellas.

Thomson had turned up the heat.

"We certainly do realize it's embarrassing and we sincerely apologize. But please, with respect, sir, understand that the design of this airship is entirely new—much of it experimental," Colmore said with uncharacteristic boldness.

"But *Burney's* people seem to be doing so much better, do they not?" Thomson snapped.

"They don't have the glare of publicity like we do, sir. We are trapped by it."

"So, it's all this publicity that is causing the airship to be so overweight, is it? Don't be ridiculous, man. I'm required to play the press every day like a damned Stradivarius—justifying your existence. Now, I'm forced to go before the House, cap in hand, and explain why it's necessary to tear the damned thing apart and rebuild it!"

"But sir, all this is easily explainable—" Richmond began.

Thomson's face became contorted with anger.

"I've favored you people from the start, giving you every advantage. Despite that, it looks as though the Howden ship is still the superior ship."

"We don't know that yet, do we, sir?" Colmore said, his face showing hurt.

"If that ship rolls out and flies rings around you, we're all going to have egg on our faces," Thomson snapped.

"I'm sure that won't happen," Richmond said.

"When is it coming out?"

"Howden's ready to launch now, sir," Colmore replied.

"If I secure funding, how long will these modifications take?"

"Three months, sir," Richmond said.

"We'll need time for testing after that," Colmore reminded them.

Thomson calmed down. "The Prime Minister's Conference is scheduled to begin next October. I want to make the trip to India and arrive back in time for that."

Thomson noticed Richmond's eyes dart back and forth to the painting of the Taj behind him. He seemed mesmerized by it. But overall they seemed to be getting comfortable again, believing the worst was over.

"That ought to be do-able, sir," Colmore said, now actually smiling.

"The Commonwealth Prime Ministers will have traveled for weeks to get here. I intend to demonstrate how airships will improve their lives and the lives of their citizens."

"I understand, sir. And you will be demonstrating your point brilliantly. It will be a major coup on your part," Richmond said. The meeting had gone according to plan, but Thomson wasn't quite done with them yet.

The weather conditions at Cardington had worsened, with winds up to 60 mph. Rain continued pounding the airship, but still more MPs arrived. By 11 o'clock, Lou had counted one hundred. He returned to the control car, where Scott and the captain were in a heated discussion. Atherstone was also present, but saying nothing. Irwin looked round at Lou.

"What's the count now?"

"One hundred, sir, plus forty-eight crew."

"I'm well aware of the count. I've given orders not to allow any more on board. Now, are you ready to depart?" Scott asked.

"This flight's canceled. The weather's worsening and we're overloaded."

"This flight certainly is *not* canceled, Irwin," Scott shouted angrily.

"I'm the captain of this ship and it will *not* be taking off today."

"Now you see here. I'm your superior and I demand you prepare for take-off."

"Indeed you are my superior, sir, but you are not the captain of this ship. *I am!*" Irwin and Atherstone stood shoulder to shoulder facing Scott, their arms folded, guarding access to the ship's wheels. "To take off in this weather with a hundred and forty-eight people on board would be suicide—unless, of course, it's your intention to wipe out half the British government in one fell swoop. I suggest, sir, with the *greatest* respect, that you return to the dining saloon and have yourself another drink with the other gentlemen." Irwin's words sank in. Scott, his face red with fury, was beaten. He turned abruptly and headed back upstairs. Irwin turned to Lou again. "Tell Hunt to drain off half the fuel and half the ballast we have left. And tell him to make sure and keep the gas bags charged all afternoon. Then instruct the chief steward to serve lunch."

"Aye, aye, sir!" Lou said.

Thomson stared at Colmore and Richmond for some moments, reminiscing and carefully considering his words. He was going to enjoy this.

"I'm going to tell you a story, gentlemen. During the Boer War, we received a message: 'CLEAR THE LINE IMMEDIATELY. I AM COMING THROUGH. I knew who 'I' was—it was Lord Kitchener. Now I realized, 'doing my best' would not be good enough. Saying 'I tried' wouldn't work either. Clearing the line and getting him through would be the only measure of success. I assembled a force of a thousand men and personally supervised the pulling of twenty railway cars off the tracks onto their sides. Kitchener got through, and from that day forth, he never forgot my name."

Thomson got up from his chair and, resting his hands on the desk, leaned over Colmore and Richmond. His piercing eyes bore into them.

"*Kitchener* did not recognize the word 'impossible.' *Kitchener* did not accept the concept of 'failure' …and neither will I. Your mission is set in stone. Do I make myself clear, gentlemen?"

Thomson stood up straight. Colmore and Richmond jumped up and came to attention. "Yes sir, very clear, sir," Colmore answered.

"Perfectly clear, sir!" Richmond echoed.

They froze as the telephone rang. It was Thomson's private line. He picked it up and listened. "Yes." A look of disbelief came over his face followed by fury.

Am I surrounded by fools?

"What time was this? On whose order? Find out and let me know."

He replaced the receiver and glared at them. "Someone up there has canceled the flight. I want to know *who* it was and *why*. There was a lot riding on this. Now, in front of the Government up there, we're being made to look weak—a if airships can fly only in good weather. They must be shown to be capable of flying in *any* weather! Got that?"

"Yes, sir!"

Thomson nodded for them to leave and sat down. No handshakes. He was done with them for now.

After Lou informed Pierre that the ship would not be leaving the tower, within minutes, an army of stewards laid out a lavish buffet on silver platters with every conceivable type of British food, only seen on the aristocratic tables of the finest houses and restaurants: pheasant, duck, grouse, turkey, chicken, beef, lamb, pork, baked potatoes, mashed potatoes, Brussels sprouts, peas, broccoli, carrots, runner beans, turnips and parsnips. And to go with that, an array of complementary sauces: white sauce, cheese sauce, mint sauce, Oxo gravy, Bisto gravy, cranberry sauce. The collection of wines available was worthy of a fine French restaurant.

A line formed and everyone attacked the buffet then made their way to the lounge to sit. They enjoyed themselves immensely and, although the ship was being buffeted by sixty mph winds, she was very stable. The cover leaked badly, but buckets were strategically located above the passenger area ceilings to catch the water, and efficiently rotated and emptied by crewmen. Lou prayed no one would fall through the ceiling onto the diners.

After lunch, a variety of exotic desserts was served: crème brûlée, chocolate soufflé, honey wine pears, and sherry trifle, as well as some not-so-exotic: spotted dick, date pudding, jam roly-poly, bread and butter pudding, rhubarb and custard. A handful of MPs went to the smoking room, including Churchill, where they smoked their Cubans. Lou saw to it that this operation was supervised by Pierre as before, keeping the door locked from inside with finished cigars properly doused. Lou made observations and reported to the captain every fifteen minutes, as instructed.

The feast was over by 4 o'clock and passengers began leaving. Irwin stood at the exit door of the lounge with Lou and Scott, who was in the same state of inebriation as their guests. Lou and Irwin felt Lady Luck had been kind and they were relieved it was over. The MP for Staines shuffled up to Scott with a group of other gentlemen. They shook hands.

"Thanks for a splendid flight, old man."

"Didn't feel a thing."

"Smooth as a baby's bottom, sir."

"I'll definitely fly with you again."

"If this is a sample of the food you'll be serving on these voyages, you can put my name down, Captain," the MP for Barking said.

Irwin grinned.

"Let's have some pretty gals on board next time, what!"

"Yes, wonderful."

"Reserve me a berth on the first India flight."

"Yes, and me, and me ..."

Scott's replies were just as daft and incoherent. Irwin and Lou shook their hands, all the while trying not to collapse with laughter. The flight of 100 MPs had been *a smashing success!*

PART SEVEN

Howden R100 flies over Howden Minster. December 16, 1929.

THE DUEL BEGINS

50

THE LAUNCHING OF HOWDEN R100

December 16, 1929.

It was ten minutes past two. The air over the Howden shed was dead calm, the sky, deep midnight blue, fading to black at its outer edges. Lou stood at the shed doors studying the full moon and scattered stars. He never failed to be amazed. He wondered where the animals were tonight. His question was answered by an owl tawit-ta-wooing off somewhere in the distance, followed by a chilling vixen's scream. Even after all these years, this place still had a magical, almost holy feel. He reminisced, recalling his first visit in '21 with the Navy, and then his many subsequent visits in the middle of the night, leaving Charlotte sleeping peacefully in their bed. Once here, he'd communed with nocturnal animals and ghostly memories of his dead buddies, to whom he felt he owed a heavy debt. Footsteps behind interrupted his thoughts.

"What are you up to, Lou?"

"Ah, Nevil."

"Barnes got back last night."

They glanced across the frost-covered field toward the bungalows. All the lights were on; everyone was up and around. Lou had traveled up by train with Billy the day before, having received word from the Cardington meteorological office that the weather would be settled enough for launching. When Norway met them in his three-wheeled sardine can, they squeezed into the thing and drove to the shed where cots had been set up for them to sleep in Lou's old office.

The works canteen would be operating during the evening and throughout the night. There'd be plenty of cold, hungry people around in the coming hours. Lou called and spoke to John Bull who agreed to pick up Billy's mother, Fanny, in Goole at 3:30 a.m. and bring her to see Billy off. John told Lou there was no way he'd miss out on seeing the launch of *Howden R100*.

After the flight of the 100 MPs, *Cardington R101* had remained on the tower under a condition of 'Storm Watch.' Due to windy conditions, it'd been impossible to walk her into her shed until the end of November. *Howden R100*, although completed and ready since early November, couldn't be launched until the Cardington tower was available.

The weather had remained unsettled until today: 16th December, 1929. A whole contingent of R.A.W. people, including Colmore, Scott and Inspector McWade, traveled to Howden and were ensconced in the Railway Station pub and one or two bed and breakfast establishments around the village. The ship's officers, Capt. Booth and Capt. Meager had been in Howden for over two months.

Out of the darkness, John Bull's Humber came chattering across the gravel driveway, up to the parking area beside the shed. Another car followed, carrying George Hunter and a photographer from the *Daily Express*. They also had a reporter from the *Hull Times* with them. After saying hello, Lou found Billy and sent him to the canteen to bring tea and toast for John and Fanny.

He then took John and Fanny to the office for half an hour, where it was warm. Norway disappeared on board the airship with Booth and Meager. The aerodrome was coming alive. Two buses arrived with the crew of riggers and engineers. Shortly after that, another, smaller bus with Cardington R.A.W. staff appeared. Next came a convoy of twenty-two buses from the barracks in York, carrying five hundred soldiers. The narrow road leading to the air station became choked with traffic.

John and Fanny retreated to the edge of the field and stood with the tiny crowd from surrounding areas. The hundred and fifty foot high shed doors were opened, revealing *Howden R100's* silver bow in the arc lights. Soon, Molly Wallis came and took John and Fanny back to her bungalow, out of the bitter cold for more hot drinks. Wallis, in a smart black overcoat, entered the shed to prepare for the extraction with Capt. Booth and the riggers ballasting up. Though gaunt, Wallis looked in good spirits and greeted Lou warmly.

"How are you, sir?" Lou asked.

"Wonderful, thank you, Lou."

Norway had told Lou that Wallis had been in Harrogate with Molly trying to relax, but had been suffering, not only from migraine headaches and insomnia, but also nausea and lack of appetite.

"I just had a huge breakfast, and once the birth of this creature is over, I shall feel even better," Wallis told him.

The R.A.W. officials gathered in a group at the front of the shed where they were joined by Wallis, Norway and Lou. There were no pleasantries, no handshaking, no attempts at cordiality; they merely swung their arms trying to keep warm and ignored each other. They had reached a critical period in the fight to the death between the dueling airships—a moment of truth. Lou wondered would this ship fail its initial tests, too.

Unlikely!

The ground rules were laid down by Scott, in charge of the operation on behalf of the R.A.W. However, he'd allow Wallis to oversee the removal of the ship from the hangar before taking over. Wallis and Scott met with the army colonel and a sergeant to discuss the formation of the walking party. Scott set things up as he'd done at Cardington in October.

The crew of ten riggers, including Billy and Jessup, six engineers, and three ship's officers, one of them Lou, climbed on board through the control car. Norway followed and went upstairs to the observation windows. Lou remained in the control car, which was much larger than that of *Cardington R101,* since the chartroom formed part of the control car itself.

Everybody was in position. Wallis gave the order through the bullhorn for the soldiers to take up the ropes. Floodlights made the scene surreal; clouds of exhaled breath from straining shadows and silhouettes; ten thousand footprints in the frost. The ship, over two football fields long, was eased out into the darkness to weak cheers. It was 6:20 a.m.

Once the airship's stern had cleared the doors, Scott took command, directing soldiers in lockstep to pull her out to the middle of the field. Wallis stalked off to one side where he watched them manhandle his creation. The bow was turned from the shed and pointed toward the open fields.

Molly rushed forward from the crowd and hugged Wallis, kissing his cheek, while people clapped and cheered. He showed no emotion, except embarrassment. They stood together for a few minutes, surveying the magnificent, silver structure, like its womb, overwhelming and gargantuan, gradually becoming bathed in the rising sun's glow.

The soldiers formed a line around the perimeter, keeping hold of the ropes while Scott checked the ballasting of the ship. The engines were started and warmed up. When Scott was satisfied, he stepped aboard, beckoning Wallis to join him in the control car. Wallis left Molly with a brief nod and trudged to the ship. Before disappearing inside, he turned and waved to her and at that moment, the cheer of approval rose to its loudest. Lou smiled at Wallis and shook his hand as he came aboard.

How proud they are of this man—and rightly so.

Wallis and Scott remained in the control car.

"Are you ready, Captain Booth?" Scott asked.

"Yes, sir."

"Then let's get the hell out of here!" Scott grunted.

Booth opened the sliding window and instructed the sergeant to be ready to cast off and then to Lou, "Drop half ton at bow and stern simultaneously, Commander Remington," he ordered.

"Aye, aye, sir," Lou answered. Water gushed from the outlets of the ballast tanks, causing soldiers to scatter and the ground to become slick. The ship was immediately drawn upwards by invisible forces.

"Let her go now!" Booth called. "Thank you, sergeant; thank you all."

The soldiers cheered and shouted up to them.

"Hooray!"

"Good luck!"

"God bless!"

Howden R100 lifted into the pale blue sky. All faces on the ground were raised heavenward in wonder.

"Go to slow ahead on Engines 1 and 2," Booth ordered. With increase in momentum, the elevator coxswain eased her bow up to six hundred feet. The rudder coxswain, following Booth's orders, circled over the village of Howden as they gained height. Lou admired the old minster in the early sunlight—a stunning sight from the air.

"How's she feeling on the wheels?" Booth asked.

"Light as a feather, sir," the rudder coxswain replied.

"Like silk, sir," the height coxswain confirmed.

Lou looked at Wallis and Scott. They must have heard this, but their faces remained impassive. Lou would tell Norway when he got a chance. His calculations concerning steering assistance must have been on the money.

Thank God! I guess ol' Nevil ain't as dopey as he looks!

Booth called back to Johnston at the chart table. "Johnny, what's the bearing for York?"

Johnston looked at the chart. "Steer three hundred and forty degrees and look out for a big cathedral," he said.

Twenty minutes later, they were over York, flying at an altitude of thirteen hundred feet in a radiant, clear blue sky. People on the ground were excited and waved at the ship. After a salutary thirty-minute flight, Booth came back to Johnston.

"We need the heading for Bedford now, Johnny."

Johnston already had the answer. "Steer due south for now. I'll give you corrections on the way."

Wallis stirred himself. "I'm going for breakfast."

"Good idea. I could use some coffee," Scott said. He turned to Booth before mounting the stairs. "Send me word of any problems, Captain Booth."

"Yes, sir," Booth replied. "Why don't you join them, Lou? Captain Meager and I'll be fine."

People from the R.A.W. and the Howden team filed into the dining room and sat down to breakfast in two separate groups. The atmosphere was cold, with no attempt at communication beyond icy stares. The journey south was uneventful. Lou spent much of the time with Wallis and Norway on the observation deck. Though it was winter, the views of the pastures and towns of England were truly beautiful.

Charlotte expected Lou home for dinner and for Norway to join them. At noon, she went to the butcher's at the parade of shops and bought a loin of pork. As she left, a milkman was unloading crates of milk and carrying them into the dairy. Irwin, who'd stopped in to buy cigarettes at the corner store, walked out, bumping into Charlotte.

"Charlotte—how nice to see you."

"Oh, hello, Captain Irwin," Charlotte said. A droning in the sky in the distance interrupted them and they glanced up. The milkman put down the crate and dashed to the door of the corner store.

"Alan, the other ship's 'ere, come and see!"

The butcher, in his bloodied, blue and white apron, also came running out to join them and so did the owners of the dairy and greengrocer's. The sound of four of the six crackling Rolls-Royce engines got louder as the airship approached from Bedford.

"Now here comes trouble, eh, Captain?" the milkman said, looking at Irwin, who was getting his first glimpse of the Howden airship.

"I wouldn't say trouble, no," Irwin said. "She looks like a very fine ship to me."

The kids poured out from the school across the street. They crossed the road toward the shops and gathered around Charlotte and the shopkeepers, staring at the airship, jabbering with excitement.

"It's the other ship from up north," a kid yelled. The airship roared directly overhead. "That's *my dad's* airship. He's going to fly in that one," another shouted in a north-country accent.

"It's not as good as *my dad's*."

"My dad's is *bigger*."

"No, it's not, *my dad's is bigger!*"

"And my dad's is *faster!*"

"*My dad* says that one's going to crash and burn like this," one kid yelled gesturing with his hand, showing it crashing into the ground. "Boom!" he yelled. The first kid jumped on the other's back and they rolled on the ground in a fierce fight, the rest urging them on.

"Stop that, immediately!" Irwin shouted, grabbing them both by the scruff of the neck. One boy's eye was puffed and closing up. The other's nose was dripping with blood.

"You should be ashamed of yourselves. Don't *ever* talk like that!" Irwin scolded.

"See what I mean?" the milkman said. "It's been bad around here lately and it's getting worse. Those Yorkshire crewmen have been causing a lot of trouble in the pubs and the kids are fighting in the schools."

"Now be careful what you say, mister! I'm from Yorkshire. There's been a lot of bad feelings on all sides," Charlotte snapped, her own accent loud and clear.

The milkman held up his hand. "Sorry, miss, no offence. I meant nothing by it."

"All this conflict has spilled out of the offices and into the streets and schools," Irwin said to Charlotte.

"It's sad, if you ask me. I'd better go. I've got more shopping to do," Charlotte said, trying to force a smile.

"See you again, Charlotte. I'll tell Lou when I see him, not to be late home."

She went to the greengrocer's further along the parade to buy Lou's favorite roasting vegetables, tears running from her eyes as she went. After that, she went into the off-license for wine.

Lou was much later than he should have been. It took three hours to dock the ship, mostly due to everyone's inexperience with the mooring gear, but Scott's interference made matters worse. It reminded Lou of Freddie. They were forced to make multiple attempts at landing, leaving the mast and flying out and returning three times. When they finally docked, Wallis left the ship immediately and was driven to Bedford Station. A meeting had been prearranged for five thirty to assess the flight and schedule another test.

Since they'd time to spare, Norway asked Lou to show him *Cardington R101*. Lou was happy to oblige, interested himself to see how the lightening operation was going. Upon entering Shed No.1, they ran into Richmond. Surprise and contempt for Norway showed in Richmond's face.

"May I ask what you're doing in this shed?" he demanded.

Lou thought Richmond must be embarrassed—'caught in the act' by his rival. "You know Nevil Norway, Assistant Director of Engineering at Howden," Lou said. Richmond glanced at Norway. Norway stuck his
hand out. Lou glared fiercely at Richmond, daring him to be rude. After a brief hesitation, Richmond begrudgingly shook Norway's hand as though he were infected with 'Spanish Flu'.

Perhaps this visit wasn't such a good idea.

"I was going to show Nevil around—unless you have any objections, of course?"

"Er, I suppose, if you must. But don't be long. They'll be shutting down for the day."

"That's aw-awfully g-good of you," Norway said. Richmond smirked and hurried away without another word.

"What's the matter with him?" Norway asked.

"You'll see," Lou said. "Don't worry. We'll take a quick gander."

The ship had been handed back to the Cardington works staff. She'd been degassed and her gas bags removed. The hangar looked as though a bomb had dropped—parts and pieces everywhere. Glass removed from promenade decks was propped against the shed walls. A line of workmen, carrying toilets, lavatory basins and bunk beds, filed past Lou and Norway. The first one, carrying a toilet on his shoulder, smiled and winked at Lou, did a little jig, and broke into song. "Oh, we puts the toilets in, we takes the toilets out, we puts the toilets in and we shake 'em all about, we do the Hokey Pokey, we turn around and that's what it's all about—oi!"

Norway looked around, puzzled, but didn't comment. Lou called across to the shop foreman and waved. The foreman nodded. They had no beef with Lou.

"How's it going, Ronnie?"

"Oh, same ol' same ol'."

"You know what you're doing?" Lou said, grinning.

"Yeah, we gotta get the fat lady's weight down."

"We're just going to take a quick look, if you don't mind. You're closing up in a few minutes, right?" Lou asked.

"Not any time soon, no, sir."

Lou and Norway spent thirty minutes wandering around inside the ship. They went through the passenger quarters, the dining room and the sitting areas. Norway's eyes scanned everything. He admired the gold-leafed columns and other finishes, nodding his head in approval. During their tour, Norway inspected the servo assistance mechanism and frowned.

"That looks damned heavy," he said.

Later, by the light of the rising moon, they walked over to Cardington House. With the exception of Capt. Meager who was on watch, the key players gathered in the conference room. These included Scott, Colmore, Richmond, Inspector McWade, Irwin, Atherstone, and a few R.A.W. staff members. The day's flight was dissected and a list of defects drawn up: a leaking cylinder on one engine, a possible big end problem, and a vent that allowed in too much air, causing the gas bags to blow around. That would be sewn up. It was agreed that if these issues could be dealt with tonight, another test flight would take place in the morning, meaning they could take advantage of the favorable weather. In less than an hour, Lou and Norway headed home for dinner on Lou's motorbike—Norway looking like cartoon character in a furry, fleece-lined 'teddy' from the ship.

51

HOME FOR DINNER

December 16, 1929

Delicious aromas wafted up from the kitchen to greet them as they walked in the front door, just after 7 o'clock. Norway had brought a bottle of Scotch. He handed it to Charlotte.

"Ah, there you are. Thank you Nevil," she said as he kissed her cheek. "Dinner's been ready for some time."

"Sorry we're late, honey. We had to go over the flight at a conference," Lou said, giving her a hug and a kiss.

"That's okay, you're here now. It's a bit dried out, I'm afraid."

"I've got to take Nevil back later. He'll be working most of the night."

"I've made a bed up for you in the spare room, if you need it," Charlotte said.

"I'll have a snooze in one of the cabins, if I get a chance," Norway said.

Charlotte had laid the dining table on the middle level beside a blazing coal fire. She struck a match and lit the candles. "Sit down. I'll bring dinner up. Lou, there's a bottle of Claret on the sideboard if you'll open it, please," she said.

Lou did as he was asked and Norway sat down. Charlotte made a couple of trips bringing up the meals on a tray. The meat was dry, but Lou and Nevil were too hungry to notice. Lou suddenly put his hand to his head and laughed.

"There's something I've been meaning to ask you, but forgot, Nev."

"What?"

"When *R101* flew over the Howden shed, you and Barnes stood there gnashing your teeth … Remember?"

"How could I not? It was a pretty poor show."

"Barnes looked like he was about to blow a gasket."

"He was damned annoyed."

"What was it you shouted in his ear?"

Norway put down his knife and fork, casting his mind back. "Hmm. Ah yes, I remember. I said, 'Methinks they bite their thumbs at us, sir!'"

"What the hell's that all about?" Lou asked.

"It's Shakespeare—Romeo and Juliet," Charlotte said.

"Look, I'm just a dumb country boy. Did Barnes know what you meant?"

"Of course he did."

"And what did he say to that?"

"He shouted 'Let them bite them till they bleed!'"

Lou got the picture. "That's all he said?"

"Actually, no. Barnes is a religious man, but I've never heard him use such foul language before. Words I couldn't repeat in front of a lady," Norway said, eyeing Charlotte.

"Enemies for life?" Lou said. Norway nodded.

Charlotte refilled their glasses. "This is all going to end in tears," she said.

"So, what the heck's going on up in that shed, Lou?" Norway asked.

"They're removing stuff to lighten her."

"That's why he got so nasty?" Norway said.

"You caught Richmond with his pants down. He was humiliated."

"I can see that. But I'll tell you this—the work I saw in that shed, was magnificent. Puts *us* to shame," Norway said.

"Oh, how he'd love to hear that."

"Was Barnes on the flight down with you?" Charlotte asked.

"Yeah, but when we landed he got out of town immediately," Lou answered.

"I cooked enough food in case you brought him home."

"He wants to get back to his aeroplanes," Norway said.

"And Molly?" Charlotte asked.

"Yes, and Molly. He's been spending too much time away from her lately."

"Not good," Charlotte said.

"All he wants to do is organize Christmas with family. He loves Christmas," Norway said.

"Good for him," Charlotte said. "I'm *not* looking forward to Christmas—not one bit." She looked away into the flickering flames in the fireplace. Lou noticed.

"The docking took far too long today," Norway said.

"That gear will work okay once everyone learns how to use it—as long as Scott stays out of it," Lou told him.

"They seem to have too many experiments going on at the same time. Everything's complicated. They've got too much money at their disposal," Norway said.

"So were you pleased with the way she behaved, Nevil?" Lou asked.

"She was splendid. I was relieved about the servo gear."

"Barnes didn't say a word," Lou said.

"Oh, I can tell you he was pleased all right. That ship flew just the way he intended. I *know* he was satisfied."

"So do you think he'll make the trip to Canada?" Lou asked.

"I know he wants to go, certainly," Norway replied.

Without a word, Charlotte got up from the table to clear things away.

About 9 o'clock, Lou took Norway back to the mast to supervise the minor repairs. A huge amount of activity was taking place, both on board and on the ground. The gasbags, fuel tanks and ballast tanks were being topped up for next morning's flight.

Lou returned home, thankful to be with Charlotte and not on that frigid airship. He was due on watch at 6:00 a.m. When he reached the chilly bedroom, he saw the candle was lit on Charlotte's beside table and she was sleeping. He smiled as he stripped off his clothes and, with his teeth chattering, carefully lifted the bedclothes and snuggled down against her warm, naked body. She felt wonderfully comforting.

"Man, I'm so lucky," he whispered.

"You're bloody freezing. Don't you *dare* put your feet on me!"

By the time Lou went aboard the ship next morning, Norway and his mechanics had made the repairs. Norway was nowhere to be found. He'd crawled under some blankets in one of the cabins in his teddy.

Speed trials had been planned during this flight test, but in one of his in-flight inspections Norway had discovered a loose sealing strip across the rudder hinge, causing the cover to flap. Speed trials would have to wait and more repairs made. *Howden R100* was brought back to the mast in the afternoon in freezing fog without fuss. She was then walked to the shed and put away for the Christmas holidays.

When they were leaving the hangar, Norway came up with a brilliant idea—at least *he* thought it was brilliant. And the more Lou thought about it, the more he liked it. Norway said he was thinking of asking his girlfriend, Frances, to go skiing in Switzerland for Christmas and suggested that Lou and Charlotte join them. "You can be chaperones," Norway said.

"We can be your *cover*, you mean, you dirty dog!" Lou said.

"No, I d-don't mean that at all. Come on, it'll be fun."

"I like the idea, Nev. It would be a nice break for Charlie. We haven't had any get-togethers since Freddie died. I know over Christmas she's gonna sit around moping."

"So you'll come?"

"Yes, I expect so, but there's one proviso: no screwing around. No creeping about in the middle of the night—you got that?"

"I'm sh-sh-shocked you'd even s-suggest such a thing!"

Since it was dark, Lou couldn't see Norway blushing from ear to ear.

52

HOLIDAYS IN SWITZERLAND & PARIS

Christmas 1929.

F ive days later, after rushing around to get Charlotte a passport, all four were in Murren, Switzerland having a wonderful time. Most importantly for Lou, Charlotte got back to her old self. They'd traveled through France by train, during which time, she'd became more subdued. But once they'd crossed the border into Switzerland, the sheer beauty of the place took her breath away and her mood changed. Throughout the days after that, Charlotte was in high spirits, especially when learning to ski (much of the time on her behind). On the last night, she played the piano in the hotel and a group of vacationers gathered around for a singsong. It was the best vacation Lou and his party had ever had, and they said so. For Lou and Charlotte, it was like a second honeymoon. It lasted ten days.

When the holiday was over, Norway was happy to get back to work, resuming the tests on his airship. Lou had mixed emotions. He saw the pain the Cardington people were going through. He also knew Charlotte's mood would likely falter.

Just after the New Year, Thomson moved into a larger flat in Ashley Gardens with room for a study. He took on a parlor maid, to complement his present staff. Naturally, Sammie the cat went, too. Thomson sat at the credenza in the living room from where he usually wrote Marthe, her picture positioned in front of him, as always. Outside, the weather was foul; wind shook the window frames and rain beat on the glass.

Dearest Marthe,
Being a bone fide Englishman, naturally, I must talk about the
weather. The New Year has burst upon us with a vengeance, with howling
wind and torrential rain. I apologize for not replying sooner, but my schedule
has been quite muddled. I'll be in Paris on Tuesday of next week on the
pretext of attending a dinner at the Chamber of Commerce. This is a blatant
lie, of course. My reason for being in Paris is to be with the woman I adore.
Fondest love always and forever, your Kit.

The following week, Thomson set off in high spirits for Paris aboard an Imperial Airways flight, with thirteen other passengers. It turned out to be a bumpy ride and an even bumpier landing. On approaching Paris, they ran into impenetrable fog and had to turn back over Beauvais Ridge where they were violently buffeted about. One poor soul bumped his head on the ceiling. They landed safely in a field near Allonne with several mighty thuds.

A local man, with other peasants, led the passengers and crew to their humble cottages and gave them shelter. Eventually, a car took Thomson to Beauvais Railway Station and he made it to Paris from there, arriving at Marthe's apartment four hours late. Marthe had gathered a few mutual friends from Bucharest to see him. The trip turned out to be pleasant and successful regarding his official duties and his romantic ambitions.

Thomson spent four blissful days with Marthe, strolling the streets and parks of Paris. They walked along the bank of the Seine, crossing the bridge to Notre Dame, where Marthe prayed fervently and lit four candles—for her father, her maid, her priest, and one for someone else—she wouldn't say who. Thomson hoped it was for him. She knew he was wondering and looked at him with that maddening half smile. Did he detect a trace of guilt, too? He wasn't sure.

They climbed the hundreds of steps to Montmartre and went into Sacre-Coeur Basilica, where Marthe prayed again. They had splendid meals, some simple, some lavish. A whole day was spent in the magnificent Musée du Louvre, soaking up its treasures. In all that time, although he longed to, he never brought up the subject of his marriage proposal. He stayed at the British Embassy for one night and the rest of the time at Marthe's apartment at Quay de Bourbon. After these few days, which filled Thomson's soul with almost total contentment, it was time to get back to the daily slog of helping MacDonald run the Empire, and to continue driving the Airship Program forward. He left Marthe a note before departing.

Dearest One,

My sincerest appreciation for your gracious hospitality. As always, you have encouraged me to carry on in the fight we call 'life.' These days with you have been magically calming and I'm ready to carry on and meet the challenges that lie in wait. Again, I thank you, darling Marthe. I hope you are able to come to England for Easter.

Au revoir. My eternal devotion,

Kit.

53

BACK TO WORK

January 1930.

Upon his return to London, Thomson went to the House of Lords to make his report. He'd be breaking the bad news during this speech. He hoped the hostile lords would either be absent, or not pick up on all his statements. He spoke as softly as he could, since most were deaf.

"I'm here to deliver a progress report concerning the Airship Program I introduced in 1924," Thomson said. Aggressive mumbling and sneering began around the chamber. Smirks appeared on jowled faces. "I must remind you, we never claimed to be building two airships that would take to the skies and circumvent the globe immediately. No, that wasn't the case at all!"

"*I* thought you did," someone muttered.

"What *did* you say, then?" asked another.

"What did he say? I can't hear him."

"If any blame is to be cast concerning the lateness of these projects —I stand here ready to accept that blame. Please understand such aircraft are experimental and cannot be rushed. Overseas testing is due to begin this year with *Howden R100* flying to Canada in June and *Cardington R101* flying to India in September after insertion of an extra bay ..."

There was silence in the chamber until that sank in.

"Extra bay!"

"What extra bay! What's that for?"

"What's he up to now?"

"More expense!"

"Good money after bad!"

"What did he say? Speak up man!"

Jeering broke out on all sides as Thomson attempted to justify his policies. It became deafening when he announced how much more money would be needed to continue the program.

The weight reduction of *Cardington R101* continued and as soon as the weather allowed, resumption of flight-testing *Howden R100* began. But before that, all remedial work had to be completed. The major issue was the repair of the outer cover securing system. It was found that the wires holding the cover in place chafed on the traverse girders, causing them to break and the cover to become loose and flap around. This meant the wiring had to be replaced and rerouted and the cover had to be laced up again. It was a massive task, but a vitally important one. On Norway's birthday, January 17th, Lou called him in York, where he'd returned for a break.

"Happy birthday, pal! You need to get your ass back down here pronto. We're taking your big balloon for a ride tomorrow morning. You need to be here by 5:00 a.m. sharp."

"Oh, bugger! The weather's bloody awful."

"It'll be calmer than a monk on morphine in the morning, 'ol buddy —first time in weeks."

"All right. I'll be there," Norway said.

"They're leavin' with you, or without you," Lou told him.

"Let Burney know—he wants to go."

By the time Norway got there, *Howden R100* had been pulled out and moored at the mast. Norway had bought himself a newish car, a Singer Coupe. It was covered in ice, inside and out, and so were Norway and his passenger, a calculator from Howden.

"Oh crap, Nev, look at you!" Lou exclaimed.

"The weather's been atrocious—ice and freezing fog all the way. We've been driving at twenty miles an hour all night," Norway said.

"Well, at least you've got *four wheels* now. You're late, but don't worry. They were two hours behind schedule walking her out."

They went to the tower and boarded the airship where Norway thawed out in the dining room with Burney over breakfast. The usual unfriendly R.A.W. officials were on board. A top speed requirement was stipulated in the contract and Cardington was anxious to find out if the airship could meet that requirement. Half an hour later, the captain gave the order to slip and they climbed above the fog into clear blue sky. Airspeed indicators had been set up and during the course of the day Booth pushed the ship to full speed. Scott appeared displeased. They were well over the speed requirement.

"What's the reading?" Burney asked.

"Eighty-one miles an hour," Norway called back.

"Must be something wrong with the instrumentation," an R.A.W. official said.

Scott scowled. "Something strange is going on with this cover. Look at it!" The cover was fluttering. They peered at it though the windows.

"I'm sure this isn't anything serious," Burney said.

"She must be under a lot of stress, I'd say, looking at that," Scott grumbled.

"Nevil, get some riggers and inspect this ship from end to end," Burney instructed.

"There's something seriously wrong with this airship," Scott persisted.

"Now steady on. Don't get carried away!" Burney cautioned.

Norway climbed about inside the airship with a gang of riggers, including Nervous Nick. They checked every inch of the structure and Norway determined that under full power no part of the airship became overstressed. Lou, McWade and Atherstone and two other R.A.W. officials joined them for the inspection and they, too, agreed. When they returned to the control car with their findings, Scott still wasn't satisfied.

"What we h-have is a har-harmonic con-condition caused by the eddying w-wind currents at high speed. It's n-nothing serious," Norway explained.

"As far as I'm concerned, this airship is substandard," Scott snapped.

Burney had the answer. "This is easily solved. We're ten miles an hour over specification requirements. By the way Scott, while we're on the subject: what top speed did your ship reach?"

"You have no business asking such questions," Scott snarled.

"Here's what we'll do. I'll instruct my team to put restrictors on the throttles so she'll only be able to reach a maximum speed of seventy, in accordance with the contract requirements. At cruising speeds up to seventy, the cover is completely normal with no signs of fluttering."

"You'll do *no such thing*," Scott growled.

"There's nothing wrong with this airship and you're trying to make out there is—and I wonder why!" Burney said. "We've met our obligations— which is more than I can say for you people at the Royal Airship Works!"

The final acceptance trial for the Howden airship began on January 27th and lasted until January 29th, amounting to fifty-four hours of continuous flight. The designated *Howden R100* flight crew was on board, including Jessup and Billy as riggers. Lou, since his promotion, served on both ships as third officer. Sky Hunt also flew in both on an 'as needed' basis.

Howden R100 left the mast around 8:00 a.m. in mist, which turned to rain with winds over fifty-five mph. These were the worst conditions Lou had flown in to date, but he didn't find the motion of the ship unduly worrying. She pitched slightly, but behaved obediently to her controls. They traveled to Oxford, unable to see the ground, and then toward Bristol and down to the southern tip of Cornwall.

Some hours later, they flew over the Channel Isles toward the North Sea, where they spent the night cruising around in the dark. A four-hour watch-keeping routine was in place, and Lou got plenty of rest in a comfortable cabin. He slept for much of the night over the North Sea and found they were crossing the coast over Norfolk on their way to London when he emerged for breakfast. Over London, they peered down into thick, greasy fog. It cleared for a minute, revealing Tower Bridge and the Tower of London. They headed south again for Torbay in Devon. In the vicinity of Eddystone Lighthouse, turning trials were carried out on both port and starboard helm, using the light as a point of reference. They spent that night cruising the English Channel between England and France, traveling to Portland and then on to the Scilly Isles in the Atlantic.

In the morning, Lou was in the control car as the ship traveled over Cornwall, the south west peninsula of England. It was a beautiful sunny morning—a delightful contrast after so much lousy weather. Mist floated in the valleys like fluffy clouds in varying colors of white, gold and pink. Lou wished Charlotte could see it. Over the Bristol Channel, they traveled through more rain squalls. By afternoon, they were back in Cardington, moored to the mast. Lou and Norway were home at a reasonable time for dinner with Charlotte.

Norway was able to stay the night this time and they spent the evening together. However, the happy mood Charlotte had exhibited in Switzerland had disappeared. She'd returned to her moody self once the ships had taken to the air again.

Trials were concluded and *Howden R100* officially accepted by the Air Ministry, whereupon the penultimate stage payment of forty thousand pounds was paid to Vickers. The final payment of ten thousand pounds would become due after a successful voyage to Canada. After more visual inspections in the air, the fluttering cover wasn't mentioned again. *Howden R100* was put into her shed for more remedial work and maintenance. There she would remain until May.

54

THE DINNER PARTY

April 1, 1930.

A t the end of March, Princess Marthe returned to London and Buck drove her to her favorite suite at the Ritz, where more of Thomson's special roses waited with a card of greeting.

Beloved Marthe,

I am sorry I could not meet you and that I'm unable to be with you this evening. Cabinet meetings till late, I'm afraid. Tomorrow I'll send the car to pick you up at six-thirty to bring you here for dinner with our distinguished guests. I am longing to see you. Until tomorrow evening then,

My deepest love, Kit.

The following evening, Thomson, dressed in a black, woolen overcoat and matching trilby, waited in the shadows outside his apartment building in Ashley Gardens, close to Westminster Cathedral. Big Ben began striking seven. His breath came out in white puffs and he had heart palpitations. Bitterly cold, he rubbed his hands together. Presently, he spotted the headlights of his limousine and edged to the curb. The car drew up and Thomson opened the passenger door. Marthe, swathed in mink, eased her way out. He took her hand.

"My dearest Marthe."

"So lovely to see you, Kit," Marthe responded, her cheek pressed to his, her French accented whisper warming his frozen ear and arousing him. He kissed her delicate hand.

"Come, dear lady, let me take you to my new flat. Our dinner guests are waiting."

He led Marthe through a marble entrance hall to a small elevator and they traveled up to the flat. Daisy, the new parlor maid, opened the door. The princess swept into the reception room, pausing for Daisy to remove her furs. Underneath, Marthe wore a pale blue, narrow-waisted, chiffon dress, which almost reached her silver, open-toed shoes. Deep red nail polish perfectly matched her lipstick. Around her neck, she wore a necklace of diamonds, which complemented her diamond earrings. Her shining, dark hair was gathered up tight to the head and crowned by a small diamond tiara.

"You are truly magnificent, darling!" Thomson said, kissing her hand again. He turned to Daisy. "We'll go in now."

Daisy obediently pushed open the double doors, revealing the spacious, bright yellow and white accented sitting room. MacDonald and his companion sat opposite each other on couches positioned each side of a statuary marble fireplace, where a log fire blazed in the hearth. Between them was a coffee table laden with half-finished cocktails. A huge guilt mirror hung above the mantel. Thomson studied Marthe as she briefly gazed at her own reflection as she approached MacDonald, who sprung to his feet. Lady Wilson remained seated.

"Thank goodness you're here at last!" MacDonald exclaimed. "Thomson's been a bundle of nerves—and I can't say as I blame him! You look positively stunning." MacDonald raised her hand to his lips.

"Ramsay," Marthe whispered, her eyes burning into his. "So lovely to see you again."

"You know Lady Wilson, don't you, Marthe?" Thomson said.

"Yes, of course. We're *old* friends," Marthe answered, giving Lady Wilson a sincere smile. After greetings and more cocktails, everyone moved to the dining room where Gwen served a fish starter course.

"I was just admiring your carpet, CB," Lady Wilson said.

"It's precious to me. It was presented to me in Kurdistan," Thomson said grandly.

"The funny thing is—I used to own its identical twin," Marthe said.

Thomson withered visibly. He hated mention of it.

"Really. And don't you still?" MacDonald asked.

"No, it perished in the flames when the wretched Germans burned down my house in Romania during the war."

"Good Lord! What reason did they have to do such a thing?" Lady Wilson asked.

"They believed I was keeping British secret documents there—which, of course, I was. This was in the early days of our friendship, wasn't it Kit?"

"Yes, and very nearly the last!" Thomson said.

"Oh, you poor thing!" Lady Wilson said. "It must have been awful for you."

Thomson appeared sheepish. He wasn't proud of the episode. For years after the war, he regretted storing those documents at Marthe's house. It was foolish and naive. He worried it may have diminished him in her eyes.

"It was a dreadful occurrence. Now, Marthe shares this one with me. It's my talisman. As long as I possess it, Marthe and I shall remain close."

MacDonald lifted his glass. "Then I say God bless you, CB. Guard it with your life!"

"Hear, hear!" said Lady Wilson.

Gwen served duck à l'orange for the main course and Daisy recharged their glasses.

"I'm trying to talk Kit into coming to Paris for Easter," Marthe said.

"Why don't you both come to Chequers? The blossoms will be bursting out in all their glory," MacDonald said.

"I cannot be here at Easter, but will you ask me in July, Ramsay?"

"July! That's a long way off. Do you think I'll still be in office, Marthe?"

"Of course. Tory friends of mine have said so."

"You can't believe a word they say," MacDonald said, with an ironic smile.

Lady Wilson glanced at Thomson. "Tell us about your recent trip to Paris, CB. Did you have fun?"

"Wonderful!"

"Tell them what happened on the way over, Kit," Marthe said.

"We ran into fog and couldn't land in Paris. We ended up having a bumpy ride over Beauvais Ridge, then a rough landing in a field near Allonne."

"How dreadful!" exclaimed Lady Wilson. "Were you all right?"

"You didn't tell me about this," MacDonald said with surprise.

"Oh, everything turned out well. I didn't want to tell you. I know how you worry. And you might ban me from flying—which might be embarrassing for the Minister of State for Air."

"What happened?" MacDonald asked.

"A delightful little rabbit poacher—a Monsieur Rabouille!—came running out of the woods and led us to some old, stone cottages, where these wonderful peasants took us in. What a place! Desolate and unforgiving, but wonderful just the same. He kissed my hand when he saw me. Monsieur Rabouille, the rabbit poacher! Splendid fellow! I hope we meet again, someday."

"So you actually went inside one of the cottages?" Lady Wilson asked.

"Yes, I sat huddled by the fireplace while this wonderful lady kept me plied with wine. What an experience it was! I was so touched by it—those people are the salt of the earth. I pulled out my wallet and said, 'Let me pay you for your kind hospitality, dear lady.' 'Non, non, non. I have had the pleasure of your conversation, monsieur,' she said. Nevertheless, I tucked a franc under the seat cushion for her to find later."

"Oh, that was so sweet of you," Lady Wilson exclaimed.

"'You are the luckiest of folk to live in this place, Madam. You have peace,' I said to her. She just said, 'Plutôt un très grand isolement.' Total isolation, more like. 'I love your people, Madam. This country is so good and so beautiful—someday I shall come here to die,' I told her."

"Oh Kit, how could you say such a thing!" Marthe said, her eyes filling with tears. "You should never speak that way." She looked in desperation at Lady Wilson. "He didn't tell me he'd said that."

Daisy cleared the dinner plates while Gwen served a dessert of rhubarb tart and cream.

"Come, Marthe, let me take you in the other room. You can compose yourself and we can talk," Lady Wilson said.

The two women went into the sitting room while Thomson and MacDonald ate dessert and drank their coffee. After that, they drank brandy and smoked cigars. The ladies' desserts remained untouched.

"I'm astonished it upset her so much," Thomson said.

"She cares about you a lot, you know. I can see that," MacDonald said. Thomson sat in silence, pondering Marthe's emotional outburst—it'd seemed genuine.

Maybe it's time I spoke to her again.

Later, when the dinner guests had gone and the servants had finished clearing away, Marthe and Thomson sat beside the fireplace drinking liqueurs.

"Have you considered my proposal any further, Marthe?" Thomson inquired gently.

"Oh, Kit, you know it's impossible."

"If the voyage to India is successful and I'm appointed Viceroy, anything will be possible, my dearest, I can assure you of that. The viceroy position requires him to be married."

"What do you mean, '*if* it's successful'?"

"Promise me, Marthe, that we'll discuss the subject before the voyage. I haven't spoken of it for nearly a year and I will not speak of it until then."

Marthe sat up and looked directly into his eyes. "Kit, will your airship *really* be safe? Please tell me the truth."

"Marthe, this whole voyage is about my destiny and I hope yours, too, my darling."

He knew power was her aphrodisiac. She turned to him and he took her forcefully into his arms. He kissed her passionately—more passionately than he'd ever done before.

55

THE WHISTLEBLOWER

Sunday June 29, 1930.

The guns raged on both sides. Boom! Boom! Boom! Lou lay there in the darkness alongside twenty-five other combat-weary soldiers. Boom! Boom! Boom!

Suddenly, a tremendous explosion ripped through their deep bunker, blasting a mountain of rubble, earth, wood whalers and body parts everywhere. He was entombed and couldn't move his legs. A terrible pain in his chest and pressure in his lungs made it hard to breathe and he was freezing cold. He tried to suck in foul-smelling air and smoke, realizing he'd been hit. Reaching into his top pocket, he pulled out his lighter and spun the flint wheel with his thumb. The blessed flame burst before his eyes. He looked down in horror at his chest and watched blood oozing from a gaping hole. It spread over his shredded tunic and over the ground like a creeping red blanket. The torso of another buried man lay across his legs, trapping them. He tried to scream for help, but he had no breath and no sound came. His thin flame was replaced by a bright shaft of light penetrating the dust and smoke. He watched a gloved-hand pulling away rubble from outside his tomb. A grotesque giant fly's head pushed its way through the hole babbling at him in guttural gibberish. As his eyes focused, Lou realized it was man wearing a gas mask with goggles over his eyes and a German helmet. Had he come to rescue him, or to kill him?

Boom! Boom! Boom! There it was again.

"Lou, Lou, wake up, wake up!" Charlotte urgently whispered, shaking his arm. "Someone's banging on the door."

"What? What's happening?"

Lou, unable to move, gasped for breath. He felt sticky, warm blood running down across his stomach and could taste it in his mouth.

"Lou, Lou, wake up."

"What? What? What time is it?"

"After midnight. Something awful must have happened."

Lou opened his eyes, beginning to come round and put his hand to his chest with dread. It seemed dry, but the awful pain remained. He pulled back the covers and, clutching his chest, rolled out of bed. He switched on the bedside lamp and looked at his chest. No blood. He slipped his dressing gown on over his pajamas.

"See who it is, but do be careful."

After switching on the dim landing light, he moved down the creaking stairs, clinging to the banister.

Boom! Boom! Boom!

"All right! All right! Damn it. I'm coming."

Lou, on opening the front door, was surprised to see the rotund figure of Inspector Fred McWade. He was hopping from one foot to the other. He looked frantic. The night was warm. McWade wore what he always wore—white shirt, grey sports jacket, tie, and flannel trousers—held up from his ankles with metal bicycle clips. It looked like he was wearing plus fours, ready to play golf. He pulled off his tweed cap.

"Fred! Whatever's wrong?"

"I've got to see you, Lou. It's very important."

"Come in, come in. What's going on?"

"I'm sorry, laddie, I know it's late, but I *must* talk to you," McWade said, pulling out a handkerchief to mop his dripping face and brow. Speech was difficult. He was wheezing and his breathing, labored.

Charlotte leaned over the railing on the top landing in her nightdress. She called down. "Lou, who is it? Is something wrong?"

"It's okay, honey. Fred McWade's come for a chat, that's all. It's only about work. Go back to bed. Everything's all right. Don't worry."

McWade stepped into the hallway. Lou pushed the living room door open. "Let's go in here. You can tell me what's eating you," he said, switching on the table lamps. Fred followed him and Lou silently closed the door.

"I'm sorry to come here like this, Lou. I hope I haven't upset Charlotte, but it couldn't wait."

Lou motioned for McWade to take a seat. "What the hell's the matter, Fred?"

"Lou, you're special," McWade said, sinking into an armchair. "I saw it ever since we pulled you off that wreck in the river up north. Someone upstairs thinks you're special, too."

"Charlotte?"

"*Almighty God!*"

"Oh, …yeah, right."

"I don't want to see anything happen to you, especially after what happened over the Humber. I want you to get out!" The more agitated McWade got, the thicker his Glaswegian accent became. Lou went to the sideboard and poured two full tumblers of Johnny Walker.

"Fred, you're gonna have to talk a bit slower for me." He handed the Scotch to McWade.

"Oh, thank you, son. I need this."

"Now calm down, Fred. What's up eh?"

Charlotte had slipped silently down the stairs and was now sitting on the bottom step. She could only make out odd words here and there, but what she heard alarmed her. She felt a desperate need to run out the front door. To be swallowed up by the darkness.

"Take the advice of an old man who's been in airships all his life. Get out of this business, fast." McWade pointed toward Cardington. "That thing up there is *a bloody deathtrap!*"

Lou knew McWade was one of the most experienced men in the country. He'd trained at the School of Military Engineering and joined the School of Ballooning in the Royal Engineers before Lou was born. He'd worked on airship construction for government for years, becoming a senior man in the Airship Inspection Department—the A.I.D. Lou sipped his whisky and peered into his glass.

Both ships had been laid up in their sheds for most of the winter and into the spring. *Howden R100* had problems of her own, but fixable. The cover leaked. Water had shorted out the electrical systems and damaged the gas bags. The tail structure needed rebuilding after collapsing during one of her endurance test flights, and the second-hand engines caused trouble—just as Wallis knew they would. They'd need replacing.

By early summer, some modifications to *Cardington R101* had been completed, though not all. The rotting cover had only partly been removed and insertion of the extra bay hadn't even begun. Padding where gas bags rubbed against the structure had been attempted, haphazardly. In places where the cover hadn't been replaced, reinforcing strips of canvas had been glued over weak, friable areas, giving the ship a 'patched up' look.

Under the pretext of testing the ship after weight-reducing modifications, *Cardington R101* had been rushed out of her shed in questionable weather. In reality, she'd been brought out to participate in a publicity stunt. That June, the Royal Air Display took place and Air Ministry big shots thought it'd give the public a boost if *Cardington R101* came out and did a party piece in front of the King.

The airship was moored at the tower and immediately a ninety-foot tear was discovered on the starboard side and a forty-five-foot tear on port. Riggers dangled on ropes for hours in wind and rain in soft-soled shoes with needles and thread making repairs.

That week, the ship made several flights. Lt. Cmdr. Atherstone had gone to Canada to make preparations for *Howden R100's* arrival. Capt. Booth and Capt. Meager covered for him while Maurice Steff acted as second officer. Lou was on board for all these flights. It proved to be an unnerving experience, especially for Booth and Meager, not being used to *Cardington R101's* unpredictable behavior.

McWade had been on board with the A.I.D. and Lou could see he was unimpressed. On practice day, with Booth acting as first officer, Lou watched in horror as the ship, required to come in low over the crowd and dip her nose to the royal box, almost collided with an adjacent building. Cameron, the height coxswain, lowered the bow in salute, but it continued to drop sharply and he had difficulty bringing her back up. The journey home had been grim, the ship becoming increasingly heavy and uncontrollable. Irwin managed to get back to the tower by dumping fuel and water ballast as he'd been forced to do the year before.

The following day, Lou was on board with Meager as first officer this time. They needed to be over Hendon Aerodrome at 3:50 p.m. After spending several uneventful hours over London and Southend, Irwin brought the ship through rain showers to Hendon for the display, where Cameron managed to perform the salute to the Royal Box over a crowd of a hundred thousand people. It had been touch and go. Lou thought diving to within five hundred feet and pulling up sharply in front of the King was sheer lunacy—a stunt which could have easily resulted in catastrophe for the nation.

The homeward journey turned out to be as bad as the day before. As they passed through rain squalls, the bow kept dropping without warning. Water ballast and fuel were dumped all the way home. Irwin, Meager and Lou knew something was radically wrong. The loss of lift was dramatic— even after burning two tons of fuel, it was still necessary to drop another ten tons of ballast. In this condition, lightened or not, this airship could never make it to Egypt—let alone India.

Lou took another sip of whisky. "Fred, I can't just up and walk away. I represent the U.S. Navy. Besides, I couldn't leave the men, or Captain Irwin."

"Och, Lou, we fished you out of the bloody river once." He took a gulp of his drink. "You might not be so lucky next time. You should take Charlotte and go back to America." McWade put his hand to his head. "Oh, I'm sorry, that's none o' my business."

"And what about *you?*" Lou asked. "You'll be flying in both ships— to Canada and then India."

"It doesn't matter about me. I'm old. It's all those young boys I'm concerned about. I don't want them on my conscience."

"Look, Fred, I think you're just upset. Granted these flights this week didn't go so well—"

"Go so well! They were *a bloody disaster!* She nearly dived into the ground nine times by my reckoning. I don't know how that boy held the damned thing up. I've had enough—something's got to be done. You're the only person I can talk to." With that, McWade took out a white envelope from his inside pocket and held it up. Lou figured it must be his resignation.

Ah, this is why he came at this ungodly hour!

"I want you to read this," McWade said. "I finished it half an hour ago."

He leaned forward in his armchair and held it out to Lou. Lou switched on the table lamp behind him as the clock on the mantelpiece (a wedding present from Charlotte's parents), chimed prettily. It was 2:00 a.m. He began reading. His eyes widened when he saw the title of the addressee. As he read the beautiful script, Lou heard McWade's broad Scottish accent accompanied by the gently ticking clock.

> 86, Barmeston Rd.
> Bedford.
> 29th June, 1930.

The Director of Aeronautical Inspection,
Air Ministry, Whitehall,
London.

Re: HMA CARDINGTON R101

Dear Sir,

Owing to the very serious state of affairs concerning His Majesty's Airship Cardington R101, I am forced to write directly to you. On the 26th of June, I issued a 'Permit to Fly,' dated 20th June and valid until 19th July 1930. Due to modifications of the harness system in an effort to increase gas capacity, the gas bags are now tight against longitudinals and rubbing against nuts and bolts and all parts of the structure. In my opinion, these modifications have led to a dangerous situation with thousands of holes being made, causing loss of gas at an alarming rate.

Over the years, padding has been an acceptable method of repair in isolated instances. Padding to the extent required in this case is totally unacceptable. The gas bags in this airship were recently removed and repaired, but after recent test flights, they are full of holes again. When padding is installed, these areas become hidden from view and corrosion of the structure usually ensues, which is another reason why padding is unacceptable.

Until this matter is taken seriously, and an acceptable solution put forward, I cannot recommend to you an extension of the present Permit to Fly or any further Permit or Certificate.

Yours Respectfully,
F. McWade,
Inspector-In-Charge,
Airship Inspection Dept.(A.I.D.)
Royal Airship Works, Cardington.

Lou put the letter down in his lap and rested his head on the back of the armchair. "My God, Fred, you're taking a hell of a risk, aren't you?"

"I know this could cost me ma job and ma pension, but that's nothing compared to the risk they're taking."

"I'm not sure this is a good idea."

"Are you advising me not to post it?"

"No, I'm not saying that. If you feel this strongly, then you must— but understand you will become the most hated man in Cardington."

"I needed your opinion."

"I wouldn't dissuade you, Fred, and I have to say, I admire your guts."

"That makes me feel better, laddie."

"But look, Fred, these men aren't fools. They're gonna add an extra bay. It should perform a lot better then, don't you think?"

"Nay, laddie. They committed a grave mistake when they let those harnesses out. Those valves might become detached. She's unstable now— the bags are surging up and down and back and forth. And adding an extra bay will only weaken her resilience. That ship's damned now. I have to tell you in all candor: these bloody geniuses at Cardington are outmatched." McWade swallowed the remnants of his glass and got up. "I'll be off, then. This letter is going in the post-box first thing in the morning."

Lou smiled weakly. At least McWade would have time to sleep on it. Maybe he'd change his mind by morning. "All right, Fred. Ride home safely. I can take you home on my motorbike, if you like?"

"No, no, son. I'll be fine."

Lou stood at the front door and watched the old man peddle off down the street, wobbling as he went. When Lou got back to the bedroom, he found Charlotte sitting on the bed staring at the floor.

"I thought you'd be asleep, honey," Lou said.

"It didn't sound good. That man is worried sick, isn't he?"

"He'll be all right, once the modifications are done."

"I told you—that ship's cursed!"

They climbed into bed. Lou lay on his back reflecting on their approach to the tower on Saturday, minutes before the arrival of a violent storm. They'd got the ship moored just in time.

When they reached the tower, Colmore was waiting with Richmond, Rope and Scott to make an inspection. Sky Hunt was already on board. Colmore was anxious to know if the modifications to lighten her had made any noticeable difference. During these past few days the ship had no load to speak of, so these flights should indicate clearly if the ship was airworthy. When the extra bay was inserted, the additional lift would be used up by the weight of passengers and extra fuel. If she couldn't fly now, she *never* could.

Once locked onto the tower, the gas hoses were connected to recharge the gas bags and a thorough inspection carried out from bow to stern with everybody in attendance. With the wind blowing a gale and rain coming down in torrents, this was the perfect time. The first obvious thing was that the cover leaked badly. In no time everybody was soaking wet. The damp atmosphere accentuated the smell of cattle's intestines.

As the ship rolled and was buffeted about, deep sighs from the gas valves were loud enough for all to hear. The creaking and squeaking of gas bags rubbing against the structure was no less unnerving. Richmond's face expressed disappointment. He spoke to Irwin first.

"Captain, assuming your calculations are correct, you're losing ten tons of lift every day. Is that correct?"

"Absolutely correct. Commander Remington can attest to that."

"We're pumping in more than 300,000 cubic feet of gas a day just to keep her afloat at the tower," Lou said.

Richmond looked at Sky Hunt for confirmation. "That's correct, sir," Hunt said.

"This is all *very disturbing*, indeed," Richmond declared, glaring at the officers.

Lou saw McWade about to explode.

"It's more than *disturbing*, sir. When you let out the harnesses, you allowed the gas bags to become riddled with holes throughout this airship. That's why you're losing gas at an alarming rate and why she's unstable. This situation is *totally unacceptable!* I cannot allow this."

"What are you trying to say? Speak up, man!" Richmond erupted.

McWade replied as though speaking to a child. "I'm saying that, as far as I'm concerned, this airship is *totally* unsafe."

Richmond was enraged. "Just who the hell do you think you are?"

"Who do I think I am? I'll tell you exactly who I am, sir. I'm the man who stood and watched *R38* break in two and blow up, killing dozens of British and American young men, decapitating them, dismembering them, blowing them to bits, drowning them and burning them to a crisp. I'm the man who's trying to avoid more of our boys sharing the same fate. That's who I am, sir!"

Richmond stormed off down the catwalk. Lou figured he was about ready to break down.

Lou lay in bed with Charlotte beside him. He was sure she wasn't asleep even though she lay perfectly still. He remembered feeling sorry for Colmore; the man's troubles seemed to be multiplying daily. When McWade made his damning statement, Colmore stood there at a loss, water pouring from his hair, running down his face, and dripping off the end of his nose. Scott remained quiet. Rope cradled his chin, deep in thought.

A couple of days after McWade's late night visit, *Cardington R101* was returned to her shed and work resumed on replacing the cover. The question of the holes in the gas bags still needed to be addressed. Lou visited the shed to see how work was progressing. He stopped by McWade's office in the corner.

"Hi, Fred. How're things?"

Fred closed the door, his manner conspiratorial. "I posted that letter," he whispered.

McWade had just brewed a pot of tea and poured a cup for Lou, his chin stuck out defiantly.

"Brave man," Lou said.

"Och, I'm not brave at all. I just don't want to see bad things happen to these men—or this city, come to that."

Lou sipped his tea, feeling awkward and disloyal. Sometimes he knew too much. He wished people wouldn't confide in him, but they did. He'd keep it all to himself and see what happened. No doubt Colmore would bring it up with him.

"I expect you've got Whitehall in a flurry, Fred."

"I bloody well hope so," McWade said.

Lou laughed. "Maybe they'll scrap the whole program, eh?"

"Better now than later," McWade replied. He finished his tea and put down his cup. "I told yer, I've been in airships all my life. The older I get, the more futile it all seems to me. It's all been for nought."

As Lou expected, Colmore confided in him the next day. He told him the chief of the inspection department at the Air Ministry had called him and told him he'd received Fred McWade's letter. They were 'all in a tizzy about it' down there.

"He asked me if this was as serious as it sounded," Colmore said.

"Did you tell him it was?" Lou asked.

"How could I do that? We're our own judge and jury here. How would it look if I said 'Yes, actually, we've built an un-flyable airship.'?"

"Sir, who cares about looks. We're talking about people's lives. Here was a chance to buy more time."

"Easy for you to say. Heads would roll."

"So what did you tell him, sir?"

"I told him it was nothing we couldn't handle."

Lou was frustrated. "How?" he asked skeptically.

"By padding. It's done all the time. And we'll do it again."

"McWade's a highly experienced man. Maybe we should all listen to him."

"Lou, I'm in an impossible situation. Can't you see that? Can you imagine his Lordship—he'd go stark raving mad."

"That would be his problem, sir. You should remind him of his own 'Safety First' policy."

Colmore put his hand to his forehead and sighed. "Lord Thomson told us a story—something that had happened in his early life involving Lord Kitchener in South Africa. I won't go into details, but it was intended as a warning, or a threat—an ultimatum really. I'm haunted by it."

Lou was fascinated and wanted to find out more, but the phone on Colmore's desk rang. Colmore picked it up. "Sir Sefton, how nice to hear your voice, sir ...Yes, hmm, okay ...Yes, I'm sure that can be arranged. Right you are ...Ah yes, I'll bring him along, too," Colmore said, looking at Lou as he hung up. He lowered his voice. "That was the Director of Civil Aviation—Sir Sefton Brancker."

"Yes."

"He's calling a meeting. Very hush, hush. He said Thomson's girlfriend is coming to town next week and they've been invited to Chequers. While he's out of the way, he wants me, Irwin and you, to meet with him at his home in Surrey. He's very concerned about what's been going on this week with the ship—and about McWade's letter."

"Okay, sir. Sure, I'll come, if I can be helpful."

"He thinks a lot of you, Lou. Saturday morning, 9:00 a.m."

"Sir, may I ask you something?"

"By all means."

"Suppose you were asked to judge *Howden R100?* I mean, suppose the ships were reversed and they had *Cardington R101* and you had theirs. What would you do?"

"I'd declare their ship unsafe and forbid them to fly it."

"Then you should do the same thing with your own ship."

Colmore screwed up his eyes and then looked down at his desk. "We're in a box. We're stuck. We have to do as we're told—do our duty."

Lou understood Colmore's dilemma. It would be interesting to see how it played out.

Later that week, Lou was in Shed No.1 again. An Air Ministry dispatch rider came striding into the shed toward him. "I'm looking for a Mr. Frederick McWade, sir," he said, reading from a white envelope. Lou pointed to the end office in the wooden structure in the corner of the shed. He watched the man walk over and knock on McWade's door. McWade opened it, surprised at first. He took the letter and closed the door. A few moments later, McWade came bursting out, his face crimson.

"Lou, come and see this," McWade said, disgusted. They went back to McWade's office and closed the door. McWade handed the letter to Lou. He read the envelope:

Director of Aeronautical Inspection,
Air Ministry, Whitehall, London.

Lou scanned the letter. He read aloud when he reached the heart of it:

".....I have discussed the matter you raised at length with the Director of Airship Development, Wing Commander Colmore. Naturally, I understand it is absolutely essential that contact between the ship's structure and the gas bags is eliminated. I am sure you understand it would be quite impossible to change the framing of the airship at this juncture. Therefore, the only solution is to install padding. It will be your responsibility to ensure all points of contact which could cause damage are properly padded."

Yours Truly - Da-dee-da-dee-da!"

Lou whistled. "Nice!"

"*Bastards!*" McWade whispered.

"You put Colmore in a bind," Lou said.

"He's gutless. He'll go along with anything they say."

"He's in a difficult position, Fred."

"This seals our fate," McWade said, almost to himself.

"What are you going to do?"

"I'll oversee the padding, I suppose. And they'll all be laughing at me while I do it. I'll do everything in my power to make the damn thing safe. I'll not walk away—not yet."

"You're a damned *good man*, Fred."

"Aye, *'damned'* is right!"

McWade was close to tears.

56

CHEQUERS & A MEETING WITH BRANCKER

Friday & Saturday July 4 & 5, 1930.

Marthe returned to London in July and this time Thomson was able to meet her at Victoria. He took pleasure in standing on the platform under his umbrella, waiting for her glistening train to come gliding in. He patiently watched it grind to a halt. Marthe alighted from the train, minus the irritating Isadora. They greeted each other warmly, but formally, and were driven by Buck across London and Buckinghamshire to Chequers. Marthe was in an excitable mood, chattering like a young girl. Thomson couldn't remember seeing her this bubbly for a long time, if ever. She made him feel elated, too. She'd certainly warmed to him this past year.

"There's something special about Fridays, don't you find, Kit?" Marthe said.

Thomson took her hand. "Even for princesses?"

"Yes, I'm happy to be here and I'm so looking forward to seeing your dear friend."

"*Our* dear friend! He's dying to meet you again, Marthe."

Forty minutes after leaving the northwest suburbs, they reached the winding lanes of Buckinghamshire, flanked by hedgerows and swaying beeches, leading up to the imposing mansion. Marthe was in a dream as they entered this magical place—a place where prime ministers relaxed, played and sometimes made policy. This was where they met with the most important men in the world and came to agreements. It was also where they entertained and bedded their mistresses.

Thomson took pleasure in watching Marthe's darting eyes. She took in every detail. Soon she'd be writing it all down. She stared up at the red brick building looming above them. Thomson knew the façade's air of enchantment cloaked an underlying menace. This came from its long history —no doubt bad things had happened within these walls. The car reached the impressive wrought-iron gates and a nondescript man in gray appeared.

"Afternoon, Lord Thomson, nice to see you back, sir," he said in a Cockney accent.

"Hello, Robards," Thomson said.

"Who is that?" Marthe whispered.

"The policeman in charge of the Prime Minister's security."

The gates were opened by two roughly dressed men.

"And here are two more, disguised as gardeners—imported from Lossiemouth," Thomson explained.

Marthe gave him a teasing look. "You British are so cunning."

"I've told him he needs more security out here, but he won't listen."

The limousine cruised slowly past the center lawn and Hygeia, the health goddess, up to the entrance. The gravel driveway crunched under their wheels in welcome. The main front door opened and Ishbel came out to greet them, while the gardeners unloaded their luggage. Thomson kissed Ishbel's cheek and turned to Marthe to make introductions.

"Ishbel, this is Princess Marthe Bibesco. Our lives have been inextricably linked since before the war."

Ishbel was shy. Marthe took both her hands. "Ishbel! What a beautiful name. Oh, I can see a striking resemblance. You are so very lucky —your father is such a handsome man."

This made Ishbel more shy and embarrassed. "Welcome. Please come in and I'll show you to your rooms, Princess," she said.

"Please call me Marthe."

"Very well, Marthe. My father told me which rooms you're to have."

"And you speak just like him. *Captivating!*" Marthe exclaimed, pressing her hands together. Ishbel smiled and led them upstairs and along a wide corridor that creaked underfoot. The walls were decorated in flowery, brown and tan wallpaper. She stopped at Thomson's room.

"Christopher is in here—where he usually sleeps." She moved on to the next room. "And you, Marthe, are in here—the Lee Room—reserved for special guests, or heads of state."

Ishbel gestured for Marthe to enter. Marthe's eyes lit up when she spotted the hand-carved four-poster bed. "I'm so honored," she said.

The room was decorated in floral pink and green wallpaper with coordinating drapes and cushions. Marthe went to the window and looked across the gardens, which were bursting with color. MacDonald had not exaggerated their beauty.

"There are two bathrooms, one each end of the corridor. There's plenty of hot water if you'd like a bath after your journey," Ishbel said.

Thomson and Marthe spent the rest of the afternoon settling in. Marthe relaxed in a hot bath, savoring the place she hoped would become part of her life, as it had for Thomson. She was soon looking her best for MacDonald's arrival and for cocktails before dinner. She wore a long, tan, satin cocktail dress with a subtle, sculptured floral design showing a hint of silver and pale-blue. The dress, from her Parisian dressmaker, was low-key and understated, narrow at the waist and covered her slender neck. She kept with her a designer wrap in a slightly darker shade, to throw around her shoulders later.

Once Marthe was ready, she sat down at a writing table in her room. She wrote down her thoughts in a leather-bound diary, together with vivid descriptions of her observations since arriving at Victoria. She'd use them in a future memoir, hopefully a best seller.

After half an hour, Thomson knocked on Marthe's door dressed in a black evening suit with a pale-blue tie. He kissed her hand. "Marthe you look quite lovely, my dear." He breathed in. "And your perfume is divine."

Just after 5 o'clock, they heard MacDonald's blue Rolls-Royce crackling over the driveway. Marthe went to wait in the reception hall and Thomson joined her. He watched as the butler opened the front door and MacDonald walked in, his face beaming, not taking his eyes off Marthe. He raised her hand and kissed it, looking into her face. Thomson felt quite invisible. MacDonald let go of her hand and she stepped closer for him to kiss her on both cheeks. He, too, breathed in her perfume.

"Dearest Marthe, welcome to Chequers. I am most honored to have you as my guest."

"I've been so looking forward to this visit, Ramsay."

"The feeling is mutual, my dear."

"*And* you're still in office!"

"You bring me good luck, obviously."

Ishbel joined them as MacDonald turned to Thomson.

"Come. This deserves a celebratory drink!"

They went into the Great Room, where they sank into the huge armchairs. Amid the splendid paintings and lofty ceilings they drank cocktails served by the butler, a kindly Scot dressed in black, also from Lossiemouth. The room dwarfed the small party, making them feel out of place. Later they moved to the cosier dining room, where dark oak paneling was brightened by late afternoon sunshine through leaded windows. As in other rooms, original paintings hung from the walls and over the carved mantel. They sat down to a three-course dinner and polite small talk, after which, Marthe faded fast.

"Well, Ramsay, as thrilled as I am to be in your company, I'm longing to climb into that four-poster bed," she said, her eyelids fluttering wearily.

"You must be terribly tired, my dear, after your journey. Be off and get your beauty sleep. Tomorrow we'll take you for a long walk," MacDonald said.

Thomson and MacDonald stood and Marthe kissed first MacDonald and then Thomson. Ishbel excused herself and the two women went upstairs while the men moved to the Hawtrey Room, a comfortable drawing room, overlooking the gardens. The butler brought a bottle of Courvoisier and glasses on a tray, closed the curtains and left.

"Are you making headway, CB?"

"I couldn't be happier, Ramsay. I believe the planets are aligning."

"Good."

"And if it's any indication, Marthe's stopped bringing her confounded maidservant, Isadora. She's left in Paris these days."

"That must be a relief."

"She's like a damned watchdog."

"Any progress on the matrimonial front?"

"Marthe has become closer and more loving of late. I pushed too hard last year, which had a detrimental effect, but she seems to be coming around, although I can never be sure."

"How do you mean?"

"I'm never sure if there aren't others ... well, I know there *must* be, she's such a vibrant woman ... in the *'social sense'*, I mean ... she's been so terribly damaged on the *'physical side'*, if you know what I mean ..." Thomson's voice petered out in embarrassment. MacDonald understood and nodded sympathetically. He frowned, looking up at the ceiling considering what Thomson had just divulged.

"Perhaps the viceroy position will bring things to a head," MacDonald said.

"I'm hoping for her answer before I leave for India in September, but she may not let me know until I return."

"You're definitely going, then?"

"Yes, I am. I must say, I've been rather touched by Marthe's concern of late."

"We're all concerned, CB. Must you really go?"

"I've stated publicly since 1924 that I'll be on *Cardington R101* when she makes her maiden voyage. I *will* go, and by golly, I'm looking forward to it. Please don't worry, Ramsay."

MacDonald left it at that.

The sun shone brightly the following morning and MacDonald and Ishbel were up with the larks. For Marthe, waking up at Chequers seemed like a fantasy. She lay happily in bed, wide awake, studying the room and its floral décor. She enjoyed the aromas and birdsong drifting through her casement windows from the garden—so unmistakably English! How she loved this place. She was aroused from her musing by Thomson's gentle knock and his entrance with a tray of tea and biscuits. He wore a silk dressing gown over his pajamas.

"Good morning, my dear," he said brightly.

"Ah, there you are, Kit."

"I thought perhaps we could spend a little time together before we go down to breakfast," he said coyly as he put the tray down.

The idea was met with coolness.

"I don't think that would be appropriate, or respectful to our host, Kit, do you?"

He was used to being rebuffed.

Later, they came down to the breakfast room looking well-rested, although Thomson didn't quite have the spring in his step that he'd hoped for. The two men ate their bacon and eggs and drank coffee. Marthe and Ishbel had porridge and fruit.

"I'll show you around the gardens this morning, Marthe," MacDonald said.

"I've been looking forward to this, Ramsay," Marthe said.

"I see you're suitably attired for a walk."

"They're her walking shoes," Thomson said.

"I'm a country girl at heart. I love the mountains."

"We used to walk in the Carpathians," Thomson said.

"You must come to the Highlands," MacDonald said.

"Indeed we must," Thomson said. "I remember my first visit to Lossie. I had an affinity with the place immediately."

"Sounds delightful," Marthe said.

"And the house—such peace," Thomson said.

"I built the house for my mother and my dear wife. They both died within the same year. The place brings me solace, but with it dreadful sadness ..." MacDonald faltered, his eyes filling with tears.

"Oh Daddy," Ishbel said, moving toward him. Before she could embrace him, he got up and moved to the window.

"It's a beautiful morning and we must get out there, before it clouds over, as it usually does by midmorning," he said.

"I won't come if you don't mind. I have things to do," Ishbel said.

"Just as you wish, my dear," MacDonald said. "She's a busy girl. Runs this house and Number Ten like clockwork. Heaven knows where I'd be without her."

While Thomson and Marthe were having breakfast at Chequers, Lou and company were traveling to Brancker's home, near Warlingham. The house, a black-beamed, white-stucco Tudor, was situated on a hill overlooking the Surrey woods and pastureland. The imposing, oak-planked, steel-studded front door was opened by a young maid in black with a frilly white apron. She showed them into a spacious study with magnificent views from leaded windows. The room was full of antiques and shelves stacked with books. The walls were filled with framed pictures of aeroplanes, airships, aviation personalities, big game kills in East Africa, as well as aviation artifacts, which included a huge wooden airship propeller, stained and varnished. There was one apparently special picture at center, of Auriol Lee, signed in bold lettering. It read:

'With much love and thanks to my dear Branks'.

Grouped around Auriol were photos of some of the Kenyan big-game crowd. Denys Finch-Hatton and his mistress Karen Blixen with his soon-to-be mistress, Beryl Markham (who would become an aviation legend within seven years), then a shot of Brancker and three shining natives standing proudly beside a slaughtered buffalo. Alongside that, there were photos of Edward, Prince of Wales with Finch Hatton, who'd taken up promoting the use of cameras for shooting animals instead of guns.

The three men studied it all in fascination. The door flew open and Brancker came bounding in, full of vim and vigor—a vortex of pure energy. He shook hands with each of them.

"Good of you to come. I thought it better we meet here. Too many big ears and wagging tongues in Whitehall—what!" He turned to the maid at the door. "Bring us a pot of tea and plenty of biscuits, Mable, please." Brancker caught Lou looking at a picture of him (much younger) beside a plane. "I made that flight solo to Persia," he said proudly.

"*Solo!* Gee!" Lou said.

"Yes, I followed the railway lines most of the way—excellent navigation tool, my boy. You should remember that. Please sit down. We have lots to talk about."

Brancker went and threw himself down in a worn, brown leather chair behind an ornate desk. They took their places in easy chairs in front of him.

"I got you down here to plan our strategy." He picked up a silver cigarette case on the desk and offered them around. Irwin took one and Brancker lit it for him with a desk lighter. Lou was tempted, but resisted. He'd quit smoking after the war when he joined the airships branch of the Navy. Brancker sat down again and stuck a cigarette in a long black holder and lit up. He immediately started coughing. They waited for him to stop.

"We need to sort things out. I didn't ask Scott—he's not the man he was—you're people I trust," Brancker said. Smoke billowed everywhere.

"Sir Sefton, I …" Colmore began.

"Yes, Reggie you're in a very difficult position. We all are." Brancker stood up and pushed the casement window open behind him. "We need to discuss our options and use our damned intelligence!" He paused to think. "The situation with that inspector fellow—McWade—he certainly set the cat among the pigeons, I can tell you!"

"He put me in a bind all right," Colmore said.

"I know—but he might just come in useful. Let's start from the beginning. What's the prognosis on the Howden ship?" Brancker looked at Irwin for an answer.

"I've spoken to both Booth and Meager and they're satisfied with that ship—and Lou's flown in both."

"She's well balanced and handles pretty well," Lou said.

"It's got its share of problems though ..." Colmore said.

Brancker looked quizzical. "But not to the degree of being un-flyable?"

"No. I couldn't quite say that. They've had a lot of trouble with the cover and its securing system. I'm still uncomfortable with it. A ship's only as good as its cover, after all."

"Their tail collapsed on her twenty-four-hour test, didn't it?" Brancker reminded them.

"Yes, and we just rebuilt it for them," Colmore replied.

"That's big! We need to play up that issue as much possible," Brancker said.

"How?" Colmore asked. The maid came in with a tray, set it down on the desk and tiptoed out.

"I'll get to that. When is *Howden R100* scheduled to leave for Canada?"

"At the end of this month," Lou said.

"Then we don't have much time," Brancker said. He stared across the room, admiring Auriol Lee for a moment, drawing on his cigarette.

"And you're scheduled to sail in her?" Brancker asked Lou.

"Yes, he is, and so am I," Colmore answered, with a frown. Brancker removed the lid from the teapot and slowly stirred the tea. He banged the drips off before replacing the lid.

"I'll be mum," he said, pouring milk from a jug into flowery, bone, china, gold-rimmed cups. He carefully placed the silver tea strainer over each cup and poured out the tea. Lou couldn't help but smile.

What a character: the toupée, the monocle, the cigarette holder. Hell, this is like the Mad Hatter's tea party!

Although sunny, it was cool. Each wore a sweater. MacDonald led them along a narrow, gravel walk between the house and a high brick wall enclosing the kitchen garden. It contained a variety of bushes, flowering plants and herbs the chef (also from Lossiemouth) used in his dishes. The path was bordered each side by manicured grass. From here, MacDonald showed them the lawn tennis courts. Marthe walked between the two men, slipping her arms into theirs.

"Doesn't he look *divine* in his plus fours, Kit?" Marthe said.

"Why, thank you. I find them most practical," MacDonald said.

"You must get some," Marthe said to Thomson.

"I don't think they'd suit me half as well," Thomson said.

"Ramsay, you're my Lord of the Manor and Kit—he's my Lord of the Air!"

"Come, I must show you our tulip tree," MacDonald said. They went to the entrance court and admired the tree.

"I've never seen anything like it—it's magnificent!" Marthe exclaimed.

"It's actually a type of magnolia," MacDonald said, picking one of the blossoms with a leaf attached and giving it to Marthe.

"Thank you, I shall send this to Abbé Brugnier, my close friend."

"He's Marthe's spiritual advisor in Paris. He's a very fine fellow," Thomson said.

MacDonald picked another and gave it to her. "Then he shall have his own. Send him this one. This tree has deep religious connections," MacDonald said, his eyes full of fun.

"Do tell me more," Marthe said, sensing she was about to be teased.

"I have it on the highest authority that when Eve—in her naked state —was being run out of the Garden of Eden by God's angels, she desperately grabbed hold of the last piece of foliage hanging over the wall from a tree—a magnolia tree identical to this. The leaf she held in her hand was just large enough to cover her private parts and thus, she was able to maintain her respectability."

Marthe giggled. "You're obviously very well-versed in botany," she said.

"Not to mention Eve's private parts. It all comes from the Scottish version of the Old Testament," Thomson told her.

They laughed and then made their way round to the Lavender Terrace on the south side, where Marthe admired a huge lavender bush and commented on its overpowering aroma. Stone steps led down from the terrace to the rose gardens, flanked by perfectly-cut box hedges. Marthe stood, hands on hips, staring up at the ancient, red brick façade.

"This is the stuff of ghost stories, Ramsay. It really is!"

"We should import some ravens from the Tower of London," Thomson suggested.

"We do have our share of ghosts here, you know. You'd better keep your head under the covers tonight," MacDonald said.

Marthe gave him a knowing smile. "Oh, ghosts appearing in the night don't bother me."

"I shall remember that, Marthe," Thomson said.

She caught the scent from the rose beds and breathed deeply. "Mmm, that fragrance!"

"Not quite as nice as our special roses, my dear," Thomson said.

This tweaked MacDonald's interest. He looked at Marthe.

"Kit always buys me very special roses—*Variété Général Jacqueminot.* They're extraordinary. We refer to them as our own," Marthe explained.

"I didn't realize CB was so profound in matters of love."

"Don't give my all secrets away, Marthe," Thomson said.

"Do you send flowers to Lady Wilson?" Marthe asked.

"Once in a while I send flowers to friends, but not such exotic varieties as Thomson's, obviously."

"I thought we might be seeing something of her this weekend," Marthe said.

"We both have busy schedules. Besides, I wanted to focus exclusively on you and CB."

"She is such a lovely lady," Marthe said.

"She is, indeed."

Brancker lit another cigarette and continued, "Okay, first things first. Get Richmond to write a memo to be read by all, saying neither ship has been designed to carry enough hydrogen and therefore neither provides adequate lift. Describe this as a massive safety problem," he said, as he handed a cup to Colmore. "It'll say it's not the designer's fault. The blame belongs with the Air Ministry, since they wrote the specifications."

Colmore stirred his tea. "I had a hand in that," he said, his expression pained.

"Don't worry about that, Reggie—so did lots of *other* people." Brancker held out tea to Lou and Irwin. "I want you to put it out there that not only does *Cardington R101* require an extra bay, but so does *Howden R100.* You can say drawings are on the boards and an additional bay is being designed for both ships, *right now.*"

"That's a *very* good idea—after all, we own them *both* now," Colmore said.

"Then I want you to get Rope to write another memo to everyone and his dog, saying the covers on both airships are in terrible shape, making them both less than airworthy. He's to say that it'd be better to postpone the flights for six months—no, make that a year—rather than take unnecessary risks with peoples' lives for no damned good reason."

"They'll gladly comply. It's *exactly* what they think," Colmore said.

Brancker smiled. "I know it is, Reggie." He turned to Irwin. "The next thing I want is for you, Captain, to write a report on the dismal performance of *Cardington R101* this week. That document is also to be read by all and sundry."

"I've already written it, sir," Irwin said.

"*Excellent!*" Brancker responded, rubbing his palms together.

The three companions strolled down to the meadow south of the rose garden, past the gate house and through the five-bar gate, stopping to admire the countryside. MacDonald pointed down the hill.

"We used to own a small house not far from here before I became a Member of Parliament. My wife and our five children used to come up this way for walks to Beacon Hill. I wrote to Lord Lee for permission to cross this land. He was here renovating the house in readiness to make it a deed of gift to the government for the use of future Prime Ministers—"

"Such as yourself!" Thomson said.

"Yes, indeed. He invited us for lunch on the terrace and told us all about it. Wonderful fellow!"

"And now you're enjoying his gift—little did you know!" Marthe said.

"Funny how things work out," Thomson said.

"Now you practically own it," Marthe said.

"Everything's only ever on loan, Marthe," MacDonald said.

Marthe looked back toward the trees. "I could swear I just saw someone up there behind that tree."

"Oh, it's only Robards. He's there to protect me."

"I see, and who will protect *me?*" Marthe asked.

"Why, *CB*, of course!"

They walked along a wide grassy pathway between lines of flowering lime trees. MacDonald looked more serious and stopped. He disengaged his arm from Marthe's and turned to face them.

"Marthe, you know I've asked CB to take up the post of Viceroy to India?"

Marthe beamed. "Yes, Prime Minister, I think it's a wonderful opportunity for him."

"Then you'd support such a move on his part?"

"*Wholeheartedly!* I know he's a great leader of men, and returning to the land of his birth in that capacity would be a huge triumph."

"It's a vitally important position."

"Without doubt," said Marthe.

"He's the one man in Britain most suited to the position."

"A very wise decision, if I may say so, Ramsay."

Thomson said nothing.

"And you'll visit him there, Marthe?"

"Indeed, I shall. What an adventure that'll be! Oh, how I long to visit the Taj Mahal."

"A testament to Shah Jahan's love of his wife, Mumtaz Mahal, who died in childbirth," MacDonald said. Marthe stared at MacDonald, amazed at his knowledge. Thomson remained silent, deep in thought.

My love for Marthe is as strong as Shah Jahan's. And someday I shall prove it.

MacDonald resumed. "Good. Good. I know you love to travel, Marthe."

"She does, she's Romanian!" Thomson said, himself beaming now.

MacDonald chuckled. "You're saying because she's a gypsy. How romantic. Bring on the violins!" He rapidly became somber again. "I shall also visit when I can. He's my wisest and most trusted friend. I'll miss him sorely."

Thomson perked up. "Don't look so down, Ramsay. We'll have a regularly scheduled airship service to India by then. You'll be able to travel in comfort."

"Perhaps one day we shall all visit the Taj together," Marthe said.

"*Splendid!* That's all settled, then. I propose we have a spot of tea on the terrace in the sunshine, followed by a game of croquet," MacDonald said.

"Wonderful idea," Thomson said. They turned back to the house.

Brancker had called for more tea and was pouring them another cup.

"Now there's another little wrinkle. If we can delay parting *Cardington R101* and thereby throw Lord Thomson off his schedule with the Prime Minister's Conference thing, he may let it slide and not care if we postpone her voyage to India till next year. That'd give us time to test these ships and do things right. So, the tactic is for us to hold off parting that ship on the pretext we're holding it in reserve for the Canadian trip. Bear in mind, *Howden R100* has yet to do another twenty-four-hour test since her tail was rebuilt. You never know—she might fail, especially if they have any more trouble with the cover."

"That's unlikely, sir," Irwin said.

"I'm waiting for the official word to begin work on the extra bay," Colmore said.

"I know you are. Don't do anything until you are expressly ordered to. I have someone working with us on delaying that. Unfortunately, the bean counters are with Thomson—they want results, and they want them *now*."

"It'll be tough, but we'll delay things if we can," Colmore said.

Brancker smoothed out his mustache with his thumb and forefinger, narrowing his eyes. "*Delay! Delay! Delay!* It'd be easier if we could get Howden to postpone. That's the goal. It'd take pressure off Cardington to make the India voyage." He looked at Lou. "This is where you come in, Commander. I'd like you to reach out on behalf of your boss, Wing Commander Colmore here—*unofficially*—and request they do the right thing."

"You want me to ask them to postpone their flight, sir?" Lou asked.

"*Exactly!* I know you have a wonderful relationship with Howden. You're a godsend! I want you to set up a meeting as soon as you can."

"I'll be glad to try, sir, but I know Mr. Burney is anxious to fly to Canada immediately," Lou said.

"No more '*Mr. Burney*'!" Brancker exclaimed. All eyes widened. Lou wondered if Burney had been sacked. "He's *Sir* Dennis now—he's just been knighted," Brancker said, laughing. They all rolled their eyes. "Anyway, arrange a meeting as quickly as possible and see if you can pull it off and don't forget to call him *Sir Dennis*!" Brancker said.

"I won't forget, *Sir Sefton*," Lou said.

"You're going to need to appeal to his better side. I'm sure he must have one. You know: 'We're all in this together, old man' and all that. If none of that works, try telling him that new designs for bigger and better ships are on the boards and Vickers will be expected to play their part. Tell them Brancker very much wants Vickers's involvement. For now, we seek their cooperation, their patience and their understanding. We're all *airshipmen* and we're all *gentlemen* and we'll return the favor and look out for them in the future—tell Burney he has Brancker's word—the word of one knight to another." They all stood up, preparing to leave. "One last thing," Brancker said. "It's important testing is carried out thoroughly—not cut short for any reason *whatsoever.* Be firm. Stick to your guns!"

Lou was dazzled by Brancker's brilliance. But would any of it work? He decided to try and track down Burney as soon as they got back to Cardington.

Nevil will give me his home number.

Tea was served on the Lavender Terrace. They sat round a wooden garden table under an umbrella. Clouds were rolling in and it was getting muggy. MacDonald took off his sweater. After tea, they played croquet until a cloudburst soaked them. They dashed back to the terrace, giggling like college chums.

Later, while MacDonald spent time at his desk in his study, Thomson took Marthe on a guided tour. They went to each room, inspecting the furnishings and paintings. She was especially taken by the oak Regency pedestal table used by Napoleon and with Nelson's watch in a display case. A ring belonging to the great Queen Elizabeth filled her with wonder. Cromwell's death mask she hated on sight—he'd been responsible for the death of so many good Irish people. But the library filled her with joy. As a highly acclaimed writer, she was able to appreciate the first illustrated edition of Milton's *Paradise Lost* printed in 1688. To hold such ancient books in her hands gave her a special thrill.

57

CHEQUERS & A MEETING WITH BURNEY & CO.

Saturday July 5 - Sunday July 13, 1930.

As soon as Lou got back to Cardington, he tried calling Norway in York, but got no answer. After an hour, he gave up and went home. He would've preferred to make this call without Charlotte around. On arrival, he found her coming in with some shopping. She didn't look happy. Her mood was always sour these days. After kissing her, Lou used the phone on the small table in the living room. Norway answered.

"Nev, where the hell've you been? I've been calling you for the *last two hours!* "

"I just got home from the flying club. What do you need, old man?"

"I need Burney's number."

"What do you need that for?"

"I want to talk to him."

"What about?"

"Nev, I can't say right now. I'll tell you later."

"Keeping secrets, eh? I can guess … Here it is …"

Lou wrote down the number as Charlotte entered the room. "Thanks, Nev. Look, I'll speak to you later. Okay?" He hung up the phone.

"What's going on?" Charlotte asked.

"I've been asked to talk to Burney and get him to postpone their flight."

Charlotte said nothing. Lou knew she understood exactly what was going on. He picked up the phone and dialed Burney's number. A well-spoken woman answered. Charlotte stood at the doorway, listening.

"May I speak to Sir Dennis, please."

"And who may I say is calling Sir Dennis?" she wah-wahed.

"Commander Remington, ma'am."

Lou heard the woman calling, "Darling … a Commander Remington is on the phone."

A few moments later, Burney came on. "Lou, this is a surprise. What can I do for you, my dear chap?"

"Good of you to take my call, Sir Dennis. I have a favor to ask."

"Of course, fire away."

"I'd like to meet with you. It's important."

"I see. I'm going to the Continent on Monday. I'll be back in ten days. We can meet then, if you like."

"Oh, dear. I'd hoped to see you on Monday."

"Well, if it's that important, I can meet you tomorrow morning in Westminster."

"Splendid, sir. Could you have Barnes and Nevil attend?"

"Don't see why not. I'll instruct them to be there."

"That's awfully kind of you," Lou said, realizing he was lapsing into British jargon.

"What's this all about, Lou?"

"I prefer to tell you tomorrow, if you don't mind, sir."

"All right. 9 o'clock. Sunday morning—Vickers's office on Broadway."

"Thank you, Sir Dennis."

Lou put the phone down. Charlotte looked at him and shook her head sadly. She gave a deep sigh, turned and went upstairs to the bedroom. Lou called Norway back, but didn't say what the meeting was about. He said he'd tell them in the morning.

That evening, Thomson and Marthe sat down to dinner with MacDonald.

"What did you do with your friend's flower?" MacDonald asked.

"I have it pressed in my journal. I'll send it to him next week with a letter describing my delightful stay at Chequers with you," Marthe replied, smiling warmly.

"Will he approve of you sleeping under the same roof as a couple of ne'er-do-well British politicians?"

"I'm sure he would. He's met Kit and loves him to death. Kit took us on a tour of Westminster Palace a couple of years ago."

"He's quite a wit," Thomson said. "On entering the House of Lords, he said he understood why politics is like a religion to us."

"He said that?"

"He said it's because we practice our politics in a cathedral!"

"I'm glad to hear he approves of CB," MacDonald said. MacDonald's observation had implications, but Marthe didn't respond. "What do you think about this proposed flight of CB's to India in September, Marthe?" MacDonald asked.

"He feels it's his destiny. I wish he wasn't going, but I wouldn't try to dissuade him."

"I *must* go. It'll give the troops a boost. Look, when your time's up—that's it. I'm a *fatalist*."

"You mean everything's preordained?" MacDonald asked.

"I told you about the boy at Cardington, didn't I?" Thomson said, looking at Marthe.

"Yes, that was a pity," she said.

"No, you didn't tell *me* about it," MacDonald said.

"Ramsay, I thought you had enough to worry about."

"I seem to have heard that before. What happened this time?" MacDonald asked.

"I met this boy in the ground crew. He stood out. He had this pair of old boots he'd shined like glass. There was something about him. I put my hand on his shoulder and complimented him. He had a beautiful young face —*angelic*."

"So what happened to him?"

"We went out for many hours—marvelous flight! I had a desk put on board and worked up there in perfect solitude. It took ages for them to land at the mast and when they did, that boy ran and grabbed the mooring line and fell down dead."

"My goodness gracious! That's terrible! What happened?" MacDonald exclaimed.

"There's always a burst of static electricity when they throw the line down."

"And he didn't know that?" Marthe asked.

"Well, everyone thought he'd been electrocuted, but it turned out, he had a weak heart and his great run for the line finished the boy off."

MacDonald looked distraught. "That poor, wee laddie."

"The point was, at the time, none of us knew anything about it. The press told me. But when they said it, I sensed immediately who it was."

"You mean he was marked for death?" MacDonald said.

"I'm saying—it was his time."

"Did he know, do you think?" Marthe asked.

"Oh no, he was a happy, young fellow. Dead keen! Very sad. I often think about him."

MacDonald said nothing for a few moments and then, "Perhaps it was his boots that marked him. God must have said, 'Bring me the boy with the shiny boots.' They'd been shined so His angels would know him."

"Oh, that's lovely, Ramsay," Marthe said. "He's such a poet, isn't he Kit?"

The weekend was spent in a state of contentment, enjoying each other's company despite the dreary weather; they were three souls in perfect harmony, at one with the universe. In Sunday morning drizzle, they were driven to St. Peter and St. Paul, the old parish church overlooking the tiny village of Ellesborough. They were greeted by the vicar and exchanged respectful nods and smiles with members of the congregation. Although Marthe found the service different, she enjoyed it.

That Sunday morning, Lou traveled down to London by train, wearing a sports jacket and slacks under his raincoat—this was unofficial business. He arrived at the Vickers offices just before nine. A security man let him in and showed him into an ornately-furnished board room on the ground floor. Soon, Norway came blundering in, out of breath, worried he was late. Wallis arrived a few minutes later, looking fit and relaxed. They made pleasant small talk, reminiscing about the good times at Howden. Punctually at nine, Burney entered the room and after shaking hands, sat at the head of the table.

Burney glanced at Wallis and Norway. "Sorry to drag you fellows out on a Sunday like this. The Commander called this meeting. Apparently, he has something important he wishes to discuss. Perhaps you'd be good enough to enlighten us, Lou."

"Yes, sir. But first I want to congratulate you on your knighthood. Sir Sefton Brancker mentioned it yesterday and sends his congratulations and kind personal regards." Lou glanced at Wallis who appeared irritated, looking down at his hands on the table. Burney beamed, while Lou continued. "Wing Commander Colmore asked me to make an approach to you, *unofficially*."

"*Really?* How strange," Burney said, appearing puzzled, but obviously enjoying this.

Is he play-acting?

Wallis and Norway remained expressionless.

"He's suggesting both transcontinental voyages be postponed until next year."

Wallis was aghast. "On what grounds?"

"Colmore's view is that both ships haven't been sufficiently tested. He thinks they have flaws, making the risks unjustifiable and doesn't feel comfortable putting men's lives in danger unnecessarily."

"What flaws is he talking about?" Burney asked.

"The R.A.W. is worried about the outer covers on both ships."

"Our cover will be in p-pretty good shape prior to our d-departure," Norway said.

"*Cardington R101's* cover is also being replaced. The tail collapsing on *Howden R100* caused a great deal of concern," Lou said.

"That's been fixed by the Airship Works staff. Nevil will be looking at that on Tuesday when he's there for the preflight conference. I understand the R.A.W. took it upon themselves to redesign the tail section. So there shouldn't be anything to worry about, should there?" Wallis said, without hiding his displeasure at their tampering with his design.

"I think they'd like to see more testing done, just the same," Lou said.

"Lou, we all like you, you know that. But I'm going to cut to the chase, as they say in Hollywood." Burney smiled at his own little joke. "The truth is, it's *they* who don't feel ready, do they?"

Lou paused. This was the crux of the matter. It was time to go into the 'old Sir Sefton routine.' "You're perfectly correct, Sir Dennis." Lou stole a glance at Wallis and saw him grimace. "And quite honestly, I think they'd admit that to you. They're making an appeal to you as fellow airshipmen."

Burney lifted his eyebrows. "It's a bit late for all this old chummy stuff, isn't it?"

"Yes, it is, and that's regrettable," Lou said.

"I told you what was happening ages ago, Lou," Wallis said.

"You were right. But do you really have to put the boot in? It couldn't hurt to be magnanimous, could it, Barnes?" Lou chided him.

"So let us understand this—they're asking us to postpone *our* flight to Canada to allow *them* time to get *their* ship into a flyable condition and in the meantime have the world believe *Howden R100* is in the same pathetic state," Wallis said.

Lou looked kindly at each man around the table in an attempt to appeal to their better sides. "Sir Dennis, Sir Sefton told me that if you do this, Vickers will be well rewarded. He regards Vickers as part of the team—an indispensible part. New designs are on the boards at Cardington for even bigger airships and he says it's *imperative* Vickers plays a major role. He asked me to tell you that, and for the moment, he seeks your cooperation, your patience and your understanding. He knows this project has been a loss for Vickers, but he'll see to it you come out whole at the end of the day. I'll tell you exactly what he said: 'We're *all* airshipmen and we're *all* gentlemen. We *will* return the favor and we *will* look out for Vickers in the future.' He said, 'Tell Sir Dennis they have Brancker's word—the word of one knight to another.'"

Burney seemed impressed. Lou sensed he'd won him over, but Wallis and Norway appeared unmoved. The 'one knight to another' part certainly didn't go down well with Wallis. Norway sat frowning.

Then Burney's demeanor changed. "I'm skeptical for one simple reason. Short Brothers used to build airships. They had a nice little business going until the government decided they'd take it," Burney said.

"What do you mean, *take it?*" Lou asked.

"They nationalized the business and renamed it the 'Royal Airship Works.' It has a nice ring to it, doesn't it? We could do all the right things, and yes, get more airships rolling out of our sheds, and then—*hey, presto!*—we're nationalizing your company! We don't trust these people. It's what they do!"

"Well put, sir," Norway said.

"Maybe the next damned socialist who comes along and can't get himself elected will call himself Lord Karl Marx of Howden!" Burney quipped.

"I can't believe it," Lou said.

"You're an American. Things like that could never happen in America," Norway said.

"There is another way," Wallis said. "They own both airships. We're merely trying to fulfill our contractual obligations. They could instruct us not to fly to Canada—announce a postponement. It's really as simple as that, Lou!"

"Easier said than done. They'd lose face with their masters at the Air Ministry—and with the public, of course," Lou said.

"The main problem is, Thomson's got his own personal agenda and schedule, which shouldn't get mixed up in the development of experimental aircraft," Wallis said.

"Surely, their ship can't be that b-bad, can it? They've removed all the unnecessary weight and they're building in an extra b-bay. That should solve their p-problems," Norway said.

"Let's hope so. But there's still not enough time for testing. Lord Thomson is insisting they leave at the end of September," Lou said, putting his hand to his forehead—he'd lost this battle and his disappointment showed.

"There you have it. They're in a mess of their own making. It's a pity, but I vote *NO* to postponement," Wallis said.

"Hear, hear," Norway said. Lou wished he'd not asked Burney to invite them now. That was a mistake. He may have pulled it off, one on one.

"They must postpone and not fly until their ship has been properly tested—or throw in the towel. It's our judgment *Howden R100* is ready. Remember, government officials were on board for all our tests and accepted the ship. It only remains for us to make our intercontinental voyage and we will have fulfilled our obligations," Burney concluded.

They all got to their feet. There was no animosity, only total detachment between Wallis and Burney. Lou shook hands sadly with each of them.

"I'll see you on board then," he said, looking at Burney and then Wallis. Wallis said nothing. He just smiled. Lou knew Wallis well enough to know there was *more* to that smile.

Lou returned to Cardington and delivered the bad news to Colmore who took it hard, although he wasn't surprised. Colmore had seen to it other parts of Brancker's plan were being put into effect. Richmond, Rope and Irwin would have their reports ready early in the week for dissemination to all interested parties. The only trouble was, there *were* no interested parties that Lou could tell. The Air Ministry didn't want to hear about any more delays, no matter how bad the reports, or who wrote them. The only person who believed the negative reporting was McWade and, as recently proved, his view didn't count for much. Lou was frustrated; the R.A.W. wanted the Howden people to make the move so they'd appear blameless themselves.

Howden was having none of that. After the debriefing, Colmore called Brancker to update him. After that, Lou went home and gave Charlotte a sanitized version of events of the past two days. She remained silent.

      Thomson and Marthe stayed at Chequers for almost two weeks. They had a lazy time reading and walking the estate or going out in Thomson's limousine for rides in the country. When MacDonald was home, they played croquet or cards and had lively conversations. During this time, Thomson received reports of disturbing rumors. He was also told work hadn't yet begun on parting *Cardington R101*. He decided not to let this spoil his time with Marthe—he'd give them some stick on his return the following week.

58

CANADA PREFLIGHT CONFERENCE

L ou was at his desk in his office at Cardington House when he heard a small plane go over. He went to the window and looked out. *That must be him.*

Lou rode down to the field outside the sheds on the *Brough Superior* in time to see Norway's plane flaring down onto the grass. It turned and taxied toward him from the St. Mary's end of the field. Lou grinned. This man Nevil was 'a bit of a lad', as the Brits would say, landing here at Cardington like this. Lou had informed Colmore, who was much too decent to object, but others would be extremely irritated; no one at the Royal Airship Works could fly a plane. And by now, they'd heard Colmore's overtures to Howden had failed. Lou strolled out and cast a skeptical eye over the Gypsy Moth.

"Methinks 'tis made of sealing wax and string!" he said.

Norway scrambled out of the cockpit. "It's lovely to see you, too, old man," he said.

"They sent me out to meet you," Lou said.

"Have they put out the welcome mat?"

"They'd rather welcome a case of the pox, old buddy."

"Thanks," Norway said.

"You wanna take a look at her rear end first?"

"Okay, let's take a peek."

They rode over to Shed No. 2. Once inside, they walked to the end of the building and Norway stared up. His jaw dropped.

"Oh, bugger me! That's so b-bloody radical! Wallis will have a f-fit."

"Don't get your knickers in a twist. It ain't that bad!"

They climbed aboard and inspected the work from the inside.

"Nothing wrong with the workmanship," Norway said. "It's bloody good—much better than ours!"

They drove across to Cardington House where they drank coffee in Lou's office before heading to the conference room. The R.A.W. people were assembled: Colmore, Scott, Richmond, Rope, McWade, Booth, Meager, Atherstone, and about ten others from the design office. Lou and Norway walked in and sat at the table. Lou was surprised at the expressions of pure hatred on their faces. He knew Norway hadn't bargained for this. It was as if Lou had brought in the devil himself. Norway filled and lit his pipe. They didn't like that pipe. They didn't like the Harris Tweed jacket. They didn't like the leather elbow patches. They didn't like the leather edging on his breast pocket. They thought he was attempting to look older than his years, create the impression he was a mature, studious thinker.

Colmore cleared his throat. "We're here to discuss *Howden R100's* flight to Canada. We'll talk about preparations Commander Atherstone has made in Montreal. He'll give us an update later. We'll go over the preparation of the ship—provisioning, fueling, ballasting and gassing up, and the final twenty-four-hour test flight this week. We'll talk about the crew and her officers and their roles." At this point Colmore looked purposefully at Scott before continuing. "We'll go over the intended schedule and routing in detail. This will take three or four hours. We'll break for lunch at 12:30 and resume this afternoon." Richmond raised his hand.

"What is it, Colonel?"

"Before we get into details, I'd like to ask Mr. Norway a few questions, if you don't mind, sir," Richmond said.

"You can—providing Mr. Norway has no objection," Colmore said. No one had been able to bring themselves to look at Norway, but suddenly their accusing eyes were upon him.

Norway removed his pipe from his mouth. "N-N-Not at all."

Richmond stared down the table with contempt. "After the collapse of the tail of *Howden R100* and the subsequent repairs and design corrections done by the Royal Airship Works—are you confident you can make it across the Atlantic, Mr. Norway?" Richmond asked.

Norway swallowed hard, blinking like an owl. "W-We knew there were some p-p-problems with the tail s-section and—"

Richmond rested his elbows on the table and leaned forward holding his head, as though perplexed. "You *knew* there were problems and you brought it to the Royal Airship Works, anyway? I don't understand, Mr. Norway."

"W-We knew we m-may have a p-problem as something had shown up in the testing m-m-model, but we thought we'd r-resolved the issue. But they b-broke down the model b-before we could do more t-t-tests. We—"

"So you delivered an untested airship to the government, knowing there was a good chance it still had structural problems?"

"They weren't m-major—"

Richmond sat back. "I'd call the collapse of the tail in mid-flight a major problem! How do you know other structural flaws won't surface en route to Canada—when it's too late? And what about the wiring system holding down and securing the cover? I hear that was chafing and falling apart."

Colmore was listening intently with alarm.

"We redid all the z-zigzag wiring and remedied the s-situation."

"Remedied the situation! That cover has a very weird look about it, if you ask me."

"There's nothing wrong with the c-cover. We conducted s-six f-flight tests—more than a hundred and twenty hours—c-covering s-six thousand miles, many in adverse w-weather c-conditions."

"And then the tail collapsed. What's going to collapse next? Maybe your ship's getting tired, Mr. Norway. I believe a hell of a lot more testing is necessary."

"I-If that's your o-opinion …" Norway was struggling for breath, his mouth puckering up like a goldfish, "you should order us n-not to under-t-take this f-flight. The ch-choice is entirely yours, s-sir," Norway said, stabbing the air with his pipe.

This set off much eye-rolling and sighing among the R.A.W. officials, frustrated at being beaten by someone they considered to be a stuttering fool with no airship experience. The audacity of Norway's last statement had surprised and silenced them. Colmore glanced at Richmond.

"Any more questions for Mr. Norway?"

"No! We might as well talk to the *wall*," Richmond said.

"Very well then, let's continue," Colmore said, shaken by this exchange.

At the lunchtime break everyone got up and went to the dining room. No one offered Norway lunch. Lou and Norway were left sitting at the table.

"No lunch invite for you, Nev, old buddy," Lou said, grinning.

"It doesn't matter. I'm not hungry."

"Just as well—it might be laced with rat poison, mate."

"Thanks."

"Come on. Charlotte's got sandwiches and a nice warm beer for us. Let's go."

Fifteen minutes later, they entered 58 Kelsey Street where Charlotte waited. Although very pale, she looked starkly beautiful, stunning in a tight black dress and high-heeled shoes. She was expertly made up. Lou studied her gorgeous face and perfect derriere. She'd made a big effort, probably because Nevil was coming. Even after nine years, she still made Lou's heart race. It'd been ages since they'd made love. He wished he could take her to bed for the afternoon, instead of returning to that oppressive conference room. She kissed Norway's cheek and Lou on the lips. They sat downstairs at the kitchen table looking into the garden.

"How's the meeting going?" Charlotte asked, placing a plate of ham sandwiches on the table.

"Brutal," Lou said. "Look at him—he's black and blue!"

"I think they're warming up to me," Norway said with a silly grin.

"Hell, I must have been in the wrong room," Lou said.

Charlotte poured their pale ales. They were parched after Norway's grilling and took a few welcome gulps before attacking the sandwiches.

"Maybe you can't blame them," Charlotte said, fixing Norway with an icy stare.

"Charlotte, they can elect to postpone our flight," Norway said gently as he chewed.

Charlotte pouted in annoyance, her full red lips emphasizing the whiteness of her skin. She flashed her eyes at him. "Nevil, you're right, but these men have their pride and you people are bloody-well wiping the floor up with them!"

"Not you, too, Charlotte? I'm really sorry, but their fate's in their own hands."

"And what about the fate of *my husband?* How will you feel if anything happens to *him?*"

"But *I'm* going, too."

"And *you're* crazy! The tail might fall off again."

"It didn't f-fall off. It only b-buckled a bit. It's f-fixed now—"

"You're forcing them to fly *their* ship! It's a bloody *deathtrap!* And *you* won't be on that one, will you!"

"Not t-true. We're n-not f-f-forcing anybody to do *anything.*"

"You're like a bunch of school kids. I'm sick of it!" Charlotte said, getting up.

"We'd better get back. We don't want them getting upset," Lou said.

"If anything happens to them all ..." Charlotte began. Lou gave her a disapproving look. She picked up their two empty bottles and threw them in the bin with a *clunk*, turned away and went upstairs without kissing them goodbye. Lou and Norway left the rest of the sandwiches and rode back to Cardington House.

They entered the empty conference room.

"They're not back yet," Lou said.

"I didn't expect them to be, but I'd sooner f-face this lot than your wife," Norway said as he filled and lit his pipe.

"You know Charlotte loves you really, Nev. She's worried, that's all. She'll be all right once these two voyages are over with."

They sat and waited in silence until the R.A.W. crowd filed in. The rest of the meeting went as planned and at the end Colmore passed out sheets of paper. "This is the proposed list of officers and crewmen for the flight to Canada and is subject to the approval of Captain Booth, as *pilot in command*," Colmore said.

A copy of the list was given to everyone—except Norway. Lou passed one to him. Lou scanned it: Sir Dennistoun Burney ...Barnes Wallis

...Nevil Norway ...Fred McWade ...Billy Bunyan ...William Jessup and Sqn. Ldr. Archibald Wann, (from *R38*, which came as a big surprise to Lou). Scott's name was at the very bottom.

"*Howden R100* will be under the command of Captain Booth, with Captain Meager as first officer. Flying Officer Steff will serve as second officer and Commander Remington as third officer and American Observer." Colmore paused to glare at Scott. "Major Scott will be acting Rear Admiral, a ceremonial role limited to issues concerning routing and scheduling and nothing more." This last statement was lost on most people in the room, but to Lou, it was telling—Scott couldn't be trusted. Lou glanced at Scott who as clearly furious. "This meeting is adjourned," Colmore announced.

There were no pleasantries when Norway left. Booth and Meager trooped down to the field with Lou and Norway to see him off the property. A few *Howden R100* crewmen joined them, including Nervous Nick. They stood around chatting for a while before Norway set off.

"They're all up at the windows watching you, Nev," Lou said indicating Cardington House behind them with a sideways nod.

"Perhaps they'd prefer to remember me as 'C-Crash-and-B-Burn' Norway."

They all thought this was pretty funny. Nervous Nick gripped the propeller and Norway gave the word to swing. The engine caught and he turned the plane out to the center of the field. Soon he was bouncing along and lifting off.

"He's a brave soul," Booth said.

"Sooner him than me in that thing," Meager answered.

A few minutes later, Norway was at two thousand feet and making a banking turn toward them. He roared over their heads, waggled his wings and disappeared into the clouds.

"Well, if they weren't mad before, they will be *now*," Lou said.

Two days later, another small plane, this one bearing Brancker, piloted by one Miss Honeysuckle, dropped in on Cardington. Brancker loved having this leggy blond as his personal pilot and chauffeur. Brancker showed Miss Honeysuckle around Shed No.1 with Colmore and Lou for half an hour. Brancker hadn't popped in for the sake of a jaunt.

"What about a spot of tea, Reggie? Anything doing?" he asked.

"Of course, sir." They left the shed and walked to Cardington House.

"I was sorry to hear about their damned poor attitude, Lou," he said.

"I did my best. They were nice and very polite, actually," Lou said.

"It's a shame. Thanks for giving it 'the old college try.' I'm grateful to you."

"They're businessmen," Lou said.

Brancker stared through his monocle at the sky, as if that thought had never crossed his mind. "I suppose you're right." He turned to Colmore. "When we get to your office, I want you to track Burney down."

"He's away on the Continent this week, sir," Lou said.

"We'll need to find out if he left a contact number."

When they got to the building, Miss Honeysuckle was left in the grand reception hall, Brancker telling her he'd be in conference. The three men went to Colmore's office, a suite with a secretary's office leading into his. He had a large room overlooking Cardington Field. Colmore closed the outer door to the corridor and spoke to his secretary. "Doris, I want you to get hold of Sir Dennis Burney. Try the London office first," he said. "Please arrange for tea to be sent to Miss Honeysuckle and we'll have some, too. Thanks."

They went in, closed the door and sat down. Doris soon came on the line on the speaker. "Sir Dennis is out of the country and cannot be reached."

"Hmm. All right, try and locate Mr. Barnes Wallis. Not sure where he's based these days," Brancker said.

"Right sir. The tea lady's here."

Ten minutes later, Doris came on again. "I managed to locate Mr. Wallis, sir. He'll be on the line in a moment."

The speakerphone crackled. "Hello, Wallis here."

"I have Sir Sefton here and Commander Remington," Colmore said.

"Good afternoon to you all," Wallis said.

Brancker leaned forward in his chair. "My dear Barnes, Sefton Brancker here. As you might have guessed, this is a follow up to your meeting with the Commander, which he kindly conducted on our behalf. I've been discussing the issues concerning both airships with Wing Commander Colmore—you know, the covers on both, the structural issue with the Howden ship, the weight issues with the Cardington ship. I think it would be beneficial to all parties if we came together as a team and recommended postponement. Then all these things can be resolved, and we can move forward knowing we've done *absolutely everything* in our power to ensure both ships are perfectly safe."

Wallis's tone was cool. "As far as *Howden R100* is concerned, I can say the problems have been minor in nature and everything's been rectified."

"But I don't feel these ships are ready. They're not fully tested, are they?"

"It's not actually up to me to make that judgment, Sir Sefton. I don't know whether you've heard, but I'm based at Weybridge now, working on aeroplane designs."

"Not officially, no. I thought this was just in the interim between airships," Brancker said. "You know we have plans to get going on more designs for much bigger airships."

Colmore was itching to speak. "How do you feel about crossing the Atlantic, or making the voyage to India in one of these airships, old man? I don't think they've proven themselves yet, do you?" he said.

"You're asking me, as the engineer of *Howden R100*, if I am confident in the ship I've designed. I have complete confidence in that airship. She has more than fulfilled my expectations and met every requirement of the contract."

"So, you're one hundred percent confident in making the Atlantic crossing in her, then," Colmore asked. There was a long pause at the other end and they took it to mean that *maybe* he wasn't.

Wallis eventually responded. "Actually, I won't be going."

This came as a horrible blow to Colmore who was unable to conceal his shock. He looked betrayed.

"What! Why ever not?"

"I wish I could."

"What do you mean?"

"I'd love to go, but I'm forbidden to fly in airships by the chairman of our board."

"Why? You're on the list of passengers!" Colmore exclaimed.

"Apparently, my safety is of paramount importance to the company."

There was a long, awkward silence and Colmore looked sick.

"Barnes, will they consider holding off for a spell?" Brancker asked.

"I don't think they'd entertain the idea for a moment, Sir Sefton— and why should they, after the way they've been treated by Cardington all these years?"

The following Sunday afternoon, Buck drove Thomson and Marthe from Chequers to the Ritz, where Marthe was dropped off. She had much writing to do. Thomson returned to Ashley Gardens. He usually found Sunday evenings depressing at the best of times, but tonight it was worse. After such wonderful company, he felt lonely. He played his gramophone and sat on the chaise longue studying his ministerial papers in preparation for a busy week. Time was slipping away. He needed to get after Colmore.

He shut his eyes, soothed by the sounds of Mozart's *Don Giovanni* and Sammie's purring. He soon dozed off and found himself wandering the rues of Paris, searching for the girl in the white carriage. The streets were empty.

59

ENEMIES IN THE CAMP

Monday July 14, 1930.

The next morning, Thomson went to Gwydyr House. After his initial snooze on the chaise, he'd stumbled off to bed, but couldn't get back to sleep. He'd spent a sleepless night stewing about *Cardington R101*. All his personal plans depended on that ship being ready for the India flight. He instructed Knoxwood to call Colmore to Whitehall immediately. Colmore, rather shaken, arrived before lunch and was led into Thomson's office. He had no idea why he'd been summoned. He'd explained to Knoxwood he wasn't in uniform and was told it didn't matter.

"Just get down here, at once, Weggie," Knoxwood had said.

As soon as Colmore walked in, Thomson calmed down. The man was harmless; no point in scaring him to death. But he did want to confront him.

"I got you down here—and thank you for coming, by the way—as I've been hearing things which give me cause for concern. I thought it best to talk to you directly." Colmore gave a start. "Rumors are circulating of a concerted effort to delay the airship program."

"Er, h-how, sir?"

"They're trying everything in their power to postpone both voyages." Colmore swallowed hard and his eyes bulged. "A series of memos and reports were written and disseminated by people in your organization last week suggesting neither airship is ready for their flights."

"It's true reports were issued by—"

"I'm aware of who wrote them, Colmore, and what they say," Thomson snapped.

"Yes, sir."

"We have enemies in the camp. I trust you're not playing a double game—not part of a conspiracy, are you?"

"No, sir."

Thomson paused, his eyes fixed on Colmore. "I'm sure I know where this originated—it's coming from right here in this building, isn't it? Tell me who it is!"

"I don't know anything."

"No one has approached you?"

"No."

"I *will* find out. And you'd better *not* be involved."

"No, sir. *I'm* not involved."

That had to be a slip right there!

"You're not involved in *what?*"

"I've never heard of any conspiracies."

Thomson sat and stared at Colmore again. "I understand one of the inspectors has been stirring up a lot of trouble?"

"I wouldn't say that. He's concerned the gas bags are full of holes."

"And are conditions so serious to warrant him writing letters directly to the Air Ministry—going over the heads of you and your staff?"

"He's a bit of an alarmist, that's all."

"He wasn't put up to it by you, or someone in this building, was he?"

"No, sir, absolutely not!"

"This problem he talks about—can it be rectified or not?"

"Oh, *definitely*, sir.

"He's not part of a conspiracy?"

"Oh Lord, no, sir, *certainly not.*"

"I understand you've put him in charge of correcting these deficiencies?"

"Yes, it'll be his responsibility to oversee and inspect the work."

"Good. Perhaps it'll make him feel important."

"Quite, sir."

"That'll keep him quiet. Has work begun on the extra bay?"

"Er, no, sir."

Now there was an edge of menace in Thomson's voice. "And *why* is that, Colmore?"

"I haven't received instructions from my superiors to proceed."

Thomson studied Colmore with suspicion, his eyes narrowing. "I see."

Colmore went on. "It's my vague understanding the Cardington ship is being held in reserve until *Howden R100* completes her final test—in case she fails. Then *Cardington R101* would be available—"

Thomson looked incredulous. "To fly to *Canada?*"

"That's my understanding, yes, sir."

"To hell with the Canadian flight. You're not making any sense, Colmore. They're not going to fly to Canada in a ship in need of an extra bay. That's all hooey!"

"I think they were trying to maintain flexibility, sir. Then *Howden R100* would be available for the flight to India, if necessary."

"What is my name and title, Colmore?"

"Lord Thomson of Cardington, sir."

"I'm not Lord Thomson of *Howden?*"

"No, sir."

"I do not want to arrive in India in a ship constructed by the Vickers Airship Guarantee Company in Howden."

"I understand completely, sir."

"Nothing must delay my flight to India in *Cardington R101* built by the *Royal Airship Works!*

"Yes, sir."

Thomson spun round in his chair to face the painting of the Taj Mahal on the wall behind him. He raised his hand grandly to it, as though talking to a schoolboy. "The *India* flight, Colmore! Do you understand? *India!*" He turned back to face the beleaguered man. "*Got that?*"

"Yes, sir," Colmore said weakly, staring with dread into the Indian summer heat—but then noticing the airship, his eyes opened wide with surprise. Thomson smiled inwardly. Churchill had done a nice job. The man was quite a painter—for a *damned Tory!* It had certainly spooked Colmore.

"Make it happen! Everything clear?"

"*Perfectly* clear, sir. Yes, sir."

"Don't fail me. All right, get out."

Thomson was more convinced than ever that his suspicions and the rumors had been correct.

Thomson and Marthe spent the remainder of their time together enjoying London and their friends, with trips to country houses and dining in fine restaurants. Thomson usually went to the Ministry in the mornings, while Marthe worked on her writing in her hotel suite at the Ritz.

They spent many pleasant hours walking the streets of the West End, visiting museums and parks, their favorite being St. James's, where they fed the ducks. Like other things, this had become a ritual in this special place, the discord of last year forgotten.

Thomson didn't bring up the subject of marriage. He'd wait until just before Marthe's departure on Monday. As the week went by, he sensed this time she might give him a positive answer—she'd been exceptionally sweet this visit. On the last Saturday morning, since the weather was nice, they drove to Lord's Cricket Ground where Marthe made an effort to understand and enjoy the game.

While Thomson and Marthe were at Lord's, Lou was traveling back from the Scilly Isles in the Atlantic Ocean aboard *Howden R100,* completing her final twenty-four-hour test. The ship had behaved perfectly. Shortly after she returned to Cardington, her departure for Montreal was confirmed for 3:30 a.m. Tuesday morning.

Lou and Charlotte had seen little of one another over the past few weeks. She'd been on night duty at the hospital and asleep during the day. He was awakened by her in the mornings as she climbed into bed just before dawn; usually tired and irritable. She rarely spoke. Lou had been working long hours, getting the airship ready for the twenty-four-hour final test and the flight to Canada. In the evenings, he arrived as Charlotte was leaving. They gave each other a smile and a peck on the cheek, like passing strangers.

Charlotte had lost weight and settled into a never-ending state of despair, speaking in monosyllables, if at all, her vitality gone. There was no animosity between them and Lou was patient and affectionate. He remained convinced Charlotte would snap out of it once the two ships had made their intercontinental flights and were up and running, confident their closeness would return.

Charlotte still kept the house immaculate and the kitchen cupboards well-stocked. She'd put his things together for the Canada voyage and his side trip down to Virginia to see his family. Lou got the impression she was glad he was making the effort to see them. Pity she couldn't be with him. They'd love her. Still, there'd be plenty of time for that. Perhaps they'd make a trip to New York next year—he'd suggest they start planning as soon as he got back.

When Lou returned from the final test on Saturday evening, Charlotte was home. She appeared brighter. She told him she had time off to help him get ready for his departure on Tuesday. "Does your family know you're coming?" Charlotte asked.

"I sent them a telegram," Lou replied. "I expect they'll be at Union Station." The atmosphere was difficult to comprehend; although she was more communicative, there remained a distance between them as wide as the Atlantic Ocean. They'd become polite strangers.

"I've washed plenty of socks, pants and shirts for you. And your spare trousers are on the bed. Shall I put them in your kit bag?" Charlotte asked.

"No, no. I can do it."

"It's no trouble."

"If you could dig out one or two photos of yourself and of us together, I'd like to show them to my parents," Lou said.

"I'll put some on your bedside table."

"Thanks, honey."

"I put a book there for you — 'Great Expectations.'"

"Dickens. Super! I'll read it on the ship. Thanks, love."

"So, it's definitely on for Tuesday, then?"

"Yes."

"What happened with Fred McWade and all that late-night carry-on?"

"Things blew over. I told him they would."

"So everything's all right now with the Cardington ship?"

"Yes. I expect it'll be fine. Fred's overseeing the problem now—he'll make sure things are done right." As he said this, Lou wondered if any of Brancker's tactics had worked.

Nothing had been started on extending the ship. He thought someone had to be pulling strings to prevent Colmore moving ahead. It was mystifying. He assumed the reports written by the R.A.W. team had fallen on deaf ears, since he'd seen no reaction from any quarter. If ordered to insert the extra bay, would they still be required to meet Thomson's schedule? If so, they were losing valuable time for testing. Irwin had drawn up a comprehensive schedule of tests to be done after modifications were complete. Lou had never told Charlotte about any of this, knowing she'd worry herself sick. He had to admit it worried him, too.

"And they're putting in an extra bay—shouldn't be any problems then," Lou told her.

"What about the Howden ship? Were your tests okay?" Charlotte asked.

"They went without a hitch. She's a good ship. The flight to Canada will be as easy as pie."

"I expect you'll be glad to see your family. That'll be nice. How will you get down to Virginia?"

"I'll hop on a train in Montreal. It'll take me through New York to Washington. They'll know when we arrive. It'll be big news. God, I wish you could be with me, Charlie. Next year, perhaps, huh?"

Charlotte gave a half smile. "It's been a long time. I hope they're okay. Things are very bad in America." This made Lou pause—he hadn't given the American economy much thought. "When you're with them, perhaps you might decide to stay there," she said.

Lou grabbed her shoulders and looked into her eyes.

"Hey, don't talk like that. You know I'll come back. I love you, Charlie."

She looked away as if she hadn't heard.

"The time will fly by. I'll be back in no time flat," Lou said.

"Yes, I expect so."

60

TIME TO SAY GOODBYE

Monday & Tuesday July 28 & 29, 1930

Thomson and Marthe sat on the terrace waiting for afternoon tea. It was sunny, with a delightful breeze off the river. Buck waited in the limousine on the quadrangle with Marthe's luggage stowed in the trunk. Thomson needed to be available. An important vote was coming to the floor. Prematurely, the newspapers were full of the story of Thomson's selection as next Viceroy to India. This gave him satisfaction, though he hadn't formally accepted—that could wait until his return from India. He still needed Marthe's decision. A waiter arrived with a tray of tea and cakes and set them on the table. He poured their teas and left.

"The newspapers are full of it today," Thomson said.

"This will be your crowning achievement. After that, who knows what the future may bring? Perhaps *even* higher office someday," Marthe said.

Thomson didn't want to concern himself with that today, although the thought had often crossed his mind. "I'm still uneasy about leaving Ramsay to deal with the radicals in the party. It's a lonely life being Prime Minister. Our talks give him solace. It's all perhaps too much to ask for the sake of what—*ambition?* Five years is a long time to be away—*"*

He was cut off by one of the ushers from the chamber rushing up and the sound of Big Ben striking the half hour: five-thirty.

"Lord Thomson—it's time to vote, sir."

Of all the times!

"Marthe, wait for me. We must talk before you go. I won't be long."

"Don't worry. I'll be here. Go and cast your vote."

"I'll meet you in the Hall in twenty minutes," he said, glancing at his watch.

Thomson set off for the House at a brisk pace. Marthe strolled down to the river wall and peered at the rippling water, lapping the embankment. A tug hooted as it passed, towing empty barges toward the docks. She was jarred back from her reflections on Thomson's overtures by the pitiful calls of a seagull which landed on the wall beside her.

A warning?

She turned away from the river and headed for the lobby. Once inside Westminster Hall, she glanced across the flagstones to the spot where Charles I had been sentenced to death through Cromwell's treachery. She thought of his horrible death mask at Chequers.

Go away morbid thoughts!

"This is the place where they bring the dead to lie in state," Thomson had told her once.

She shuddered and went to the wall to study a picture of the beleaguered King in a gilt frame, his head still defiantly on his shoulders. Wherever she stood, his accusing eyes followed her. She was disturbed by the sound of someone entering at the bottom of the hall. The crash of doors echoed across the space a hundred feet away. She turned to look, hoping it might be Thomson, but it was a paunchy, old gentleman with long, white hair who strode toward her.

"I'm sorry. I thought you were somebody else," Marthe said.

"Who are you waiting for? Perhaps I can be of assistance," the man said.

"Lord Thomson."

"Ah, you must mean our precious Lord of the Air!"

Is this man being sarcastic?

"Er, yes."

"If I were you, Madam, I'd talk him out of all of his grandiose schemes. It can only end in disaster. It's all just an *impossible dream*, you know."

"And who are *you*, sir?"

He raised his hat. "Lord Scunthorpe at your service, Madam. Good day to you."

He walked off toward the north entrance. Thomson entered from the other end, carrying his hat. He noticed Marthe looked ruffled. "Did that man speak to you?" he said.

"Oh, he just asked if he could be of assistance, that's all."

"Did he say anything else?"

"Nothing *important*."

They walked across the room and he stared up at the ceiling as he always did.

"Yes, I know, it's the most magnificent Gothic room in all of England," Marthe said. He smiled. They stopped for a moment at the center, his eyes earnest. "Marthe—"

She raised her hand to stop him.

"Kit, I've given the matter a great deal of thought. Your voting gave me a final moment to reflect." She placed her hand on his arm. "Fly your airship to India and on your return, I promise, you shall have my answer."

Thomson was disappointed, but perhaps a triumphant return aboard *Cardington R101* would seal things. When they reached the exit doors, they kissed cheeks and said their goodbyes. He led Marthe to the curb, Buck opened the car door and Marthe slipped into the backseat. They exchanged waves and smiles through the window as Big Ben was striking six, Thomson watched her driven away. The car turned onto Parliament Square and disappeared on Victoria Street. He put on his hat and walked back toward Westminster Hall.

As Thomson and Marthe were saying their farewells, Lou was checking progress at the tower for *Howden R100's* departure next morning. The area around the tower swarmed with ground crewmen pumping gas, water, petrol and carrying provisions on board. Since the ship had behaved flawlessly, no repairs were required.

Lou spoke with Capt. Booth and First Officer Meager who told him to go home and be with his wife—*'everything was under control.'* Norway confirmed the same thing, saying he planned to stay on the ship all day and through the night until departure. He sent his love to Charlotte. Lou went to bid farewell to Irwin and Atherstone in Shed No.1 and find out if there were any new developments on their front. Lou entered the shed as a commotion started.

The works foreman stood in the corner yelling. "All right, you lot." The men shuffled toward him. "Okay, boys, it's time to cut the lady in half."

"Oooo-bloody-ray!"

"It's about bleedin' time!"

"Been standin' around 'ere for weeks waitin'."

"Bunch o' wankers!"

Lou normally would've smiled, but morale and discipline had slipped steadily over the past few weeks—not so much with the Howden group, but it was out in the open in Shed No.1. They were looking in his direction.

"Not this bloke. He ain't a wanker," one said.

"What? The commander? No, he's all right."

"This bunch 'ere don't know if they're comin' or goin' half the bloody time."

Hundreds of men gathered equipment and wheeled scaffold into position, ready to break the ship at its center. Utilities and controls inside the airship would need to be detached, lengthened and reconnected on completion—itself, a daunting task. Workmen climbed aboard to get started. Other crews were getting ready to detach the exterior cover.

Lou knocked on Irwin's door and went in. Irwin appeared gaunt. Atherstone sat behind a dilapidated desk in the corner. He looked just as weary. Irwin stood at a high table reviewing drawings for the modifications.

"Looks like something's happening out there, sir," Lou said.

"They just got word," Irwin replied.

"They've been hanging around for weeks without pay," Atherstone said.

"At least someone made a decision," Lou said.

"Now it's gonna be *rush, rush, rush*," Irwin grumbled.

"There'll be plenty of overtime," Lou said.

"For them, it's feast or famine," Atherstone said.

"I want to make sure this ship gets tested properly when they're done," Irwin said. "I heard your test went well, Lou?"

Lou nodded.

Irwin stuck out his hand. "Charlotte okay?"

Lou pursed his lips and waggled his head from side to side. "Not really."

"I'll make sure Olivia keeps in touch with her. Lou, have a safe flight."

"Thank you, sir."

"Good luck, Lou," Atherstone said.

Lou returned to the shed floor, running into Ronnie the works foreman and McWade.

"They're happy now, aren't they?" Lou said.

"This lot's *never* 'appy."

"At least they're back to work."

The foreman shook Lou's hand. "Best of luck, sir."

"Thanks, Ronnie."

"You'll be all right," Ronnie whispered.

"You're still coming right, Fred?" Lou asked.

"I suppose I am," McWade answered.

As Lou was leaving, Potter, Binks, Church and Disley gathered round him. They shook his hand, wishing him a safe journey. Cameron arrived, out of breath.

"What's up, Doug?" Lou asked.

"I've just been told I'm going to Canada."

"You lucky devil! What happened?" Binks asked.

"Their coxswain's gone down with mumps."

"Well, don't look so bloody miserable, mate," Church said.

"It's money in yer pocket, ain't it?" Binks said.

Lou glanced at Cameron, understanding his dilemma. He hurried home to Charlotte.

The day was hot. Lou sat outside on one of the deck chairs he'd bought the previous summer. Fluffy lay lazily in the shade beside him. Charlotte brought out corned beef sandwiches and a beer for Lou. They sat listening to the insects buzzing around Charlotte's flowers, conversation impossible.

Later, Mr. and Mrs. Jones popped their heads over the garden fence and spent a few minutes wishing Lou a safe voyage. Sensing tension, they didn't linger. When they'd gone, Lou and Charlotte resumed their awkward silence. In the end, they went to the living room on the second floor and Lou read the newspaper. Fluffy followed and sat on the couch beside him. After twenty minutes Charlotte went to the kitchen to prepare dinner, peeling potatoes and carrots. When Charlotte had left the room, Lou rested his head back while he stroked Fluffy.

"You want to come for a ride in an airship, Fluff? The cat mewed softly, jumped down, and went out. "No, I don't suppose you do—sorry puss, I forgot," he said.

This was all too painful. Lou wished he was on the airship over the Atlantic—anywhere but here right now. That wasn't fair. He knew how Charlotte would feel as he drove off on his motorbike in the morning.

She'll be damned lonesome.

They ate dinner and went to bed early. Charlotte did something she hadn't done for a long time. She lit the candle on her bedside table. He made love to her. She wasn't responsive, nor was she cold, just preoccupied—in some other place. She let him do whatever he wanted. He took pleasure in re-exploring every curve of her beautiful body. How long had it been? Weeks—perhaps months. He couldn't remember. After an hour, he cradled her in his arms until it was time to leave. He got up and washed and put on his uniform. He went downstairs and left his kit bag by the door. Before going back upstairs, he took the framed photograph of Charlotte from the mantelpiece in the living room, wrapped it in a shirt, and slipped it into his kitbag. He searched for Fluffy, but she was nowhere to be found. He opened the back door. She wasn't there.

Charlotte got up and put on a long, white, silk nightdress and came to him at the center of the bedroom. She stared at him and put her arms around his neck. She kissed his lips slowly and deliberately, seeming to savor the moment. He held her and took a handful of her hair, running it through his fingers at her back. She gazed at him with those huge, blue eyes, as if for the last time. He sensed she believed she'd never see him again.

God, you're so beautiful!

"Oh God, I love your hair," he said softly.

"Make the most of it," she whispered.

"I *am* coming back, you know—I promise you."

Doubt showed in her eyes.

"Better go," he said, letting go of her.

She slowly removed her arms and followed him down to the door. They embraced and kissed again on the recessed front porch.

"See you in about three weeks, honey," he said. "I love you."

Her voice was barely audible. "Goodbye, Lou."

He descended the steps to his motorbike, fastened his kit bag on the luggage rack and kicked it over. He climbed on and turned to Charlotte standing in the doorway, her long, white nightdress backlit by the overhead light. She looked like an apparition of a Greek goddess, her flowing, black hair shining in the moonlight. He felt sick leaving her now, and guilty. He wished he could stay another hour, or just not leave at all. He bowed his head to her and waved. She didn't move or make any gesture. Like a statue. He drove away believing he could never feel more miserable than this. But he was wrong.

PART EIGHT

Howden R100 Approaches Montreal. July 1930.

CANADA

61

LIVERPOOL

Tuesday July 29, 1930.

L ou arrived at the Cardington tower at around 2:00 a.m. The place was a hive of activity; gear, mechanical parts, gas valves, fuel tanks and ballast tanks had to be checked and rechecked. Ground crewmen carried luggage and last-minute items aboard while the gas bags were given a final top up. A crowd of two thousand spectators watched the floodlit ship from the fence. Lou's mood lifted. Next to their black Austin, Meager kissed his wife and small son goodbye. Mrs. Meager laid the child on the back seat and got in, blowing a kiss as she drove away.

Lou noticed Jessup assisting the ground crew, carrying boxes of provisions to the elevator. He gave Lou a hateful glance over his shoulder. Lou climbed off his motorbike as Binks came up.

"What's *he* doing over there?" Lou asked, nodding toward Jessup.

"He's working with the ground crew."

Lou was puzzled, but said nothing.

"Shall I take care of the bike, sir?" Binks asked.

"That'd be nice of you, Joe, thanks. Leave it over by the admin office. Oh, I've another favor to ask." Lou pulled out a brown envelope from his kit bag containing a flat box. "Would you mind putting this in the postbox next Monday? It's a birthday card for Charlotte. Her birthday's on the sixth of August. I'd like it to arrive the day before."

Binks tucked the envelope inside his coat.

"I'll do that with pleasure."

"Thanks, Joe."

"I wish I was coming with you, sir."

"Won't be long now. We'll all be off to India in *your* ship soon."

Binks climbed on the *Brough Superior*. "Good luck. I'll be right here with your bike when you get back, sir," he said.

Lou headed toward the customs shed for clearance before boarding. Colmore got out of the Works' Humber in front of the building, dressed in a sports coat, collar and tie. He'd had his hair cut for the trip—an extreme short back and sides. His face had a grey pallor, matching his jacket. He looked sick with fright.

Lou went over to him. "Is everything all right, sir?"

Colmore raised a trembling hand, wiped his forehead and grunted. Lou put his kitbag over his shoulder and took Colmore's small suitcase from the driver and walked with him. Inside, crewmen and a few civilians were being checked for prohibited items. On the wall was a notice with red lettering:

ABSOLUTELY NO MATCHES OR LIGHTERS ALLOWED

WEIGHT RESTRICTIONS:

Passengers and Officers 30 lbs
Crewmen 15 lbs

Lou stood at Colmore's side. When asked questions, Colmore answered in monosyllables. Scott appeared behind them, tapping Colmore on the shoulder. Colmore's face brightened slightly and he let out a deep sigh.

"I came down to get you, Reggie. You'll be all right. It'll be a lovely trip, you'll see. The views along the St. Lawrence will be spectacular," Scott said.

Lou emptied his kitbag for the customs officer and was surprised to find a black leather writing case at the bottom. Charlotte must have put it in there. After clearance, he walked with Colmore and Scott to the tower elevator.

"Coming?" Scott asked.

"No, I'll take the stairs, sir," Lou answered.

Lou was glad to get away to his assigned cabin in the officers' section. He hated to see men of high rank paralyzed with fright—he'd seen plenty during the war. The passenger section accommodated one hundred, with eighteen four-berth cabins on the upper level and fourteen two-berth on the lower level. Cabins were situated above the crew's quarters over the control car. The officers' cabins were grouped together—small but comfortable, measuring seven feet by eight, with paper-thin, beige, fabric walls.

Lou's narrow bed, tight to the wall, consisted of stretched canvas over aluminum framing and beside the bed, a writing table against the head wall—both immovable. On the bed was a 'teddy' and a Sidcot flying suit with a fur collar, neatly folded beside them, a sleeping bag, a blanket and a sheet.

A curtain concealed a small closet in the corner with two shelves. Lou removed the framed photograph of Charlotte from his kit bag. He'd taken the picture in Switzerland at Christmas: she posed beside a snow-laden fir tree wearing her ski outfit and a big smile. He studied her suntanned face.

She'd been happy on that trip. He carefully placed the frame on the bedside table next to his binoculars. He emptied his kitbag on the bed and picked up the writing case. He flipped it open. Inside he found a leather-bound diary embossed with gold lettering and a pad of fine, white writing paper, together with a pen, but no inscription or note. Charlotte must have wanted him to keep a journal.

A nice going-away present. Good girl. Great idea!

He placed it on the writing table with *Great Expectations* beside her photograph. He suddenly had a horrible sinking feeling. Those old feelings of panic and depression swept over him. She was his rock. He didn't want to leave.

Damn, I miss her already.

Lou took the shirts and hung them in the closet with his work clothes and stowed his socks and pants on the shelves below. He heard a nervous cough outside and then that familiar voice.

"Hello, *Lou?*"

"That's me."

Lou opened the curtain. Norway stood there grinning, his unlit pipe clamped between his teeth.

"All set?" he inquired.

"I guess."

Norway showed Lou where he was berthed. Burney was in the next cabin. He came out and shook hands with Lou.

"You still want to do this, Sir Dennis?" Lou said.

Burney didn't say much—perhaps he'd got the jitters now, too, Lou thought. Along the corridor, Scott stood at Colmore's door. Hopefully, Colmore was feeling better. When Scott saw Norway's pipe, he charged down the corridor and gave him a shove.

"Get rid of that damned thing!" he yelled.

"It's not lit," Norway protested.

"I don't care, just get rid of it!" Scott grunted.

Norway put the pipe in his inside pocket and wandered back inside his cabin.

"He's right, Nev, you'll scare everyone to death," Lou called after him.

Scott took Colmore's arm. "Come on, Reggie. Let's go and get some coffee in the dining room, shall we?" he said.

There were half a dozen passengers in and out of their cabins, getting settled in along the corridor, including R.A.W. officials. Inside some berths, people snored, a few having come aboard early and retired. After chatting for a few minutes, Lou made his way to the control car, passing McWade, whose face was like a mask. Since McWade had received the letter from the Ministry, neither of them had mentioned his late-night visit again. Lou was sure he was frustrated and highly embarrassed. Lou reached the wireless room above the control car and poked his head in on Disley, who glanced up.

"Evening, sir."

"How you doing, Dizzy?" Lou said.

The meteorologist's room was next door and occupied by Mr. Giblett, whom Lou had met at Cardington House a few times. Giblett was working on weather maps and data. Lou descended into the spacious control car incorporating the chartroom, passing Johnston, busy with his charts. Capt. Booth and Capt. Meager stood nursing mugs of coffee, waiting for the last passengers to arrive. The two coxswains were stationed at their wheels.

Lou smiled at the officers. "Good morning, Captain," he said, nodding.

"Morning, Lou. I'll take the first watch until 6:00 a.m. We'll rotate in four-hour stints throughout the voyage. We've got a lot of experienced officers on board. We can split some of these watches up."

"Very good, sir."

Giblett entered the control car holding up a sheet of paper. "I've just finished the weather chart. As I said earlier, a small depression is centered over the north of Ireland. If we work our way around to the north, we'll pick up a favoring wind that'll push us west."

"*Excellent!* Exactly what we need," Booth said.

"That won't last, but I'm working on another system over the Atlantic, which might come in handy."

"Keep us posted." Booth turned to Lou. "Ask the chief coxswain to let us know when everyone's aboard. We're ready to cast off."

"Aye, aye, Captain," Lou said.

On his way to the stairs Johnston looked up. "Hey, Lou."

"This is the *India* flight, right?" Lou said.

"Oh, non, non, non. You're on der wrong sheep," Johnston said, chuckling. "Dis sheep is for Montreal, *French Canada!*"

Lou headed to the central corridor and found the chief coxswain, who reported they were still waiting for one R.A.W. official. All first watch crewmembers were at their stations. Second Officer Steff was in the main corridor with a crew of riggers ready to set the gas bags on take-off. As the ship ascended, the gas would expand and bags would need careful repositioning to prevent damage to them. The rest of the crew sat in their quarters drinking coffee, or slept in their bunks. Lou returned to the control car and relayed the information to Booth.

"We'll give that man ten minutes," Booth said.

They stood around waiting until the chief coxswain called down.

"Everyone's aboard, sir, save the one. Thirty-eight crewmen and six passengers present and accounted for. Crewmen are at their stations awaiting orders!"

"Then we shall wait no longer. Start engines and pull up the gangplank," Booth ordered.

Lou wondered what had happened to the R.A.W. guy. Perhaps he'd got cold feet. He remembered his engineer Wiggins who missed *R38* when his car broke down.

That was Wiggins' lucky day! Is this the 'Wiggy thing' all over again?

Engines were started and in no time they'd slipped the mast. In the half darkness, the ship floated upwards. Booth gave instructions for ballast to be dumped at the stern to bring the tail up. There was just enough light to make out the fields and the roads below. They heard cheers from the ground crewmen on the tower and on the field through the open windows. The ship turned slowly and cruised very low across the front of Shed No.1, while *Cardington R101* crewmen and construction workers stood at the doors shaking their fists at them.

Booth smiled. "Now it's *their* turn. And they don't like it."

"Do we bite our thumbs at you, sir? *Damn right we do!*—I've been polishing up on my Shakespeare," Lou said, smiling at Meager, who laughed.

Booth ordered more power and the ship ascended to one thousand feet. They turned toward Bedford. Lou was able to make out Kelsey Street and then their house, which was in total darkness. He presumed Charlotte had gone back to bed. He thought about how lovely she'd looked on the front step in the moonlight. Already, he couldn't wait to get back home to her.

I'll make it up to you, I swear.

After passing over Bedford, Johnston called out the heading for Liverpool and they were soon at fifteen hundred feet and on their way, riding smoothly on three engines at forty-five knots. Lou was tired. He went to his cabin, changed into his work clothes and lay down, covering himself with the sleeping bag and blanket. The ship was eerily quiet, seeming perfectly still— the engines far enough aft of the control car to make them completely silent. Before drifting off, he thought of Charlotte, then *R38* and his dead crewmen, and then Josh and *Shenandoah*. It all seemed so long ago. He slept while the ship cruised across Midland towns toward Liverpool.

Lou was awakened just before 6:00 a.m. by music from the gramophone in the crew's quarters below. They had the volume low—at least they were being considerate. At first, Lou had no idea where he was. He listened to the music for a few minutes, looking at Charlotte's photograph on the bedside table. He hoped she was okay and able to sleep.

Although still tired, he went to the toilet room and washed his face in cold water and brushed his teeth. A steward brought him hot water in a tin can for shaving. The floor of the washroom was covered in brown linoleum and echoed hollow underfoot. There were two small shower stalls with a sign

'Please Conserve Water' and in a separate area, two WCs with privacy curtains and an extractor fan in the ceiling. By the smell, they had already been used extensively.

He looked in on the control car where Meager had just taken over the watch from Booth. They passed over the Roman-Saxon town of Chester. Off to starboard, they saw the smoky haze over Liverpool and turned toward it. The ship flew directly over the impressive, white city hall building and then the sandstone cathedral. As they went over, train whistles, car horns and steamer sirens in the port, wished them well

62

TIIE IRISII SEA

Tuesday July 29, 1930.

They left the English coast at Formby Point at 6:20 a.m. and headed out into the Irish Sea toward the Isle of Man, passing Morcambe Lightship on starboard. Lou decided to stretch his legs before breakfast and climbed to the upper deck.

From there, he could look down onto the promenade decks, equipped with loungers, wicker seating and matching low tables. He turned and went to the center and leaned on the white railing around the perimeter of the forty by forty foot, two-story dining room below. It was bright and airy with windows allowing plenty of natural light—a departure from previous airship design. This room was the largest space on the ship, seating fifty-six.

Stewards, in white coats and black trousers, were serving breakfast. The chief steward, Pierre, looked up at Lou and smiled. Lou gave him a nod. He admired the tablecloths and flatware—not as expensive as the other ship's stuff. Not the Ritz exactly, but not bad—a reasonable restaurant in town, perhaps. The room was busy with a buzz of whispering, punctuated by clattering plates in the galley. The smell of eggs, bacon and coffee wafted up —it all seemed surreal, hovering above the Irish Sea like this.

He returned to the control car as they entered a heavy rain shower and flew blind for a few long moments. When they came out, a mountain on an island appeared dead ahead.

"What's this island, sir?" Lou asked.

"It's Isle of Man and *that* is Sugarloaf Mountain—which I think we should take pains to avoid," Meager replied. They altered course to fly along the coast of the island toward the point of Ayre Lighthouse and Scotland beyond. The green hills of the Lake District lay to starboard.

"I'm going for breakfast. Do you need anything?" Lou asked.

"Johnny and Steff are relieving me at eight. I'll join you then, thanks."

Lou went to the dining room where Colmore sat with Scott and Sqn. Ldr. Archie Wann and a couple of R.A.W. officials. Colmore looked more relaxed. McWade sat at a table with Giblett the meteorologist. Lou nodded to McWade and went over to Wann, who got up from the table to greet him. Lou hadn't seen him to speak to since leaving him in the control car on *R38* just before it broke in two and fell from the sky. Lou had been down to visit Wann in the intensive care ward just before he left the hospital, but Wann was swathed in bandages, unconscious. He was surprised how much Wann had aged, his hair now pretty grey. They shook hands while everyone looked on, understanding their connection. It was a touching moment. Neither man spoke. Lou left Wann and went and found an empty table. They'd talk later.

Lou felt drained due to lack of sleep and worry about Charlotte. It'd been a wrench leaving her. He'd burdened himself with all her emotions and added them to his own. It felt like a hangover. Norway entered the dining room as Lou was finishing breakfast. He was smiling and pretty jazzed.

"You're looking mighty pleased with yourself there, buddy," Lou said.

"I just s-saw the lighthouse at P-Point Ayre. It's b-blowing a gale out there."

The steward came to take Norway's order.

"I'll have c-coffee and the f-full English breakfast and t-toast p-please," Norway said. "And yes, I'm very p-pleased with the sh-ship."

Meager appeared and joined them. The steward looked at Meager.

"I'll have what he ordered. Sounds good to me," Meager said.

"We've a long way to go yet. Don't get too cocky," Lou cautioned.

Lou glanced around the room as though appraising it for the first time—for Norway's benefit. "It looks pretty good, I suppose," he said.

"You slept well?" Norway asked.

"No complaints."

"An airship is the best place in the world to fall asleep," Meager said.

"What happened to our friend?" Lou asked.

"Who?" Norway asked.

"Jessup. I saw him at the tower, but I haven't seen him since."

"He got the b-boot."

"Who by?"

"Captain Booth."

"Why?"

"Someone told him Jessup was a b-bad lot," Norway said.

"Who told him that?"

"Me." Norway grinned.

"You!"

"Yes. I didn't want to d-deal with that n-nut. We've got enough to worry about."

"We can do without that," Meager agreed.

"Who broke the news to Jessup?" Lou asked.

"Sky Hunt. He said he was p-pretty annoyed."

"He'll blame me for it. Not that I care," Lou said.

The steward arrived with a plate of eggs and bacon in each hand. Norway and Meager began eating.

"I'm starving," Meager said. "I'm going to take a look on top later. You might as well come with me, Lou."

"I've got to pump petrol first. Can we do it after that?"

"Sure."

Norway looked envious. "Should I c-c-come, too?" he said.

"No, no need," Meager answered.

"All right, I'll take a look round inside then," Norway said, disappointed.

After breakfast, Lou went with Norway to transfer petrol with hand pumps to the gravity tanks above the engine cars. They were assisted by Billy, Cameron, Nervous Nick and Disley. Everyone was expected to do his part and Lou thought he might as well get used to it. There'd be plenty of this grunt work to be done if they wanted to reach Canada.

"I can't believe you people were too cheap to install a couple of damned electric pumps," Lou grumbled. "And you didn't put pumps in the WC's either did you? It's gonna get pretty nasty in those rest rooms, mister."

Norway grinned his silly horsey grin. "We didn't have money for luxuries," he said.

Later, Lou followed Meager up the cat ladder to the forward hatch on the roof.

"Keep your eyes open for damage to the cover. If the rain gets in, you know what happens to the gas bags," Meager said.

"Yes, sir."

"Hold on tight. Let's go."

They climbed out of the envelope onto the twelve-inch-wide reinforced catwalk on the roof, holding onto a bitterly cold, steel cable. The cable stretched over seven-hundred feet from bow to stern, lying alongside the catwalk. The conditions were blustery and cold, and they were surrounded by scattered, swirling clouds.

"Where are we?" Lou shouted.

"Over the Mull of Galloway."

Lou looked out to the starboard side and saw the rugged terrain of Scotland in the distance.

"Come on, follow me!" Meager yelled above the howling wind.

They crawled on their hands and knees up the slope of the never-ending catwalk, making their inspection. Lou thought of Charlotte; if she could see him now, she'd die! He wondered how many airshipmen had been lost doing this. If they were blown away, no one would even know. They'd just be unaccounted for. When they reached halfway, violent squalls peppered them with showers of hail, which felt like razor blades on their faces and hands. It was as if Mother Nature was trying to pry their hands off the cable. By the time they reached the stern, they were soaked through and chilled to the marrow. Neither of them had spotted any damage to the cover or intakes. Meager opened the trap door and they climbed down, their hands so numb it'd become almost impossible to hold on.

"Well, that was invigorating!" Lou said.

"Let's go and dry out," Meager said.

They returned to their cabins and changed into their second set of work clothes. Lou put on his teddy, which was aptly named. They took their wet clothes to the cook in the galley for him to dry. Pierre admired Lou's outfit.

"Very nice, my dear. *Very cuddly*, if you don't mind me saying."

Meager roared with laughter. Lou went off to look for Norway and found him amidships.

"You look sweet," Norway said.

"Now don't *you* start!"

"How's everything on the roof?" Norway asked.

"Bloody freezing! But everything looked good. No leaks—*yet*."

"I'm going to take a gander at the engines," Norway said.

"Come on then, let's go."

They climbed down the ladder to each of the three nacelles, the menacing, grey Atlantic only twelve hundred feet below. Lou admired his friend, who showed no fear. Climbing down was no problem for Lou, but once inside the engine car, he felt uncomfortable. His heart rate accelerated and he began to sweat. He kept an eye on the exit to reassure himself there was a quick way out.

In each of the three cars were two, brand-spanking new Rolls-Royce Condor IIIB liquid-cooled, V-12, 650 bph engines, in tandem—a total of six. They were barely broken in, having been installed only recently for the final test flight. The Air Ministry had decided, without fuss, to change the reconditioned engines Burney had forced on Wallis.

To a mechanic, or anyone with a love of engines, these monsters were impressive and sounded sweet. After a few hand signals between themselves and the engineers, they left the engine car and went to the ladder, where they paused to look at Rathlin Island on port. It looked wild and remote in this force eight gale. They climbed back into the hull. Norway went to his cabin to write up his log and Lou changed into his uniform, ready for an early lunch, before going on duty.

Lou returned to the empty dining room. One steward stood by the wall, his arms folded. Pierre greeted Lou with a welcoming smile.

"It's lovely to see you again, sir," he said.

"Thank you," Lou said, sitting down.

"You look much smarter in uniform, Commander, but I must say I *did* like you in your teddy."

Lou nodded modestly, noticing the other steward scowling.

Pierre put a jug of water on the table. "We have beer, if you prefer?"

"No, I'm going on watch. Water will do."

"For lunch we have mushroom soup, beef stew, mashed potatoes and peas."

"That'll be fine, thank you."

Pierre hurried off to the kitchen with the steward following him. After hearing raised voices and grumbling, the sour-faced steward returned and placed a bowl of soup and a basket of bread in front of Lou without speaking. Lou got started.

Pierre reappeared as Lou was finishing his soup. He picked up the plate and empty soup bowl. "Was the soup to your liking, sir?"

"Yes, thanks."

"I was on the promenade deck earlier looking at the Scottish scenery. It's lovely. Have you seen it?" Pierre asked.

"Yeah, I saw it from the roof when I was up there."

"You were on the roof! Oh my goodness, you must be *ever so* careful."

"I was holding on, don't worry."

"I'd love to go there. I've never been," Pierre said.

"On the roof?"

"Oh no, no, silly! *Scotland.*"

"Scotland, yeah, right."

"I expect you must be missing your wife, sir. I heard you were married to a most *beautiful* lady."

Lou cleared his throat, pretending not to have heard. He picked up his glass and swallowed a mouthful of water and Pierre scurried out. The steward returned, carrying Lou's stew on a tray. He set it down and disappeared. Lou stared after him as Pierre reentered the room. He noticed Lou's expression.

"Oh, don't worry about him. He's got the 'ump," and then conspiratorially, "He can be a right little 'you-know-what' sometimes!"

Lou finished his lunch and Pierre returned.

"For dessert today we have greengages and custard," he said.

Greengages and custard!

"I'll take a pass on that."

"I thought you would," Pierre said, puckering his lips.

Hell! Now what have I said!

"Oh, I do love your accent—I could listen to it *all night*," Pierre said.

Lou raised his eyebrows, but didn't respond.

"If I can do anything to make your voyage more pleasurable, I'm at your mercy ... er I mean at your *service,* er sorry. My name's Pierre, but you know that. If you're in need of anything, I mean *anything*, please let me know …"

Lou got up. "That's very kind of you, Pierre. I don't anticipate anything, but thank you just the same."

"What about *coffee?* Aren't you staying for coffee?"

Lou made his escape.

Lou reported for duty at 11:45 a.m. in the control car with Cameron and one of the regular ship's rudder coxswains. They'd picked up the favorable winds promised by Giblett around the Head of Islay and were heading due west along the last stretch of Ireland's north coast. They'd stopped the aft engines and were now cruising on three at forty-five knots. With the favoring wind, the ship's ground speed was now sixty-five knots. Steff and Johnston stayed with Lou and the two relief coxswains for ten minutes, lingering to look at Tory Island, five miles in the distance, before going for lunch.

"Say goodbye to the Emerald Isle, lads," Johnston said, putting on an Irish accent. That's the last dry land you'll see for seventeen hundred miles —'til we reach Newfoundland."

Johnston turned one of the clocks back one hour to 11:00 a.m.

"We just entered Greenwich Mean Time, Zone One," he said.

When they'd gone, Lou looked down at the ocean ahead. It was foreboding. He felt fear in the pit of his stomach, which caught him by surprise. He looked at the two coxswains. He knew they'd be having similar thoughts.

"You lads okay?"

"Yes, sir," Cameron said gloomily.

Lou wasn't convinced.

"Fine, sir," the rudder coxswain said more brightly.

63

THE ATLANTIC

Tuesday July 29, 1930.

L ou returned his gaze to the ocean below. They were so low—at times it felt as though they were actually on the water. It looked pretty damned desolate and unfriendly out there. He wondered if they could've made it to New Jersey in *R38* if she hadn't broken in two.

That's a good question.

And what happened to that pilot and the heiress who'd attempted to make this crossing in a small plane? Lou had met the guy in Cardington with his wife, there to ask for assistance from the Meteorological Office. That was when Lou had first met Giblett, the weather guy. After the pilot and his wife had discussed weather patterns over the Atlantic with Giblett and Johnston, a whole crowd had gone with them to the Kings Arms pub. It was like a celebration—a send-off. Pretty soon the pilot and Richmond got into a dust up about whether planes or airships would prevail.

Not long after that, the pilot and his heiress copilot took off from Cranwell Aerodrome and disappeared. The newspapers had been full of it and the public became totally engrossed. It was a weird story. Following their disappearance, the pilot's wife went on a crusade in a bid to end the airship program—supposedly put up to it by her dead husband. Lou glanced at the whitecaps below and shook his head.

Crazy people! What was their name? Hinkley? ... Hinchliffe—that was it!

Lou heard footsteps on the stairs. It was Scott and Colmore.

"How's everything, Commander?" Scott asked.

"Everything's fine, sir. We've a following wind now, giving us a boost. Should last for a couple of hours. We're running on three."

"Three? Excellent! Any problems?"

"Everything's fine at the moment, sir."

Colmore stood motionless, his face frozen, listening to the howling wind. Lou guessed Scott must've brought him down to make him feel at ease, but it was having the opposite effect. Colmore's eyes darted around the perimeter windows. The craggy cliffs on Ireland's northwest coast were rapidly disappearing behind them. Ahead, an endless, angry, grey sea.

Colmore peered up at the hull above them. Its dull silver cover reflected the sun intermittently as they ran through the underside of swirling black cloud. He stared down at the engines suspended in space behind them.

"You don't want to visit the engine cars, eh Reggie?" Scott said, winking at Lou.

Colmore ignored Scott's silly joke. "Let's go back upstairs," he mumbled.

"Okay, Reggie. Keep up the good work, Commander. Let me know if anything needs my attention, I've done all this before, you know!"

"I most certainly will, sir."

The two men began climbing the stairs. "You need a strong Bloody Mary, Reggie. Come, it'll settle your stomach," Scott said, as they went.

Lou and Cameron exchanged glances.

"I could do with one of them myself," Lou said.

The two coxswains remained silent.

An hour later, Norway appeared, with mugs of tea for Lou and the coxswains. "Here. I mustn't stay long or I'll be in trouble with ol' Captain Bligh up there," he said, putting the tea tray down.

"I was just thinking about those two people in the plane who attempted this flight—you know Hinchliffe and the chick—whatsaname—the heiress?" Lou said.

"Elsie Mackay. She was a corker!"

"I'll take your word for it."

"I must admit, I used to have those grand notions of trying it myself, once," Norway said.

"We'd have been reading your obituary, too, pal."

Norway studied the ocean again. "Yes, from here—it looks like sheer madness."

"I guess there were a lot of bucks riding on it?"

"Enough to retire on, I reckon."

"A lot of people tried it," Lou said, after a swallow of tea.

"Many died in the attempt."

"His wife's still campaigning to stop the airship program with messages from the grave."

"She's often in the newspapers and on speaking tours. She's got no chance. After this voyage and the India trip—airships will be part of everyday life," Norway said confidently.

Lou finished his tea.

Norway squeezed past Giblett on the stairs.

"It's bad luck to pass on the stairs," Giblett said.

"Don't be s-superstitious, Mr. G-Giblett. All will be w-well."

"Don't listen to him; he's just the design engineer," Lou said.

"I'm a man of science, too, and I *am* superstitious," Giblett answered.

"Do you have good news?" Lou asked.

"A high pressure area has developed in the Atlantic to the south. We need to head in that direction to get another favoring wind. I'll ask Johnny to work out the new heading."

"Thank you. I'll brief the captain when he comes on watch," Lou said.

The rest of Lou's spell on duty was uneventful. After giving Booth the information, he went to the dining room for tea and sandwiches. He sat talking with Wann, Colmore and Scott. Alcohol had calmed Colmore down to some extent. They didn't mention *R38,* not wishing to upset him again.

After tea, Lou went to lie down. The crewmen below were playing the gramophone, louder this time. Strains of "Can't Help Loving That Man O' Mine" came up through the floor. Lou gazed at Charlotte's photo—the blues seemed fitting. He listened, remembering the songs she liked to play. She hadn't played for ages; Freddie's death had put a stop to the parties. As sad as Freddie's death was, the grief *had* to end. Fun and laughter must be brought back into their house. Children would bring joy back into her life. Yes, children were the answer. The song ended and Al Jolson sang "Blue Skies" in his upbeat vamping style. Lou spoke out loud, not caring if anyone heard him. "That's right, Mr. Jolson. You sing it! It's gonna be blue skies from now on, ol' buddy."

During the next two days of the crossing, Lou had an epiphany. His spirits rose and he became euphoric. This voyage had given him time to reflect in solitude. Whenever he came to rest, or attempt to read the book Charlotte had given him, he had similar thoughts.

How could I have been so thoughtless?

Everything became crystal clear. He'd selfishly put his career above all else—while she'd met his every need. He'd failed her miserably! He knew what he must do on his return. They'd begin the adoption process, but beforehand, he'd get checked out. He'd stubbornly refused before, hoping for a miracle. He dreaded being found to be less than a man.

Lou's love for airships returned during the crossing and this flight proved airship travel could be safe. It'd certainly go down as a landmark flight. The ship had behaved magnificently with only a small repair necessary to one engine. Lou was glad he'd stuck to his guns, sure Charlotte would come around, especially after they'd made a few intercontinental flights. Perhaps, one day he'd be able to take her to America by airship—a pleasant three-day voyage!

On Wednesday morning, Colmore invited Lou to join him on the promenade deck. They sat at one of the wicker tables in comfortable easy chairs, encompassed by the sea. Colmore appeared fairly relaxed, well-scrubbed and shaved, his graying hair slicked down and shiny; he was well-dressed as always—sports jacket, collar and tie. He ordered tea. Lou ordered coffee.

"I'm going to confide in you, Lou. Hope you don't mind."

"Not at all, sir."

They were interrupted by people gathering at the windows, watching a whale ploughing through the waves, water spouting from its blowhole. Lou and Colmore got up and joined them for a few minutes to enjoy the awesome sight. The massive creature disappeared and they returned to their seats. Pierre set down a tray of tea, coffee and biscuits.

"I wasn't always like this, you know. Oh, always nervous about flying, but not this bad. I got on with it—strange thing for the Director of Airship Development to admit, eh."

"We can only admire your courage, then, sir."

"It's ridiculous. I get so annoyed with myself," Colmore said, sipping his tea.

"Regardless, many think you're the best man for the job."

Colmore sighed. "I hope so. My fear got worse after Captain Hinchliffe's wife came to Cardington with Sir Arthur Conan Doyle last year."

"What happened?"

Lou picked up his coffee and Colmore offered him a biscuit.

"She claimed she'd had messages from her husband—the pilot lost with Elsie Mackay—right out here, somewhere." Colmore waved his hand vaguely at the foreboding sea.

"What did she say?"

"The Airship Program was too dangerous and would end in horrible disaster."

"I expect she was upset after losing her husband, sir."

"She and Doyle showed up after the briefing—you know when Lord Thomson came up after he got back in office. They were in the garden when Thomson gave his speech."

"Yes, I remember. I couldn't figure out what was happening. We couldn't hear—someone switched off the mic. It looked like she was making some sort of protest," Lou said.

"She asked a lot of embarrassing questions."

"Lord Thomson looked irritated," Lou said.

"It was astonishing how much she *knew* about the Airship Program —top secret technical stuff. Lou, it was *unnerving!*"

"I bet."

"But you see, it made the woman *so bloody credible.*"

"But it's a bit weird, sir. Conan Doyle has a reputation for being an eccentric—what with the fairies and all that stuff."

"Yes, but how the hell did she know so much?"

"People talk. They find out things. I shouldn't worry about any of it, sir."

"She has a lot of powerful people on her side, you know."

"Well, there you are. They probably fed her the information. Poor woman was being used. It's all politics."

"I'm sure you're right," Colmore said, his smile half-hearted.

"Sir, may I be blunt?"

"Please do, dear boy."

"If you're not sure the ship's ready, regardless of how well *Howden R100* does, you must put your foot down, be strong and stand up for what you believe. *Postpone* the voyage to India!"

Colmore looked frightened by the prospect. He scratched his chin and gazed at the surrounding ocean. "We'll have to see, but I do value your council, Lou. You know that."

Lou drew a deep breath. "I've cheated death a few times. I guess I was spared for a reason—but when our time's up, that's it. We meet our Maker—but I think we must do all we can to prevent that day coming *prematurely!*"

"You're lucky. You're *bloody fearless!*"

"I wish that were true, sir."

"Somehow, you always manage to make me feel better, Lou," Colmore said, pausing to watch a rusty freighter heading in the opposite direction. "And you give me much to ponder."

"You started telling me about Lord Thomson and his experience with Lord Kitchener."

"Oh yes, I did."

"I'd love to hear that story."

Colmore smiled fully for the first time and Lou listened in fascination to the tale of Thomson's ruthless obedience to Kitchener's orders during the Boer War, as well as his recent threats. By the end of the story, Colmore was back in the doldrums, and Lou understood why.

It was important for the officer on watch to be a skilled navigator and, during the crossing, Meager and Johnston gave Lou instruction. All he had learned in books over this past two years, he put into practice. He accompanied both men when they took sun sightings with the sextant on the roof. They left him to calculate their latitude using these observations. Sometimes, if the stars were visible, they showed him how to fix their position by taking astronomical sightings. They also taught him to use the Pole Star to ascertain their latitude.

Lou was shown how to make drift, wind speed and directional calculations using targets dropped on the water from the control car. During the day, they used 'dust bombs,' small boxes filled with aluminum dust, which exploded when they hit the sea, leaving a perfect sighting target. At night, they dropped calcium flares, which burst into flame on contact with the water.

The aspect of navigation Lou found most interesting was the use of ships at sea. During the crossing, Lou sent a signal to the *Montclare*, which sent *their* position and the airship's bearing back to the airship. Moments later, the same information was received from the *Caledonian*. By getting two bearings at almost the same time, they determined the 'cut' and hence their own exact position. At that time, they were at fifty-three degrees north —twenty-one degrees, zero minutes west. Lou believed he'd be a competent navigator by the end of this voyage, having been instructed by the best.

Norway out-did himself on Wednesday afternoon. Meager was on watch and the ship was now positioned seven hundred miles east of Belle Isle, where the St. Lawrence enters the Atlantic, about a thousand miles south of Greenland. After visiting the engine cars with Lou, Norway decided to go up to the roof. Lou followed him. Norway opened the bow hatch and popped his head out. The rushing, damp wind hit them full force. They were making fifty knots and Norway, in his Harris Tweed jacket and green woolen polo-necked sweater, clambered onto the roof and sat down. Lou stuck his head out.

"Icebergs!" Norway shouted, pointing into the distance.

"Some of them are huge," Lou said, looking southwards. "I guess the Titanic must have hit one somewhere south of here."

"Over there in iceberg alley. Four hundred miles off Newfoundland," Norway said. They both stared at the inhospitable landscape. Norway began crawling away.

"Hey, where the hell d'you think you're going?" Lou yelled after him.

"I'm going to see if I can make it to the stern!"

"What are you, crazy? Stop! It's too dangerous."

Lou stood on the top rung of the cat ladder and watched Norway inch away on his belly along the narrow catwalk up the incline, holding the steel cable. After Norway had gone about a hundred feet, Lou was astonished to see Nervous Nick heading toward them from the other direction. He wasn't crawling, but walking upright with his hands in his pockets, leaning into the wind. His lips were pursed—he was whistling!

Now what?

When Nervous Nick reached Norway, Norway looked up, startled at first. Then he turned sideways, making himself as small as possible. Nervous

Nick stepped over Norway without breaking stride and on toward Lou. He grinned. "Afternoon, sir," he said on reaching him.

"Out for a stroll?" Lou asked.

"Just getting a little air, sir, are you going?"

"Not today," Lou said, climbing down the ladder to allow him to get down. "You've progressed a bit since we first met, Nick."

"Oh yes, sir—thanks to you. I love this job!"

"I take it everything looks good on the roof?"

"No serious damage, sir, but I think those intakes might be leaking."

Lou made a mental note to pass that on to Meager and moved on to make an inspection of the structure and gasbags. He'd check on Nevil later. Amidships, he ran into Wann.

"Good afternoon, Commander. Working on anything special?" Wann asked.

"Just a routine inspection."

"Then I'll join you. I could use the exercise. It's damned boring around here. *No crises.*"

"I don't think we need *another* crisis, do we?"

"I apologize—stupid joke. Boring is *always* best."

They progressed along the catwalks, peering up at the helically wound girders. "Pretty damned impressive," Wann said.

"Barnes Wallis," Lou said.

Wann nodded approval. "I'm surprised he's not on board."

"Vickers wouldn't allow it."

"Very wise of them."

They reached the stern and found one of the riggers making repairs to a small chafe in the cover on one of the fins. They watched him for a few minutes. After complimenting him on his work, they moved on.

"They're a conscientious lot, this crew," Wann said. He stopped and turned, holding onto the rail. "How are you, Lou? Have you got over that bloody catastrophe?"

"I guess, but it took a while," Lou replied.

"Some of us were spared. God knows why. I never got over the guilt of that," Wann confessed.

"I saw the control car lying in the water. I didn't think anyone could've survived."

"They say everything happens for a reason."

"There's the rub," said Lou.

"Do you know your purpose?"

"I *think* so."

"Good. You're lucky. I heard your testimony in court was excellent," Wann said.

"Oh, I don't know—"

"You saved the commodore's reputation."

"I just told it the way I saw it."

"I'm not sure he deserved it. You were very gracious." Wann said as he stared up into the ship's structure. "We continue to believe in these damned things—or pretend to."

"I think we're getting them sorted out," Lou replied. He suddenly remembered Norway. "Oh hell! I'd better go up and look for Norway. He went on the roof. I'd better make sure he hasn't been blown away."

"Yes, you better had," Wann said. "The R.A.W. would *never* get over the loss!"

Lou made his way to the stern hatch cat ladder, climbed up and opened the hatch. He was disturbed by what he saw. Norway stood fifty feet away, arms outstretched, facing the horizon, hair blowing riotously around his head. He reminded Lou of the Christ the Redeemer statue under construction in Rio de Janeiro.

The master of all he surveys! Dumb S.O.B!

"Nevil! What the *hell* are you doing? Get back down here. Right now!"

Norway turned around slowly, as though coming out of a trance.

"Ah, Lou."

Norway walked carefully toward Lou at the hatchway.

"*Exhilarating!*" he shouted.

"Life's dangerous enough without you pulling a silly stunt like that."

"It felt so good and I wanted to prove I could do it," Norway said.

"If you fall off, there'll be a lot of disappointed readers out there."

"I can just see the headlines. 'Hated airship designer mysteriously disappears over Atlantic. Royal Airship Works staff helping with enquiries.'"

"*Very funny,*" Lou said smiling.

Norway looked at his watch. "Come on, Lou, it's time to pump petrol."

"It's time you pumped the toilets out, too—they're getting pretty smelly, pal."

Later that day, Lou made an entry in the diary Charlotte had given him:

Wednesday July 30th 1930.

Saw icebergs this afternoon. Some of them collapsing. Awesome sight. All I could think about was the Titanic. I thought about that beautiful ship on the bottom, not far away. And all those poor, wretched souls! Sad to think about. Was it an iceberg that killed them, or someone's stupid pride?

64

NEWFOUNDLAND

Wednesday July 30, 1930.

I *see a light!*" Everyone rushed to the windows at the front of the control car.

"Yes, there it is."

It was 9:45 p.m. Wednesday evening—Meager's watch. Lou, Johnston, Booth and Wann had gone down to join him. Johnston spotted it first. On the port bow, they saw a flashing light—the lighthouse on Cape Bauld on the northern tip of the island of Newfoundland.

"The crossing from Ireland to Newfoundland has taken ..." Johnston hesitated carefully reading his watch. "Thirty-seven hours and forty minutes or ..." He looked out into the darkness. "Forty-six hours and twenty-eight minutes from Cardington."

Everyone shook hands and smiled gleefully.

Within half an hour, they were passing directly over flat, scrubby Belle Isle. Gradually, fog closed in as they traveled along the Belle Isle Strait. Below, they heard plaintive foghorns. The fog cleared when they reached the Gulf of St. Lawrence. Low clouds impeded visibility, but once in a while they spotted a ship moving smoothly through the black water and later, a pod of glistening blue whales breaking the surface in the moonlight.

By the midnight to 4:00 a.m. watch (now Thursday), the cloud cover had gone and it became beautiful and clear. Giblett warned these conditions wouldn't last, and as usual, he was right. Next watch, Scott being anxious to get to Montreal before dark, they put on two more engines. They ran on all six engines, though not at full power, at fifty-eight knots, bumping against headwinds, which reduced their ground speed to thirty-six knots.

Lou visited the control car at 4:00 a.m. They'd reached well inside the Gulf of St. Lawrence, between Anticosti Island and the coast of Quebec. At dawn, with the sun coming up on the water, the scene was spectacular, with quaint fishing villages set in treed hillsides along the riverbank. Lou spent much time studying the landscape through binoculars. That morning, he wrote in Charlotte's diary:

Thursday 31st July 1930.

What a great place the Gulf of St. Lawrence is! Teeming with wildlife. Saw a black bear at the water's edge with her cubs this morning. She stopped to look up. I wonder what she thought of us. We've also seen blue whales and bright, white belugas, elk and moose (good swimmers). No icebergs. Wish C was here to see this.

Later in the day, two magnificent steamships, their hulls stately dark blue, topsides gleaming white, moved majestically along the seaway below toward Montreal. Disley entered the control car, waving two wires.

"We have two messages. The first is from the *Empress of Scotland*, the second the *Duchess of Bedford*. Both captains send their best wishes and congratulations." The ships sounded their sirens as they passed over, their decks lined with madly waving passengers. Freighters and fishing boats, swarming with seagulls, joined in, adding to the fuss, and then came the roar of engines, as a Canadian flying boat came by to make its own inspection.

"It's getting busy around here. Show these to Captain Booth. I expect he'll send a response," Lou said, handing the messages back to Disley.

A damper was put on all things when the chief coxswain reported gas leaking from bags seven and eight. With Johnston left in control, Booth, Meager, Lou and Norway went to investigate, after easing off the power. The riggers, led by Nervous Nick and Billy, clambered around on the radial wires making an inspection, without the possibility of using safety harnesses. They found six slits in each bag, three inches long, some out of reach. Booth ordered the ship up to three thousand feet to make the bags move toward the riggers as the gas expanded. That worked, and Nervous Nick completed the repairs. About that time, Disley brought another message.

Montreal Police Department Montreal, Canada.

Understand your position to be 50 miles from Quebec. Please advise us of your ETA so that we can manage the traffic and welcoming spectators gathering at St Hubert Aerodrome. Sincerely Chief of Police Montreal.

Meager asked Lou to show the message to Booth, at lunch in the dining room.

"This wire just came in from the Montreal Police, Captain," Lou said laying the wire on the table. Booth read it. Scott was sitting on another table nursing a brandy.

"What have you got there?" he grunted. Booth showed him the message. "Tell them we'll arrive before sunset." Then, checking his watch, "One-thirty. What's our speed?"

"Fifty-eight knots."

"Right, crank 'em all up to full power."

"I don't think that's wise, sir," Booth warned.

"*Just do it!* We need to get our skates on to make it before dark."

"I don't like it. It'll put unnecessary strain on the ship. She's already taking a pounding. We're up against a twenty knot headwind, sir."

"Maybe that's not a good idea, Scottie," Colmore said.

"Reggie, we've got to push on. Booth, just do as I say, there's a good chap."

McWade, who'd been sitting with Giblett, got up and left the dining room shaking his head. Lou returned to the control car with Booth.

"*Damn!* He's not supposed to give orders," Booth said.

"What do you want to do, Captain?" Meager asked.

Booth looked at Lou. "Do as the man says. Full power, all engines."

Lou relayed instructions to the engine cars and within a few minutes all six engines were up to full power, slogging against the wind. Lou and Meager left Booth fuming in the control car with Johnston. Meager went to inspect the gas bag repairs. Lou went to his cabin and wrote in his diary:

Thursday July 31ˢᵗ 1930.

It's a beautiful day with a clear blue sky. Coming up to the Saguenay River, which flows out of the spectacular Laurentian Mountains on the north side. Engines on full power against 20 knot wind on the nose. We've been ordered by Major Scott to reach Montreal before dark. Saw steamers today. What a sight! Decided this is definitely the way I'll bring Charlotte when we come by sea. Then from Montreal to Washington by train. She's gonna love it!

Lou lay on his bunk while Mr. Jolson belted out his song for the umpteenth time. He thought about Charlotte until he drifted off to sleep. He dreamed she was holding up a baby's shawl she'd made and was looking at it, her face like alabaster. There were tears in her eyes and they were running down her cheeks. He woke with a start with the sickening smell of mothballs in his cabin. After that, he couldn't get the baby clothes out of his mind. She hadn't made any for a long time, nor had she opened the 'baby drawer', where she kept them wrapped in tissue. He assumed they must still be there.

Charlotte, I promise you, your labor of love will not be for nothing, my darling ...

He fell into another deep sleep.

At 2:40 p.m. Lou was dumped out of bed. The ship was slammed by what felt and sounded like a freight train. The gargantuan *Howden R100* had rolled onto her side and was rolling back upright as Lou came round. He struggled to his feet, the ship pitching wildly up and down and yawing to and fro. He staggered into the corridor holding onto the railings and grab bars. The dining room was in total disarray—cups, saucers, plates, bottles of ketchup and sauce, cutlery and food scattered all over the floor, chairs and tables overturned. Pierre was distraught.

"Whatever is happening?" he cried.

At that moment, Lou felt real sorry for him. "Don't panic, Pierre. It's just turbulence, that's all," he assured him in the most calming voice he could muster. People emerged from all corners of the ship with the same question, many of them, like Lou, having been catapulted out of bed. As he ran into the control car, he felt the power easing off. Booth and Johnston held on, looking stupefied.

Booth yelled at the rudder coxswain, "Steer to the opposite shore. Cold air's spilling out of this valley." He pointed to the Saguenay River valley where the mountains each side reached four thousand feet. The coxswain swung the wheel, turning the ship away from the disturbed air and the turbulence gradually eased, then ceased completely. The starboard engine car telegraph bell rang, followed in quick succession by the aft car.

"Lou, go and find out what their problem is," Booth ordered.

In the corridor, Lou ran into Norway who tagged along. Lou climbed down into the starboard engine car. The engineers pointed up through the window at the rear fins, where the cover was torn up and flapping. Lou bounded back up the steps. Meager had now joined Norway.

"Cover's all torn up on the starboard fins," Lou shouted.

They rushed along the corridor to the stern, led by Meager, with Wann, Nervous Nick and Billy in tow. Along the way, other riggers joined them. They examined the bottom fin first. Not so serious: three tears about three feet long. Meager left Wann to supervise two riggers making repairs while he, Lou and Norway climbed a transverse girder to the starboard fin. There was more damage there, but no reason to panic. A split in the cover ran along the outer fin edge about twelve feet long. Two riggers were sent with needles and thread to make repairs, with Norway assisting.

Lou and Meager moved to the fins on the port side, although they'd received no reports of damage from the port engine car. They climbed along the cruciform girder to the port fin to make an inspection. They were shocked by what they found. The fabric to the underside was in ribbons, flapping around a gaping hole about fifteen feet square. Meager sent Lou to inform the captain.

Lou climbed down and went to the speaking tube in the stern corridor and signaled the control car. It was 3 o'clock. Booth answered and Lou explained the situation. Booth sent the chief coxswain and ten more riggers to assist. Meanwhile, Booth made the ship stationary, positioned near a small island, head to wind, with just enough power to maintain their position. Lou returned to the riggers. While they worked, they heard what they thought was the howling wind on the opposite shore. It turned out to be wolves howling in the canyons.

The chief coxswain showed up with an army of riggers and a roll of canvas he'd stashed away. They were joined by Norway and his men from the starboard side, their own repairs satisfactorily completed. They stretched a system of cords over the opening, forming a mesh as a foundation. New canvas was laid over them and lashed down. It was like watching tightrope walkers at the circus, balancing on wires—their only means of support. Meager nagged the riggers to keep their safety lines fastened. The riggers were unfazed by the thousand foot drop and the bobbing Belugas breaking the surface and staring up at them. They joked that the Belugas wanted to mate with the big silver whale in the sky. The repairs took two hours.

At 5 o'clock, during the dog watch, His Majesty's Airship *Howden R100* resumed her journey, but with less haste. They proceeded toward Quebec at fifty knots against the same headwind. As they approached the city, Meager decided to inspect the top of the ship for damage, with Lou and Norway assisting. Leaks in the cover had been discovered in the past few days, requiring repairs to the gas bags.

Before going to the roof, Lou went to his cabin for his Sidcot suit. It'd be chilly up there. The room was still a mess. While picking everything up, he was upset to find Charlotte's picture lying underneath his clothes, its glass smashed, her face no longer visible. He laid it face-down on the bedside table.

At 6:00 p.m., Lou climbed the cat ladder to the roof with Norway. Meager had gone before them. They were over the city and heard the commotion below: ship's sirens, train whistles, car horns and people cheering. While Meager and Norway made their inspection, Lou waited at the hatchway, his attention fixed on the sky directly ahead. It was an alarming sight. A fifteen-mile squall of sparkling, copper cloud, like a line of fire with ominous blackness beneath, stretched across their path. Above the wall, raging cumulonimbus cloud formations reached up to the heavens.

When Meager and Norway returned to the hatchway, Lou gestured toward the storm. Meager's face showed concern. They made their way to the saloon, where Scott was drinking sherry with Burney and Colmore while stewards busily laid out a buffet on tables pushed together. Everything was spic and span once more. The meal looked delicious, with soup, salad and assorted cold cuts. Bottles of wine, stacks of plates, bowls and wine glasses sat nearby.

"There's a bad storm ahead, sir," Meager said, almost casually.

Scott sounded bored and dismissive. "Yes, they've already sent us details from Montreal advising us to go around, but we don't have time for that."

"We should discuss this with the captain. I'm about to go on watch."

Irritated, Scott drained his glass and plonked it down on the table. He strode off toward the control car. Norway and Burney went to the promenade deck to see what they could see from there. Lou and Meager followed Scott to the control car where they found Booth and Johnston standing with Giblett, studying the squall line dead ahead. They were alarmed.

"I think we need to avoid this, sir. It looks bad," Booth said grimly.

"I must agree," Giblett said.

Scott's face was as black as the storm. "Well, *I don't!* We've already lost too much time."

"What's the point? We're not going to make it before sunset anyway," Booth argued.

"A fifty-mile detour for safety's sake might be worth it," Johnston said.

"There are thousands of people in Montreal waiting for us!"

"I don't think it's worth the risk, sir," Booth said.

Scott became more irritated. "We can't bugger about. We're already late and we'll look ridiculous."

"At least we'll arrive in one piece," Booth said.

"It's just a rainstorm—nothing to be frightened of."

"But—"

"Hold your course, Captain. That's an order!"

Scott turned abruptly and when he got to the stairs he stopped.

"Let me know if you run into difficulties requiring my attention."

He went upstairs.

"That man is a *bloody* menace," Booth muttered.

"*Reckless!*" Giblett agreed.

The five men stared through the windows straight ahead. Night was falling fast as they approached the black wall.

At 7:40 p.m. they felt the first tremors under their feet. It was completely dark.

"Hold on boys. This is it!" Booth shouted.

The storm struck with a blast, rocking and shaking the ship. It was accompanied by shrieking winds, heavy rain and hail beating the windows. A mighty gust lifted the bow and ran under the ship to the stern, as though it were a paper cup, tipping the nose sharply downward. Cameron, on the elevators, did his best to counter the effects, turning the metal wheel one way and then the other, to no avail.

"*I'm losing her! I'm losing her!*" he screamed.

The altimeter dial that read thirteen hundred feet spun to three thousand in a matter of seconds. Her nose, which was pointing at the ground, slowly came back up. A few moments later, they were hit by another, even more violent updraft. Again, the ship went shooting toward the heavens tail first, and again, the altimeter spun wildly, now to five thousand feet.

Adding to everyone's distress, all the lights went out, except those on the control panels.

"Oh, bugger!" Meager said.

Lou thought of Josh and Zackary Landsdowne in *Shenandoah*.

Is this what it had been like for them?

Charlotte's alabaster face came back to him and her solemn goodbye.

Perhaps she was right. Maybe she knew I wasn't coming back.

Other thoughts raced through Lou's mind in milliseconds: Richmond's strident words shouted at Norway about the structural integrity of his ship, and then the 'Wiggy thing' clinched it. Something dripped on Lou's nose. He wiped it with his finger. In the glare of the instrument lights he could see it was red.

Blood? Someone upstairs must be badly cut.

He sniffed at it.

No, it's dope! Thank God.

The riggers fixing the canvas had left a drum of dope open up there somewhere.

Silly fools!

"Look, we're done for!" Cameron screamed, his voice breaking in fear. Everyone peered at the black horizon. A massive cross shone in the sky.

This must be Heaven!

"Okay, settle down, boys. We're not dead yet! It's the cross on Mount Royal," Johnston boomed from the back of the control car.

"Ease her gently down to fifteen hundred feet, coxswain," Booth ordered.

"Yes, sir," Cameron said, steadying himself.

Booth issued further instructions. "George, go and survey the damage. Lou, get hold of Disley and get the lights back on."

"Aye, aye, sir."

"Johnny and I will remain here. Oh, and if you run into Major Scott, inform him we ran into a little difficulty—in case he hadn't noticed."

"Right, Captain," Lou said.

"We're through the worst of it. The cross tells us we are," Booth said.

"I think I'm going to convert," Johnston said.

"So you should, Johnny!" Lou said.

Lou got Disley working on the electrical breakers and then went to the dining room, which once again resembled a bombed out ruin. He found Colmore sitting in the dark, surrounded by the buffet strewn across the floor, with broken plates and wine glasses from one end of the room to the other, and down the corridor to the bow.

Pierre sat in the corner sobbing. "Oh, my Lord. Whatever is going on? Look at my beautiful buffet … Oh my Lord …Twice in one day …"

"Pierre, it's all right. It's over now. Come on, pick everything up, there's a good fella. Everything's going to be fine," Lou said, offering his hand. Pierre allowed Lou to pull him up, whereupon he put his arms around Lou and hugged him tight, his head on Lou's chest.

"Oh, my dear Commander, what would I do without you? You're such a comfort in these perilous times."

Lou glanced over Pierre's shoulder at Colmore slumped in a chair, holding a flashlight in one hand and an empty brandy glass in the other. Lou broke free from Pierre and went over to him. Colmore was badly shaken. Scott was nowhere to be found.

Probably crashed in his bunk.

"Are you all right, sir?" Lou asked.

"What can I say? I'm at my wit's end. But I suppose if we can survive this we can bloody-well survive *anything!*"

"Quite right, sir."

"I'm off to bed. If we were going to die today, we'd already be dead," Colmore said, struggling to his feet. He staggered down the corridor toward his cabin.

"Goodnight, sir. Try and get some rest," Lou called after him.

The lights came back on.

Meager, Lou, Wann and Norway walked the ship with flashlights. The repairs made to the fins had held up pretty well, but the underside of the starboard fin had sustained further damage: two twenty-foot tears this time. A gang of riggers was assembled and patching started.

Howden R100 limped into Montreal at midnight and flew over the magnificent city of a million lights until dawn, weaving her way around numerous localized thunderstorms. At first light, Booth steered straight for the tower at St. Hubert to a cacophony of sounds. A loud brass band couldn't be drowned by a cheering crowd of ten thousand who'd waited patiently through the night. When the sun came up, the size of their welcome became apparent: flags and bunting flew everywhere, huge placards of greeting, advertisements for beer, chewing gum and motor oil posted on every available surface. All roads to and from St. Hubert were jammed. The journey from Cardington had taken almost seventy-nine hours. This was indeed a moment for celebration—and relief!

PART NINE

TROUBLE IN AMERICA

65

EZEKIAH WASHINGTON

Friday August 1, 1930.

Lou boarded the *Washingtonian* from Montreal Station the day the airship landed at St. Hubert. This had been a day to remember, but hectic and tiring. He felt glad to be alone, at last. Everyone on the airship had been treated like royalty, from the officers, to the engineers and riggers. They weren't used to being fussed over back home. The men sensed a lack of rank and class—that stuff didn't seem so important here.

Lou got the film star treatment. Girls gathered around him, some actually swooned—highly embarrassing but, he had to admit, a little satisfying. The press knew he was on board and anxious to meet the 'American hero' who'd survived the *R38/ZR-2* disaster. It was a great angle that'd sell newspapers. One reporter told him, "Son, you should take your handsome looks and fame to Hollywood. You'd be a sensation!"

Lou just laughed. He answered their questions with patience and good humor, making it plain he didn't like the hero label. On this ship, they were all heroes; he wasn't special. This made him even more popular and everyone wanted their picture taken with him. Lou was glad to get away; the focus needed to be on the British crew and the ship's designers, including his good friend 'Mr. Shute' and 'Mr. Shute's' boss, Sir Dennis, who got into top gear the moment he stepped off the ship. *Howden R100* was *his* idea, *his* design and *his* airship. As soon as Lou could escape, he sent two wires. The first to Charlotte in Bedford:

My darling Charlotte Arrived safely Thinking of you STOP Heading south today by train STOP Will wire later Love you Lou

The second went to his family in Virginia:

Dear All Landed Montreal Arriving Union Station 8 am Saturday August 2 Love Lou

When he got close to the train, a portly steward studied him from beside the door. He was dressed in a crisp, white jacket and well-pressed black trousers. He bowed his domed head that shone like a clarinet, perfectly matching his patent leather shoes. He rubbed his huge hands together.

"Good afternoon, sir. I'm honored to have you aboard my train," he said, taking Lou's kit bag. He led Lou to a luxurious sleeper suite. Lou glanced at the couch, the writing table and the pull-out bed.

"There must be some mistake—this isn't for me."

"Oh, it most certainly is, sir, yes indeedy," the steward said, flashing an enormous smile, his perfect teeth as white as his jacket.

"But—"

"My name is Ezekiah Washington the Second and I'm here to take care of you," he said, busily stashing Lou's bag in a closet.

"I can't accept this."

"Why not? The train's half empty and we've got to take care of our people—especially, *you*, sir."

"*'Our people'?*"

"Our brothers ...our brothers-in-arms." Ezekiah Washington's wide, black nostrils flared for a second. "I know you were at the Front." He pointed at the newspapers on the table. "I have the *Washington Post* and the *New York Times* here for you," he said, his huge, brown eyes shining and radiating warmth.

"How did you know who I was?"

"You're wearing the uniform of a lieutenant commander in the United States Navy—previously of the United States Marine Corps, sir—Belleau Wood right? I know exactly who you is," he said, his voice gravelly and coarse. Lou appeared disappointed. "Don't you worry, sir. I won't tell a soul. I'm a veteran, too."

"Army?"

"New York 369th. The Harlem Hellfighters, yes sir!"

"France?"

"The Argonne Forest. We were the first colored outfit in there."

"Oh, yeah, I know. You guys took a hell of a beating!"

Ezekiah beamed with pride. "The French were good to me—awarded me the Croix de Guerre with gold palm. Even General Pershing said nice things about us. I was one of the lucky ones. Still am."

"I'm proud of you, man. And you made it back!" Lou said, nodding.

"Yep, in one piece. My Lord and Savior Jesus brought me through. I was lucky to get my job back on the railway. The rest of 'em ain't looking so good."

"Why, what's happening to them?"

"Thousands are down in D.C. You'll see 'em when you get there. It's a cryin' shame, is what it is. They're camped out down there in that bog hole, tryin' to get the money the government promised 'em."

"What money?"

"When they came home they were given government bonds, promising to pay 'em a bonus for their service to the country."

Lou remembered. He'd received bonds when he got back, but since he joined the Navy almost immediately, he'd stuck them a drawer in his mother's chest and forgotten about them.

"What about you?" he asked.

"Yes, I got some, too. But I'm okay. I've got this job. The rest of our brothers are starving. They're *desperate*." Ezekiah's eyes glistened now.

Lou rested his elbow on the window ledge and looked out. This was truly depressing. He hadn't realized things were this bad. He wished he'd taken more interest.

"What about everybody else?"

"The country's in a terrible mess, millions out of work, thousands losing their homes. Banks a' takin' everythin'—hundreds killin' 'emselves. It's *pitiful!*" Ezekiah said. Tears ran down his cheeks.

A commotion started up on the platform: Whistles blew, doors slammed, multiple voices yelled "All aboard!" The train lurched forward. Ezekiah cleared his throat and wiped away the tears on the back of his hand, recovering his demeanor.

"They'll be serving afternoon tea and sandwiches, if you're hungry, sir," Ezekiah said. "I can reserve you a place in the dining car, if you like."

"That would be great. I'll come down, shortly. I'm starving."

" 'Bout half an hour then, sir. I'll have you a seat."

When the steward had gone, Lou picked up the *Washington Post*. The headlines confirmed what Ezekiah had said.

The left-hand headline read:
TEN THOUSAND MARCH ON CAPITAL

The right-hand headline:
BONUS ARMY REFUSES TO GIVE UP

There were photographs of men in rags, marching on the streets of Washington, waving banners. BONUS NOW, read one. WE ARE YOUR SOLDIERS DON'T FORGET US, read another. Lou studied the article with concern for his home town, his veteran brothers-in-arms and his country. He wondered how his parents were faring.

They must be okay, surely?

His eye skipped to the bottom of the page. A small headline caught his eye and then a photograph of himself outside the Howden Court in 1922. He remembered them taking that picture. He'd been standing with Potter, but they'd cropped *him* out.

Virginia Welcomes Favorite Son
Hero of the Airship ZR-2 due to arrive at Union Station

Lt. Cmdr. Louis Remington is expected to arrive at St. Hubert's, Montreal early today aboard one of the largest airships ever to fly, British airship, Howden R100. Remington is serving as third officer on board and will play the same role aboard Cardington R101, another monster dirigible under construction by the British government. Remington has been serving as a special assistant to the Director of Development of British Airships at Cardington in Bedfordshire on behalf of the U.S. Navy throughout design of both airships. Remington is known for his bravery as chief petty officer aboard U.S. ZR-2 when that airship crashed into the River Humber in Yorkshire, in 1921, killing all but five of the British and American airshipmen on board. The flower of the British Airship industry was lost that day and due to his valuable knowledge and airship experience, Remington was seconded as a liaison officer by the British and attached to the Royal Air Force. The Lt. Commander was born in his grandmother's farmhouse in Great Falls, Virginia in 1898. Remington is expected to arrive in the U.S. in the next day or so.

Lou scratched his head in embarrassment. He went to the dining car for tea and ham sandwiches. He studied the other travelers. No one appeared happy. Some glanced at him and smiled, seeming to recognize him, but respecting his privacy. He supposed they were Americans returning from business trips, or visiting relatives. The American immigration officer politely welcomed him home.

Later, Lou returned for dinner, where he had a decent steak. He struck up a conversation with a Canadian lumber salesman. "The U.S. economy is in dire straits," the man said. "These are desperate times we're living in. And it's all Hoover's fault!"

Lou returned to his car and sat on the couch, put his feet up, and read the rest of the newspapers. The steward reappeared and offered him a drink. He ordered black coffee and a Jack and Coke. It felt good to be home, but he found the news troubling. He slept well, lulled by the rocking motion and clicking wheels over the long North American tracks.

Lou was vaguely aware of coming into New York's Penn Station, disturbed by slamming doors and the general bustle of hundreds on the move. He faded in and out until the train got underway again. He slept deeply until there came a gentle tapping on the door. He woke up confused and disappointed, expecting Charlotte to be lying beside him.

"Sir, it's six-thirty. They're serving breakfast now," Ezekiah called.

Lou sat up. "Thanks. I'll be right there."

He got up and washed his face in the sink. An hour later he sat with his kitbag, ready for Washington D.C. The train began slowing down as Ezekiah came in.

"The train always stops here for ten minutes—sometimes longer, going into Union. You might as well relax, sir," he said.

As they came to a halt beside a stationary freight train, two men chased down and cornered two filthy wretches beneath Lou's window. He watched in horror. Despite their pleas, they were beaten mercilessly with billy clubs until blood ran from their heads and down their faces. Ezekiah stood at the window beside Lou.

"It ain't right what they do to our brothers. Look at 'em. It's disgusting."

"Who are they?"

"The ones with the clubs are railway police. They're just thugs is what they is."

"What the hell is going on in my country?" Lou said, jumping up. He rushed to the door, jumped down from the train into the gravel, and ran over to the men with the clubs. "Leave these men alone," he shouted.

"Get back on the train, sailor. We're railway police," one said holding up a badge.

"And these men are veterans. Leave them alone." Lou turned to the men on the ground. "Where you guys tryin' to get to?"

"Anacostia, sir."

"These here men have been ridin' the rails *illegally*. They're under arrest." Lou stepped forward to help one of the beaten men to his feet.

"Step away," the one with the badge ordered, drawing a gun.

Lou jumped him in a flash, putting his arm in a lock. The gun fell from his hand and Lou wrenched it upwards and bent the fingers of the gun hand backwards, breaking them. He then methodically yanked the man's thumb out of its socket.

"Ah, Jeez!" the man screamed. His partner froze.

Lou dumped the first man down like a sack of turnips and moved toward the other man.

"I don't want no trouble, mister," the second man pleaded.

Lou picked up the gun, emptied the bullets on the ground, and threw it across the tracks. "Back up, right now!" Lou shouted.

The man obeyed. Lou pulled the two veterans to their feet.

"D.C. right?" Lou asked.

"Yes, sir."

"Get on that train."

Lou led them to the door where Ezekiah waited to give them a hand up. He took them to a quiet car and gave them wet towels to clean up the blood. Lou pulled the train door shut and on cue, the train moved forward.

66

UNION STATION

The *Washingtonian* rolled into Union Station and, after trying to give Ezekiah Washington the Second a crisp dollar bill, Lou hoisted his kit bag onto his shoulder and marched down the platform with the two veterans he'd rescued. He tried to spot his brother within the crowd gathered at the barrier. Some were dressed in business suits. Many others were in tatters and disheveled—homeless perhaps. Lou assumed they were waiting for a congressman or a senator. Then he heard shouts.

"Look, this must be him!"

"Yes, that's him."

"I see him."

The ticket collector glanced at the two scruffy veterans with Lou, about to say something. "These men are with me. Any problem?" Lou said.

"Go right ahead, sir. If they're with you, that's good enough for me," the man said, waving them through.

The small crowd broke into spontaneous applause and a few cheers. A couple of men in trilbys were holding Speed Graphics. Flashbulbs went off. Lou couldn't understand what the fuss was about.

They must think I'm someone else.

Then he remembered the newspaper article. Standing apart from the crowd, he noticed two people beside a column. They looked familiar. She reminded him of his mother.

Oh my goodness, it's Anna and Tom!

The crowd swarmed around Lou before he could get to them. Reporters peppered him with questions. "Are you home to stay, Commander Remington?"

"How was your airship flight, sir?"

"How long are you here for?"

"We read you got married in England."

"Tell us about your wife."

"Have you gotten over the crash of *ZR-2*?"

"Can airships really ever be safe?"

"Are you going back to England?"

"What do you think about the Bonus Army?"

"D'you think they should get the money?"

One of the men in rags stepped forward. He reeked. People backed away in disgust, screwing up their faces.

"Lou, d'you remember *me?*" he asked, his voice plaintive.

Lou studied him. He was about his own age, but in poor physical condition; his face was filthy, hair long and greasy, a front tooth missing, the rest discolored and about to fall out.

"It's me, Henry—Saint-Mihiel—*France!*"

Good God, it's Henry Faulkner! He was behind me at Verdun somewhere in that last attack.

He hadn't seen Henry since that horrible morning of eleven, eleven. Lou had been taken to a field hospital. It was all a blur; chaos had followed the official ending of the war at 11:00 a.m. He assumed most of his buddies were dead. Lou took the man's grimy hand.

"Yes, of course I remember you, Henry. I thought—"

"No, I survived, but we might as *well* be dead. We need your help, sir —real bad."

Henry thrust a piece of scrap paper at Lou. "I've written down where you can find us—Tent City in Anacostia. Just ask for me. We *must* talk to you."

"I'll come. I promise," Lou said.

"There's so much you can do to help us, Lou."

Lou pointed to the two men he'd brought with him on the train. "Henry, do what you can for these two men," he said, slipping a few dollar bills into his hand.

The crowd listened in rapt attention, while reporters scribbled madly.

"I must go. My family's waiting for me," Lou said, raising his voice.

"Where are you staying, sir?" a reporter called.

Lou didn't answer. He smiled and moved toward his brother and sister.

"You won't *forget* us?" Henry shouted.

"I'll come as soon as I can," Lou yelled back over his shoulder.

Before Lou got away, a man and a woman stopped him. They were about fifty-five, dressed casually, but decently. The man put his hand on Lou's arm. "Excuse me, Commander Remington, I'm Daniel Jenco— Bobby's father—*Bobby Jenco*—you remember our Bobby, don't you?"

Lou's heart skipped a beat. This was exactly what he'd always dreaded.

"Bobby was on *ZR-2* with you," the man said, his eyes sad and penetrating. Lou could see the resemblance to Bobby. The crowd closed in around them once more, the reporters wide-eyed, eager like wolves.

"Josh Stone told us what you did—how you threw Bobby your own parachute ..."

"Oh, er, Josh, well—"

"We came down from Baltimore to personally thank you for trying to save our boy."

They put their arms out and hugged Lou. He suddenly remembered the two pregnant girls at the court of inquiry. "Did you know you have a grandchild?" Lou said. They looked stunned and thrilled at the same time.

"No, nobody told us—"

"I talked with your son, just before the ship broke up. He told me he was going to ask the girl to marry him that same evening—a nurse."

Overwhelmed, Bobby's mother began to cry.

"The child would be about eight or nine now, I guess," Lou said.

"What was the girl's name?" Bobby's mother asked, her eyes pleading.

Lou thought for a moment. "It was *Elsie*. Write to Hull Infirmary. They'll help you. You can contact me at the Royal Airship Works in Cardington if you need to."

The couple was thankful for the information. Bobby's father wrote down their address and gave it to Lou.

"I must go. My folks are waiting." Lou left them knowing he'd given them something precious—something from Bobby. Their eyes shone with hope.

Lou broke away from the crowd, finally reaching Tom and Anna. Tom, now 26, was a couple of inches shorter than Lou, with the same broad shoulders and muscular arms, obviously put to good use. Tom's hair was already starting to recede like their Dad's. His bone structure was also similar, chiseled, and his eyes as intense. He was a man, not the boy Lou had last seen. Anna was a couple of years younger than Tom, with long, light brown hair, most of it hidden under a floppy, yellow sun hat. She wore a long, white, cotton skirt and a pale blue blouse. Her eyes were ice blue and wider apart, similar to Lou's—a younger version of their beautiful mother.

Anna put her arms out and Lou embraced her, feeling her tears on his face. He turned to Tom and hugged him, too, though he sensed Tom was distant. Tom led the way out of the station. Lou put his arm around Anna and they followed. They walked toward a crowd of Army veterans, who watched them with doleful eyes. They stopped and Lou gave them all the money he had in his pockets and in his wallet. Tom appeared sullen and unimpressed.

They had an old pickup truck parked outside the station.

"Thanks for meeting me. You got my wires okay?" Lou asked.

"No, we didn't get any wires," Tom answered.

"How did you know I'd be here, then?"

"We read it in the paper—you're famous. They said you were on the airship," Anna said with a giggle.

Tom went to the pickup and pulled back the ragged canvas cover.

"This is Granddad's old Buick from the farm!" Lou exclaimed.

"Yep. A bit rusty, but still rollin'," Tom said curtly.

He threw Lou's kitbag in the truck-bed beside the shovels and picks and covered it with the canvas. It was sunny, not yet too hot. They climbed in the cab, with Lou in the middle, and Tom drove out of Union. Along the sidewalk, a crowd of several hundred waited beside a line of empty tables.

"What are they waiting for?" Lou asked.

"*Food!* That's a soup line. They're waiting for it to arrive," Tom replied. Lou detected sarcasm. He looked around, speechless.

Goddammit! What the hell's happened to my country?

Tom drove along Louisiana Avenue and on to Constitution, heading west toward Virginia, about three miles off. There were groups of men everywhere with placards and mounted police watching from a distance. On the surface, everything appeared peaceful. Lou studied their hopeless faces.

"Looks like everything's gone to hell in this town."

"These men are coming from all over, many of them with wives and kids," Tom answered with resignation, as if *Lou* had something to do with it.

"I feel so sorry for them," Anna said.

"I saw them on the railroad tracks," Lou said.

"It's a bad situation. They should give 'em the damned money," Tom snarled. They drove in silence for some minutes, until Lou spoke.

"How are Mum and Dad?"

Silence.

"*Well?*" Lou asked.

"They're okay, but you'll notice a change—especially in Dad—but don't worry, they're fine. They've both gotten older, that's all," Anna said. She sounded weary.

"We *all* have, I reckon. I'm ashamed to say it's been ten years," Lou said.

Tom smirked, but remained silent, keeping his eyes on the road. Lou was disappointed at Tom's off-handedness. He hadn't expected it—but perhaps he should've. It was only natural. Big brother back on the scene. It might take a few days.

Anna studied Lou, trying to ease the tension. "You look wonderful, Lou," she said. "If you weren't my brother, I'd take a fancy to you *myself*."

They drove past the Smithsonian Museum of Art and along the tree-lined mall. Lou thought back to when his Mom and Dad used to bring him here to see the paintings.

"We've all missed you," Anna said, her eyes resting on him again, but seriously now. "Aren't you coming home soon … for good? You really should, you know. God, we so much want you home, big brother."

Tom showed no reaction.

"Well I'm …" Lou began, but Anna knew what was on his mind.

"I'm sure you and Dad will get along. He's pretty mellow nowadays. He's a big softie. Bring Charlotte. We'd love to meet her. She looked so beautiful in the wedding photo."

Lou looked down. It was gut-wrenching to hear. "I'd love to bring her over to meet you all. I miss you, too," he said. He looked across the open lawn toward the White House in the distance. "And she'd love to come."

"Then bring her!" said Anna.

"I'm dying to see Mum and Dad, and of course, Gran. Tell me about them."

"They've been getting ready for your homecoming since 5 o'clock this mornin'," Tom grunted. He turned off the main road and onto the George Washington Parkway, the scenic country road along the Potomac River toward Virginia.

"Where you goin'? We live that way," Lou said, pointing back at the main road.

"Actually, we *don't*—not anymore," Tom said. He seemed to be enjoying this.

"What d'you mean. Did you move?"

"Yeah, had to," Anna said.

"Why?"

"They took the house," she said.

"What do you mean *they* took the house? *Who* took the house?"

"The bank," Tom said.

This was like a jab in the guts.

"They also took the car," Anna said.

"Dad's Ford?"

"Bank took everything. Everything they could get their hands on," Tom said, his eyes narrowing.

Shattered, Lou put his hand up to his forehead, unable to breathe.

"Lou, it could be worse. Dad lost his job, but—"

"That was *ages* ago!" Tom sneered.

"Dad lost his *job!* Things could be worse! How could they be *worse?*"

They motored along the high, winding road overlooking the glistening river. It was beautiful, but Lou hardly noticed.

"Dad had been with that firm for what ...twenty years?" Lou said.

"Twenty-three, actually. But they shut down. Like thousands of other companies," Tom said bitterly.

"So, where are you now?"

"We're all back at Gran's place, like the old days. Gran doesn't owe anyone a dime. They can't touch her," Anna said.

"Why wasn't I told about any of this?"

"They didn't want you to worry, dear brother," Tom replied.

"So, what do you all do for money?"

"We do jobs. Dad and I work at Arlington Cemetery sometimes, or he did 'til recently. Jeb helps me nowadays," Tom answered.

"Doing what?"

"Digging graves, doing landscaping and stuff," Tom replied.

"*My God!*"

"Lou, we're lucky. Millions are out of work. Millions are starving," Anna said.

"You just saw the soup lines, didn't you," Tom said.

"We grow stuff. We've got rabbit, deer, squirrel, bear, possum, ground hog. We'll *never* go hungry!" Anna said.

"We opened a couple of fields Gran had left fallow. We're growing tobacco for Gran, like always, and old Jeb and I are growing a stack of potatoes and carrots and peas and beans—you name it. And grain o'course. We sell some and we give a lot away. Jeb takes a load to his people in D.C. every week," Tom said.

"Plus we trade in a little of the old '*you know what.*' We like to keep the Army and the Navy and Congress happy," Anna said with a wink.

Lou smiled.

"Which brings us to another sore subject. More trouble," said Tom.

"What kind of trouble?"

"The Klan," Tom said.

Lou stared out the window at the forest. This was like walking into a hailstorm. "What the hell are those idiots up to?"

"They're enforcing Prohibition," Tom answered.

"How?"

"They're running around in bed sheets burning down bars and destroying stills all over the place," Anna said.

"And *lynching blacks*, I suppose," Lou said.

God, he wished he were here to help deal with this crap. They traveled up the Georgetown Pike. As the day got hotter, the cicadas in the trees got louder.

What a racket!

It was a screaming whine. He'd forgotten that sound.

"When you left, Gran let old Jeb build a shack down by the creek. The family's always taken care of Jeb and he does a lot for us. After Granddad went, he tended the still. He's a good man—and his whisky's every bit as good as ol' Granddad's," Anna said.

"His wife's okay, too. They ain't no trouble," Tom said.

"They have two beautiful children. A boy and a girl," Anna said.

"So, tell me what's been happening?"

"The boys in white have been around, looking for the still. It's been drivin' 'em crazy," Tom said.

"But they didn't find it?"

"Not yet. But I'm sure they will. They're determined," Tom replied.

"They've been threatening Jeb. He's terrified," Anna said.

"Poor old Jeb. I love that man," Lou said.

It was Jeb who'd taught him to fish on the river in the skiff and to beware of the current rushing to the falls. He'd taught him to shoot and skin a rabbit, expertly wring a chicken's neck with minimum suffering to the creature, plant beans, and set up and run the still, which Grandfather—known locally as 'the man from Moray'—had passed on to Father and Jeb.

"Their threats are gettin' worse," Anna said.

"They'd better not lay a finger on him," Lou said.

"What are *you* gonna do? You can't mess with the Klan," Tom sneered

"Do you know who these men are?"

Tom hesitated.

"Tom!"

"I've got a good idea," Tom said, waving his hand dismissively.

"Good. Then you'll tell me and I'll pay them a visit."

"*What!* Don't get crazy," Tom said.

"Tom, only cowards hide under bed sheets."

They pressed on along the pike, up winding hills and down through valleys between wooded banks toward Great Falls.

"Charlotte would love it here. It's so much like England," Lou said. "I'd forgotten."

"I reckon you did," Tom said.

Soon, they came to an opening in the trees on the right marked by two massive boulders. His grandfather had placed them to mark the entrance to the farm, meaning to build two fine stone pillars one day, but there'd always been too many other more important things to do. Lou wondered again how his grandfather got those boulders there in the first place. Now he'd never know. Someone had put up a sign.

REMINGTON'S FARM

"That's new," Lou said. "I like it."

67

REMINGTON'S FARM

Saturday & Sunday August 2 & 3, 1930.

They followed the winding trail through the forest for three quarters of a mile. These familiar surroundings Lou found magically calming. Although the property belonged to his grandparents, he'd lived here for many years. When Lou was twelve, his father had saved enough to put down a deposit on a home in Fairfax, and he and his siblings had been sorry to leave this place.

Presently, the Virginia, black stone farmhouse came into view among the towering oaks. Lou's grandfather had built this house in the 1870's after leaving Moray, Scotland fifteen years earlier, at age twenty-five. The roof was clad in gunmetal grey, standing seam metal, complete with snow-guards. The second story was sheathed in white clapboard. Operable green shutters set off the small-paned, double-hung sash windows. It was a Virginia classic.

As the pickup rolled around the dirt driveway, chickens kicked up a fuss and dogs barked. The arrivals got out of the pickup and the dogs, a gold Labrador and a black mutt, came with their tails wagging to welcome Lou. He patted them.

"The Lab's 'Tobacca' and the black one's 'Moonshine'—she's a sweetie," Anna said. The screen door flew open and banged shut, and Lou's mother, Violet, rushed out. It opened again, more slowly and was closed carefully by his father. Following him came Gran in her long, white kitchen apron. Then Jeb emerged from the path leading up from the river—tall and stooping, his hair and mustache turning grey.

They gathered around Lou, his mother and grandmother smothering him with kisses. His father stepped forward and hugged him, after hanging back awkwardly. They both became embarrassed. Lou turned to Jeb and shook his hand and embraced him. True, they'd all gotten older, especially Father. His shoulders were rounded and his thinning, grey hair had receded more and gone white over the ears. His deep blue eyes, under white, straggly eyebrows, were as piercing as ever, though sunken. His sallow face was gaunt, cheeks hollow. Lou was shocked. His dad had the air of a beaten man. His mother was still a pretty woman with the same wonderful smile, big, bright eyes and soft, brown hair.

They stepped inside and Lou immediately caught that familiar smell of furniture polish, tobacco and wood smoke from the bluestone fireplace, lingering from previous winters. He glanced around the room, appreciating the dark wood paneling and oak flooring, like a shadowy cave—cosy in winter, oppressive in summer. His eyes fell on a shotgun propped in the corner by the door. It jarred him for a moment. Above all else, this place was home—more home to Lou than the Fairfax house had ever been.

On one wall were a few yellowing pictures in frames: General Lee and Stonewall Jackson and a photo of Gran and Granddad taken in the 1880s. Beside them, photos of Lou: one in Marine dress uniform taken just before being shipped off to France, and the other, full of promise in his Navy uniform before leaving for England as an airshipman.

Gran scurried off to the kitchen to bring refreshments. Everyone sat down in the living room in the old, but comfortable, easy chairs. It was hard at first. Where to start? Father sat packing tobacco onto a cigarette paper. He licked the edge and rolled it.

"Tell us about the journey here, son. They say you flew the airship," Mother said.

"It was okay, Mom. Nothing spectacular really. Pretty boring most of the time."

"To read the newspapers and hear your mom tell it, you'd think he'd flown the damned thing to Canada all by himself," Lou's father said, flicking a brass lighter under his cigarette. It flamed, filling the room with smoke. He began to cough—a nasty, hacking cough. Gran came out from the kitchen with lemonade and iced tea. Everyone helped themselves except Father. Gran brought him coffee.

"We had plenty of experienced officers on board. I was just one of them."

"No, you were an officer aboard His Majesty's Airship *Howden R100* based at the British Government's Royal Airship Works in Cardington and Special Adviser to the Director of Airship Development, as well as being the Official American Observer. It says it all right here in the paper," Anna said, holding up the *Washington Post*.

"Sis—"

"Don't play it down, Lou. We're all very proud of you," Anna said. "Even Dad!"

Father remained impassive. He took a gulp of coffee and put his cup back in the saucer on the table beside him. Tom sat in an upright chair against the wall, arms folded across his chest, lips pursed, staring out the window.

"I don't know why you couldn't have settled down here and married a nice, American girl, one of your own kind, instead of going off and marrying *some hoity-toity British dame*," Father said. He stopped to cough and clear his throat. His voice was weak and hoarse."Julia sat around here waiting for you to come home in that silly damned airship. She would've been perfect. You broke that poor girl's heart, that's what you did. *Jilted!* That's what she was. She was devoted to you. And still is! She comes round here to see your mother every week and Mother treats her like a daughter. She'll die an old maid!"

Everyone sat silent. Lou felt bushwacked. That was *Father.* Nothing had changed and Tom was turning out just like him. The old animosity was alive and well. This was not exactly *The Return of the Prodigal Son.*

Mother dabbed her eyes with a handkerchief. "Cliff, you can't say that," she said. "He's got to lead his own life. Maybe it's lucky he's over there. At least he's working."

"I had every intention of coming back. After the crash, everything changed."

"Yeah, he got the hots for his nurse," Father sneered, glaring at Mother.

"It's true, Dad, I did fall for a wonderful girl, but that wasn't the only reason."

"They always fall for the nurse," Father said.

"What else was it, son?" Mother asked.

"I don't want to talk about it right now, Mom."

"He doesn't want to talk about it right now, Mom," Father scoffed in a whiny voice. He began to cough again and pinched out his cigarette in the dirty ashtray.

"Josh came to see us, you know," Mother said.

"He said he would."

"He was such a nice young man," Gran said. "Anna and Tom brought him to see me."

"He thought the world of you, Lou," Mother said.

"Anna was very taken with him. He was *so* good looking," Gran said.

Anna had become wistful and was tearing up. "He was a lovely guy," she whispered.

"It was a tragedy," Mother said.

"It was *inevitable!* That's what it was! Riding around in the air in a balloon filled with gas—you're asking for it. It defies logic. Common sense'll tell you that sooner or later you're gonna be blown to smithereens. It's the law of physics. Any damned fool could figure that out," Father said coldly.

No one said anything for a long time and Gran got up to get more refreshments. "Louis, how long are you staying for?" she said.

"I'll be here until August the eleventh—if you don't mind, Gran."

"You can stay as long as you like, my darlin' boy."

"I wish I could stay longer."

"But he's got to get back to the 'little wifey' in merry old England," Father said, smirking.

"Dad, *stop it!*" Anna cried.

Father got up and disappeared through the front door. Gran went round clearing things away.

"Don't be too upset by your Dad, Lou. He's had a rough time. He's been longing for the day when you walked through that door," Mother said.

Lou looked skeptical.

"It's true," Anna said.

"You're all he thinks about," Mother said.

"You're his favorite," Anna said.

"I don't know about that …"

Lou watched as Tom got up and went upstairs.

"Your dad worries himself sick about you, son," Gran said.

A few minutes later, someone tapped on the front door.

"It'll be Jeb," Mother said. "Come in."

Jeb stepped into the living room. "Shall I bring up anything special for dinner, ma'am?"

"Bring up a nice, plump chicken, Jeb, and some beans and carrots. Oh, and some squash, please," Gran said.

"Jeb, is my husband down there with you?" Mother asked.

"He's sitting on his seat by the crick as usual, Mrs. R."

Lou strolled down the pathway past the old barn to the paddock. He paused to pat the draft horse before moving past rows of lettuces and carrots in a small adjacent field. It was getting hot and insects were buzzing around. His movements were followed by three blackbirds wheeling overhead. He continued along the well-trodden path down to the creek, passing Jeb's shack on the right-hand side, among the trees. Lou stopped to inspect it. Though basic, Jeb had done a nice job. It had a small verandah across the front and window boxes full of yellow flowers. The wood siding was painted white and the roof was clad in corrugated iron sheeting. On each side sat a painted wooden barrel under a downspout. Everything seemed perfect and in its place. Instinctively, Lou got the impression that Jeb was a happy man, or at least he would be if the KKK left him alone. A plume of blue smoke came from the chimney.

Jeb's wife must be inside.

Mother had written to say that Jeb had got married late in life to a younger woman. He'd asked if he could bring her to Remington's Farm. The three blackbirds swooped down and landed on the roof and began to strut along the ridge, cawing noisily, heads bobbing, their eyes beady and wicked. The door opened and a big woman, about thirty, wearing a full-length, bright blue dress and a white turban emerged. She held a boy in her arms, a towel in her one hand. A little, brown-eyed girl peeped from behind a clutched handful of her mother's skirt. The woman gave Lou a stunning white smile.

"You must be Mr. Lou. It's good to see you, sir," she said, standing above him on the edge of the porch.

"It's *Alice*, right? My mother told me all about you. How are you?"

"I's fine. Everybody's bin lookin' forward to seein' *you*, Mr. Lou."

"It's good to be home," Lou said.

But the blackbirds were causing a distraction. Alice looked up at them, vexed. "Ah don't know what's got into them darn birds. Carryin' on an' fussin' like 'at. She waved the towel at them. "Go on shoo!" The startled crows took off and circled the shack before flying off toward the river.

"Perhaps they're welcoming me home," Lou said.

"No, they're bad luck—a warning more like. I don' like 'em on our roof. Yer daddy shoots 'em when he has a mind to."

"Now, who are *these* little people?" Lou asked, peering at the children.

"This is Doris, she's four and this guy is Benjamin, he'll be three next week." Alice looked down at the kids. "Say hello to Mr. Lou."

The girl smiled, but was too shy to speak.

The boy was more bold. "Hello Mr. Lou-Lou," he said, giggling.

"How long is you stayin'? You stayin' for good, ain'tcha?" Alice asked.

" 'Fraid not."

"Yer daddy's down there by the crick. He sits there most of the time these days—thinkin' 'bout you I reckon."

"How do you know?"

"Oh, I jus' do."

"I'll go on down."

"He ain't bin too well lately."

Lou walked along the pathway past a chicken run with about fifty chickens clucking and carrying on, and then on past more plots where vegetables were thriving. His dad was sitting on a bench on the dock. Lou went over and eased himself down, trying not to disturb him.

"Dad, I'm so pleased to see you. You don't know how much."

Father said nothing—as if he hadn't heard. He looked away across the creek, took out his lighter and re-lit a half-smoked roll-up, exhaling a cloud of smoke that hung in the still, humid air. Two ducks splashed into the water and swam past them. Finally, Father nodded as if Lou's words had just sunk in. He wiped the sweat off his forehead with his hand and rubbed it on his checked shirt.

"I'm sorry about the house, Dad. I didn't know."

"How *would* you know?"

This stung, but Lou tried to ignore it. "It's *terrible*," he said.

"It really doesn't matter," Father said, staring at the dark water.

"I was shocked when I heard about it this morning."

"Well, you needn't concern yourself."

"I want to help."

"We'll manage."

"I'll help some way."

"How?" Father said his lip curling into that old familiar sneer.

"I'll find a way."

"Don't worry. *Tom'll* look after things. He's a good boy."

"He's a wonderful son and wonderful brother."

"As long as *he's* around, you can do your thing. You don't need to give us a second thought."

"Dad, I love you, you know. I love you all. I've been a rotten son. You're right."

Father didn't argue. He raised his eyebrows as if to say, '*It really doesn't matter.*'

"Dad, Tom told me you've been having trouble with the Klan."

This irritated Father. His eyes narrowed. Now he was mad at Tom.

"Goddammit! I told him not to tell you about them fools."

"What do they want?"

"You know what they want. Don't pay 'em no mind. I got the twelve. I'll deal with 'em. I'll have them sons o' bitches in the ground faster'n you can spit."

Lou exhaled and looked away. He didn't doubt his father on that score. No point in arguing. "I'm going back to sort a few things out." He got up and moved away. "See you later, Dad." Father nodded without turning his head, continuing his gaze into the creek. Lou walked back up the path past Jeb, who was weeding one of the vegetable gardens.

Lou called to him, "Jeb, you okay?"

"Yep, Mr. Lou. I'm fine."

"No, *really?*"

"Yeah, everything's good."

"What about them damned night riders?"

"Nah! They ain't nothin'. Don't you worry about *them* none. We got it covered, sir."

Back at the house, Gran served a ham salad at the massive kitchen table. Lou loved this room with its old, wood-burning range and huge, white porcelain sink. He opened the pantry door and looked inside. Lots of jars and homemade stuff. He looked at Gran.

"We don't buy much. We grow everything."

"What about things like toilet paper and milk?"

"We get the local newspaper once in a while," Gran replied, with a little smirk.

"We trade with Jonesie up the road; he's got Jerseys at his place," Mother said.

"You'd be surprised how much bartering goes on around here," Gran said.

"We're very blessed," said Anna, putting her arm around Lou's neck and kissing his cheek. "Oh, my darlin' brother, it's *so* good to have you home."

That first evening, a Saturday, the family gathered around the big oak table in the rarely-used dining room and ate the roasted chicken and vegetables Jeb had brought up. Gran took out a bottle of elderberry wine she'd made a year before—said she'd been keeping it for a special occasion. Anna poured some out and they raised their glasses.

"Here's to you, Lou—to your safe return in your airship," Anna said.

"And the rest of your flights," Mother added.

Father lifted his glass and took a sip, saying nothing. Tom did the same. Dinner was over by nine. Father said he was tired and went to bed, waving a hand to Lou as he left the room.

Well, at least that's something.

"Tom, can you take me into Georgetown on Monday morning?" Lou asked.

Tom frowned at first and then said, "Sure."

"I've a few errands to run. Wanna come, Sis?"

"I want to be with you every moment you're here, Lou."

"Do you still have the guitar and banjo somewhere? Or did the bank get them, too?" Lou asked, looking at Tom. But Mother seemed ready for this question.

"No, I hid them away and brought them here. I dug them out of one of the attic bedrooms and cleaned them up last week. I knew you'd be looking for them."

"So many times I've thought of how Dad and I used to play together, on good days."

"You should get him to play with you," Gran said in a whisper as though her son upstairs might hear. "Since you left, he hasn't played a note."

When Lou went to his bedroom, he saw Mother had stood the guitar and banjo against the wall in the corner. He undressed and fell asleep in his old bed, wishing Charlotte was there.

The next day, they all went to church, except for Father. He said he didn't feel like it. He used to go regularly, but his churchgoing, like his faith, had dropped off. Mother said she was surprised Julia wasn't in church—she'd kept up her attendance at this church after her family had moved away.

On Monday morning, Lou went with Tom and Anna in the pickup back along the river and over the recently completed Key Bridge, into Georgetown.

"This is all new," Lou said as they passed a streetcar gliding its way over the river.

"There's a lot of stuff round here you ain't seen," Tom said.

Lou turned and faced Tom and spoke across Anna who sat in the middle. "You still mad at me, little brother? What's eatin' you, huh?" Lou said. Tom paused, mulling things over. "Come on Tom, *spit it out!*"

"You show up here like you're '*the man*'. Giving money to the poor. Who the hell do you think you are? Some big shot!"

"Tom, I was just tryin' to help my   "

"And to tell you the truth, Louis, it irritates me, how everyone's had to suffer because of *you! Virginia's Favorite Son—my ass!*"

"Who?"

"Dad, and Mum, although *she* won't admit it—"

"I'm sure Dad doesn't care that much—"

"He does so! It tears him up worrying over you."

Lou was surprised, but glad it was all coming out.

"And then there's *Julia*," Tom added.

"*Julia?*"

"Yes, *Julia!* She believed, and the family thought, it was a foregone conclusion you'd come back and marry her."

"It's true, Lou. Tom's right," Anna said.

Lou glanced at Anna.

Not you, too, Sis.

"Now you show up like the big hero and we're supposed to fall at your feet, while you act all surprised at what's been going on in this country."

They traveled along M Street in silence for a time. It was getting busy with private cars and trucks on the road. Lou had brought Charlotte's photo, wrapped in the newspaper he'd read on the train. Lou asked Tom to stop outside a glass and mirror shop and went in. Ten minutes later, he was back with a smile on his face. He climbed back into the pickup.

"Look guys, I'm sorry. I really am. I don't know what to say. I'd fully intended to come home, believe me." He unwrapped the package. "Look at this," Lou said, as if it might explain things a bit. He handed the frame to Anna. "It fell down and got smashed on the airship."

"How did that happen?" Anna said.

"It just fell off my bedside table."

"Oh my, she's gorgeous. I can understand why you never came home!" Anna said. "Although, you did hurt poor Julia somethin' fierce."

The next stop was the post office. Lou went in and sent a wire to Charlotte telling her he'd arrived in Virginia and wished she were here. They drove on to Riggs Bank, parked and went inside. The bank building was cool under its domed, copper roof. The interior was ornate with hardwood and marble finishes. Lou found a sub-manager and explained they needed to open a joint account in their three names. This was done and Lou deposited ninety seven dollars and thirty-cents into the account after converting the bank draft he'd brought with him from the Midland Bank. Lou told them he'd be sending money to the account as an emergency fund. After Lou had drawn out thirty-five dollars, they climbed back into the pickup. Tom had become irritated again. "What are you doing all this for? We don't need your damned money! You think you can just pop back into everyone's lives, leave some money and go flying off again, huh! What the hell d'you think we are?"

"Tom, please don't be like that, brother, I just want to help. Seriously I do," Lou said.

"Well, we don't need your help. We've done all right without you for the last ten years."

"Oh, Tom—" Anna said.

"I need to call in at Fort Myer," Tom said.

"Okay, Tom. After that, I'd like to run by Anacostia Flats to see my army buddy, if you don't mind."

"Right," Tom answered.

They retraced their route and re-crossed Key Bridge. Fort Myer formed part of Arlington Cemetery. They passed white gravestones on their left and wove their way up the steep hill to the top, where stately, red brick buildings stood and pin oaks lined the street on the plateau. The place had the feel of a college campus and the smell of horses in the air. They slowed to a walking pace as a flag-draped caisson drawn by six white horses approached, on its way to a new grave down the hill. Four soldiers in blue rode four of the horses.

Tom drove past the officers' club to the morgue at the end of the street and around the back to an adjoining building. He unlocked the door and he and Lou entered. It was dark inside. When his eyes adjusted, Lou made out an old coffin on the floor. Tom took out a key and unlocked the padlock, opened the hinged lid and propped it against the wall. He went back to the pickup and threw back the canvas, revealing six cardboard boxes full of booze. Without speaking, Tom and Lou carried them inside and placed them in the coffin. Tom closed the lid and locked the padlock. They came outside into the sunshine and Tom relocked the door.

"That'll keep the fellas at the officers' club happy for a day or so," Anna said with a smile and a wink.

68

TENT CITY

Monday August 4, 1930.

Tom drove them down through Rosslyn back to the George Washington Parkway, then crossed the river again into the city. They motored along Constitution Avenue, passing the George Washington Monument, toward the back of the Capitol Building. Scenes on the street were much the same as before, with mounted police keeping a watchful eye on the poor wretches lining up for food or carrying placards. They crossed the Anacostia River into Anacostia Flats, where another miserable scene greeted them.

Hundreds of ragged, makeshift tents and shanties had been set up. At the moment, the ground was hard and rutted. Lou knew that after a rainstorm this place would be an unpleasant mud hole. Anna was visibly appalled at the squalor. Tom parked the pickup in the first open space he found. The place looked like a slum settlement in some distant country and smelled as bad. The conditions reminded Lou of the Front. Human misery! Although, due to his war experience, he perceived some semblance of order in all this chaos.

The camp was divided into rows, with street names daubed on wood slats nailed to posts: Ypres Row, Argonne Avenue, Somme Street, Verdun Road, Belleau Wood Boulevard. Saint-Mihiel Street. They watched kids playing in the dirt and blacks and whites together, chatting. They nodded as the Remingtons walked by, as if they were sitting on their old front porch.

Lou stopped a man passing by and asked where he could find Henry Faulkner. The man was polite and took them to a shack fifty yards away and called through the doorway.

"Henry, folks here to see you."

Faulkner appeared. His weary face broke into a warm smile and he ushered them inside, where there was a table consisting of packing case boards nailed together, old 4 x 4 legs and planks each side for seats. Two men were seated at the table—one black, one white, ill-kempt and dirty, faces glistening with sweat, their body odor overpowering. Lou regretted bringing Anna. The two men jumped up and stood erect when Lou entered. Tom looked surprised at the respect shown to his brother.

"This is Sergeant Terry of the 307th and this is Gunny Jackson of the New York 369th. This, gentlemen, is Commander Remington, formerly of the United States Marine Corps," Henry said. They all shook hands.

Lou spoke directly to Sgt. Terry. "You were in the Lost Battalion?"

"Yes, sir. Now I'm lost in Tent City," Terry said bitterly.

"Can I get you coffee or water?" Henry asked.

To be polite, Lou said he'd have coffee. Anna and Tom declined.

"What's going on, Henry?" Lou said.

"We've set up this camp as the First Expeditionary Force of army vets. We need the money they promised us. We need it bad and we need it now."

"How long can you last?"

"We've nowhere to go. We'll be here 'til we get the money—or until we starve or freeze to death, I guess."

"How many of you are there?" Anna asked.

"Right now, ten thousand. We expect that number to increase to fifty thousand. Hundreds are pouring in every day."

Sgt. Terry poured out coffee from a pot into a tin mug and gave it to Lou.

"It'll be a public health nightmare," Lou said, taking a sip. The coffee was lukewarm and bitter. He'd had worse in the trenches—*much worse*.

"We're pretty disciplined—we're running this place like an army camp, as we were trained. We have latrines dug and supervised, and kitchens of sorts."

"I'm here for a week. Tell me what I can do to help."

"You're well known, sir. Could you write or meet with a congressman or two? And write to the President on our behalf?"

Lou saw Tom looking at him with new-found respect, with perhaps a hint of remorse in his eyes. Anna and Tom couldn't believe what they were hearing.

"If I can help, I will. There must be a lot of things you need."

"What about medicines and food and stuff like that?" Anna said.

"Yes, all of that, and water, and soap. We need doctors and nurses, and some decent tents. We could use some lumber."

"What about the people here? Are they peaceful?"

"We've been trying to establish good relations with the police. There are elements trying to stir up trouble—they want a full-blown revolution."

"*Communists?*"

"Yes. But there are only a handful."

"It's important no one makes trouble, or your cause will be lost," Lou said. He pulled out his wallet and put twenty-five dollars on the table.

"Take this. It's not much, but it'll help a little," he said.

Henry was humble, but delighted. "Thank you, Lou. You don't know what it means to have your support," he said.

Lou finished his coffee and stuck out his hand. "We must go now. I'm staying with my folks in Virginia. Let me think about this."

They drove away from the camp depressed.

"We must help those poor people. Did you see those kids?" Anna said. "We must take food over there."

"They need more food than you've got, Sis," Lou said.

Tom remained deep in thought. It was his turn to be speechless.

Back at the farm, they found a black Ford sedan parked near the house, a driver at the wheel. A woman in her early thirties stood on the porch talking to Mother.

"This is Helen Smothers from the *Washington Post*. She wants to talk to you, Lou," Mother said.

The lady looked more like a fashion model than a reporter, her face exquisitely made up. She wore a white, wide-brimmed hat with a blue band, slightly cocked to one side, and a white jacket with wide lapels. Her skirt, to just below the knee, pinched at the waist, accentuated her graceful figure. She stepped forward, a perfectly manicured hand outstretched, her French perfume overpowering. Intense brown eyes held him in her gaze.

"Commander Remington, I'm so pleased to make your acquaintance," she announced, in a distinct Chicago accent. This woman was a *go-getter*.

Lou took her hand. He looked around at Tom and Anna who signaled that they'd leave him to it.

"Please, sit down," Lou said, pointing to the couch and easy chairs on the porch.

Mother reappeared. "Can I get you some iced tea?" she asked.

"A pitcher would be nice, with lemons, if you have any, Mom," Lou answered. He turned back to his visitor. "How can I help you, Miss Smothers?"

"Commander, there are so many questions our readers have about you. First, I'd like to ask you about the *ZR-2/R38* crash. Are you over that now?"

"Yes, completely, but I don't talk about it anymore."

"Of course. You have been in England for ten years now. Will you stay there? You're married to an English lady, I believe?"

"I'm pretty well settled, but you never know what tomorrow will bring. I love England almost as much as I love my wife, Charlotte."

Helen Smothers pressed Lou with questions for half an hour. He answered them carefully, taking his time while she took notes on a stenographer's pad. He thought this woman could be helpful.

"I was a marine before I went to England," he said finally.

"Ah, yes, you were in France, I believe?"

"Yes. I went to see some of our veterans today."

Helen Smothers stopped scribbling for a moment and sat back. He had her full attention. Lou knew this'd add dimension to the piece she'd write.

"What was your impression?" she asked.

"I was deeply saddened by their plight and the appalling conditions they've been reduced to live in. I was *totally stunned*, if you want to know the truth, Miss Smothers."

"You feel they should get the money?"

"Have you been to Anacostia Flats?

"No, not personally."

"Then you should. I think the country should do everything in its power to help and protect the men who faithfully served this nation and made great sacrifices."

"Perhaps I'll do that, Commander."

"Please write down this name: Henry Faulkner. Ask for him when you go. Sit down with him and have a cup of coffee," Lou said. "And please, *don't* go dressed as you are now."

"I understand."

"Prepare yourself, Miss Smothers. It isn't pleasant," Lou said.

Lou answered a few more questions and Helen Smothers thanked him for the interview. There would most certainly be something in the paper tomorrow and a feature article in the Sunday issue, she told him. She also intimated that she'd like to meet him again in the future—perhaps in more '*unofficial capacity*'.

69

JULIA

Monday August 4, 1930.

Lou spent the rest of the day helping Tom and Anna work on the vegetable gardens. He found it enjoyable and relaxing. Father, in his old, straw sunhat sat in a deck chair contentedly watching them and smoking cigarettes. Mother and Gran toiled in the kitchen making jam and bottling fruit. Later, they decided to have a quiet night, although Mother did warn Lou that Julia usually came by on Monday evenings. He sincerely hoped she would.

Julia had lived next door to Gran's place until she moved away twelve years ago with her parents to a big house in Georgetown. Over the years, her father had made a lot of money in business with his brother. Julia's father died of leukemia three years after moving to Georgetown. She now worked with her uncle, attempting to take over her father's shares in several businesses, including the largest lumber yard in Fairfax County—Tyson's Lumber & General Hardware Corp.

After dinner, Julia arrived in her burgundy Chrysler Imperial. They heard the sound of her tires on the driveway and the car door slam.

"That'll be Julia. She's later than usual," said Mother. "Why don't you kids sit on the porch and catch up."

The three siblings went out as Julia was climbing the wooden steps. She wore a simple beige cotton dress in the latest fashion, tight at the waist with short sleeves.

Lou was taken aback. She'd blossomed into an exceptional woman, exuding class and style. Her blond hair fell to her shoulders and across her face, causing her to toss her head every so often. Her almond-shaped, hazel eyes radiated wisdom, confidence and patience. She wore a hint of blush, accentuating high cheekbones and perfect skin.

"Well, look at you!" Lou said. "You're *so* beautiful, Julia." While Tom and Anna looked on, they embraced, holding each other tightly. Lou kissed her cheeks. She'd never been one to show much emotion—always calm and collected, but for her, he sensed this was a big moment.

"Look at her, Tom—isn't she *absolutely gorgeous!*" Lou said.

He saw a flash of jealousy in Tom's eyes.

"She's the most beautiful girl I know," Tom replied.

Lou knew instantly his brother was in love with her. Father stepped out onto the porch and smiled at Julia. He pointed at her.

"Now *that's* the girl you should have married—*that girl right there!* But what do you do—*you* go off to become a big shot with your uppity *British* friends. They don't make 'em like this one anymore. You made a *big* mistake, boy!"

Lou was mortified. He glanced at Tom and saw both acquiescence and annoyance in his eyes. But Tom had already made his feelings plain earlier in the day. Father looked at Tom and turned around and went back inside the house, shaking his head in disgust. Everyone continued without comment, but Father's words hung in the balmy air like a bad odor on this hot, still night. Julia's eyes glistened.

"Let's sit down, shall we?" Anna said.

Lou sensed Julia and Anna were close and suspected they confided about most things. Mother appeared with lemonade on a tray and put it down on the table in front of them.

The four chatted long after dark. Lou went over the events of his life since he'd seen Julia in 1920. Lou expressed sympathy about her father's death and she was grateful. His passing had been a blow and now, according to Anna, her uncle had seized control of everything, including most of the family fortune. Lou got the impression Julia wasn't all that fond of Uncle Rory.

A full moon had risen, casting a pleasant light across the drive, paddock and river beyond. The noise of the night insects and cicadas started up all around them in the trees, some with an overpowering ratcheting sound, accompanied by a loud purr. This subtropical racket was hypnotizing, coming and going from area to area as the swarms took their turns. Anna made excuses, saying they'd things to do, and got up, silently signaling to Tom. Tom reluctantly followed her into the house. Lou realized he'd been set up. Well, it didn't matter. He loved Julia very much. *Always had.*

"We used to have a swing under that tree, remember?" he said, gesturing toward the large oak on the edge of the paddock.

Julia nodded and smiled. "You kissed me there as the darkness fell."

He detected animosity in her voice. "Yes, I did."

"I remember it well, Remy," Julia said flatly. "That was the day I fell in love with you … the day I made up my mind to have your children."

This came as a serious blow. He was being pummeled from all sides. He sensed Julia had a lot more to say and was mulling things over. This was going to be a serious reprimand.

"Lou, when you went off and joined the Marine Corps, I was devastated."

"It was a dumb thing to do," Lou said.

"I decided to wait for you."

"Julia, I'm …"

She held up her hand to silence him. "No. I want to tell you—so you fully understand."

Feeling small, Lou sat silently, worried about what was to follow.

"I knew you'd joined up under age and thought for a long time you wouldn't be sent to war, and then I heard you were on a ship bound for France. I prayed to God He would return you home safely."

"And He did," Lou said.

"Yes, and I thanked Him for it. I was truly grateful. And I waited. Then you joined the Navy." She rolled her eyes and laughed sarcastically. Lou felt horribly guilty, appreciating the extent of her bitterness and his perceived betrayal. She hadn't shown these feelings at the time—or had he been too blind and dumb to notice?

"You went off to England and I was happy for you. You were doing exactly what you wanted and you'd soon come back in a new airship. I longed to see you. I went over everything time and time again. I'd be waiting at the hangar in New Jersey and watch you descend from the heavens—and later, I'd become the proud wife of an airshipman."

Lou's mind was racing. Had he lead her on when he'd last seen her? Surely not. At least not to that degree. *She* obviously thought so. And so did his family.

"Julia, I'm so sorry."

She held up her hand again and went on, her breast heaving with uncharacteristic emotion as she relived events. "And then came the accident over the river in England. I went to church that day—it was a Wednesday— and lit a candle and prayed to God. I begged, 'Please, God, spare Lou's life again and I will never ask for anything—I will have no claim on him. I promise You'. And He did. Miraculously, you lived and you stayed and I was happy."

"Julia, after the crash, I couldn't face coming home. I was riddled with guilt," Lou said.

"I understand completely. It was God's will. He kept you from me."

Julia was calming down as if God had truly spoken to her. Lou felt wretched. She'd squandered her young life on him—such a magnificent girl. It was as though he'd left her at the altar. It felt strange and bizarre as he remembered thinking of her briefly at his wedding in St. Cuthbert's. All the things his family had said about her spilled over him.

What a heel!

"Julia, what can I say?"

"There's nothing to say. God kept His bargain and so will I."

Lou looked at her. She was so different from Charlotte—so un-needy. He dreamed of what might have been for a moment and caught himself. They sat in silence with nothing more to be said. Lou admired her candor, her acceptance. She appeared to be at peace with her agreement, without self pity, at least on the surface.

Suddenly, above the roar of the cicadas, they were disturbed by a commotion down in the trees on the path from the creek. In the flickering shadows, Lou could make out three horsemen riding toward the house. He stood up. Julia sat motionless.

The riders were led by a squat, heavy-set figure on a striking Appaloosa, its head and front half jet black, its rear, black and white leopard-spotted. They were clad in white sheets, fluorescent in the moonlight, with pointed hoods over their faces, their narrow eye slits, satanic. The last Klansman, on a black quarter horse, had a rope attached to his waist, the other end knotted around Jeb's neck. Jeb stumbled along behind, the whites of his eyes projecting his terror. Alice followed, carrying their two wailing children, all of them crying hysterically.

"Please, don't hurt him!" she screamed. "*Please! Please! I beg you.*"

The other Klansman rode a chestnut mare. He stopped about twenty yards from the porch and planted a cross in the ground lashed to a spike. Lou smelled diesel. The ten-foot cross went up with a whoosh as it was lit. The flames accentuated the whiteness of their robes, making them more phantom-like—calling up the fires of hell. The first Klansman, stopping at the porch steps, spoke in biblical tones with the cadence of the South. While he delivered his ultimatum, the shining Appaloosa fidgeted with its feet, swishing its tail, nickering softly, the bit clinking between its teeth.

"It's come to our attention an illegal still is operating on this here property. The making of moonshine and the distribution of liquor is prohibited by federal law and will not be tolerated!" He lifted his arm like Moses, pointing at Lou. "You there, boy, tell this here nigger to lead us to that still right now, or tonight he'll be hung by the neck from that tree over yonder, until he is dead!"

He pointed to the oak tree where Lou had kissed Julia years ago. Alice let out a bloodcurdling scream, "*Aaaaah, no! Please don't! … No, no, please!*"

Jeb fell down on his knees, sobbing. At that moment, the two frenzied dogs came rushing from behind the house barking ferociously. Lou figured Father or Tom had let them out the back door. Lou eased his way along the porch and down the steps. The Klan could see clearly in this light, he was unarmed. He stared up at them—all high and mighty on their horses. The old black mutt kept barking up at the leader.

"You shut this mangy flea bag up, right now!" the Klansman yelled at Lou.

"Moonshine, shut up!" someone called. Lou wasn't sure who.

"Moonshine!" the Klansman shouted in a fury.

He drew a silver six-shooter and shot the dog through the head. Her bark trailed off into a scream as she fell down dead.

"A dog with a name like that deserves to die," the Klansman roared.

Lou ran round to the back of the last Klansman and grabbed the rope, yanking it hard. The horse rose high in the air on her hind legs. The Klansman rolled backwards over the mare's rump into a heap at Lou's feet. Lou leapt onto the man's back and pulled his wrist up over his head tugging the arm out of its shoulder socket. The man screamed in agony. The first Klansman raised his gun to shoot, but was shaken by a deafening shotgun blast. Now, the Appaloosa reared up with a snorting scream.

"Keep those guns lowered," Father shouted from the open front door.

The two Klansmen sat still on their horses. "So what you gonna do now, mister? You got one left. My friend here an' me, we'll finish all a yer, including this punk down here."

Another voice screamed from a bedroom window. "Keep still, mister." It was Anna. "I got two in this here twelve to blow both yer heads clean off."

"And I got another two, right here, you demons from hell," Gran yelled from a ground floor window.

"Go home, Uncle Rory," Julia said calmly. "Go home right now."

"You don't know who we are," the leader shouted back.

"It's not hard to figure, Uncle Rory. You're on my damned horse. Now go!"

Lou untied the noose from Jeb's neck and lifted the third whimpering Klansman from the ground and laid him over his horse on his stomach. He took the rope and lashed his feet and hands under the horse's belly. He tugged on the man's hood, and yanked his head up by the hair, exposing his young face.

"Why you hiding that pretty little puss, huh?" Lou said. "Best be on your way now, boys, and don't let the bogeymen getcha on the ride home." He gave the horse's rump a hard slap, making her start forward violently. While the fiery cross crumpled and smoked and its light diminished, the three Klansmen rode off into the night without further threats. Lou took Jeb back to the shack with his wife, who had settled down some.

"They'll come back. I just know they will," she kept saying over and over.

Lou went back to the house where Julia was getting ready to leave. He put his arms around her and gently kissed her lips. She closed her eyes with pleasure. Tom watched silently.

"You must take care," Lou said.

"Don't worry. I'll be fine."

"I *am* worried about you, Julia."

"Who's the young one?" Father asked.

"He's my cousin, Israel, Uncle Rory's son. He's just as crazy as his father."

They walked Julia to her car.

"Make sure you come to us if you need help," Father said.

The next day, Tom and Jeb loaded the pickup with three consignments of whisky. Jeb had the appearance of a man whose spirit had been crushed—overnight his hair seemed to have become more grey. Lou, today in uniform, rode with Tom and Anna in the pickup to make deliveries, first to the Navy Yard across the river from the tent city, the second to the Capitol Building and the third to Fort Myer. At Fort Myer, above Arlington Cemetery, Lou reluctantly decided there was another place he really needed to visit.

"I need to find Captain Maxfield's grave," he said.

Anna smiled, realizing why Lou put on his uniform.

"I know exactly where it is," Tom said.

"How come?"

"Jeb and me dug that grave, amongst others. We all went to the funeral. Dad insisted he was going, so we all went."

"For God's sake! He didn't tell me."

"It changed Dad," Anna said. "Made him ill."

They drove round the circular gravel road flanked by thousands of white gravestones. Tom pulled up abruptly. They climbed out of the pickup and Lou stood in silence at the grave with a tombstone bearing the captain's name. Anna put her arm through his and they stood in the sunshine in silence, facing the new Lincoln Memorial across the river in the distance. Before leaving, Lou stood rigidly to attention and saluted the tombstone. Tom looked on in stunned silence.

That night, Lou dreamed he was aboard *R38*. Capt. Maxfield's voice came through loud and clear in the darkness.

Remington, look to your crew!

The ship was on fire and breaking up. Lou came round. He opened his eyes in a daze. The room was brightly illuminated. He leapt out of bed, realizing he was in Gran's house and ran to the window. The sky was lit by orange flames rising down by the creek. He understood immediately. He pulled on his pants and boots and ran out onto the landing as his whole family spilled out of their bedrooms.

"They're back. Come on," Lou shouted. "They got Jeb's place."

"You stay with Gran," Father yelled to Mother and Anna, grabbing his shotgun.

When they got down to the shack, the roof was falling in. There was nothing they could do. Jeb, his wife and two children sat under a tree in tears, safe from the flames, watching their home burn.

"I tol' yer they was comin' back. ... I tol' yer," Alice sobbed. "They got the still. They held a gun to my baby's head. Threatened to blow his brains out."

Lou glanced at Jeb who kept nodding, unable to speak. Everyone stood in silent disbelief until Father spoke. "Jeb, Alice, bring the kids. Come up to the house. Nothing we can do here."

The following morning Lou, Father, Tom and Anna went down with Jeb to inspect the smoldering ruin. Jeb led them to what was left of the still. It would've been hard to find. Jeb had constructed a huge dugout with a roof covered with dirt, grass and shrubbery. The barrels, copper piping and all parts had been smashed beyond repair.

In the afternoon, a military vehicle drew up outside Gran's house. Anna came out. A sailor in uniform leapt out and stood at attention.

"Pardon me, ma'am," he said. "I'm looking for Commander Remington. We understand he's visiting the family."

Anna went in and got Lou. The two men exchanged salutes.

"Chief Petty Officer Brown, sir, at your service. Commander, I've been ordered to bring you to the Navy Yard at your *earliest* convenience, sir."

"Like *right now?*"

"*Yes, sir!*"

"Give me five minutes."

Forty minutes later, Lou was escorted into a room in one of the Navy Yard Buildings in Washington, D.C., where he was introduced to a Capt. Yates. Lou sat down and they made small talk. The captain was familiar with Lou's history. They talked about the Canada flight in *Howden R100* and his upcoming voyage to India. After a few minutes, the captain cocked his head on one side, choosing his words carefully.

"This brings me to a rather delicate matter," he said coyly.

"It's come to my attention from different quarters that the source of the finest whisky in Virginia has just dried up!"

The captain looked mischievous, raising his hands in the air as if to say 'How could such a thing happen?' Lou was dumbfounded. The captain went on. "I've been asked to intercede, as this situation is going to have a severe impact on a few people—from a *medicinal standpoint*, you understand."

"I do indeed, sir."

"There's been some sort of a fracas, I hear."

"News travels fast, sir. Some gentlemen in white hoods paid my family a visit."

"*Bastards!* Anyone hurt?"

"No, but they terrorized my folks and did substantial damage."

"If you require any help in that regard, you must tell me."

"I could use a few good men, sir," Lou said.

"*'A few good men'*—I like that! Nice ring to it! On your way back to Virginia, tell Chief Brown exactly what assistance you need."

"I'll *do* that, sir."

"Now, as important as that issue is, *that* wasn't the main purpose of asking you here—although I know the folks in the Officer's Club will be pleased we had this conversation. The Army Chief of Staff, General Luby, is coming to talk with you about what's going on in Hooverville."

Lou gulped. "The Army Chief of Staff! .... Hooverville, sir?"

"Tent City, across the way." The captain waved his hand in the general direction of Anacostia. "Don't worry about the general. He's paying an informal visit. Wants to meet you."

Just then, the door swung open and they were joined by an imposing two star general in khaki, a briar pipe clenched between his teeth. Both Lou and Capt. Yates jumped up, snapped to attention and saluted. The general gave a casual return salute.

"At ease," he said. He removed his hat and pipe, and when he spoke he reminded Lou of a Shakespearean actor. He extended his hand to them both.

"Commander, I'm Ray Luby. Congratulations on your historic flight —well done, son. You make all of us proud!"

"Thank you, General."

"Sorry we've called you here at such short notice. Across the river here, we have a huge potential crisis."

"Yes sir. I visited the camp as soon as I got here."

"We know you did, and we don't have a problem with that. Maybe you can be of assistance to us."

"How, sir?"

"The situation must be kept under control."

"We know you met with one of their leaders," the captain said.

"I served with him in battle at Saint-Mihiel and then the Verdun sector, sir."

Respect showed in the officer's faces.

"We're anxious this camp doesn't turn into a festering sore, rife with violence and disease. I'd like to hear your views on the subject, since you were in the place and you know some of them personally," the general said.

"These people are desperate, sir, and it's going to get much worse," Lou said.

The two senior men looked startled.

"They're poverty-stricken, hungry, without medical help, and they've no place to go. They were *better* taken care of at the Front. This winter, they'll freeze to death."

The officers shifted uncomfortably in their chairs and Lou caught fleeting glimpse of compassion in the general's eyes.

"Do you have any suggestions, Commander?" Capt. Yates asked.

"Yes, sir, I do. Set up food banks within the camp. Send them decent tents and lumber they can use. Build temporary medical facilities in the camp. Send in medical supplies and assign them army doctors and nurses. Supply them with clean water and plenty of soap. Assign liaison officers to work with them and with the city's police chief on a *daily* basis. Most important of all—make sure these men are *not* forgotten!"

The two men stared at Lou. He'd given them more than they'd bargained for—so much to think about. But there were other factors to consider.

"There're people in this town who are concerned we have communist agitators in this camp fermenting revolution, encouraged by Marxist bastards from Britain and Russia," General Luby said.

"I understand, sir. Right now this is a public relations nightmare. I'm concerned if things aren't handled properly, you may have an unmitigated disaster on your hands—perhaps a full blown revolution."

"Yes, yes, but if there is the slightest hint of violence, they'll be cleared out, ruthlessly, without hesitation. We'll send tanks in there and flatten that place if necessary. Ex-military or not—traitors will not be tolerated! Make sure they understand that, Remington. This is the Army's mess. We own it, and we'll deal with it as we see fit," General Luby warned.

"There's a small element of trouble makers, sir. Ninety-nine percent of those men are patriots—true-blue Americans."

"There're blacks and whites in that camp living together—all getting along like pigs in shit. That's making a lot of people around here mighty nervous. Seems unnatural to them!" the captain said.

"There is racial harmony—something many of them learned at the Front in the Army, which could be seen as a positive thing, sir."

The general relit his pipe and puffed out some smoke.

"So, Commander, how come you went to the camp?" he asked.

"They met me at Union Station and asked for my help, sir."

"What are you going to do?" the captain asked.

"I thought about writing my congressman and perhaps even the President."

"I strongly advise you not to get political," General Luby said. "I read your comments in the *Post*. That's already raised a lot of hackles up on that hill."

"Even though it's not due, I'd give them the damned money," the captain said.

"You're getting into politics," the general said, standing up. "I've a meeting. I must go." He shook hands with Lou. "I like what you said just now. Your advice is sound. Good luck on your flight back to England."

"The Commander here," the captain said, smiling at Lou, "has kindly agreed to look into that '*other matter*' we talked about."

The general broke into a broad grin. "*Excellent!* He's a good man, this one," he said.

The three officers saluted before the general left. When he'd gone, the captain asked Lou to sit down again.

"Your progress in England has been followed by some of the top people here, including Admiral Mottet himself. I should tell you, your name's come up in connection with the *Akron* and the *Macon* being constructed in Ohio, but more importantly, they've been following your work with the British engineer Barnes Wallis and, of course, with the Royal Airship Works. They see you as a potential player in our own program. I thought you might like to know that, Commander. There could be a bright future for you here."

Lou wasn't sure if this excited him or not. He tried to look pleased—it was inevitable the Navy would want him back sooner or later.

70

A FEW GOOD MEN

Thursday, August 7, 1930

The following morning Lou pulled up on the dirt road outside Tyson's Lumber & General Hardware with a truck full of marines. This was Vienna, seven miles from Remington's Farm, ten miles from Washington. They were all in fatigues, including Lou. The marines jumped down from the truck and moved into position with planned precision. The site was a sprawling fifty-acre compound surrounded by woods. It contained concrete products, pipe and lumber in a huge, fenced-in yard bordering the road. A buzz came from a sawmill way off in the distance at the back of the property.

Lou had planned this operation with these men at the Navy Yard after reconnoitering the premises the previous afternoon. He hoped serious violence wouldn't actually be necessary. His distaste for that hadn't changed. Permanent behavioral modification in a few individuals was the goal, as well as the negotiation and procurement of some serious compensation for damages. For the sake of his own family, for Jeb's and for Julia, he needed to make this count—not to mention the matter of keeping the brass in Washington happy—another major concern relating to family business.

Lou, carrying a rolled-up newspaper and a bullhorn, strode into the huge metal building, which was sectioned off and included an enclosed general hardware store within the shed itself. A rough wood stairway led up to a complex of offices high up near the roof, with windows overlooking the contractor's sales areas. The marines spread themselves out between stacks of lumber and architectural millwork. Lou nodded to one of them who blew a whistle. The staff of four yardmen and a handful of customers eyed them nervously. Lou stepped into an open area and raised a bullhorn to his mouth.

"Attention! Attention! Everybody, listen up! This business has been closed down. This is a danger zone. Leave these premises immediately. I repeat, this business has been closed down."

"What's the matter?" a concerned storeman asked.

"Everybody out!" Lou shouted.

Startled employees and customers obeyed, sensing trouble. They moved quickly to the entrance doors. Lou collared the last employee before he left.

"Bring me six lengths of chain about four foot long and six padlocks. Right now!"

The man scurried off as fast as he could without asking questions. He was back with the items in a few minutes. "Okay, get out. And speak to no one," Lou ordered, and then to his marines, "Get going, men!"

The marines started pulling down the stacks of lumber and architectural millwork into disorganized piles. There was a shout from the top of the stairs. Two men, red-faced and angry, were peering down, having heard the commotion.

"What the hell's goin' on dun 'ere?"

The one doing the shouting was built like a little bull, his voice familiar. Lou put on his pleasant face and smiled. He raised the bullhorn.

"This business has been closed down. Store's being evacuated, sir. This is a danger zone."

"What are you talkin' about? For what?"

"On account of the fire, sir."

"What fire?"

"The fire that's gonna gut this place ten minutes from now."

The man came racing down, tripping and struggling to regain his balance.

"You crazy bastard. Get the hell off my property, you son of a bitch!"

"Take this man into custody," Lou ordered, handing a pair of chains to two marines.

"*Yes, sir! Yes, sir!*"

The marines grabbed the man by the arms and forcefully backed him into a steel column, making him yelp and knocking the wind out of him. Another marine wrapped the chain around his neck and padlocked it snuggly. A second chain was wrapped around his ankles and locked. The other man was also grabbed and chained in the same fashion. Both were now terrified.

"Uncle Rory! Remember me? I'm the punk with the black dog."

Lou took another chain and gave it to another marine.

"Chain the back doors," Lou said. "We don't need anyone coming to the rescue."

The marine marched off to the rear entrance doors. Lou held up and swung the last piece of chain from side to side.

"This one's for the front doors, for when we leave."

Four more marines came in carrying tanks of gasoline. The Klansman's eyes protruded from his head. "What you gonna do?" he screamed.

"Give everything a good dowsing, men," Lou ordered. The marines spilled the gas over the piles of lumber and across the concrete floors. Lou took one of the cans and held it over their heads, thoroughly dousing them from head to toe. They quaked with terror.

"Sorry we don't have a cross, boys. I know you like to have one for this type of occasion."

"What are you gonna do?" Uncle Rory wailed his hair and face glistening with gasoline, the smell overpowering.

"Notice we don't use diesel. Gasoline burns *so* much better, don't you think?" Lou said.

"Please, mister. Please, don't. I'm begging you," the Klansman screamed.

The second man was blubbering and wailing, too.

"I'll make it right. I'll make it right!" the Klansman yelled.

"What are you gonna do about my family's dog, huh? Oh, how they *loved* that dog!"

"I'm sorry. I'm *so, so* sorry, mister."

"You're sorry! Sorry for *what?*"

"I'm sorry. I'm sorry," he wept. His pants had become saturated with urine and gasoline. A pool formed at his feet.

"Sorry for *what?*" Lou screamed into his face, his nose almost touching the Klansman's.

"I'm sorry for what I did, sir." The little bull screwed up his eyes and tears flowed down his cheeks, like a child.

"*What* did you do?" Lou shouted. He stepped back, took the newspaper, lit the end and held blazing it in the air. "I asked you, *what* did you do?"

"I burned your place down! And I killed your dog. Oh, please, please, no."

The marines stood glaring, their faces emotionless.

"You burned Mr. Jeb's place down. That man helped raise me, *by God!*"

"I'm so sorry, sir."

"How's it gonna feel to see *your* place burn down—with *you* cooking inside, fat boy?"

"Bad, bad …Oh, please, no …have mercy, sir."

"And what *else* did you do?"

"I destroyed stuff."

"You've made a lot of people in this town mad as hell. And when *they* get upset, bad things happen—property gets destroyed, *people die!*"

"I'll make it right. I beg you. Give me a chance. Please … please …"

The Klansman broke down, weeping uncontrollably. Lou handed the burning newspaper to a marine who took it outside and stomped out the flames.

"So *what* are you going to do? *How* are you gonna make things right?"

"I'll rebuild the house and send all the materials you need. I'll pay for everything and for labor. I'll rebuild the still."

"Let's recap. I just heard you say, you will send every scrap of material to rebuild Mr. Jeb's house, *bigger and better*, along with the other thing—right? Is that what you said?"

He nodded his head up and down vigorously, "Yes, yes, sir, I promise …bigger and better."

"Did I hear you say you would pay Mr. Jeb the sum of one thousand dollars—no make that two thousand dollars—compensation for pain and suffering you caused him and his family?"

"*Absolutely*, yes, *absolutely*."

"And deliveries will begin tomorrow morning?"

"Yes, sir. Yes, sir. Tomorrow."

"You will send laborers and carpenters on Monday morning at 6:00 a.m. sharp."

"*Absolutely*—anything, sir."

"You got three months to rebuild that house to his satisfaction—*bigger and better!*"

"Yes, sir, *bigger and better*."

"I don't wanna hear any bitchin' or squawkin'."

"No, sir, you won't, I promise you."

"You know Anacostia Flats—Tent City?"

"Yes, I know it."

"You're to donate and deliver six—no, make that twelve—loads of lumber to that location by tomorrow."

"Yes, sir. No problem at all."

"2x4's—2x6's—2x8's with nails and a hundred sheets of canvas," Lou said.

"I don't have any canvas."

"Then *find* some dammit! And fifty paraffin heaters. Deliver it all to Henry Faulkner. Got that?"

"Yes, absolutely. To Henry Faulkner, sir."

"Another thing. Your niece. She's family to me. If you harm her in any way, I will come down here and I will kill you. I'll *roast* you alive like a pig on a spit!"

"I won't. I won't, I promise you."

"I'll be looking into her finances. You'd better not be stealing her father's fortune. See to it she and her mother are cut in fair and square, *fifty-fifty*. I want audited accounts *every year* and details of who owns what including all previous records. Do you understand?"

"Yes, yes, sir, *every year*. I'll see to it."

The Klansman had begun to relax. Sensing they were off the hook.

"We'll be talkin' again. Okay, men, let 'em loose." Lou handed the various keys to the marines. He turned to one. "Marine, find me a long-axe and some rope."

The marine strode into the hardware section and re-appeared a few minutes later with the axe and rope.

"This brings us to the matter of the family dog," Lou said, uncoiling the rope.

Uncle Rory began quaking again.

"Bring him over here," Lou said. Lou tied the rope around the fat man's wrist and laid him face down on his belly on a pile of lumber. The marines held him down and Lou lashed his right hand into position.

"This is the hand you used to shoot the dog. The *right* hand, wasn't it?"

"Oh no, no, no. Please no. Not my hand!"

The Klansman screamed and blubbered for a few moments and then gave up and put his head down. Lou took the axe and swung it over his head, bringing it down full force, but twisting it at the last moment, smashing the Klansman's hand with the blunt head. Uncle Rory screamed in agony and terror, believing his hand had been severed. When he opened his eyes, the bones were well and truly crushed, but his hand still remained attached to his wrist.

"Now you think about '*Moonshine*' every time you raise that hand, mister," Lou said. And then, leaning forward he whispered in the Klansman's ear, "I'll be watching you—don't make me come back again …And remember …*mum's the word*."

71

GOODBYE MY FATHER

Friday August 8 through Monday August 11, 1930.

The day after his lawless actions at Tyson's Lumber & General Hardware, Lou went with Tom and Anna to visit the city police chief. They found him to be warmhearted and sympathetic to the veterans. Lou spoke of the meetings in Tent City and at the Navy Yard. It turned out to be a worthwhile exercise in public relations. Lou assured the chief the men in the camp wanted to cooperate with him.

From the police station, they went to Tent City to update Henry. They also delivered a load of vegetables from the farm. Lou told the veterans he'd urged the general to give them support. Three truckloads of lumber had already been delivered. Henry was thrilled and very touched by the generosity of Tyson's Lumber & General Hardware. Helen Smothers had visited the camp and planned to write a feature article for Sunday's newspaper. Lou wished them good luck, urging them to keep the peace, relaying the general's warning. He promised he'd write to the President and the Congress on his return to England.

On Saturday, the first consignments of lumber began arriving at Remington's Farm for the reconstruction of Jeb's home. The truck driver confirmed Julia's uncle would be sending men to start the work on Monday. Anna and Tom sketched some drawings on sheets of paper with Jeb and Alice. Father had taken an interest and promised Lou he'd keep an eye on the construction. The new place would be bigger, with four bedrooms, a nice living room, a decent kitchen and a wrap-around porch with aspects over both the creek and the river—more a real home than a shack.

Lou spent much of the day with Anna, Tom and Jeb, cleaning up and removing the old parts of the building and making a junk pile for burning. They'd need to build some new piers for the extended sections. The driver from Tyson's Lumber was told to be sure to bring plenty of red brick and cement on Monday morning and, of course, bricklayers to lay them.

On Sunday, Lou's last day, spirits were low. Lou was torn; being in England away from family, was rough. Before leaving for church, Tom asked Lou to walk with him and Anna down to the river, just beyond the creek.

There was something they needed to tell him. With the sound of overpowering birdsong surrounding them and the smell of charred wood in the air, they ambled down, past the remains of Jeb's shack to the misty river. Lou had a bad premonition.

"Lou, we're not supposed to tell you, but we decided you should know," Anna said.

"What is it?"

"Dad."

Lou realized immediately. He stared across the water at the distant Maryland shore. Lenny's face filled his mind. *The cough.*

How did I not see this?

"He's dying," Tom said.

Lou's throat became dry and tight.

"Cancer."

"What type is it?" Lou whispered.

"Lung cancer. It's spreading all over his body."

"How long?"

"Three months, maybe four," Anna said.

Everything became clear—his appearance, his attitude, his bitterness, his sadness.

"God, I wish I could be here with you all. Damn it!"

"We thought it important you knew tonight, as it'll be special," Anna said.

"Probably my last night with him on this earth," Lou whispered. He closed his eyes, grief already taking its toll and understanding Tom's irritability.

Anna put her arm through his. "Yes, Lou, 'fraid so."

Julia arrived in the Chrysler, and Mother, Gran and Father (all in their Sunday best) climbed in with her. Lou, Anna and Tom followed in the pickup. Jeb and Alice and the children were already in the church, nicely dressed in many colors, when they arrived. Throughout the service, Lou could think of nothing but Father, regretting he'd not spent more time with him. He looked at Julia standing at his side holding a hymnal. Did she know? Sympathy showed in her eyes when she returned his stare. *Yes, she knew.* All week they'd not told him—protected him. He felt like a spoiled brat.

He glanced across at his dad standing next to Mother. Dad never sang hymns, but he was valiantly doing his best, in his blue serge suit, his wife clinging to his arm. Lou looked around the church. He saw it clearly. They'd bring in his coffin and lay him down on trestles in the center aisle and say prayers for him. His mother, grandmother, Tom and Anna would hold on to one another, weeping—and *he* wouldn't be here to comfort them. He closed his eyes and tears flowed down his cheeks. Julia squeezed his arm to comfort him. He looked into her eyes and they held each other's gaze for a few moments.

What an incredible woman she is.

She had his profound and absolute respect.

After the service, the vicar stood at the door. He told Lou the community was proud of him and wished him well. After that, the congregation made a big fuss over Lou, gathering around him, while his family, including Father, watched with pride. Lou felt numb.

In the early afternoon, Mother came up to Lou's bedroom to get his uniform. "How long have you been married now, son?"

Lou thought for a moment. "Eight years."

"Eight years and no children?"

"Unfortunately no, Mom—but all that's about to change."

Mother picked up Lou's uniform from the chair and put it over her arm. "You must try and bring Charlotte to see us ...before he goes."

That evening, they had a special dinner of roasted venison prepared by Gran and Alice—a farewell feast with nearly everyone in the world Lou cared about, including Julia, Jeb and Alice and the children. They made a feeble attempt at jollity.

At the end of the meal, Father rose from his seat at the head of the table. "I'm not one for speeches, but I want you all to know this." His eyes rested on Lou. "I've said things I shouldn't have said, *especially* when you were growing up. I pushed you hard, son. And I drove you out. I want to say in front of all of you—I'm truly sorry. I was out of line—but only because I cared about you. I haven't always made that plain. I want you to know, no father could be more proud of his son than I am of you. I wish you well on your journey. Good luck and may God bless you and protect you, *always.*"

Lou was stunned. This had come out of the blue. Everyone had tears in their eyes. Anna hurriedly got up and poured more elderberry wine. She sat down and raised her glass.

"Safe trip, my darling brother."

Everyone drank to that. After dinner they moved to the porch where Lou and Father played the guitar and banjo together. It was like those rare good old days, except those days were gone, forever.

The next day, Lou got up before dawn, put on his uniform, expertly steamed and pressed by Mother. He went down to breakfast as the first rays of sunshine poured into the kitchen. Outside, a lumber truck arrived along with a dozen workmen. Tom went out and directed them down to Jeb's ruin. Father said he'd go down, too.

A few minutes later, Julia appeared. Lou rushed down to his father who was directing the men. They shook hands and Father gave Lou a long hug goodbye and kissed him. Father looked at the activity going on and the piles of delivered materials and then back at Lou.

"You did Jeb mighty proud, son."

"I love you Dad."

"I love you, too, son."

Lou walked back up to the house and Father followed him. He embraced and kissed Mother and Gran and then his father again. Before climbing into Julia's car, Lou had them pose for some photos including Jeb and his family. They drove off, with Anna and Tom following in the pickup. Lou was barely able to look at them standing there waving. Lou and Julia traveled in silence to Union Station, slowed by demonstrators on Constitution. There were no words to be said.

At the station, they walked to the barrier where they said more hurried goodbyes—they were late. Lou kissed Anna and shook Tom's hand, but Tom grabbed him and gave him bear hug. Lou put his arms around Julia and held her tight. She closed her eyes as he kissed her cheek.

"I'll continue to pray for your safety," she said. "I will always love you."

Calls echoed through the station. 'All aboard that's going aboard!'

Lou went back to Tom and cupping his hand, whispered a message in his ear. He grabbed his kit bag and ran for the train.

"Come back soon," Anna called after him.

"I will, I promise—*very soon!*" Lou yelled back.

Lou reached the train. Ezekiah Washington was standing by the door.

"Ah bin waitin' here for you, my dear sir," he said.

Lou glanced back at the barrier. Tom stood with one arm around Anna and the other around Julia. All three were in tears. The two women waved sadly as he boarded the train.

"This *is* a coincidence," Lou said.

"If you *believe* in coincidences, sir," Ezekiah said.

Lou smiled.

"Got your same suite, Commander."

"I got you all figured out," Lou said.

"How's that, sir?"

"You're my guardian angel."

"Maybe I is, sir. Maybe I is."

Lou didn't protest this time. He followed Ezekiah down the corridor to the suite where the *Washington Post* lay on the table. He looked forward to reading what Helen Smothers had to say. He sat down and the train pulled away.

"I went to the camp," Lou said.

"Yes, I heard you did. That's good. I also heard you put a little hurt into our brethren under the sheets."

"How the hell—"

"Oh, you'd be surprised what I get to hear, sir. Now, here's a nice cup o' coffee. Nice and black, just the way you like it."

"Thank you, Ezekiah. Thank you very much."

"Not at all, sir. It's my pleasure."

PART TEN

Bringing in the hay while *Howden R100* is moored at the Cardington tower

THE DAYS BEFORE THE
INDIA VOYAGE

72

WELCOME HOME!

Wednesday August 12 - Saturday August 16, 1930.

L ou talked with Ezekiah and thanked him as the train approached
Montreal. Ezekiah wished him luck and told him to 'stay strong.' For
Lou, this whole trip to North America had been like a fantasy—
another world. Norway was waiting on the platform.

"How was your trip?" he asked.

"Oh, pretty quiet," Lou grunted.

The return voyage had been uneventful, except for one night on
Lou's watch. After everyone had retired, Cameron fell asleep. Lou suddenly
realized the ship was descending rapidly toward the water and grabbed the
elevator wheel, slapping Cameron around the head. Lou didn't report the
incident, realizing Cameron had lost a lot of sleep over Rosie lately. Apart
from this incident, the journey turned out to be boring, and the Canadian
journalists who'd been invited to travel with them, said as much. Scott kept a
low profile the entire voyage.

On the way home, Lou lay in his bunk hoping the feelings of
euphoria would return, but all he could think about was his father. His
mission became clear: as soon he returned from India in October, he and
Charlotte would take a steamer to Montreal and travel down to Washington
by train.

Wouldn't it be great if Ezekiah was our steward!

Aside from the worry about his dad, he was glad he'd gotten things
straight in his mind. He'd had plenty of time to think. Things were going to
be different from now on. They'd pay their visit to America. On their return
they'd start a family—adopt if necessary. Everything was going to turn out
swell!

They got back to the Cardington mast around 11:00 a.m. on
Saturday, August 16th. The journey home had taken less than fifty-eight
hours. Two hundred cars were parked on the field when they arrived and a
crowd had gathered—tiny compared to the reception in Montreal. Lou was in

the control car for the docking with Booth and Meager. He scoured the fence, hoping to catch a glimpse of Charlotte, but couldn't see her anywhere. Mooring the ship took an agonizing forty-five minutes. Lou was scheduled to be on duty at noon the following day. He hurried off the ship behind Booth and Steff, leaving Meager on watch with a skeleton crew. Thomson waited with Brancker at the foot of the gangplank where they shook hands with each man, uttering words of praise and welcome.

From the top of the tower, Lou could see a BBC crew waiting with their broadcasting equipment in front of Shed No.1. A small brass band was playing a march. Thomson was obviously planning to make a speech and Lou didn't intend to stick around, anxious to get home to Charlotte. He glanced over the tower rail. No Binks. No motorbike.

Dammit! He's late as usual.

But then Lou looked across the field and saw Binks roaring toward the tower. Lou went down. Binks raced up to him.

"Here she is, sir, good as new," he said, chirpy as ever. "Voyage okay?"

"Yeah, not bad."

"Someone put sugar in your tank. I 'ad her in the shop and me and Mr. Leech stripped her down. She's all right now, sir."

"Damn! Who would do such a thing?" Lou asked, knowing *exactly* who.

"And I mailed the envelope a week after you left, just like you asked me to."

"Thanks. I owe you a pint, Joe."

While Thomson and the crowd moved toward Shed No.1, Lou strapped on his kit bag, and after dropping Binks off in Shortstown, drove to the florist's at the parade of shops near Kelsey Street. He bought a big bunch of violets and tied them on the gas tank. Then he nipped into the corner store and bought a box of Cadbury's chocolates—her favorite. He slipped them in his side pocket and rode slowly home.

Thomson went from the tower to the front of Shed No.1. The doors had been opened to reveal the bow of *Cardington R101*. The public turnout for *Howden R100's* return had been disappointing, but the broadcast would give things a boost and the usual battery of journalists and photographers had been summoned. The publicity derived from this little homecoming event would pressure the R.A.W. to keep up with the schedule he'd imposed on them for the *Cardington R101*.

Thomson stood at the microphone with Capt. Booth and Second Officer Steff, a small group of R.A.W. personnel on either side. The crowd that had been at the fence was allowed in and people gathered around to listen.

"It is with pleasure that I welcome you home from your voyage to Canada," Thomson said, smiling at Colmore and Scott and then at Burney and Norway who were standing off to one side. "I want to congratulate the Howden team and Vickers for their magnificent achievement. This will be recorded as a landmark flight in the history books. In undertaking this journey across the Atlantic Ocean to North America, you have succeeded in taking a giant step in the development of a new generation of British airships."

Thomson looked directly at Capt. Irwin standing beside Lt. Cmdr. Atherstone. Irwin appeared thin and drawn. "We shall now move forward with complete confidence toward a successful conclusion of this grand experiment."

Thomson turned his gaze on Colmore, Richmond and Rope. "All that remains is for this great airship behind us to make its *own* landmark voyage. This will demonstrate to the Dominion Prime Ministers the advantages of this mode of travel—a demonstration of *incalculable importance!* Thank you."

Thomson signaled to the BBC announcer it was time to end the broadcast. The brass band struck up again with the rousing "Royal Air Force March Past," heard by thousands all over Britain.

On reaching home, Lou looked up at the front door step, remembering the image of Charlotte when he'd last seen her there. He'd had it imprinted on his mind for the last fifteen days. He bounded up the steps and knocked on the door. While he waited, he removed the present, the wine and the card from his kitbag, ready to hand them to her. He'd hastily bought Charlotte a small, white marble replica of Abraham Lincoln from a gift shop at Penn Station when the train stopped en route to Montreal. At the station, he'd also bought a bottle of Cabernet from Napa Valley and a gift card. They'd celebrate. She'd like that. He stood at the door and studied the brass knocker. He'd never seen it polished so brightly.

Must be looking forward to seeing me. She's been busy. Bless her heart!

He knocked again and waited.

No answer.

She must be in the garden.

He put down his kit bag and, holding the flowers in one hand, the gift box and the wine under his arm, and the card between his teeth, he searched for his key. He finally fished it out, dropping the wine as he did so. The bottle smashed and the wine ran down the concrete steps. Lou cursed under his breath as he unlocked the door, pushing it into a pile of mail scattered about the floor. His heart sank. He put the flowers on the hall table with the present, chocolates and card and gathered up the mail. His birthday card in the brown envelope was the first thing he spotted with the two telegrams he'd sent from North America. Something must have happened to her.

Oh my God, I hope she's all right!

His mind began to race. He thought of the sugar in his gas tank ...

What if Jessup's been round ...Damn that son of a bitch!

He called out, although he realized it was futile. The place felt like a morgue.

"Charlotte!"

She obviously wasn't home.

Maybe she went up north.

Everything in the house was pristine and in its place—*too pristine*. He went down to the kitchen. Again, all was clean and perfect. Even the rubbish bin was spotless. The sink shone white with nothing on the draining board or table. He peered inside the metal bread bin. Empty, not even a crumb. He heard Fluffy at the door mewing and let her in. She wanted fussing over, but he didn't have time for her. He bounded up the stairs, two at a time, Fluffy on his heels.

Their bedroom door was ajar. He pushed it open and gazed around the room. *Immaculate*. The bed was made, not a crease anywhere. His guitar hung on the wall on his side of the bed where it always was. Shined to perfection. A dead bluebottle on the windowsill seemed out of place. The candle holder, usually on her bedside table, had disappeared.

He opened the wardrobe. All her things were gone. His clothes, newly washed and ironed, hung on his side. His heart began to pound.

"Oh, no, oh no," he gasped.

He went to the chest of drawers, without noticing the envelope, and opened 'the baby' drawer. Empty. He yanked open the rest of Charlotte's drawers. All empty. The house looked as if Charlotte had never set foot in it, except for a few photos—that said it all.

Reminders she doesn't want.

"Oh, Charlotte. What's happened to you?" he whispered.

Suddenly, he noticed the white envelope propped against the photo on the chest of drawers. It came like a hammer blow. He knew instinctively what it was and froze, staring at it with dread. The way it was placed in front of *that* particular photo in its special gold frame had to be a statement. His name was in her hand. He snatched it up, tore it open with shaking hands and pulled out the letter. He sank down onto the bed, his hand against his head in despair.

Dear Louis,

By the time you read this, you will have been to Canada and returned safely—I hope. I am sorry to tell you I have left you. I am not cut out for this life. All I ever wanted was for us to be an ordinary family with children and a dog—and we both know how that turned out.

We have had good times and bad—mostly bad for me, though. I have given it all much thought, and I must face the fact that I no longer love you. Please do not come after me, or contact me. That would be futile. I wish you all the luck and happiness in the world doing what I know you love most.

Goodbye – Charlotte

He had a vision of her standing on the doorstep the night he left—like a goddess.

"Goodbye, Lou," she'd whispered.

How had he missed that?

Fluffy jumped on the bed beside him, mewing and purring, wildly happy he was home.

"She's left us, Fluffy," Lou said quietly, his eyes fixed on Binks' three pencil portraits on the wall: he, the intrepid airman, she, the stunning flapper. Binks had portrayed her beautiful, full lips perfectly. Her smile so captivating. So chic … Then it hit him.

Robert!

"Son of a bitch," he whispered.

He must have materialized from somewhere.

"No, surely not …"

She's obsessed with getting pregnant.

Suddenly, his incredulous eyes blazed and his anger erupted.

"God damn it!"

He leapt to his feet and smashed his fist through the wardrobe door, splintering it.

"Bitch! Bitch! Bitch!"

Fluffy flew out the bedroom door in terror. Lou stumbled after her down to the kitchen in a daze, holding his bleeding fist. He held it under the cold tap. It hurt like hell. He opened a cabinet and pulled out the Scotch Norway had brought before Christmas. He ripped the top off, poured some in a glass and swilled it down. He tried to think. This wouldn't help, but he needed something to numb the shock and the pain in his hand. His wild thoughts went to Charlotte, his father and back to Charlotte again. *Agony*. He sat at the table with his head in his hands. A monotonous wood pigeon cooed from a tree in the garden. He wished he could kill the damned thing! He poured out another shot and put the bottle on the counter. No point in drinking any more. He finished his glass and went back up to the bedroom and laid down, his face in her pillow, her familiar scent now replaced by soap powder.

At Shed No.1, with the broadcast over, the journalists were ready with questions. They raised their hands. Thomson pointed to one. "It's Tom Brewer—the *Daily Telegraph*, if I remember correctly?"

"Quite right, sir. When do you propose setting off for India—I presume you *are* still going, are you?"

"Yes, of course. As to the date, I leave that to my team."

"If you go, don't you have a deadline to be back to attend the Prime Minister's Conference?"

Thomson smiled at Colmore. "I have every confidence we'll be back by 20th October."

Thomson singled out another journalist.

"Bill Hagan, *Daily Mail*. When do you anticipate completion of the modifications?"

"I'm told by R.A.W. the extra bay will be completed this month." Thomson glanced at Colmore who nodded.

"And ready to fly when?"

"In September."

"So you'll definitely leave for India in September, then?"

"I expect it'll be *late* September, yes," Thomson said, eyeing Colmore again. He pointed at another reporter. "Mr. Haines with the *Times*, over there, yes, sir."

"Will that leave adequate time for testing?"

"I shall be guided by my Cardington team."

"It doesn't seem to me like you're allowing enough time. Is it wise to go flying off to India without the airship being properly tested?" Haines asked.

"As I said, I'll be guided by the experts." Thomson glared at Irwin, sure he was in agreement with the premise of that question. "Look, I want to make myself perfectly clear. While I'm in charge, unnecessary risks will not be run and lives will not be sacrificed."

Bill Hagan came back with another question. "Sir, you said yourself in your speech 'this is all experimental.' Does it make sense for you to be flying around in an *experimental* aircraft?"

"I'll just say this: I will not ask of others what I won't do myself."

Thomson pointed at another reporter, remembering him as the troublemaker with the five o'clock shadow.

"George Hunter, *Daily Express*, sir. Has the fact that *Howden R100* has flown to Canada affected the R.A.W.'s judgment? Are they now obligated to fly to India when, perhaps, their ship isn't ready? Do you *really* think this ship's up to the task?"

Thomson frowned.

Damn this man!

"I'm completely confident in this airship and in the Royal Airship Works staff and its officers. That's why I'll be on board when she casts off. One last question—you're Jacobs with *Aeroplane Magazine*, I remember."

"*Sixty tons* of disposable lift. That was the stipulated requirement if you remember, sir. I remember distinctly you telling us—"

"Yes, well, er—"

"They've managed to achieve only thirty-five tons—that's *twenty-five tons* short."

Thomson gave a dismissive wave of his hand. "The team is working hard to rectify that—"

"Wouldn't it be wiser to stop the clock and the schedule until the ship is proven—just to be on the safe side?"

Thomson saw Irwin exchange glances with Brancker. He wondered if these questions had been planted. Irwin actually nodded his head as he glanced at Atherstone.

The nerve of the man!

"I've already stated my feelings on all this."

Another journalist raised his hand.

"All right, one more."

"Sir, stories are filtering out to the press about morale: that it's at an all-time low and there's a breakdown of discipline at Cardington. Would you care to comment?"

"Who are you, sir?" Thomson asked. He'd been caught wrong-footed and cast around helplessly toward his R.A.W. team. They gazed at him blankly, while Irwin stared at the ground.

"Edmund Jones, *Daily Mirror*, sir," the reporter replied.

The Daily Mirror! I thought these people were supposed to be on our side.

"Edmund Jones," Thomson said, filing that name away. "I haven't the slightest idea what you're talking about, sir. Good day, gentlemen." Thomson marched off.

From the car, he watched the reporters gathering around Burney and Norway. They appeared eager to talk.

They would be!

73

OLIVIA

After Lou had climbed on his motorbike and left for the Cardington tower in the middle of the night, Charlotte returned to the bedroom. She removed a blanket from the bed, went down to the kitchen and opened the French doors. After turning off the lights, she sank into one of the deckchairs. She remained in a semi-catatonic state until she heard the sound of Lou's airship passing over. It was as if it were trying to seek her out. She glared at the massive, black shape, droning like a prehistoric insect.

Damn you! You can't see me here in the dark.

The airship passed over, its red navigation light clearly visible. She watched it vanish into the darkness. She felt relieved—never wanting to set eyes on the thing again. That chapter was over.

Charlotte sat in the deckchair through the rest of the night, wrapped in the blanket, staring at the stars. At dawn, she went back to bed and slept until noon. Three times she'd been woken by someone knocking on the front door, which she ignored. When she finally got up, she washed and dressed and walked to the Irwin's house on Putroe Lane. She rang the doorbell and stood on the front step like a waif. Olivia opened the door.

"Come in, you poor dear. I came round to visit you earlier, but you weren't home."

Charlotte's face was grim. "I'll not stay long. There are things I need to tell you, Olivia."

Olivia put the kettle on and then sat down with Charlotte.

"I'm leaving Lou," Charlotte said.

Olivia's eyes widened and her mouth dropped open. "What do you mean? You can't be serious. Have you told Lou?"

"No. I thought it better he didn't know. I'm leaving Bedford this week."

"Charlotte, are you *sure* about this? You're such a lovely couple. Come and stay here with us while he's away and think about it."

"Olivia, you can't imagine what I've been through. It's made me so ill." She broke down and began to cry. "I can't go on. I tried to warn him. I wanted to persuade him. I'd made up my mind last year to tell him how I felt. I had it planned when he came home that day when Thomson came up after he'd got back in office. I'd worked it all out; what I was going to say. We would quit all this and go back to the cottage like he promised. Mr. Bull would take him back. But when he came home he was so happy—he got two promotions that day. I *just* couldn't do it."

"Oh, dear, Charlotte. But I think you should wait until Lou returns."

"No, my mind's made up. Truth is Olivia, I don't love him anymore. I can't be the wife of an airshipman—*not for one more day.*"

Charlotte wiped her eyes and blew her nose. They sat in silence for a few minutes. Charlotte became mesmerized, dulled by her thoughts.

"I was *there*, you know. I saw everything," she said finally, her voice flat.

"Where, love? What did you see?"

"When his ship went down in the Humber."

Olivia put her hand to her mouth in disbelief. "You were there?"

"I was standing right there on Victoria dock."

"You *saw* it?" Olivier closed her eyes.

Charlotte gazed at the wall, experiencing the horror again.

"*Everything*—that thing on fire and breaking in half, the control car breaking away, spinning in the air like a top, men on fire, men falling, bits of bodies flying everywhere—"

"Dear God! I didn't realize you'd actually witnessed it."

"We never talked about it."

They ignored the whistling kettle in the kitchen.

"They laid out the bodies in the garden next to the hospital—too many for the morgue—dozens of them—or what was left of them. We had to chase the kids off. They were peeking through gaps in the fence. They must've had nightmares for years after that. They had to post policemen outside to keep them away. Later, from the ward, we watched a massive funeral pass along the waterfront. It was a dreadful sight."

"Oh, Charlotte. You poor dear."

"When he left last night, I thought to myself, 'I have no idea whether you'll come back.' I will not live my life this way anymore, Olivia. It's over. I don't want to witness another funeral like that."

The kettle continued its howling.

"I'm sorry," Olivia said, getting up. She went and made tea and returned to let it brew.

"Olivia, You're the first person I've told."

Olivia sighed and sat and thought for a while. Charlotte sensed Olivia was deciding whether to confide in *her*.

"I spoke with Captain Booth's wife about Bird. We're pretty close. All this with the Cardington ship is making *him* ill. I asked her what would happen if Bird decided to give up flying—maybe we'd go and live in Ireland."

"What did she say?"

"She asked Captain Booth and he said they'd make *him* fly it to India."

"I suppose they would. That's obvious, isn't it?"

"Bird knows that and he wouldn't shirk his responsibility and put it on another man like that."

"So, you're worried?"

"Yes, I am. It's become a nightmare. The other day, before he went to work, he sat down on the edge of the bed, in his uniform, staring at the floor. I sat down beside him and put my arm around him and put my face against his. I begged him to give it up and he said 'I must go on with it, Olivia, it's my duty.'"

"He really *should* give it up," Charlotte said.

Olivia went to the window, glaring at the overcast sky. When she turned, Charlotte saw, she too, had tears in her eyes.

"Duty! Duty! I'm bloody *sick* of it!" Olivia said, as she shuffled wearily into the kitchen. She returned with a tray of cups and a pot of tea. Olivia obviously had more on her mind.

"He told me Emilie Hinchliffe came and spoke to him. You've heard of her?"

"Yes, she's always in the papers. What did she say?"

"She'd asked to meet him. He didn't tell me at the time. Nothing in it, of course. He didn't want to worry me. Bird and Captain Hinchliffe had been friends. She gave him messages from her husband telling him airships were a lost cause. Gradually, it told on him. It's dragged him down ever since."

They sat and commiserated for another hour until Charlotte got up to leave. They hugged and Charlotte went home, leaving Olivia in a similar state of misery, but feeling her own now had resolution.

Charlotte took a bus to Bedford Station after leaving Olivia's house, to check on train times to Wakefield. While at the station, she ordered a taxi for Friday morning. On her way home, she went into the chemist's shop and bought a large pair of scissors.

She got home around 6 o'clock and sat in front of her dressing table mirror with the scissors. After swinging wildly at a bluebottle intent on annoying her, she began snipping. With Fluffy watching closely from the bed, she started at the top by her left ear and cut her hair off in great swaths. Charlotte turned and glared at the cat.

"What are you looking at Fluff?" she said.

The cat remained silent.

"You really miss him, don't you? I guess you're his cat. I wonder if you'll miss *me*."

Her thick, shiny locks fell to the floor around her feet and after half an hour they looked like the remains of a dead animal lying there. An hour later, she had a bob-cut, finally—short as a boy's. She took a hand mirror from the drawer and inspected the back. It was pretty uneven, but it would have to do. She picked up the hair and threw it in a brown bag and placed it in the bottom of a suitcase on the bed. What would Lou say? It didn't matter.

She spent the evening sorting out drawers and clothes and items to wash, including some of Lou's things. She went to bed early and slept soundly for the first time in months. She got up at six and cleaned the house from top to bottom until late into the night, stopping occasionally to chase the irritating bluebottle that was always just out of reach. It became a battle of wits.

"Damn you!" she shouted.

The following morning she stripped the bed, washed the sheets and pillowcases and hung them on the line in the garden. By midday, they were dry, before the rain came. She ironed them and put them back on the bed and then spent the rest of the day packing.

That evening, Charlotte laid a small, black suitcase on the bed. She opened the 'baby's drawer' and pulled out the clothes she'd made over the years. While rummaging around and pulling out a collection of old Christmas and birthday cards, she found Bobby's message from *R38*. It was still in its cardboard tube buried at the back of the drawer. She pulled out the note, wincing as she read it.

Marry me and come away. I promise to love you forever. Bobby.

"Pathetic! Wasted lives!" she said aloud.

She replaced it in the tube and put it on the bed, making up her mind to find Elsie and give it to her. Though pointless, she owed it to that foolish girl.

Her child must be almost ten now. God!

She held up a woolen shawl, examining it through tears, her face deathly white in the mirror. The shawl smelled of mothballs. She roughly folded it and flung it into the suitcase. She did the same with the rest of the clothes, unwrapping them and throwing them in the case. After screwing up the tissue, she took it down to the dustbin and threw it out with the cards and a heap of half-used cosmetics. Dumping the cards was bit of a wrench, but there was no point in keeping them, and that was not half as bad as what she had to do next.

Around midnight, she put on a headscarf, left the house with the suitcase and walked to the ancient bridge, and although the roads were deserted, she sensed she was being watched. She walked to the middle and looked down into the river, swollen by rain. She listened to the swirling, babbling water. After looking around and seeing no one, she dropped the suitcase over the stone balustrade. She leaned over and watched it splash into the water in the moonlight. It floated for a moment and then moved from side to side in the current before disappearing into the depths. She stood staring at the spot for a few minutes feeling drained—as after an exorcism, or more accurately, a water burial. She wept.

There, it's done. It's over at last.

She felt a weight, or not so much a weight as an expectation, had been lifted and torn away—one that couldn't be fulfilled, but which had finally been confronted and eradicated. Charlotte trudged home and slept fitfully on the couch, grieving for her phantom child and for a husband who was as good as dead.

The next morning was overcast and chilly. She spent time going around making sure everything was in its place with no sign of her existence. The exception was the collection of framed photos, which she had dusted and left where they were. She didn't want them. She took down his guitar from the wall in the bedroom and dusted and polished it until it shone. She stared at it before carefully replacing it. That thing had made him so happy and she'd worked so hard to get it for him. She could hear it now. Oh, how he could play! He made it sing. He made it cry. The sound of it had often made her weep. But not now. Not anymore.

The last thing she did was to dust and polish her precious piano. She made that shine, too. When she'd finished, she stood back to look at it. She thought about taking it somehow, but couldn't cope with it. Maybe when she was settled he'd have it sent to her. The thought of leaving John Bull's present behind made her feel bad about John—like a spit in the eye.

The taxi arrived ten minutes early. She put on her cloche hat and went down and asked the driver to take her cases. She was standing at the bottom step when she heard a familiar voice behind her.

"You're leavin 'im then, ain'tcha?"

Charlotte spun around and stared into the face of Jessup. For the first time in years, she studied that face, noticing the scar. It was on the opposite side to Lou's. She found him attractive in a repulsive way, as many women did, even with his twisted jaw. Strange. His manner was humble. This was certainly new.

Maybe he's changed.

"He's no good, you know. He done me out of my rightful place on that ship. I was in the crew an' everythin'. He got me kicked off."

"I don't know anything about that."

"It wasn't right what he done to me."

"That has nothing to do with *me*."

"I want you to know, I still love you, Charlotte, despite all the beatings and suffering he put me through. I'd endure it all again for you. I love you and always will. I want to say how sorry I am for all the upset I've caused you. I'm a changed man. I walk with the Lord now. I have accepted Jesus Christ as my Savior."

The taxi driver approached them. "And *this* one, too, miss?"

"Yes, please."

The driver worked his way around Jessup, who stood in his way. He gave Jessup and irritated glance as he picked up the other case.

"Will you *both* be traveling, miss?"

"No, just me."

"Charlotte, give me a chance. I'm not really a bad person, you know. I never 'ad much of a chance really, what with me dad an' all," Jessup begged.

Charlotte showed him mild indifference—not the usual complete brush off.

"I've got the baby clothes. I rescued them from the river. They're all at 'ome with me landlady, dryin' out. I saw you throw 'em in the river last night. I dived in and saved them for you, Charlotte."

"You did *what!*" Charlotte screamed, her eyes wide in disbelief.

The taxi driver was getting impatient. He kept looking over at them. Jessup responded with a venomous glare. The driver looked away, scared stiff.

"You need to be with me, Charlotte. We could 'ave a family. There's nought wrong with *me,* you know."

Charlotte shut the front door with a bang and walked toward the taxi. Hearing Charlotte's front door, Mrs. Jones came out and stood on her top step. Jessup hung around, following Charlotte with pleading eyes. Then Church's girlfriend, Irene, showed up. She gave Jessup a funny look and rushed to Charlotte as she was climbing into the taxi.

"Charlotte—"

"I'm sorry, Irene. I can't stop," Charlotte said, not meeting her eye.

"Are you all right? I just—"

"I've got a train to catch. I'm really sorry," Charlotte said, slamming the door.

As the taxi pulled away, she glanced at Mrs. Jones and Irene, who both looked very concerned. Fluffy sat on Mrs. Jones's windowsill staring at her with accusing, green eyes.

74

ROSIE

At 9 o'clock Sunday morning, Lou woke up with a groan as the alarm clock made its ugly sound. He'd slept uneasily and when he came round, the nightmare hit him again, sending him into a freefall.

She's gone.

Fluffy lay beside him. She stretched herself and nuzzled his face. He stared at the photo on the chest of drawers with both sadness and bitterness. He remembered exactly when the picture was taken. Charlotte had sat on the five bar gate opposite her parents' house on Station Road during his first visit to Ackworth, while he stood beside her. They both looked very happy—and they *were* happy. It was Lou's favorite photo, and he'd put it in a special gold frame. Charlotte's dad had snapped it with his Brownie.

He went down to the kitchen and let Fluffy out, then made coffee. A knock came at the front door. Mrs. Jones stood on the step with a shopping bag of groceries. By her expression, she must have been aware of events of the past couple of weeks.

"There was a lot of glass on the steps. I cleaned it up," Mrs. Jones said.

Lou had forgotten. "Oh yeah, I dropped a bottle of wine. I'm sorry."

"Lou, can I—" she began.

"Sure come in, Mrs. Jones. Come and have a cuppa Joe with me."

"All right. Your milk's here on the step. I'll bring it in," she said. She handed him the shopping bag. "I picked up a few things for you." They went down to the kitchen. "Charlotte told me the milkman would start delivering again this morning."

"That was *real* nice of her!" Lou said. He placed the groceries on the table, poured out the coffee and put the milk in a jug.

"I'm so sorry, Lou."

"Did she talk to you?"

"I knocked on the door the morning you left, but I got no answer."

"Probably asleep," Lou said.

"She came and talked to me the Friday before she left in a cab. Gave me money for cat food. Fluffy's been living with us while you were away. She's such a sweet cat."

Lou kept his face expressionless.

"Charlotte didn't say a lot, except she was leaving and wasn't coming back."

"Did she say where she was going?"

"No, I didn't like to pry—but I wish I had now."

"Don't worry. Did she say *why*?"

"She said she'd been unhappy for a long time—that was all. And I must say she looked very sad. But you know, she often seemed like that to me—like something was gnawing away at her inside."

"She was desperate for a kid."

"I don't know, Lou. It seemed more than *that,* to me."

Lou felt depressed hearing all this from a neighbor. Charlotte had been low, but he hadn't realized the extent of her unhappiness. Now *everybody* knew.

"I thought we could sort things out. I guess I was wrong."

"If you find out where she is, you can talk to her—you *must!*"

"She's probably at her mom's place. She said clearly in a letter her mind's made up. She's a stubborn Yorkshire girl."

"Oh, dear. Lou, please don't give up."

"You're very kind, Mrs. J."

"She gave me the key and asked me to get some shopping in for you. I didn't bring it in. I didn't like to."

"Thank you."

She finished her coffee and stood up. "The girl's mad, going off like that," she said.

"She's unhappy, and *I'm* to blame," Lou said.

"Takes *two* to tango, love—that's what I say."

When Mrs. Jones had gone, Lou stared out the window at the sunlight on the flowers. Charlotte must have planted them this spring. He hadn't noticed them before. He took out the pad from the writing case she'd given him and sat trying to put his thoughts together while the mind-numbing tap dripped in the sink. Finally, he began.

My Dearest Charlotte,

I found your note when I came home and I was devastated. I looked forward to coming home and seeing your lovely face at the door. You have no idea how much I have been longing for you. I had lots of time to think and wanted to surprise you with some definite plans when I got back. I suppose that's all out the window now—unless you don't mean the things you said. When you said in your letter you didn't love me anymore, it was unthinkable to me—I believed our love was forever. Please say it isn't true and please meet me and let's talk—I'm sure we can work things out, if we try ...

Lou glanced at the time: 11:30 a.m. already. He needed to get going. He'd finish it later. He put on his uniform and went down to the front door, gathering up the dying violets on the hall table. He took them out and threw them in the dustbin. When he reached Cardington, the gatekeeper glanced at him with what Lou took to be sympathy. He wasn't sure.

"Mornin', Lou," he said.

"Hi, Jim. What's up? Everything okay?"

"I'm not sure. I'd been expecting another officer this morning, but no one showed up. The watch crewmen are on the ship, though."

"I'm supposed to come on at noon."

"Something else is a bit funny."

"What's that?"

"That Mrs. Cameron came through here earlier dressed up to the nines. Said she had something for her husband. I'm certain he's not on the base—bit fishy if you ask me."

"I'll find out what's going on. Thanks, Jim."

Lou rode up the driveway passing Cardington House and coasted silently over to the fence. He left the motorbike and walked across the field to the tower, climbing noiselessly up the stairs and gangplank. He heard shouting and laughing as he moved along the ship's corridor.

The place was a disgusting mess. Empty bottles of Canadian Club, various bottles of spirits and beer lay on their sides on the dining room tables on a carpet of bread crumbs, crackers and scraps of cheese. The noise was coming from the promenade deck on the port side. He stood at the opening.

Disheveled, unshaven watch-crewmen sat slumped on the loungers, couches and easy chairs, their feet on tables. It was Jessup's crowd. A fat lout in his twenties spotted Lou. He downed the remnants of a beer and released a loud belch.

"Aye, look what the cat's dragged in, lads," he said, his mouth curling into a sneer.

"It's our old mate, *Lucky* Lou," a tall, skinny one said, waking from a stupor on a couch.

"What's 'appened to the other big shots? No one's been 'ere all day but us," said one with a Birmingham accent, his face sallow and spotted like a frog.

"But you don't need to worry, mate. Everything's under control. Come and have a drink," the fat one said.

"What the hell do you men think you're doing?" Lou shouted.

"Easy, Lou, me old pal—or should I say, Lieutenant Commander, Third Officer, United States Navy, *sir!*" the skinny one said.

"You're supposed to be on watch," Lou said.

"Yeah, so we *are* on watch, ain't we? See us 'ere!" said another with rotten, goofy teeth.

"We're just having a little drink. It's Sunday—the day of rest. Relax. Come on, sit down and 'ave a drink, me boy."

"He's got nothin' to go 'ome for, 'as he?" the fat one said, roaring with laughter.

"You men are a disgrace," Lou said.

The fat one and the goofy one got up and moved toward him.

"Perhaps the fancy Navy man's going to get us all in trouble," the goofy one said.

"Trouble? You have no idea what trouble you're in," Lou muttered.

"We're not in your precious bleedin' Navy, Lou, me old cock," the goofy one said, putting one hand on his hip and shaking his backside around.

"Go on, Micky, give 'im one!" someone said.

Goofy moved in, but Lou stopped him with a blow under the chin which lifted him off his feet. He crumpled to the floor out cold, minus a few teeth, which fell on the floor like gravel. The other five rushed at Lou, but were surprised by a great shout from the dining saloon.

"*That's enough!*" It was Capt. Irwin. "Step back and get in here, all of you," he bellowed.

"*Very* merchant service!" Sky Hunt, shouted from behind Irwin.

"Very merchant service *indeed*, Mr. Hunt!" Atherstone echoed.

The five crewmen did as they were told, rapidly sobering up, fear registering in their faces. Hunt tilted his head back, sniffing the air.

"Apart from whisky and beer, there's *something else* I smell," he said.

The five sorry crewmen glanced at one another, their worries compounded. Sky Hunt left the dining saloon and marched off to the officers' cabins. In a few moments, he was back, dragging Rosie Cameron by the wrist. She wore only her brassiere and a pair of pink knickers. In her other hand she clung to the rest of her clothes and a pair of high heels. Jessup slunk behind, putting his braces over his shoulders. He glanced across at Lou and smirked.

"Out, you little whore!" Sky Hunt roared.

Rosie bolted.

"You might have let her put some clothes on, Mr. Hunt," Irwin said.

"*I did*," Hunt replied.

"There's gonna be an inquiry and charges," Irwin thundered.

"They've broken into the ship's bar and all the officers' lockers—add that to the charges. They've stolen all Steff's Canadian Club," Hunt said.

"And drunk it, by the looks of it," Atherstone said, surveying the empty brown bottles lying everywhere.

"He struck one of our crewmen," the skinny one whined, pointing at Lou.

"And you men are all *drunk!*" Irwin said.

"All right you lot, on yer bikes!" Hunt snapped.

Later, Lou went home to finish his letter. Irwin had asked him to come by Putroe Lane later for something to eat, but he declined. He sat at the table with a mug of coffee, brooding. His dark thoughts were interrupted by Mrs. Jones knocking at the door again. She came in carrying a plate of sandwiches covered with a clean tea towel.

"Lou, there's something else I must tell you," she said, following Lou into the kitchen. "The morning she left, a young man showed up and was talking with her. I couldn't hear what they were saying—but it seemed odd to me."

"What was he like?"

"Blimey, if I didn't know better, from a distance, I'd swear it was *you*—must be your ugly twin. I didn't like the looks of him. About your build … scar down his face … 'orrible greasy hair. And his eyes … satanic—like one of them hyenas. His chin was crooked to one side, like this … Oh, and he had a limp."

Lou got the picture.

"He came around here once or twice while you were away. Once, walking past and another time on a motorbike. Does he sound familiar?" Mrs. Jones asked.

"Nothing to worry about, Mrs. J. We're old friends."

"Oh good," she said, relieved. "Oh, yes, and a girl showed up. She's been here with one of your crewmen. Don't remember her name—nice looking girl."

"Long blond hair?"

"Yes, that's it, and a lovely face."

"Probably Irene," Lou said with a frown.

Everybody knows.

"Lou, there's something else."

"What?"

"Charlotte has cut her hair."

Lou shrugged.

"No, I mean *all* of it. All that beautiful hair! I couldn't believe it. I saw her from the window when she was pegging the sheets on the line."

His heart sank. "You're kidding me!"

When Mrs. Jones left, Lou made more coffee and ate the sandwiches. He hadn't eaten all day. He was deeply saddened about Charlotte's hair. She knew how much he loved her shining locks. He sat down to finish his letter, but couldn't think of anything to say. He was lost for words.

Lou got up at 4:00 a.m. the following morning. It was Monday. He went to Cardington field where he assisted in the removal of *Howden R100* from the mast and 'sticking her back in her box.' He returned home at 9 o'clock and put on his best suit, a clean shirt and a tie.

He went to the post office and sent a wire to his family in Virginia letting them know he was still in one piece. Next, he paid a visit to the bank to check their joint statement, not from a mercenary standpoint—he wanted to understand Charlotte's frame of mind. He saw where she'd taken out fifty pounds on July 31st—about a quarter of the total. He pondered this.

She didn't even take half of it—some women would have taken everything!

He left the bank and drove to Bedford Hospital, feeling like a cuckold and a sleuth on the trail of an unfaithful spouse. But maybe she wasn't unfaithful, just devious and deceitful in planning her escape, which she'd carried out with precision.

Did I deserve this? Was I so bad? Perhaps I was ...

He asked for the matron on Charlotte's ward. After about ten minutes, a pretty nurse showed him to Matron's office. She sat at a table in the corner of the room, her uniform stiff and white, like her personality. She gave him an accusing glare.

"This is—" the nurse said, giving Lou a furtive glance.

"I *know* who he is, nurse. Go out and shut the door. What can I do for you, young man?" she said unsmiling.

"I've come to speak to you about my wife, Charlotte."

"I've been expecting you."

"I got back from abroad on Saturday and Charlotte wasn't home."

"She gave me her notice three weeks ago, Mr. Remington."

Lou almost choked. "*Three weeks* ago!"

"Yes. Said she was leaving Bedford."

"Are you sure?"

"Of course I am. No, it was more than that." She consulted her log book. "She gave in her notice on the 15th of July. Her last day was July 25th and it's now the 18th of August. She'd been working nights."

She'd given in her notice two weeks before he left and served her last shift while he was still with her. He was stunned. How did he not see this coming? He'd missed this and the fact that his father was dying. He was usually so perceptive. Matron sensed his terrible disappointment and self blame. Her attitude softened.

"Don't be too hard on her, or yourself, son. She is a wonderful girl and she has really suffered—she had a *lot* of problems—believe me, *I know*. She was trying, in her own way, to be kind. Maybe one day, you'll understand that. Not all these girls are cut out to be the wives of airshipmen, you know."

But while the matron was speaking, all he could think about was how they'd made love the night he left. She'd even lit the candle for cryin' out loud!

How could she do that?

What he'd learned about Charlotte's actions over the past few weeks was the *coup de grace*. He got home feeling utterly betrayed. He sat down and read his unfinished letter and realized he had nothing more to say. If he put down what he thought at this moment, he'd certainly make matters worse. He signed the letter curtly, 'Fondest love,' addressed it to Charlotte's parents' home and stuffed it in an envelope. He walked to the pillar box on the corner and dropped it in the slot. At that moment, he realized how Julia must have felt.

Poor Julia!

75

SUNDAY PAPERS

Sunday August 17, 1930.

T homson had a restful Sunday. He rose at 8 o'clock, donned his silk dressing gown and went to the breakfast room, which was bathed in morning sunshine. He opened the *Sunday Sketch*. He enjoyed these Sunday mornings, leisurely going through the newspapers while Gwen served him tea and toast with his favorite thick-cut marmalade.

Every newspaper had a photograph of *Howden R100* arriving at the Cardington mast and some had pictures of him welcoming home the officers and crew. The articles were fair with the questions and his answers reported accurately, though he perceived the right-wing papers were a little snide in talking about the Cardington ship, whereas the rest appeared more objective, more even-handed.

He opened the *Sunday Express* to find a picture of himself shaking Burney's hand—like best friends; they stood together smiling happily. The interviews with Burney and Norway he found annoying—they were crowing. But then he had to admit, they'd done what they set out to do—he had to give them full credit. Now it remained for him to drive the R.A.W. to better this achievement. A voyage to India and a safe return would do just that.

The caption read:

HOWDEN R100 AIRSHIP WELCOMED HOME
SIR DENNIS SAYS HIS SHIP PERFORMED FLAWLESSLY
THE BAR HAS BEEN SET—NOW IT'S UP TO CARDINGTON

Thomson scoffed out loud. "Huh! We'll show you, *Sir* Dennis!" he said.

He turned to the *Sunday Telegraph*.

HOWDEN R100 AIRSHIP BACK FROM SPECTACULAR TRIP
WILL CARDINGTON AIRSHIP BE READY IN TIME?

The Times, business-like, alluded to the 'great competition.'

VICKERS FULFILLS CONTRACT WITH HOWDEN R100.
CAN ROYAL AIRSHIP WORKS COMPETE?

The Sunday Pictorial appeared more light-hearted:

HOWDEN AIRSHIP WOWS CANADIANS
WE DID IT. NOW IT'S YOUR TURN! SAYS SIR DENNIS

Overall, publicity was satisfactory. Thank God, no mention had been made of that damned fool's question concerning morale. He considered the issue again. What were Irwin and Brancker up to? Was there still some undermining going on? Was Irwin demoralizing the whole damned organization? He went to the bedroom and, with Buck's help, got dressed. Later, he sat in his new study overlooking the rear courtyard and worked on ministerial papers for the rest of the day. In the evening, he sat in his spacious living room at his credenza and wrote to Marthe, while listening to a sad violin on the gramophone. Marthe smiled down from her picture frame.

122, Ashley Gardens.

17th August, 1930.

My Dearest Marthe,
Thank you for asking, but I cannot get over to Paris this month. I could come in September if you're there, say during the first week.
I have moved from No.100 (as you can see by my new address) to a larger flat No. 122 with room for a comfortable study, a nicer aspect, a bigger kitchen—which pleases Gwen—and since I plan to keep it a long time —a longer lease. Now all that's necessary is for you to bestow your blessings upon it, along with me and Sammie, who misses you almost as much as I. So, dearest, I hope we can be together before I leave for India so that you can work your magic upon my spirit and fortify my soul for the journey. Please let me know soonest.
Ever my devotion, Kit.

Thomson received Marthe's reply a week later. She wouldn't be available since she'd be in Romania attending a reception for a group of professors from America. After that, she'd be hosting a garden party for them at Posada. These arrangements had been made a long time ago. Marthe sent her love and best wishes, remarking that she'd been 'outwitted by Fate.' Thomson had a rash of unhappy thoughts about a herd of virile, good-looking

American intellectuals in Marthe's house. He hated the thought and tried to push it aside. He wrote back immediately.

122, Ashley Gardens.

25ᵗʰ August, 1930.

My Own Dear Princess,

No, it is I whom Fate has outwitted. I hope these headwinds we are up against abate soon. Though you are not actually with me, please know that you shall be forever present in my heart throughout my journey. Let's hope we return from India in triumph, and that all our new days are glorious. If only we had a crystal ball to glimpse the future. Meanwhile I shall sit helplessly by, watching for hopeful signs.

Always and Forever, Kit.

76

QUESTIONS

Lou carried on with his life as best he could. He constantly wondered what Charlotte was doing and what she was thinking, not to mention where she was. He got home each evening hoping for a letter. But none came. He asked Billy to move in with him. Work would be nearer for Billy and Lou could keep and eye on him, as he'd promised Fanny. The lad would be company, too; he was miserable being in the house alone. Lou decided to write John Bull. Perhaps he had news of Charlotte. He dashed off a note.

> 58, Kelsey Street,
> Bedford.

> 22nd August, 1930.

Dear John and Mary,
I don't expect you have heard—or maybe you have? When I was in Canada, Charlotte left Bedford (and me) and did not say where she was going. I wonder if you have heard from her? As you can imagine, it came as a terrible shock. I guess it's my fault. We are preparing the other ship to fly to India in September. Please drop me a line as soon as possible.
> *My fond regards, Lou.*

Lou received a letter from John Bull three days later.

> *Croft Cottage, Brough, Near Hull,*
> *Yorkshire.*

> *24th August, 1930.*

My Dear Lou,
Mary and I are deeply shocked. We had not heard a word about this until your letter arrived. We have heard nothing from Charlotte. You are a wonderful couple and you know we love you both very dearly. We hope you can resolve everything and get back together soon. Please let us know if there is anything we can do. Anything at all!
> *Much love, John and Mary.*

Lou spent the rest of August and most of September in Shed No.1 monitoring the alterations, as he'd done during construction. As the deadline loomed, a toll was exacted on everyone, nerves fraying, tempers flaring. Furious activity continued around the clock in an atmosphere of general panic. Morale and discipline sank to new lows.

A preliminary inquiry had started regarding the altercation between Lou and the drunken watch crewmen, but nothing of consequence was expected from it. The man Lou had knocked out was still off with a broken jaw—a reminder for Jessup to stay out of Lou's way, which he did conscientiously. One afternoon, Lou tracked him down in the crewmen's locker room lavatories. Lou had been worrying about Charlotte and brooding about Jessup's visits to Kelsey Street all morning and was in foul mood. Lou worried that if Charlotte was in Ackworth, Jessup might go up there and harass her. He was also sore about the episode with Rosie. He'd not acted on any of this until now. Jessup was standing at the urinal trough. Lou came up behind him, grabbed his neck and slammed his face into the brick wall, causing Jessup to spray himself.

"Mr. Jessup. Question: I understand you were hanging around my house when I was away." Jessup made babbling noises. Lou leaned against his ear and yelled. "What were you doing there, shithead?"

Jessup remained silent.

"Cat got your tongue, boy?"

"I was passing by, that's all," Jessup whimpered.

"I warned you to stay away from my wife," Lou said, letting him go.

"She's gone. She's fair game now."

"You stay away from her!"

"Don't come near me. I'll have you up for assault. I'm gonna lodge a complaint with my union. We'll go on strike and you'll be court martialed."

Lou knew these things were possible, particularly the way the mood was in the shed just now. He didn't get too rough. He'd bide his time.

"Watch yourself, Jessup," Lou said, walking out of the locker room.

"Yes, an' you watch yourself an' all," Jessup muttered.

During the last week in August, Thomson summoned Colmore, Scott, Richmond, Rope, Irwin, Atherstone and Lou to Gwydyr House for a progress meeting. Knoxwood took minutes. Thomson was showing his most affable side.

It was the first time Lou had been to the Air Minister's office. The first thing that struck him was the Taj Mahal in its ornate gilt frame. He smiled when he saw Churchill's airship and wondered who the 'daubing fool' was. The painting looked pretty damned good. He noticed Richmond studying it, too. He looked mystified—as though he was seeing things.

"Good morning, gentlemen. I have a few questions about your progress and the schedule. First of all, update me on the modifications, Colmore," Thomson said.

"The work on the extra bay is almost complete, with the additional gas bags being installed and inflated. The bags with holes are being repaired.

"What about the padding issue?"

"Padding is almost complete—and monitored by the inspector."

"The fellow who caused the rumpus?"

"Yes, sir, Fred McWade."

"Good. When do you expect to schedule the re-launching?"

"Hopefully mid-September—leaving two weeks for tests."

"So, we'll start for India before the end of September?"

"Providing the tests are satisfactory."

Thomson glanced at Irwin, sitting behind the others. "What testing is required? I thought most of it was done last year?"

"Captain Irwin has drawn up a comprehensive schedule of tests. I'll let him brief you," Colmore said, turning to Irwin.

Irwin stood up. "First of all, I must stress this ship's only *ever* flown in near-perfect weather. Initially, a flight of twenty-four hours will be conducted in *moderately* adverse weather, followed by forty-eight hours in *adverse* conditions—six hours of this flight at full speed, the rest at cruising speed. After that, the ship must be put in the shed for a thorough inspection."

"This all seems rather extravagant, after all the flying this ship's already done." Thomson growled.

"After the insertion of the additional bay, she'll be a different ship with different characteristics—we'll need to start from scratch. These tests are required in order to be declared '*fit to fly*'," Irwin said.

"Seems to me we're asking an awful lot of the weather—we want conditions '*dead calm*' to bring her out—'*windy* and *rough*' for seventy two hours, then '*dead calm*' to put her back in the shed. What are the chances of *that* in your two-week window? *Zero*, I should think!" Thomson sniffed.

"We'll have to play it by ear, sir and adjust the schedule, based on experience," Colmore said, his eyes shifting to Scott.

Scott was glad to step in. "I'll keep an eye on the situation, Lord Thomson. We'll make these decisions as we go along. We can be flexible, I'm sure."

Thomson saw Irwin didn't appreciate Scott's accommodative tone. *Irwin is a spoiler!*

"One request: I want you to lay a nice blue carpet from the bow to the passenger public area. The interior needs dolling up a bit," Thomson said.

Colmore winced.

"What's that for, Colmore? You don't like *blue?*"

"It's *weight* I'm worried about, sir."

"Come on, Colmore! It won't weigh that much. What's the story with the cover?"

Richmond wanted to answer this one. "Most of the cover's been replaced and waiting to be doped. The rest of the areas are under inspection," he said.

After the meeting, Thomson left Gwydyr House where George Hunter from the *Daily Express* and Edmund Jones from the *Daily Mirror* were lying in wait outside. The *Cardington R101* saga had become a drama closely followed by the public.

"Lord Thomson, do you mind if we ask a few questions?" Hunter asked.

Though caught off guard, Thomson smiled broadly. "By all means, gentlemen."

"We're getting reports *Cardington R101* may not be ready in time for the voyage in September."

"My staff from the Royal Airship Works informed me less than an hour ago, she *will* be ready to fly."

"Will that leave time for testing, Lord Thomson?" Hunter asked.

"We'll have to *make* time won't we!" Thomson snapped, but then caught himself and smiled pleasantly.

"What about morale and discipline? Apparently, an inquiry is being held to look into brawling and drunkenness. Can you tell us about that, sir?" Jones asked.

"I've no idea where you're getting all this. Morale, gentlemen, has never been higher," Thomson said. "Good day to you."

The next day the two newspapers carried headlines.

The *Daily Express* asked:

WILL R101 BE READY IN TIME FOR VOYAGE TO INDIA?

The *Daily Mirror* would not let go of the morale and discipline story:

AIR MINISTER DENIES RUMORS OF BREAKDOWN IN MORALE

77

RACE AGAINST TIME

September 1930

They toiled through September at a feverish pace. Richmond arranged to make an inspection before bringing the ship out, with Lou, Rope, McWade, Irwin, Atherstone and the shop foreman, Ronnie, in attendance. The group trooped around the ship's interior, looking at the padding.

"They've done a *fine* job, Mr. McWade," Richmond said.

"They did what you asked. Not *my* idea of a fine job!"

"You've carried out your instructions. That's all that matters."

"What matters sir, are the lives of these young men. I maintain padding is *not* a satisfactory solution."

"Yes, yes, Mr. McWade, we're all aware of your feelings on the subject. Let's move on, shall we? I want to examine the cover."

They moved to the exterior of the ship and stood looking up at the canvas. The foreman pointed out that the cover had been replaced with the exception of the area between Frame 1 and Frame 3 at the front end. Richmond stood under the frames in question.

"What about the rest, then?"

"It's in fairly good condition. We would replace every piece, but we don't have time," replied the foreman.

McWade wasn't satisfied. He made them follow him up on the scaffold. "I want you people to focus your eyes on *this*," he said. "You think you've removed all the rotten fabric from this ship. Well, you haven't." He led them around poking his finger at the cover. Sometimes the cover held, other times his finger went clean through, like rotting paper.

McWade glared at Richmond. "So, *now* what?"

Richmond addressed Rope and Ronnie. "Get the *whole* crew on this. Put patches over the holes and weak areas and anywhere it looks doubtful," he told them.

"It's *all* very doubtful, if you ask me. I'll be surprised if you make it to Dover!"

Richmond stormed off.

"This ship's gonna have more pads, bandages and sticking plasters than the bloody Red Cross," McWade sneered. Lou worried about Irwin. He looked physically ill.

The Air Ministry decided *Howden R100* would also receive an extra bay. Norway came down to discuss these modifications, although he didn't believe it was necessary, and told Richmond as much. Naturally, his views were not well received. But he was glad of the work; Vickers was still paying his salary, for the moment anyway. Most of the staff at Howden had been laid off and he expected the axe to fall at any time.

New designs for bigger and better dirigibles were on the boards at the R.A.W. Many in government urged a freeze until the two existing airships proved themselves before committing more money. One successful return trip across the Atlantic could've been due to sheer luck.

While in Bedford, Norway stayed with Lou on Kelsey Street. Since their triumphant return from Canada, Norway had been treated with even more disdain by the R.A.W. (if that were possible). His only safe haven was in Booth's office in Shed No. 2, where *Howden R100* was presently housed. After Richmond's inspection of *Cardington R101*, Lou took a piece of the cover to show them. None of them seemed happy when Lou stepped inside.

"Come in, Lou. Nevil's complaining because no one loves him," Booth said.

"There's tea in the pot," Meager said.

Lou closed the door and poured himself a cup.

"They're treating me like a b-bloody leper," Norway complained.

"What do you *expect*, Nev? You've caused all this panic, all this worry and all this misery," Lou said.

"Many a true word spoken in jest!" Booth said.

"Everything's rubbed off on *us*. They won't include us in anything either," Meager grumbled. "We're sitting in here with nothing to do all day. It's all *his* fault."

"We upped the ante. Now you're the enemy, too," Norway said.

Lou laid the cover sample on the table in front of Norway, without a word. Norway put on his thick-framed reading glasses and carefully picked up the fabric in two hands. As he did so, it crumbled to pieces.

"Oh, my good Lord!" Norway gasped, while Booth and Meager gathered round. "W-w-what the hell is this? Where did this c-come from?"

"Don't panic, Nevil, it's not off your ship. This is part of the old cover from *R101* next door," Lou replied.

Norway turned the remaining piece over in his hands. "Look at this. They've stuck tapes on the inside as reinforcement and the adhesive is having a chemical reaction to the dope."

"You could be right," Booth said.

"I hope they d-don't leave any of this on that ship."

"Most of the cover's been replaced—they're patching the rest."

"They need to remove *all* this r-rubbish!"

"They're trying to, but they're running out of time," Lou said.

In late September, while the October fair was arriving in the village and setting up opposite Cardington field as usual, *Cardington R101* was going through her lift and trim tests, which came out as follows:

Fixed Weight	118 tons
Gross Lift	167 tons
Disposable Lift	49 tons

These results were as expected, although still shy of requirements originally laid down by Thomson in 1924. The good news was that the two forward engines, Nos.1 and 2, were both now reversible, so they would no longer be carrying one engine as dead weight and had the benefit of much needed forward power on all engines. This would increase dynamic lift and help them stay airborne.

78

TRAIN RIDE NORTH

September 25 - October 1, 1930.

The ship was handed over to the flying staff a week behind schedule, but now the weather was taking the final bite out of allotted time for testing. It remained atrocious for the next five days. As the departure date loomed, Lou felt the need to make an effort to try and meet Charlotte. She hadn't responded to his letter and Charlotte was all he thought about.

Who knows? Maybe she didn't receive it. Perhaps she hasn't gone to her parents' home. Maybe they haven't heard from her either. Maybe she's with this Robert guy. At least I'll be able to talk to her mom and dad if I go up there.

Lou went to Capt. Irwin and asked for permission to be away for one, possibly two days. Irwin encouraged him to go. Lou also spoke to Colmore, who was kind and sympathetic and wished him well. On October 1st, the weather abated and Lou went with Norway to witness the handling party walk *Cardington R101* to the tower. Once moored, *Howden R100* was brought out of Shed No. 2 and put into the longer shed for work to commence on the insertion of her own additional bay. This would be the first time the two ships had actually been visible together and Norway wanted a photograph.

Afterwards, Norway ran Lou back to Kelsey Street, where he put on his best suit, clean white shirt and a smart red tie. Before leaving, he placed the writing case Charlotte had given him on the bed to take with him. Maybe he'd draft some letters home during the train journey. Then, as an afterthought, he removed the photo of them together from its gold frame and stuffed it in an envelope. He put it in the writing case. Lou wanted to travel by rail so he could dress decently. He decided against wearing his leather greatcoat.

On the way to the station, Norway aired his employment woes.

"I met with Richmond this morning," he said.

"How did *that* go?"

"I asked him if they'd put me on the payroll while they insert the extra bay and do the modifications to our ship. I offered to stay here as consulting engineer for half my salary."

"I'm sure that went over *real* big!"

"He flatly refused!"

"You're out of work then, basically?" Lou said.

"They're talking about more ships—but goodness knows when that'll be."

"I don't think they like you much, Nev."

"I know."

"This is the perfect opportunity to write another novel!"

"I'm out of ideas right now," Norway said.

"Hey, I got one for you. How about this: An American naval officer flies to Canada in a British airship. After escaping death twice on the way, he goes to visit his family in the U.S.A., ravaged by the Depression. He finds he's run into a shit-storm; his family have lost everything; he gets mixed up with moonshine, the Ku Klux Klan, his old Army buddies in Shanty Town, the government and the military—and then his *old girlfriend* shows up!"

They arrived outside the station.

"Lou, Lou, Lou!" Norway said, shaking his head. Lou got out and stuck his head in the window. Norway continued. "I don't know where you come up with these silly ideas. They're daft! That kind of ph-ph-phantas-m-mag-g-goria would never appeal to my readers. They're f-far too sophisticated for that kind of unrealistic silliness."

"You're probably right—whatever that means."

"Lou, I wish you the very best of luck today," Norway said. "I'd ask you to give her my love but it might q-queer your p-pitch."

"Make sure Billy's okay. Tell him to get his stuff ready for *India*."

Lou bought two dozen red roses at the florist next to the station before purchasing a ticket. He arrived in Wakefield two hours later and waited for the local train to Ackworth. Pretty soon, a steam train trundled in. The journey to Ackworth took twenty minutes.

A wave of nostalgia overcame him. He remembered arriving there the first time with Charlotte to meet her parents. It was this same time of year—leaves on the ground rustling underfoot—their colors as bright as daffodils and plums in the sunshine. All the thoughts he'd had at that time rushed into his head. Now here he was, back to ask what had become of his bride. *Humiliating!*

Under heavy cloud and spitting rain, Lou, clutching the roses, walked up the dirt road between the stone houses. As he got closer to Charlotte's house, he had feelings of both dread and excitement. Would she be there? Perhaps she'd be thrilled to see him on the doorstep. Maybe she wasn't there. Maybe she *had* found someone else. What sort of reception would her parents give him? Would they blame *him* for everything?

His whole life depended on this unrequested (and perhaps unwelcome) visit. But the more he thought about it, he believed he was right to come. He should've come before now. Staying away meant he didn't care. He felt confident and his spirits rose with every step.

This is what men do—pursue. It's what we're meant to do.

At last, he stood at the front gate. He glanced up at the rooftop. Smoke was coming from the chimney. The net curtains in the front window were drawn, preventing him from seeing in.

The room where she was born!

He hesitated for a moment, looking at where Charlotte's swing used to hang from the oak tree. It was long gone—but he could see marks on the bough where it'd once been tied. He pushed down on the gate latch. The gate squeaked as he opened it. They'd surely hear it. He figured the whole neighborhood must have. He went to the front door, sensing an aura of unfriendliness. He felt like a stranger, his confidence began to dwindle. He lifted the brass knocker and gingerly knocked once. He waited. Perhaps they couldn't hear it if they were in the kitchen. He waited patiently for a few more minutes, his heart racing. No one answered.

He knocked again, louder, twice. He waited, but no one came. He knocked three times, this time much louder. Hell, all the neighbors must have heard that! Still no one came. He carefully put the flowers down on the grass next to the stoop. They were beginning to droop and some of the petals had fallen off.

He bent down and peered through the letter box. A few coats were hanging on hooks in the hallway—he spotted Charlotte's—the blue one she wore in Switzerland. Beyond the foyer, the coal fire glowed in the grate in the living room—probably stoked less than half an hour ago. On the coffee table in front of the couch, he noticed a cup and saucer.

Someone's home.

There was nothing next to Father's easy chair on his shelf. No cup and saucer. No cigarettes.

He must be at work.

Lou left the flowers on the ground and went back to the front gate and into the street. He walked along the stone wall, past the house next door and into the alleyway leading to the back of the houses. He felt like an interloper. He'd ridden his motorbike round to the backyard many times. This place used to feel welcoming. Not anymore.

He got to the back of the house, passing the outhouses, and went to the kitchen door. Hearing Lou's footsteps on the gravel, the dog behind the fence next door started barking, while nearby chickens clucked and carried on. The curtains had been drawn across the window over the sink.

That means they're out—or they know I'm here.

He knocked with his knuckles and got the same response. He tried the door. Locked. He glanced up at the windows next door. The curtains were also drawn, but he could swear they moved. Probably someone had been asleep. Many of these people were miners on shift work who slept during the day. Now the neighbor would be irritated. He thought about knocking on their door and asking about Charlotte.

No, that would only make her mad as hell.

Lou retraced his steps along the alley and returned to the front stoop and peeped through the letter box again. He could swear the cup and saucer had been moved. He was sure someone was home and knew he was there.

Well, if they're home and they won't open the door that tells me all I need to know. No point in sticking around here.

He scanned the windows again on the second and third floors— nothing. It began to rain. He took out a sheet of paper from the writing case and wrote:

Dear Charlotte

I had hoped to talk to you before leaving for India. Please remember I always loved you, and always will. I guess old Mrs. Tilly got it wrong.

Lou signed the note, smudged by raindrops and put it in the envelope with the photograph of them together at the five-bar gate across the road. And then, on an impulse, he pulled off his wedding ring, slipped it in the envelope and sealed it. He pushed it through the letter box and, leaving the wilting flowers on the ground, left the front garden. He walked off toward the station, collar up, shoulders hunched against the cold rain. He wished he'd worn his leather greatcoat.

"Go after him!" Charlotte's mother implored.

Mrs. Hamilton had spotted Lou first from her bedroom on the second floor as he came in the front gate. She rushed down to Charlotte who was sitting in the living room on the couch, reading and drinking tea.

"Lou's coming to the front door," she whispered hoarsely. She didn't know why she was whispering, but had anticipated Charlotte's reaction.

They heard a light knock on the door.

"Don't you *dare* open that door," Charlotte hissed.

Charlotte got up and went to the kitchen and pulled the curtains across the back window over the sink and turned the key in the lock. It was stiff. She couldn't remember the last time it'd been locked. She returned to her mother in the living room and picked up her cup and saucer, and then put it back down. He must've seen it there.

"Come on, we must go upstairs," she murmured, her eyes determined. The two women sneaked up the staircase, to Charlotte's parents' bedroom, overlooking the front garden. They peeped down through the net curtains and saw Lou standing at the door. There were two more knocks.

"Charlotte, why don't you go down and talk to him."

"No, I won't!"

"Oh, Charlotte, he's come all this way. You can't leave him standing out there in the rain."

"Mother, I will *not* speak to him. I don't want any more to do with him."

"How can you be so cruel? He's such a lovely fella."

"I don't love him anymore. There can be no happiness with an airshipman."

"Perhaps you could talk him out of it."

"No, he's committed. You don't understand. I've tried a thousand times. He has his reasons. I've no control over that. Now leave it be."

They followed Lou's movements as he tried the back of the house. They saw him returning to the front door. A minute or two later, they heard the letter box snap shut. They watched him walk off up the road toward the station.

"Oh, Charlotte, go after him. He's so thin and gaunt. Look at him! He's your husband. You made a vow—for better or for worse." Tears were springing from her eyes. "Go after him! I can't bear it—it breaks my heart to see him like this."

"Let it be, Mother!"

It was raining hard now, with gusty winds. The leaves fell on the road, leaving a slippery, mustard and brown carpet. Surreal, ominous clouds shifted overhead, occasionally revealing vivid blue sky and shafts of sunshine, illuminating fields each side in patches.

He trudged up the deserted street toward the station. Rain soaked through his jacket, chilling him to the bone. A spectacular rainbow arched over his road ahead. The vicious irony of it infuriated him, and with every step he took, he became more angry. When he got to the station, the stationmaster told him the next train was due in twenty minutes. He slumped down on the bench in the empty waiting room, fuming. He was mad at himself for bothering to come. She'd made it plain she didn't want him to make contact.

Stubborn Yorkshire b...

He couldn't bring himself to say it again, even to himself.

Charlotte's mother came downstairs, wiping her tears with a handkerchief. She went to the vestibule and picked up the envelope from the mat, then opened the front door and warily peered outside. Petals were being beaten off the roses by water cascading from the roof. She gently scooped them up and took them to the kitchen table. She was cutting the stems and placing them in a vase when Charlotte entered the room.

"Where did these come from?" she snapped.

"He left them for you."

"I don't want them."

"I'll not leave them out there. They came with his love. I'll keep them, even if you don't want them," Mrs. Hamilton said.

"Do as you please."

"And there's a letter for you."

"I said leave it be!"

"You've *never* done right by him, you know. You kept him in the dark all this time. It wasn't right!"

"Don't go on about *that*, Mother …anyway, it doesn't matter now."

Charlotte sat down at the kitchen table, scowling at the envelope.

Later, Mr. Hamilton returned from Ackworth Colliery. After getting them to unlock it, he came through the back door wearing his bicycle clips on his overalls, grimy with coal dust.

"What's that locked for?" He noticed the flowers, "Hello, hello. What's all this? Have you got a secret admirer, Mrs. Lena Hamilton?" he said, smiling at his wife and then Charlotte. But then he saw they were both upset.

"Lou's been here and left them for our Charlotte. She wouldn't open the door to him."

His face lit up for a second and then fell. "*What!* Has he gone?"

"He was on foot. He walked back up to the station. Poor Lou, he looked so sad." She started to cry again.

"How long ago was this?"

"He left about fifteen minutes ago. Oh, that *poor* boy …"

"I'll go up and see if I can catch him. I'll bring him back."

"Don't you dare, Dad!" Charlotte said.

But Mr. Hamilton was resolute. He put his cap back on, rushed out the back door and jumped on his bicycle. He began peddling like mad.

Sick at heart, he returned twenty minutes later. The station had been empty. Mr. Hamilton got washed in the kitchen, changed, and went to sit in his armchair by the fire. Mrs. Hamilton brought him a cup of tea and sat down. He lit a cigarette. Charlotte came and sat on the couch with Lou's letter. It felt stiff and there was something else inside making it bulge. Mr. Hamilton turned on the radio beside him in time for the news. Charlotte tore the letter open and Lou's ring fell into her lap. It stunned her and she felt a knife in her heart. She clasped it into her palm and closed it, hoping her father hadn't seen it. But he had. She caught a glimpse of sadness in his eyes. After the sound of Big Ben striking the hour, there were six beeps on the radio and then the familiar BBC announcer's voice. Charlotte was surprised to find the photograph as she pulled it out with Lou's damp note. She read his brief words before raising her head to listen.

'This is the BBC Home Service. It was announced today by the Air Ministry in Whitehall that His Majesty's Airship Cardington R101 is expected to leave her mast in Bedfordshire on the 4th of October to begin her passage to India. The Secretary of State for Air, Brigadier General, the Right Honorable Lord Thomson of Cardington, will be on board for this, her historic maiden voyage…'

Charlotte left the room with Lou's letter, his ring still in her palm, and went to the attic bedroom where Lou had once slept. She sat on the bed and pulled out the photograph and studied it. Lou looked younger. He wore a sweater (she remembered it was light blue) and black trousers. She looked closely at his face. He was looking into her eyes and smiling with such love. She lay down, burying her head in the pillow. She thought about the things old Mrs. Tilly had said on her deathbed and remembered kissing the palm of her hand where his tears had been on that horrible, beautiful night in Hull. She opened her hand and looked at his ring.

Lou's anger simmered throughout his journey back to Bedford Station. He sat alone huddled in a carriage with his feet up on the seat opposite, trying not to shiver. On the journey up to Yorkshire earlier, he'd mulled over the idea of foregoing the voyage to India and quitting airship business altogether. He had a good excuse. He could've said he needed to rush back to see his dying father. He'd thought about taking Charlotte with him. They would've taken a steamer from Liverpool to Montreal (as he'd dreamed of doing) and then hopped on the train to Union. But that would've meant deserting his captain and his crew and leaving them to their fate with that damned airship. Would he have done it? For her, yes. For *her,* he would've done it! Then he thought about the guilt that would've been associated with that—especially if something happened to them all. But she wouldn't open the door, so it was all moot. And, in some ways, he was glad.

What the hell! It doesn't matter. I'll fly with them and take my chances. I could care less now anyway.

He couldn't help thinking of Charlotte's words when Freddie died.

That ship is cursed! And this city is cursed. And we're cursed, too.

He looked at the impression on his ring finger where his wedding ring had been. Perhaps she was right. He dwelt on what she'd said as the train approached Bedford. He thought about *Cardington R101.* It wasn't up to *Howden R100*—although that ship was Spartan and without frills—it didn't even have any damned fuel pumps for God's sake! *Cardington R101* was ornate and bloated, a testament to overspending and a desire to impress.

I'll talk to Colmore again. I'll give it another try. You never know, he might grow a set of balls—but I doubt it. Time's getting short.

Richmond had conscientiously done his best to design a strong airship that wouldn't break in two, and this and the extravagant touches, had caused her to come out heavy. And now they'd added an extra bay—what had that done to all their calculations and to the factor of safety? Lou still didn't know if the ship was really and truly airworthy. He hoped they'd find out more during the twenty-four hour test. But the lack of testing was crazy! And for what? To satisfy an old martinet, hell-bent on using it as his own personal plaything! It was maddening. *Colmore* was maddening! They were *all* maddening!

This just ain't no way to run an empire!

Had *Cardington R101* become the symbol of the Empire—too big, too heavy, too vainglorious to fly?

Lou got home late, after stopping at The Swan in Bedford near the old bridge, where he downed a pint of bitter and a couple of double whiskies. He didn't expect them to be up, but Norway and Billy were waiting to hear his news. Lou sat down with Norway while Billy made a pot of tea.

"We're dying to know. Did you see her?" Norway asked.

"They wouldn't answer the door."

"What!"

"I'm positive she was home. I saw her coat hanging in the hallway. The fire was burning. Place was locked up tighter than Dick's hatband."

"Who's Dick?" Billy asked.

"You tried the door?" Norway asked.

"I tried the *back* door."

"It was locked?"

"Yes."

"Nobody locks their doors up there. Especially the *back* door."

"I guess somebody must've seen me coming."

"Probably. Did you try the *front* door?"

"No. I didn't."

Lou was mad with himself. "You know something—if she'd let me in and said 'Give it all up,' I'd have done it right then and there. She obviously doesn't care for me anymore and that's that," Lou said.

"Damn!" said Billy.

"What happened with the flight test?" Lou asked.

"Irwin took his ship up today. They had the new AMSR on board— Air Vice-Marshall Dowding. He knows absolutely nothing about airships."

"Sounds a lot like you, Nev. Are they doing the twenty-four hour?"

"It got shortened to sixteen hours. Booth told me this afternoon."

"What about the forty-eight hour?"

Norway put on his most exasperated face. "No time for that."

"Irwin's gonna be mad as hell. It's flat calm out there. No use at all!"

79

A FEW LOOSE ENDS

October 2, 1930.

T he following day, Lou sat at the kitchen table and wrote some letters. The first was to his mother. After delivering the bad news, he'd try to keep the rest positive.

58, Kelsey Street,
Bedford,
England.

2nd October, 1930.

Dear Mom,
I am heartbroken and I have only myself to blame. Charlotte has left me and gone away. Please keep this to yourself, for now. I guess Dad was right. Perhaps it was all a mistake. I hope he is not feeling too bad. Tell him I think of him always and I will be with him soon. I am praying for a miracle. I hope he is taking an interest in Jeb's new house.
We are off to India this Saturday aboard Cardington R101. I hope, all being well, to see you on my return. I will come home for good after we get back from India. My job here will have been done and there is no reason for me to stay—although I will miss this place and these people more than I can say.
There's a chance of a place on the U.S. Akron or Macon and I will probably try for one of them, unless I become a farmer! Give Dad my love— and also Tom, Anna and Julia, and of course, Jeb and family.
Fondest Love, dearest Mother,
Your son, Lou.

He took a long deep breath before addressing his next letter.

President Herbert C Hoover,
President of the United States of America,
The White House,
Pennsylvania Avenue,
Washington, D.C. U.S.A.

58, Kelsey Street,
Bedford, England.

2nd October, 1930.

Dear Mr. President,

 Please forgive me for taking the liberty of writing to you, sir, but I believe it is important I do so. I served in France during the war with the Marine Corps and now I am serving as an airshipman with the U.S. Navy, seconded to the British Airship Program.

 I recently flew in the British Airship Howden R100 from England to Montreal and came to Washington, D.C., where I was met by a delegation of Army veterans who asked me to intercede on their behalf. I promised I would do my best to help. As you know, they are camped out in Anacostia and are lobbying for their Army Service Bonds to be paid now instead of later, due to the hardship caused by the depressed state of the economy.

 Therefore, I am respectfully appealing to you to help these men, who have done so much for our country, by urging the Congress to pass a bill which will give them financial relief and ease their suffering.

Yours faithfully,
Louis Remington Lt. Cmdr. United States Navy,
Chief Petty Officer U.S.N. Airship ZR-2,
Third Officer HMA Howden R100 and HMA Cardington R101,
Special Assistant to Director of Airship Development of Great Britain.

 Lou wrote a similar letter to the senator in his grandmother's district. Lou sealed the letters and took them to the pillar box on the corner. He next went to two insurance agents on the High Street in Bedford. At the first one, The Prudential, he took out a life insurance policy on himself for the sum of one thousand pounds, the beneficiary being Charlotte Remington of 11, Station Road, Ackworth, Yorkshire. The second, with the Pearl Life Assurance Company for the same amount, but with Mrs. Louise Remington of Remington's Farm, Great Falls, Virginia, U.S.A. as beneficiary. The premiums were high, due to his occupation, but he paid the money willingly.

Lou stopped next at Midland Bank, also on the High Street, where he arranged for a draft of one hundred pounds to be sent to the new account he'd set up at Riggs Bank in Georgetown. This left him with ninety pounds in the joint account with Charlotte. No activity, apart from his own, had occurred in the account since she'd gone.

Lou went from the bank to Needham & Finley, Solicitors-at-Law, where he asked the receptionist if he could get a will drawn up immediately. She told him to come back in an hour—Mr. Needham would take care of the matter personally.

On his return, he was ushered into the white-haired solicitor's office, a dark room surrounded by leather-bound books. Lou explained the will would be simple—he had few assets. Lou told the solicitor he was an airshipman aboard *Cardington R101,* which intrigued the old gentleman. On leaving, Mr. Needham asked Lou if he wouldn't mind paying his bill before leaving the premises.

At 6:00 p.m., Thomson sat at his desk at Gwydyr House. Knoxwood looked in to tell him his visitors had arrived.

"Send them in and come in and take minutes, would you?" Thomson instructed.

Colmore and the new AMSR (Air Member for Supply and Research) entered. Dowding was a tall man in his late forties, with graying hair and strong features. Thomson, though tired, perked up as soon as they came in, taking their hands and greeting them with warm smiles.

"Come in, gentlemen, come in! Just a few loose ends to sort out this evening. How did the test go—well, I hope? That was her final—yes?"

"Major Scott reported the test went well. 'Wonderfully,' actually. No major problems, except for the oil cooler," Colmore replied.

"Anything serious?"

"Oh, not too serious, but it prevented them from doing the speed test."

"And what about the additional bay?"

"The extra lift has helped considerably. No question," said Colmore.

"You were on board, Dowding?"

"Yes. I must say, it was a *most pleasant* experience—surprised me!" This pleased Thomson.

"I should point out that Air Vice-Marshall Dowding had to be back by 8 o'clock this morning, so it meant the ship only did sixteen of the twenty-four hour test. And of course, we've not done the forty-eight hour test —required in rough weather," Colmore said.

"Required by *whom?*"

"The schedule drawn up by Captain Irwin."

"Oh, *Irwin* …" Thomson said, waving his hand dismissively.

"I did ask the Air Ministry—which comes down to the Air Vice Marshall here—for permission to reduce the test durations," Colmore said.

Dowding shifted uncomfortably in his chair. "The problem is, I'm not fully in the picture. As you know, I've only just assumed this position. I must be guided by the experts at Cardington."

Colmore explained, "We agreed that if Major Scott felt satisfied, there'd be no objection to shortening the twenty-four hour test to sixteen."

"And forgetting about the forty-eight hour?" Thomson asked.

"Providing *Scott's* comfortable. The test durations are really arbitrary. This'll allow us to depart Saturday—providing you still want to proceed, that is—" Colmore said.

They were interrupted by a knock at the door. Brancker popped his head in. "Ah, CB, I didn't realize you were in conference. I've been trying to reach you all day. It's important I talk to you," Brancker said.

Thomson waved him off. "Not now, Sefton. Come back about eight-thirty this evening. I should be free by then." Colmore and Dowding appeared uncomfortable. Thomson had skillfully avoided Brancker all day and didn't want him hanging around—he'd be eager to join this meeting and knew he'd have far too much to say. Brancker nodded and closed the door.

Thomson picked up exactly where they'd left off.

"Well, of course we're going to proceed. We can't delay the voyage any longer. I need to be back by the twentieth!"

"We'll make preparations, then," Colmore said.

"Can we get away on Friday, instead of Saturday?"

"That wouldn't be possible. It'll take until Saturday to get the ship prepared, fueled and gassed up. And the crewmen need rest. They've been flat out for weeks."

"Yes, yes. Of course they do," Thomson said.

"It's important we arrive in Ismailia around sunset—we need the smoother air," Colmore explained. "If we leave Saturday evening, everything should work out just right."

"Look, I don't want to rush things, Colmore. I bow to your superior judgment." Thomson glanced at Knoxwood, to make sure he was taking all this down. "Where are we with the documentation?"

Knoxwood held up the paperwork triumphantly. "The Airworthiness Certificate and Permit to Fly are here, Lord Thomson," he said.

Dowding had been thinking. "About these tests: Would it be possible to complete some of them around Cardington when you leave the mast on Saturday evening before heading south?"

Nobody spoke. On the face of it, it seemed like a daft idea. Thomson turned to Colmore. "Let me consult Scott," Colmore said.

Thomson slipped on his spectacles and shuffled his papers. "Let's go through the passenger list." He ran his finger down the names. "O'Neill. Who is he again?"

"He's the new Deputy Director of Civil Aviation in Delhi…Sir Sefton requested—"

"Oh, yes, and Palstra?"

"The Australian."

"Yes, right. I don't see Buck's name here," Thomson said frowning.

"Buck! Who is Buck?" Colmore asked.

"My valet, of course."

Colmore became flustered. "I didn't know anything about a valet, sir."

"I can't do without Buck! And what about the blue carpet?"

Colmore grimaced. "Yes, sir. We had to remove the parachutes and cut down the crew's luggage limit to ten pounds to accommodate that—in part, anyway."

"Colmore, we've just spent thousands on installing a new bay. Now you're fussing over a bit of carpet and my valet!"

Colmore kept his mouth shut.

"Okay, let's talk about the banquet. As you know, I'll be entertaining the King of Egypt during our stopover in Ismailia. No refueling operations will be allowed in Egypt—understood?"

Colmore couldn't hide his astonishment. His eyes popped and his jaw dropped.

Dowding came to the rescue. "You planned to carry *only* enough fuel to reach Egypt and then refuel there, Wing Commander—is that right?"

"Yes. Of course. It's a weight issue."

"Impossible! You will not be permitted to refuel in Egypt. The stench of diesel fuel would be intolerable—we're entertaining the King of Egypt, man!" Thomson snapped.

"I'd need to s-stand down the whole third watch crew to s-save that kind of weight, sir," Colmore stammered.

"Right. Then do it!"

Colmore slumped back in his chair, dazed.

"One more thing. I want you to arrange for my luggage to be picked up Saturday afternoon. I'm bringing a Persian rug to lay down for the banquet. Send a couple of crewman with a van."

"I'll make arrangements, sir," Colmore answered weakly.

"Everything's settled then!" Thomson said, jumping up and rubbing his palms together. He shook hands and dismissed them.

As Colmore trudged out, he looked as though he had the weight of *Cardington R101*, including the fuel—now increased by 100%, the crew—reduced by 33%, *plus* Thomson's valet, on his shoulders.

80

THE ALMIGHTY BLOODY ROW

Thursday October 2, 1930

At 8:30 p.m., Thomson was still at his desk. The light had faded and the table lamps had been switched on. He was writing comments on the draft minutes of his meeting with Colmore and Dowding, which Knoxwood had left before going home. There was a gentle tap at the door.

Must be Brancker. Damn! I'd forgotten about him.

"Come!"

Thomson continued scribbling. Brancker approached his desk.

"Something on your mind, Sefton?" Thomson said, without raising his head.

"Yes, as a matter of fact, CB, there is."

Thomson continued writing. "And what is that?" His tone disinterested, patronizing.

"It concerns the airship."

"Which one?"

"*Cardington R101,* of course."

Thomson finally raised his head. Brancker appeared fidgety and nervous. Thomson, being calm, had the edge.

"Ah, *Cardington R101*—what about *Cardington R101?*"

"I'm very concerned. I've been trying to speak to you all day," Brancker said.

"I heard you've been chasing around after me. So, here I am. What's the problem?"

"The airworthiness of that airship."

"Whatever do you mean? They've issued an Airworthiness Certificate and a Permit to Fly. What *more* do you want?"

"Bits of paper issued by a department under your control—that's meaningless!"

"I don't make these people do things. I'm guided by them."

"Look CB, the R.A.W. and the officers don't have confidence in that ship."

"How do you *know* that?"

"I hear things."

Thomson got to his feet and drew himself up to his full height.

"From *whom?*"

"The ship's overweight."

"I was informed the lift and trim tests were satisfactory."

"She's *still* heavy," Brancker said.

"It's got forty-nine tons of lift now."

"Your own requirements were sixty tons. *Remember?*"

"*Howden R100* had only fifty-four," Thomson said.

"But that ship was still much lighter!"

"Well, their *engines* were lighter."

"It doesn't matter why. It's still a lighter ship. *Cardington R101* is too heavy."

"I'm guided by the R.A.W.," Thomson said, his voice trailing off.

"The gas bags were full of holes."

"They've all been fixed."

"And they'll be full of holes again before we reach the English Channel. They're still rubbing against the ship's frame."

"They're all padded now," Thomson said.

"They're *still* rubbing!"

"The inspector's satisfied."

"I don't think so. He only confirmed the padding installation is complete. He's dissatisfied with the method of addressing the problem. Then there's the cover—"

"They've assured me that's been taken care of."

"Not a hundred percent."

Thomson grunted in annoyance.

But Brancker kept on. "Their biggest concern is that the ship's untested—and is therefore unfit for this journey."

"I've just had a long discussion about the tests with Dowding and Colmore."

"Dowding knows absolutely *nothing* about airships. He'll be the first to tell you that—and as for Colmore, bless his heart, he'll do whatever you ask of him."

"They put the testing business to Scott and he's perfectly satisfied—that's *his* domain."

"*Scott!* You can't rely on Scott! He's not the man he was."

"What do you mean?"

"Did you read the report on the flight to Canada?"

Thomson looked vague.

"No, I *thought* not. Read it and you'll see why you can't rely on his judgment. The man's *totally* reckless!"

"They tested the ship yesterday," Thomson said.

"For sixteen hours? Sixteen hours!—before going off on a ten thousand mile voyage. That's insane!"

They stopped speaking and stared at each other. Thomson's jaw was set, his face grim, his eyes like lead bullets.

Brancker spoke softly now, coaxing. "CB, people confide in me— tell me things they're afraid to tell you."

"This is Irwin!"

"As a matter of fact, I did speak to Irwin, amongst others. Irwin is an excellent skipper and a very fine man with an *impeccable* record."

"He's a *whiner* and a *complainer*. He's spread dissatisfaction and discord throughout the ranks. *He's the one responsible for the breakdown in* morale."

"I know you're angry. All this doesn't change the fact that the ship is untested. You must think about postponing this voyage."

"I will not even *consider* it. We'd become the laughing stock. I've announced this ship will leave on her maiden voyage to India on October 4th —and leave we shall!"

"That doesn't make it a reason to leave. Just because you've announced it—you can *un-announce* it! You also announced to the world the ship would be adequately tested. Face the fact—the ship is unfit until it is given a clean bill of health by its captain."

Thomson leaned over his desk on the palms of his hands.

"Listen to me, Brancker. I know what's been going on. If you don't want to go, or you lack the courage, then don't. Show the white feather! There're many others who will jump at the chance to go in your place."

"I will go, CB—and I'll tell you why," Brancker said evenly. "I encouraged people to fly on this airship—people like O'Neill and Palstra— believing it'd be built and tested properly. I believed all your rhetoric about 'safety first.' I didn't think you'd use this airship for your own personal aggrandizement, for your own personal agenda, set to meet your own personal schedule. People like O'Neill put their faith in me and my word. I will *not* abandon them now."

Thomson sat down and resumed his scribbling. Brancker turned and left, silently closing the door behind him. But Brancker had shaken him.

81

A DAMNED GOOD BOLLOCKING

Friday October 3, 1930.

The next day, at 7:50 a.m., Irwin found himself waiting in the reception area of Thomson's outer office. He sat with a fixed stare, his dark uniform accentuating his pale, drawn face. Thomson marched in at 7:59 a.m. and swept past Irwin, into his office.

"You and I need to have words," he growled as he went by.

Irwin got up and followed. He stood before Thomson.

"You've become something of a liability, Irwin."

"I don't know what you mean, sir."

"You're insubordinate—getting way above your station."

Thomson sank into his chair, glowering.

"I'm not sure—"

"You've been speaking to Sir Sefton Brancker—the *Director* of Civil Aviation!"

"Sir, I only—"

"You're a man with no confidence in what he's doing," Thomson sneered.

"Sir, I'm responsible for my crew and my—"

"I don't need a lecture from you about your responsibilities, Irwin. Keep your mouth shut and listen. Everyone who comes in contact with you leaves with a bad case of melancholia!"

"Sir, that's not—"

"You've spread malicious rumors about *Cardington R101*. You've attempted to sabotage the inspection procedure, delay the Howden ship's voyage to Montreal, and thus put off your own flight to India. Well, you haven't succeeded. All you've done is cause a breakdown in discipline and morale. You think I don't understand what's been going on? If you lack the courage to fly this airship—*resign!* I don't believe you've got the guts— that's the crux of the problem."

"Sir—"

"An inquiry is underway regarding the brawling and drunkenness caused by the general breakdown in discipline—which may result in a court-martial. And *you* might be next for insubordination, insurrection, mutiny and cowardice!"

Irwin's eyes opened wide in horror and his jaw dropped.

"What—"

"If this flight to India isn't a success, there'll be no more funding for airship development—none will be asked for! That'll be the end of it. Do you get that?"

"Yes, sir."

"You've never understood, Irwin. There are careers to be made. Honors to be won."

"I do understand, sir. But for me, my crew and my ship always come first."

"*Wrong*! Your country comes first. This whole country's honor is at stake. …If that means anything to *you!* …"

Thomson let that barb sink in.

"Yes, it does sir."

"Get a grip on yourself. Do your duty. You're dismissed."

Irwin marched stiffly from Thomson's office to drive back to Cardington. He appeared to be in a state of shock.

82

FIXING SCOTT

Friday October 3, 1930.

That morning, Lou got word that Colmore would like to meet with
him. Lou was at the tower checking on the ship's preparations with
Atherstone and Steff. He went straight to Cardington House on his
motorbike. He was a little surprised to see an RAF man on guard at the door.
The pretty, blonde receptionist smiled at him and told him Wing Cmdr.
Colmore was expecting him. Lou proceeded to his office, where Colmore
was in conference with Scott. The partition between Colmore's room and the
secretary's didn't reach the ceiling. He could hear voices. Doris, put her
finger to her lips and gestured for Lou to sit. They listened.

"I want to make this perfectly clear. Your role will be limited,"
Colmore said.

"To nothing in particular, I suppose," Scott answered.

"*Irwin* will be in control as the commander. You'll be a passenger."

"I seem to be the one who always gets blamed."

"You'll have no significant role—symbolic only—that of Executive
Admiral, pertaining to route and the time of departure. I hope you understand
that, Scottie?"

"Executive Admiral! Is that supposed to make me feel good? A
meaningless title!"

Lou and Doris exchanged glances.

"I was the first man in the world to fly the Atlantic and land on
American soil—and return—as pilot in command! I was awarded the Air
Force Cross."

"Yes, yes, Scottie—and it was well-deserved."

"Alcock and Brown did it the easy way, a month earlier, *from* Canada
and landed nose first in an Irish bog. One way! And *they* got knighted for
that!"

"Yes, there was no justice."

"No justice! You got *that* right."

"Scottie, my dear fellow, we'll give Thomson what he wants. He can
impress his girlfriend. He'll be set for life. And so will *we!*"

"Yes, yes—"

"He's promising the world, so you never know …keep the faith. Oh, and yes, one other thing—no uniform."

"What do you mean, *no uniform?*"

"You're *not* to wear your uniform under *any* circumstances. You'll be a civilian on this flight, just like me."

"Look, the mishap on the Canada flight was just bad luck—"

"Yes, yes, Scottie, leave everything to Irwin. *He's* the commander, not you."

They heard Scott's chair scrape the floor as he got up.

"I want to tell you—I don't like what you're doing. You told the Secretary of State the fitness of the ship was up to *me*—whether the flight testing could be shortened, or waived. You put those decisions on *me*. Now you're telling me I don't have a role. So, I'll be the scapegoat when things go wrong. No, sir. If Irwin's in command, you should have made those decisions *his*. But you didn't. You made them *mine!*"

There was a long silence until Scott came rushing through the outer office and went storming off down the corridor. Doris glanced at Lou and raised her eyebrows.

"Not a happy camper," she said.

"Commander Remington's here," Doris called.

Colmore came and stood in the doorway. He appeared bashful, realizing Lou had heard everything. Colmore glanced at Doris. "Do you mind organizing some tea for us, Doris?" he said. She got up and went out, closing the outer door, realizing he wanted privacy.

"Lou, thanks for popping over. I have a favor to ask you in a minute, but first, I wanted to say, you don't have to make this voyage, you know."

"Yes, I know—but I'm committed."

"Are you *sure?*"

"Yes, of course, sir."

"How do you feel about the ship now?"

"From what I can tell, they've done a good job, but I would've preferred it if they'd completed the tests as laid down by Captain Irwin," Lou answered. "It would make more sense."

Colmore ignored this. He leaned forward earnestly and lowered his voice.

"How are things with you, Lou? At home, I mean?"

"Not particularly good, sir."

"Not giving up?" Colmore asked.

"No, of course not."

"You don't have a death wish or anything like that?"

Lou laughed. "No, no."

Who knows, perhaps I do.

Lou realized the implication of Colmore's question.

"Sir, will you please think about what I just said about testing?"

It was as if Colmore hadn't heard. "Was the guard at the door when you came in?"

"Yes. Never seen that before, sir."

"We've had the pilot's wife here again. Wants to meet with me."

"Mrs. Hinchliffe?"

"She's trying to get the flight stopped."

"So, you're not going to meet her?"

"Lord no, I've got enough problems."

Lou nodded, understanding; she'd probably push him over the edge again.

"Lou, you'll probably be in command of your own ship soon. I think you should stick around here with me tomorrow—it'll be good experience. Come in early and we'll check the weather and make the final decisions." Colmore paused and looked at Lou, his eyes skittish. "I was told by Thomson to stand down the third watch so we can carry a full load of fuel."

"Why?"

"He doesn't want us refueling in Egypt. I've asked the new AMSR to appeal the decision. If Thomson won't budge, we'll stand them down tomorrow."

Lou didn't comment, but thought the situation totally ridiculous.

"You mentioned a favor?"

"Oh, yes. Would you mind taking a van over to Lord Thomson's flat in Westminster tomorrow afternoon with a couple of your best men?"

"Sure. What does he need?"

"He's got a carpet he wants picking up, and his luggage."

"Sounds heavy."

Colmore winced, putting his hand to his temple, as though this hadn't occurred to him. "Dear God," he said.

"I guess we'll find out, won't we," Lou answered. Things were becoming more absurd by the hour.

"Sorry, but I don't want to send them unsupervised in case they muck it up—you know how he is," Colmore said.

"Fine. I'll take Binks and Church."

"Thanks, Lou. That's another load off my mind."

The phone on Colmore's desk rang and he picked it up. Lou heard Knoxwood at the other end. "Weggie, it's Wupert ..."

Colmore listened and turned deadly serious.

"Yes, I'll let them know ...forty minutes ...Right. I'll make sure they're standing by and ready to go ...Goodbye." Colmore put the phone down.

"That was Rupert Knoxwood. Thomson is sending his chauffeur. He wants to see you, Richmond and Scott. He'll pick you up then bring you back. He said it's going to be a very short meeting."

"What the heck about, sir?" Lou asked.

"Blowed if I know. It's weird. Sounds to me like he's got the wind up —but that wouldn't make sense—all I know is, Irwin looked dreadful when he came back from seeing him earlier."

Lou already knew that to be true. Perhaps they were going to get an ass-kicking, too.

The driver appeared on time and the three men were whisked off to Gwydyr House where Thomson was waiting for them. Knoxwood hustled them straight into Thomson's office without delay. Each of them glanced at the painting of the Taj Mahal as they filed in. They understood its significance, and that of its airship, at this moment.

"Ah, gentlemen, I apologize, but I felt it important to lay a few things to rest."

"Will you need me to take minutes, sir?"

"No, no, Rupert, no need. This is just an informal chat, thanks anyway."

Knoxwood went out and closed the door. Lou, Scott and Richmond made furtive glances at Thomson wondering what was coming. Thomson graciously ushered them to the easy chairs arranged around the fireplace where an electric fire glowed in the grate. He went to the sideboard. He was at his most benign.

"Scottie, my dear chap, what'll it be? Gin, whisky …? I thought we ought to have a little drink and a talk."

"Er, make it a whisky, straight, sir, thank you," Scott said, unable to hide his relief.

Lou watched Thomson reach for a bottle of Macallan.

Nothing but the best. Must be a special occasion.

Thomson began pouring. "And you, Richmond and Remington, what'll it be?"

They asked for the same to keep it simple. Thomson poured three more out and handed them out. He took his own and held it up.

"Your very good health, gentlemen."

"Yes, sir, good health," they all said.

Lou took a sip.

Very nice—as good as Granddad's—the man from Moray!

Thomson sat down. "I didn't get you down here to discuss the pros and cons of *Cardington R101*. All I want to know is this: Are you fellows comfortable and confident we can make this voyage without undue risk? I want the unvarnished truth. I thought it only right and proper you should be given the opportunity to let your feelings be known. I've been hearing all sorts of scuttlebutt and I want to get it all cleared up and out in the open." Thomson looked from Richmond to Scott. "After all, you, Richmond, have been responsible for its design and you, Scott, are in charge of flying operations …"

Scott and Richmond sat looking at Thomson with stony faces. Not sure what to make of it all. They'd had the jitters on the way down. Lou sat there astonished. Surely Thomson wasn't going to let them call it off? He'd soon get his answer.

Thomson went on. "I want you to both reassure me that this airship is capable of flying to India and back. I want to know you both have full confidence. And you, Remington, I brought you here as a highly experienced airshipman—I thought it worth hearing what you had to say about it all as you are, in way, an unbiased outsider—a *trusted* one, I might add."

Richmond put his drink down and was about to speak, but Thomson continued.

"We must all understand what's at stake: the country's honor. *Cardington R01* has become something of a symbol of the British Empire itself. Naturally, I want this voyage to be a rip-roaring success. It's absolutely imperative. The world is watching. Also, I should mention that the rewards will be huge for everybody. ...What were you going to say Richmond?"

Richmond sat up primly. "I was going to say that I believe the airship is now in tip-top condition ... or, well almost. We've had our problems, now with the extra bay and all the padding ..." Thomson waved his hand. He didn't want to hear about all that. "I think this journey can be accomplished quite safely, sir," he said.

"So you have *absolute* confidence?"

"Yes, sir, I do."

Thomson turned his gaze to Scott. "What about *you*, Scott? Do you feel the same way? Please understand, I'm not trying to put you chaps on the spot."

Scott boosted himself with another slug, draining his glass. "I do sir, yes. I see no reason to feel anything but confident now. We just ran her around the countryside for sixteen hours and she performed magnificently."

"What about the rest of Irwin's tests? Do you feel we're running any risks here? You know we're talking about people's lives and I feel very much responsible?"

"Oh, I think she got through a lot of tests last year and we took care of all the issues. I don't think we've got anything to worry about, not really, sir," Scott said. "And look at it this way: the Howden ship made it to Montreal and back without too much fuss in their bare-bones machine. I'm sure we can do the India run without a problem in *R101*."

That made Lou smile. He was unimpressed with this whole performance. Did Thomson think he was going to reinforce all their statements? Thomson got up and refilled Scott's glass and handed it to him.

"Now, what about you, Commander? I value your opinion."

"My feeling is this ..." Lou paused for some moments, moistening and licking his lips. "You're right, I *am* an outsider. And I see things from a much different perspective."

Their eyes were riveted on him.

"I don't share your urgency to get this voyage accomplished. I see the risks as being too great—for your long-term goal. I'd urge you to slow down and carry out the full schedule of tests Captain Irwin has proposed. With so much riding on this voyage, I think you have far more to lose than to gain. You're maximizing the risk of failure by *not* doing them. You're putting all your chips on black, Lord Thomson."

Richmond and Scott were stunned and extremely irritated. Thomson showed no emotion, keeping his eyes in a fixed stare at Lou.

"I see… That's one way of looking at it, I suppose," he said. "Now, here I have you disagreeing with my two most senior men."

"I'm sorry, sir, you asked me and I gave you the *unvarnished* truth, the way I see it." Thomson turned away to Richmond. "Can I get you another, Richmond?"

"Oh, no, sir, I don't usually imbibe during the day, thank you."

Thomson stood up; their cue to leave. "Well gentlemen, this has been useful. I'll think on what you've said." He turned to Lou. "Commander, you are under no obligation to make this journey, you know. If you're uncomfortable …"

"Sir, I'm committed to the ship, to the crew and to our captain."

Thomson put his hand on Lou's shoulder. "Admirable, sir! Admirable! First class attitude, if I may say so."

They left Thomson's office and made the silent journey back to Cardington in just over an hour. Thomson sat back down in his easy chair and contemplated the situation. The young commander might be right. His two yes-men had said what he wanted to hear. He derived no comfort from their words. Lou's only worried him further.

… *But he's young.*

83

CELEBRATION & FAREWELL AT THE KINGS ARMS

Friday October 3, 1930.

A smoky haze hung over the excited crowd of well-wishers in The Kings Arms opposite the green, on Church Lane. The place was full of airship construction workers and crewmen with their families and girlfriends. Their frenzied chatter over the honky-tonk was deafening to any sober person, of which there were few. Lou entered around 9 o'clock and fought his way to the bar where Potter, Billy, Cameron, Binks, Disley, Church and Irene were tightly gathered. Among the crowd, Lou noticed a lot of faces he'd never seen before.

Probably press and spectators.

He was surprised to see the piano player was George Hunter from the *Daily Express.* Hunter gave him a wink. He was one hell of a pianist, presently knocking out "Putting on the Ritz." Church and Irene looked especially happy, with goofy grins on their faces.

"What are you two looking so pleased about?" Lou shouted.

Irene shyly buried her head in Church's shoulder and then held her left hand up in the air displaying a tiny diamond ring.

"Irene and me are getting married as soon as I get back!" Church proclaimed.

The room erupted into cheers and applause. "This calls for a drink," Lou said. He ordered another round and a bottle of champagne. The barman poured the champagne and they raised their glasses.

"You're a lucky man!" Cameron shouted. He looked down in the dumps. The incident with Rosie and Jessup on the ship had been the last straw. His marriage was over.

"Here's to you both," Lou said.

Three girls in the bar had their eyes on Lou, including the busty blonde from the Cardington House reception desk. They knew he was a free agent and on the market, or hoped he was. He smiled pleasantly at them, but kept his distance. Then he noticed Mrs. Hinchliffe loitering next to Hunter at the piano. She glanced over at him and he suspected she wanted to talk. He wasn't in the mood. Life was much too complicated as it was.

Hunter broke into "I'm Sittin' On Top of the World" and everybody sang at the top of their lungs—everybody except Lou and Cameron. Lou glanced at the door and imagined Charlotte walking in—just like that—kissing him on the lips and telling him how much she loved him, and asking him not to go, and he would say, 'Okay honey, I'll quit right now.' Even Colmore would understand …But Charlotte *didn't* walk in.

After half an hour of trying his best to look happy, Lou decided he needed some air. He walked out the door as Hunter was transitioning seamlessly into "Blue Skies." On his way through the smoky haze, he nodded politely to the three girls who gave him yearning glances. He left the pub and walked across the cobblestone road onto the damp, grassy field toward the fairground.

The sound of the out-of-tune honky-tonk drifted through the mist behind him with sounds of laughter, singing and chinking glasses. Soon, the carousel drowned out the pub sounds, reminding him of Freddie and the clown's head. He stood for a few minutes staring at the ominous shape riding at the tower bathed in searchlights. He heard rustling footsteps behind him in the grass and then a woman's voice.

"Do you think she's beautiful?"

Lou turned around. *Mrs. Hinchliffe* was beautiful. She had long, blond hair and deep blue eyes. She reminded him of Julia. There was something about her face he could only describe as spiritual. She was around his own age and as tall as Charlotte.

"No, I wouldn't call *that* beautiful," he said.

"*My* husband flew away, too."

She paused and stared sadly into the night sky, as if remembering the last time she'd seen him. "Every day since then I've wished I'd stopped him." She closed her eyes, reliving the awful pain. "Oh, how I've wished it!" she said.

Lou felt her regret. "Do you really think you could have?"

"That's a good question." She stopped to consider. "I think so." She paused again. "But I didn't even try." Lou sensed her self-blame. "He was so confident and to me, he was invincible."

"Now you warn others?"

She glanced down at his hand.

"Yes. I see you're not wearing a wedding ring. Aren't you married?" she asked.

He automatically raised his hand and looked at his ring finger. It came as a shock to see his ring missing. "Technically, I suppose I am."

"Then give this up for her sake."

"I would, but it's too late."

"I'm sorry."

"I met you and your husband just before he left," Lou said.

"Yes, I remember you. We were all right here in this pub."

"It must be tough for you to set foot in the place," Lou said.

"He wants the Airship Program stopped," she said.

"Your husband, you mean?"

"You must think I'm crazy?"

"I'm not sure what to think."

"Take it from me. I'm not crazy," she said.

God, what grief does to people!

"Mrs. Hinchliffe, I must go. I have a busy day ahead."

"I suppose I'm wasting my time?"

"I don't think you've a snowball's chance in hell of stopping that thing taking off tomorrow."

She took his hand to shake it and then clasped it with the other.

"I'll be here to see you all leave," she said, looking into his eyes.

"Goodbye, Mrs. Hinchliffe."

Lou sensed, like him, she was a lost and lonely soul. He put his arms around her and they hugged. She put her lips to his.

"Are you going back to the pub?" she asked.

"No, I think I'll call it a day.

She kissed him again, her lips soft and wet.

"Come with me," she said, her voice an urgent whisper.

"You want to save me from all this, huh?"

"Yes, I do."

"Perhaps we'll meet again, Mrs. Hinchliffe," he said.

"Yes, I hope so. Good luck, and may God be with you … And next time we meet, please call me Millie."

"So, you're confident I'll make it back?" Lou asked, with an amused grin.

"I don't know, but I pray you do, Commander," she said.

Lou nodded. "Okay, Millie."

He left her and walked across the field toward the fairground. The music and laughter grew louder, the lights more dazzling. Hundreds were milling around, enjoying the fun of the fair.

Minutes later, Lou reached the gypsy's tent. The old woman was standing outside. "I've bin waitin' for you, my lucky lad."

"To tell me my fortune, right?"

"Cross me palm with silver and I might give yer something."

He followed her into the tent, breathing in the familiar, musty smell of damp hay. Being dark this time, the place seemed more ominous. Flickering candles lent a sinister atmosphere. He laid a silver half-a-crown on the table. She stuffed it in her apron and gazed at him intently.

"I see you've used up more lives." She chuckled wickedly. "You might have one left. I ain't sure."

Lou's mind flashed to *Howden R100's* two mishaps over the St. Lawrence. His brush with the Klan. Did that count? And then Cameron nearly put them all in the drink on the way home. That was close. The old crone's crackly voice brought him back.

"She left yer, didn't she? The woman you brought to me last year. Your wife, wasn't it? Longing for a baby she was. I don't see 'er around you anymore. She had things she couldn't share. There was much troubling her—another victim of war—she was a very brave girl, that one. It all just got too much for 'er."

Lou had no idea what the woman was babbling about and though it sounded curious, he didn't answer. He really didn't want to know.

Yes, and probably you had a lot to do with it, dammit!

"But I do see another woman who patiently waits. I see her in your family." Her eyes opened wide as if looking at a portrait held up to her. "Another beautiful woman! My, oh my, you do attract the lovelies, doncha!"

Lou knew exactly who she was talking about. Still, he kept his mouth shut.

"You're wonderin' about this journey. Well, you will go, sunshine. And you deserve what you get! But just know this: The impatient one you all follow blindly is ruled by fire. He's surrounded by it. Always has been. So beware! Those who don't heed my advice, do so at their peril. Curses shall be 'eaped upon 'em!"

Lou stared into the gypsy's penetrating, watery eyes. In the flickering supernatural light, they appeared luminous green, flecked with red. He felt energy radiating from that old body into his like an electrical current. He became paralyzed, sensing her strange and powerful force, not sure if she was good or evil, or neither.

"Now, there's one who seeks to do you harm," she went on.

Lou realized she must be talking about Jessup, but then she looked away into a dark corner and dismissed that image with a flick of her bony fingers and a sneer.

"A message of ill and one of truth—these two shall be conveyed. At the end of the day, that's what this saga's about." Suddenly, her head slumped with her eyes closed. She was spent. She sat motionless for a few moments and then opened her eyes as though from a deep sleep. She seemed surprised. "Oh, you're still 'ere. Did you get what you wanted?"

Lou smiled. "Yes and no. You talk in riddles, lady."

"Have an interesting trip—might be good for yer soul," she said, getting to her feet with a sly grin.

At 10 o'clock, Thomson and MacDonald emerged from MacDonald's study on the second floor at No.10, having gone over the agenda for the Imperial Conference of Dominion Prime Ministers, scheduled to begin later that month. They stood on the wide landing overlooking the grand staircase. MacDonald put his hand on Thomson's arm, his eyes intense.

"Forgo this trip. I need your wise council for this conference. Do this for me, CB."

"Are you *ordering* me not to go, sir?"

"No, I'm asking you as my dearest friend."

They held each other's forearms and Thomson looked into the Prime Minister's face. "How can I not go? I'm committed. And besides, the troops are expecting me. I need to rally them." Thomson moved to the top of the stairs. "Don't worry. I'll be back for the conference—have I ever let you down, Ramsay?"

MacDonald's eyes, moist earlier, now glistened. Thomson saw this before he started down the stairs. When he got to the bottom, he stared up at MacDonald and waved. Thomson crossed the black and white checkered floor, stopping at the door.

"Farewell, my good friend," MacDonald called down.

Thomson's voice echoed up the stairway. "Don't look so glum, my dear chap. Don't you remember? Our fate is already written."

MacDonald stood hunched like a man watching his brother going off to war. He wiped his eyes with a handkerchief. "Yes, I do," he whispered. "Yes, I do."

"Ramsay, if the worst should happen, it would soon be over."

As Thomson left, the door slammed behind him, the sound echoing around the great hall like thunder.

Thomson left Downing Street and crossed Whitehall to Gwydyr House. He passed the nightwatchman, giving him a curt nod. His office was in darkness. He switched on the picture light over the huge oil painting of the Taj Mahal and sat down, staring at the airship he'd had superimposed upon it by Winston Churchill. He hoped for some sort of divine affirmation. But he got none. He got up and went to the window and peered out over the river, faintly glimmering under the dim street lamps. The bitter taste and the feeling he had was something akin to buyer's remorse. Brancker's words continued their stinging assault:

I will go CB—and I'll tell you why. I encouraged people to fly in this airship—people like O'Neill and Palstra—believing it'd be built and tested properly. I believed all your rhetoric about 'safety first.' I didn't think you'd use this airship for your own personal aggrandizement, for your own personal agenda, with everything set to meet your own personal schedule. People like O'Neill put their faith in me and my word. I will not abandon them now.

Then he heard the young American's voice like an echo, depressing him further.

You're putting all your chips on black, Lord Thomson... You're putting all your chips on black...

Then to cap it all, Wallis's words from six years ago gave him a jolt.

You're planning to build airships by committee?

What if all these people were right? Did they have justification for being nervous? Were there indeed things he didn't know? Was he pushing them too hard?

He tightened the knot in his tie.

Come, come man—it's your destiny! No, I mustn't fall victim to negativity. Stay positive ... But ... no reason not to be cautious.

He went back to his desk and sat down again, opened the drawer and took out his address book. He picked up the phone and dialed the number. Knoxwood answered.

"Ah, Rupert, I'm so glad you're home. I want you to do something for me. Call Colmore immediately and tell him I've reconsidered. He *may* refuel in Egypt, but only after the banquet. If it delays taking off the next day, so be it. Tell him to stand the third watch down anyway—that'll be a double saving in weight."

Thomson replaced the phone and sat back for a moment. He pulled the drawer open, revealing Marthe's photograph. He stared at it wistfully. What was she doing? Was she with anyone? Were any of those damned American professors still hanging around? Had she got shot of them? He hoped so. He pulled out a sheet of paper and placed it on his blotter. He stared at it for a few moments then wrote forcefully in the shadows from the picture light behind him.

Air Ministry
Gwydyr House, White Hall, London.

Last Will and Testament

On this Friday, Third Day of October, Nineteen Hundred and Thirty, I declare that in the event of my death during my return voyage to India aboard HMA Cardington R101, I leave all my worldly goods and possessions to my brother Colonel R. Thomson, currently residing in Widdington, Essex.

Christopher Birdwood Thomson,
Brigadier General Lord Thomson of Cardington,
Secretary of State for Air.

After signing his will, Thomson thrust it into an envelope and put it in the top drawer. Knoxwood would find it and know exactly what to do, if required.

84

GO BREAK A LEG

Saturday October 4, 1930.

Lou woke with Fluffy beside him. He missed Charlotte most just before he closed his eyes and again when he first opened them at dawn. The bed was empty and, at times like this, he wondered what the hell he was doing in this place. The thought of flying to India no longer excited him and feelings of futility haunted him. He grieved for her. Soon, he'd be grieving for his father. He'd get this voyage over with and return to the States, immediately.

He'd enjoyed having Norway around, but he'd gone back up north. He rolled over and switched on the bedside lamp. His kitbag, already packed, lay on the floor. Mrs. Jones had helped him and Billy get their clothes ready.

While he boiled the kettle, he heard the letter box snap and the newspaper hit the mat upstairs. After pouring himself a cup of tea, he sat down and opened the *Daily Mirror*. Under a photograph of *Cardington R101* at the mast, the headline read:

GIANT AIRSHIP'S MAIDEN VOYAGE

The newspaper was full of praise for *Cardington R101*—previous negative stories forgotten. This was a great moment in British aviation history and the press was not about to spoil things. A knock came at the front door. Mrs. Jones appeared with her shopping bag.

"I've come to cook breakfast for you lads," she said, pushing her way down to the kitchen. "Can't have you boys going off to India on an empty stomach."

Lou poured a mug of tea and took it up to Billy, who had a thick head. The smell of eggs and bacon permeated the house. When they'd finished, Mr. Jones arrived to wish them well. Time was getting short. They hurriedly put on their uniforms and said their goodbyes, leaving Mrs. Jones to clean up. Before leaving, Lou picked Fluffy up and kissed her nose. Mrs. Jones would take good care of her.

They grabbed their kitbags and, after wiping off the wet saddle, set off on the motorbike in the rain at speed. As they approached the junction at the parade of shops, a painter's van, laden with ladders, turned out in front of them. There was nothing Lou could do. The bike skidded and they rammed the side of the van. The riders sailed over the hood and landed in the middle of the road. The van driver, realizing his error, swerved to the right, causing the vehicle to flip over and its doors to burst open. Paint and ladders were scattered everywhere. Lou came down on his left side, not badly hurt, except for a few bruises and a grazed hand. Billy lay groaning, his right leg bent at a sickening angle. Hearing the crash, corner store owner, Alan Rowe, rushed out. He recognized them and knelt down beside Billy.

"Well, *you* won't be going anywhere, sunshine. It's Bedford Hospital for you."

After checking on Billy, Lou went to see the driver of the truck, a middle-aged man in painter's whites. He sat on the curb holding his head, rambling incoherently—perhaps he had a concussion. Lou inspected the motorbike. The front tire was blown out, the headlight broken. He suspected the forks were twisted. He removed the kitbags from the carrier and put Billy's under his head and sat down beside him.

"Rotten luck, Billy," he said, holding the boy's arm.

"Damn, Lou, I was looking forward to going," Billy said. He winced in pain and then threw up.

So much for Mrs. Jones' breakfast.

"I'll have to go, but I'll call your mom and tell her what's happened."

"What about the bike?" Billy asked.

"I'll put it behind the shop," Alan said. "I'll take care of it 'til you get back, don't worry."

He got up and wheeled the motorbike down the alley. Lou stayed with Billy until the ambulance arrived. He watched them load Billy onto a stretcher and put him inside the ambulance with the painter. Before they closed the doors, Billy held up his hand.

"Lou, Jessup's out to get you. Everyone knows it."

"I'll be fine, Billy. I'll send word to Mrs. Jones and Irene. They'll come up and make sure you're okay."

"I wanted to be around to guard your back. He's been bragging all week—he's gonna kill you."

"You don't need to worry, Billy. His crew's gonna be stood down—but keep that to yourself—okay!"

"Good," Billy said.

He laid his head down thankfully as the ambulance doors were closed. Lou stood on the curb until Billy had gone before walking to the bus stop. He felt a twinge in his guts. Was this the 'Wiggy thing' all over again? He went and stood behind four waiting crewmen. Lou nodded and smiled at them. Pretty soon, a green bus arrived with the same cheery bus conductor Lou had come to know.

"Hell, you must live on this bus, Luke!" Lou said.

"I do indeed, sir, and I know where *you're* going."

The bus rattled and groaned its way along the country lane in the drizzle to the next stop, where more men in uniform were standing in line. Sam Church was among those waiting, with Irene, his mother and father, Joe Binks and Fred McWade. The men carried pith helmets and small bags. The bus conductor rang the bell after they boarded.

"Next stop, Cardington Gate, then Cardington Tower, then Ismailia," he said. He went around taking fares, stopping beside Binks. "Hello Joe, where you off to—the Kings Arms is it? Bit early for a pint, isn't it, mate?"

"No, I'm off to India with this lot."

"I know you are, lad—otherwise I'd need another penny," he said, and then with a grin, "Just don't pith in your helmet that's all!"

Lou glanced at McWade, who turned away with a scowl. He had the look of a condemned man. Lou had seen a few of *them* lately. The bus drew up to Cardington Gate and a crowd got off.

"This is it, ladies and gents—'ave a lovely time," the conductor shouted.

As they walked toward the gatehouse, Irene turned to Lou. "We're seein' Sam off in case we don't see him later. We'll be back this evening."

Church grabbed Irene and gave her a passionate kiss and the crewmen walking by clapped and cheered. Lou laughed. Even McWade cracked a smile. Lou glanced over at Binks and Church.

"We're going on a mission this afternoon. I'll tell you about it later," he said. He looked at Irene, "Irene, Billy and I just had an accident on the bike."

Her face fell. "Are you all right?"

"*I* am, but Billy's broken his leg. Could you tell my neighbor, Mrs. Jones, what's happened and ask her to go and see him in hospital?"

Everyone listened, shocked.

"We'll go straight up there, won't we, Mum?" Irene said. "Poor Billy."

"*Lucky* Billy, if you ask me," McWade mumbled.

When they arrived at the gate, the gatekeeper called to McWade.

"Got a message for you, Fred. Wing Commander Colmore wants a word."

"*Now* what?" McWade groused.

"I'll walk up with you," Lou said.

Two cars entered the gate. The first contained Capt. Irwin in his Austin Seven, his face deathly white, and behind him, Scott in his Morris Oxford, in full dress uniform. Lou wasn't surprised, especially after yesterday's meeting with Thomson. When Lou and McWade got to Cardington House, Scott and Irwin had already gone inside. An RAF man was still posted on the door. Lou and McWade went in and made their way to Colmore's office.

"Ah, Fred, do come in," Colmore said. "Come in, Lou. Bad news I'm afraid, Fred. I'm standing you down. We have to cut down on weight."

McWade appeared insulted at first, then visibly relieved.

"Standing me down? It's no disappointment to me, I can tell you that. Standing me down, indeed! Saving weight! I think you need to stand the whole bloody lot down!"

"Yes, Fred. Thank you," Colmore said, in his gracious manner.

"And I'll tell you something. If left to me, they'd *never* have got that Permit to Fly!" McWade left the room and went down the corridor muttering to himself. "Standing me down! Saving weight! I've never heard such nonsense in all my life. ..."

"I do love old Fred," Colmore said. "Hey, what've you done to your hand?"

"Had an accident on the way here. That's why I was late—sorry."

"Anybody hurt?"

"My passenger broke his leg."

"Who was that?"

"Billy Bunyan."

"He was in the crew?"

"Yes," Lou answered.

"Better inform Sky Hunt."

85

THE THIRD WATCH

Saturday October 4, 1930.

Lou and Colmore headed down the corridor in the north wing to the office of Giblett, the meteorologist on this flight also. Irwin, Johnston and Scott were already there, talking with him. Lou watched Colmore for his reaction to Scott showing up in uniform. Colmore did a second take, but said nothing.

Maybe he'll talk to him later.

Lou peered out of the window into the gardens. The wind was picking up. Giblett had chalked up weather graphics on a blackboard on the wall. Next to that, he'd pinned up a map of Europe and Asia. This showed the route Johnston had marked in black, dotted lines, from Cardington to London, over Kent to the town of Hastings, across the Channel, north of Paris, west of the Rhone Valley, Toulouse, then over the sea at Narbonne, along the Mediterranean to Ismailia, Egypt.

"How are things looking, Mr. Giblett?" Colmore asked.

They gathered around the map. "Right here, in the Newcastle area, there's a shallow depression moving into the North Sea and over here an associated cold front moving east, across France. I'd say, at present, things are looking pretty good," Giblett said.

"Okay, I'll report this to Lord Thomson's personal secretary. What time are we casting off, gentlemen?" Colmore asked, eyeing Scott and Irwin.

Scott glanced at the time. "No later than nineteen hundred hours. You can tell him his Lordship should be here an hour prior to that."

Back in Colmore's office, Lou and Colmore sat behind closed doors. Colmore dialed Knoxwood's telephone number in Gwydyr House and put on the speakerphone.

"Rupert, Good morning to you—it's Reginald."

"Morning, Weggie—big day!"

"Yes. I have Commander Remington with me. We've just been to the met room and checked the forecast."

"How's it looking?"

"Pretty good, they think."

Colmore repeated what Giblett had told them.

"So, it's definitely on?" Knoxwood asked.

A sudden wind gust shook the windows and Colmore turned in surprise. "Yes. Unless anything unexpected occurs with the weather."

"What time shall I tell Lord Thomson to be at the tower?"

"We're scheduled to depart at 7 o'clock," Colmore said. "Tell him to be here an hour earlier."

"His lordship won't like to be kept waiting. I'll tell him 6:15."

"Just as you wish, Rupert."

"Have you arranged for a van to deal with the luggage?"

"Yes. Thank you for dealing with the fuel issue, Rupert. I feel much better about that situation."

"Think nothing of it, Weggie," Knoxwood said and hung up.

"I need to call Billy Bunyan's mother in Goole and tell her what's happened," Lou said.

"Perhaps she'll be relieved," Colmore said.

"Then, I'll get over to the ship, if you don't mind. I want to set myself up in a cabin and talk to the crewmen I'm taking to London with me," Lou said.

"Let's meet again in the met office at noon. We can have lunch in the officer's mess after that," Colmore said. Before Lou left, Colmore had Doris type a bulletin for him to post in the crew's locker room.

Lou went to his office and called the hospital in Goole.

"Fanny, it's Lou Remington."

Lou heard Fanny gasp. "Is Billy all right?"

"Billy's fine. We had a spill this morning on the bike and he broke his leg. He's in hospital."

"So, he's not going to India today, obviously?"

"No."

"Thank God for that! If you want to know the truth—I'm glad. I've been worried sick. What did Charlotte say about it?"

"She doesn't know yet," Lou answered. Technically, it wasn't a lie, but Fanny had told him what he had wanted to know—Charlotte hadn't contacted her, either. He needed to get off the phone before Fanny asked any more questions.

"Look, Fanny, I'm sorry. I have to go. Just wanted to let you know about Billy. Please don't worry. He's gonna be fine."

"Oh, er, how is Char—"

"Bye for now, Fanny. I'll call you when I get back from India."

"Yes, er, all right. Good luck, Lou—"

Lou hung up and sat thinking. He rested his chin in one hand and drummed his fingers on the desk. Charlotte hadn't contacted John and Mary, or Fanny, her closest friend. And Charlotte's parents wouldn't open the door.

She must have gone off with some other guy.

Ten minutes later, Lou picked up his kitbag and hopped on a bus from the main gate down to the tower gate and went into the customs shed for kitbag inspection. He put it on the table.

"Hello, sir. Let's see what you've got here, shall we?" the customs officer said, pulling everything out: a pair of work trousers, a pair of soft-soled shoes, four sets of clean underwear, four pairs of socks, three clean shirts, a bag of toiletries and a small, gold picture frame.

"It took me all morning to pack that bag!" Lou said.

"No lighters or matches, sir?"

"No, and no *parachutes*, either," Lou said with more sarcasm.

"Let's hope you won't be needing 'em, eh, sir."

Lou noticed Potter's accordion on the table behind the customs officer. "What's *that* doing there?" he asked.

The customs man shook his head. "Too heavy. They won't let him take it on board. All right, sir, this bag's cleared," he said, marking the bag with a chalk cross.

Lou went to the elevator at the foot of the tower, where Bert Mann, the operator, was supervising food and drink being loaded by a steward and galley boy. First, it had to be weighed, and then logged in by the R.A.W. chief storekeeper. The provisions included barrels of beer, cases of champagne and wine, an assortment of huge cheeses wrapped in cheesecloth and different types of biscuits in big tins.

"Won't keep you, sir," Mann said. "We're just getting the booze and grub aboard for the banquet. Hurry up, lads, make room for the commander."

"No, it's okay. I'll use the stairs," Lou said.

Lou eyed all this stuff. It looked heavy. Mann shut the concertina gates with a crash and Lou watched it travel up the tower before he started up the stairs. At the top, he found Scott standing with his hands on his hips, glaring with red eyes into the elevator.

"Just been doing the lift calculations with Captain Irwin. I need to lose four tons." He waved to the stewards. "Put this, this, and this on," he said, pointing at the beer, wine and champagne, "but take the tins and throw them out. It's all unnecessary weight. Put all these biscuits in paper bags."

Lou grinned.

This man's got his priorities right.

Leaving the biscuit tin dilemma in safe hands, he went on board and found Sky Hunt in the crew's mess giving instructions to the riggers about stowing materials and luggage. Lou took him aside and told him about Billy. He also mentioned Thomson had ordered the third watch stood down and that he'd be posting the bulletin in the crew's locker room. Hunt told him he'd meet him there, as some might make trouble.

Lou went to his assigned cabin. *Cardington R101* felt much different from the Howden ship. Odors of recently applied dope to the cover and overpowering diesel fumes combined with a strong smell of Axminster carpet to assault his nose. He'd miss Norway—but not pumping fuel by hand every few hours! This time, he'd brought a photo of his family taken at Remington's Farm. He stood it on the small table and smiled cynically to himself. It was the frame that used to hold the photo of him and Charlotte at the five bar gate.

'I no longer love you'—welcome home, pal!

He held up the frame for a closer look. Tom was smiling, Anna shading her eyes, Dad forcing a smile with his arm around Mom   more like *holding on* to Mom, he realized now. And then there was Gran, sweet and kind—*but don't mess with me!* Julia was smiling demurely, classy as always. And last, at the edge of the photo, Jeb with Alice and their two kids, a sad weariness in Jeb's eyes. Lou wondered if Jeb would forgive and forget. He replaced the frame on the table and returned to the tower where Scott was in conversation with a reporter.

"Ah, Lou, this is Major Robertson with *Flight Magazine*. He's an old friend of mine. Major, this is Commander Lou Remington. I brought Lou on board in 1924. He survived the *R38* crash," Scott said, slurring.

Robertson stuck out his hand. "Indeed. Yes, of course. Honored to meet you, Commander."

"We lost so many of our finest airship people on that ship. We were lucky to get him. He'll represent the United States on this trip. We also have others representing India and Australia."

"You don't say," Robertson said.

"I'm going to show the major over the ship. He's writing an article about us. Why don't you come, Lou?" Scott said.

"Sure thing, sir."

Scott led them around from bow to stern, through the passengers' quarters, the chartroom and then down into the control car. They stood at the windows studying the overcast sky. The ship rolled and shifted with the wind.

"I must say she's most impressive. Are you satisfied with her since the modifications?" Robertson asked.

"She's a very fine ship now and I'm sure it's going to be a marvelous flight," Scott answered.

"And what will your role be on this flight, exactly, Scottie?" Robertson asked.

"I'm *officer-in-charge* of the flight. That's why I'm in uniform, of course."

Lou glanced at Scott's hat, which sported 'R101' stitched in gold, set crookedly on his head. Lou couldn't believe what he was hearing.

"I decide such matters as time of departure, course, as well as speed and altitude. The captain will command the crew and maintain discipline—carrying out my orders, you understand."

Robertson shook hands with them. "Well, gentlemen, I wish you a safe flight and look forward to a full report. Thanks for showing me around."

"We'll meet again when we get back. We'll celebrate," Scott said, beaming confidently. Robertson glanced dubiously at Scott as he left.

Lou left the ship and went over to the locker rooms, where crewmen were awaiting orders. When they saw Lou they stampeded to the bulletin board and gathered around. He posted the notice. Someone at the back shouted. Lou wasn't sure who, but suspected it was Binks.

"Well, somebody read it out then!"

Lou took the bulletin down and faced them. "Okay, guys: 'A demonstration flight will commence today, the 4th of October 1930, at 1900 hours GMT with a return flight to Karachi, India via Ismailia, Egypt. Dress uniforms shall be worn at all times when embarking and disembarking and for all official functions on board. Riggers and engineers of first and second watches shall report for duty at 1300 hours today. Note: The third-watch crew has been stood down. Luggage is restricted to ten pounds per man.'"

Pandemonium broke out among third-watch crewmen, led by Jessup, with much shouting and slamming of locker doors. The disgruntled men were about to leave as Hunt entered. He leapt up onto a bench. Everyone stopped to listen. "Don't you go anywhere, Jessup. I'll be needing you tonight, my lad," he growled.

Jessup, his confidence shattered, sat down sullenly at the back of the locker room. Lou glanced at him. He'd need to watch his back tonight, after all. Hunt pointed at the third watch crewmen. "All right you lot, be on your way. The rest of you, listen up! You heard the commander. Go home and get packed, if you haven't already done so. Ten pounds is all you're allowed to carry. That amounts to a change of underwear and a toothbrush. Catch an hour's shut-eye—you're gonna need all the rest you can get."

Lou went over to Binks. "We're going to London. Where's Church? Ah, there he is. Church!" Church came over. "You're both coming with me. We're taking the Air Ministry van to London to pick up the Air Minister—"

"I'd 'ave thought he would've come in 'is limo—" Binks said.

"Let me finish, Joe, —to pick up the Air Minister's luggage. I'll come and find you on the ship. Gas up the van and bring it to the tower. We'll leave at 2 o'clock."

"Have we got to be in uniform, sir?" Church asked.

"Wear your work clothes."

Lou returned to the administration building, where he met Colmore in his office.

"I see Major Scott's in uniform, then sir," Lou said.

Colmore shook his head wearily. "Yes, I know. Silly damned fool!" But, of course, Lou knew Colmore had seen him earlier.

"He's just been telling Major Robertson he's in overall command of the ship."

Colmore shook his head. "He's just sounding off, I expect. I'll keep an eye on him. If I send him home to change, he won't come back."

"That might be a good thing, under the circumstances, sir, don't you think?" Lou said. Colmore didn't respond.

Lou realized just how reliant Colmore was on Scott, for all his faults; like a broken crutch. They headed to the meteorological office, where they met Atherstone. Giblott reported conditions had deteriorated somewhat. A low pressure trough was moving from western Ireland, bringing winds of ten to fifteen mph, and expected to increase up to thirty mph across northern France, accompanied by heavy rain.

After lunch, Lou and Colmore returned to Colmore's office. Remembering Colmore the night he boarded *Howden R100*, he seemed a different man.

"I must say, you look very well, sir."

"You mean compared to the Canada trip? Yes, Lou, I must tell you, I feel much better this time. I think if we could survive the St. Lawrence, we can survive anything—especially in *this* ship with all her improvements! And thank God Thomson relented on the refueling. I'm *fairly* confident everything's going to be all right."

"You seem to have convinced yourself. But look, there's still time to postpone this voyage, if you're not one hundred percent sure. Finish all the testing—do things right—stand up to him. You'll have Brancker and Irwin standing behind you, and the other officers, and me, of course."

Colmore considered for a moment and then shook his head sadly.

"It's just not possible, dear boy—besides standing up to Thomson and the Air Ministry, we'd be up against Scott and Richmond—both have their eyes set on knighthoods—and then there's the Treasury. I just have to have faith in the ship. We've addressed all the problems, after all—at least, I think we have."

Lou looked at him skeptically, knowing they sure as hell hadn't.

Colmore took out a piece of paper from his drawer and gave it to Lou.

"Here's Lord Thomson's address."

"Thank you. I have a map. It'll be no problem."

86

THE MAGIC CARPET

Saturday October 4, 1930.

Lou headed back to the tower to locate Binks and Church. Binks had gone to his engine car—No. 5. Lou made his way there and descended the ladder as Binks was pouring a drum of oil into the engine. All parts of the engine, its pipes and valves, gleamed.

"You're a thirsty girl, ain't you," Binks was saying.

Lou raised his eyebrows. "Talking to the engine now, are we, Joe?"

Binks turned, embarrassed. "Oh, sorry, sir, I didn't hear you comin.' I already put one drum of oil in and she still needs more." He was about to stop.

"Take it easy, Joe. Finish what you're doing. We've got plenty of time. Meet me by the van when you're done. Seen Church?"

"He's in the crew's quarters, having a fry up."

The crew's quarters was a mess hut at the foot of the tower, where crewmen could cook something to eat. Church was finishing a 'bacon sammy.' Seeing Lou enter, he got up and wiped the grease from his mouth with the back of his hand.

"Can I get you one, sir?" he said.

"I've just eaten, thanks. Ready?"

"Ready when you are, sir."

With Lou giving directions, they motored from Cardington through the country lanes to Shefford and then on through Henlow, Hitchen, Welwyn Garden and onto Potter's Bar.

"Have you decided on a wedding date, Sam?" Lou asked.

"Irene wants to get married at Christmas at St. Mary's," Church answered.

"That'll be a wonderful time."

"And you're invited, of course, sir."

"D'you remember what that old gypsy told yer, Sam?" Binks said.

Church choked. "Yeah, I remember."

"You didn't tell Irene, did you?" Binks asked.

"Nah, 'course not. I told her after this flight, I'm only gonna work in the shed. But this one voyage will 'elp pay for the weddin'—then that's it."

They continued south through Barnet, Whetstone, Swiss Cottage and past Lord's Cricket Ground.

"What about you, sir? Are you staying in England?" Binks asked.

Lou knew they must be wondering. They'd been upset when Charlotte cleared off.

"Not sure. My life's a bit up in the air."

"Nicely put," Church said.

"We all loved Charlotte, sir," Binks said, shaking his head sadly.

Lou didn't respond. He stared out the window wondering what she was doing. Was she thinking about him? Probably not. He reached for his map of London. They passed Regent's Park and drove down Portland Place toward Regent Street. At the end of Regent Street, they moved through Piccadilly down the Haymarket, passing His Majesty's Theater, and around Trafalgar Square.

"Take a good gander, guys. We might pass over this way tonight," Lou told them.

"I love London," Binks said.

They drove slowly down Whitehall, the mounted guardsmen in their red tunics at the Horse Guards Parade on their right. Church studied them in awe. "There's somethin' about this place ..." he said.

They passed Gwydyr House. "That's Lord Thomson's office in the Air Ministry Building," Lou said. They stared at the brick and stone mansion.

"Hey, there's Big Ben and the Houses of Parliament," Binks said, gleefully pointing at Westminster Palace.

"And here, in front, is Westminster Hall with Westminster Abbey across the street," Lou told them. "Okay, we're here. Turn here. This is Ashley Gardens."

At 3 o'clock precisely, they drew up outside Block No. 9 and parked the van just as Knoxwood arrived in Thomson's chauffeur-driven Daimler. The three men got out and went through the lobby, where Knoxwood joined them. Knoxwood motioned them to the birdcage elevator, with its black iron concertina gate and brass pull, just big enough to carry four.

They crammed themselves in. Lou felt uncomfortable and began to sweat. He closed his eyes. They traveled up the open, steel-framed elevator shaft to the third floor and found flat 122. The Great Caruso's voice was belting through the door from Thomson's gramophone. Knoxwood rang the bell. Thomson opened the door himself immediately, dressed ready for off: dark, pinstripe trousers, grey waistcoat, white dress shirt, wing collar, black and white-spotted tie. Gwen the housekeeper, Daisy the parlor maid and Buck the valet, hovered behind him. Lou sensed an atmosphere of excitement as they stepped inside. He felt sorry for the staff—Thomson must have run them ragged all day.

"Ah, here you are, gentlemen. Good day to you all," Thomson said grandly.

"Good afternoon, Lord Thomson. How are you, sir?" Knoxwood asked.

"I'm in superb shape! We'll need all hands. It's in the living room. Follow me."

Lou had never seen Thomson so exuberant. Knoxwood went first, followed by Lou and the two crewmen. The furniture had been pushed back against the walls to make room for Thomson's pile of belongings—cases, trunks, leather bags, bulky canvas bags, packing cases and cardboard boxes. Alongside the luggage, was a roll wrapped in brown paper, tied up with string. The ends were visible, showing part of its vivid red and black pattern and fringe. A dress sword sat atop the mountain.

Lou, Binks and Church stood motionless, unable to believe their eyes.

"My good Gawd!" Binks mumbled in a daze.

"And this must be the magic carpet, sir?" Lou said.

Thomson's magic carpet had become a legend around Cardington. Lou wasn't sure why.

"Yes indeed, *that's* my famous Persian rug—all the way from Sulaymaniyah. We'll lay it down for the banquets in Egypt and India."

Sammie, the big black cat, padded into the room and rubbed itself against Lou's uniform trousers, mewing mournfully. It was the biggest cat he'd ever seen. Like a damned panther.

"Could be good luck, I reckon," Binks said, eyeing the cat.

"Yeah, looks like you've got a new friend there, sir," Church said.

"Sammie can't resist a man in uniform," Thomson joked.

"That cat might be a bit queer. I'd watch out, if I were you, sir," Binks muttered.

"Actually, you're perfectly safe. We used to think it was a 'he', but we recently discovered 'he' was a '*she*'. Hence, we changed her name from Samuel to Samantha," Thomson explained.

"Well, I'm glad we got that one sorted out, sir," Binks whispered.

They spent the next hour taking everything down in the elevator to the van. Knoxwood, Buck, the chauffeur, Gwen, Daisy and even Thomson himself, pitched in. The two trunks took four men to carry. The Persian carpet was manhandled by all six down the stairway, being too long and too heavy to go in the elevator. Finally, it was pushed into the van alongside cases of wine and champagne and Thomson's dress sword. Binks closed the van doors with a big sigh.

Lou stood catching his breath with his crewmen, Knoxwood and Buck, waiting for Thomson to reappear. Finally, he emerged from the building in a black overcoat and matching trilby, carrying a brown leather case, his walking stick hooked over his arm. He was followed by Daisy and

Gwen, who held the cat in her arms. Thomson said his farewells and rubbed the cat's nose with a gloved finger.

"Now, I want you to be a good girl, Miss Samantha, do you hear?" Thomson whispered. The cat wriggled from Gwen's grasp and ran under a hawthorn bush. She glared at Thomson and mewed wildly, scolding him. Binks was unnerved and glanced at Lou for reassurance.

Before climbing into the car, Thomson handed the case to Lou.

"Here, Commander. Guard this with your life. This is part of my personal record collection. We shall have music on the ship to brighten our spirits throughout the voyage."

Knoxwood climbed in with Thomson. Buck sat in front with the chauffeur. Thomson gave a royal wave to the two women and the Daimler set off with the van behind. Thomson told them he had two stops to make on the way. On Victoria Street, the convoy drew up at the post office. Thomson marched up to the clerk at the counter.

"I'd like to send a telegram to Romania, please."

"Romania!" the clerk exclaimed, handing him a telegram form.

Thomson scribbled a few lines.

Princess Marthe Bibesco, Posada, Par Comarmic Prahova, Romania
En route to board Cardington R101 for India STOP The Persian accompanies us STOP As always I am thinking of you STOP Yours ever Kit

Thomson handed the message to the clerk.
"When will this be received?" Thomson asked.
"Monday, I should think, sir."
"Thank you. You're very kind."

Thomson next requested the chauffeur to stop at the florist's shop a few hundred yards up the street. He jumped out and went inside. Thomson was a regular customer and the florist greeted him warmly.

"I'd like you to arrange to send fifteen roses to Paris, if you please," Thomson said

"*Fifteen,* sir? You'd have to pay for two dozen, I'm afraid."

"Yes, yes, that's okay. The number has significance."

"Certainly sir, I quite understand. Any particular color?" the florist asked.

"They *must* be red *Général Jacqueminot,*" Thomson answered.

"Ah, yes of course, sir, *the usual.* They might be a bit hard to come by."

"You'll have plenty of time, my dear fellow."

Thomson solemnly wrote a note for the card to accompany the bouquet. When finished, he handed it to the florist with Marthe's address and delivery instructions. After paying by check, he bade the florist 'good day' and strode out. In the car, Knoxwood was waiting with the red box full of ministerial documents.

"Now, what have we got?" Thomson asked.

"Here's a cable from Egypt confirming the High Commissioner is coming to the banquet on Monday night. As are the other ten you invited."

"Excellent."

"The secretary of the Royal Aeronautical Society, the chairman of the Royal Aero Club and a few others all send their good wishes."

"How nice."

"You have a message from the Prime Minister wishing you a safe journey."

"Good. Please reply. Say: Thank you for your kind wishes. I'm confident this voyage will be a great success and I look forward to seeing you on the twentieth."

"And here, sir, is the latest weather report from the Air Ministry."

Thomson took it from Knoxwood and read it aloud, nodding as he did so.

"Anticyclone centered over Balkans. ...Depression over Eastern Atlantic moving east. Occluded front running from shallow low centered near Tynemouth to South of France moving east. ...Winds tonight over France likely to be west or south-west moderate strength over Northern France light over Southern France. Weather mainly cloudy. ...Western Mediterranean: light and variable or south-west winds probable tomorrow with fair weather. ...Central Mediterranean: light easterly or variable winds. Weather fair. ...Eastern Mediterranean: winds northerly or easterly Athens to Crete lighter toward Egypt. Weather mainly fair perhaps local thunderstorms."

Thomson handed the report back to Knoxwood. "Well, that doesn't sound too bad."

"That's a blessed relief, sir," Knoxwood said.

Thomson peered outside. The weather over London was cloudy, but calm. They continued the journey northwards, retracing Lou's route down.

In the van, Binks and Church were anxious to find out what recordings Thomson had brought. Lou allowed them to take a peek. Church held the case on his knees and pulled each record up and read the label. The first three were operas, which he'd never heard of. He was disappointed, but then he got excited.

" 'Ere look at this! "I Wanna Be Loved by You", "Bye, Bye Blackbird", "Happy Days Are 'ere Again", "Puttin' on the Ritz", Wow, ee's a gay old dog!" Church exclaimed. "Who would have thought? And here's "Somebody Stole My Gal" and "Singing in the Rain"—"

"Sounds like we're gonna have a party," Binks said. "Yes, sir!"

The lads in the van continued on with new respect for the Minister of State for Air.

They reached the village of Shefford as light was failing. Thomson checked his watch.

"Ah, we're running early and I'm dying for a cup of tea. What say you fellows?"

"I don't see why not, Minister," Knoxwood said.

"Look here. Teas and Hovis," Thomson said, pointing at a small inn. Its black and white façade, tiled roof and soft, warm lights looked inviting.

"The White Hart Inn. How quaint. Let's stop here, driver," Thomson said.

The Daimler pulled into the gravel carpark with the van behind.

"Bring all those chaps, Buck. Least I can do is buy everyone a cup of tea. I expect they could do with one."

At dusk, they reached the top of Hammer Hill on the Bedford Road. Thomson asked his driver to stop again. They were still early.

"Let's see how she looks from up here," Thomson said, climbing out of the car.

He walked to the crest of the hill. Everyone followed him. Two hundred and fifty feet below, the colossal, silver airship was a dazzling sight. She floated head to wind at the tower, bathed in light. Faint thumping sounds of a brass band were carried on the increasing winds from the west.

Thomson turned to Lou. "Now, *there's* our magic carpet, Commander! It's taken almost a decade to fulfill this dream. But there she is in all her glory. Look at her. See how the light catches her—how she sparkles!"

"You must be proud, sir," Lou said.

PART ELEVEN

Passengers board *Cardington R101* from the tower

INDIA

87

GRAND FAREWELL

Saturday October 4, 1930.

Thomson's Daimler slowed at the gate on the road to the tower. A cheer went up from the crowd. He waved grandly to everyone while the brass band hammered out another inspiring march. Today, he felt almost like royalty—perhaps this was the beginning of greater things to come. The airfield was surrounded by vehicles of every description, the atmosphere was one of celebration, despite the blustery weather.

The multi-colored lights of the fair grew vivid in the falling darkness and carousel music added to the gaiety, as it competed with the *um-par-par* and *thump-thump-thump* of the brass band. Thomson glanced up and listened to laughter and screams from girls on the Ferris wheel.

Their view of the ship must be wonderful.

Thomson scanned the multitudes huddled along the fence, bundled up in overcoats, scarves and hats, backs to the wind. Those lucky enough to have cars remained inside, wrapped in blankets. Some dozed, having traveled many miles. Small clusters gathered around vendors selling hot chestnuts and jacket potatoes cooked on steel braziers over glowing coals. The tasty aroma wafted across the field, filling Thomson's nostrils. It was comforting, and for a moment, he was reminded of his mother's kitchen in Devonshire.

Other vendors, unfortunate souls without the comfort of heat, attempted to sell mementos from tables or boards lashed to the fence. "Postcards! Postcards! Come an' get yer postcards 'ere. Two for threepence, ten for a bob," one cried.

"Keyrings and flags, only a shillin'. Come and get 'em!"

"Lovely souvenirs, commeneratin' this 'istorical event!"

Thomson sympathized with the poor wretches. In this chilly wind, they were having a devil of a time preventing their wares being blown away. And in such hard times, few spectators had money to fritter away on souvenirs. Clowns mingled with the crowd, handing out flyers, enticing people into the fairground. One, in a bowler hat high above the crowd, wore colossal, billowing, black-and-red-striped trousers over stilts. Flowing white locks blew around his head. Thomson admired the man's skill in such awful conditions.

The Daimler slowed while the gate was opened and the clowns gathered around the car, laughing and waving at Thomson. Amongst them, Thomson spotted Mrs. Hinchliffe, barging her way to the car. Obviously, she had something to say to him. He was irritated.

"Driver, *don't stop!*"

He glanced at Knoxwood, who'd seen her, too.

"I don't want to talk to *that* woman!" Thomson grunted.

The driver put his foot down and they sped through the gate. Another cheer went up.

A BBC crew was waiting under the tower for him to make his appearance, ready to do a commentary on the departure of the airship and ask for his comments. Many in the nation were glued to their radios and millions around the world were following this extraordinary event.

The car drew up. Thomson pulled out his wallet and took out a ten shilling note. "Here, Buck. Go back to the gate and pick up a few souvenirs. Get a couple for yourself, too," he said. And then as an afterthought, "And don't speak to that Hinchliffe woman, whatever you do."

"Right you are sir, absolutely."

Buck scampered off, clutching the money. The chauffeur opened the door and Thomson got out and waved to the crowd. Binks parked the van. As Thomson walked toward the BBC crew, his hat flew off and rolled on its rim across the field. Embarrassed, Thomson watched ground crewmen chase it down. He received the hat gratefully and replaced it on his head. He stood close to the BBC van and leaned on his walking stick. The reporters moved in.

"...Lord Thomson has emerged from the limousine and many reporters are gathering around. We'll listen to some of their questions ..." the commentator said, moving closer. He thrust the microphone out toward Thomson and press photographers took pictures for tomorrow's Sunday newspapers.

"How do you feel about the flight, sir?"

Thomson gazed up at the airship. "All my life, I've prepared myself for this moment."

"Any second thoughts?"

"Absolutely *none*. There's certainly nothing to fear," Thomson answered.

"The weather is kicking up, sir. Sure she can take it?"

"This airship is as strong as the mighty Forth Bridge!"

"Do you think your departure will be delayed?"

"The experts will be looking at the weather. They'll make that determination."

"Will you be making the whole voyage, bearing in mind you have a tight schedule?" George Hunter asked.

"The Prime Minister has given me strict instructions to return by the twentieth of October. Yes, I'll make the entire journey in this very fine airship."

Ground crewmen gathered around Lou, Binks and Church behind the van. Church flung the doors open.

"Gordon Bennett!"

"Cor blimey!"

"S'truth!"

"Bloody 'ell!"

"Holy smoke!"

"I don't believe it!"

"Someone's gotta be jokin'!"

Lou knew he'd better inform the captain—this would affect all his calculations. He climbed the tower steps, carrying Thomson's case of records. He went to the lounge, where he locked it in the gramophone cabinet, then proceeded to the chartroom.

Since early that morning Irwin, Atherstone and Johnston had been busy working on the ship's lift calculations. Its lifting capability had to be weighed against many complex issues which constantly affected it: air temperature, atmospheric density, purity of gas, fullness of gasbags, gas bag leakage, fuel load and projected rate of usage, ballast requirements and usage, likelihood of collecting water ballast (from rain) en route, duration of journey, altitude and the airship's relation to terrain they'd be crossing, and of course, the weather. The task was daunting.

Lou entered the chartroom as the three men poured over their figures. "Captain, we've just returned with Lord Thomson's luggage. It's quite a load. He's brought everything but the kitchen sink."

Exasperated, Irwin threw down his pencil, went down the steps into the control car and glared down at the van. "Get all that stuff weighed. Don't load anything before you let me know the *exact* weight and *I* give you permission," he said.

"Yes, sir."

Lou went down the gangplank to the tower, where Sky Hunt leaned on the rail watching the activities. The ground crew laid Thomson's carpet down on a tarpaulin. Buck stood keeping an eye on it as though it were the *Shroud of Turin*.

"*That* could be the straw that breaks the camel's bleedin' back," Hunt muttered, shaking his head. Lou nodded in agreement and descended the stairs. He went to the stores foreman making out the load sheet.

"Don't put anything on board until it's weighed and cleared by Captain Irwin," he said. "*Nothing!*"

On the ground, Lou found himself surrounded by much hugging and kissing and tearful goodbyes. It made him sad and a little bitter. He looked for Charlotte's face in the crowd, even though he knew that was futile, but then a young RAF man came to speak to him.

"Sir, are you Commander Remington?"

"Yes."

"There's someone at the gate asking for you—says he's your father. Should I let him in, or will you come out? We know most of these people," he said, gesturing to the crewmen's families, "but we haven't seen this gentleman before and he has a north-country accent."

"I'll come and talk to him," Lou said. Obviously it wasn't his dad, but maybe it was Charlotte's father. His spirits soared as he marched quickly toward the fence. It was John Bull. He couldn't help feeling disappointed, but didn't allow it to show. The two men hugged.

"John, you shouldn't have driven all this way down here," Lou said.

"I had to come. I've been brooding all week. Mary said 'Go on, John, you go and see him off.' So here I am."

"That was thoughtful of you—you know I'm pleased to see you."

"Charlotte isn't here anywhere, I suppose, is she?" John asked, peering around.

"No, she's washed her hands of me."

"I can't believe that. I hope you'll try and see her when you get back."

"I tried. I went to her parents' house, but they wouldn't open the door."

"Oh, no ..."

"I'll definitely visit you when I return. Then, I guess, I'll head back to the States."

John was heartbroken. "God, I'm so sorry. Look, if anything changes —the cottage will always be yours, you know that."

"Thank you, John."

They shook hands and hugged again. John's eyes filled with tears.

"Good luck, son. Make sure you come back safe," he said and then, turning away abruptly, he disappeared into the crowd.

God, I'll miss that man!

A familiar voice spoke up behind him. "Good evening, Commander."

Brancker magically appeared next to Lou in John's place. He carried a small case and held a pith helmet under his arm. With the flat of the other hand, he tried valiantly to hold down his toupée while screwing up his face to keep his monocle in its socket.

"Sir Sefton!" Lou said, forcing a smile.

Then, to his surprise, among the crowd near the gate, Lou spotted her dark, shining hair—no mistaking those long, flowing locks down to her waist. She stood next to a young man about Lou's age and build, her arm through his. Lou's heart raced.

Damn, she's been in Bedford all this time!

"Excuse me, Sir Sefton, I'll be right back as soon as ..." Lou said, marching over to where she stood.

"Charlotte!" he shouted as he approached.

Her companion at first became confused and then hostile. The girl turned—she was nothing like Charlotte. In fact, her hair was auburn when he got up close—the light was wrong. He was bitterly disappointed, but relieved. Then he remembered—Charlotte had cut all her hair off.

"I'm sorry, no offense. I thought you were my sister," Lou said, holding up his hand.

He returned to Brancker and they were joined by Mrs. Hinchliffe, who stepped out of the crowd. "Good evening, gentlemen," she said.

"Millie. What on earth are you doing here?" Brancker said. "I'd give you a hug, but my hands are rather full."

"Then I'll kiss *you*," she said planting a kiss on his cheek. She smiled at Lou and kissed his lips. "I've come to tell you what Ray— " she began.

Brancker exploded. "Millie, Millie, don't! Just go home! The ship will leave tonight. Thomson has decreed it." He turned away from her. "Come, Lou, we must go. *Goodbye*, Millie!"

Lou gave Mrs. Hinchliffe an apologetic smile. He'd not seen Brancker so on edge and the poor woman didn't deserve it. He took Brancker's case and they marched off through the gate to the tower with others who ambled trance-like toward the great beast. Maybe they were all under its evil spell. A clown appeared with a handful of flyers and stuffed one in Lou's hand. Lou couldn't help grinning as he read it.

LET THE GREAT CLAIRVOYANT
MADAM HARANDAH
THE ROMANIAN GYPSY
TELL YOUR FORTUNE
PSYCHIC READING
PALM READING
TAROT CARDS
3d each

"What's that?" Brancker asked.

"It's an invite to talk to a fortune teller from the Elephant and Castle," Lou said. "Would you like to meet her?"

"No, I don't think I would."

"Mrs. Hinchliffe mentioned Ray ...that's her—"

"Dead husband. I love Millie dearly, and she may be right, but we have our duty to do. Can't be listening to all that stuff tonight. I'm depressed enough already."

"I guarantee you don't need a session with Madame Harandah, in that case," Lou said.

"I had my fortune told in Paris once ..." Brancker began. He stopped in mid-sentence, seeming to think better of it.

"What did they say, sir?" Lou asked, but Brancker didn't answer.

They walked to the tower, passing Thomson, who was just finishing his press conference. His well-wishers were gathered around him shaking his hand. In that group were Dowding and his predecessor, Higgins, Richmond, Scott, members of the press, Knoxwood and many from the R.A.W. Colmore stood apart with his wife, seeming more relaxed than she. Lou moved to the elevator with Brancker where Bert Mann, the elevator man, waited with a cheery smile.

"Good evening, Bert. I'm expecting a lady friend any time now—Lady Cathcart. When she arrives, show her to the gangplank. Tell her to follow the blue carpet, would you? Inform her I'll be waiting. We're having a little leaving party," Brancker said winking.

"I can do that, Sir Sefton. No problem at all, sir."

"Before I go up, I'd better have a word with Lord Thomson," Brancker said. But Thomson had already spotted Brancker and was approaching with hands outstretched. They greeted each other like long lost brothers.

"Ah, Sefton, good evening! Lovely to see you, my dear chap." The two men stood smiling and shaking hands while photographers' cameras flashed.

"Come on, everyone. Gather round. Let's get some nice group pictures. Get as many crewmen in as possible," Thomson instructed.

While they were taking a third picture, eight ground crewmen trooped past with Thomson's Persian balanced on their shoulders. Irwin appeared from the tower staircase, his face contorted with anger, vividly pale in the searchlights' glare. Thomson was quick to spot him marching stiffly toward the men with the carpet. Thomson raised his voice above the wind, spiking Irwin's guns.

"Ah, there you are, Captain Irwin. Please join us."

"What the hell is *this*?" Irwin demanded, gesturing at the heavy roll in disbelief.

"Why, this is my talisman. It flies with us. We'll lay it down for the banquet in honor of the King of Egypt. We'll do things in style. Now come and stand next to me Irwin, there's a good chap."

Irwin fumed, but did as he was told. Everyone dutifully gathered around for more photos. In the next few hours, Lou would come to fully appreciate what a truly intimidating presence Thomson could be and what a skilled manipulator he was. Brancker picked up his belongings and headed for the elevator.

Lou stood posing until he could slip away. He went over to Colmore and his wife, who had her arm linked through his. Colmore grinned. "Not sure if you've met Mrs. Colmore, Lou," he said.

"You were in church last year—for the blessing," Lou said.

Mrs. Colmore smiled. She had a sweet face and she obviously doted on her husband. Her eyes shone with love each time she looked at him.

"I'm always relaxed when *this* man's around," Colmore said.

"I know you are, my darling." She glanced at Lou, seeming almost convinced.

"He's my special assistant and our third officer. He's also our American observer, as Zachary Lansdowne had been on Scottie's voyage to America."

"And where is Mr. Lansdowne these days?" Mrs. Colmore asked innocently.

Lou bit his tongue, remembering.

Killed on the Shenandoah with Josh.

"Er, if you'll excuse me, I think I'd better check on that girl over there. She'll have news of my injured crewman. It was good seeing you again, ma'am," Lou said, with a slight bow, touching his cap. Irene and Church were locked in a tearful embrace, while Church's mother and father stood by. Irene noticed Lou approaching and tore herself away.

"Lou, I went and saw Billy this morning and this afternoon. He's got a compound fracture, but he'll be okay. He said to tell you not to forget what he said to you this mornin'—especially now. He said you'd know what he meant. His mum's coming down from Goole tomorrow morning."

"Thanks, Irene," Lou said.

Someone must have told Billy that Jessup had been picked as his replacement. He thought about Fanny again and how she'd rather her son had a broken leg than be on this flight tonight. Suddenly, he remembered and his stomach turned over. What was it Madame Harandah had said to Billy a year ago?

Go break a leg!

Lou was shaken. Church kissed his mother and shook his father's hand.

"We'll be back by the twentieth. I'll see you all then," Church said. Before heading to the ship, Church grabbed Irene and they kissed passionately. "I love you, my darlin'," he said as he let her go. He turned toward the tower and as he retreated he raised his arms triumphantly, shouting at the top of his voice. "You're gonna be the most beautiful bride in all of Bedford, my darlin'!"

Once again, Lou felt uneasy.

What else did that old gypsy crone say?

While the Churches waved to their son, Sky Hunt was saying his own goodbyes. His wife held a baby in her arms and their son stood beside her. "Albert, if anything happens to me, you must take care of your mum and the baby. You'll be the man in the family, son," Hunt said, kissing each of them. He stood and watched them troop off to the gate.

For Lou, this was tough; never had he felt more alone. All around him were similar scenes: young men in uniform kissing their wives and girl friends; Richmond and his wife; Atherstone and his wife; Olivia Irwin looking earnestly up into her husband's face.

Harry Leech's wife tucked a piece of heather into his lapel while he smoked a last cigarette. "Here you are, Harry," she said. "For luck." She patted his chest and kissed him.'

"I'll be all right now then, won't I? You go on home, love," Leech said, peering up at the swirling clouds. "Goodness knows what time we'll leave—that's if we leave at all."

He stamped out his dog-end on the ground. Mrs. Leech agreed and, showing not the slightest sign of anxiety, kissed Leech again and made for the bus stop.

Leech glanced over at Lou. "No point in 'er hangin' around 'ere," he said.

Lou agreed. Binks arrived at his side.

"Where's your missus, Joe? Isn't she coming?" Lou asked.

"Nah. I told 'em to stay home. I don't wanna go through all this rigmarole. I told 'em I'd be back in a couple of weeks."

But Binks seemed upset.

"What's up, Joe?"

"Sir, some of the blokes have been talkin'. Jessup's carrying a bloody great stiletto. He 'ad it in customs. Jessup told 'em a lot of old bollocks about needin' it for emergencies."

"He's got a point, Joe."

"Sir, everybody knows he's got it in for you."

"All right. Thanks. I appreciate it—but don't worry."

"Oh and sir, they weighed the old geezer's stuff. It was over two hundred and fifty pounds."

"Jeez! Thanks for your help today, Joe."

"Welcome, sir."

Lou re-joined the main group just as Thomson was ushering them into the elevator.

"Come along, everyone. We'll have a farewell drink on board," he said.

While they were piling in, Knoxwood handed Thomson a telegram. Thomson stopped to read it, waving the group on. He thought it might be from Marthe. Mann slammed the accordion gate shut. The wives stood watching their husbands sadly.

"Keep the old flag flying, Florry, my dear," Richmond called to his wife. Standing behind the steel bars of the elevator doors, they reminded Lou of men on death row.

Thomson tore the telegram open.

A word to wish you good luck on your historic flight STOP kindest regards Burney

"That's decent of him," Thomson said, disappointed.
He handed the telegram back to Knoxwood.
"Send him a reply."
Knoxwood pulled out his notepad.
"Thank you for your very kind wishes. Indeed, this is a wonderful day. We're looking forward with excitement to flying down Marco Polo's ancient route—sign it CBT."

Lou was about to take the stairs when he spotted a chauffeur-driven Rolls-Royce approaching the tower. Perhaps it was Sir Sefton's lady friend. The limousine stopped and a pair of elegant legs stepped out. The finely-dressed woman made her way toward Lou, clutching her long, dark coat tightly to her breast.
"Lady Cathcart? Lou inquired.
"Yes, I'm here to wish Sir Sefton Brancker *bon voyage.*"
By now, everyone was onboard the ship. Feeling obligated, Lou led her to the elevator gate. "This is the lady who Sir Sefton is expecting. Please take us up, Bert," Lou said.
"Right you are, sir."
Lou closed his eyes as the elevator ascended.

88

ON BOARD RECEPTION

Saturday October 4, 1930.

W hen Thomson had arrived at the tower gallery minutes earlier and climbed the gangplank, he was reminded of that New Year's Eve of 1923, on the train crossing the Firth of Forth on his way to meet MacDonald—a truly wicked storm. He listened to the intermittent rain beating on the ship's cover and felt the wind's fury.

I survived that night and I shall survive this one.

Thomson made his entrance into the lounge with great fanfare— shaking hands, giving nods of encouragement and expressions of thanks. Tables had been set up for a brief farewell celebration. R.A.W. passengers had gathered, along with Higgins and Dowding and the Deputy Director of Civil Aviation for India, Squadron Leader Bill O'Neill and his wife. Thomson sensed Mrs. O'Neill was in serious distress about this flight. He couldn't abide such feelings of negativity and, with a stony look, moved away to speak with Squadron Leader Palstra and his colleague from the Australian Embassy.

Lou led Brancker's terrified visitor up the gangplank and then past a group of crewmen struggling to stow the Persian carpet at the bow, between Frames 1 and 2. Lou and Lady Cathcart continued unsteadily along the main corridor, over the blue carpet. The ship rocked and rolled from side to side to the sound of rain, belting down in torrents. Lady Cathcart found all this unnerving and took hold of Lou's arm. The deeper into the airship they got, the more uneasy she became.

At last, they arrived at the entrance to the magnificent dining salon, its brass wall sconces casting light onto slender, white columns, each with its own shining, gold leaf ornamental head. Lady Cathcart peered around helplessly, not noticing or caring about the beauty of the room. Brancker came rushing over.

"So good of you to come, my dear," he said, taking both her hands and gallantly kissing her on both cheeks.

"Oh Branks, will you be safe in this *bloody thing?*"

"Safe as houses, my love. Don't you worry—old Sefton's going to be all right."

"Dear God—are you sure? I'm scared to death."

"Let me get you a glass of bubbly and we can go and have a little chit chat." Brancker left Lady Cathcart with Lou and nipped off to the table. He returned with a tray and four glasses of champagne and a few brandies. "Come along, my dear, let's go this way, where it's quiet. We'll have a drink and you'll feel so much better," Brancker said. He gave Lou a smile of thanks and another of his little winks as he led the lady off to his cabin. Lou grinned.

Not the most private place in the world—what the hell—it could be The Last Supper.

In the lounge, the stewards came round with trays of champagne. Thomson took one and moved to the center of the room.

"Ladies and gentlemen, well-wishers and fellow travelers. Please take up your glasses. Here's to this historic voyage—to our success—*to India!*"

"To India!" everyone repeated, and swallowed it down.

With that, Thomson went over to Colmore. "What's the latest on the weather?"

"We're waiting for Mr. Giblett, sir. He'll have the updated weather report in his hands shortly," Colmore replied.

"Good. We'll meet and discuss it after the reception—somewhere private."

"The chartroom would be the best place, sir. We can just about squeeze in there."

"Schedule that meeting in half an hour," Thomson said.

After Brancker and the woman had gone, Lou poked his head in the lounge. Colmore stood in the corner talking to Thomson, Richmond and Scott. Scott was drinking heavily. Colmore still appeared relaxed. He smiled at Lou and beckoned him over.

"I've told Lord Thomson that we'll have the latest weather report any time. Would you tell Captain Irwin we'll meet in the chartroom in half an hour?"

"I'm on my way there now, sir. I'll relay your message," Lou said.

Lou headed along the corridor passing the passenger cabins. Sounds of passion were coming from what he guessed had to be Brancker's cabin.

God bless the old dog!

When Lou reached the end of the corridor, he ran into Jessup lurking with two others, listening to Lady Cathcart moaning with delight.

"Oh Sefton ...oh Sefton ...oh, oh, oh, yes, yes, *yes, yes, yes!* ...Aaaaaaaaahhh!"

The crewmen laughed and sniggered.

"Okay, you lot. Get away from the passenger quarters. Immediately!" Lou said.

"Yes, sir. Sorry, sir," one of them said. "We've just been turnin' down the beds."

Jessup gave no lip, but he had a glint in his eye. The three slouched off toward the bow. Jessup turned back to Lou and with a crooked smile said, "See you later … *sir.*"

After they'd gone, Lou went to the chartroom overlooking the control car. Although doubling as the control room, it was usually referred to as the 'chartroom.' It was from here the ship was managed, including the production of weather charts, navigation and load calculations. Johnston was studying the weather charts with Giblett. Irwin had returned and was going over the load sheet with Atherstone, inputting additional data—Thomson's luggage.

"Two hundred seventy-four pounds," Irwin said.

Atherstone entered the number onto a load sheet.

"We'll have to adjust the ballast for that," Irwin said.

Irwin continued with the figures. As he called them out, Atherstone repeated them and wrote them down.

"Okay, fuel 25.3 tons ...lube oils one ton ...water ballast 9.25 tons ...drinking water 1.1 tons ...crew and passengers 3.8 tons ...food and provisions .33 tons ...luggage .53 tons ..."

"Including Thomson's?" Atherstone asked.

"Yes. Crew kit .8 tons ...furnishings and equipment 1.25 tons ..."

"That bloody Axminster carpet weighed more than half a ton," Atherstone muttered.

"We'll call it permanent ballast. We'll tear it up and throw it in the Channel, if we have to," Irwin said. Lou knew Irwin meant what he said. "Okay, so, lift available, with bags filled to ninety-six percent, is 161.75 tons. Lift needed is 162.1 tons. We'll need to dump 1.35 tons of ballast to slip," Irwin concluded.

"All very nice, but we have no margin for safety," Atherstone said.

Irwin glanced up at Lou for a second, giving him a nod. Lou went to the rail and peered down into the control car. Steff stood on watch, his face frozen. These men were under almost unbearable stress. Lou had seen faces like this before aboard *R38*. His uneasiness returned.

"Lord Thomson wants to have a conference before we leave," Lou said.

"Where?"

"Right here," Lou answered.

Irwin nodded again. "Okay," he said absently.

While Lou was in the control car, Thomson walked along the corridor with Buck to his cabin. Thomson was mystified by grunting and moaning noises coming from one of the cabins. He said nothing.

Surely that can't be what it sounds like!

Buck was impassive as he stopped and held the curtain of Thomson's assigned cabin open, although Thomson detected a hint of a smile at the corner of Buck's mouth and mirth in his eyes.

"This one's *yours*, sir," Buck said. "I'm next door."

Thomson surveyed the cabin. It was double size, having had one partition removed. A large desk and a comfortable chair had been installed for him to work on affairs of state.

"This one's bigger than the others, sir," Buck said. "So's the bed."

Thomson nodded with satisfaction. Buck had laid out a clean shirt and underclothes for a change before dinner. Although it was chilly without heating, Thomson removed his overcoat and Buck hung it in the closet behind the curtain.

Thomson picked up the postcards Buck had bought from the souvenir vendors and left on the table. He browsed through colored pictures and photographs of the airship floating at the tower. They were emblazoned in red letters with *Cardington R101* alongside the Union Jack. Each had been date-stamped: 4th October 1930. Pleased, Thomson laid them back on the table. He picked up the two key rings, each of which had a chain and the metal shape of an airship attached with HMA *R101* pressed into the metal—one red, one blue. Thomson nodded with satisfaction and handed Buck the blue one along with three postcards.

"Here, some mementos for the trip," he said.

"Thank you, sir. I shall always remember this," Buck said, genuinely grateful.

Thomson slipped the red keyring into his trouser pocket.

89

THE WEATHER CONFERENCE

Saturday October 4, 1930

Fifteen minutes later, everyone trooped into the chartroom. Five chairs had been placed at the bow end, where Thomson, Knoxwood, Colmore, Scott and Richmond sat, with Thomson at center. This left the officers and Rope standing. Lou stood next to Irwin at the back with Atherstone and Johnston. It was cramped and oppressive. There was no sign of Brancker, still in his cabin recovering from Lady Cathcart's '*bon voyage*'.

Colmore stood up. "Minutes ago we received a new weather forecast. Why don't you give us an update, Mr. Giblett?"

Giblett leaned against the chart table holding the latest information, his eyes darting back and forth across it. "Around one o'clock today, the occluded front over France moved eastwards, leaving a trough of low pressure off the Irish coast to move in, causing rain to spread over England this evening and throughout the night. Therefore, we can expect increasing southwesterly winds over the south of England and northern France."

"And the velocity of these winds, Mr. Giblett?" Thomson asked.

"They're forecasting surface winds of ten to fifteen miles an hour, freshening later. Upper winds above two thousand feet are expected to be from twenty to thirty miles an hour."

"At what altitude will we be flying?" Thomson asked, looking at Scott.

"Between one thousand and fifteen hundred feet, sir," Scott answered.

Giblett continued, "On the basis of what we're being told, we don't expect a huge increase in wind strength tonight—but I must stress, we *can't* rule that out."

"So you're saying it *could* increase ... and if it did, by how much?" Thomson asked.

Brancker entered the room, soaking wet, embarrassed, and a little the worse for wear. His toupée was askew and his monocle splashed with rain. Lou wondered if he'd been wearing it in his bunk with Lady Cathcart. He couldn't help grinning at the thought.

I'd like a snap of that!

"Ah, Sefton, it's so very good of you to join us," Thomson said.

"I'm terribly sorry, Minister. I didn't realize you'd called a conference."

Thomson looked down his nose. "I don't suppose you did. We were discussing the weather. Mr. Giblett has been telling us of the possibility of the winds increasing."

"I just saw someone off to the elevator—it's *bloody awful* out there!"

"I asked Mr. Giblett how much the winds might increase and he was about to tell us." Thomson turned to Giblett.

"That's not possible to predict, sir, but—"

"Might they increase to, say, thirty or forty knots?" Thomson pressed him.

"It must be blowing twenty-five knots *right now!*" Brancker announced.

"I have to tell you anything's possible. I can't give you the odds. Weather forecasting is not an exact science, sir," Giblett said.

"All right. Let's suppose the winds do increase to 40 knots." Thomson's eyes fell on Richmond. "Would that be too much for this airship, Colonel Richmond?"

"No, Lord Thomson, not at all. She's proved herself on that score."

Thomson's gaze was transferred to Scott, whose red face became animated.

"No, sir. *Absolutely not!*" Scott affirmed.

Irwin's voice projected from the back of the room. All heads turned in his direction. "I must remind you this airship has *never once* been flown in foul weather and its tests have *never* been completed," Irwin said. He sounded almost detached.

"So, Captain, you don't have confidence in your ship. Is that it?" Thomson snapped.

"That's *not* what I said, sir. I was merely pointing out the fact that this ship has *never* flown in anything more than a ten-knot breeze—and *never once* under full power."

"Captain Irwin—" Scott started, but Irwin stubbornly continued.

"And I should mention the gas valves are pumping out gas at an alarming rate every time the ship rolls. The gas bags are rubbing on the padding, which will wear holes in them in no time …and the cover was never completely replaced."

"So, are you proposing that we postpone this voyage, Captain?" Thomson asked.

"I'm saying we should definitely consider that possibility, yes," Irwin replied.

Scott tried again. "I don't think—"

"You *do* realize we'd become the object of ridicule. Thousands are camped out around this field—people who've come from all over England, Scotland and Wales to witness history in the making—not to mention the distinguished passengers we have on board. The eyes of the world are upon us and on British engineering. If this flight is postponed due to the weather, we'll be announcing that airships are fair-weather aircraft. I should also remind everyone here that the Treasury is looking for a glimmer of hope—some small success."

"Sir, I think—" Scott began again.

"So, I ask you: Is it to be that the government's revered airship *Cardington R101*, which has cost millions of pounds, cannot match the splendid performance of the men at Vickers, who did *what* they said they would, *when* they said they would—for a fixed sum of a mere three hundred and fifty thousand pounds—despite efforts to coerce them into a postponement."

"Sir—" Richmond began. Thomson cut him off, too.

The tirade was over. His voice became soft and cajoling. "I will say just this, gentlemen: Reward for success will be great and honors bestowed. Careers and reputations will be made with financial rewards beyond your wildest dreams …" Here Thomson paused. Everyone in the room waited while the wind howled and rocked the ship. Then came the knife, silent and smooth. "…But there will be no reward for failure. No more government funding—none will be asked for."

Richmond leapt to his feet followed by Scott.

"I'm completely confident this airship can handle it, sir," Richmond said.

"I agree," Scott said.

"What about the gas bags and valves and the cover the captain is referring to?" Thomson asked.

"All airships lose a certain amount of gas. It's to be expected," Scott said.

"The cover was thoroughly inspected and approved. We've been over this time and time again, sir," Richmond said.

Another long pause.

"So, from what you're saying, we have *nothing* to be concerned about?"

Brancker stirred himself, stepping forward from the back of the room. He'd composed himself somewhat, his toupée now on straight. All eyes turned toward him. He carefully finished wiping his monocle with a handkerchief and stuck it back in his eye. "Lord Thomson, I'm going to make a suggestion, if you'll allow me, sir. We depart on schedule and flight test the ship around this area of Bedford. And then, if, and only *if*, Captain Irwin and Major Scott are satisfied—we *then* strike a course for London and France."

"Oh, yes, I heartily agree," Richmond said.

"And if not?" Thomson said.

"Then we'll return here to the tower," Brancker said.

"That certainly sounds like a pwudent plan, sir," Knoxwood said brightly.

Suddenly, people were smiling and nodding—but not Irwin, Atherstone, Johnston and Lou. Colmore's mood had deteriorated over the last thirty minutes, but now he was perking up again. Lou had paid attention to Irwin while Brancker was putting his suggestion forward.

"Easier said than done." He'd muttered to Atherstone beside him.

"Why can't this test be done en route to London? It all sounds like a waste of fuel," Thomson asked.

"It'll give us a chance to test her on all headings under full power, sir," Scott said.

"I do remember Dowding suggesting this at our meeting," Thomson said, glancing at Colmore. "But won't people be wondering why the dickens we're flying around in circles?"

"Everyone'll think we're making a grand tour—in honor of the city," Scott said.

Thomson peered at the wall clock.

"What time do you propose getting started, Major Scott?"

"Immediately, sir. Immediately!"

"*Splendid.* I'm going to sit in the lounge with Wing Commander Colmore. Carry out your testing and keep us informed."

Knoxwood stood up and shook hands with everyone. "I wish I was coming with you," he said. "Bon voyage!"

While the meeting was breaking up, Hunt entered and whispered into Irwin's ear. Irwin became concerned and left. Lou followed. Irwin raced down the corridor and down the gangplank. Lou heard the captain's rapidly descending feet on the steel stairs. Lou stayed on the upper gallery and looked down. He could see Olivia Irwin some distance away, standing beside their small black car. She was dressed in a long, hooded, black cloak, which swirled around her in the wind, her face stark and white in the floodlights.

Lou watched Irwin rush out of the tower and into her arms. She hugged him to her, crying and speaking into his ear—pleading. He laid his head on her shoulder, doing his best to hold back his own tears. He drew back, obviously trying to reassure her, perhaps telling her of Brancker's plan, which Lou knew he had no faith in at all.

Olivia didn't appear convinced, but finally seemed resigned. They kissed again and he helped her into the car. Irwin stood and watched her drive slowly away, the wind churning the autumn leaves as she went. He turned and trudged back to the tower and up the staircase. Lou noiselessly retraced his steps, his heart heavy for the captain and his wife.

90

SALUTE TO BEDFORD

Saturday October 4, 1930.

L ou checked the wall clock: it was 6:32 p.m. On this day, the 4th of October, the clocks were scheduled be set back one hour at 1.00 a.m. Irwin had posted a duty schedule on the wall in the control room:

*CARDINGTON R101 DUTY ROSTER INDIA FLIGHT:
FIRST LEG TO EGYPT*

WATCH	HOURS	DUTY OFFICER
Evening	*16:00 – 20:00*	*F/O M. Steff*
1st Night	*20:00 – 23:00*	*Lt. Cmdr. Atherstone*
Middle	*23:00 – 02:00*	*Capt. C. Irwin*
Morning	*02:00 – 05:00*	*F/O M. Steff*
2nd Morning	*05:00 – 08:00*	*Lt. Cmdr. Atherstone*

*Lt. Cmdr. L. Remington Relief Duty Officer and Navigator
This rotation will continue throughout the voyage.*

Steff had been officer of the watch since 4 o'clock with Potter as height coxswain. Lou leaned on the rail overlooking the control car, alongside Johnston, Brancker and Scott.

Irwin's face was grim, his jaw set. "Start engines," he ordered.

"Start engines," Steff repeated.

Steff relayed the order via the telegraph, first to engine car No.1 and then through the others to No. 5, where Joe Binks was located with Ginger Bell. Atherstone was also in the control car, shining a flashlight on the propeller of engine No.1 to check it was turning. It wasn't. The two coxswains were ready at their wheels. Suddenly, everyone's attention was diverted by a woman's scream carried on the wind across the field from the gate. Irwin beckoned Lou down.

From the control car, they recognized Rosie, rushing toward the tower, waving something in her hand. Some distance behind Rosie, a policeman was in pursuit, blowing a whistle, his black cape gleaming in the rain.

"Lou, go down and find out what's going on," Irwin said calmly. "Looks like she's got a letter for her husband. Take it to him."

"We don't have time for this nonsense," Scott shouted.

Irwin glared at Lou. "Do as I say!" he snapped.

Lou left the control car as the first propeller began to turn on engine No. 2. The crowd cheered. As each engine was started, a cloud of black smoke spurted from its exhaust into the floodlights, sending a greasy, diesel odor across the field. Lou rushed down the corridor to the gangplank three hundred and fifty feet away. Church was about to assist another crewman in pulling up the gangplank.

"Hold it, Sam. I've gotta go down. Something's going on," he said, dashing out into the steady rain. He bounded down the stairs to the bottom where he found the now obviously pregnant Rosie Cameron pleading with Bert Mann. She was a sorry sight; her clothes, hair and face, soaking wet. Lou's heart went out to her.

"Please, Bert, let me go up and talk to Doug," she sobbed.

"No, 'course yer can't, Rosie. Ship's about to leave," Mann said.

Seeing Lou, Rosie turned to him, her eyes imploring. "Oh, sir. Can you get Doug for me? Please, I beg you. I *must* talk to him."

The out-of-breath policeman arrived on the scene. Lou held up his hand.

"It's all right, officer, we can deal with this." He turned back to Rosie. "That's not possible, Rosie. What you got there?"

Rosie grabbed Lou's arm, burying her face in his shoulder. "It's a letter for Doug. Can you give it to him—*please, please?*"

"Sure I can, Rosie."

She handed over the soggy letter. Lou put it in his inside pocket.

"I'll make sure he gets it. Don't worry."

"You must go home now, Rosie. You can't stay here," Mann said.

"Come along, miss," the policeman said.

Rosie nodded and walked off toward the gate, the policeman following. Lou glanced up at the ship. A bright, amber light shone down from the long windows of the promenade deck and her red navigation lights flashed on the port side where he stood. Three engines were up and running now, their blades spinning. Torrents of water ran down the ship's outer cover and spilled to the ground. A black cloud shot from engine No. 4. He bounded up the stairs. At the top, Mann followed Lou to the gangplank where a concerned Capt. Ralph Booth stood bundled in rain gear.

"What are you doing here, Ralph?" Lou asked.

"Just wanted to wave you fellas off. Take care of yourselves," Booth said, shaking Lou's hand.

"You wanna trade places?" Lou shouted above the wind and engines.

"Can't tonight—gotta wash my hair."

Lou went aboard. Church and Hunt pulled up the gangplank and closed it from inside.

"You might save a marriage, sir," Church called after Lou.

"I think it's a bit late for that, Sam," Lou replied.

Lou went to the crew's sleeping quarters, passing Jessup in the crew mess having his evening meal of bread, cheese and cocoa. He'd missed the commotion with Rosie, which Lou figured was a good thing. Lou found Cameron on his bunk reading a magazine. He handed him Rosie's letter.

Cameron screwed up his face. "What's this?"

Lou spoke kindly. "Rosie's been here. She asked me to give you this. She wants your forgiveness, Doug."

Cameron snorted with disgust and threw the letter down on his pillow. "Stupid bitch!" he muttered.

By the time Lou got to the control car to report what had happened, all engines except No. 1 were running smoothly, their propellers whirring in the sparkling raindrops. Lou went back up to the chartroom.

In the control car, Irwin glanced across at Atherstone. "Take over the elevators from Potter. Let me know how she feels."

Potter went up and stood in the chartroom beside Lou with Johnston, Brancker and Scott. The speaking tube whistle sounded and Steff put it to his ear. "They're having trouble with No.1, sir. Hunt says they can't get the starting engine going," Steff said.

"Tell them to keep trying," Irwin said. He raised his eyes and glared at Scott as if it was his fault. Scott stared back with bloodshot eyes as he paced back and forth along the rail. Finally, engine No.1 fired up with a shower of sparks in the blackness and all five engines were humming smoothly. Lou had concerns about weight, especially since the cover was totally saturated. The process of ballasting up began, so the ship could rise when they slipped from the tower.

"She's nose heavy. Drop two half ton bags at Frame 1," Irwin ordered.

This was done. A fine mist appeared in the floodlights.

Irwin wasn't satisfied. "Not enough. Drop two more at Frame 1 and two half tons at Frame 6," he snapped. That seemed to do the trick. Irwin appeared more comfortable the ship could rise. "Okay, slip now!" he ordered.

Lou marveled. This had to be the toughest getaway ever undertaken, lifting more men and dead weight into the air than any craft in aviation history—and in the foulest conditions. As the bow lifted and was released from the tower, the crowd roared. Pushed by engines 1 and 2, the airship drew backwards and rose above the tower, falling off to starboard.

"Cut engines 1 and 2 and convert to running forward. All engines at seven hundred rpm's." Steff telegraphed the instructions.

"She's still heavy. Drop another ton at Frame 6!" Irwin ordered.

The mighty *Cardington R101*, dangerously low over the crowd, slowly pushed forward, spewing water from her ballast tanks, wallowing into the night. From the control car, they saw signals from loved ones on the ground who were using flashlights. Car headlights flashed on and off and horns sounded nonstop.

"Okay, Captain, get all engines up to eight twenty-five," Scott ordered from the rail above. Irwin nodded to Steff who relayed the order by telegraph.

"How's she handling, Captain?" Brancker called down.

Irwin turned to Atherstone who muttered something inaudible.

"Heavy as hell," Irwin replied.

"Let's try her on another tack," Scott said.

"Turn ninety degrees to starboard. Steer forty-five degrees toward South End," Johnston called down.

"That's good, Johnnie," Scott said, pacing to nowhere.

The ship pitched and rolled. Nobody spoke.

"How is she now?" Scott asked finally, leaning on the rail again.

"Like the *Titanic*," Irwin replied.

The ship, traveling downwind, moved along a northeasterly track. Lou turned to the chart table. Johnston pointed to the map. "We're over the captain's house on Putroe Lane."

They'd barely reached six hundred feet. Lou wondered if Olivia had reached home and how she was feeling.

If she's watching this, she'll be horrified.

Irwin called up to Lou. "Take a look round the ship, Lou."

Lou passed through the lounge, where Thomson sat in silence opposite Colmore. Neither of them spoke as he went by. He walked into the dining salon. The tables had been set for dinner. Some had been pushed together, forming a head table at one end. Pierre entered and smiled nervously at Lou, hoping for his approval.

Lou nodded. "Everything looks good, Pierre."

"I'm waiting to hear if they'll be dining this evening, sir," he said.

"We'll know soon enough," Lou said, on his way out.

He headed out onto the catwalk where Leech and Rope were making an inspection. The wind had picked up. Rain beat like gravel on the cover in squalls, while the valves expelled gas in great puffs. Lou eyed the surging gas bags and wondered if they'd have any hydrogen left by the time they reached Egypt—*if* they reached Egypt! He got level with Leech, who no longer seemed so carefree. "She's pitching a bit, isn't she?" he said, glancing at Rope.

"She's bound to in this weather—but I'm not unduly worried," Rope replied.

They heard someone behind them and turned. It was Jessup. He stood on the catwalk holding the rail.

"What's up, Jessup?" Leech barked.

"Just making some inspections, sir," Jessup responded, glancing at Lou.

"Good man," Rope said.

Lou nodded and went to engine car No. 5 to check on Binks and Bell. The flap was already open. When he peered down the ladder, he noticed the propeller was still. He returned and got Leech, keeping an eye out for Jessup—but he'd disappeared. They made their way down, clinging to the slippery rungs. They could see by lights on the ground, the ship was turning a hundred and eighty degrees to port. They squeezed into the engine car.

"What's up?" Leech asked.

"She was running okay for a while then the pressure dropped—so I shut her down," Bell replied.

"All right, I'll let your foreman know," Leech said.

"Could be something wrong with the gauge," Binks said. "The engine sounded fine."

Lou and Leech left Binks and Bell to wait for their supervisors. Lou went back to the chartroom while the ship now traveled in an easterly direction—still within striking distance of the tower.

"What's going on?" Scott demanded.

"No.5's down. Oil pressure dropped, sir," Lou said.

"They'll fix it," Scott said.

Irwin scowled up at Scott. He raised his voice to Johnston. "Where exactly are we, Johnny?"

"We're over Marston Thrift Wood. Let's turn ninety degrees to port, Captain, while you decide what we're gonna do," Johnston said.

Just then, Colmore arrived from the lounge expecting a report. "The weather appears to be worsening," he said. "Are we going back to the tower?" He looked down at Irwin and then at all the other faces. Everyone ignored him.

Finally, he got an answer. "She seems all right to me. I suggest we make tracks for London. Anyone disagree with my decision?" Scott said.

Colmore looked forlorn. "But Scottie, what about the engine? I hate to start a voyage with one engine down already," he said.

"They'll get it back up, don't worry," Scott said.

"But the weather's—"

"You're right—it's getting worse. It's too dangerous to attempt a landing at Cardington now."

"Wait, Scottie, I think we should discuss this."

"What do *you* think, Captain Irwin?" Scott shouted down to the control car.

"It'd be much too dangerous. But let's face it, that was obvious from the start, wasn't it. Now, we have no choice," Irwin replied.

Lou glanced at Colmore. He'd been outwitted. He understood how both Colmore and Irwin had become virtually powerless. Scott had usurped them—enabled and sanctioned by Thomson, since their last-minute meeting with him in London.

Scott's mind was ticking over. "Look, Reggie, if anything goes wrong, we'll make contingency plans to land in France, that's all."

"Do you really think we could?" Brancker said.

"Oh dear," Colmore mumbled, wiping his forehead with his handkerchief.

Lou knew this was a false hope for Colmore to cling to—if they couldn't dock in Cardington, they couldn't possibly land in France in this weather without facilities or huge teams of trained men.

"What's the heading for London, Johnny?" Scott asked.

"One hundred and eighty five degrees," Johnston answered.

"Steer one hundred and eighty-five degrees. Full speed on all engines," Scott ordered.

"This is ridiculous. My ship's been commandeered from under me," Irwin muttered.

"Captain Irwin, I'm the senior ranking officer aboard this ship. You *will* obey my orders without question," Scott shouted.

Irwin glanced up at Lou. "Commander, inform the chief coxswain the flight test is over. Tell him to get down to scheduled watch-keeping routine."

"Yes, sir."

Over Clophill where the A507 crosses the A6, the airship turned south. Brancker and Colmore appeared beaten. "Come on, Reggie," Brancker said. "Let's grab a couple of stiff ones."

Thomson sat patiently in the lounge, staring straight ahead, listening to the rain beating on the ship and cascading down the promenade deck windows. He felt it gently pitch and roll. With the engines running, the heat was on, and it was nice and cozy. Thomson thought it amazing that even in weather like this, airships were smooth and comfortable. He had no qualms about imposing his will on these men.

They just need leadership.

Again his mind went back to the night on the Forth Bridge.

Well, the Tay Bridge came down, but not the mighty Forth. They'd learned by experience—as we did with the crash of R38. We'll sail on to victory through all the storms and torrents the gods can throw at us.

He smiled with satisfaction as Scott came bursting into the lounge. He was able to speak freely, since the passengers were out on the promenade decks, where Disley had dimmed the lighting so they could see lights on the ground.

"I've decided to press on, sir. I'm going to drive her hard. We'll outrun this storm."

"*Bravo,* Scottie! It's times like this when the men are sorted from the boys, momentous decisions are made, and great things are achieved."

"Nothing ventured, nothing gained, sir. That's my motto."

"I shan't forget this. You've shown leadership and courage tonight."

Colmore and Brancker entered the lounge.

"Scott informs me he's decided to push on to London and beyond. We shall ride the storm!" Thomson said, unable to conceal his pleasure.

"Yes, sir," Colmore mumbled.

"What time's dinner? I'm famished," Thomson asked, glancing at Colmore.

Pierre was hovering in the doorway. "We can be ready for you in thirty minutes, gentlemen," he said.

"I think it's time we had some music, don't you?" Thomson said.

91

EVENING (DOG) WATCH
16:00–20:00 HOURS

Saturday October 4, 1930.

A fter Scott's announcement at 8:20 p.m., Thomson went to his cabin to change. Fifteen minutes later, with assistance of his valet, Thomson appeared—pressed and dressed in a new, lightweight, black evening suit made by Anderson & Sheppard. He'd also bought some expensive white shirts and splendid ties. With a blood-red rose in his lapel, tonight he looked fine indeed. He thought back fondly to the afternoon in July when Marthe had dragged him to Savile Row, insisting he had new clothes for the voyage. She'd helped him choose the materials—money he could hardly afford—but he was glad he'd splurged. Marthe would be proud of him tonight.

Thomson headed for the dining room. Buck went to the crew's quarters for bread and cheese. Thomson chatted with passengers on the promenade deck. They stared nervously out into the night, occasionally lit by a half-moon showing itself between squalls and scudding cloud.

Everyone had dressed for dinner. Pierre unlocked the record cabinet and showed the galley boy how to operate the gramophone. When the music came on, Thomson, Brancker and Colmore moved to the lounge for cocktails. Brancker appeared rigid—his way of masking his inebriated state —his monocle immovable, as if screwed into his head. Colmore was showing apprehension, but the alcohol had taken the edge off. Thomson didn't care how much they drank as long as the ship pushed on for India. Some would feel lousy in the morning—that was their prerogative. He anticipated enjoying the view of the Mediterranean with a clear head the following day. How beautiful that was going to be!

The first recording the galley boy put on (no one knew if it was intentional) was "Singing in the Rain", sung by Cliff Edwards. Everybody had a good laugh, which helped ease the tension. Most people sat down around 8:40 p.m., but it wasn't as formal as Thomson would have liked, since some of the officers were tied up with their duties. VIPs and special guests were served by the stewards as they arrived in the dining room—the more senior VIP's (including his 'Top Three'—Colmore, Scott and Richmond) sat at the head table with Thomson. Seating had been designated with white cards embossed with silver lettering, bearing their names at each place setting.

The first course was a tasty oxtail soup with crusty bread rolls, followed by meat cold cuts. Now Miss Helen Kane was giving her all on the gramophone with her smash hit, "I Wanna Be Loved By You."

In the chartroom, Irwin, Johnston and Lou studied the maps while Steff remained on duty below them. The evening watch would be over in half an hour. Potter had taken back the elevator wheel from Atherstone.

"What's the elevation of the ground ahead?" Irwin asked.

They checked the maps. They were coming up on Bendish, a small hamlet on rising ground just east of Luton, west of the A1.

"Four hundred feet above sea level," Johnston answered.

"After that, we've got the South Downs to contend with," Irwin said. The ship was still dangerously low.

"Bring her up as much as you can, Steff," Irwin shouted over the rail.

"Aye, aye, sir," Steff said and then, "You heard the captain, Potter."

Potter turned the elevator wheel. "She's heavy, sir. She's stayin' right where she is."

"We're going to have to dump ballast and quick, sir," Steff shouted to Irwin.

"Do it! Right now!" Irwin replied.

While Thomson and his fellow passengers were enjoying their first course, Church was keeping an eye on Jessup, who was still on the prowl. Church had checked the duty roster and knew Jessup was scheduled to be on the next watch. The villain was snooping around at the bow for no apparent reason—he had no business there.

Church and the others were very concerned about Lou. While the big shots had been having their conference, a few of the crew were having a conference of their own. They knew Lou was capable of snapping Jessup's neck in a second. Jessup would only get one chance—they reckoned he'd lie in wait and strike from behind. They'd taken turns watching him ever since leaving the tower. The time had come to put their plan into action. Jessup approached amidships toward Church. Church put two fingers in his mouth and gave him one of his own wild whistles from the lower catwalk. "Hey Jessup, I got something for you, me old cock," Church yelled.

Jessup was outraged. He stared down, his hateful eyes narrowed. "Who you whistling at, you little shit? What's that you got there?"

"A letter for you from Charlotte Remington. She sent someone to the ship with it tonight. Must be stuck on you, eh! Who would 'ave thought?"

Everyone knew there'd been a bit of a 'to do' over a girl at the tower earlier, but not the details. Jessup's infatuation with Charlotte was common knowledge.

"Give it 'ere, you little punk," Jessup shouted, rapidly climbing down a ladder.

Church ran off toward the oil storage room, laughing like a crazy man with Jessup in pursuit. Church slipped inside, closing the door behind him. Catching his breath, he leaned against the door, taking in the smell of lubricants and sacking piled in stacks. Jessup pounded with his fists, throwing himself against the door. Church stepped away and Jessup came stumbling in. Clearly, it wasn't what he'd expected. Church stood at the other end of the room waving the envelope in the air, taunting him. Church sang the words.

"Oh, Jess ...up ...come ...and ...get ...it."

Then too late, Jessup spotted the others. With the sounds of "boo hoo beloo" drifting from the dining room above, he realized he'd been set up. He took in the faces of Disley, Binks, and now, closing the door behind him and blocking his escape—Cameron. Jessup turned toward him in time to see the high-speed blur of a lead pipe coming toward his head. The pipe connected with his front teeth with a sickening crunch.

"You won't be smilin' at my wife again, boy," Cameron said.

Jessup spat his teeth on the floor mixed with gobs of blood and phlegm. Cameron hadn't finished. He brought the pipe back, swinging it up into Jessup's groin, crushing his testicles.

"Nor will you be doin' her anymore," Cameron whispered.

Jessup sank to his knees holding his crotch and groaning, his face contorted in agony. His eyes rolled up in his head and he threw up. Cameron reached to his back pocket and pulled out Rosie's letter. Cameron held it up, glaring at Jessup, his eyes murderous.

"*This* is the letter delivered tonight—you destroyed my Rosie. She's really buggered now and so are you—you piece of shit!"

Cameron unhurriedly and methodically stuck the envelope back in his pocket. He swung the pipe high in the air and brought it smashing down on Jessup's skull. His head exploded. Blood, brain and bone fragments flew in all directions and Jessup went down like a side of beef.

"Dammit, Doug, you've gone and killed 'im now!" Binks said incredulously, wiping splatter from his face with his sleeve.

"Yer don't say," Cameron said.

"You weren't supposed to *kill 'im*, were yer," Disley said.

"The plan was to put him out of action—not *this*," Binks said.

"Shit—now what are we going to do?" Church said.

"You've made a right mess of 'is 'ed, look," Binks said, standing over Jessup.

"Drag him over here while we figure this out," Disley said, stepping out of a pool of blood that had soaked one of his canvas shoes. They pulled Jessup across the room and pushed him up against the shelving stacked with cans of oil. They wiped up the blood from the floor with sacking and covered Jessup's torso with it.

"We're gonna have to get rid of 'im," Binks said.

"We'll have to dump him overboard," Church said.

"He might land in someone's back yard," Disley said.

"Or on somebody's roof," Binks said.

"Come *through* somebody's roof, more like," Church said.

"That wouldn't be very nice," Binks said.

Church took a rag and wiped blood from his face, jacket front and sleeve and then his hair, now an unruly mess. He took out his comb, put his foot up on Jessup's chest and began combing his hair back into place, while Jessup's demonic eyes stared vacantly up at him. When he'd finished, he threw a sack over Jessup's face.

"You're such an *ugly* sod!" he muttered.

Moggy Wigglesbottom loved cats, hence her nickname. She sat in her 15th century cottage in the quaint hamlet of Bendish finishing the last of her delicious baked trout. On a chair beside her, a majestic, white Persian, named Queen Isabella, sat watching and licking her lips. Moggy was a contented woman. Her tranquil life had never been better.

Suddenly, to her bewilderment, a bloodcurdling scream emanated from the kitchen. The cook and the maid must surely be under some kind of attack. Without hesitation, Moggy jumped up from her upholstered antique chair, snatched up the white ball of fluff, grabbed the poker from the fireplace and raced to the kitchen. She found both women staring, trance-like, out the garden picture window over the sink. Moggy couldn't believe what she saw.

Coming toward them, up her garden path, was the largest object she had ever seen in her entire life—a monster with flashing red and green eyes and yellow rays spilling from its sides. All she had worked for was about to be erased from the map and she, Queen Isabella, and her staff faced certain death.

"Come on! We can't stay here," Moggy yelled. She dropped the poker and rushed to the back door clutching the cat, the cook and maid close on her heels. All three ran full gallop down the path and leapt over the fence —a remarkably clean effort, worthy of a trio of Olympic hurdlers. They landed together in a heap on the other side in a pile of the gardener's horse manure. The area was suddenly lit like a stage set by an eerie, amber glow and flashing, green lights that made it even more surreal. The once white Persian howled in disgust.

"Oh, bugger!" Moggy exclaimed, surely echoing the Persian's thoughts, while picking manure out of her hair.

The women stared up in horror as His Majesty's Airship *Cardington R101* sailed over their heads. They were mesmerized by the sound of thumping railway engines accompanied by "I Wanna Be Loved By You". More annoying was the sight of men in dinner jackets and bow ties casually moving around the promenade deck as if they were in some swanky hotel bar, oblivious to the plight of Mrs. Wigglesbottom and her staff.

Then came another unwelcome sound—gushing water—two tons of ballast released by Steff. The beleaguered women were saturated by the freezing deluge as it spilled down upon them. They struggled to their feet, shivering.

"Shit and bugger!" shouted Moggy. The maid and the cook were shocked. They'd never heard such profanity fall from the lips of their mistress, church deaconess, Moggy Wigglesbottom.

The airship passed over, just clearing the thatched roof. It did, however, scrape the clay pot from the ancient chimney stack, which crashed onto the driveway on the other side of the cottage and smashed into tiny pieces.

"Damn you!" Moggy screamed at the dirigible's rear end. The twinkling lights, the roaring engines and Helen Kane singing her song faded gently into the night. She took a deep breath, her teeth chattering in the howling wind. It could've been worse. Much worse—they could all be dead and her beloved cottage destroyed. She would get down on her knees tonight and thank God her home had been spared and, after that, she'd write to the Air Ministry. She'd read earlier, with mild excitement about the airship leaving for India—but didn't expect to actually set eyes on it, let alone get close enough to be touched by the diabolical thing!

Dinner jackets indeed!

In the oil storage room, the crewmen were still debating the situation.

"We'll have to dump 'im in the sea," Disley said, at last.

"How long before we're over the Channel?" Church asked.

"I dunno. We'll 'ave to find out," Binks answered.

"It's gotta be a couple of hours," Disley said.

"I'm on watch in ten minutes," Church said.

"So am I," Binks said.

"Me, too," Cameron grunted. Until now, he'd remained mute.

"You gonna be all right to go on duty?" Binks asked.

Cameron didn't answer.

"Yeah, it'll be better if he does," Disley said.

"We'll 'ave to do it after 23:00, when we get off," Church said.

"We could dump 'im from the hatch above No. 5," Binks said.

"We'd have to lower 'im down the ladder on a rope, so he doesn't hit the car or the prop and make another bloody mess," Disley said.

"There's plenty of rope over 'ere, look," Church said.

"We'll have to wait till they've fixed my engine," Binks said.

"Won't they spot us from the control car?" Disley asked.

"They're usually looking where they're goin,' not backwards," Binks said.

"As long as the navigator ain't there, buggering about," Church said.

"We'll have to make sure the coast is clear," Disley said.

"And time it just right," Church said.

"Gettin' 'im to the 'atch without anybody seein' is going to be difficult," Disley said.

"We'll need more help. He's a big bugger," Binks said.

"I'll get Potter. He hates the bastard," Church said.

"They'll hang the lot of us for this, you know," Cameron said.

"Shut the hell up, will yer? No one's gonna find out," Binks said.

"Besides—you were the silly arse what clobbered 'im," Church reminded him.

"What 'appens when they can't find 'im?" Binks asked.

"He's on the next watch. They'll be lookin' for 'im," Church said.

"They'll think he's hiding somewhere," Binks said.

"We can say he must've committed suicide. Jumped out or got blown away," Church said.

"Here, grab this tarpaulin," Disley said.

They pulled out a folded tarpaulin and wrapped Jessup into a bundle, tying it with rope.

"A nice, tidy package," Disley said.

"He's humming a bit," Church said.

"What if people come in 'ere for oil and stuff?" Binks asked.

"Let's hope no one notices," Church said.

"We'll have to keep an eye out," Disley said.

In the control car and the chartroom, the officers had had a few nervous moments approaching Bendish. They'd heard the control car strike Moggy Wigglesbottom's chimney pot. They'd managed to gain altitude, but it was insufficient and too late. Lou realized the captain was worried about dumping more. The ship would get lighter and they could rise too high over the following days as the weight of fuel diminished. Then they'd be forced to valve off gas and not have enough to last the voyage. It was a vicious circle, but in this weather, the ballast tanks were being replenished with rainwater for the moment.

"Make a note, Johnny. We owe somebody a new chimney pot," Irwin said.

"Better than a new house," Lou said.

"We should go in to dinner. His Lordship will be expecting us," Irwin said. Lou, Irwin, Giblett and Atherstone trooped off to the dining room, leaving Johnston and Steff in control.

Dinner was well underway when they arrived. The diners were finishing their first course, oblivious to the near catastrophe just beneath their soft-soled shoes, which they all had to wear. The mood was upbeat and Brancker was relating tales of his world travels and wild affairs, his face flushed with the four glasses of wine added to the whisky, brandy and champagne. Everyone laughed and enjoyed his stories, or appeared to—Lou put it down to nerves. He'd seen all that before.

"...so there we were, stranded on the bloody lake in Jinja with the lady standing on the plane's floats in the most delightful pair of the shortest shorts with the damned crocs and me eyeing those beautiful legs. I think they were thinking about lunch—"

"And you were a tad hungry yourself, I suspect, Sefton, what!" someone said.

"Yes, I was getting hungry all right. Damned hungry!"

The room erupted. Thomson smiled at the four officers who'd just arrived.

"There you are, gentlemen. Is everything under control?" Thomson peered at Irwin, who was trying to suppress a yawn. Atherstone appeared just as tired.

"Yes, sir," Irwin answered.

"Will we be showing ourselves over the West End?" Thomson asked.

"Over the city, actually."

"What a pity."

"If you like, I'll ask Johnston if we can divert course slightly," Irwin replied.

"Would you? That would be such a wonderful gesture. It's Saturday night and the revelers will be out. It would give them such a thrill," Thomson said.

"I'll see what we can do, sir," Irwin said.

Irwin explained they didn't have much time and the stewards rushed off and brought the three late arrivals soup and bread rolls. The officers refused wine for water and tea.

"I wonder, will we be passing over Beauvais?" Brancker asked, looking at Irwin. "Treacherous place!"

"Ah, Beauvais. I made an unscheduled stop near there last year," Thomson said.

"An emergency, sir?" Richmond asked.

"Yes, the weather was rough and we couldn't get into Paris due to fog."

Thomson related his adventure of landing near Allonne in the dark and being taken to shelter by a funny little rabbit poacher named Rabouille, while they waited for transport to take them to the station.

"So, will we be passing that way, Captain?" Thomson asked.

"The navigator has us maintaining a safe distance from the ridge."

"We must be careful," Thomson said.

"They will be, sir, I'm sure," Scott said.

The officers finished their soup.

"We must go. It's time to change the watch," Irwin said, getting up.

"Yes. I'm on duty," Atherstone said, following Irwin back to the control car. Lou remained behind to finish his coffee. Pierre switched off the gramophone and put the wireless on. The BBC News came on after the sound of Big Ben striking the hour and the familiar signal.

Beep Beep Beep Beep Beep Beeeep.

'This is the BBC Home Service. Here is the nine o'clock news. This evening, at seven thirty-six, precisely, His Majesty's Airship Cardington R101 left the tower in Bedfordshire to begin the first leg of her maiden voyage to India. The airship will travel across France toward Paris and then down to the Mediterranean and on to Ismailia, where a banquet will be held aboard in honor of King Fuad—the King of Egypt. From Egypt, the airship will fly across the Arabian Desert to Karachi in Northern India. A number of dignitaries are on board for this historic flight, including the Secretary of State for Air, the Honorable Lord Thomson of Cardington, Sir Sefton Brancker, Director of Civil Aviation and Major Herbert Scott, the first man to command an aircraft making its return flight to America. Also on board, are other high-level staff members of the Royal Airship Works along with representatives from Australia, India and the United States. The weather forecast for the first leg of the journey promises a stormy passage, but it will be plain sailing once the airship reaches the Mediterranean tomorrow ...'

92

FIRST NIGHT WATCH
20:00–23:00 HOURS

Saturday October 4, 1930.

Atherstone had taken over the watch and was busy writing up the hourly report when Lou returned to the chartroom. Pierre followed him, bearing a plate of roast beef sandwiches. He placed them in front of Johnston at the chart table with a mug of tea. Johnston thanked him and ate ravenously. Leech came and reported that the pressure gauge had been replaced and No. 5 was running smoothly once again.

"What's our position, Johnnie?" Irwin asked. Lou leaned over the map with Irwin. Johnston continued eating. Pierre hung around. He liked to be aware of their position so he could inform Thomson, if asked.

"We've covered thirty-nine miles over the past hour. We're up against a virtual head wind varying between twenty and thirty miles per hour. We're over Hadley Common, approaching Alexandra Palace—after that, we'll be looking for the Cattle Market."

"His Lordship wants to fly over Soho. What do you think?" Irwin asked.

"What's he wanna wave to his old girlfriends?"

"Be nice, Johnny," Irwin chided.

"Okay, since it's his show, we'll continue down to the West End and make a left turn at Big Ben and Westminster Hall, then along the river toward Greenwich," Johnston said.

"Johnny, you really are the best," Lou said.

"Yes, he's lovely," Pierre agreed, before returning to the dining room with Johnston's plate.

"I'm gonna lie down," Irwin said. "Come and get me if you need to."

"Aye, aye, sir," Lou said.

Five minutes later Atherstone called up from the control car. "We're coming up to the Cattle Market, Johnnie."

"All right. Time to change course. Steer 210 degrees. That'll take us over Piccadilly and down to Westminster."

Johnston marked the time down on the chart—9:15 p.m.—as he'd been doing throughout the flight. The rudder coxswain brought the nose round onto the new heading. The ship 'crabbed' against the weather to stay on course. As they closed in on London, Hunt arrived in the chartroom to make a strange announcement.

"Excuse me, gentlemen. We seem to have lost a crewmember. He's supposed to have come on watch, but no one can find him. I had to put someone else in his place."

"Who's gone missing?" Atherstone asked.

"Jessup. No one's seen him, I suppose?"

Everyone shook their heads.

"Wait 'til I find that bugger, I'll kill 'im. He's ruining my kip," Hunt muttered, as he left to resume his search.

Lou was suspicious. Maybe Jessup was lying in wait somewhere.

The whistle on the speaking tube sounded. Atherstone listened, exasperated. "Damn! The bloody oil pressure on No. 5's dropped again."

Lou left the control car to inspect the engine himself. He climbed down the ladder in the atrocious weather and entered the engine car. It was warm and quiet—too quiet. Binks had taken over from Bell and stood glaring at the engine with Leech and another charge hand.

"What's up now?" Lou asked.

"There was nothing wrong with the gauges. We're gonna have to inspect the big end bearing and main bearings. After that, we'll check the relief valve," Leech said.

In cramped conditions, Binks began removing the eight inspection covers. Lou wished them luck and climbed back up the ladder into the ship to give Atherstone an update. After that, he walked the ship from stern to bow, moving around carefully on the catwalks in case Jessup was lurking somewhere. There was no sign of him.

In the dining room, Thomson and his party were finishing their coffees and enjoying brandy and port chasers. Their stimulating conversation covered aviation, war, women and horses. Pierre came and stood beside Thomson.

"Sir, I've been informed we're coming up to the West End, if you and your guests would like to remove to the promenade deck."

Thomson jumped up. "Oh yes, mustn't miss *that!*"

With "Blue Skies" belting out by Al Jolson from the gramophone, everyone followed Thomson's lead. Colmore, Scott, Brancker and Richmond stood with Thomson.

"We'll have blue skies when we get to the Med, sir," Scott said. "That, I can promise you."

"Champion, Scottie!"

They stared from the windows into the bright lights of London, startled to see the roof tops so close. On the glistening streets of Piccadilly, cars were stopping to get a better look. People peeped at them from under umbrellas in swirling rain. Hundreds sheltered in doorways gazing upward while the airship pushed on relentlessly. Thomson caught sight of His Majesty's Theater. He knew *Bitter Sweet* was still playing. He couldn't read the billboards, but he knew what they said. Marthe had so enjoyed that musical. He'd been by the theater many times and read them since—treading the precious ground she'd walked on. Sadness seized him. He smiled wistfully—such fond memories, and yes, they were indeed bitter sweet! What was she doing at this moment?

Those Romanians like to stay up half the night!

He glanced at his watch: it was 9:22 p.m. They were two hours ahead in Bucharest. He knew she'd now be back at Mogosoëa. He doubted she'd be in bed yet—she may be entertaining. So many admirers! The thought depressed him, but he fought it off as he usually did. At times like this he thanked God she wasn't the over-sexed siren they made her out to be.

Maybe she's writing—who knows, perhaps to me.

Over Trafalgar Square, Thomson peeked out at the wet lions guarding the fountains. And then at his idol, Lord Nelson, standing high on his column, looking in their windows.

Oh, that I would someday be as revered as thee!

A red double-decker stopped below for the passengers to get a good look. The conductor stared up from its exterior, curved staircase. He was, no doubt, excitedly announcing that *Cardington R101* was overhead on her maiden voyage to India!

How rapidly the world is changing! Thank God I can play my part.

The ship traveled down Whitehall toward the luminous, white faces of Big Ben standing mute next to Westminster Hall, his most favorite Gothic room in all of England!

Just before 9:30 p.m., Lou and Giblett composed a message to Cardington using the ship's call sign.

CROW: 20:21. GMT. Crossing London. All is well. Rain moderate, heavy at times. Low cloud. Base ceiling 1500 feet. Winds 25 mph at 240 degrees. On course for Paris via Tours, Toulouse and Narbonne.

Lou showed the message to Atherstone. After taking it to Disley for transmission, he rejoined Atherstone in the control car where Johnston was giving Atherstone the new course for Greenwich. Lou winked at Cameron, but he didn't respond.

Poor guy's still upset about Rosie.

Lou figured Cameron had read Rosie's letter. The envelope was sticking out of his back pocket, its flap ripped open, its edges stained with blood. Lou was puzzled.

Must have cut himself.

The time had come to gain altitude. The ship turned over Westminster Hall and flew east toward Greenwich, along the river. They passed over Greenwich Observatory and the Royal Naval College, then Greenwich Park, where they turned onto a heading of one hundred and ninety-five degrees, toward Blackheath Park Station. Atherstone ordered Lou to dump a ton of ballast from Frame 6. They'd replenished plenty from the rain now. The ship became lighter as they burned fuel. They dropped another ton and Cameron brought the ship up, keeping an eye on the altimeter. They were soon up to twelve hundred feet. The North Downs, Johnston told them, would rise to eight hundred feet. Their concentration was high and intensifying—there'd be no room for error.

Twenty minutes after leaving Greenwich, they thundered on toward Eltham and Crockenhill. Over Lullingstone Park, Johnston had them turn the ship through forty-eight degrees to starboard and from here they traveled along the Darent Valley through the Downs. Lou marveled at Johnston's navigational skill as they wove their way between the Kentish hills— especially in such foul weather with little or no visibility.

Lou returned to the chartroom, where Disley came in with a message. Giblett read it and laid it down silently in front of Lou and Johnston. They leaned over reading the contents together with growing alarm.

To: CROW. From: Met Office, Cardington.
A trough a low pressure along coasts of British Isles is moving east. Ridge of high pressure over southern France forecast for next 12 hours. SE England, Channel and Northern France Wind at 2000 feet will be from 240 degrees at 40 to 50 mph. Low cloud with rain.

Johnston scowled. "I wish we'd known this three hours ago."

"These winds will be double what we were told," Giblett said.

"What's going on up there?" Atherstone called up.

"They're now telling us the winds are going up to fifty miles per hour," Johnston replied. Fear showed in the coxswains' faces.

Atherstone winced. "You'd better inform the captain," he said

Lou went to the captain's cabin adjacent to the chartroom and called from behind the black curtain at his door.

"Come in, Lou. What's up?"

Lou pulled back the curtain. Irwin was lying on his back, wide awake.

"A weather report just came in, sir."

"I presume it's bad news."

"The winds are expected to kick up to fifty miles an hour."

Irwin swung his feet down off the bed and sat up. He rested his head in his hands, rubbing his eyes and sighed. "This is turning into a full-fledged gale," he said. Lou knew he must be thinking about Olivia. "There's not much we can do—we're stuck."

"'Fraid so, sir."

Lou returned to the chartroom where they were still engaged in negotiating their way across the Weald through the Downs. He went back down to assist Atherstone in the control car. As soon as they reached Sevenoaks, they made a right-angled turn to fly due east, passing Kemsing on port. The ship was turned again to pass through another gap between Borough Green and Ightham and then onto a southerly track for Tonbridge.

Atherstone turned to Lou. "D'you mind checking No. 5 again, Lou?"

"Not at all. I *love* it out there."

Lou put on his topcoat and disappeared along the gangplank toward the problem engine. He climbed down the cat ladder. It felt like the winds had increased a lot. Inside the car, Binks had removed the inspection covers. Leech was examining the big end bearings and main bearings. Lou waited for Leech to speak.

"Can't tell you anything yet, sir," Leech said. "Might know something in another hour."

"I'll come back later," Lou said.

Back in the control car, Lou attempted to see through the rain.

"Where are we now, sir?" he asked Atherstone.

"We're passing Tonbridge on starboard."

Lou looked across at the lights, but ascertained little in the blinding rain. He checked the altimeter. They'd dropped to eleven hundred feet. Atherstone spotted it, too.

"Cameron, bring her back up to twelve hundred. *Concentrate!*" he snapped.

Lou stayed in the control car on watch, while Atherstone took a break. When Atherstone returned, Lou checked with everyone and then went to rest in his own cabin. He'd be back and forth as relief watch and navigator for most of the night. Irwin remained in his cabin and as Lou passed by, he noticed light under the door curtain. He worried about the captain. He thought he heard a sob.

Lou lay down with a light on over the night table. He'd dreaded this. It reminded him of the Canadian voyage. He'd been so euphoric then. All those times while he'd lain in his bunk thinking of her and making plans, she'd been cleaning up and getting the hell out—but God, how he still loved her. The agony of being separated was too much to bear—especially tonight. He wondered what she was doing—if she'd listened to the 9 o'clock news. Maybe she's out with someone else—perhaps this Robert guy. The thought was intolerable. He felt like a failure—he'd not measured up.

Maybe she's got someone who can give her what she craves. A kid.

He glanced at the time: it was 10:20 p.m. They'd soon be coming up to Bodiam Castle. He could faintly hear the sound of the gramophone above. "Sittin' on Top of the World" was playing.

That's a laugh! She could be right, though. Perhaps this is the end. No—the thunderstorm over Montreal was worse. We survived that. I'll take John's advice and try to see her again when we get back—if we get back!

He glanced at the picture frame on the bedside table—the family, Julia, Jeb and Alice. Somehow, at this moment, the frame had more significance than the photo. Even the sight of it caused him pain. Why the hell had he used the same frame? He studied his father, trying his best to smile. He wondered how he was doing. What was it, six weeks since he'd seen him? Did he look worse? Many of Lou's boyhood days with his father had been rancorous, but they'd gotten closer that last day than during his entire life. Lou switched off the light and lay back.

The darkness accentuated the movement and sounds of the swishing, buffeting wind and rain. It sounded like the ship was being peppered with shards of glass. The engines were noisy, too—more intrusive than *Howden R100's.*

Ol' Nev and Wallis would love to hear that!

He missed Nevil and Billy being around. But at least Potter, Binks, Church, and Dizzy were on board. His mind wandered to Mrs. Hinchliffe. Perhaps he should have taken her up on her offer!

She's a beautiful woman.

He thought about Julia. He wondered if it was time to start taking an interest in other women. He didn't feel ready for that. His mind changed the subject. He thought about the American airships and the interest expressed in him in Washington. Perhaps he should retire from this crazy life and help his family make moonshine and grow carrots and corn—and keep the Klan at bay!

That'd be more sensible and probably a lot safer!

Lou missed Virginia. He lay there, finding it impossible to relax. Then the gypsy's words began tormenting him.

She had things she could not share ...Another victim of war.

After all her deceit, he figured cheating would have come easy. After half an hour, he got up and went back to the chartroom.

While Lou had been trying to rest, Thomson and his group were sitting comfortably in the lounge, most of them well oiled and quite numb. Pierre approached Thomson again.

"Sir, we're coming up to Bodiam Castle. They tell me we'll be crossing the English coastline in a just few minutes."

"Come on, Sefton—time to say goodbye to Dear Old Blighty," Thomson said, getting up from his floral-cushioned, wicker armchair. Everyone got to their feet. Thomson's choice of words upset Colmore and Thomson wished he'd been more careful.

The airship passed over Bodiam but they couldn't see much, save a light shining from a crofter's cottage. They flew over Ewhurst Green, crossed the River Brede, over Guestling Green and then the village of Pett. Everyone gathered at the windows on the promenade decks.

When they reached the coast, they passed over the *Olde Cliff End Inn*, its illuminated sign on the gable plainly visible. Outside, braving the weather, revelers stood wrapped in raincoats by their cars, under umbrellas—those that hadn't been blown inside out. Some waved mugs of beer up at them, to wish them luck. Now, "Blue Skies" was being repeated from the lounge and dining room speakers. Thomson hoped the inn patrons could hear it.

Our crabbing attitude must appear awfully strange.

The ship swept out over the raging sea at a weird angle, still minus an engine, its colored navigation lights reflecting intermittently on the turbulent water. The sound of music gradually faded. Soon, the throbbing engines were gone, the glints of red and green swallowed by the darkness. Now, only the pounding surf on the rocks and the vicious wind in the swaying poplars could be heard by the pub crowd at the cliff edge.

Thomson, surrounded by his entourage, stared back at England's receding lights, Hastings and Bexhill on starboard, Rye and the Dungeness Lighthouse on port. Colmore couldn't hide his gloom. "Perhaps the air will be smoother over the water," he mumbled, almost to himself.

"Don't you worry, Colmore, it'll all be here when we get back—and we'll get a rousing reception, the likes of which you couldn't possibly imagine!" Thomson reassured him. "Gentlemen, I think the time has come for a fine Cuban cigar to round off this very special occasion."

The thought of that only increased Colmore's depression.

"Good idea, sir," Scott said.

"*Rather,* CB," said Brancker.

A party of six, including O'Neill, the Indian representative, went with Thomson to the smoking room, led by the reluctant chief steward. Richmond and Rope excused themselves, needing to make another inspection. Colmore went back to the lounge with the Australian and a couple of R.A.W. officials for tea. Thomson shook his head.

That's what some British do to make themselves feel better—while the rest get drunk!

In the smoking room, everyone settled down in easy chairs around the perimeter. Brancker took off his dinner jacket and sat next to Thomson on the long couch against the wall. Pierre served yet more port and brandy in fine crystal glasses to everyone, except Thomson, who requested coffee. Once they had drinks, Pierre came round with the box of cigars, cutting the caps off and assisting with the lighter chained to the trolley. Soon, the room was filled with smoke, causing Pierre to cough and his eyes to stream as before.

The ship ploughed on toward mid-Channel and Johnston came down into the control car followed by Lou, who carried a box of flares. Johnston, his clipboard under his arm, also carried his sighting instrument. Lou put the flares on the sill and Johnston opened the window, causing a blast of cold air to rush in.

"Sorry, gentlemen," Johnston shouted above the howling—not sorry in the slightest.

"That's okay, these boys need waking up," Atherstone said, eyeing Cameron.

Lou threw the flares down into the thrashing sea at fifteen-second intervals, where they burst into flames on contact. Soon, a line of bobbing flames lay behind them, visible intermittently.

"Look at the angle we're flying at. *Bloody ridiculous!*" Johnston exclaimed.

"She's taking a beating all right," Lou said.

Johnston took his sightings, noted them on his clipboard, then closed the window.

"Are you done, Johnnie?" Atherstone asked.

"Yes, sir."

"Check how they're doing with No. 5, Lou. We need that engine," Atherstone said.

"Aye, aye, sir," Lou said.

Lou left the flares on the windowsill. He and Johnston went back upstairs. As Lou was putting his coat on, he glanced down at the altimeter. It'd dropped to nine hundred feet. Atherstone had also noticed.

"Wake up, Cameron! What the hell's wrong with you? You need some more cold air!" He took the wheel and brought the ship up to a thousand feet. "Keep her right here."

"Yes, sir, I'm sorry." Cameron looked more miserable than Lou had ever seen him, unaware he'd just committed cold blooded murder.

That boy shouldn't be on the wheel tonight.

Lou left the control car and went down the catwalk to engine No. 5, keeping an eye out for Jessup. Rope was still making inspections. They both nodded without smiling. Lou pulled back the flap to the cat ladder. The wind lashed his face and head. He clung on and climbed down. Inside the car, they were wrapping things up. Leech gave Lou a half smile, confident now. He leaned down and peered out the window.

"Blimey, look at them whitecaps. Who the bloody hell's on the elevators?"

"It's a bitch of a night, Harry," Lou said. "You guys done?"

Binks screwed the last of the inspection plates back on.

Leech answered, "Should be all right now. I'm going up to the oil storeroom. As soon we dump in some more oil, we'll crank her up and find out."

Binks jumped up. "Stay where you are, Mr. Leech. *I'll* get the oil," he said.

"That's damned good of you, Joe," Leech said. "I'll wait here."

Binks went out and up the ladder like a squirrel up a tree. Lou's eyes followed him.

"He's a damned good fella. So willin'," said Leech.

Lou nodded, wondering what Binks was up to and where the blood on his collar and sleeve had come from. A few minutes later, a shaken-looking Binks was back with drums of oil in a sack tied on his back. Leech poured oil into the engine. Binks got the starter engine going and cranked up the Tornado. After a few moments, the engine was running sweetly with its familiar, deafening rumble, the oil pressure perfect. Leech gave Lou and Binks the thumbs up.

"I'm going up for me cocoa," he shouted.

"Wish I could come," Binks said.

Lou checked his watch: 11:45 p.m. "You've only got fifteen minutes, Joe."

Leech and Lou climbed back up into the ship.

93

MIDDLE WATCH
23:00–02:00 HOURS

Saturday October 4, 1930.

Lou got back to the chartroom at ten minutes to midnight. Irwin had arrived to take over the watch with two fresh coxswains, who'd already taken over the wheels. Cameron and the rudder coxswain hung around while they got the feel of the ship. Irwin looked positively ill. The voyage had hardly begun. Exhaustion was already taking its toll.

"Okay, time for cocoa and then a kip," Atherstone said.

"I hope *you* can sleep," Irwin said.

"I've just requested bearings from Le Bourget and Valciennes," Johnston told them. "As soon as I have them, we'll reset the course and I'll take a nap myself."

At 23:00, Cameron glanced at his relief coxswain who nodded to him.

"Okay, I've got it, Doug," he said. Cameron scuttled off. Lou thought everyone seemed too damned jumpy this evening.

At midnight, a wireless operator popped into the smoking room. The smoke-laden air and cigar odor was overpowering. "Gentlemen, would anyone like to send a message to friends or loved ones?" he asked, trying not to sneeze. He held up a notepad and pencil. Thomson was profoundly pleased.

This will delight Marthe. Why not, I'll send her another one.

He took the pad and pencil and wrote in his bold scrawl.

M Bibesco Mogosoëa Palace, Romania
Dearest M We are making good progress STOP Now over the English Channel en route to Paris STOP Thinking of you as always K

Brancker was next to take the pencil. He leaned close to Thomson.

"I must drop a line to my dearest love, Auriol Lee in New York. She's producing a play on Broadway, you know," he whispered.

Thomson gave him a funny look while Brancker scribbled a few lines. When he'd finished, O'Neill wrote a note to his wife. The wireless operator took the messages and hurried out.

Church was tense. He'd waited five long minutes for the others, who slipped in one by one—Cameron, Binks, Disley and then Potter who'd joined the party.

"About bloody time!" Church growled.

"Keep yer wool on," Binks said. "I came in 'ere twenty minutes ago for some oil an' there's two bleedin' riggers sitting on Jessup's carcass drinking beer." Everyone gasped. "I told 'em the foreman was comin' and they scarpered, right quick."

"Best get moving. We've only got twenty minutes. We're near the French coast," Disley warned.

"We gotta be careful. Where is everyone?" Church asked.

"No. 5's fixed now—Mr. Leech is out of the way," Binks said.

"Where is he now?" Church asked. ''He's always making the rounds.''

"He's 'avin' his supper in the mess," Disley answered. "Where's the navigator? Has he finished with the flares, Doug?"

"Yes, he left the control car," Cameron mumbled.

"What about the chief?" Church asked.

"Sky Hunt's asleep in his bunk," Potter said.

"What about them two officers with the R.A.W.?" Binks asked.

"They're up in the tail, climbing around," Church said.

"Let's hope they stay out the way. Sammy, make sure the coast's clear. We'll get him ready," Disley said.

Church went to the door and switched off the light before opening it. After poking his head out, he moved stealthily along the catwalk and then amidships to the hatchway at No. 5. No one was around. He scampered back to the storage room and slipped back inside.

"Come on—it's all clear," he whispered.

They'd pulled Jessup into the center of the room, nicely wrapped, and tied ropes to his ankles, which were sticking out the bottom. The corpse was lifted among them and they carried it along the catwalk, Church holding the feet. Up ahead, Church spotted Richmond, approaching.

"Whoa! Watch it. Someone's comin'," he hissed.

"Quick, under here," Disley said, gesturing to an area off the catwalk. They laid the body down and threw a sack over Jessup's feet. They stood in front of the bundle until Richmond arrived.

"Evenin', sir," Church said, giving Richmond a sweet smile.

"Evenin', sir," the others said together.

Richmond was pleasantly surprised by so much respect. "Good evening, gentlemen," he said. "What are you fellows up to?"

"Just stretching our legs, sir, and saying what a wonderful airship this is," Binks said.

Richmond smiled. "And what's in the bundle?" he said, eyeing the tarpaulin behind them.

"We wrapped Lord Thomson's carpet and brought it up here from the bow to distribute the weight better, sir," Church answered.

"Excellent! I must confess that did concern me. Well done!" Richmond spotted drips of blood. "What's that trail of red liquid along the catwalk and down here?"

"Oh, that's just dope. Someone spilled some, sir. Horrible stuff," Binks said. "Don't worry, we'll clean it up."

"Dope, right. Ah, well, I'm off to the promenade deck to take a peek at the coast of France. Keep up the good work, chaps," Richmond said, walking off.

"Come on, we'd better hurry," Church said.

Around 12:15 a.m., one of the stewards reported the sighting of the French coast. Thomson waited while Pierre put out the last cigar in a pail of water, switched off the lights and shut the doors. Thomson followed them to the promenade deck. Some were in a bad state. Brancker, his jacket over his arm, was having difficulty negotiating the corridor. When they reached the promenade deck, they joined Colmore and the Australian at the window. Brancker collapsed into an armchair. Up ahead, the lights of France beckoned in the darkness.

"Gentlemen, the lights you are seeing ahead are on Point de Saint Quentin," Scott announced proudly.

"Bravo," someone said.

As soon as Richmond had disappeared, the five crewmen resumed their unpleasant task. They grabbed Jessup in his tarpaulin shroud and marched rapidly to the flap over engine No. 5. Church shimmied down the ladder to warn Bell and make sure the coast was clear. He checked the control car. Irwin and the coxswains were facing forward.

Church returned and they got themselves in position. Jessup's body was lowered head first down the cat ladder, while Cameron, Disley and Binks held the ropes tied to his ankles. Awkward to the last, Jessup became snagged between the engine car and the ladder and Church had to go down and push him out until he was clear. Soon Jessup was dangling free in space below the engine car. Church came back up the ladder.

"Okay, let him go," he whispered.

"Anyone gonna say a prayer for him?" Binks whispered.

"You're jokin', right?" Church asked.

"Yeah, I'll say a prayer for him, all right," Cameron said.

They unraveled the ropes from their wrists and let go. The bundle and rope was gone in a flash. They heard nothing but howling wind.

"Go straight to hell, you worthless sack o' shit!" Cameron shouted down the ladder.

"*Amen!*" Binks echoed.

At 12:20 a.m., the wireless operator handed a message to Johnston in response to his request to Le Bourget and Valciennes for bearings to fix their position. Lou and Johnston referred to the chart, calculating an adjustment to the course. Johnston drew a new line.

"We need to steer two hundred degrees. This'll bring us nine miles southwest of Abbeville and four miles west of Beauvais," Johnston said. He wrote the heading down and gave it to Irwin.

Scott entered the chartroom a little unsteadily. "Commander, do you mind coming with me? I need your assistance." Lou followed Scott past the dining room, now laid for breakfast, to the lounge.

"Have a seat. We must write a communication to Cardington," Scott said. He had some *Cardington R101* stationery on the table. Lou sat down.

Scott held out a pencil. "Here, your writing's better than mine."

"Okay, sir. What would you like to say?"

Scott sat thinking.

The passengers were still gathered on the promenade deck with Thomson, Colmore at his side with Richmond. Brancker remained slumped in his chair.

"Well, gentlemen," Thomson said, "having seen the welcome sight of France, I must now bid you all a *very* good night!"

Amid a flurry of 'good nights' and brimming with satisfaction, he drew himself up to his full six foot five inches and marched away—every inch a brigadier general. Tonight, he'd accomplished something great—this would go down in the history books. Thomson entered his cabin. He took out the red keyring from his pocket and put it on his desk. He then changed into his pajamas and put on his silk dressing gown. Before sitting down to write his journal, he picked up the keyring to examine it closely. Satisfied, he slipped it into his dressing gown pocket and began to write.

Saturday October 4th, 1930.
A successful day. Airship standing up to gale admirably. Having crossed the Channel, we are now heading toward Paris. Tomorrow, I anticipate enjoying sunshine over the Mediterranean. Today, we have put an end to the naysayers.

When Thomson had gone, Colmore appeared at Lou's table in the lounge, Pierre at his side. "Lou, please give Sir Sefton some assistance. He's a little bit under the weather," Colmore said, squinting as if to say, 'Let's not make a fuss.'

Lou went to Brancker and held out his hand. Brancker took it and Lou pulled him to his feet. "Can't seem to get my legs going, old man," Brancker mumbled.

Lou put an arm around Brancker's back and under his arm. "Quite all right, sir," Lou said. They walked crablike down the corridor, joined at the hip, with Pierre leading the way, holding Brancker's jacket.

"It's awfully good of you, Lou," Brancker said.

Pierre pulled back the curtain to Brancker's cabin and Lou manhandled him to the bunk and gently laid him down. Lou pulled off Brancker's shoes and stood over him. Colmore remained at the doorway. Brancker tugged at his tie and collar, revealing a St. Christopher on a silver chain. He pulled it over his head and held it out to Lou, smiling happily.

"See that? Belongs to Lady Cathcart. Took it off and gave it to me, she did. *Insisted* I wear it. Sweet gal—said it'd keep me safe."

"I'm sure it will, sir."

"Wants me to give it back to her when we get back," he said with a devilish grin.

"I expect she's making sure she sees you again soon, sir," Lou said.

Brancker grinned at that. He wanted to confide more, but speech was difficult and his eyelids were beginning to flutter. Lou was sure he wouldn't remember any of this in the morning. Brancker revived for a moment.

"Lady Cathcart is a close friend of Lord T's lady love—Princess Marthe, you know."

"Interesting, sir," Lou said.

"But you know *Auriol* is the one I love the most. Oh, how I miss my Auriol. She understands me …I'm not *perfect* you know ..."

"That's nice, sir."

What came next stunned Lou. It was as if Brancker was merely continuing their earlier conversation and he'd just decided to answer Lou's question. "Yes, as I was saying, I had my fortune told once. The woman said she couldn't see a damned thing in my palm after 1930 …Precious little time left now, what!"

Brancker faded out and was sound asleep, snoring gently. He clasped the St. Christopher to his chest. Lou carefully removed his monocle and laid it on the side table.

Pierre hung Brancker's jacket in the closet. "You're such a good man, sir," he whispered. He took a blanket from the closet and covered Brancker with it. "I must be off to bed myself," he said with an impish smile. Lou came out into the corridor where Colmore shook his hand.

"That's why I switched to tea; otherwise you'd have been putting us *both* to bed," Colmore said.

"Maybe *I* should have 'one too many'," Pierre said playfully.

Lou ignored this and bade Colmore goodnight. He smiled at Pierre and returned to the lounge, where he found Scott waiting, brandy glass in hand and a bottle of cognac on the table.

"I think I've got it now," he said.

While Lou wrote, Scott spoke slowly—having difficulty getting his tongue around some words. "After a lovely dinner—"

"How about ...after a splendid supper?" Lou suggested.

"Yes, that sounds nice ...our important guests—"

"Our distinguished passengers?"

"Okay ...smoked another cigar—"

"How about ...smoked a *final* cigar?"

"Yes, that's good ...and having reached France—"

"What about ...having sighted the coast of France?"

"Right ...have gone to bed to rest—"

"Okay, sir."

"...after all the stress of saying goodbyes to their—"

"How about this ...after the excitement of their leave-taking?" Lou suggested.

"Right. And then ...all essential services are functioning," Scott said.

"You could say ...all essential services of the airship are functioning normally and the crew has settled down to their normal watch-keeping routine?"

"Yes, right, that's very good." Scott glanced at the time. "Show it to Captain Irwin and send it to Cardington. Everyone'll read it in the Sunday papers tomorrow. I'm off to bed." Scott yawned.

"Good night, sir," Lou said.

Lou showed the message to Irwin and then took it to the wireless room, where the radio operator was trying to decipher the messages Brancker and O'Neill had scribbled earlier. Lou studied them and dictated what he thought they said.

Miss Auriol Lee Manhattan Hotel New York NY
Darling Auriol On board R101 to Paris Egypt and India STOP Just thinking of us in Jinja STOP Told my traveling companions about you STOP Love always Your Sefton

O'Neill's was easy:

Mrs O'Neill West London Hospital Hammersmith London
Wishing you the best for a speedy recovery STOP Cardington R101 progressing well STOP Love W O'N

Lou went to Irwin in the control car. "How are things now, sir?"

"She's at least three tons heavy."

"Should we dump ballast?"

"Running with the engines at full bore, she's developing enough dynamic lift like a plane, so it doesn't matter right now—unless we ease off."

Lou checked the altimeter. They were maintaining 1500 feet without too much problem. Outside, they were enveloped in darkness, no lights or landmarks to use for navigation. He hoped they were on course.

"Sir, something weird's happened," Lou said.

"What?"

"One of the crewmen disappeared earlier," Lou said.

"Disappeared? Who?"

"Jessup."

"Hmm. Must be on board somewhere," Irwin said.

"He was missing for his watch at eight o'clock. No one's seen him."

"Did you check the engine cars?"

"I'll ask Leech. He's been in and out of the cars all night."

Later, a groggy Johnston returned from his cabin. He went down to the control car and stared out. He spotted a landmark in the distance. He told Lou he was familiar with the area.

"This is Poix. We've been blown *way* off course again, damn it!"

Johnston returned to the chartroom and worked out a new course to make the correction. After a few minutes, he went back to Irwin and handed him the bearing.

"Here, you need to steer two hundred and ten degrees toward Orly," he said.

The coxswain reset their course.

In his humble cottage outside Allonne, in the gloomy half-light, Monsieur Eugène Rabouille, the button maker, sat huddled by the fireplace in a threadbare armchair. He smoked a rolled cigarette and stared into the dying embers of his log fire, listening to the din.

"God, I hate this weather," he muttered.

Violent gusts roared down the chimney, pummeling the tiny windows, making them whine and rattle and tree branches to scratch at them like ghosts' fingernails—a sound that had terrified him as a child living there with his mother. And it terrified him still. Adding to his misery, a violent clap of thunder shook the cottage and the tiny room was lit by lightning.

Lightning or not, he had no choice. There was work to be done, bellies to be filled. Rabouille wearily pulled himself up and donned his scruffy brown overcoat and flat cap. He picked up his sack of paraphernalia. The metal parts inside rattled as he threw it over his shoulder. He blew out the lamp and opened the front door. The wind blew the door open with such force it smashed against the stone wall, almost tearing it off its hinges. He had difficulty pulling it shut behind him. He trudged up the road and across the field toward Therain Wood. Oh, God, how he hated the struggle.

Rabbits by night and buttons by day—that's my miserable life!

Lou gingerly opened the smoking room door and closed it tightly behind him. He opened the second door and peered inside. The odor of stale cigars and brandy filled the air. Leech was lying on the couch previously occupied by Thomson, smoking a cigarette. Lou closed the door.

"Still wearing the wife's lucky heather, I see, Harry," Lou said.

Leech glanced down at his lapel. He'd obviously forgotten about it.

"I thought I was gonna get blown away once or twice, tonight—it must be powerful stuff!"

"Taking a break?" Lou asked.

"Yep, a fag before bed, sir," Leech said, taking a long drag.

He swung his feet off the couch, sat up and killed the dog-end in the ashtray. He picked up his glass from the floor beside him and took a sip.

"You having one, sir? I'm having a whisky and soda."

"You deserve it. No, I'll fall asleep. Seen anything of Jessup?"

"No. I expect that sod's hiding somewhere."

"He's not in one of the engine cars?"

"Definitely not. I would've seen him. I've been in all of them four times tonight."

"He'll turn up when he gets hungry. I'll say goodnight. Great job tonight, Harry."

"Thank you, sir."

Lou returned to the control car.

It was a beautiful day. The sun streamed in through the café windows. Thomson sat at his usual table, engrossed, watching the girl in the carriage. He couldn't see her face—her wide-brimmed hat obscured part of it and its shadow hid the rest. But somehow, he was able to imagine it, as though he knew her and had seen her beautiful face many times before—though perhaps not in this lifetime.

He hesitated, knowing if he rushed outside that damned coachman would snap the reins and she'd be gone. He studied the girl's slender, white neck and dark brown, almost black hair with tinges of red, tumbling around her shoulders. He caught a glance of her magnificent profile as she turned toward the shop next to the café. She was waiting for someone.

A short, dumpy, Slavic woman wearing a drab, brown headscarf came into view. She marched to the carriage carrying a large package tied

with pink ribbon. She opened the door and clambered in. Thomson leapt to
his feet, charged outside and sprang to the curb. The coachman leered down
at him from his lofty seat with that sickening, cocky smile of his. The
maidservant's back was to Thomson—she sat facing the girl. The coachman
snapped the reins and called to the two beautiful, white beasts with long
flowing manes.

'*En avant! Walk on!*'

The carriage moved toward Thomson in slow motion. He desperately
wanted to take in the features of this girl—to know her, make sure that
beautiful face was etched in his mind forever. As she drew closer, she looked
directly at him. She'd never done that before. Her eyes lit up and she gave
him the smile of an angel, moving her head as she passed, so they shared
each other's gaze—a moment of pure love. It was *her*! No doubt about it. She
could be no more than fourteen years old and so beautiful he was overcome.
He cried out her name.

"*Marthe!*"

She lifted her white-gloved hand to her lips and blew him a gentle
kiss as she passed, still smiling. He noticed her drop her eyes to his neck for
a moment, taking in the insignia on his collar—the flames of the Royal
Engineers.

The carriage gathered speed and she turned her head back toward
him, not removing her eyes from his. The carriage turned the corner and she
was gone. Thomson turned back and stared at the cloistered shop and read
the words over the door from which the maidservant had come. He was
devastated!

MADAME DUPREE

Haute Couture Bridal Gowns.

94

MORNING WATCH
02:00-05:00 HOURS

Sunday October 5, 1930.

Head down, Rabouille pressed on across the sopping field toward Therain Wood, pulling his soaking overcoat around him. "It doesn't get worse than Beauvais Ridge," he grumbled, his words swallowed by the beastly wind and driving rain.

He became conscious of a distant droning behind him. He turned. A mile away, the dirigible glistened in the intermittent moonlight and lightning flashes. The sinister sight made him shudder. He stopped, open-mouthed, for a few moments, staring in astonishment. Even far off over the city, the horrible thing appeared enormous. The ship was struggling to make headway. He caught its green navigation light between fast moving clouds. Thunder rolled across the angry skies all around him. Rabouille turned and continued his tramp toward the woods, where he hoped it'd be less miserable, sheltered among the trees. He cursed as he moved through a bleating flock of terrified sheep suddenly lit up like day, bells tinkling and clanking around their necks.

Lou and Irwin stood side by side, staring at the beautiful city, which, under normal circumstances, they would have appreciated—but not this terrible night. The magnificent Cathedral of St. Peter of Beauvais with its tall, flying buttresses rose before them, glistening between lightning flashes. Too close for comfort! Lou checked the altimeter: twelve hundred feet. They had just adequate clearance over the rising ground. The winds increased the closer they got to Beauvais Ridge. He glanced at Irwin, who was shaking his head, not believing they'd arrived in *this* of all places! The town hall clock was striking two. It was time to change the watch. Steff and Hunt came down into the control car with two fresh coxswains, one of them, Potter.

"We're approaching the ridge," Irwin said. "You can take over once we're clear of this damned place. Hopefully, the wind's gonna die down once we get by." But for now, it was growing more violent by the minute. The four newcomers peered out of the windows over the city with concern.

"Okay, sir," Steff said. "I'll do the hourly report. Let me know when you're ready for me." He took the log and went upstairs to the chartroom. Hunt stayed in the control car and the fresh coxswains took over.

Binks was snoring in his bunk when he was awakened by his foreman.

"Come on, Joe, wake up! You should've been on watch by now. Bell's waiting for you." Binks sprang up and sat on the edge of his bed.

"Oh, bugger!" he exclaimed.

The foreman thrust a cup of cocoa at him. "Here, take this."

"I don't have time for that, Shorty. Bell's gonna be mad."

"You'd better drink it, mate, or *I'll* be mad!"

Binks swilled the cocoa down, nodded his appreciation and took off along the catwalk. He collided with Richmond, on his way to the bow to do another inspection. Apologizing over his shoulder, Binks ran to the hatchway and slid down the ladder. He clung on to prevent being blown away like a leaf, stunned to see the ground so close. He slipped into the engine car. Bell gave him a nasty look, eyeing the engine car clock, which said 02:03 a.m.

"I'm really sorry, mate," Binks shouted.

Bell shook his head in disgust. Then something caught Binks's eye out the tiny window.

"Oh, my God!"

"What?"

"I just saw a church steeple in the lightning—just *yards* away."

Bell pushed Binks out of his way and peeked out into the darkness. He saw nothing.

"You silly sod, you're still asleep!"

Just inside the tree line of Therain Wood, Rabouille was checking his snares. He came upon a trap with a creature caught in its jaws, its leg broken. He released the dripping animal and held it up roughly by the scruff of the neck. The sky lit up again. The rabbit shivered with fright.

"You'll do for dinner," Rabouille muttered.

His attention was taken from the rabbit by that infernal droning noise again—louder this time. He looked up in shock, believing *he'd* now become the hunted one. The airship was coming straight at him at about five hundred feet. The covering material at the front was torn and flapping wildly. Vicious winds were rushing inside the hideous contraption.

The shrill speaking tube whistle sounded in the control car. Irwin grabbed it and listened; his eyes widened in horror and the blood drained from his face. He shot a glance at Lou and winced, mouthing, "Oh, my God!"

Lou sensed his panic. Something catastrophic must have happened. Irwin listened a few more moments and then began yelling.

"We have an emergency! Richmond says the cover at the bow's torn and the first gasbag's getting destroyed and more are gonna be. Sky, go and see what's going on. Take some riggers with you. Try and close it up. We'd better get prepared for a crash landing—just in case. Be ready to warn all hands." Hunt dashed up the steps toward the crew's quarters and Steff came down into the control car. Irwin shouted, "We've got to try and save the rest of the gasbags. Lou, dump emergency ballast at Frame 2 and Frame 6. Steff, be ready to dump fuel."

"Aye, aye, sir."

Lou grabbed the toggles on the control panel and released emergency water ballast. At the same time, Irwin released additional ballast with the valves on his side. Now bow-heavy from the loss of gas and the breakdown of airflow over the nose, and aided by vicious downdrafts, the bow dipped violently.

When Thomson cried out "*Marthe!*" in the dark, the sound of his own voice woke him with a start. His mouth felt like sandpaper. He coughed, unable to swallow, trying to remember the dream before it was gone. He was brought back to reality by the buffeting wind, which caused the airship to buck and dive. Alarmed, he jumped out of bed and switched on the light. It was near impossible to maintain his balance. His watch said 2:07 a.m. He hurriedly slipped on his soft shoes and dressing gown and made his way unsteadily along the corridor to the chartroom. His feelings of satisfaction and well-being had evaporated.

Something must be seriously wrong!

Rabouille couldn't budge. He remained staring at the airship, which seemed to lose buoyancy, its nose dropping without warning. Suddenly, water spewed from its front end and it came back up, leveled out and continued to fly straight for him at about two hundred feet. He could see both the red and green navigation lights. The tear at the front had grown into a gaping orifice, like the mouth of a great fish. He clung tightly to the rabbit. Now, two sets of bulging eyes stared up at the monstrous creature coming to devour them. Rabouille prayed the damned thing would clear Therain Wood.

Thomson clung to the railing and hurried down the steps into the control car. He was thoroughly displeased.

During the dive, Irwin shouted to Potter, "Bring her up!"

Potter reacted immediately. He spun the elevator wheel forcefully, until it refused to turn anymore.

"That's maximum elevators, sir!" Lou shouted.

The speaking tube whistle sounded again. Irwin grabbed it and listened intently, his face ashen. He replaced the tube with resignation.

"What the deuce is going on, Captain Irwin?" Thomson snapped.

"That was the chief coxswain. The cover's failed completely at the bow. We have a massive hole. Un-repairable! He confirmed we've lost Gasbag 1 and Bag 2's deflating fast. Bag 3 is soaked and getting ripped away from its valves. Bag 6 has also ripped away at one side. He thinks more are coming loose due to the surging. We got caught in the vicious winds. It's all over."

"Is this Beauvais Ridge?" Thomson asked, desperately struggling to hold on as Potter tried to bring the ship back up to her original altitude. It felt like a roller coaster.

"Yes, it is," Irwin answered.

"But you *knew* this place was treacherous!"

"We got blown miles off course by the gale. We should never have left the tower—but you *all* overruled me, didn't you!" Irwin shouted, not hiding his contempt.

As the ship finally leveled out, a loud crack vibrated throughout like a harmonic chord. Potter swung the elevator wheel in dismay—all resistance gone.

"We've lost elevators," Potter yelled.

"That was the elevator cable," Irwin said calmly.

"What's happened to it?" Thomson asked, his eyes finally registering fear.

"It snapped under the strain of full elevators."

More unnerving noises followed, slowly at first—creaking, groaning, popping, snapping—sounds all too familiar to Lou. He could only think of Charlotte. The image of her when he'd last seen her standing on the front step in the moonlight filled his mind. A Greek goddess. He was brought back by Irwin.

"Now you're listening to the sounds of her back breaking," Irwin said, matter-of-factly. "Add an extra bay! Loosen the harnesses. Huh!"

Richmond jumped down into the control car in a state of panic.

"Ease off power! Some girders are buckling," he shouted.

"It's worse than that!" Lou shouted, pointing out of the windows toward the bow. Through lightning flashes, they saw the hull slowly sagging. When they turned to look at the stern, the same thing was happening—she'd gone limp from head to tail.

"Oh, no. She's done for!" Richmond cried.

"Her back's broken," Irwin said.

Thomson was speechless. He thought of Marthe—and all his carefully laid plans.

"Prepare for crash landing! Dump *all* ballast at the bow," Irwin ordered. "I'm gonna try and put her down."

Lou blew down the speaking tube. Someone answered. It wasn't Church.

"Where's Sam? Find him and tell him to dump the emergency ballast. *Right now!*"

"Bring her head to wind!" Irwin ordered.

The rudder coxswain swung the wheel, bringing her bow into the wind to slow her down.

"Signal all engines to SLOW," Irwin shouted.

Lou rang all telegraph bells, relaying the order to the cars.

"Dump all fuel!"

Steff grabbed the emergency fuel tank cutters, emptying many of the diesel tanks instantaneously.

"Lou, go and wake Disley. Tell him to be ready to pull all breakers as soon as we're on the ground. Find Hunt. Tell him to warn all hands. Steff, go and warn Atherstone and the passengers."

"Can I send Potter? I'll stay with you, sir," Lou asked.

"No! Get out of this control car. Everyone above decks!" Irwin ordered, grabbing the rudder wheel from the coxswain and pushing him toward the stairs. The two coxswains rushed upstairs. Lou and Steff hesitated. Potter stopped at the chartroom railing above, to wait for Lou.

"*Go!* All of you! That's an order!"

Before following Steff upstairs, Lou turned to Irwin, making eye contact.

"Good luck, sir," he said. Irwin nodded. But Thomson wouldn't budge. He stared straight ahead through the window into the blackness of Therain Wood.

Irwin glared at Thomson. "And *you!* This is the most dangerous place on the ship—you'll have a chance upstairs." Thomson and Irwin faced each other, neither backing down.

Lou rushed upstairs to the chartroom where Potter was waiting.

"I'm gonna stick with you, Lou," Potter shouted.

"Come on then."

As the ship dived, Binks was thrown backwards against the engine.

"Oh, bloody hell!"

"Don't panic, Joe. It's only the storm. She's done this 'undreds of times," Bell said.

But then, stampeding feet and yelling above their heads increased Binks's fear.

"Something's very wrong, Ginger, I just know it. I'm really scared," Binks whimpered.

The ship leveled out again and as it did so, they felt the harmonic vibration and then the creaking and groaning as her keel compressed and other parts were pulled apart. The telegraph bell rang. They watched the indicator move to SLOW.

Bell grabbed the throttle lever and eased the power.

"Oh, no! What now?" Binks groaned.

Steff had already set off for the passenger cabins, having roused Atherstone. Lou rushed to the switch room, Potter on his heels. Lou burst in, finding Disley asleep on a cot, his chess set in disarray on the floor next to a blood soaked shoe. Lou leaned over and shook him

"Dizzy, wake up! We're making a crash landing. Be ready to pull the breakers as soon as we're down."

Disley leapt out of bed in a daze. Lou turned and ran off to the crew's quarters, Potter close behind. There, he found Hunt, who'd already begun rousing the sleeping crewmen.

"I took riggers to the bow, but it was hopeless. She's done!" Hunt said.

"Yeah, the skipper's putting her down, Sky. You felt it go, didn't you?"

Hunt nodded.

"We gotta warn all hands," Lou said.

Hunt hollered at the sleeping crewmen. "We're down, lads. Come on, shake a leg!" He turned back to Lou. "The bags are full of holes again and the valves have been puffing their guts out. We could never 'av made it anyway," Hunt said.

Crewmen began sitting up, bleary-eyed. Lou looked in cabins adjacent to the crew's quarters and roused the men inside. He rushed into Pierre's cabin. Pierre was snoring in his bunk, his hairpiece lying on the table beside him.

"Get up, Pierre. The captain's putting the ship down—try and save yourself. Run to the stern!" Pierre became wide awake immediately, springing bolt upright like a jack-in-the-box, shielding his balding head from Lou's eyes. He cried out in anguish, eyes wide with terror.

"Oh, no. God no! Save me, Commander, please save me!"

Lou suddenly remembered Leech in the smoking room and rushed off in that direction. Potter was slower off the mark this time. The ship dived a second time as Lou dashed down the corridor, his momentum increased by the ship's acute nose-down angle. He grabbed the railing and hung on, glancing back to see what had happened to Potter. Potter was twenty yards behind, also clinging to a railing, unable to move. Lou felt the bow gently touch the ground and heard the unnerving squeaking, squealing sound of the nosecone scraping the earth down to bedrock. It put his teeth on edge.

The floor fell away beneath Lou's feet, and then leveled out. The ship settled, while continuing to move forward. The hull shuddered and shook violently, as though in an earthquake, grating and juddering over the rocky ground, before telescoping into itself. The sound was deafening and the vibration rattled every tooth in his head.

We're down now, all right!

Just after the lights went out, massive explosions erupted at the bow and behind Lou (where Potter had been), knocking him to the floor. Stunned, momentarily blinded and almost deaf, he struggled to his feet, grabbing the railing again. He hung on, looking desperately for Potter, trying to see through the wall of fire. His face and body were seared by the heat and much of his hair burned away. His uniform smoldered, scorching his back, chest and legs. For a few seconds, a gap appeared in the curtain of fire and smoke. Potter was gone. At that moment, he realized how much Potter meant to him and how much Potter depended on *him*.

I must go back and find him.

Lou let go of the railing, which had blistered his palms and fingers, and started back toward the inferno. A hand roughly grabbed his shoulder, pulling him back.

"No, sir. This way!" a voice shouted behind him.

Leech had emerged from the smoking room.

"I've got to find Potter!" Lou cried.

"He's got to be dead. He couldn've survived that."

"I can't just leave him."

"No! You're coming with me."

Potter filled Lou's mind—aboard *R38* and at their wedding at St. Cuthbert's. Overcome by a sense of profound loss, he began to weep. He felt himself gripped in a bear hug from behind and dragged down the corridor. All the while, above the roaring fire and rolling thunder, he heard piercing screams that made his blood curdle. Lou was too weak and in too much pain to fight. Moments later, they were in the smoking room, lit by flames from outside. Utter chaos reigned. Most furniture had slid against the bow-end wall. The remaining chairs lay on their sides with the drinks trolley, from which glasses and bottles had been flung like missiles. Leech grabbed a soda siphon and sprayed Lou's smoldering clothes. Then he slammed the two doors shut, leaving them in pitch darkness. Once inside, the rumbling inferno surrounded them. Lou's heart pounded and unbearable panic rose in his chest and throat. The moment he'd dreaded all these years had come.

Moments earlier, Thomson had stepped up beside Irwin at the wheel, reconciled to his fate. "The fault is all mine. I stand beside you, Captain Irwin," he said. Nothing but bitter regret filled Thomson's heart.

Was all this for Marthe? Never will I see her again—not in this lifetime.

He looked at Irwin and saw terrible sadness in his face.

He's thinking of his wife. What have I done! Dear God, forgive me.

Irwin turned to him, and as if reading his mind, nodded his forgiveness. They shook hands. Thomson stared at the ground coming up to meet them. The bow gently kissed the earth and the ship balanced on its nose for an eternity, ploughing a deep furrow into the woods.

Perhaps we can survive this. Maybe God will allow us live, after all.

The hull settled slowly down—so very, very slowly, moving forward at a snail's pace. Everything unfolded in milliseconds with astonishing clarity. The forward port engine propeller made contact with the ground, causing the car to be twisted round on its supports and driven up into the hull. Its exhaust pipe was glowing red and shooting a spray of beautiful sparks, like the sparklers he'd had as a child in India during the Diwali Festival of the darkest night. The massive explosion that followed at the bow blew out the control car windows, the shards ripping flesh from their faces and bodies. The flares Lou and Johnston had left on the windowsill dropped to the floor.

The gigantic bulk gradually sank on top of the control car, pushing it into the sodden ground. Irwin went down with a moan and Thomson fell backwards to the floor beside him. He held up his arms to protect his bleeding head and face, but the structure came down upon them and the flares burst into vivid white flame as the ballast water mains over their heads ruptured with a great whoosh.

In that instant, Thomson's life played out before him. He heard his own first cries as he left his mother's womb in Nasik …every word he'd ever uttered and every word spoken to him …his early childhood in India and then England …growing up with his siblings …Cheltenham School …the Royal Military Academy …the Army …the Retreat from Mons …Ypres …the girl in the carriage on Rue de Rivoli …meeting Marthe at Cotroceni Palace …his sorry attempts in her boudoir …having dinner and blowing up oil wells with her husband, George …Palestine ….Versailles …campaigning for a Labour seat and failing …riding the Flying Scotsman …meeting MacDonald at Lossiemouth …battling Lord Scunthorpe in the Lords …witnessing the launching of *R101* …his meetings with Colmore and Richmond …all his bullying …and all his arrogance. It all took less than a second before his chest was crushed under the collapsing structure. He gave himself up to the blinding white light.

In engine car No.5, during these last moments, Binks's terror had increased. Their car vibrated with the urgent, pounding feet of crewmen above.

"Oh, blimey, now what?" Binks sobbed.

Both men were thrown backwards a second time as the ship dived again. Hunt's voice above them in the crew's quarters reached them loud and clear.

"Oh, no, that's Mr. Hunt. We've had it now!" Binks cried.

Though it might have meant certain death, Rabouille stood rooted to the spot, paralyzed with fear. The monster moved toward him against the wind, balanced on its nose, carving its deep furrow and clearing a wide swath through the trees. The smell of diesel, spilling from the ship's belly, overpowered him and he was enveloped in a cloud of fuel and water vapor. With relief, he realized the ship was going to miss him—just barely, having turned away during the last moments. He could now only see the starboard green navigation light. It settled to the ground like a beached whale, still moving, the hull telescoping in on itself for a hundred feet. Sparks flew as the structure and the propellers tore at flints in the rocky earth. In horror, he watched the massive bulk settle onto the control car, squashing it like a tin can, along with the two doomed men he'd seen inside.

As with Thomson, Rabouille experienced events in slow motion. Engine No.2 hit the dirt, its propellers still turning, forcing the car upward into the envelope. The ship was ripped apart, the flaming cover torn to shreds. Broken guy-wires and cables whipped and lashed about. Sparks showered in all directions, from severed wiring torn from electrical devices and from smashed light bulbs. All went dark for some seconds after she'd come to rest and then a deafening explosion shook the ground and knocked him down. He sat clinging to the rabbit like a child with a stuffed toy, as flames burst hundreds of feet into the air, lighting up the French countryside for miles.

Rabouille wept uncontrollably as he watched screaming figures perform a terrible, macabre dance of death inside the inferno. The heat scorched his face. He choked on the smoke and acrid fumes of burning diesel, oil, carpet, wood and canvas. Brilliant white columns with golden heads withered away to ash, along with the poor creatures trapped within.

He tried to block out their screams, sticking his fingers in his ears, letting go of the terrified animal. He cried out in horror and his rabbit hopped lopsidedly away, leaving him alone. The ship's cover blazed from stem to stern, revealing the grand lounge and dining room, fine furniture and upholstery gutted with vivid intensity. Curtains to the passenger cabins were aflame, along with bedding and bodies, giving off suffocating, black smoke and the odor of burning flesh. High on the stern, the scorched red and blue ensign fluttered defiantly in the howling wind.

Rabouille watched a flaming super-human struggle out of the blazing structure, jump down and run toward him, falling at his feet, screaming in agony. He heard the poor wretch cry out a woman's name as he fell: "Florry!"

Rabouille leapt to his feet and dashed through the forest like a madman chased by the devil, wet branches tearing and lashing his face. He ran out into the tussocked field, tripping and stumbling among the wildly bleating, clanking sheep and crossed the Meru Road. He didn't stop until he reached the cottage, where he barricaded the door and fell down on his knees beside the bed. He prayed he'd forget the horror of this night. He crossed himself and climbed into bed, pulling the covers over his head, listening to the rolling thunder dying away over the ridge. There, he remained for the next three days, his bed becoming like him, grubby and smelling of diesel fuel and acrid smoke.

Binks stared out of the window of the car from the center of the inferno. No sooner were they hearing the commotion above their heads and the signal given to SLOW, than the ship became a blazing wreck on the muddy, wooded plateau. For them, there was no jarring crash as the ship came to ground. All *they* witnessed was the rapidly disappearing cover devoured by fire and the vast skeleton exposed in blinding light. Blistering hot walls turned their cocoon into an oven. Flames licked their feet and legs through holes in the floor.

"Safety first. What a *bloody* joke!" Bell shouted.

"Sweet Mother of Jesus, save us," Binks cried.

"We've got to get out. This petrol tank's gonna blow any second," Bell screamed.

Binks suddenly remembered the old gypsy. A vision of her filled his head and he clearly heard her voice.

"Hey, hold on a sec, Ginger. Trust me on this," Binks shouted, putting both his hands on Bell's chest. Bell frowned at Binks, but didn't move. A few moments later and without warning, one of the ballast tanks above ruptured, sending a torrent of water cascading over them and the car. The flames were doused and the car cooled momentarily. The two men picked up their wet coats and threw them over their heads.

"Come on Joe, let's get out of here."

"Thank you, dear merciful Lord God in Heaven!" Binks exclaimed. "Through fire, rain and fog she said! Yes! Yes! The old witch was right."

They climbed out onto the car's entry platform into the intense heat and blinding fire and jumped. They fell down on their hands and knees into the mud, then dashed, slipping and sliding through smoke and steam to a safe distance. They collapsed on the ground, burned, but alive.

"I owe you one, Joe. Thank you for being late, mate!" Bell croaked. "But how did you know water would come down on us like that, eh?"

Binks smiled. " 'Ee who 'esitates ain't always lost, is 'ee!"

Lou's worst claustrophobic nightmares had materialized. In this tomb, at the center of hell, in total darkness, they'd surely be cooked alive. His fear was increased when the rumbling floor above collapsed. They were knocked down as the ceiling fell, leaving them four feet of headroom. Aside from his phobias, Lou was in a bad state. Burns to his body and face stung with salty sweat. What was left of his hair smelled singed.

"This ain't no way to die, is it, sir?" Leech said.

"We've got to get out," Lou yelled.

"I'll try the door." Leech crawled to the first door. The frame and structure of the opening were askew. The door wouldn't budge. He found the drinks trolley, ripped off the cigar lighter and lit the space with the flame.

"Cigar, anyone?" Leech said, holding up the cigar box.

"Nice, Harry," Lou croaked.

Leech stuffed two cigars in his inside pocket.

"We've got to break through this wall," he said.

In insufferable heat, they crawled on their hands and knees through broken glass around the sheet metal-lined walls. Lou heard Leech pulling on a settee screwed to the wall on the starboard side. He scrambled across the floor to help him and they yanked it free.

"I need a knife," Leech said.

Lou reached gingerly inside his pocket and pulled out his old *R38* switchblade. He opened it and passed it to Leech. Lou held up the flaming lighter while Leech went to work on the hot wall. He was able to pry away the sheeting at one of the seams, exposing asbestos boards behind it. He frantically beat the asbestos with his fists and stomped it with his heels until it cracked and fell to pieces. After more furious moments of clawing and pulling, he'd made a hole big enough for them to pull themselves through. Leech went first. As Lou struggled out, he ripped a deep gash in his left arm on the jagged metal sheeting.

Outside, the cover had disappeared entirely, but the fire was still raging. Making their way through the flames to the perimeter of the structure, they stepped on red-hot girders, burning the soles of their feet. Once there, they had no choice but to jump for it. Lou guessed the ground was thirty or forty feet down, although he couldn't see for smoke. Again, Leech went first. Lou heard crackling sounds, and then Leech shouting up to him.

"It's okay, sir. There's a tree there. Jump for it."

Lou leapt out as far as his strength would allow. He could just make out branches and leaves that shook cold water over him as he jumped. He caught hold of one branch, but it snapped. He grabbed wildly at others, but they slipped through his grasp, tearing his face. He fell to the ground head-first, strangely evoking a vision of Irwin reading the lesson in church. He hit the ground with a snap, as his right arm was broken. He rolled across the grass and lay there feeling like Jonah spat from the whale onto the dripping shore. Irwin's gentle Irish voice filled his head. *"...And the Lord spake unto the fish, and it vomited out Jonah onto the land ..."*

Water continued to shower upon him.

Ah, blessed cool water!

Leech knelt down beside him. "Are you okay, sir?"

"You know what? I reckon we're gonna get to smoke those cigars you stole from His Majesty's airship, Harry."

"Damned right we are! Powerful stuff, this heather, sir."

Leech helped Lou to his feet and they limped away from the smoke and flames. From out of the haze, they heard a shout.

"Anybody out there?"

"Me, Leech!"

Two men, their heads covered, emerged like desert tribesmen in a war, their faces black and blistered, clothes burned. But Lou recognized the voices. "Thank God, you're all right, sir," Binks said. "And you, too, Mr. Leech."

"Anyone seen Potter or the captain or Pierre?" Lou asked.

They shook their heads. Three additional men approached out of the smoke: more engineers who'd escaped from their aft port and starboard engine cars. Two of them were supporting their companion, who looked close to death.

"Who are you?" Lou asked.

"I'm Cook, sir, and these are Savoury and Radcliffe." Cook nodded to Radcliffe. "This man's hurt pretty bad."

"You two lay him down over here and stay with him. We'll go and see if we can find anyone else," Lou said.

Radcliffe was burned all over his body, face and hands. He cried out in agony as they laid him down. Both Lou's arms throbbed and blood ran from the cut he now realized was deep. He held on to his broken arm as they moved along the wreck, feeling dizzy and nauseous.

"Hey look, there's another one," Binks said.

"Who are you?" Leech shouted.

"It's me, Disley."

Disley, his hands badly burned, was in terrible pain. He, like the others, was hardly recognizable, being black with soot and oil. He grimaced and moaned. They came to the position where the control car should've been. Not much was left. It was flattened into the ground.

"If the captain was in there, he had no chance," Leech said.

"Thomson stayed with him 'til the end," Lou said.

"I guess you gotta hand it to the man for that," Leech said.

Lou had been in that control car only minutes ago. All this was *déjà vu*—he'd survived again. He felt wretched. They moved on toward the ship's bow in the woods. Someone was on all fours, trying to crawl away from the intense heat.

"Sammy, is that you? Yes, it's Sammy!" Binks cried, sinking to his knees beside Church.

"Oh, Sammy, thank God you're alive. Are you all right?"

Church was far from all right. He, too, was barely recognizable—his hair completely gone, face and hands horribly burned, his jacket smoldering.

"Get me jacket off ..." Church mumbled, fighting to breathe.

Church cried out in pain as Binks and Bell gently turned him and sat him up to remove his jacket. They lifted him carefully and moved him further from the burning wreck.

"Oh, Sammy," Binks sobbed.

"Get me cigs," Church whispered, his eyes beseeching.

"He wants a cigarette," Lou said.

"In me jacket," Church said.

Binks fished through Church's jacket pockets and found a tin of Players. He lit one from a piece of burning wreckage on the ground. He stuck the cigarette in Church's mouth and took hold of his injured hand, but had to let it go. Church winced and took a long drag and blew the smoke out. He looked thankful for a moment, nodding to indicate they should help themselves. They each took a cigarette. He looked up at Lou.

"I'm sorry sir, I tried to release that ballast, but I got there too late," Church whispered.

"Don't worry about that, Sam. It wouldn't have made much difference," Lou told him.

"I was so looking forward to a life with Irene," Church said, looking up at the swirling clouds.

"You'll have that life, Sammy," Lou assured him, knowing it was a lie.

"Not now. They don't call me 'Bad-Luck Sam' for nothing." He closed his eyes. "I shoulda stayed home. Joe, me cards. You take 'em."

Binks fished out the playing cards loose in Church's coat pocket. "Don't worry, mate. I'll look after 'em for yer."

Lou hobbled away coughing and holding his broken arm. He beckoned to Disley with his head to follow him.

"Dizzy, can you make it to that town over there?"

"Yeah, I reckon."

"Call the Air Ministry. Tell them what's happened."

"The police station's the best bet, sir," Disley said. Despite the pain, he stumbled off across the field toward the lights of Allonne.

Lou sank to the ground as an army of villagers approached—there must have been a hundred of them. They moved slowly up the hill in the darkness, carrying lanterns and rescue equipment. At last, they arrived. Nuns, nurses, doctors, firemen, policemen and farm workers made up the procession. They carried stretchers, first aid supplies, picks, shovels and digging bars. The fire had died down some and Leech implored them to help him try to find his shipmates inside the wreck. Lou didn't have the strength to assist them. He lay on his side watching, until he faded into blackness.

PART TWELVE

Passengers board *Cardington R101* from the tower.

AFTERMATH

95

MOGOSOËN

Sunday October 5 & Monday October 6, 1930.

While Thomson had been enjoying a cigar in the smoking room and scribbling a message, Marthe was kneeling beside her sumptuous bed praying to God for Him to watch over Thomson and his airship and for his voyage to India to be a resounding success. She shuddered with cold as she climbed into bed and burrowed under the bedclothes. As she drifted off, she considered Thomson's marriage proposal. Had she, deep in the furrows of her subconscious, already made up her mind? She prayed again in a whisper for an answer. Guilt and depression hung over her like a guillotine.

Please God help me, please help us all.

Marthe woke in the darkness Sunday morning and let out a piercing scream. Isadora burst in from the adjoining room.

"My dear baby, what's the matter?"

Marthe sat up clutching her chest, her face screwed up in agony.

"I'm dying. I'm dying. Fetch the doctor! The pain is terrible!"

Isadora rushed off and telephoned Marthe's doctor, asking him to come at once. She also called Marthe's husband, who was in bed fast asleep with this mistress. George arrived before the doctor.

Isadora sat with Marthe on the bed, her arm around her. Other servants came and joined the vigil. Gradually, the searing pain subsided, only to be replaced by despair. Just before dawn, the French windows to Marthe's bedroom burst open and the sheer curtains flew out from the wall. To the women gathered around Marthe's bed, this was a dreadful, supernatural sign.

"Oh, my God! Oh, my God!" Marthe moaned.

"It's only the storm," Isadora assured her.

"No, no, it's not."

"What is it, my darling?"

"It's Kit."

"What about him?"

"It's him—he's dead," she whispered.

"Oh, Marthe. Don't be so dramatic."

"He's dead! Isadora, I know he's dead ..."

The next day, the pain had subsided and despite her anguish, Marthe wrote in her journal.

Sunday October 5th, 1930.

    Last night, I was awoken by Kit's voice calling to me in a dream. So loud, it woke me. I managed to get back to sleep, but was awoken again by a dreadful pain in my chest. It felt so bad, I thought I would surely die. I called for Isadora, and she sent for George, who came immediately. He is very good these days. The doctor came at last, but found nothing. A heart attack, perhaps. He gave me pills to sleep, but they did no good. I could only think of Kit. I long for him to be back from his voyage and for us to meet again in Paris. Oh Kit, my dear friend, Kit. May God preserve you.

The following morning, Isadora came to Marthe's bedroom with two telegrams—both from Thomson. One was from the post office in Westminster on the evening of departure and the other from the airship itself, during the early hours of Sunday morning. Marthe derived no comfort from them.

Half an hour later, Marthe was informed Prime Minister MacDonald was on the telephone. She knew the reason for his call. Her heart sank.

"Good morning, Prime Minister."

"Marthe, I'm calling with news which breaks my heart ..." He sounded shaken.

"Yes, Ramsay?"

"His airship has crashed in France."

"He's dead?"

"I'm afraid he is. All but nine perished."

"It happened at just after 4 o'clock Sunday morning?" Marthe said, managing to stay composed.

"Yes, my dear. Today they'll lie in state in Beauvais. They'll be brought home tomorrow from Boulogne and thence by train to Victoria. I shall be there to meet him ..." his voice faltered.

"He'll be glad of that."

"I've arranged for them to lie in state in Westminster Hall."

She pictured Thomson's handsome face as he stood in the center of Westminster Hall, staring up at the structure before they parted, as he always did.

"When?" she asked.

"Friday ...The damned blabbermouths have already started with their mischief."

"What do you mean?"

"Some newspapers are asking questions. They're blaming him. He hasn't even been identified and buried ..."

She heard him draw in his breath as he choked up.

"You think they'd leave a man *something* …" he whispered.

"Sickening!" she said.

He rallied suddenly.

"I shan't allow his name to be tarnished. I'll not *stand* for it!"

"Has the funeral been arranged?"

"Saturday. Will you come?" MacDonald asked.

"I wish that were possible, but I'm feeling quite ill."

"I understand. Please take good care of yourself, Marthe."

"Will you do something for me?" she asked.

"Anything."

"Place a single red rose on his coffin from me."

"I shall make a point of obtaining one of his special roses—*Variété Général Jacqueminot*, I believe."

"Bless you, dear Ramsay."

They said their goodbyes and MacDonald promised to keep her informed. Marthe retired to her bedroom, where she remained for the next three days.

96

THE NUNS OF BEAUVAIS

Monday October 6, 1930.

Lou found himself riding into the Cardington Fairground on the *Brough Superior*. The colors were vivid, unnaturally so, the cloudless sky a deep sapphire, the sandy ground, violent ginger. Above, he heard unnerving screams of girls on the Ferris wheel, not of joy, but of horror and behind him, more screams…those of crewmen trapped inside *Cardington R101*. He looked back over his shoulder at the tower. The ship, shining like polished silver, was enveloped in orange flame from end to end. He turned the bike and stopped. He saw no one, but could hear their cries inside. Turning away from that miserable sight, he coasted on through the fairground toward the carousel, its music gently playing. Sound came intermittently, as though from a speaker with a bad connection.

He passed the crimson tent where Madam Harandah stood with her hands on her hips. She gave him an off-hand look as he neared the gilded, red and gold carousel of bobbing horses. He stopped to watch it. Charlotte was the first person he spotted, with her parents standing beside her. She rode a white horse, her eyes vacant. She took no notice of him. Others were seated behind her on multi-colored horses: his own father and mother, Tom and Anna, Julia, old Jeb, his hair dazzling white, and wife, Alice, and their children dressed in fluorescent colors. Following them, from *R38* was Josh, Capt. Wann soaked in blood, Capt. Maxfield and Commodore Maitland horribly burnt. They were in uniform. The commodore looked ridiculous, wearing a black Napoleonic bicorn hat. Lou's dead German boy, with the broken neck, sat beside New York Johnny, Bobby and Gladstone the cabin boy—all dripping wet. Three satanic Ku Klux Klansmen followed in flowing, white robes. The leader, on a black and white appaloosa, held a blazing cross. Lou sat motionless, realizing why no one would acknowledge his presence—they all hated his guts. He couldn't contain himself any longer.

"Dad!" he screamed in desperation, but not one head turned in his direction. They remained like tailors' dummies, riding up and down and round and round, in a slow motion parade.

Then, off to one side, he saw two women. They were both gorgeous and beautifully dressed and made up, unreal, like shop-window mannequins. One was Helen Smothers (in her magnificent hat), and the other, Mrs.

Hinchliffe. "Hey, Commander Remington, come ride with us," Helen Smothers called.

"Yeah, come on, Remy," Mrs. Hinchliffe said.

But he knew they didn't mean it. They were taunting him.

"Come on Lou, I was hoping we'd meet again," Helen Smothers said, her voice silky and inviting.

"Don't forget to call me Millie when we meet again, Lou ..." Mrs. Hinchliffe shouted.

Lou rode away from them, over to the coconut shy, where he found Potter at the entrance, playing his accordion. He smiled as he squeezed the bellows, playing a polka. On the ground in front of him was his airshipman's cap full of coins. Lou tossed in a silver half crown. Potter smiled and nodded his thanks. At the rail, Church stood holding Jessup's grimacing head high in the air like a trophy. Disley, Binks, Cameron, Freddie and Billy fell about with laughter while the fairground attendant angrily shook his fist. Behind him, the heads of Jessup's friends cried out from their coconut cups, tears streaming down their cheeks.

"See, I told you those 'eads were glued in, didn't I, boys!" Church was yelling.

Beside Lou, there was more laughter. The clown's head in its glass box stopped its cackle and glared, and as Lou rode away, it threw its head back and roared.

The carousel music and Potter's accordion were drowned out by sounds of sita, flute and beating percussion. A group of Indian musicians in national garb sat playing their captivating music. In front of them, a huge silver cobra reared up and swayed from side to side, its evil eyes on Lou, ready to strike.

Lou drove away through the chestnut fencing and was overpowered by the smell of fish and seaweed-filled air. Finding himself on top of a sand dune, he left the bike and began to walk, hoping to find relief from all this weirdness and misery. Directly ahead, in the distance, he saw an airship. It was black. He knew it was *Howden R100* by its rippling cover. The gentle surf monotonously sucked the seashore, while gulls sounded their warnings overhead. Lou's eye traced the curved, sandy beach stretching to a low-lying headland, where the great Egyptian Pyramids stood silhouetted against a rising sun. In the opposite direction was another headland where the dome and minarets of the Taj Mahal stood in shining orange against another, dying sun. The airship passed directly over his head and disappeared behind him.

From the direction of the pyramids, a tiny, open-topped vehicle approached. As it drew nearer, he saw four figures inside, woodenly upright, rocking to and fro. The vehicle sped up the sand dune and came to an abrupt halt in front of him, the figures' heads bobbing and jerking comically. The car and its occupants were made of molded red and blue plastic. Lou recognized

Scott as the driver. He wore a tall pointed hat with the letters R101 embossed across the front. Next to him, was Irwin. Thomson sat in the back, complete with overcoat and trilby, Brancker beside him, wearing his pith helmet. Each of them appeared weary and forlorn.

"I say old man, could you tell us, which way to India?" Scott called.

Lou pointed along the beach toward the Taj Mahal on the other headland. With a wave of Scott's hand, they sped off in their strange contraption, doomed to an eternity of searching—melded together for all time. Lou felt abject pity for them.

The sound of Potter's accordion in an overlapping dream woke Lou from his morphine nightmare. He was glad to be released from that, but overwhelmed by loneliness. Voices of dead crewmen screamed in his head. The sickening horror of the ship's last moments flooded back to him—the massive boom and blinding light, not being able to breathe or hear. Then, more detonations as the rest of the gas bags ignited in succession. He couldn't get Potter out of his mind—in plain sight one moment, gone the next. Again, there was the accordion.

Damn it, Walt—why didn't you stick close to me?

Lou wished he'd waited for him, perhaps even shared his fate. He wondered where Leech was—he owed that man his life.

There'll be so many devastated families in Bedford.

He thought about Church and Irene and hoped Church was going to make it. Was he still alive? Then Captain Irwin ...

Poor Olivia.

Did Charlotte know yet? She'd been right all along. Who could blame her for getting out?

I should have listened. She knew something others didn't know—except for that damned gypsy ...and Mrs. Hinchliffe ...Millie!

Lou couldn't see—his eyes and ears had been covered, further impairing his hearing. He hoped he wasn't blind and dreaded the thought of the nuns removing the bandages. When the French villagers had come to their aid in Therain Wood, he'd felt as if he was coming around from a deep sleep. His eyes hurt from being blinded by the hydrogen fire, and he was still half deaf—he supposed his eardrums had been damaged. He wondered if this would be permanent. Would his hair grow back?

I'm a wreck—but most of the others are dead. Oh God, why do you do this to me?

The nuns and nurses had been caring and gentle on the field—so reassuring, although he couldn't understand a word they said. They'd lifted his arm carefully and tied it in a sling and bound up and bandaged the cut on the other arm. They applied cool lotion to his burning face and head. He was in and out after that.

The journey in the field ambulance had been agony. It bounced and squeaked across the field, jarring his injured body. A couple of others were with him—probably Radcliffe and Church. He heard their cries and whimpers.

The next thing he remembered was the removal of the bandages; the brightness was blinding—overhead lights above the table, glistening white walls, smocks, headscarves. They washed his wounds and burns. That hurt like hell. They also stitched the cut on his arm. Other victims had been in the room. He could tell by the chatter of nurses and doctors close by, and from groans on their creaking gurneys.

The nuns have been kind and soothing—with voices of angels.

Lou slept for what seemed like ages, in and out of consciousness, depending on the morphine doses they gave him. It caused him to seriously lose track of time; he drifted off to sleep for a minute and think he'd slept for an hour or two. During one of his conscious moments, he heard the voices of his men—those not too badly hurt—probably Binks talking to Bell. They must have thought he was asleep. One of them was mumbling close by his bed.

"...Jessup ...'is 'ead exploded, you should 'ave seen it ...it was 'orrible! ...Damn! ...I couldn't ..." Then more muttering—most likely Bell. Lou drifted off to sleep, those phrases repeating themselves over and over, like an infuriating recording that just wouldn't stop. Sometimes, he sensed the guys hovering by his bedside only to be shooed away by nuns.

Allez-vous en! Go away!

He thought about Disley. He hadn't heard his voice. He wondered if he'd managed to call London. The smells of the hospital got to him, particularly the disinfectant. Once, he smelled the perfume of one of the nurses. Though not the same as Charlotte's, it made him think of her. She'd always worn the same perfume, which he loved. He'd first noticed it in the hospital in Hull when she leaned over him and stitched his face. He'd concentrated on her perfume to block out the pain as she stuck in her needle and pulled the thread.

What seemed like a week later (he had no way of knowing), he thought he smelled the scent Charlotte used. It came to him so strongly, it was jarring.

Must be another crazy dream.

He faded back to sleep again, sensing the aroma of Balkan Sobrani and he thought of Norway. It was all a confusing muddle. Then, that same damned recording began playing over and over again in his brain, " ...Jessup ...'is 'ead exploded, you should 'ave seen it ...it was 'orrible ...Damn! ...I couldn't ..."

He came to, smelling the same perfume and shook his head, trying to snap out of it. He felt delusional, saddened and comforted at the same time. There was more mumbling and he strained to listen; first a woman's voice then and a man's, possibly two. Then nothing. Now, a soft woman's voice which he figured had to be a nun. He drifted back to sleep. When he awoke, the muttering continued and he caught the smell of that magnificent perfume once more. What was it called? Who could it be?

If only she were here—if only it were she!

He breathed in the scent and wept and lay there listening to those incoherent voices. Someone wiped the tears from his cheeks and gently took his hand.

Must be a nun—thank God for her.

"Can you hear me, my love?" a voice said.

But the voice was *English*—perhaps even *Yorkshire!*

"It's me," the voice whispered close to his ear. A soft loving kiss covered his mouth—the lips moist and luscious. There could be no mistaking those lips, or that perfume.

Damn these dreams! Damn the morphine!

One of the nuns spoke and his bandages were gently unwrapped. Though hazy, Charlotte's face came into focus, appearing more beautiful than he'd ever seen her—her lips full and red and her eyes so huge and clear and sparkling and blue. Short hair accentuated her elegant neck and high cheekbones.

Thank God, I can see, but is any of this real?

And she looked so well—she had an aura about her—not the same Charlotte he'd last seen. Behind her, he made out Norway and John Bull standing against the wall. He was overwhelmed.

"*Je Reviens*," he said softly.

"*Je Reviens*," she repeated.

Lou didn't speak again for some moments. A cloud descended over him. He stared blankly at Charlotte in a daze, remembering. He wrapped his bandaged arm around his head. His shoulders shook and he fought for breath. Charlotte embraced him, believing he was overcome with joy at the sight of her. But it wasn't that emotion which had enveloped him. He'd finally collapsed under his burden and his demons. Her appearance fuelled the agony caused by burgeoning guilt, smothering him with feelings of self-loathing and unworthiness. Again, why hadn't he been allowed to die in peace with the others? He gasped for breath.

"I threw myself down, you know," he said at last.

She leaned over him. He was obviously delirious.

"I didn't black out. That was a lie."

"What, my darling? What do you mean?"

"The machine guns cut my buddies down. I didn't black out."

She understood perfectly. In that moment, she knew all there was to know about Lou Remington. He wasn't worthy to live, or to have her return to him. It was all too much.

"I cheated God. He'd sent me to that front line that last day as punishment for killing the German boy. I really didn't have to kill him. I should've died that morning with the rest."

"No, Lou. You did what any man would've done."

"They said I was a hero. I was a cheat and a liar who deserved to die —and now my punishment is to live."

"Oh, Lou, please don't say that, my darling."

"Julia's prayers saved me …She made a pact."

"*Julia* …a pact?"

"With God," he said.

She waited.

"And look at her—she has *nothing!*"

Charlotte was thrown even more off balance. "Who is *Julia?*"

The nun came to Lou's bedside and glared at Charlotte and then at Norway and John, who was himself, choking up.

"*Ça suffit! Vous le contrariez. Il est temps de partir.* That's enough! You're upsetting him. It's time for you to leave."

And then something happened that astonished Lou and Norway, but not John Bull. Charlotte smiled and turned to the nun and spoke perfect French.

"*Je vous supplie de me laisser rester. Je suis une infirmière. Je connais bien cet endroit. S'il vous plâit, laissez-moi rester un peu plus longtemps, j'ai des choses importantes à dire à mon mari.* I beg you to let me stay. I'm a nurse. I'm familiar with this place," she said, lifting her hands and gesturing to their surroundings. "Please allow me to stay a little longer. I have important things to say to my husband."

The nun's manner changed as she looked into Charlotte's face. She showed a hint of recognition and relented. Norway pulled a chair up to the bed for Charlotte to sit close. He and John went into the corridor. Charlotte took Lou's hand again.

"Julia—she was waiting for you back home, wasn't she? I always had the feeling there must be *someone.*"

"Charlotte, she's a wonderful person. She asks for nothing."

"I'm sure she is. She deserves you more than I, especially—"

"My darling, don't …I missed you so much," he said.

"Lou, I'm so sorry I didn't let you in that day—"

"I came to tell you I was ready to give it all up."

Charlotte felt sick.

"Kiss me again," he said.

She leaned over, kissed him and then took out a folded, white handkerchief from her handbag. She opened it, revealing his gleaming gold wedding ring. She gently slipped it back on his finger and kissed him again. He became calm.

"I figured Robert had shown up again and you'd run off with him."

She was shocked at the suggestion. She held up her ring finger.

"I never took mine off," she said. "Poor Robert is dead—long dead, poor boy."

For the first time, Charlotte pronounced 'Robert' the French way (Ro-bare), which strangely, she'd never done, even in her own mind.

"I love you, Charlie," Lou said.

"Now, there's something I must tell *you*, Lou," Charlotte said, pausing to recall dreadful memories, her voice a whisper. "I was at the Western Front, too."

It took a few moments for it to sink in. He was speechless.

"What …!" he stammered. "Where? …When?"

"I was at different field hospitals …the last one was at Saint-Mihiel …near you."

"Oh, my God …" Stunned, Lou put his hand to his head, it explained a lot of things.

"I decided you should know."

Tears welled up in Lou's eyes.

"Many of *them* were American," Charlotte told him. "So many died. I'll never forget their pleading eyes …they were so far from home. I couldn't talk about it. I'm sorry. I've never spoken of the horror of that place to anyone." She wiped her eyes with a handkerchief smudging her eye makeup and then blew her nose.

"Baby, I'm so sorry. I wish I'd known. A fine pair, huh. So that's where you learned to stitch—and speak French!" He closed his eyes and smiled as he remembered.

She had things she could not share …Another victim of war …She was a brave girl that one …And the Red Cross pin!

Charlotte smiled now, too. They consoled each other until the nun returned and told them visiting would be suspended for a couple of hours. Lou's dressings had to be changed and he needed rest. Before leaving, John came in and patted Lou's shoulder, overjoyed Lou had survived and that he and Charlotte were reunited.

97

BLACKOUT IN BEDFORD

Sunday October 5, 1930.

Around 6.00 a.m. on that chilly Sunday morning of the crash, Charlotte and her parents were roused by pounding on the front door that shook the whole house. When Charlotte heard it, a feeling of doom overcame her and her heart began to race. Instinctively, she knew. She *had* listened to the 9 o'clock news the night before. Her heart had skipped a beat when she heard it mentioned that a representative from the United States was on board. She put on her dressing gown and went down to the living room where her father was already on his way to the front door. Charlotte's mother followed her. Mr. Hamilton nervously switched on the vestibule light and opened the front door. Two familiar figures stood on the step: Norway and John Bull. Their faces said it all.

"W-we're s-sorry to d-disturb y-y-"

"Lou's ship went down," John said.

Charlotte felt as though she'd been stabbed in the chest. She let out a gasp and her mother caught her and led her back into the living room. They followed. Mother eased Charlotte down into an easy chair.

"What happened?" Charlotte's father asked.

"I got a c-call from George Hunter of the *D-Daily Express*, he's a r-reporter," Norway said.

"What did he say?" Charlotte asked.

"He said the airship had crashed in France."

"Where?"

"B-Beauvais," Norway answered.

"Beauvais!"

"There are survivors. I'd been following it all night on my short wave radio. I don't speak French, but I was able to pick up parts of it," John said.

"What about Lou?" Charlotte asked.

"We d-don't know."

"All we know is that nine survived and they're in hospital," John said.

Charlotte's father went to the radio and switched it on. There was nothing but church music on and a program about birds in Newfoundland on the other station. He looked at the clock.

"We must listen to the seven o'clock news," he said. It was twenty minutes to seven.

"When did you last see Lou?" Charlotte asked.

"I saw him off last night," John replied.

"From Cardington?" Charlotte's mother asked.

"Yes. I was worried when I left. The weather was shocking. I got home and sat by the radio all night. It came on in France at four o'clock this morning."

"And they said there were survivors?"

"Yes, they said *neuf survivants*—that's nine," John said.

Charlotte nodded.

"George Hunter confirmed nine," Norway said.

"And all the rest are dead?" Charlotte asked.

"Yes, but we've got to keep our hopes up for Lou," John said.

"His luck may've run out," Charlotte said. She remembered the nine lives he joked about.

"We're going to f-f-fly down to Cardington and then F-France. Depending on what we f-find out," Norway said.

"Depending on if he's dead, you mean?" Charlotte said, her eyes flashing at Norway, who looked away, badly stung.

"There were a l-lot of good people on that flight. P-people I liked," Norway said.

"It's all *your* bloody fault!" Charlotte snapped.

"Char-Char-Char ..."

"I'm coming with you," Charlotte said.

"I'd hoped you'd say that. Bring your passport," John said, "and don't forget your door key."

"We're going over to Sh-Sherburn to pick up a plane," Norway said.

"Okay, I'll make you breakfast before you go," Charlotte's mother said, rushing off to the kitchen. There was now a great sense of urgency. Charlotte dashed up stairs to get dressed. Mr. Hamilton put the radio on just before 7 o'clock.

"They'll make an announcement, I'm sure," he said.

They listened closely to the news while they ate breakfast, but the BBC didn't mention a word about *Cardington R101*. It made them wonder if it'd all been a cruel hoax. There'd been false stories put out when *Howden R100* flew to Canada—rumors it'd gone down in the Atlantic. Within half an hour, they were on their way to Norway's flying club in John's car. Once there, they found that the plane they needed was already rented, but the club-member allowed them to take it when he heard the news. Everyone at the club was deeply shocked.

Two hours later, they landed on Cardington Field, parked the aeroplane close to St Mary's Church and tied it down. That morning, the weather was perfect for flying; the wind had dropped and the sky was clear. Charlotte stared at the leaves stuck to the damp, autumn-smelling ground. Their colors reminded her of khaki blankets and dried blood. Across Church Lane, they heard the congregation singing. There wasn't much gusto in the voices; it was supposed to be Harvest Festival with worshipers there to give thanks. Charlotte remembered being in church with Lou last year, this very day. She looked across at the Ferris wheel. It was still. The fairground, like the aerodrome, was empty and quiet except, for the sound of birds in the hedgerows and men dismantling the rides. Perhaps the gypsies knew there'd be no business here now—maybe never.

They walked across the field, past the sheds and up to Cardington House. The doors were locked. Booth's Sunbeam Talbot was parked outside next to Scott's Morris Oxford and two other cars. Norway pounded on the door. Eventually, they saw Booth through the glass, walking toward them. His face was grave. He reluctantly let them in.

"Look Nevil. I can't tell you anything and you're the last person they want to see around here right now!" Booth whispered.

"What are *you* d-doing here, then?" Norway asked.

"They called me at four-thirty this morning."

"I got a c-call from a reporter at the *D-Daily Express* at four o'clock," Norway said. He pointed at John, "And he heard it on shortwave radio."

"Most people round here don't have radios," Booth said.

"So people in Bedford don't know?" John said.

"They didn't, but a rumor has spread like wildfire," Booth said.

"Are you sure it's actually *true*?" Charlotte said.

Booth nodded. "Disley, the electrician called from the police station in Allonne."

"But there *were* survivors?" Charlotte asked.

Booth wouldn't say, but he did nod his head slightly.

"What about Lou?"

Charlotte could see, Booth was in a terrible position. He kept looking nervously toward the corridor behind him. "I'm so sorry I can't …Orders have come from the highest levels," he said. "The *very* highest!"

"I need to know if my husband's alive!" Charlotte whispered, her eyes like daggers. Booth nodded his head silently so that others listening couldn't tell he was communicating. Charlotte closed her eyes in relief.

"Is he going to live?"

Please God.

"*That,* I can't say. I don't know. Honestly, I'd tell you if I knew," Booth murmured. And then, in a loud voice, "Nevil, you must leave! You really shouldn't have landed here, you know."

"I'm s-sorry if I hurt anyone's f-feelings, but this was important to Mrs. Remington. We're going on to F-France tomorrow morning," Norway said.

"So am I. I'm leaving this morning," Booth whispered and then in a loud voice, "I'm sorry I can't tell you anything. They'll put out a statement later, when in possession of the facts." Booth opened the front door. "That's all I can tell you. Goodbye."

Booth's face was more kindly than his words sounded down the corridor

"We'll see you over there," Norway muttered.

Booth shut and locked the doors behind them.

They left Cardington House and walked the half mile down to the gate, where a crowd had gathered. Norway went to the gatekeeper.

"Jim, what's going on?"

"Mr. Norway, they've 'eard something about the airship. They keep asking me. I can't tell 'em anything. No one's told me a damned thing and they won't come down 'ere and talk to these people. It ain't right, keepin' people in the dark like this!"

The gatekeeper unlocked the small side gate and Charlotte and her companions stepped outside. The desperate crowd surged forward. Charlotte found it heartbreaking to see people in such a state. They rushed at Norway.

"Is it true, sir?"

"What can you tell us?"

The crowd surrounded them.

"You've h-heard something about the air-sh-ship?"

"You heard it went down?" Charlotte said.

All eyes centered on Charlotte.

"Yes, we 'eard a rumor, m'am, my boy's on that ship," one desperate man said.

"Look, I'm going to be honest with you. My husband's on that ship, too. We heard it went down and there are a few survivors. That's all we know. I'm so sorry. We must go."

A bus drew up nearby.

"Oh, yes. You're the American's wife."

"God Bless you, miss. I hope your 'usband's all right," someone said.

The crowd parted for them as they went for the bus. They climbed aboard and looked back at the unhappy faces. Charlotte wondered when they'd be told the facts.

They got off at the top of Kelsey Street and walked to No. 58. It felt strange seeing her old house again. Charlotte was desolate—she'd betrayed Lou. She found herself staring at the oil patch where he always parked his motorbike. She wondered where it was now. She'd heard about Lou and Billy's accident from Fanny, who'd been to see her the previous evening. After receiving Lou's phone call at Goole Hospital, Fanny had been shocked to learn from other sources that Charlotte had walked out on Lou weeks earlier. She dashed over to Charlotte's parents' place to find Charlotte. After catching up, Fanny told her about their collision with the painter's van. Charlotte had been relieved the boy was safe and *not* aboard that damned airship.

As she walked across the concrete parking area in front of the house, she looked at Mrs. Jones's window. Fluffy was sitting on the windowsill, inside. She'd seen Charlotte and was making a fuss. Soon, Mrs. Jones appeared at the window. Her face lit up.

Charlotte stood at the foot of the steps and looked up, noticing the stains. She had no idea what it was. It looked like dried blood. It made her shudder. She unlocked the door and they went in. There was a white envelope bearing her name lying on the hall table. She slipped into the living room and opened it. The card simply said,

> *My Darling Charlotte,*
> *I'll take you to see the full-size statue one day soon.*
> *God, I've missed you!*
> *All my Love*
> *Lou XXXX*
> *Many more kisses to come!*

She wasn't sure what it meant until the clock chimed on the mantelpiece. Next to it, was the Sitting Lincoln statue he'd bought for her. She felt empty inside. They trooped down to the kitchen where Charlotte opened the window to let in some fresh air. Everything was tidy. Mrs. Jones knocked on the front door and came down stairs with Fluffy, who was making a hell of row—admonishing Charlotte.

"What's happening, Charlotte? Are you back?" Mrs. Jones said.

There was an awkward silence. Mrs. Jones looked from one to the other. Then she realized something was up.

"What is it, dear?"

"There's been an accident," John said.

"The airship?"

"It crashed," Charlotte said.

"What about Lou?"

"We think he may have s-survived," Norway said. "But we d-don't know for sure."

"What about the rest of 'em"

"Nobody knows, or at least they ain't telling anybody," John said.

"Well, there's been nothing in the paper about it," Mrs. Jones said.

"It happened in the night, so there won't be," Charlotte said.

"George Hunter said the *Express* stopped the presses early this morning and was doing a special late edition. Maybe we can get one," Norway said.

Charlotte said, "Look, if you don't mind, I'm going to walk round to Olivia Irwin's house. I must see her."

Before leaving, Charlotte went upstairs to their bedroom. It was tidy, but not as tidy as she'd left it. Their portraits were still on the wall. She spent a moment studying them. Lou looked handsome. Happier days. Then she noticed his guitar was missing from its hook on the wall on his side of the bed—then the gaping hole in the wardrobe door. She pictured the scene, feeling regret she'd caused Lou so much pain.

Oh, God, that must have hurt. My poor dear Lou.

She opened the wardrobe door and peered inside. Her heart sank. In the bottom was the guitar, or what was left of it, in a thousand pieces. It broke her heart. She realized just how much she'd hurt him. She sat on the edge of the bed and wept. She got up and went to the sink in the bathroom, washed her face and re-did her makeup. He was all that mattered.

Please God, let him live.

Twenty minutes later Charlotte was on Olivia's doorstep ringing the bell. It was some minutes before Olivia appeared in her dressing gown, her eyes cast down. There was both rage and sorrow in her lovely, ashen face. She held the door open in silence for Charlotte to enter. As soon as the door was closed, Charlotte put her arms around her and they both cried bitterly. They went into the living room.

The house felt dead. Only the ticking clock on the mantelpiece made any sound.

"How did you find out?" Charlotte whispered.

"We both knew he wasn't coming back …" Olivia dropped her head. "…Booth was here early this morning."

"You both sensed all this coming?" Charlotte asked.

"Yes. I went back to the ship last night. I begged and pleaded with him."

"But he *still* went?"

"Yes. How could he not? They made him go. They damn-well forced him!"

Charlotte didn't want to talk about survivors. It'd seem cold. But Olivia brought it up. "Booth said Lou's alive," she said suddenly. "He's injured. He said some won't live."

Charlotte let out a sob. "Oh God!"

He could still die.

She was brought back by Olivia's weary voice.

"I went and saw that damned gypsy last week." She sounded bitter.

"Oh, Olivia!"

"I just couldn't resist. Fat lot of good it did. She said, 'the bells will toll for them'."

"She was right."

"And then, that pilot's wife came to see me."

"Mrs. Hinchliffe?"

"Yes. She came knocking on the door just before they left. She told me they had no chance of survival. She said her dead husband had told her this."

"I wish I'd known."

"What could you have done? You were gone. Anyway, it wouldn't have made a difference. That bloody Thomson had his own agenda. It was all *his* damned fault!"

"I suppose he's dead, too," Charlotte said.

Charlotte left Olivia and walked back toward Kelsey Street. On her way, she went past the corner store to see if she could get the *Sunday Express*. Inside, there was a crowd of nervous people with the same idea. News of the crash was out. People in the corner store were desperate and very angry.

"We need news," somebody said, as if Alan, the store owner, had influence with the press. He held up both his hands, trying to quell the storm.

"I made a phone call. The *Sunday Express* has printed a late edition, but we've not been able to get any yet. The *Bedford Circular* is printing a late paper right now. It should be getting here any time," he told them.

Somebody saw a *Daily Express* van slowing down outside. A bundle of newspapers tied up with string was thrown out on the ground from the tail gate and it tore off up the street. Everybody stampeded from the shop and grabbed at the newspapers like crazy people. In seconds, they were all gone. The lucky ones stood reading the front page with people gathered around them. Charlotte read the headlines of the *Sunday Express* over someone's shoulder.

CARDINGTON R101 CRASHES ON FRENCH HILLSIDE
Air Minister Lord Thomson and Director of Civil Aviation Among the Dead
Nine Survivors: Some Severely Injured In Beauvais Hospital

Charlotte's heart sank. She kept thinking of how she'd refused to let him in her parents' house. She'd deserve it if he died now. She couldn't help thinking of old Mrs.Tilly's last words.

You'll find someone special. I just know you will. And when you do, you grab 'im and 'old on to 'im and never let 'im go.

In despair, Charlotte headed for the *Bedford and District Circular's* office on the High Street in town. As she approached the square, she heard a brass band playing Chopin's "Funeral March."

Damn! As if people aren't depressed enough.

She walked round the square to the newspaper office where a crowd had gathered. This'd become a command post for news and exchange of information. She spotted John on the other side and went over to him. He'd come here, leaving Norway at home in case the phone rang.

Bundles of newspapers were being unloaded from a van and put into a stack for people to take free of charge. A blackboard had been chalked up with survivor's names. Charlotte read them, knowing most of these men. Their faces came to mind. The reality of seeing Lou's name made her stomach turn over.

Dear God, please let him live. ...They all die someday, Charlotte.

<u>Survivors as of 10 a.m. this morning – Unconfirmed.</u>

L. Remington	3rd Officer USN
A. Disley	Electrician
H. Leech	Foreman Engineer
J. Binks	Engineer
A. Bell	Engineer
W. Radcliffe	Engineer
V. Savoury	Engineer
A. Cook	Engineer
S. Church	Rigger

While everyone gathered around the blackboard in hushed silence, the Salvation Army band marched up the road spreading the gloom. There was little or no traffic and people spoke reverently in whispers, as if in church. People sobbed into their handkerchiefs. A bell tolled close by. As soon as one stopped, another started elsewhere. And so it went. It was unnerving to hear the howling of someone's dog.

There was one girl Charlotte recognized after a few moments. It was the pregnant Rosie Cameron. Well, that was no surprise. She wondered whose child it was.

"I'm walking with the Lord," Jessup had told her.

What a laugh!

Charlotte wondered what had happened to him.

They're probably both dead. ...Poor Doug.

She watched Rosie trudge off up the road in tears and felt enormous sympathy for her.

Silly little fool! Where's the justice?

A man came out of the newspaper offices and whispered behind his hand into the ear of the man at the blackboard. He picked up a damp cloth and rubbed out Radcliffe's name. A great moan went up in the crowd. One woman let out a terrible scream.

John put his hand on Charlotte's shoulder. "Come on, let's go home," he said.

"I must go and see Sam Church's girl, Irene, on the way. She's probably at his parents'."

"Okay, I'll come with you," John said.

They talked as they left the square. It was good to see John again. Charlotte realized how much she'd missed him.

"I must say, Charlotte, you're looking well."

"Yes, I'm getting better and I feel stronger."

"And you still love him?"

"Yes, of course I do."

John appeared relieved. "You can tell him when we get to Beauvais."

John was easy to talk to, caring, as always. It was then, that it all came spilling out, like a dam bursting, surprising her and shocking John.

"Beauvais …I know it …only too well," Charlotte said dreamily.

"What d'you mean?"

"I was *there*."

Now she screwed up her face as though in terrible pain. John put his arm around her shoulder, totally confused.

"You mean you were at Cardington Tower when they left last night?"

"No. I was a nurse in *France* during the war."

Her voice was a whisper, her eyes fixed on his. This came as a hammer blow to John. His face expressed horror as he remembered his son.

"Dear God! When?"

"I got there in 1917, before the Americans arrived."

Charlotte described how, at the age of seventeen, after working at Pontefract Hospital for two years, and after being inspired by Red Cross recruitment posters, she'd joined to do her bit for King and Country, to care for her sick and dying countrymen. No one in her village, except for her parents and an aunt, knew where she'd gone. They thought she was working in Guy's Hospital in London. After additional training, she'd been sent to various front-line field hospitals, the first near Arras.

Morale was in decline; it looked as though the war was lost. The Germans were pounding on the gates of Paris. For French soldiers, Aisne was the last straw—tens of thousands of them were slaughtered—their lives counted for nothing. One regiment mutinied and it spread like wildfire throughout the French Army.

Nothing could have prepared Charlotte for what she encountered in the squalor of those khaki tents. Hundreds of seriously wounded men lying on cots in states of agony and distress, lingering for days; arms and legs blown off, faces and jaws gone, gaping bleeding wounds—all made worse by plagues of rats and lice. It was their cries that got to her the most: cries for their mothers, cries to be put out of their misery. She'd been proposed to by many soldiers. She'd usually accepted. They always died within a day or two.

As soon as she arrived at the Front, she assisted a weary, irritable surgeon with amputations and stitching wounds, things she'd never done before. It was a horrific baptism, but she carried on while enemy guns roared close by. She spent eleven months in the field with little or no rest, except for short breaks in Paris, when all she could think of was getting back to care for those poor wretches.

Charlotte didn't tell John everything. During one of her Paris breaks she'd met a young French soldier. He'd sat next to her on a bus. His face was beautiful, but full of despair. It broke her heart to look into his mournful, grey eyes. His name was Robert. They'd struck up a conversation. Her French was improving, and he was able to muster a few words in English. He looked at her nurse's uniform with admiration, as if she were holy.

"Ange de la miséricorde. Angel of mercy," he said. "Vous êtes magnifique!"

They spent the day trudging the streets amongst weary Parisians whose faces registered the same despair, while German guns boomed only forty miles away. They sat in a café drinking coffee where Robert told her sadly that the war was lost. Many in his regiment had torn off their uniforms and thrown down their rifles. Dozens had been shot for desertion.

"Lâches! Cowards!" he called them. *He* wouldn't do that. He'd rather die in the mud of no man's land than leave France to the barbaric Boche. He was due back at the Front the next morning and reconciled to his fate. After a light meal, they walked in the park, chatting. His mood was elevated. At the end of the day, just before dark, he bade her farewell and kissed her tenderly on the lips.

"Thank you for everything, angel," he said. "You have lifted me up. I now go goodly."

"You mean, gladly."

"Yes, *gladly*," he said with a slight bow and a smile.

He saw her onto a bus to her pension. She watched him as it pulled away. She never saw him again, although she looked for him in every crowd and at the café when she returned to Paris. She knew he was dead.

When the Americans entered the war, Charlotte was sent down from the north to the Château-Thierry/Saint-Mihiel arena with British Forces. A new American offensive had been opened led by General Pershing, along with the revitalized French Army.

When the war ended, she was sent to Beauvais Hospital to care for those too ill to be moved, or who were chronically sick from the influenza pandemic nicknamed the 'Spanish flu'. She remained there for six months. When she got back to Ackworth, she never spoke of her experiences, and people, including her parents, knew well enough not to broach the subject. On her arrival, they tried, but she lifted a finger to her lips, and they understood. Soon after that, one of Charlotte's aunts brought up the war and Charlotte flew into a rage—out of character for her. The war became like the mad relative in the attic—ignored and never to be mentioned. Charlotte erased the horror from her mind. Or so she thought.

John was deeply touched. "Does Lou know you were there?"

"No."

"My Goodness! You must tell him."

"Perhaps you're right."

"What about Fanny, did she know?"

"No. The only person that knew was the matron at Bedford Hospital. I forget how it came up, but it turned out that she'd been at the Front herself —and somehow she just knew. I confided in her and she completely understood. She was very kind to me."

They walked in silence for a few moments and then Charlotte spoke again. "Do you know why I really hate airships, John?"

She went on to relate how during her first week of training at Guys Hospital, she'd taken a bus ride to Westminster. Suddenly, the bus in front exploded—bombed from the air. Charlotte jumped from her bus and looked up in time to spot the guilty culprit: a tiny, silver Zeppelin lurking high in the sky. She watched it disappear behind a cloud. Seven died that sunny afternoon and eight were severely injured. Setting up a triage station had been her introduction to the war and she knew she'd made the right decision to go to France to help beat this evil enemy.

After baring her soul, Charlotte felt indescribable relief. She was now, more than ever, desperate for Lou's survival. A massive load had been lifted. Yes, she'd tell him everything. He'd understand why she'd held it back.

Please God let him live.

They were interrupted by a great rumbling. They looked round. Coming toward them on the London Road was a gaggle of motorcycle dispatch riders dressed in Air Force blue, helmets and goggles. When they reached the main square they split off and went their separate ways. Charlotte looked startled.

Angels of Death!

After a fifteen minute walk, Charlotte and John reached Church's parents' house on Doctor Street. It was on a run-down, working-class row of terraced houses on a narrow, cobblestone street. Charlotte lifted the old black knocker and rapped gently on the door. Church's father answered, and by the look of his haggard face, he obviously knew. Irene stood behind him.

"Mr. Church?"

"Yes, that's me."

"I'm Charlotte—"

"It's Charlotte, Dad—Sam's commander's wife," Irene said.

"Come in, love," Mr. Church said.

They followed Irene down the narrow, dark passageway into a small back room with brown lino and a small piece of faded carpet in front of the fireplace. On the way, Charlotte caught the smell of a dog, and a roast cooking in the oven. In the tiny living room, a coal fire burned in the black iron grate. On one wall was a small crucifix and on another, a painting of The Holy Virgin with Child. The dining table under the window was set with a white table cloth for Sunday dinner. Church's mother came out of the kitchen in her apron. All eyes in the Church family were red and swollen.

"We've got to keep our strength up, 'aven't we?" Church's mother said, apologizing for cooking dinner in these circumstances. Charlotte put her arms around Irene and Irene's tears started again. An old, black mongrel in its basket in the corner, trembled uncontrollably, watching them with sad, knowing eyes.

"That's Sam's dog. He won't come out of 'is basket. *He* knows," Mr. Church said.

"I was down at the newspaper office earlier," Mr. Church said. "They've got Sam's name up on the board as a survivor—I hope it's still up." He almost broke down again.

"Yes, it is, Mr. Church," Charlotte said.

Irene looked down and shook her head. "God, I'm so thankful," she said, "If anything happens to him, I don't know what I'll do."

"There's nothing on the bloody wireless. It's disgusting," Mr. Church said.

"What about your 'usband, Miss?" Mrs. Church said.

"They've got his name up, too. We hope he's going to be all right," John said, although he hadn't been introduced.

"This is Mr. Bull—he's a close friend of ours," Charlotte said. Everyone nodded. "We're flying over there tomorrow. Another friend has a plane—"

They were interrupted by the sound of a motorbike outside in the street and then a loud bang on the front door. Mr. Church disappeared. They heard muttering. Irene ran up the passage and Charlotte heard them talking. They came back a few moments later. Mr. Church was holding a letter.

"It's from the Air Ministry. It says the airship crashed and Sam's been severely injured and he's in Beauvais Hospital…" He broke down and couldn't speak for a few moments. "…It says his condition is …'grave'."

Irene began sobbing. "We've got to get to him," she cried.

Mr. Church stopped crying. He was suddenly calm. He had a plan.

"We'll go to Henlow in the morning. I'll borrow the money and charter a plane. We've got to be with the boy."

Charlotte and John headed back to Kelsey Street. After they'd mounted the front steps, a dispatch rider drew up on the road outside and parked his motorbike. He shuffled through some envelopes in his shoulder bag and pulled one out. He came up the steps to Charlotte.

"Excuse me, m'am, I'm looking for a Mrs. Remington."

"I'm Mrs. Remington."

"This is for you. Please sign for it."

He held out a clip board and Charlotte signed her name.

"I'm so sorry, m'am," he said.

Charlotte's heart missed a beat. He turned away and went back to the curb. His words worried Charlotte, had something happened to Lou? Was he dead? She opened the front door and they went into the living room. John stood by while Charlotte ripped open the envelope. Her eyes quickly scanned the letter. John waited.

Air Ministry,
Gwydyr House,
Whitehall, London,

5ᵗʰ October, 1930.

REF. HMA CARDINGTON R101 G-FAAW.
Voyage to India. Departure 4ᵗʰ October 1930.

Dear Mrs. Remington,

Regretfully, I must tell you that at nine minutes past two this morning, His Majesty's Airship Cardington R101 crashed into a hillside in Beauvais, France. Your husband, Lt. Cmdr. Louis Remington U.S.N. survived the crash and is in hospital in Beauvais. Your husband's injuries are extensive. His chances of recovery are favorable.

Yours truly,
Hugh Dowding,
Air Member for Supply & Research. (AMSR)

"Thank God. He's still alive," Charlotte said.

They went down to the kitchen, where Charlotte showed Norway the letter. John switched on the wireless.

Beep Beep Beep Beep Beep Beeeep.

This is the BBC Home Service. We interrupt this program to bring you a special news bulletin ...'

"Here it comes. It's about bloody time an' all!" John growled.

...it has just been confirmed by the Air Ministry in Whitehall, that His Majesty's Airship Cardington R One hundred and One crashed on a hillside in Beauvais, France at nine minutes past two last night. The airship had been in the air since leaving Cardington at seven thirty-six on Saturday evening in weather conditions not thought, at the time, to be severe enough to delay the flight. However, weather conditions grew steadily worse over Northern France. There are nine survivors. Among the dead are, Brigadier General, Lord Thomson of Cardington, Secretary of State for Air, Air Vice Marshall, Sir Sefton Brancker, Director of Civil Aviation, Wing Commander Reginald Colmore, Director of Airship Development ...'

The following morning, Charlotte, flew with Norway and John to Beauvais. Weather conditions were extremely unpleasant. Charlotte was badly shaken and wondered how Irene and Mr. Church were faring with their charter flight. When they got to Allonne, Norway took the plane over the crash site before landing.

The wreck looked like the skeletal remains of a massive, prehistoric sea creature. The front section had ploughed into the woods and crumpled up. The rear portion appeared intact. They could see the ensign fluttering in the breeze on the tail—the only fabric left on the entire craft. Hundreds of people stood around the edge of the site, with police keeping them as far away as possible—a virtually insurmountable task. Charlotte hoped all the bodies had been removed. Norway put the plane down at Beauvais Airport and they took a taxi to the hospital.

98

THERAIN WOOD

Monday October 6, 1930.

After she'd decided to unburden herself with Lou, Charlotte had been transformed. Her crushing depression was gone. Liberation had made her radiant. Lou had survived, knocked about, but he was going to be okay. In all this devastation, there were positive signs which she couldn't dwell on due to the terrible price others had paid—people she'd come to love. She left the ward and went into the corridor where she found Norway and John chatting with Booth and McWade.

"Fred and I walked the wreck site yesterday afternoon and this morning," Booth said. "We came here to speak to survivors and take statements."

"We can't go back in the ward for a couple of hours," Charlotte said.

"I'd like to take a look at the ship," Norway said.

"The bodies have been removed," Booth told them. "When we arrived yesterday they were pulling them out and laying them under sheets along the edge of the wood. It was bloody gruesome."

"Horrible!" McWade said, shuddering.

Booth glanced at Charlotte. "He had a lucky escape, this one," he said, pointing at McWade.

Charlotte remembered first meeting him on Victoria Pier nine years ago. She went to him and put her arms around him. "Fred, Fred, Fred," she said, burying her head in his shoulder.

"All those men. I warned them," McWade said, his eyes welling up.

"If you're going, I'm coming with you," Charlotte said.

"Are you *sure* you want to do that?" John asked.

"Yes, it's important we bear witness. We'll need to tell people what we've seen," Charlotte replied.

"I should warn you. Four more Air Ministry officials flew in today. They're probably over there right now," Booth said.

They took a taxi to the wreck site and asked the driver to wait. They trooped across the field toward the blackened and twisted structure. It stood higher than the tallest trees of Therain Wood, alien and tragic. The odor of diesel and other burnt substances hung in the air. For Charlotte and Fred

McWade, the scent of death brought back awful memories of a sunny evening on the waterfront in Hull.

Gendarmes stopped them and asked for ID. Booth was in uniform and Norway held up his Cardington pass. They were waved on without argument. Charlotte walked between Booth and Norway to the stern. She stared up at the Air Force ensign attached to the crow's nest, still fluttering nobly in the breeze. The rudder above them swung from side to side, squeaking. One of the workmen came to them, appearing friendly and wanting to talk.

"Messieurs et Madame, were any of zeese people your friends or family?" he said in passable English.

"Friends," Charlotte said.

"*Ah, vos amis.* What a conflagration! They were so burned they were small like children, their 'eads shrunken like zis," he held his hands together indicating the size of an orange. "There wasn't much left of zem, Madame. They were light as a fever when we put zem in zee coffins."

"Have all the remains been removed now?" Booth asked.

"*Oui, oui*—to zee town 'all. Possessions we found—we found all sorts of fings er—watches—all stopped at ten minutes past two, er fountain pens, cuff links. We put everyfing in boxes and give zem a number—zee same as on zee coffin."

The Frenchman stooped down and picked something up and held it out to Charlotte.

"Look at zis," he said.

She stared at the blackened, rubbery object, puzzled. He was holding the remains of an old-fashioned, black and dark green, steel beaded, kid pump with a Louis heel. The workman threw the shoe down in disgust.

"Pah!" he muttered.

My God, was there a woman on board?

The man drew her attention away from the shoe, pointing up at the ensign.

"Do you want it? I can get it for you."

While they were gazing up at the ensign, Norway hurriedly picked up the shoe and stuffed it in his pocket.

"Yes, please. We'll take it home," Charlotte said.

"I will have it for you before you leave," the man said, going off to find a big ladder.

They moved on to look around the wreck. Charlotte stuck close to Norway the boffin, intensely interested from a technical standpoint. McWade stayed with them. John followed on behind, silent and forlorn, hands behind his back. No one from the Air Ministry appeared to be around. They went to the bow, where the remains of a bundle of fabric was still smoldering. McWade poked at it with a steel bar he'd picked up.

"Look—a carpet," he said.

"It's a Persian," Charlotte said.

"What's left of it," Norway said.

"Probably worth a few bob—or was," McWade said.

"I wonder what it was doing there," Charlotte said.

"Strange place to s-stow it," Norway said.

Charlotte glanced at the ground nearby. Something red caught her eye. She picked it up. It was half of a playing card, burned and blackened at the edges; the Jack of Hearts. She slipped it into her handbag.

They proceeded through the wreck with plumes of smoke rising from the ground around them. They gazed at the remains of the fluted columns, some still bravely standing, their little gold-leaf heads mostly gone. Charlotte felt sad; those false columns represented false hopes and misguided dreams. The group stopped and stared at the starboard engine car—now a melted, tangled piece of wreckage driven up into what used to be the envelope.

"The poor devil in this thing didn't have a chance," Booth said.

"Must've been blown to kingdom come," McWade said.

They went next to the location of the control car, its structure crushed, the silver coxswain's wheels bent and twisted, along with the instrument panels and telegraph board. The water ballast main piping above the car and leading down to the valves in the car was mangled and broken. The floor was covered in a layer of black ash and soil washed in from the field by rain and ballast.

Something caught Charlotte's eye. "Nevil, what's that?"

Norway pulled out his knife and opened the blade. He poked around to expose the object—a ring with a red metal plate attached. Norway wiped the dirt off. "It's a key ring with *Cardington R101* on it. Look."

"I wonder who it belonged to," Charlotte said.

Norway slipped the keyring into his pocket. They left the control car and arrived next at a tree standing mysteriously in the middle of the wreck, undamaged, save for burn marks.

"This tree is clear evidence of how gently this ship settled down," McWade said.

"They must've b-been head to w-wind, t-traveling at virtually z-zero," Norway said.

They stood looking at the tree as if it were sacred. They were joined by two more Englishmen, dressed in raincoats and trilby hats. Charlotte presumed them to be from the Air Ministry. They appeared officious, but not overly so. McWade seemed familiar with them. Charlotte and Norway wandered away into what Norway explained was the passenger cabin area. Charlotte spotted a glint in the dirt. She pointed it out to Norway who took his knife out again. He carefully unearthed a chain with a silver medallion attached. He cleaned it off, squinting closely.

"Look, it's a St. Christopher," Charlotte said.

Norway got down on his haunches once more and poked around.

"There's something else here," he said. Pretty soon he had another object in his hands—a monocle. "Oh my goodness. Brancker must have died on this very spot. Oh, dear," he said, painfully closing his eyes. He didn't know Brancker personally, but the man was legendary and so was his monocle. He gave both objects to Charlotte. "Put them in your handbag." They moved on and joined the others, where McWade showed them a broken cable on the ground. "Look at that, s-snapped clean in two," Norway said.

"We saw this earlier. That's the elevator cable," McWade said.

"I expect the heat of the fire and the explosion caused that," an Air Ministry man said.

"Maybe and m-maybe n-not," Norway said.

"What do you mean?" the man said.

"C-could have been caused by t-too much strain on the elevators, if they were t-trying to get out of a steep d-dive," Norway replied.

The Air Ministry man said nothing. They moved and stood between frames 8 and 9, where the extra bay had been inserted.

"And that c-could've been what broke her b-back," Norway went on.

"Broke her back! I don't see any evidence of structural damage," the second Air Ministry man said.

"She's *hogged*. Look here," Norway said, pointing at the keel structure. "She's compressed at the keel, but the top members are stressed and broken apart, look. See that!"

Two more Air Ministry officials joined them, obviously desperate to know what assumptions were being made. Both were dressed in black overcoats and bowler hats. The tall one had a beaky nose and the short one, a limp. "May I ask if you're authorized to be in this location? Who *are* you, exactly," the short one said curtly.

Booth stepped forward. "I'm an officer with the Royal Airship Works. I was sent here yesterday to carry out an inspection and make a report after interviewing the survivors."

"And what about *these* people?" said the tall one with a smell under his beak. Charlotte stepped forward, ready to let him have it, her eyes blazing.

"My husband was an officer aboard this airship. He's severely injured, lying in Beauvais Hospital. I came here to visit him and to see this bloody wreck—and, I might add, he was a representative of the United States government!"

The tall man's face showed little emotion, but she perceived a trace of caution in his manner. He turned to Norway and McWade. "I just heard you making statements about structural damage. Be *very careful* what you imply."

"We're n-not *implying* anything. The f-facts speak for themselves," Norway said.

"And who are *you?*" the short one said, glaring at Norway.

"My name is N-Nevil N-Norway."

"With whom?"

"V-Vickers Aircraft Company."

The man's eyes bulged in horror. "What the dickens are *you* doing here? You're *certainly* not authorized!"

"He brought me here. He's my pilot," Charlotte said.

The man turned his gaze on John. "And *you*, sir? Who are you, may I ask?"

"I'm taking care of Commander Remington's wife. They're my family," John said.

"He came and got me in Yorkshire and informed me about the crash —unlike you people at the Air Ministry, who failed to tell anybody what was going on for more than *twelve hours!*" Charlotte snapped.

The short one glared at Norway. "You have no business being on this crash site. Are you here to gloat?"

"H-how d-dare you, sir! M-many of the men on this ship were good f-f-friends of mine."

"Well, you need to leave. Immediately."

"You d-don't have any j-jurisdiction. This is F-France, not W-Whitehall. And I should have thought you'd have been p-pleased I am here. I'm one of the last remaining airship engineers in England. Anyhow, we've seen enough," Norway said.

"Remember what I said—do *not* talk to the press," the tall one said.

The French workman came to Charlotte holding out the folded ensign. "Madame, pour vous," he said.

"I'll take that," the short one said, putting out his hand. "Give it to me at once."

The Frenchman sneered in disgust. "Non, non, non. First, I give it to zee lady. I got it for 'er. She can give it to you, *if* she pleases." He handed the ensign graciously to Charlotte, as though it were a ceremonial relic, bowing his head. Charlotte received it solemnly, hugging it to her breast.

"Merci, monsieur. C'est très gentil de votre part. Vous êtes un gentilhomme." Then, turning to the Englishman, she said, "You shan't have it! My husband will take the flag home."

Norway took out the red keyring and placed it in the man's upturned palm. "Here, you c-c-can have this s-souvenir instead," he said. "And by the way, w-were there any w-women on board?"

"Of course not," the tall one grunted.

Norway fished out the woman's shoe and thrust it at him.

"I s-suggest you do m-more investigation," he said.

99

CHURCH

After Charlotte's party had arranged for somewhere to stay, Charlotte spent the afternoon visiting hours with Lou. He told her about his trip to Canada—not so much about the trip as the plans he'd been making. He'd had a lot of time to think, he said. He mentioned his encounter with Bobby's parents at Union Station. He was surprised when Charlotte told him she'd tracked Elsie down and given her Bobby's message, still in its cardboard tube attached to its parachute, just as the girl on the waterfront had found it. Charlotte said Elsie had never married and had 'matured into a fine-looking woman' and her daughter 'was a sweet lass'. When Charlotte showed up at her door, Elsie had been touched and thankful. Charlotte was happy to find out that Bobby's parents had already made contact and were making plans to visit England to see their granddaughter. Elsie was looking forward to seeing them. Bobby's note in the tube, she said, had seemed like a miracle from heaven, coming when it did.

While Lou and Charlotte caught up on events, the others sat and talked with Leech, Binks, Bell and Disley. They were all able to sit up in bed, despite dressings on their burns, mostly to their hands, arms and faces. They were delighted to see Charlotte. Church lay in an adjacent room at death's door, swathed in bandages. Charlotte was granted permission to go in and see him.

"He's very ill, madame," the nun whispered.

"Can I speak to him?" Charlotte asked.

"He *may* hear you. You can try."

Charlotte leaned over Church. Only his eyes and blistered lips were visible. His eyelids fluttered.

"Sam, this is Charlotte. Irene and your Dad are on their way. Please wait."

Church made a little noise in acknowledgment and blinked his eyes. He moved his head slightly from side to side.

"Dear Sam, try to get better," Charlotte whispered.

The nun shook her head. "He may last until tomorrow," she whispered.

Charlotte wondered what had happened to Irene and Church's father. *They should've been here by now.*

She returned to the main ward where Norway and John were chatting with Lou, who seemed much brighter. Lou's face dropped when he saw in her eyes that Church was not long for this world.

Church hung on bravely through the night. Irene still hadn't arrived by morning and Charlotte was worried. Later in the day, after spending a couple of hours with Lou and visiting with survivors, Charlotte, Norway and John went to the town hall, where the dead lay in state in pine wood coffins, each draped with a small Union Jack.

Charlotte counted five as having been identified, their names on the coffins. Walter Potter was the only name she knew. It made her cry. The rest had a number written on the end in large numerals. A small, wooden box rested on each coffin with its number. The back wall had been draped with black fabric.

Four solemn French guards stood to attention with two Red Cross nurses. A line of people carrying flowers filed past, their heads bowed. A huge crowd had gathered around the square. It was time to load the coffins onto carriages, drawn up at the bottom of the steps. Charlotte and her companions left the town hall and stood at the curb in the crowd. Soldiers brought the coffins down and laid them in pairs in the backs of the twenty-three open carriages, each drawn by four magnificent horses. By 11 o'clock, forty-six coffins had been loaded.

John tapped Charlotte's shoulder. "Look—the survivors, who are well enough."

Binks, Bell and Leech were led to a place of honor in the procession. Charlotte pitied them. *Those poor devils didn't ask for this.*

As a band played *God Save the King* and the *Marseillaise,* a hundred and one gun salute was fired.

"Lord Thomson is getting the full treatment today," Charlotte muttered.

"While the w-world watches," Norway replied.

The procession of firemen, policemen and all branches of the military moved off around Beauvais Square toward the railway station. A formation of aeroplanes flew overhead.

They returned to the hospital in the middle of the afternoon. Lou was making progress, but Church was slowly slipping away. Charlotte couldn't believe Irene still hadn't arrived. The funeral procession to the station ended and Binks, Bell and Leech returned to the ward to rest.

Later, a priest carrying a small case was led into Church's room by the Mother Superior. Charlotte, Norway and John went in, too. Binks, Bell, and Leech stood along the wall beside Church's bed. The priest put on a sash and took out bottles of holy water and oil and put them on the side table and administered last rites.

Church opened his eyes, appearing fearful at first, then at peace. Charlotte took Church's bandaged hand. She felt him squeeze hers weakly. Ten minutes later, Church breathed his last. The priest put his bottles away, took off his sash and put it in his case. He nodded his head and left. A nun pulled the sheet over Church's head. Binks sobbed.

Not an hour later, Charlotte heard hurried footsteps in the corridor. She jumped up and went to the door, stopping Irene and Mr. Church in their tracks.

"We couldn't get a plane. They said the weather was too bad."

"Irene."

"We took the boat train to Calais …"

"*Irene!*"

"…and we've been travelin' by car …"

Irene's voice trailed off as she stared into Charlotte's face—the truth dawning on her.

"Oh, no, no! Please, no!"

Irene and Mr. Church wept as they were gently led away by the Mother Superior.

MacDonald called Marthe on Wednesday, as promised.

"Dearest Marthe."

"Ramsay."

"He came home last night. I was at Victoria at midnight to meet their train."

"So many times, he met me there."

"They crossed the Channel aboard *Tempest* yesterday afternoon," he said. "The strange thing is—there's one man they cannot account for."

"How odd. Perhaps the fire …"

"They're in the Westminster morgue trying to identify them."

"What about *him*?" she asked.

"No."

She heard him choke up. "I shall miss his friendship and his counsel …" he said.

"Yes, he always said he protected you."

"Aye, he did that."

"You know you can count on me, Ramsay."

"Thank you, lassie."

"He'd want that."

100

ΛΝΟΤΗΕR FUNERΛL

Friday & Saturday October 10 & 11, 1930.

T he airshipmen lay in state in Westminster Hall the following Friday, their coffins draped in Union Jacks smothered with flowers. Thousands filed past in silence, paying their respects, including Lou, Charlotte and John. Lou had barely recovered, his head and arm in bandages, his other arm in a sling, but he insisted on being there. Lou was in awe of the place. The room was so massive. He stood at center looking up at the enormous roof beams. The scale reminded him of one of the sheds. He read a plaque on the wall. It said this was where King Charles I had been tried before being executed. Lou was enthralled. Now, he supposed they'd install another plaque dedicated to the victims of the *Cardington R101* disaster.

Later that day, memorial services were held in both St. Paul's Cathedral and the Catholic Westminster Cathedral. Lou and Charlotte sat with the heartbroken Olivia Irwin. Before the service began, Lou gave Mrs. Richmond the ensign. "I know you'll remember his last words to you from the elevator," he said. She received it gratefully and asked the chaplain to lay it on the altar.

Lou and Charlotte took part in the funeral procession the following day, riding in a car with Binks, Bell and Leech behind the twenty-four gun carriages. Each was drawn by four black geldings, their coats groomed to a sheen that glistened in the autumn sun. The number of coffins had risen to forty-eight, now including Radcliffe and Church. Disley was not up to taking part and Lou couldn't help marveling that he'd managed to get to a phone in Allonne that night, despite his injuries.

The two-mile procession wended its way from Westminster Hall, past Gwydyr House, to Whitehall, around Trafalgar Square and on to Euston, passing hundreds of thousands of grieving people. All flags were flying at half-mast. At Euston, the coffins were loaded onto a train, itself covered in wreaths. The mourners made the slow journey to Bedford, passing thousands standing silently beside the tracks, at railway crossings, on railway stations, on their allotments and in their back gardens.

On reaching Bedford, the coffins were placed on trucks and taken to St. Mary's Church, where a single grave had been dug in the tiny cemetery within sight of Shed No.1, where the hated *Howden R100* remained in her prison, awaiting sentence. As the procession passed by, the bells of Bedford's churches tolled. Hundreds of thousands of mourners stood in stunned silence.

While prayers were being said by the RAF chaplain, coffins were walked slowly down a ramp into the grave and laid side by side. Lou thought it ironic that Thomson's coffin wasn't marked. He hadn't been identified. He was just one of the unknown airshipmen.

Lou and Charlotte stood at the grave's edge with Olivia, Rosie, Irene and Sam Church's family. Charlotte made a point of holding her hand out to Rosie and giving her a hug. She invited her to stand with them. Binks, Bell and Leech stood behind them with the legend of the airship world, friend of Brancker, Scott and Richmond—Hugo Eckener, the great German Zeppelin designer.

Lou spotted Norway standing in the crowd with Barnes Wallis and John Bull. What must they be feeling right now? No one in the crowd recognized Wallis, who was wearing a flat cap. Where was Burney?—probably in America. Lou wondered about his own family in Great Falls. He'd write to them this week. He'd already sent them a wire to let them know he was okay. He and Charlotte needed to arrange a visit as soon as possible.

Across the mass grave, he saw Prime Minister MacDonald in a black overcoat, hat in hand—with his mane of white hair and magnificent mustache—but, like everyone else, he looked desolate. When the last hymn ended, MacDonald walked slowly down the ramp to the coffins. He seemed lost, not knowing where to place two vivid, red roses he was clutching. Finally, he laid them down on the nearest unmarked coffin, where he stood, head bowed.

After a few moments, he turned and walked up the ramp, glancing at Charlotte as he passed. Charlotte began to shake, as if he were an apparition. She'd seen MacDonald's picture in the newspapers over the years, but it wasn't until this moment that she recognized him. It was the same face she'd seen years ago, eyes full of bewilderment and sorrow as he'd approached her dressed in black, carrying his hat, then as now, in a casualty clearing station in Arras in 1918. She heard the voices of those two officers escorting him as plain as if it were yesterday.

Our future Prime Minister!

Preposterous!

She was jarred back to the present by a covey of crows breaking from a tree. They swarmed across the cemetery above the mourners' heads, a swirling black cloud, twisting and turning, over the gravesite and away across the vacant fairground. But for the sound of their wings, they were completely silent. Their disturbance had been caused by an approaching squadron of aeroplanes.

As the service ended and the shadows grew long, the crowd stood in the chilly wind and watched MacDonald climb wearily into the blue Rolls. Everyone had a sense, not only of profound loss, but of uncertainty, which added to their misery. They knew this was the end of 'Airship City'. They'd been cut adrift.

Before leaving, Lou and Charlotte placed flowers on Freddie's grave. They were driven home by Booth and his wife and, after an early dinner, went to bed. It was the first time they'd been in their own bed together since Lou had left for Canada aboard *Howden R100*. In spite of the dreadful events of the day, Lou's injuries and weariness, it was a joyful occasion for both. Never before had Charlotte been so gloriously satisfied as she was that night —with all her mind, with all her heart and with all her soul. The airship was out of her life; so was Jessup; she knew she was going home; the unspoken had been spoken. At last, she was free.

On Sunday, there was a knock on the door. The person standing on the step was someone Charlotte had never seen before. She introduced herself as 'Mrs. Beasley'. She said she was William Jessup's landlady. In her hand, she had a large, white paper bag, which she handed to Charlotte.

"These belong to you," she said. "I laundered them myself. I know the whole story. I wanted to make sure you got 'em back."

Charlotte was mystified. She opened the bag and peeked inside. She gasped.

"Now, don't you worry, Mrs. Remington. You take 'em. No telling when you might be needing 'em."

"Let me give you something," Charlotte said.

"Don't you dare think about that, my girl," the woman said, turning away.

When she reached the bottom step she stopped and shook her head. "That Jessup was a bad lot. Got what he deserved I reckon—the only one that did."

She left with a nod. Charlotte closed the door. Lou was standing behind her. "What you got there, Charlie?" he asked.

She opened the bag for him to look. He was puzzled.

"The baby clothes! I thought you'd taken them with you," he said.

"It's a long story, Remy," Charlotte said.

Lou smiled, "I've got plenty of time, honey."

Later that day, Lou wrote to his mother.

58 Kelsey Street,
Bedford.

12ᵗʰ October, 1930.

My Dearest Mother,
    I hope you and Dad are holding up. Tell Dad I think of him always and that I am praying for him. I want you to know I am doing okay. I will make a full recovery. I am so sorry if I caused you and Dad and everyone a lot of worry. Charlotte is with me! She came to Beauvais in France immediately after the accident.
    Please write to me often and tell me how Dad is doing. Not quite sure what the future will bring, but I guess I will leave the Navy soon. We plan to visit you and Dad as soon as possible via New York.

Fondest Love,
Your loving son, Lou.

During the following week, his arm in a sling, Lou went to Cardington on the bus and wandered around. He looked inside the customs shed. Potter's accordion was still on the back table where he'd last seen it. He picked it up. It made a few wheezing sounds. Terrible sadness washed over him.

With the accordion slung over his good shoulder, Lou went to Shed No. 1 where he met Booth and Meager. They preferred to sit around next to *Howden R100* than in Cardington House. They'd had no direction and went through the motions of going in each day and filling out pointless daily reports. He asked Booth if he wouldn't mind dropping the accordion off at Kelsey Street. He'd take it to over Potter's wife later.

Lou went next door to Shed No.2 and looked inside. It was empty but for two men sweeping the floor. Lou stood quietly for a few moments remembering the noise, echoes, shouts, singing and laughing ... The silence was now absolute. He stood at the shed doors staring at the tower, remembering his morphine dreams. He turned away. It was all over. This was a milestone in his life, one also marking the end of an era in British aviation.

He walked to Cardington House between the autumnal trees. Everything had a depressing air about it. His first visit, when Thomson had made his grand announcement had been enveloped in optimism. When he got to the great house, he saw two grey Air Ministry vans parked outside. A gang in grey boiler suits were busy loading them with file cabinets and office furniture. He went to Colmore's office. It was bare: furniture gone; lockable filing cabinet gone; wall pictures gone. There were only clear patches where things had been and impressions in the green carpet where his desk had stood.

Lou went to his own office. His files and logs were being removed, the operation supervised by two men in bowler hats—a tall one with a beaky nose and a short one with a limp.

"And who are you, sir?" the short, officious one said.

"Commander Remington, U.S.N., Special Assistant to Wing Commander. Colmore, Third Officer, Royal Airship Works, Cardington."

"Hmm, I see. Got any documents in your drawers or at home—any records pertaining to airships *R100* and *R101*, including any memos, instructions, letters, logbooks, photographs, reports, progress records, drawings, calculations …?"

"No, I don't."

"Are you quite sure?"

"Yes, I'm quite sure. What's happening to all the files?"

"Going up to Central Filing. They'll be available on an 'as needed' basis by request after special approval."

"Right."

"There is one other thing. There was a lady. I presume she'd be your wife, who brought back the Royal Air Force flag. Do you know where it is?"

"Yes, it was on the altar in St. Paul's. Now it's on the altar of St. Mary's," Lou said.

"I see," the man said. He seemed resigned and turned briskly away.

Lou went home.

PART THIRTEEN

Cardington R101 Court of Inquiry

EPILOGUE

101

ANOTHER COURT OF INQUIRY

November 1930.

The Court of Inquiry began a month after the crash. It was held in the auditorium of the Institution of Civil Engineers on George Street, close to Westminster Hall. Lou sat with Charlotte and Olivia Irwin. The hushed room was full of Air Ministry officials, government bureaucrats, world press reporters, French witnesses and survivors, Binks, Bell, Disley, Leech, Savoury and Cook.

Some aspects of the proceedings bothered Lou. He often saw small groups gathered around the entrance lobby or about the corridors engaged in deep conversation. The feeling of conspiracy was heightened when he saw the two bowler-hatted Air Ministry men jawing with Thomson's secretary, Knoxwood, on various occasions. One time, he saw the same men in a deep conversation with Leech. They appeared to be bullying him, laying down the law, pointing fingers in his face. It all seemed irregular. These people seemed intent on keeping control of the evidence, lines of questioning and testimony.

Furthermore, Lou heard the president of the court complaining on more than one occasion that the Air Ministry hadn't provided requested documents. They were usually 'about' to send them, or 'trying' to locate them, or declared the said documents had been 'mislaid' or simply 'gone missing'. It was unfortunate, they said. The court would just have to glean information through witnesses. But, of course, most of the people who knew the answers were dead.

No meaningful discussion was had about the 'grand competition' set up by Thomson, pitting the teams against each other. The two most qualified and experienced airship designers in the country, Wallis and Norway, weren't consulted, invited to testify or offer an opinion. They may have shown government as incompetent, or Thomson in a bad light. Instead, they preferred to interrogate people like their German airship competitor, Hugo Eckener or Monsieur Rabouille from Allonne, button maker by day, rabbit poacher by night. Wallis and Norway and the Vickers team were excluded, just as they'd been from the great funeral.

Lou and Charlotte listened patiently while forty-two witnesses were cross-examined, charts explained, and models displayed. It was all terribly well-managed, but devoid of any real research. The ground rules were set early in the proceedings by the president of the court, who praised the design team and all those in government having anything to do with the structural integrity and vetting of the airship—clearly the structure wasn't in question and therefore, not worthy of any discussion at all. The notion that the airship could have broken or deformed in the air, besides being painfully embarrassing, would have been intolerable to the public, especially after all the hoopla. The court and the public were skillfully directed by the President away from the subject and any notion that the crash may have been caused by or contributed to a massive structural failure. The press eagerly took this and disseminated it as truth. At least, they said, we can rest assured the ship didn't break apart like *R38/ZR-2* or *Shenandoah*.

Lou believed, however, as did Capt. Irwin and McWade, that with the additional bay, her resilience had to have been diminished to some degree. Under 'full elevators' she'd broken her back—just as *ZR-2/R38* had done under 'full rudders'. The one thing Richmond had striven to avoid at all costs had occurred. But still, none of that would be examined—it'd all been under the government's care and control and, therefore, off limits. Lou knew that if her back hadn't broken, she might have made it out of Therain Wood, but only just; all that was moot. With the cover damaged beyond repair and the catastrophic loss of gas, both gradual and sudden, there was no hope for this ship's survival and the officers knew it. The crash was inevitable. McWade had sounded the warning, but no one would listen.

No questions were asked regarding the airworthiness of the ship or its fitness to make this journey. No mention was made of the fact that the ship had never flown in adverse weather conditions, nor been properly tested at full speed. No one questioned the qualifications of the main players, including the Minister of State for Air himself. No one asked what all these civilians (including Thomson) were doing on board this untested, unproven, experimental aircraft, making a ten thousand mile return trip to India. Neither was there any discussion concerning the fitness of Scott, Colmore, Richmond, or Rope to oversee this project or supervise or schedule such a voyage.

Of course, despite the move afoot to create a whitewash, someone would have to take the fall. Lou sat fascinated when he realized just who'd been selected for that honor. It was a logical choice—one that the public would buy into. He remembered Commodore Maitland and he smiled to himself.

Not on my watch, good buddies!

The president of the court reminded Lou of the president of the court in Hull—another Oxford man, or was it Cambridge? Beautifully spoken, beautifully dressed. Lou watched as he addressed his own questions to one of the faceless senior Air Ministry bureaucrats.

"What we need to know is: Who made the final decision to fly? Who was the man in charge of this airship?"

"Captain Irwin, sir."

"He was the pilot in command. Is that correct?"

"Yes."

"But Major Scott was on board, also. Is that correct?"

"Yes, he was, but—"

"In what capacity was he on board?"

"As Rear Admiral or Commodore—a ceremonial position."

"He was a uniformed officer?"

"He was wearing his uniform on the night in question, yes."

"He outranked the pilot in command, did he not?"

"Yes, technically, but he was wearing his uniform more as a ceremonial thing."

"So, if he was the most senior uniformed officer ...I'm confused."

"It sounds confusing, sir, but really, it's not."

"All right. Let's look at the flight to America in 1919. Who was the pilot in command of that ship?"

"Major Scott."

"He was the captain?"

"Yes."

"Was there a commodore or rear admiral on board that voyage?"

"Yes, Commodore Maitland, sir."

"But Scott, as the captain, had full control?"

"Absolutely, sir."

"Then it follows that this logic applies to this voyage to India. Captain Irwin was in full control. If he thought it imprudent to attempt to fly this ship to India then he should have—"

A terrible shriek erupted in the courtroom. Olivia Irwin jumped up beside Lou. *"How dare you! How dare you!"* she screamed.

Lou and Charlotte stood up and helped Olivia, now in a state of total collapse, out of the courtroom. Officials directed them to the library where she fell into a leather armchair, sobbing hysterically. A doctor was sent for and Olivia was given a sedative. Lou and Charlotte sat beside her and she took Lou's hand. "Please, Lou, don't let them destroy my husband. They forced him to do what he knew was suicide. It was insane and he knew it. Now, they intend to destroy his memory." She buried her face in her hands. "Oh my poor Blackbird, what are they trying to do to you," she whispered.

The following day, it was Lou's turn to take the stand. He was examined by the same solicitor general who'd cross-questioned him in Hull in 1922. They exchanged pleasantries, the solicitor general showing much respect for Lou. He questioned Lou about his role at the Royal Airship Works and his experience aboard *R38*. Then Lou's perspective on the voyage to India was discussed in detail. Finally, Capt. Irwin's role was called into question. It was what Lou had been waiting for. He was quick jump to Irwin's defense.

"You are *not* here, Commander, to give Captain Irwin a character reference!" the solicitor general snapped.

"That may be the case. *Nevertheless,* sir, I shall give one to this court, just the same." The court was stunned into silence. The solicitor general fumed. "Captain Irwin was one of the most skilled officers it has been my honor and pleasure to serve—and he was one of the finest human beings I've ever known. I would not be standing here today, if it were not for him. No blame should be cast on him, *none* whatsoever! The world must know that."

"So are you trying to say the captain was *coerced?*"

"Yes, *absolutely* he was coerced!"

The court went silent. No one asked by whom. No one needed to. That ploy turned out to be a miserable failure and abandoned immediately. Capt. Irwin's name would be preserved for all time.

When the court adjourned the next day, Lou caught up with Binks and took him in the library, having asked Charlotte to wait for him in the reception hall. They went in and stood by the window.

"Tell me what happened on the ship that night, Joe."

"What d'you mean, sir? When?" Binks replied, his eye and cheek twitching furiously. This almost made Lou break into grin, but he managed to remain stern.

"What did you do to Jessup?"

"I don't follow you, sir."

"Joe, you had blood on your jacket, Cameron had an envelope in his back pocket smeared with blood and Disley had blood on his right shoe. And if I'd seen Church, he probably had blood on him, too."

"Not much gets past you, does it, sir?"

Lou held both his hands out, curling his fingers to his palms.

"Come on, Joe, let's have it!"

"Well, before we left, we got together and decided we'd put Jessup out of action—just hurt him a bit."

"On my account?"

"Yes, but Doug got a bit carried away and bashed 'is 'ead in and killed 'im."

"His head exploded, did it?"

"Well, yeah."

"Just like the gypsy said it would?"

"That's right."

"What did you do with his body? It wasn't found in the wreck."

"We cast him into the sea—just like *Jonah,* sir."

Lou screwed up his face. This was a conundrum, or was it? Maybe not.

"I s'pose you're gonna have to tell 'em, sir, aren't you?"

"I have no idea what you're talking about, Joe. I thought Jessup had been incinerated."

Binks sighed in relief then smiled fondly at Lou.

"Oh, Joe, I want you to do something for me. You're a good artist. Do some sketches for me of the goings on over these past years: the *R100* the *R101* and all the characters involved."

"Sure I can sir, I've done loads already. What do you want 'em for?"

"I thought maybe we'd put them in a book someday," Lou said.

Lou and Binks came out of the library as Big Ben was striking four. Lou stood a moment, as he'd done many times in the past, admiring Charlotte from a distance. She was looking out of the window at the traffic, unaware of him. She looked so beautiful. He shook his head in wonder of her. Even though he'd used up all nine lives, he was still the luckiest man in the world! As he was thinking this, he put his hand in his pocket and pulled out the burnt remnants of Church's Jack of Hearts. He'd brought it for Binks to put with the rest. But then, he decided to keep it. He put it in his wallet, where it would remain always. Church wouldn't mind.

The day after the Court of Inquiry ended, Lou received a telegram from Great Falls.

Dearest Brother STOP Regret to inform you Father died last night at 3 am STOP Letter to follow STOP Love Anna

A letter arrived three weeks later.

Remington's Farm,
Virginia U.S.A.

Dearest Brother,

I am sorry to tell you that on December 5th, at 3 a.m., our beloved father died at home on Remington's Farm. During that last day, he asked Mother and me to tell you he loved you. He asked that you forgive him. He said he is thankful you are safe and that Charlotte is with you. A funeral service will take place at St. Peter's this Saturday. We know you will be there in spirit. I will place a wreath on his coffin from you and Charlotte.

You'll be happy to know Jeb's house is finished and they are pleased with it. Dad saw it when it was nearly complete and he liked it very much. Jeb is a lot better now, but his hair is snow white.

Julia came and sat with Dad every day and during many nights over the last month. We all long to see you and Charlotte soon.

Your ever-loving sister, Anna.

P.S. In all this sadness and grief, there is some good news. Julia is to become our sister-in-law. (Father knew about it and it made him a very happy man.)

P.P.S. What was it you whispered in Tom's ear at Union Station?

Lou smiled. He remembered word for word what he'd whispered:
'Put your arms around Julia and never let her go. Thank you for everything you've done. I am very proud of you. I love you, my dear Brother'
When he'd got home to find Charlotte gone, he'd had a few moments of regret for uttering those words, but he knew he'd never have gone back on them. Would he answer Anna's question? He would need to think about that.

102

CHRISTMAS EVE IN PARIS

December 24, 1930.

O n Christmas Eve, Marthe was joined by Abbé Mugnier, her Catholic priest, spiritual adviser and friend, in her Paris apartment on the Left Bank. It was a frigid day. They sat drinking coffee at the window overlooking the stone terrace, bright in the morning sunshine. They reflected on their trip to the wreck site on Beauvais Ridge earlier that month.

Marthe had dressed in black from head to toe and worn a veil. What a miserable day it'd been—cold and blustery—not unlike the conditions *he* must have faced that terrible night. It took them a long time to find the wreck, but in the end, after making enquiries, they discovered it some distance from the Meru road. Half of it was in a field, the rest in the woods— woods infested with rooks, their ghostly calls rasping and mocking. The birds were irritated still by the great incursion of the flaming beast and all the activity ever since.

Marthe had taken a dozen red roses with her and laid them on the ground. A workman had shown them the exact spot in the mass of tangled steel where Thomson had died. Of course, Marthe knew this was impossible, but gave him a franc anyway. The man was helpful, but much too descriptive about the scene the morning of the crash. Marthe got down on her knees on a blanket while the Abbé conducted a short Requiem Mass for Thomson and all those who'd perished. After that, they visited Beauvais Cathedral where Marthe lit a candle for Thomson and said more prayers.

"I shall miss him so much. No one could ask for a better friend," Marthe had said, sadly.

"Indeed. He was a very fine fellow, and now he is with God," said the Abbé.

Their reverie was interrupted by the sight of a boy entering the courtyard and climbing the steps. He carried a basket of flowers. He crossed the terrace with its stone balustrade and knocked on the door. Isadora ushered him in and told him to place the basket on the table in the circular entrance hall. Marthe was disturbed. They were *Général Jacqueminot* roses—only *he* sent her those... She jumped up and pulled out the card. Her eyes became wide with astonishment as she read the words.

If I cannot be at your side on this joyous Christmas Eve, then my love comes to you with fifteen of our special roses, one for each of the splendid years I have known you since the banks of the Cotroceni—years which have given me exquisite pleasure and exquisite pain; pain which I have endured happily. Until we meet again, your eternally devoted love and friend.
        Now and forever,

                Kit.

103

A NEW DAY

July 1931.

It was a magnificent new day—a beautiful morning in July. Marthe delighted in the song of the larks drifting through the open windows. Ah, how she loved that sound.

Yes, yes, so unmistakably English!

She reflected on how beastly the last year had been.

Thank God this year is showing signs of improvement.

Luxuriating in the enormous bed, she stretched her limbs and let out a sigh of pleasure. The fine silk sheets felt good against her naked body.

This bed is the very center of power. The most powerful place on earth! Kit was right. I am Cinderella! And who knows—perhaps the wife of a British Prime Minister one day…

MacDonald, dressed in his black and burgundy silk dressing gown, awkwardly pushed the door open with his elbow. He entered slowly, concentrating on the tray of tea and buttered toast he held out before him.

"What a darling man you are!" Marthe exclaimed.

"Made it all ma self, in the scullery."

"Even the toast?"

"Aye and I buttered it, too," he said. "There's marmalade and honey if you want some." They sat in silence for a few minutes, enjoying their breakfast.

"We owe everything to *him*, you know," she said suddenly.

"Aye, we do. It was he that brought us together."

"Dear Kit, I do miss him," she said.

MacDonald looked genuinely pained. "No one misses him more than I. He was the only person I ever confided in."

She gave him her most endearing look of compassion. "Then, from now on, you must confide in *me*, mon chéri."

"I shall. And I will confide this to you: When I first saw you with him at the House of Lords that day, I fell hopelessly and passionately in love with you. I felt so desperately guilty. I was beside ma self," he said, shaking his head, re-experiencing his pain.

"And I felt exactly the same about *you*," she said.

"And when we all played croquet together, I'm ashamed to say, my longing was unbearable. It was pure *agony!*"

"And me," she said, clapping her hand to her breast.

"But I have to tell you, in all seriousness, if he were still with us, none of this would be happening," MacDonald said.

"Of course not! ...He was such a dear, dear man. Now, *I* have two confessions of my own to make to *you*."

"Oh, how I love these love-bed confessions!" MacDonald said, chuckling

"When Kit came to Paris that Christmas, we went into Notre Dame and I lit four candles. One was for my beloved father, one was for Isadora, one was for Abbé Mugnier and the other was for someone else. Kit was dying to know who, and I wouldn't tell him."

"Who was it for?"

"It was for *you*."

MacDonald blinked in disbelief. "Good grief!"

"I felt so bad about it afterwards."

"And what else are you going to tell me?"

"Kit always had a recurring dream about this ..."

"Girl in the carriage! Oh yes, he was mesmerized by it," MacDonald said, his face lighting up.

"He dreamed of it time and time again and told me about it over and over—it was an obsession!" she exclaimed.

"Aye, it was that."

"He swore it was me, but in the dream the coachman always drove off before he could get a closer look."

MacDonald pursed his lips and dropped his head. "Poor Kit," he said sadly.

"I told him it couldn't possibly have been me."

"No, of course not, my love."

"But Ramsay ..." She faltered, her beautiful bosom heaving, about to burst into tears. She pressed the heels of her palms into her eyes. "...it *was* me!"

"Oh, my goodness gracious!"

"I never owned up to it. It would've been too painful for him. I was there in Paris with Isadora to pick up my wedding gown. I was to be married in Bucharest the following month, on my fifteenth birthday."

"Well, I never did!" MacDonald exclaimed.

"The sad thing is: I never remembered seeing a young officer on Rue de Rivoli that day."

"Poor CB. He loved you so much, sweet lassie." She watched him reminisce. He looked away into the garden and his face clouded over.

"I blame myself. I wondered if he was driving them all to their deaths, including his own. It was foolhardy and somehow I *knew* it. I should've put my foot down and stopped him. Now, I doubt my own motives. I canna help myself! It's something I'll have to live with. Did I feel about him, the way he'd felt about your husband—hoping for the worst? Nay, I had my doubts and I stood idly by and let it happen. It makes all this bitter sweet." He put his hands to his head.

"Oh come, my precious. You tried to stop him—you know you did! Don't blame yourself. He did what he did of his own free will. He truly believed it would all turn out well. But it just wasn't to be."

Bolstering a man's spirits was one of her most unique skills. His face brightened; his depressing thoughts banished, for now.

"What happened to his precious painting?" Marthe asked, changing the subject.

"It's hanging in Mother's room up in Lossie. He loved that room."

"Good," she said.

"Do you want it in your flat? I'll send it over to Paris, if you like?"

"Dieu non! God no! It would remind me of that detestable, bloody airship."

"Mr. Churchill came back and painted some clouds over the damned thing before we took the painting down."

"Dear old Winston …" she said.

"So you *wouldn't* see it," he reassured her.

"No. *I'd* know the beastly thing was lurking behind those clouds. I don't want it! There's just one thing, Ramsay …" Her voice tapered off.

"I was just thinking the same thing, my darling. When you come up to Lossie, I'll have to find a new home for it."

"Would you dearest? I'd appreciate that."

"Perhaps we can stick it out in the shed," he said.

Having unburdened themselves, they sat in silence for a few moments. Marthe lay back down on the pillows with a sigh of contentment—and now, exquisite longing.

"You know, my darling Marthe, from the moment we met, I knew you were a passionate woman—*and very highly sexed*—if I may say so!"

To her, when he said this, his Highland accent, sounded like beautiful music, pleasing and seductive—as sweet as Eros' lyre.

"You're such a perceptive man. I always *knew* you understood me perfectly."

"And now, I do believe our wee friend is beginning to raise his head yet again," MacDonald said, leaning over and gently kissing her hardening nipples. She sighed with pleasure.

"He is *relentless*, and we shall not disappoint him. Come back to bed, Ramsay."

"Oh, my dear Lassie. Love is all …"

"Come to me, you sweet, gorgeous man," she purred.

104

THE TOMB

July 1931.

Lou and Charlotte stood in silence, reading the names on the tomb. They hadn't wanted to visit previously; they'd put off coming to pay their respects until it was finished. The dedication ceremony had taken place the day before, but Lou could not bring himself to attend. Red wreaths from that ceremony lay under the carved spread eagle. Lou placed a bouquet of white roses at the foot of the monument, beneath Captain Irwin's name.

Each name on the seven-foot-high edifice brought a face vividly to Lou's mind. At some, he smiled wistfully, at others, he felt intense sadness. Potter was such a name …and Capt. Carmichael Irwin …and Peter 'Pierre' Higginbottom. Lou was pleased they'd had the decency to put up the name he preferred. He was unable to suppress a smile when he remembered Pierre telling him his last name was Higginbottom. "No saucy remarks from you, sir, if you don't mind," he'd warned with one of his cheeky looks.

Lou forgave those whom he knew had made wrong decisions. They were all human—*only* human. It was pride that killed them, ultimately. He realized why Scott drank too much; who could blame him? Deep down he must have been a worried man—perhaps scared—caught in a trap not entirely of his own making, like everyone else. There was also the possibility that he was actually a sick man—something Lou had never considered until this moment. Perhaps he should've been knighted back in 1919 when he'd astonished the world with his two-way Atlantic flight. Who knows? Perhaps they wouldn't be standing here now if he *had* been.

He thought about his own role in this saga. Had he done enough to try to prevent it? He remembered his own irrational guilt over *R38*—which obviously he knew he couldn't have prevented. He considered all this and finally felt guilt-free. He'd tried his damnedest. It must've been Fate. He was satisfied about that. One of life's big learning experiences!

Lou was brought back from his thoughts by the sound of footsteps on the gravel. Turning, he was surprised to see the Prime Minister with a beautiful lady on his arm—and by the way they looked into one another's eyes, they were pretty darned close. MacDonald's blue Rolls was parked outside the iron gate in front of John Bull's van. Two men in dark suits hovered nearby. The woman carried a bunch of exquisite red roses.

"Good morning, laddie. I hope we're not disturbing you," MacDonald said, while Marthe placed their flowers in one of the tomb's stone flower pots.

"Not at all, sir."

"How old is your baby?" Marthe said, coming close to Charlotte and peering at the newborn in Charlotte's arms.

"He's two weeks," Charlotte answered.

"Oh, how *adorable!* Such thick, black hair. May I hold him?"

"Yes," Charlotte said.

She carefully transferred the infant into Marthe's arms.

"Just look at those *blue, blue* eyes. He's so sweet. What's his name?" Marthe asked.

"Christian—Christian Carmichael."

"How lovely. Did you have friends aboard the airship?"

"Yes," Lou said, "...*many* good friends."

"He was on board *this* ship and *R38*," Charlotte said.

MacDonald and Marthe were taken aback. MacDonald studied Lou thoughtfully for a moment. "You must be the *American* I've heard about."

"Yes, Prime Minister. Formerly, Lieutenant Commander Louis Remington, U.S. Navy."

MacDonald put out his hand. "I'm *very* honored, sir," he said. "This is Princess Marthe Bibesco."

"I heard Lord Thomson speak of you once, ma'am," Lou said. "This is my wife, Charlotte."

Charlotte smiled.

"He spoke to you of *me?*" Marthe asked her eyes full of curiosity.

"No, ma'am, I *overheard* him speaking to Captain Irwin, by accident really."

"How nice."

"He spoke very highly of you."

Marthe seemed delighted. Even in death, Thomson complimented her.

"Tell me, laddie, with all your experience: What do you think of airships now?" MacDonald asked.

"Sir, if you want to know the truth—I'd have to say: The concept is flawed—at least for the present."

MacDonald was thoughtful.

"Fate has had a hand in me running into you like this. There is much you have simplified for me today with just those few words. I must say, I had reservations myself and I was told I was worrying unduly. What are you going to do now, son?"

"I'm going back to fixing cars and pumping gas in Yorkshire, sir, and living a comfortable, quiet life in a lovely cottage with Charlotte and Christian."

"That's a noble thing to do."

"And maybe I'll write a book—a novel—about these airshipmen with some sketches—like a tribute," Lou said, nodding toward the monument. "I asked a writer-friend of mine to write it once, but he wouldn't. Perhaps I'll do it myself."

"Wonderful idea," Marthe said. "Let me know if I can be of any help to you."

"The Princess is an acclaimed writer," MacDonald said.

"And what will you call this book of yours?" Marthe asked.

"*The Next Big Thing*," Lou said, without hesitation.

"Yes, wonderful!" MacDonald said. "I look forward to reading it."

After a few more pleasantries, Marthe eased the baby back into Charlotte's arms and Lou and Charlotte turned to leave. As they did so, Charlotte whispered to Lou.

"Charlotte has just reminded me of something, Princess. I understand you are you a friend of Lady Cathcart."

"Yes, indeed I am."

Lou put his hand in his pocket and pulled out the silver St. Christopher on its chain.

"Charlotte found this at the wreck site in Beauvais. I've had it in my pocket ever since. Sir Sefton Brancker proudly showed it to me on the ship. He said he'd promised to return it to Lady Cathcart on his return from India. I wonder if you'd be kind enough to give it to her—I know he'd appreciate that."

"I shall make a point of it."

"Thank you, m'am."

"It will be my pleasure, Commander Remington."

Lou and Charlotte made their way out of the cemetery to their restored motorcycle, now with a shiny, new sidecar attached. Lou held Christian while Charlotte tied her white headscarf under her chin over her now almost shoulder-length hair. She put on her sunglasses and climbed in. Lou kissed Christian's forehead and carefully slipped him into her arms. He covered them both with a blanket, tucking them in snugly before leaning over and kissing Charlotte's lips. He waved to John and Billy sitting in the van with Fluffy in her cage on the seat between them. Potter's accordion was in the back of the van with the furniture. He'd taken it to Potter's wife, but she'd refused to take it.

"You keep it safe for Walt—he thought the world of you—and the kids ain't musical," she'd said.

He vowed to himself that he'd learn to play it—if he could bring himself to try. Perhaps Walt would look over his shoulder and show him how —he had *promised*, after all.

Lou kicked over the engine, put on his gloves and goggles and climbed aboard. They drove away slowly up Church Lane in convoy, careful not to dislodge the small, black and white Jack Russell sitting in the dicky seat behind Charlotte. With his chest out and his nose in the air, Spot sniffed the chilly breeze like some little, but very noble, lord.

Later that year, MacDonald went on the floor of the House of Commons and announced that the British Airship Program had come to an end. A small amount of money was budgeted merely to keep an eye on what other countries were doing. The Germans and Americans continued with their programs until *they* too, reached the same conclusions as the British after their own similar, painful experiences.

Soon after that, the government decided *Howden R100* had to be destroyed. Lou, Charlotte and Norway made a point of going down to Shed No.1 in October to witness her execution. Norway paced around as though in pain, gnashing his teeth while Wallis's sacred creature was roughly dismantled and put to death under a great steamroller.

"If they couldn't b-bloody-well succeed, then n-nobody else would be allowed to either—despite Thomson's promise," Norway seethed.

"Calm down, Nev, maybe it was all a bad idea. Let it go," Lou said.

Charlotte remained silent, but she couldn't help smiling radiantly.

"I should remind you that on two occasions we almost lost *your* precious airship over the St. Lawrence—*we* very nearly became part of the Canadian landscape—or had you forgotten about that?"

Norway thought for a moment. "I wonder what in the world would have happened then."

"I reckon *we'd* have been the ones having a lovely funeral in Montreal and Thomson's trip to India would have been delayed for a year or two. It would've turned out to be a fabulous success and *he'd* have gotten the girl—*maybe*."

Norway calmed down, as though he'd had an epiphany. "Okay, I suppose you could be right," he said finally. "We took a huge bloody risk and we got away with it."

Lou looked across to where the fair usually stood at that time of the year. It never returned to Cardington and he never saw Madam Harandah again.

Around this time, Lou received a brown envelope from Certified Accountants, Bennett, Wicklow & Brown from an address on K Street in Washington, D.C. It contained a full report on the Holdings of Tyson's Lumber and Hardware and a number of other related companies, including real estate holdings. Julia's name appeared throughout as a fifty-one percent shareholder. The accompanying letter described Lou as an interested party representing the interests of one Mrs. Julia Remington, Joint Chairman of the Board. Lou was fairly satisfied, at least for the time being. The fifty-one percent was intriguing; maybe Julia's father had owned more than that before his death. He'd look into that when he and Charlotte paid their next visit to the U.S.A. Now that Tom and Julia were married, maybe it was time for Tom to become a member of the board. Lou was sure Uncle Rory would be agreeable to this, after they'd had one of their 'little chats'.

The Report of the Cardington R101 Court of Inquiry was issued. Though beautifully written, it did little to determine the real cause of the disaster. It was found that the crash involving His Majesty's Airship *Cardington R101* was due to a loss of gas in bumpy weather conditions. No one was to blame. It would have made any fiction writer proud.

During these months, while he sat in the garden at Candlestick Cottage with Christian asleep on his chest, Lou often wondered what became of Jessup's body. Had he washed up on a beach or floated into the marshes of some French backwater? Or was he somewhere out in the endless sea, destined to float around in the Atlantic Drift until he disintegrated and sank to the black depths of the ocean floor? He'd never know.

THE END

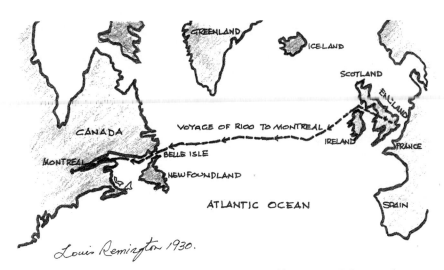

Voyage of Howden R100 from Cardington to Montreal
July-August 1930.

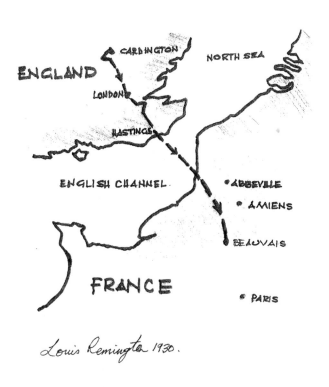

Voyage of Cardington R101 October 4th, 1930.

ST. MARY'S CHURCH, CARDINGTON

IN MEMORY OF THE FORTY-EIGHT AIRSHIPMEN WHO DIED
OCTOBER 5ᵗʰ 1930.

THE TOMB

AUTHOR'S NOTE

This is a work of fiction—pure fantasy, if you like—based on actual events. It is not a historical nonfiction documentary written to 'set the record straight'. It is my hope that this novel piques the reader's interest in this dramatic era of aviation history. Some characters are based on real people, others are fictional. Some events in the novel took place, others did not. After some years of research, I took what I thought was the essence of the characters involved and built on those qualities for dramatic effect, with fictional characters woven into the story to take part and to witness events. In the end, Lou Remington and Charlotte Hamilton became as real to me as Brigadier General Christopher Birdwood Thomson and Princess Marthe Bibesco.

I did not see any real villains in this story and did not set out to portray anyone as such. But I did see all the characters as suffering with that one trying malady—being human. The myriad symptoms of this disorder include: unconditional love, passion, ruthless ambition, pride, megalomania, greed, spinelessness, jealousy, deviousness, murderous intent, loyalty, duty, trust, obedience, honor, patriotism and selflessness.

I took liberties for dramatic effect: Scott and McWade were *not* on Victoria Dock in Hull when the *R38* went down, as far as I know. Hull Infirmary is not on the waterfront. The scenes aboard *R38/ZR-2, Howden R100* and *Cardington R101* during their flights and crashes are painted mostly from my imagination with information drawn from many books. Actual events on board those ships, as well as the dialogue throughout the novel is, of course, conjecture.

There is a great deal of truth in what I have written as a fictional account, but like the extraordinary Princess Marthe, the truth is elusive. Much I have taken from reading between the lines, exaggerating or emphasizing for dramatic effect. Some is pure speculation. The grand events are true, save for those actions carried out by fictional characters.

Lord Scunthorpe, the Tyson family and Tyson's Lumber & General Hardware Co. are fictitious entities, not based on any persons living or dead, any organization or corporation.

ACKNOWLEDGMENTS

I have been blessed with a tremendous amount of help from many amazing people while researching and writing this book. Very special thanks are due to my consulting editor at LCD Editing (lcdediting.com) who has put many years into this project and kept me focused and on the straight and narrow. Thanks also to Steven Bauer at Hollow Tree Literary Services for his expert guidance and editing. Grateful thanks must go to Edith Schorah for additional editing and proofreading. My appreciation also goes to Kathryn Johnston and Jon Eig at the Writer's Center, Bethesda, Maryland for their patient and professional coaching during workshop sessions.

I am indebted to John Taylor, lighter-than-air flight test engineer and consultant and writer of *Principles of Aerostatics: The Theory of LTA Flight,* who conducted a technical review and spent many hours reading and critiquing this manuscript and offering a wealth of advice, not only regarding airships, but also on formatting and preparing this book for publication.

Very special thanks to Eddie Ankers who worked tirelessly, consulting on book design and images. Thank you also to Bari Parrott who created the marvelous cover imagery.

Deep gratitude is due to Katie Dennington who did a wonderful job of designing and setting up the website http://www.daviddennington.com (although she is not accountable for its content). Katie was also responsible for helping me get started in the realm of novel writing. Throughout this five year process, she gave me the spiritual fortitude and encouragement to see it through.

I am also very grateful to Frank Dene at Act of Light Photography who produced the website video and assisted Katie.

I owe a debt of thanks to the people at Cardington Heritage Trust Foundation for their kind help over the years, especially Dene Burchmore and Sky Hunt's son, Albert, who showed me around Shed No. 1. Thanks also to Alastair Lawson, Alastair Reid, C.P. Hall and to Dr. Giles Camplin, editor of *Dirigible Magazine, Journal of the Airship Heritage Trust*, who kindly assisted with contacts in the airship community and photographs for this book and for my website. Many thanks to Paul Adams of the British Airship Museum and Jane Harvey of Shortstown Heritage Trust, Christine Conboy of Bedfordshire Libraries, Paul Gazis of The Flying Cloud, Trevor Monk creator of Facebook pages relative to the sheds and airships, and John Anderson of the Nevil Shute Foundation, all of whom advised on or shared photographic information.

I would like to thank the following for their help and encouragement: my dear wife, Jenny (my own special Yorkshire lass), Lauren Dennington and Lee Knowles, Richard and Katie Dennington, Dawn and Nick Steele, Alan and Violet Rowe, John and Sandy Ball, Katya and Michael Reynier, Edith and Michael Schorah, Cliff and Pat Dean, Ray Luby, Chris and Jan Burgess, John and Sally Slee, Richard Lovell,

Julie and Marty Boyd, Karel Visscher, Aaron Kreinbrook, Derek Rowe, David and Susan Adams, Commander Jason Wood, Graham Watt, brothers Karl and Charles Ebert, Ruta Sevo, Harry Johnson, Alan Wesencraft of the Harry Price Library at the University of London, and Mitchell Yockelson at the U.S. National Archives. I am grateful to Isabelle Jelinski for consultation regarding French translation (any errors are mine).

And lastly, my sincere appreciation goes to the marine who helped distill into words what I thought it must be like to search for a reason to go on after surviving horrific events and having experienced your friends and brothers-in-arms dying all around you. He confirmed that 'survivor's guilt' is all too real. He told me how once home from the war in Vietnam, he was unable to speak of it to anyone, even to the woman he married after coming out of the VA hospital. He allowed his wife to believe for years that his wounds were the result of a traffic accident. This veteran's experiences and his reactions to them are, seemingly, not uncommon.

BIBLIOGRAPHY AND SOURCES

Inspiration, information and facts were drawn from an array of wonderful books, as well as newspapers, magazines and documents of the period, including:

Report of the R101 Inquiry. Presented by the Secretary of State for Air to Parliament, March 1931.
Eleventh Month Eleventh Day Eleventh Hour. Joseph E. Persico. Random House, New York.
American Heritage History of WW1. Narrated by S.L.A. Marshall, Brig. Gen. USAR (ret). Dist. Simon & Schuster.
Icarus Over the Humber. T.W. Jamison. Lampada Press.
To Ride the Storm. Sir Peter Masefield. William Kimber, London.
Lord Thomson of Cardington: A Memoir and Some Letters. Princess Marthe Bibesco. Jonathan Cape Ltd., London.
Enchantress. Christine Sutherland. Farrar, Straus & Giroux. Harper Collins Canada Ltd.
Barnes Wallis. J. Morpurgo. Penguin Books, England. Richard Clay (The Chaucer Press) Ltd., England.
Howden Airship Station. Tom Asquith & Kenneth Deacon. Langrick Publications, Howden UK.
The Men & Women Who Built and Flew R100. Kenneth Deacon. Langrick Publications, Howden UK.
Millionth Chance. James Lessor. House of Stratus, Stratus Books Ltd., England.
Sefton Brancker. Norman Macmillan. William Heinemann Ltd., London.
The Tragedy of R101. E. F. Spanner. The Crypt House Press Ltd., London.
Hindenburg: An Illustrated History. Rich Archbold & Ken Marschall. Warner Bros. Books Inc.
My Airship Flights. Capt. George Meager. William Kimber & Co. Ltd., London.
Slide Rule. Nevil Shute. Vintage Books/Random House. William Heinemann, GB.
Chequers. Norma Major. Cross River Press. Abberville Publishing Group.

The Airmen Who Would Not Die. John Fuller. G.P. Putnam's Sons, New York.
R101 - A Pictorial History. Nick Le Neve Walmsley. Sutton Publishing, UK. History Press, UK.
Airship on a Shoestring: The Story of R100 John Anderson. A Bright Pen Book. Authors OnLine Ltd.
Airships Cardington. Geoffrey Chamberlain. Terence Dalton.
Dirigible Magazine: Journal of the Airship Heritage Trust, Cardington UK.
Aeroplane Magazine.
Daily Express October 4, 1930 newspaper articles.
Daily Mirror October 4, 1930 newspaper articles.
Daily Mail October 4, 1930 newspaper articles

IMAGES: SOURCES AND CREDITS

Cover Art   *Taj Mahal and Pyramids* by Bari Parrott.

Page 2   Girls and R101 at tower: courtesy of Martin Edwards, Roll of
                   Honour and the Bedford Borough Council Virtual Library website.
                   Photographer unknown.

Part No.
One   Launching of R38: U.S. Government. Archives.
Two   The Flying Scotsman: unknown photographer, public domain.
Three   St. Cuthbert's Church, Ackworth: photograph by author.
Four   Airship Macon under construction: U.S. Government. Archives.
Five   Cardington Shed around 1915: Simon George.
Six   R101 over London: courtesy of the Airship Heritage Trust.
Seven   R100 over York Minster: courtesy of Gary Hodgkinson, IMA-GEN
                   Productions.
Eight   R100 Approaching Toronto: City of Toronto Archives.
Nine   Klansman with horse from author's sketches and photographs
Ten   R100 at Cardington Tower: unknown photographer, public domain.
Eleven   Boarding R101: unknown photographer, public domain.
Twelve   Wreck of R101: Australian Airforce website, public domain.
Thirteen   Courtroom, R101 Court of Inquiry: Nevil Shute Foundation, public
                   domain.
Epilogue   Tomb at St. Mary's Church, Cardington: photograph courtesy of
                   Jane Harvey.

AUTHOR'S BIOGRAPHY

As a teenager, I read all Nevil Shute's books, including *Slide Rule,* which tells of his days as an aeronautical engineer on the great behemoth *R100* at Howden and of his nights as an aspiring novelist. I was fascinated by both these aspects of his life. He inspired me to write and to fly (ignorance is bliss!). The writing was put on hold while I went off around the world assisting in the management various construction projects and raising a family. I picked up flying in the Bahamas, scaring myself silly, and sailing in Bermuda. This was all good experience for writing about battling the elements, navigation and building large structures.

Many years later, I read John G. Fuller's *The Airmen Who Would Not Die* and my interest in airships was rekindled. It was time to pursue my dream—writing. My daughter was in Los Angeles, trying to get into films. I thought, stupidly, I could help her by writing a screenplay.

I had done extensive research on the Imperial British Airship Program and attended many screenplay writing workshops at Bethesda Writer's Center. I wound up writing two screenplays which had a modicum of success. The experts in the business told me the stories were good and that I just *had* to write them as novels. So, back to the Writer's Center I went to learn the craft of novel writing. Five years later, with my daughter working as my editor and muse, the book was finished.

CAST OF CHARACTERS (*Fictional)

A

*Alice—Jeb's Wife.
Atherstone, Lt. Cmdr. Noël G.—1st. Officer, *Cardington R101*.

B

Bateman, Henry—British Design Monitor, *R38/ZR-2*, National Physics Laboratory.
Bell, Arthur, ('Ginger')—Engineer, *Cardington R101*.
Bibesco, Marthe, ('Smaranda')—Romanian Princess.
Bibesco, Prince George Valentine—Princess Marthe's Husband.
Binks, Joe —Engineer, *Cardington R101*.
Booth, Lt. Cmdr. Ralph—Captain of *Howden R100*.
Brancker, Air Vice Marshall, Sir Sefton, ('Branks')—Director of Civil Aviation.
*Brewer, Tom—*Daily Telegraph* Reporter.
Buck, Joe —Thomson's Valet.
*Bull, John—Lou's Employer and Close Friend.
*Bull, Mary—John Bull's Wife.
*Bunyan, Fanny—Nurse at Hull Royal Infirmary and Charlotte's Best Friend.
*Bunyan, Lenny—Fanny's Husband.
*Bunyan, Billy—Fanny and Lenny's Son.
Burney, Dennistoun—Managing Director, Airship Guarantee (*Howden R100*).
*Brown, Minnie—Nurse at Hull Royal Infirmary.

C

*Cameron, Doug—Height Coxswain, *Howden R100 & Cardington R101*.
*Cameron, Rosie—Doug Cameron's Wife.
*Cathcart, Lady—A Friend of Brancker.
Church, Sam, ('Sammy')—Rigger, *Cardington R101*.
Churchill, Winston—Member of Parliament.
Colmore, Wing Cmdr. Reginald—Director of Airship Development (R.A.W.).
Colmore, Mrs.—Wing Cmdr. Reginald Colmore's Wife.

D

*Daisy—Thomson's Parlor Maid.
Disley, Arthur, ('Dizzy')—Electrician/Wireless, *Howden R100 & Cardington R101*.
Dowding, Hugh—Air Member of Supply & Research (AMSR), Air Ministry.

F

*Faulkner, Henry—WWI Veteran—Lou's Wartime Friend.

G

Giblett, M.A.—Chief Meteorologist at Royal Airship Works Met. Office.
*Gwen—Thomson's Housekeeper.

H

*Hagan, Bill—*Daily Mail* Reporter.
*Hamilton, Charlotte, ('Charlie')—Nurse at Hull Royal Infirmary.
*Hamilton, Geoff—Charlotte's Cousin.
*Hamilton, Harry—Charlotte's Father.
*Hamilton, Lena—Charlotte's Mother.

*Harandah, Madam—Gypsy Fortune Teller at Cardington Fair.
Heaton, Francis—Norway's Girl.
*Higginbottom, Peter, 'Pierre', Chief Steward, *Cardington R100 & Howden R101*.
*Hilda—Forewoman at the Gas Factory, Royal Airship Works, Cardington.
Hinchliffe, Emily—Wife of Captain Hinchliffe, MacDonald and Thomson's Pilot.
*Honeysuckle, Miss—Drancker's Pilot.
Hunt, George W. ('Sky Hunt')—Chief Coxswain, *Cardington R101*.
*Hunter, George—*Daily Express* Reporter.

I

Irene—Sam Church's Girl.
Irwin, Flt. Lt. H. Carmichael, ('Blackbird')—Captain of *Cardington R101*.
Irwin, Olivia—Captain Irwin's Wife.
Isadora—Princess Marthe's Maidservant

J

*Jacobs, John—*Aeroplane Magazine* Reporter.
*Jeb—Tenant and Friend Living at Remington's Farm.
*Jenco, Bobby—American Trainee Rigger, *R38/ZR-2,* Elsie's Boyfriend.
*Jessup, William, ('Jessie')—Charlotte's Ex Boyfriend.
*Jessup, Angela—William Jessup's Sister.
Johnston, Sqdn. Ldr. E.L. ('Johnny')—Navigator for *Howden R100 & Cardington R101.*
*Jones, Edmund—*Daily Mirror* Reporter.

K

*Knoxwood, Rupert—Thomson's Personal Secretary, Air Ministry.

L

Landsdowne, Lt. Cmdr. Zachary USN—Commander of *Shenandoah.*
Leech, Harry—Foreman Engineer (R.A.W.), *Cardington R101.*
*Luby, Gen. Raymond—U.S. Army Chief of Staff, Fort Myer, Arlington.

M

MacDonald, Ishbel—Daughter of Ramsay MacDonald.
MacDonald, Ramsay—British Prime Minister.
Mann, Herbert—Cardington Tower Elevator Operator.
*Marsh, Freddie—Cardington Groundcrewman, Joe Binks' Second Cousin.
McWade, Frederick—Resident R.A.W. Inspector, Airship Inspection Dept. (A.I.D.).
Maitland, Air Commodore Edward—British Commodore, *R38/ZR-2.*
*Matron No. 1—Matron at Hull Royal Infirmary.
*Matron No. 2—Matron at Bedford Hospital.
Maxfield, Cmdr. Louis H. USN—American Captain of *R38/ZR-2.*
Meager, Capt. George—1st Officer, *Howden R100.*
Mugnier, Abbé—Princess Marthe's Priest and Spiritual Advisor.

N

*Nellie—Worker at the Gasbag Factory, Royal Airship Works, Cardington
*'New York Johnny'—American Trainee Engineer, *R38/ZR-2.*
Norway, Nevil Shute, ('Nev')—Chief Calculator.

O
O'Neill, Sqdn. Ldr. William H.L. Deputy Director of Civil Aviation, Delhi.
P
Palstra, Sqdn. Ldr. MC, William, Royal Australian Airforce, Liaison Officer to the Air Ministry—representing the Australian Government.
*Postlethwaite, Elsie—Nurse at Hull Royal Infirmary, Bobby Jenco's Girl.
Potter, Walter—British Coxswain, Mentor of American Crewmen, *R38/ZR-2*.
R
Rabouille, Eugène—Rabbit Poacher, French eyewitness.
*Remington, Anna—Lou's Sister.
*Remington, Charlotte—Lou's Grandmother.
*Remington, Cliff—Lou's Father.
*Remington, Violet—Lou's Mother.
*Remington, Louis, ('Remy')–American Chief Petty Officer. *R38/ZR-2*.
*Remington, Tom—Lou's Brother.
Richmond, Lt. Col. Vincent—Head of Airship Design and Development (R.A.W.).
Richmond, Mrs. Florence, ('Florry')—Richmond's Wife.
*Robards—Ramsay MacDonald's Bodyguard.
*Robert—Charlotte's first love.
Robertson, Major—*Flight Magazine* Reporter.
*Ronnie—Works Foreman, Cardington Shed No. 1.
Rope, Sqdn. Ldr. F.M.—Asst. Head of Airship Design and Development (R.A.W.).
S
*Steel, Nick, ('Nervous Nick')—Rigger, *Howden R100*.
Scott, Maj. Herbert G. ('Scottie')—Asst. Director of Airship Development (R.A.W.).
*Scunthorpe, Lord—Member of the House of Lords, Opponent of LTA.
*Smothers, Helen—*Washington Post* Reporter.
Steff, F/O Maurice—2nd Officer, *Cardington R101 & Howden R100*.
*Stone, Josh—American Trainee Rigger, *R38/ZR-2 & Shenandoah*.
T
Thomson, Christopher Birdwood, ('Kit' or 'CB')—Brigadier General/Politician.
Teed, Philip—Chemist in Charge of Manufacture of Hydrogen, Howden.
*Tilly, Mrs. Queenie—Patient at Hull Royal Infirmary.
*Tyson, Julia—Lou Remington's first love.
*Tyson, Rory—Julia's Uncle, Proprietor, Tyson's Lumber and General Hardware Co.
*Tyson, Israel—Rory Tyson's Son.
W
Wallis, Barnes—Designer-in-Chief, *Howden R100*.
Wallis, Molly—Barnes Wallis' Wife.
Wann, Flt. Lt. Archibald —British Captain of *R38/ZR-2*.
*Washington, Ezekiah, II—Train Steward aboard *The Washingtonian*.
*Wigglesbottom, 'Moggy'—Owner of a 15ᵗʰ Century Cottage, Bendish Hamlet.
Y
*Yates, Capt. USN—Washington Navy Yard, Washington, D.C.

THE AIRSHIPMEN TRILOGY

The Airshipmen is now also available as a three part series with additional photographs and maps in each volume.

FROM ASHES   **Volume One**

LORDS OF THE AIR   **Volume Two**

TO ASHES   **Volume Three**

DAVID DENNINGTON

Amazon page: https://www.amazon.com/dp/B08SFVQ1NJ

Author's website: http://www.daviddennington.com

Made in the USA
Monee, IL
12 February 2024

53353238R10386